HEART SONG

EMMANUELLE

SNOW

Smart Lily
Publishing

Heart Song
Emmanuelle Snow

First edition - June 2024 (2025 update)

ISBN eBook: 978-1-7776150-0-0

ISBN paperback: 978-1-990429-89-7

Contains Blindsided (part 1) and Forevermore (part 2).

Editor: Shalini G.

Cover: SMART Lily Publishing inc.

Published by SMART Lily Publishing inc.

———

Emmanuelle Snow
emmanuellesnow.com

CARTER HILLS BAND UNIVERSE
(SUGGESTED READING ORDER)

Carter Hills Band series
False Promises

HEART SONG DUET
Blindsided
Forevermore

Whiskey Melody series
Sweet Agony

SECOND TEAR DUET
Cruel Destiny
Beautiful Salvation

BREATHLESS DUET
Wild Encounter
Brittle Scars

Upon A Star series
Last Hope

Midnight Sparks

Love Song For Two series
Lonesome Heart Duet
Fallen Legend
Rising Star

Two of Us Duet
Snowbound

Wicked Love

All titles available at
emmanuellesnow.com

For the best experience, read in the order as shown above

WHAT THE REVIEWS SAY

- "DAAAMN. This author can write! I mean, wow. It is not often I enjoy musician angsty romance books. But this blew me out of the park." **(Net Galley)**

- "What a rollercoaster ride! That had to be one of the most emotional and heartfelt books I've read in a long time because wow, that was both intense and sweet and just everything my romantic heart wants! " **(sara.reads.too.much)**

- "It was the sweet (and slightly steamy) little romance novel I didn't know I needed... I can see fans of Colleen Hoover enjoying this one." **(Net Galley)**

- "This romance novel had me entranced from the first chapter." **(Net Galley)**

- "Give me all the angst." **(Tanja - OMGReads blog)**

- "A little bit of Country and a whole lot of HOT. Angsty, fun, romance." **(Gina Rae Mitchell blog)**

- "It is absolutely brilliant. The emotions, the banter, the love, the chemistry - it all just works!!" **(Shalini's Books and Reviews)**

- "This book had so much heat and sizzle that I am surprised my kindle didn't melt." **(Carla Loves to Read blog)**

TRIGGER WARNINGS

Disclaimer

My books are realistic and emotional romance reads.

I'm an advocate for mental health, and some topics could be sensitive for certain readers since they are portrayed as close to real life as possible.

I've listed the potential trigger warnings for each title on my website.

Be advised that those trigger warnings could potentially be spoiler alerts for the storylines.

Those sensitive topics have been written with the utmost care and respect. Please reach out if you have questions or comments.

All books contain sexuality, mature content, and language not intended for people under 18 years of age.
For other readers' sake, please avoid spoilers in your reviews.

Thank you and have a wonderful day!

Emmanuelle

emmanuellesnow.com

To my kids and husband.
This adventure wouldn't be as thrilling as it is if you weren't cheering
me on. I love you with all my heart.
Now and forever.

———

To all the artists in the world.
Follow your own rules.
Shine the way you were meant to shine,
not the way other people want you to shine.
It's your voice.
Never lose sight of who you really are.

Nobody else can tell your story the way you're telling it.
Embrace it.
Breathe it.
Live it.

BECOME A VIP

TO NEVER MISS A THING

Snow's VIP

Join **Emmanuelle Snow's VIP newsletter** for all the cool stuff, promos, new releases, giveaways, and gifts.

emmanuellesnow.com

Snow's Soulmates

Join Emmanuelle Snow's Facebook VIP group, **Snow's Soulmates**, to chat with her and other readers, get updates, and more bonus content.

facebook.com/groups/snowvip

PINK AND COUNTRY
THE SONG

I couldn't see the light
I thought I had it all figured out
But I didn't; I had no clue
And then you came my way
You disrupted everything I've always
    known
And there you were
That night on my front porch
I never planned to fall so hard so fast
I never thought it would last

[CHORUS]

Girl, I just want you to know
There's no one else like you
You are the sunshine in my storms
You color my night sky
You are the star I wish upon every
    night

You hold my heart; I'll never let
    you go
Babe, I'm blind without you.

I still feel your lips on mine
Even after all this time
Babe, you're special; you're the one
Now all I want is to make you mine
Watch you sleep every night
And breathe you in
And watch you smile
I want to live in your pink world
'Cause you're my favorite color

[CHORUS]
Girl, I'm mesmerized by you
You are the rainbow
I never knew I needed
You're my compass
My muse and my other half
Babe, I'll never let you go
This is my promise to you

[CHORUS]
Girl, I just want you to know
I want my life to be pink like yours
Babe, I'll never let you go
You're my absolute favorite color

Music and lyrics by Carter Hills

1

APRIL

My eyes flew open. I blinked a couple of times, letting my vision adjust to the darkness. Entangled in my bedsheets, I combed the web of knots my hair had turned into with my fingers. Great, my night had been another round of tossing and turning. I stared at the ceiling, the darkness swallowing me in, wondering what time it was. Through the small crack where my curtains didn't quite meet, the moon peeked at me, a thin crescent of silver in the night sky. I propped myself up on my elbows, angled my upper body toward the nightstand, and searched for my phone with a hand numb from sleeping in an awkward position. Once I unplugged the cord, I slumped back, my head hitting the fluffy pillows. Squinting at the phone screen, I held my breath.

Three forty-eight.

No. I cringed and dropped my device beside me, where it landed on the mattress with a soft thud, praying I read the time wrong.

I needed the rest. More than ever. My novel wouldn't

write itself. Right now, I had half a mind to look for a ghostwriter. But who was I kidding? I'd never go there. I sighed, dragging my hand over my face, still heavy with sleep. All I needed was to bring my brain on board.

A few years ago, I had my first meet-and-greet with insomnia, and it was a hard cycle to break. Believe me. We were in this long-lasting relationship. Sure, the sleeping pills I took for a while helped with the sleep part, but they also made me feel drowsy during the day. After I dropped them, I tried melatonin, magnesium, meditation, breathing exercises, and lavender essential oil. Anything to help me find sleep at night. The latter had even become Zen-April's drug of choice. So much so that I turned it into my personal fragrance. I sprayed it on my pillow, misted it in the kitchen using one of those little, ten-light-setting diffusers, and kept a roll-on in my purse.

Every night, my brain was stuck in the hamster wheel for hours, with thoughts of what could have been, but remained stalled and blank during the day. Forget being productive or at the top of my game. Not happening. My disturbed nights complicated my existence. In one word, they messed with my head. And my life.

Damn thing.

I pondered my options. Get up and get to work. Or force my eyes to stay closed and bury my head under a pile of pillows, hoping sleep knocked on my door and swept me away. Yeah, right. I snorted. Sleep never knocked twice on the same night. At least, not in my case. With a sigh, I tried the pillow thing anyway. Just in case. One could still be hopeful.

My brain would not win this round. No way. Not under my watch.

Four fifty-seven.

This was an impossible situation.

How early was too early to wake up and jumpstart your day?

If I had an athletic bone inside of me, I would be a runner. Or a high-performing triathlete. Those were the people who got up early with purpose—or I supposed they did. At this time of the day, I, April Simmons, had none. To focus on my writing now was asking too much from me.

Hours ticked by.

I flipped onto one side, then rolled on the other, doing a poor job of convincing myself I'd fall back to sleep.

My mind wandered to my third novel, which I hadn't even started writing yet. My agent Jill had given me a one-month deadline to submit the first draft…my fourth deadline extension. I'd been procrastinating for the last three months, unable to focus, my fingers too stiff to type, my brain blocking my creative flow. My head wasn't in the game. Nah, it was lost somewhere, far from the place it should be. And added to my sleepless nights, that was a deadly combination. Who would ever believe I was a twenty-four-year-old fantasy—enchanted kingdom, magic spells, elves, and all—author with two bestsellers? At this moment, I wasn't convinced myself.

Blame me for my lack of organizational skills. Every minute of every day, I managed to find more ways to be counterproductive than efficient. In the past few months, I'd shattered my previous low records and now should reward myself with a medal. "Procrastination Queen." My bubbly, spur-of-the-moment personality usually fueled my creative side and made up for my mental chaos: a cluster of grief, broken dreams, and lack of restful sleep.

It worked for my second book.

Not this time.

My brain turned into a blank canvas when it came to writing eighty-four days ago and counting. Every attempt to reboot it since then had failed. Baking chocolate chip cookies, going for walks around the block, singing my heart out. Once I even tried jogging. *Yeah. Crazy, right?* Anyway, the right side of my brain, the root of creativity, had gone on strike and refused to come back to work. Regardless of the reward at the end. Stupid gray matter. Or was it white matter? Who cared? Somewhere inside me, I had locked away every single disappointment and sorrow in my life. Losing Travis, having to reinvent myself, being on my own again. That was what fueled my insomnia. And now I was failing my agent with this book. Even when I tried to keep my pain out of reach, but it always resurfaced and toyed with my mind. I guess the lock wasn't sturdy enough, and my sleeplessness only amplified my sense of inadequacy, adding to the rambling inside my head.

How pathetic had I become? I was now talking to myself as if there were two of us.

Six eleven.

Sitting, my attention drifted to the dresser on the opposite wall. The paint was chipping on the side, and I made a mental note to repaint it. And change the knobs while I was at it. It was the only piece of furniture that had followed me around since college. It used to belong to my boyfriend when he was a kid, and for sentimental reasons, I had kept it when I moved here. It matched the teal bed frame and nightstands. My bedroom was big enough to host a queen-size mattress, flanked by dual nightstands and a large walk-in closet. A dozen black-and-white framed photographs of my friends and me over the years covered the wall above the dresser, and a freestanding mirror stood in one corner, next to a large potted plant. My eyes lingered on one of the happiest days of my life for a long moment. That perfect memory now had a sour aftertaste, so I blinked and looked away, not wanting a fresh surge of emotions to ruin my day. Insomnia had already taken its toll on me; I didn't need my sobs and broken heart to be added to the mix.

Deciding I had prolonged the inevitable long enough, I got up. I put on my favorite dark-purple sweatpants and slid my arms into a gray cardigan over the white T-shirt I'd slept in. With the elastic band I kept around my wrist, I tied my jaw-length baby-pink hair in a messy half-do on top of my head. I slid my feet into my sheepskin boots—the one expensive fashion piece I'd ever indulged in—and made myself a large mug of hot chocolate, with whipped cream. Not coffee, though. No matter how tired I was, I never yielded to caffeine. The smell alone was powerful enough to engage my gag reflex. Sure, I downed a cup or two—let's be honest—in college when I knew I'd be up all night studying for mid-terms or finals, but each attempt failed at keeping me awake and left a putrid taste on my tongue. Back when insomnia and I weren't acquaintances. I filed coffee under the *You'll have to kill me first* file in my head. Along with oysters, licorice, and kissing Stevie Broderick in high school. All things that made washing my mouth with bleach seem like a viable option.

In my own twisted way of thinking, I believed hot chocolate solved everything. Heartaches, headaches, menstrual cramps, writer's block. However, the latter hadn't turned out to be true. I remained hopeful it'd work its magic. One day. Eventually. The secret was in the whipped cream. A catalyst able to multiply the *hot chocolate cures everything* effect by ten. Or I wished it could.

With my head tipped back, I crossed my fingers and mouthed a silent prayer to the God of creativity. Yeah, if he didn't exist, someone should invent him.

In the kitchen, I plopped down on a stool at the island and turned on my laptop, shutting my eyelids when the lit screen blinded me. *Ugh, too early for this.* I blinked to moisten my eyes, the back of them burning from the sudden assault of white light. Since when did I become a morning person? *April, get a grip on your life, move forward, and live a little.* How many times had I repeated the exact same words to myself in the early hours of the morning without success?

I sighed. I'd lost count.

I perused the space around me, anything to distract me and prevent me from staring at a blank page and the cursor blinking back at me. The room was small but inviting. Stainless steel appliances, chess-black-and-white tiled floor, mint-green cabinets. A wooden island topped with a concrete slab and two stools separated the kitchen from the dining room, which consisted of a square blonde wood table surrounded by four mismatched chairs in a spectrum of colors. A large window overlooked the neighbor's building and prevented natural light from getting in early in the morning. A steel-blue sofa, a square artisanal coffee table with a floor lamp, a small cactus in a pot, and a wall-to-wall bookshelf filled with my favorite titles made up the living room of the two-bedroom apartment. The whiff of lavender mixed with the sugary scent of the chocolate chip cookies I baked and left on the cooling rack last night filled the air, giving the place a homey feeling.

Bernice, my tabby cat, woke up from her slumber and jumped on the kitchen counter, her vibrant-blue eyes—almost the same shade as mine—staring at me, unblinking, as she padded on the keyboard. I pushed her to the side and caressed her head, her soft fur warming up my fingers.

"You hungry, sweet girl?"

She purred, and I rose to my feet to fill her golden bowl, set on the floor by the refrigerator. It was the one with a black fishbone etched on the side that I made in the ceramic class I took last year, when I tried to meet new people and start socializing again.

"You should grow fingers, you know. And learn how to type. Could be useful."

She arched her back and ignored me as she attacked her food.

"Keep ignoring me, Bern. Super useful." Why did I ever think getting a cat as a roommate would be entertaining?

Once back on my seat, I stared at the blank page on the screen and typed in big, bold black letters—

AMELIA'S KINGDOM – BOOK 3
I CAN'T EVEN COME UP WITH A TITLE
BY APRIL SIMMONS, LOST BUT NOT FOUND.

Before my brain could catch up, I opened a new browser tab. Procrastination much, right? I typed "Kitten pictures" and hit search. The image of a tiny black kitten yawning in the big palm of a firefighter, his gorgeous soot-covered face set in a determined expression, stole all my attention. The sight was just too damn hot. At least through the chaos my life had become, my hormones weren't dead. Good to know.

I rolled my shoulders forward, buried my face in the crook of my elbow, and let out a heavy sigh. Gone were the days when I impressed myself with my dedication. A series of yawns escaped my mouth, making my eyes water. I took a sip of my hot beverage, absent-mindedly watching Bernice groom herself.

"Hey girl, can you do that later? I need some encouragement here. Can't you see I'm struggling?" Our eyes met for half a second before she went back to licking her paws. "Never mind. I've seen beauty queens more enthusiastic than you. You won't be mentioned in my acknowledgments section this time. Shame on you." My words didn't rattle her. Not even a little.

My phone chimed, and the sound startled me. Perfect. As if I needed another distraction. I clicked open the text message my best friend Saunders just sent me as if she'd read my mind and knew I required some much-needed guidance. Or a kick in the butt. Such a seer. *Take this, Bernice.*

Wait. Why was she up at this early hour? Saunders should be all wrapped up in her boyfriend's arms at six in the morning. Not texting me. She wasn't even a morning person. Never had been.

SAUNDERS

Hey, Bubble Head, call me when you get this. Love you xx

Bubble Head was the nickname Saunders gave me during our freshman year in college when I was in too many projects and committees during our first semester. Lacking time to hang out with my friends, I told her one night I pictured myself as a cartoon character with text bubbles popping up all around my head. The name stuck all these years later.

I read her text message for a second time, wondering what she wanted. My curiosity won, and my sleepiness vanished as I punched in my best friend's number.

She answered on the first ring. It seemed like I wasn't the only one feeling impatient this morning.

"Okay. I hope you're ready for this because I have great news for you. I've got your next adventure. Something to change your mind and give you that kick in the butt you desperately need."

Yeah, Saunders knew me too well.

My heart raced at the thought she'd send me bungee jumping or swimming with sharks. "Do I really wanna know?"

"Oh, April, just trust me. When did I ever fail you?"

I inhaled, bracing myself for whatever she was about to propose to me.

"One of my clients rented a two-bedroom luxury cabin in Green Mountain for the month. He can't go because his wife got sick, and she needs to stay in the city. Anyway, I thought you could use it. Fresh air. Great for inspiration. And, oh yes, it's rent-free. Since he canceled last minute, he couldn't get a refund. Anyway, what do you think?"

"You're serious? You want me to move to the country for an entire month? They probably don't even know what wi-fi is."

"Girl, you're being ridiculous. It's a five-star cabin, not a shack. Anyway, don't be a party-pooper. Imagine writing your new book without being distracted. You know I'm a genius in disguise, right?"

"Don't flatter yourself. Genius isn't your middle name, Saund. Your super ideas don't always turn out so great. At least not for me."

"Come on. It's not like we live in New York City. We're in Ginger Creek, Georgia, April. Most people would consider it a small town."

"Except here we have malls. We have more than just one main street, and there are no deer living in people's backyards. You know what I mean." I pinched the bridge of my nose, thinking. "What about Bernice? I know you won't watch her. You hate that litter box thing."

"I already checked with the renting company, and they said you can take her along. So, you're going? You don't have any good excuses to avoid this opportunity. I'll give you one hour to think about it. If you leave tomorrow morning, you'll be there by sunset."

"Fine. Give me an hour." We hung up, and I dropped my forehead on the table. Did I just get set up? Saunders was right, though. I had no good excuses for refusing her offer. Damn it. I hated when she was right.

My phone pinged as a new text message came in. Two words.

SAUNDERS

Start packing.

I gritted my teeth. My best friend would never let it go. And telling her I feared bears wouldn't cut it. Saunders ran a vacation and retreat agency for rich folks. She booked vacation spots according to their needs in luxurious locations only they could afford, where they could unwind and have a good time without too many distractions. Over-organized—the opposite of me—she had vacation packages ready for all types of clients. Exotic destinations, mountain retreats, boathouse rentals, treehouses, or desert and jungle getaways.

Right now, she was offering me a cabin, for an entire month, all by myself. Why was I still trying to find reasons not to go?

I worked my jaw back and forth, making a pros-and-cons list in my head, weighing my options through the mental traffic jam that was my brain.

Could a change of air boost my creativity and engage my brain productively? *Yes. No. Probably.*

Plus side? No distraction. No noisy neighbors. *A definite pro.*

Would I feel lonely all by myself for an entire month? *Sure. Not so much. Maybe a little.*

No Saunders around. *A con.* No busy sidewalks. *Pro? Con? Tough call.*

Being on my own was my normal these days. Here or there wouldn't matter much. *Okay, a pro then.*

My mind raced through the possibilities. I rubbed my eyes with my closed fists. I hadn't taken a vacation in…huh… forever. When was the last time? I sighed. Too long ago. I massaged the nape of my neck with my fingertips, untying the knots in my upper back and shoulders. My pulse picked up as the idea of going on a mountain vacation took root.

I scanned my small apartment. With its ivory walls, dark ceilings, maple floors, and colorful accents, it wasn't much, but I liked it. It was home.

I'd moved here, an almost four-hour drive from Atlanta, three years ago, after graduating from college. After everything. When my life collapsed. This place was supposed to be my fresh start. The first step to moving forward. My apartment wasn't big by any means, but it suited me and it was all mine.

New me.

New life.

New career.

New home.

That was the plan back then. Did it work out? Honestly? *Not really. A bit…maybe.*

Bernice jumped on the counter and butted my cheek, purring into my ear. "You wanna go, girl?" She purred some more. "And *now* you have an opinion." Could a cat and my best friend know what I needed better than I did? With a huff, I shook my head. No, not going there. Even I had to admit it sounded silly. But maybe… *No, April. Stop.*

I dropped my shoulders and scraped my hand through my hair.

"Okay, girl, let's do this. Let's go on an adventure for a month." Bernice and I exchanged what could pass as smiles, at least in my mind.

In the last few years, I'd lost sight of who I was. It was time to get my power back. To redefine myself. To find where I belonged. To dream again. To do this whole new me, new life thing. And give it a real shot. I blew out a breath. The more I thought about it, the more enticing it sounded. I'd been waiting for a sign for so long. Could this be it?

Yeah. Time to get my groove back.

Straightening my spine with a new resolve, I typed a message to Saunders, letting her know I'd go to the cabin. I would do this. I would get out of my comfort zone. *About time*, the smart side of my brain screamed at me. For once, I agreed, and mentally gave myself a high-five.

The mountain air would clear my head. See? It was working already. Just thinking about it released years of pent-up tension from my back. I remembered reading somewhere, a while back, about how living in the mountains made you healthier and happier. Green therapy, they called it. I risked nothing by trying it out for a month.

The seclusion would help me focus. Yes, the idea grew on. A wide grin painted my face. "Time to pack," I said out loud, mostly to myself—or to Bernice, who had already retreated to the comfort of my bed.

I shut my laptop and sauntered to my bedroom with a pep in my step I hadn't experienced in a long time. Saunders's crazy last-minute idea didn't sound so crazy after all. On my tiptoes, perched on a plastic step stool, I grabbed my suitcase from the top shelf of the closet.

Yeah, I was doing this.

No more excuses.

No more procrastination.

The mountains were calling me, and I was answering.

Half-packed, I sat back in front of my laptop to find a dozen new messages from my best friend. I expected nothing less from her and imagined her doing a victory dance in her underwear when I agreed to her retreat idea. Saunders emailed me lists. Lists with an *S*. Itineraries, things to do in Green Mountain at this time of the year, the best places to eat on my way up there. She attached forms to sign, the cabin's rule book, and other documents I didn't dwell on, for now.

For an instant, I wondered if she sent these to all her wealthy clients or if she had compiled all this information for my sake only. Knowing my best friend, probably a mix of both. Part of her foolproof strategy to win me over.

I skimmed over the documents I printed and emailed back the signed forms. It looked official. It even included a non-disclosure agreement. I shrugged. Guess that made sense since Saunders only booked high-end, private destinations for her clients. Anyway, I trusted my friend. Back in my bedroom, I finished packing, adding more sweaters to my suitcase under Bernice's watchful eye, now curled up on my pillow.

Jitters filled my heart, knowing I'd enjoy one of Saunders's destinations for once. My best friend offered me a month-long vacation, and I intended to make the most of it.

2

CARTER

My smile was anchored to my face, and nothing seemed to chase it away. These days, running helped me put my thoughts in order. Not so long ago, it was a coping mechanism, to deal with stress. Not anymore. Lately, I started enjoying exercise for its health benefits. I nodded at the security guard holding the door of my building as I slipped through the opening. Instead of using the elevator, I climbed the staircase up to the top floor, adrenaline still coursing high in my bloodstream and needing to flush it out of my system.

My phone went off, and I reduced my pace, going from a light jog to a walk. My lips curled when I noticed the name flashing on the screen. "Hey, June. What's up?"

"Carter, can we talk?" Something was wrong. I could tell. Her voice was devoid of any hints of playfulness, which was unusual for our phone calls.

"Huh, sure. Gimme thirty minutes? I'll shower and eat something. I just came back from a run with Taylor."

"Listen, I just got off the phone with someone from

your record label. They heard from Savannah Prince's people. Some things we need to discuss."

"The fuck."

"Call me when you have a minute. I'll see what I can do in the meantime, okay?"

I huffed my frustration. "Yeah, I'll do that."

With my fists clenched at my sides, I threw my head back and exhaled.

Once I reached my floor, I hurried inside my apartment.

My cheerful mood had vanished, replaced by an angst that sent chills down my back. The name of Savannah Prince never rhymed with good news, but rather with catastrophe.

Discarding my gym clothes on the bathroom floor, I positioned myself under the hot stream and let the water relax my body while the gears of my brain engaged. A dozen different scenarios played in my mind. Whatever Savannah wanted, I knew, for sure, it would piss me off.

Minutes later, dressed in a pair of faded denims and a simple white T-shirt, I downed a glass of icy water before returning June's call. Like a Band-Aid, I had to rip it off and fast, or else it would pollute my thought feed, and I'd become restless.

The moment she picked up and revealed the reason for her call, I regretted ever returning it. Now that I had the confirmation June wasn't delivering good news, I wondered how anyone with a sense of decency at my record label would ask me to partake in this circus.

"No, June, I won't do it. I'm done. D. O. N. E. Been there, done that. Bought the T-shirt. Burned it. From now on, they can talk to my lawyers." I scratched my forehead with the tip of my thumb. Anger simmered inside me. *Get a hold of yourself, Carter.* "It's a no. Everything has been explained already. If they wanna prove one of them is at fault, they don't need me. Isn't this why corporate lawyers exist?" Juniper, or June as I called her, my assistant manager slash personal assistant, was my go-to girl in my music career. Sometimes, I felt like her job description could be summed up as *Keeping Carter out of trouble*.

From her five-foot-four height, with three-inch heels on, Juniper Stewarts had a lot of attitude. She stood up for herself—and me—no matter what.

With long brown hair and exotic caramel eyes with dark-green rings around the pupils, she resembled a college student more than a twenty-eight-year-old assistant to Riley Burns, music mogul and manager of some of the biggest names in country music.

I trusted her with my career. Most times. Not today, though. Today, I didn't dig it. "We broke up officially weeks ago. I'm done with this episode of my life, and I don't owe her or anyone else anything. I thought I had been clear when we parted ways. She even signed the damn papers. What more do they want from me?" I balled my hands into fists as June delivered her spiel on the other end of the line.

"Listen, Carter. It's big. She claimed Carla paid her to gather as much intel on you as possible. Seems like Savannah wasn't the only one with paparazzi on speed dial. Carla was feeding them information too. About you."

"I told everyone from the start Carla was crazy. I never trusted her. Her irises were dollar signs. I never authorized her to publish that crap about me. Or to sell me to gossip rags without my consent."

"That's why the label requires your testimony. To settle the case quickly. And to make sure it's not just another one of your devil ex's setups, but legit accusations. This is no joke. Only you can confirm the conversations that took place between you two in her office."

"Well, right now I don't care about Carla. And whatever Savannah says, it is usually a big lie. They make a great pair. Yep, two psychos I can live without." I paused to calm myself before I said things I would regret. "Without solid evidence and any other way to prove they teamed up against me, I'm not getting involved. I've turned the page. The label has enough means to deal with it on its own." A low grunt escaped my lips. I refused to be those manipulative witches' puppet any longer. "Whatever scheme they've come up with, I'm staying out of it. Both can rot in hell for all I care. And why is Carla still working if the label thinks she screwed me over? See? It's all a big joke."

June kept talking, but I turned a deaf ear, working extra hard to keep my calm.

"Tell the label's attorney I'm unavailable to meet with him or for video calls or whatever. I won't answer anyone's questions. They all know what I think of Carla. Riley does too. He can vouch for me. He was there and heard her nonsense. Where is he anyway? I would have thought he would get involved in this himself and put a stop to it before it even reached my ears."

Riley Burns was my manager. He had been by my side since before I made it big on the music scene. Over the years he had become a friend to me, a brother, someone I could always count on.

"He's been in and out of meetings all day. We're supposed to get together later, but he put me in charge in the meantime. It's over my pay grade, but for you, I'd run errands naked if it meant you wouldn't have to go through this on your own. Being the middleman is no fun, but I bark loud enough that the label is almost overnice each time they contact me."

"I get it. I swear. It's just… I thought we all had moved on and that I was free from their scheming. Word of advice. Tell everyone who wants a piece of me right now to keep me out of it. I really don't wanna have to come to the office and tell them what's on my mind. It wouldn't be good for anyone involved. Trust me."

"I'm sorry, Carter. I really thought we were done dealing with them too." June hesitated for a beat. "Let me see what I can do."

"You sure? I don't like the idea of your being stuck between all of us. It's not fair."

"I told Ry I would do it. And he knows he can count on me. I'm on your side. Always." She paused and seemed to hesitate for a moment. "And Carter, listen… I also wanted to inform you about something else." She lowered her tone. "So you're not taken by surprise when the news comes out. Huh…Savanna landed that lead role in Wesley's next movie. She'll be everywhere. Giving interviews. Rising to the top. I just wanna make sure you're ready for what it implies. Your relationship, or lack of it, will continue to feed the media. I would bet my next paycheck she'll surf on your fame for a little longer."

Evil manipulator. Torturous witch. Selfish huckster. I lacked adjectives to describe my ex-girlfriend nowadays.

"Seriously, can't I catch a break? I'm sure there are more exciting scandals out there than my personal life, which isn't interesting to anyone else right now. I'm almost a monk these days."

"Well, maybe. Some heiress will get divorced or some actor will be caught cheating soon enough, but for some reason, your love live is still the hot topic. You've always been so discreet about it in the past. It's like now the entire planet thinks they are entitled to every detail. I know it's not fair and you did nothing to deserve it, but that's the way things are. People live vicariously through you. The mysterious and brooding top-selling country artist who ended a relationship that fed the gossip trash for two years. You offered them a window to your personal life, and they jumped in with both feet. Wasn't it Savannah's plan all along? It's not like—"

"Just for the record, I don't care about her big, multi-million-dollar Hollywood contract. Or whose dick she sucked to get there. Or that she snitched to my publicist." As if my life hadn't been enough of a circus lately, now my label suspected my ex-girlfriend had been feeding info to my publicist and vice-versa. They both knew my position about fame, and they went behind my back to sell me to the press. Sharks with no respect for private lives whatso-ever. "She got the part, good for her. And bad for everyone else involved. The truth is she probably did unthinkable things to win it." A chill crossed my entire self as I thought about how Savannah would do just about anything to get to her end. Yep, there were no lines she wouldn't cross for fame or money. "Whatever went down with any of them isn't my problem anymore. I'm over that bullshit, and I have no plan to revisit it anytime in the future. And, by the way, next time, tell whoever brings it up it wasn't a separa-tion, it was a fucking breakup. I dumped her ass."

For the last fifteen minutes, I'd been pacing my pent-house back and forth from the kitchen to the living room in an attempt to calm the storm raging inside me. I stopped by the dining table and placed a hand over the backrest of one of the chairs, hanging my head low, wondering how my day had gone from amazing to this. With its high ceil-ings, straight lines, open floor plan, and honey-colored hardwood floors, I loved everything about my place, espe-cially the panoramic windows overlooking the city of Nashville in every room. My own bachelor pad. My safe haven. One that suffocated me right now the more June kept talking about the devil and her crazy sidekick.

"Carter? Are you still there?"

Angst built inside me. Why had I endured that nightmare for so long?

My fist hit the table, and the vibration echoed through the room.

I wasn't the guy to lose his cool, not usually, but any mention of Savannah Prince took me back to a dark corner of my existence. A place I wished to never return.

Bile rose in my throat at the memory of the hell I had endured for those two years.

All this time, she wore the victim suit like a second skin.

I heaved at the reminder.

We were toxic together. Poison. Before her, I avoided all relationships, and she knew it. She took advantage. And I let her. I became the worst version of myself for the length of our relationship, pushing away all the people who genuinely cared about me. The ones who had my back.

Never again would I wish to revisit that part of my existence. The one where I became sexually frustrated. And castrated—in many ways.

It still angered me that I'd been blind for so long.

Being linked to her had been my first mistake.

Dating her had been the second.

And moving in with her had been the fatal one.

A prison that took me a long time to escape from.

"Talk to me." June sounded worried now. "Cart, don't give her power over you."

June was right. My grip loosened around my phone, and I unglued it from my ear. *Relax, man. Breathe in. Breathe out. Don't let Savannah Prince ruin another one of your days. Not after she wrecked the last two years of your life.*

"Carter, try to keep your emotions out of the equation.

She's fishing for a reaction. Don't give her that satisfaction and let her antics affect you."

"Yeah, I hear you, and you're right." I pivoted on my heels, grabbed an apple from the fruit basket on the kitchen island, and juggled it with one hand until I missed, and it crashed on the floor at my feet.

"I will tell them you're unavailable. To be on the safe side, I'll run everything by Riley tonight to make sure we're all on the same page. By the way, I only found out about all this one hour ago."

A humorless laugh bubbled out of me. "Like she hadn't planned it ahead of time."

"I don't want you to suffer anymore because of her actions. She seems desperate to keep feeding off your fame and your name."

A new upsurge of anger simmered inside me, and holding back my anger, I forced my voice to remain steady as the next words left my mouth. "Miss Hollywood, like the narcissist bitch she is, can't stop painting me as the villain to gain all the sympathy and exposure she's always dreamed of by acting like a victim. Typical. Geez, why can't she set me free?" A guttural growl exited my mouth. "I'll die before I put my name next to hers of my own volition again."

"I know. Believe me, I do. It's like those two never grew a brain. Or a conscience. As long as I'm involved, they won't get away with it. I'll buy the shovel and bury them myself if I need to."

"That's why people in this industry fear you." Humor returned to my words.

"Yeah, well, I guess Savannah and Carla haven't gotten the memo they should stay away from your business."

"Well, their funerals." I breathed out, some of my left-over anger evaporating. "I'll stay put for a while and let the dust settle. When I come back, I'll be stronger than ever before."

"You promise you'll be fine?"

I swallowed. "Yeah. I'll be with my family. They always ground me. And the fresh air will do me good."

"Be safe, Carter. Just a sec, I'll be right back. Some unknown number keeps calling."

It still surprised me how I had played along with Savannah Prince all this time without questioning her motives. Either she was smarter and a better actress than anyone would give her credit for or I was so lost back then that I refused to see the warning signs.

A long sigh passed the rim of my lips.

What was done was done. I was self-aware now, and I wouldn't agree to any of her requests.

Our relationship had turned out to be the worst decision of my life. By far. Worse than the sophisticated snake tattoo I got on my upper back at sixteen.

The tattoo had been removed.

However, nobody could ever erase my relationship with the Evil Queen.

June's voice broke my train of thought. "She's relentless. I'm telling you, I bet she can feel the heat about to burn her ass."

"Who was it?"

"Carla. She just requested an emergency meeting. She just wants to save face."

My tone hardened. "I'm fucking over all of this. And I'm done with this conversation. We've already lost enough time today on a subject I have no interest in. Let's put an end to it. Get her on the phone." I barked the words at June and slapped myself mentally. *Come on, man, be nice. June is on your side.*

"Carter, forget it, you're not in the right state of mind

to talk to her. She's not in her office at the moment. She said she'd be back this afternoon."

"I don't care where she is. Mars or in the middle of the fucking jungle. Get her on the phone. She has a cell phone. Call her." I paced the room, tugging at my hair. I exhaled through clenched teeth. "I'm sorry for yelling. You shouldn't have to deal with this shit. It's not your job. I'll fucking shut her up once and for all. She's done bossing all of us around like we're her puppets. But I appreciate your help, and I swear I won't punch anyone this time." Last year, I had punched a paparazzi who was following me in New York City for no apparent reason other than I had been dealing with one of Savannah's crazy episodes and he wouldn't let it go. Six months ago, I stormed out of an interview when the host didn't stop praising Savannah's talent and charitable endeavor. *Fucking idiot.* That was my fucking money she had pledged.

June sighed and kept her tone even. "Carter, listen to me. Calm the fuck down before you talk to anybody else. Nobody wants to deal with you when you're like this. Take that break, go to the countryside as you planned, spend time with your family, then we'll talk. Green Mountain usually helps you unwind. I'll clear your schedule, and we'll only keep the engagements you can't miss. Meditate, do yoga, or any other shit that'll help you relax. Stay away from the press, don't watch the news, and let the Savannah story wear out. I'll take care of it from my end. And please keep it in your pants. Don't fuck around. The last thing you need is another scandal."

"What about Ry?"

"I'll share the new developments with him later and keep you updated. We'll figure it out. All of us. Don't worry. I have your back. Always."

With both hands, I tousled my hair, my phone now on speaker.

"Fine. I trust you, June. You better be right about this. Never let Carla near me ever again. I can't promise I won't lose it next time. And if I wasn't clear enough before, she's fired. Tell the label whatever they wanna hear, but Carla isn't on my team anymore. Effective now." We agreed to talk later, the hair on my body standing on end, an unmistakable sign I needed to walk away before I had one of my episodes.

I strode back to the kitchen and kicked a chair off balance. Lava boiled inside my veins.

When did I become so restless? My emotions usually ran the game. Not my actions. But today, it all seemed too much to deal with.

I needed a release. Something. Anything to calm my nerves down.

My hand dragged along my jawline. My beard felt weird under the pads of my fingers. I'd never kept it this long, but now I used my scrubby face as a shield to hide from the rest of the world.

I changed back into my workout gear, and with red boxing gloves on, I pounded the punching bag hanging from the ceiling of the small gym. Along with a treadmill and a weight station, it was set in the corner of one of the guest bedrooms I had transformed into a man cave. It also hosted arcade games, a large screen mounted on the wall, and an oversized leather couch. Every time my friends came over, this was the room where we spent all our time.

The exertion burned my muscles, and sweat pearled on my forehead. With my shoulder, I pushed strands of hair falling over my eyes away. With both arms around the bag, I stopped its back-and-forth motion and leaned my forehead against the slick surface, catching my breath.

Punching the sucker for one hour straight did nothing to ease my angst.

Riled and restless, I packed my guitar and a few things in the trunk, tossed a duffle bag filled with clothes on the backseat, and climbed into my SUV.

When I told Taylor, my bodyguard and chief of security, earlier that I was going to spend some time in Green Mountain, I didn't expect to leave today. But now that I thought about it, there was nowhere else I'd rather be.

The tires screeched as I exited the parking garage in a hurry.

As I replayed June's and my animated conversation in my head on a loop, I headed toward the mountains.

Once some of my wrath melted away, I gave myself a pep talk. *Get your shit together, Carter. Use this time to work on your next album and be with your family.* With the train wreck my life had become, it'd been too long since I released a new album. Yeah, the last one had been before Savannah. I had one scheduled last year but ended up pushing it back indefinitely as I worked on my dead-end relationship. The joke was on me now. It was long overdue to give in to my creative side. My fans were adamant about it. Time to go back on the road and bring the music back into my life. No more wasting my time in a relationship based on false promises and pretenses. Savannah had hardened my already icy heart and wrecked my mojo, and I was ready to leave my past behind and move forward with my life.

––––––––

Jack and Dahlia were already there, waiting for me on the front porch, when I parked my black SUV in front of the three-story log cabin at the end of the road. Located atop the mountain, it offered the perfect view of the valleys and the sunsets. At night, the lack of city lights provided a glorious sight of the constellations sprinkling the black canvas. Back when Dahlia and I formed the Carter Hills Band together with our ex-bandmate, Stud Burgess, we used to play at Green Mountain Fest every fall. We started performing on the small stages when we were kids and ended up headlining the festivals only a few years later. After her life went through the wringer, Dahlia moved here full-time. Nestled in the Smoky Mountains, it possessed all the small-town charm one would expect while being just a few hours' drive from Nashville, Atlanta, and other big cities. Green scenery, fresh air, valleys, and a quaint Main Street, it was no wonder Dahlia chose to raise Jack here.

Over the years, I'd acquired half a dozen luxury log cabins all over town—most of them nestled in the mountains—and rented them to high-end businesses and wealthy folks craving some peace of mind. No other spots beat the mountains to evade your everyday life and forget about everything making you tick.

This one cabin where I had parked, I kept it as mine.

Nobody except close friends or family was welcome here.

Its location gave me some much-needed privacy, and no picture hunters could take snapshots of me when I relaxed on the deck over the steep mountainside.

Perfect spot.

When I bought the lot at the top of the mountain, I had a gate installed down the road and a fence put around the perimeter to keep bears and other animals out—and of course, stalkers. Let's be real. I'd had some following me around over the years. I had my mountain lodge, where the view was breathtaking, built first. The following year, I added two smaller cabins next to it, both of them sitting in the gated part of the property. I used them to lodge friends who stayed overnight, while the rest of the time they were rented through agencies that conducted thorough background checks on everyone, never compromising my security. They made sure everything was in working order and always left a handwritten note in the kitchen to welcome each new guest. I never revealed my identity, but I loved the idea of offering those who stayed in one of my cabins a personal welcome. It was one of the many little details that made up the experience I was providing within my rental business.

My other properties were spread all over Green Mountain. I bought them through the years and made minimal changes to them as they were already fully furnished and ready to be rented. They just diversified my real estate portfolio. Nonetheless, all guests staying at any of my cabins always received the same little attentions to make their stay unique and memorable.

"*Carrrter.*" Jack ran my way and jumped into my arms as soon as I climbed out of my truck.

I held on to him tight and twirled him around. The long drive had defused every remnant speck of my anger. Thanks to the wide-open countryside scenery, some old classic rock music, and peppermint tea.

"Hey, buddy. It's been too long, I've missed you." I ruffled his short dark hair and put him back on his feet. With my palm raised, I pretended to measure him to my body. "You're almost a man now. You've grown at least two inches since I last saw you." Jack, Dahlia, and I hadn't spent time together in months due to the fact that I was in a very dark place and was trying not to drown in the chaos of my love life and bring the ones I loved down the rabbit hole with me.

The boy giggled, and Dahlia mouthed *Thank you* from

where she stood, her arms crossed over her chest, wearing ripped dark denims and a red flannel jacket.

"I could use some help. Show me those muscles of yours." Jack flexed his arms, and I handed him my guitar case with a grin. "Be careful. You're the only one I trust with it." I bent at the knees, leveling our faces, and whispered, "Don't tell your mama, or she'll be jealous." Jack snickered, and my voice rose as I added, "Put it in my studio."

The boy's eyes sparkled. He knew how much the guitar meant to me. I had gifted him a kid-sized replica last summer for his fifth birthday. He wouldn't treat diamonds any better. And the kid had natural talent. It flowed in his veins. He shared the same genuine passion for music that Dahlia and I did at his age.

His mama inched closer and rose to the tips of her toes to drop a kiss on my cheek. Our eyes met, and we exchanged more in our gazes than any words could ever do.

"I've missed you, Carter."

I wrapped my arms around her and pulled her closer. She felt skinnier than usual under my touch. I framed her face with both hands and leaned back to look at her. A lone tear rolled down her cheek, and I wiped it off with the pad of my thumb. "I've missed you too. So damn much. I'm sorry. I needed to heal and find my way. On my own."

Dahlia lowered her gaze, her hands stuffed in her pockets. "I know. Didn't mean I wasn't worried about you. It's okay, though."

"No, it's not, but I'll make up for it."

She squeezed my forearm, and her lips curled up.

Back when Dahlia, Stud, and I had a band together, Dahlia hated the fame, so after she found out she was pregnant with Jack, she walked away from it. Then everything went to shit, and she secluded herself here in Green Mountain and stayed out of the public eye. For good.

Lost in my toxic relationship with the devil herself, I let Dahlia and Jack down for a few months. I refused to involve them in the nasty turmoil my life had turned into. It was mine to fix. I promised myself it'd never happen again.

Was Dahlia's weight loss related to my messy existence? It wouldn't be the first time my antics affected her. I blew out a worried breath.

She stepped back, breaking our embrace, as Jack came trotting in our direction.

"Done. Your guitar is safe in your music room."

"Thanks, bud. I knew you were the man for the job." We fist-bumped, and I handed him another bag. "This is precious stuff too. Are you up for the challenge?"

"Yes, sir," he said, giving me a salute. A flicker of emotion tickled my spine. The small gesture reminded me so much of my big brother when we were younger. I chased the memory away.

"Hey, Dah. Where's your car?"

"At the mechanic's. Nick dropped us off an hour ago."

"I could've picked you two up. You know that, right?"

She flicked her hands as she added, "It's nothing. Nick had errands to run anyway. It's not like we live hours from here either." True. They lived a few miles from my cabin.

"When is he picking you up?"

"In two or three days. Haven't decided yet. Did I forget to tell you Jack and I are staying with you? Is that all right?"

The idea the three of us would spend a few days together sent a soothing feeling through me. For a second, it felt like old times.

"Oh yes, it's perfect."

I opened the back door of the truck and swung the duffel bag over my shoulder, draped my arm around Dahlia, and we followed Jack into the house.

"Hope you're hungry. I've cooked dinner. We could eat early and get Jack to bed and spend some one-on-one time together. We're long overdue." She glanced at me, one brow arched, a small curve playing on her lips. My heart swelled as I took her in. *God, I've missed her.*

"I'm starving, and there's nothing I'd like more than spend some alone time with you, Dah." I winked and kissed her forehead before leading her inside and taking all my stuff to my room upstairs. The master bedroom occupied the entire third floor. It was decorated simply with a recycled barn-wood king-size bed with matching nightstands on either side, a dark charcoal bedspread, a walk-in closet, and an en-suite bathroom. A large black-and-white picture of my first solo show—the one Dahlia herself took and gifted to me—was hung above the bed. On the second floor, Jack had his own room with a guitar-shaped bed my ex-bandmate Stud Burgess handcrafted for him after he outgrew his crib. Next were a bathroom and three additional guest rooms—one Dahlia used every time she spent the night—down the hall. Toys and clothes filled Jack's closet because my home was his too. Even Dahlia had left some of her stuff in her bedroom, so whenever she decided to stay over, she was never caught off guard.

Stud and his wife now lived in Oregon with their children, and we barely saw each other, except for a couple of times a year. I missed my friend, but he was happy, and in the end, it was all that mattered.

When Stud quit the band, soon after Dahlia did, my existence shattered. I had not seen it coming. The guy breathed music. Talented, he begged Dahlia and me to give him a chance to join our band back in the day. And he soon became family. Growing up in a fucked-up environment, I understood his need to build something else. A family. A stable future for him and his wife. Even if I wanted to, I could never blame him for offering his kids the chance he never got when he was a child himself.

While I showered, Dahlia and Jack busied themselves in the kitchen downstairs. Other than the den and my music studio, the kitchen had always been one of my favorite rooms in the cabin. It had state-of-the-art Sunset Bronze appliances, a large island with a walnut butcher-block top, and a panoramic window overlooking the valley. Like every other room here, it had hardwood floors, wooden walls, and twelve-foot-high wood plank ceilings. The cabinets were painted a soft shade of cream just like the L-shaped couch in the living room, the rug in the den, and the bricks dressing up the fireplace. A few teal accent items like pillows, vases, and paintings—the ones Dahlia insisted I needed—were scattered around. The cabin was a bigger replica of the two-story smaller ones down the road. It was a mix of rustic and farmhouse chic. Thanks to my best friend, it looked like a house and not just a bachelor pad with no personality.

On the walls were framed pictures of the happy memories of my life, and some of Jack's pieces of art through the years.

The smell of white wine sauce pasta with fresh herbs invaded my nostrils as I grabbed a clean towel from under the sink to dry myself off. Dressed in low-cut denims and a long-sleeved black shirt, I jogged downstairs. Not in the mood to tame the wild strands of my shaggy look, another side effect of my after-Savannah-Prince era, I raked a hand through my damp hair. It was freeing not to give a damn about trivial details of my appearance and just surf life for once.

"Ohmygod, Carter. Your hair," Dahlia teased with a tentative smile as I joined her by the stove. "It's so long and unruly. I wouldn't have been able to tell earlier." She studied me for an instant. "Never mind, I like it. It's a good look on you." For a second, I forgot I'd worn a beanie when I arrived.

I shrugged, half-smiling. "Let's just say grooming hasn't been a top priority lately. And it's easier to stay under the radar when I look like this." I shoved the carrot stick Dahlia offered me into my mouth.

Dahlia had always said I looked like a boy-man with my tousled hair. Like I knew she would, she ran her fingers through it, and loads of memories from our past resurfaced.

A shiver traversed me. Not sure if it was due to the mid-January crisp air or her familiar touch reminding me of my carefree days. When we used to be at the top of the world together. She and I living the dream we'd been cherishing since we were little kids. I loved my life now, but parts of me missed those early days. When everything Dahlia and I did felt like magic. Back when we still had that innocence about the rock star lifestyle and climbed the ladder to stardom one step at a time, having no clue what would happen when we reached the top. I understood the choices she had made in the last few years, but that didn't mean it sometimes still didn't sting to walk onstage on my own.

"I'm glad we're all here," Dahlia said.

"Me too. Gimme a few minutes, I'll light up the fireplace." I left the kitchen, crossed the living room and beelined toward the side door as a wave of nostalgia hit me. I wasn't in love with my best friend anymore, but sometimes, when we were alone, playing house, I got a picture of what life could have been if things between us had been different. Standing in the living room with my hand around the doorknob, I surveyed the space around me. On my right was a hallway leading to a home gym and my music studio, rooms no one visited except me, and the media room which consisted of a large screen and over-sized couch. The wooden staircase separated the living room from the rest of the main floor where the kitchen, dining room, and den were located. The latter had large windows that gave the impression we were standing outside and a second fireplace. I loved the room. It was one of my favorites, and every time it snowed, I sat there and looked outside for hours, playing music and losing myself in my creative side.

With a pile of wood in my arms, I shut the door with a kick. A shiver zipped through me. The winter this year was colder than usual.

The fire crackled as I contemplated the scenery from the bay windows in the den. A sense of calm washed over me. The sky, a pale shade of gray, threatened us with an imminent snowfall. A breeze lifted fallen leaves from the ground and twirled them around. From where I stood, I saw the silhouettes of the mountains in the distance, the peaks no doubt covered in snow. I rubbed my jaw. *Home.* Green Mountain was home. I blew out a shuddering breath. Maybe I should move here full-time. Sure, I'd miss Nashville, but here, I felt calmer. In control.

Happier.

Jack joined me and slid his tiny palm into mine. We stayed still for a fat minute, our gazes glued to the mountains afar. The tension in my back vanished. I closed my eyes, tingles of contentment rising inside me at the realization I had conquered my heartbreaks and was still standing strong. And tall. Just like those mountains that passed the test of time.

———

After I sang Jack one of my songs, at his request, Dahlia tucked him in bed while I attacked the dishes. A smile stretched my lips at the thought of being here with two of my most favorite people in the world. The ones who mattered.

No camera flashes.

No interviews.

No screaming fans.

No underdressed groupies or crazy stalkers after me.

No Savannah Prince or her toxic nonsense.

When Dahlia joined me, I handed her a glass of wine. Her floral fragrance, the same one she'd been wearing for the last ten years, reached my nostrils. The one reminding me I was home. "How are you doing? For real."

She offered me a hint of a smile. "I'm fine." Without taking a sip, she put the wineglass on the counter beside her, avoiding my gaze.

"Come on, it's me, Dah. You can tell me anything. No woman who says she's fine is ever fine."

She huffed a laugh.

"What is it?" I cocked my head to the side, meeting her watery eyes.

Her eyes brimmed with tears, and she fanned herself with a hand.

A weird sensation twisted my insides.

"I'm not sad. I swear."

I let go of the breath I was holding.

She swallowed a big gulp of air, met my eyes, and said, "Carter, I'm pregnant." Cradling her face with my hands, I stared at her. I studied her moss-green eyes, the curve of her lips, the blush on her cheeks. My lips drew into a sad upturn when, for a second, I wished this could have been the news we could have shared together. The words felt like a *déjà vu*. Something we had uttered in the past.

I cleared my throat, my mouth as dry as California during a drought. "Are they happy or sad tears, Dah?" I usually had no trouble reading her expressions. Not this time. The flow down her cheeks confused me. A lot. Women's simplest emotions were always the hardest to figure out.

"Happy," Dahlia sniffled.

"Why the tears then?" I clamped her waist with my hands and dropped a soft kiss on her forehead.

"I was…I was scared to tell you. I didn't know how you'd react." She looped her arms around my midsection and buried her face into my chest. My hands traced circles on her back. "You and I, we went through this once. It makes me emotional thinking about the last time I told you I…I was pregnant…with Jack. And the aftermath of how it changed our relationship. You. Me. Jeff. It brings back so many memories. Good and bad. I swear I'm happy about it. Nick and I, we're ready for this."

My heart quivered in my chest, and a tightening sensation wrenched at my insides. I breathed slowly. The last time my best friend announced she was pregnant, it ended up being the beginning of a very traumatic episode in our lives. But she deserved her happily-ever-after. She'd been through too much not to come out stronger on the other side. And thriving.

"If you're happy, then I'm happy for you. It's all I've ever wanted." My pulse slowed down, and the knots in my chest slackened. Air flowed in and out of my lungs easier. I had faith that this time around, her pregnancy wouldn't be a bittersweet memory. With a finger, I tipped her chin up and looked into her eyes. "What about the weight loss? You don't seem so fine to me."

"Morning sickness. Remember how it was with Jack? I couldn't get out of the house for weeks."

A lopsided smile twitched my lips at the recollection. "How's Nick?"

"Ecstatic. He's a wonderful dad to Jack. I love him, and he's good to me." Dahlia and Nick had gotten married two years ago. The summer before I embarked on my ride to hell with the one I shouldn't mention.

They had an intimate ceremony here, in the mountains, with only a few people in attendance. I shed a tear or two that day. My heart had ached at the sight of my best friend in a white dress for the second time. However, it also allowed me to let go of the feelings I'd bottled up long ago. Dahlia, Nick, and Jack were a family of their own, and I trusted Nick to care of the two people I loved the most in this world.

I sighed. On their wedding day, I wished it could've been me up there at the altar. Today, this feeling re-emerged. I wished this baby were mine.

But the news also confirmed I had made my peace with this part of my past. As much as I still loved her, my feelings for Dahlia weren't the same that had clung to me for so long. We were best friends, and I was okay with the current status of our relationship.

Entangled in blankets, we sat on the loveseat before the fireplace, just like old times. Dahlia's head rested on my lap, and I smoothed her red hair, twisting strands around my fingers.

"I love you, Carter. That will never change. Time for you to find your happiness too." She yawned, and I stayed silent. My pulse spiked at the thought.

Life would change for all of us. Things would never be the same again.

A baby.

Knots tied my stomach. Dahlia and Jack were no longer mine. Not like they used to be. Our family, as we'd known it, would be altered forever. Dahlia and Nick would have a baby. A child of their own. Even though I refused to panic at the idea, I wondered if I would still have a place in our unique family dynamics or if I would be on my own all over again. Unless… No. I refused to let myself think about the different scenarios tonight. I wasn't ready to deal with the consequences of my curiosity. Not before I was absolutely sure I could handle the outcome without the reality of it plunging me into another downward spiral. Perhaps someday I'd be ready to face the truth. Not today, though.

My throat closed, and I focused on my breathing to avoid getting unsettled by the emotions raging inside me. Now wasn't the time to have an episode.

Jack was sleeping upstairs in his bedroom, and Dahlia was here. With me.

Everything was fine. We were all fine. They would forever be my family. No matter what. That, I was sure of. Just in a different way. It was all good. The realization quieted the insecure part of my mind.

Pushing the thoughts of the unknown as far away as I could, I blinked fast to keep in the tears prickling the back of my eyes.

Tightness developed in my chest, and choosing to have faith in the unknown, I slumped back, my head sinking into the headrest, evading my flow of paralyzing thoughts, and fell asleep to the steady rhythm of Dahlia's breathing.

3

APRIL

"Girl, I'm in the middle of nowhere. The GPS is worthless," I said, hitting the steering wheel with the palm of my hand. "I'm driving around in circles. These roads lead nowhere. The navigation screen is a jumble of purple and white roads. My pantry is less messy, can you imagine? One moment I'm facing a cliff on a dead-end road and the next, I'm stuck in a labyrinth with no exit. Even the satellite is lost. Tell me again why I agreed to this."

"Relax, Bubble Head. Follow my directions, and you'll get there. It's trickier in the dark. I get it. But I'll assist you. You're lucky it hasn't snowed yet."

"Snow?" I repeated my friend's word. I sat up straight, forehead creased, scanning the pitch-black mountain road as if a bucketload of snowflakes would fall any second from the sky right on my path. "I've been on the road for eight hours. It's late, and I'm tired. Tell me you're joking."

"S-N-O-W, snow. You know, the fine white dust winter gods sprinkle on Earth during the cold months. I've heard it's quite common in the mountains at this time of the year."

I sighed through clenched teeth.

"Relax, April. You'll be fine. Don't panic over some sparkling white sprinkles."

I rolled my eyes. "I love snow. But it looks better on postcards, puzzles, or in Christmas movies."

My best friend chuckled, and I joined in.

Laughing relieved some of the tension in my back.

"Okay, I'm at the corner of Bear Crescent and Eagle Lane. Next thing I know I'll be on Weasel Boulevard. Who has given these streets their names?"

Saunders sighed on the other end of the line. "April, please focus. Stay on Eagle Lane up to Mountain Road. It should be about half a mile further on your right. Be careful, there's a sharp turn ahead."

"These roads are too narrow. Even for Miss Dolly. Tell me again why rich people vacation here. It's not safe. Don't be surprised if I drive off a cliff. Please choose a nice casket."

"Stop whining. Your car—Miss Dolly—is full of food, so you won't have to go out too much. I'm still confused you named your car. Each time you mention it, I believe, for a second, you have a passenger riding with you. Anyway, once you see the cabin, you'll never want to come back home."

"I doubt it. Remember you're lucky I still trust you, Saund." I carefully took the sharp bend along the mountainside and stopped breathing when all I could see for a second was the vertical drop of the cliff. "The last time I did, I ended up on a date with a podiatrist who had some foot fetish and asked me at least twenty times to show him my toes during dinner." I winced at the memory.

"There are no feet involved this time, and it's cold, so no one will beg you to take off your shoes. You're safe."

I uttered a bunch of curses. "You should've warned me before I came here that I needed to update my life insurance policy."

Saunders snickered but chose to ignore my quip. "Where are you now?"

I squinted and leaned forward to read the street sign on my left. "Huh, Mountain Road."

"Great, you're almost there. Make a right turn. Tell me when you see the gate."

"Gate? As in I'll be living in a gated community? In the middle of nowhere? Are you playing a prank on me?"

"Relax, girl. Blimey, I told you already. It's safe, and the view is to die for. You'll thank me later and dedicate your new book to your super-extraordinary best friend. Be real. You know I'm the most amazing girlfriend in the world." Saunders clapped her hands together on the other end of the line, sounding a lot more enthusiastic about the entire trip than I was at the moment.

What did I get myself into?

I steadied my breathing and reminded myself of the reasons I agreed to come here.

Mountain air.

Creative environment.

Free rent.

Hope for something new.

"What's the code?"

Saunders laughed, her attention not on me. She whispered something, and my cheeks flushed. Ohmygod, I had interrupted a fuck session when I called her in panic. If only I could lash myself. Not lash, ugh. Bad choice of words. No BDSM reference when my two best friends were fucking. Please… No… If only I could kick myself. There. Better.

"Saunders, I'll let you go back to your fuck marathon if you give me the code."

She giggled and brought her focus back to me. "Four-two-six-eight-five. Once you punch it in, it will be deactivated within five minutes and you won't be able to use it again. In the kitchen, you'll find an electronic key fob that will let you in and out of the gate for the length of your stay. Oh, and use your phone to unlock the cabin. I've already set up the digital key for you."

"Wait. What?"

"This morning, I added the digital key app to your device. You lock and unlock the front door with it. It's super easy, you'll see."

"*Thaannkks*," I said, stretching my word longer than I intended to.

"Call me in the morning or if you need anything before then. Love you, Bubble Head."

"Love you too, Saund. Tell Reed I'm sorry I interrupted whatever you guys were doing. I won't bother you anymore tonight." *Oh God, please don't let these images get etched into my brain.*

My friend moaned. Clearly, for my sake.

"Take care, April. Don't talk to strangers, and find yourself some testosterone-filled lumberjack to keep you warm at night," Reed said through the phone. I fought a smile. Saunders and Reed were family to me. The only ones I had left.

Once through the gate, three cabins appeared before my eyes. A three-story one so big it could be a mountain lodge, flanked by a smaller one on each side. Mine stood on the right side of the road, closer to the huge log castle.

Squeezing my steering wheel, I parked next to the front

porch and killed the engine. Back steeled and chin up, I climbed out of my car and reached the steps. Even at this late hour, the lingering smell of barbecue wafted in the air. I congratulated myself for packing warm clothes. The chilly winter air sent shivers down to my toes. With my suitcase and Bernice's carrier beside me, I tried to unlock the door using my phone.

Nothing.

With fumbling fingers, I tried twice more.

Still nothing.

I rebooted my device.

Nope.

My nipples puckered and threatened to drill holes through the fabric of my light cotton shirt. My jacket was somewhere in my messy car, but I refused to empty the trunk to find it at this late hour. At my feet, Bernice meowed, no doubt also annoyed by the cold breeze.

"Sorry, girl. I'm trying here. Stupid technology."

After three more attempts, the green light of the door lock flashed in the dark.

Hallelujah.

I sucked in a quick breath and flicked the light switch on. A dim glow lit up the room.

A fervor spread through my body. I gaped. The interior of the cabin looked nothing like how I'd pictured it in my head. I freed my cat, who purred as she butted my legs. "Go explore, girl."

Hugging myself, still freezing, I scanned the room, taking everything in and blinking to make sure I wasn't dreaming. Hardwood floors, wooden walls, vaulted ceilings —wooden everything.

Anywhere else, it'd be too woodsy, but not here. Here, it worked.

The cream sofa, kitchen cabinets, and wool rug made it look classy. And inviting.

The soft aqua accessories gave the whole place a modern yet country charm vibe.

In the living room, there was a stone fireplace with a wooden mantel above. A black wrought-iron chandelier with a rustic charm hung above the farmhouse dining table, big enough to seat eight people.

With a straight back and a hand pressed to my heart, I emptied my lungs.

Love at first sight.

Saunders was right. One month here would never be enough. I felt at home and wanted to live in this cozy log cabin for the rest of my life. A hammock chair hung in a corner, facing the floor-to-ceiling window, giving the impression it floated in the air. Without a doubt, I knew this would be my writing spot.

Like a kid, I hurried around the cabin, opening the door to every room, wanting to uncover all the secrets this place hid between its walls.

The master bedroom occupied the second floor, a mezzanine overlooking the living room downstairs. The shower alone was bigger than the entire bathroom in my apartment. It had soft-gray tiles and a rain-style showerhead.

Flutters invaded my stomach. I jumped and landed on the mattress, on my front, arms spread, giggling. This was too good to be true.

The darkness outside engulfed me. Without any big city close by to light up the night sky, it was darker than anything I'd ever experienced before. I couldn't wait for the morning to come so I could admire the view. Saunders had promised it'd be spectacular, and I believed her. After all, she'd sent me to heaven.

Back in the kitchen, I added water to the kettle and turned the stove on, in need of some herbal tea to warm me up.

A handwritten note on powder-blue paper lay on the butcher-block topped island.

> Dear Ms. Simmons,
> Hope you have a marvelous stay.
> Enjoy the view and fresh air.
> Your host,
> C. H.

Whoever this C.H. was, he or she was kind enough to welcome me personally. Everything about this place drew me in. A lone tear streamed down my cheek. Somehow, I felt as if I belonged here.

Back in the living room, I added wood to the fireplace —someone had lit the fire prior to my arrival—to cozy up the cabin. Not quite warm enough yet, it served more as an element of decor than a source of heat. I cranked the thermostat up in the meantime and went to my room to empty my suitcase.

One cup of tea later, wrapped in the duvet on the bed, my eyelids heavy, I fell asleep on the soft mattress, dreaming I was lying on the fluffiest cloud.

———

The sound of a car engine outside woke me up the next morning. One quick look at the alarm clock on the night-stand told me it was thirteen past nine. Wait. No middle of the night *I can't sleep and the minutes are ticking by* episodes? No tossing and turning in bed for hours? I blinked twice to make sure I read the time right.

Curled on my side, my body buried under the white duvet, I failed to stop the grin growing on my face.

I'd been in Green Mountain for twelve hours, and already the mountain air was working wonders on my sleepless nights.

With lightness in my chest, I jumped in the shower. Singing at the top of my lungs, I enjoyed the hot water relaxing my knotted muscles. "Red dress, high heels, la la la." Dressed in faded blue jeans and a cropped fuzzy pink sweater, with a cup of hot chocolate in hand, I sat in the hammock chair, feeling as if I were at the top of the world. Without blinking, I took in the red and orange leaves covering the ground and the clear blue sky that let me see miles ahead. The view from here was breathtaking. I took a sip of my liquid cocoa indulgence, and heat traveled from my head to my toes.

Peace spread through me, and I felt calmer than I had in a long time. And happier too.

With my mug in hand, I ventured out onto the back deck. A hot tub occupied the right-hand corner, while two wooden Adirondack chairs and a small grill were positioned on the left. The mountain air woke up all my senses, and the cold breeze stung the tip of my nose.

Saunders truly had sent me to paradise.

I snapped a selfie and sent it to her with a heart emoji.

The reception wasn't that great up here, and it took a few minutes for the message to go through.

After devouring a light breakfast, I powered my brain, excited about where my creative mind would take me. Comfortably tucked in my now favorite chair, armed with a notebook and a pen, I scribbled notes for my new book. Before I knew it, it was four o'clock.

Buried in my work, I'd lost track of time.

For dinner, I fixed myself some chicken and noodle soup I'd brought from home and relaxed with a glass of white wine on the couch, my legs folded under a fluffy blanket.

The fireplace had warmed the air, and before I could make it to my room, my eyelids got heavy. And I dozed off.

———

The next morning, I woke up at eight, on the couch, entangled in the blanket, with Bernice curled up beside me. Butterflies danced in my stomach, and tingles of excitement spread through my chest. A faint aroma of pine lingered in the air. It tickled my nostrils in the most delicious way.

I stretched my arms over my head. "Good morning, Green Mountain."

I'd slept for over twelve hours. Whoa, I'd clearly misjudged how sleep-deprived I had been.

Could a change of air have been all I needed, all along?

I got up and reached the bathroom upstairs. My eyes widened when I glanced at my reflection in the mirror. *Oh my.* My hair was a tangled mess, and I had dried drool at the corner of my lips. Who cared, right? The smile on my face had turned into a permanent fixture I couldn't shake away.

I'd spent the last three years of my life in some kind of monotonous parallel universe. I lived through them, but instead of enjoying myself, I went through the motions. Days turned into months, and months bled into years. Except for my long-lasting friendship with Saunders, I lived a pretty lonely life. Now, for the first time since the day my world had been turned upside down, I felt free.

After Travis, the love of my life, passed away, I barely got out of bed for weeks. We'd moved in together during our junior year in college, living in his closet-sized apartment for ten months before making an offer on a house. A fixer-upper dream we had planned to renovate over the years until it fit our vision fully. A little house with banana-yellow wood siding and white shutters, a backyard, and a wrap-around porch. Nothing extravagant, but a place to call our own. It was like we both felt this urge to reach for our goals early on in life. Like we knew our story came with an expiration date. We shared so many dreams together. Backpacking a summer through Australia, adopting a dog from a shelter, going bungee jumping in Europe—Travis's dream, not mine. And raising a bunch of kids—somewhere down the line. But then Travis got sick. It shattered all our hopes and plans, every single one, until all that remained was dust.

His death threw me into a downward spiral.

A dark hole that sucked me in until I crashed and burned.

I lost a lot that year. Myself included.

Freshly showered, I draped a towel around my body, my hair piled on the top of my head in a messy knot. Something—or rather someone—caught my eye outside.

From the bedroom window, I noticed a tall dark silhouette of a man standing in front of the larger log cabin, the one I thought was a mountain lodge. The man was rummaging through the trunk of a massive black SUV. I took in the over-the-top log cabin behind him.

All of it screamed money.

Way out of my league.

I wondered if the man was a tenant like me or if he

owned the place. Not that it really mattered, as long as I could enjoy the sight of him.

His attention drifted to his left. He pushed back from the trunk and pivoted around. His plaid shirt clung to his ripped chest and defined biceps.

Even from a distance, I noticed how handsome he was.

Longish, disheveled dark hair, wild stubble, broad shoulders, and high cheekbones. And an ass worthy of a jeans ad.

All male and testosterone-y.

I would've paid good money to run my fingers over his couple-of-days-old scruffy jaw.

"Hello, gorgeous," I said to myself. The part of me I'd buried years ago awoke the moment I laid eyes on him. I grinned. Green Mountain was definitely everything I needed.

A beautiful red-haired woman and a little boy traipsed down the road, hand in hand, toward him. Handsome picked the boy up and twirled him around. They shared words and laughed hard. His arm curled around the woman's neck, and he pressed his lips to her temple.

"Aww," I exhaled with a huff. "Perfect family."

That's what Travis and I thought we'd have someday. Life decided it'd never happen for us. A strong pinch tightened my chest at the memory.

I'd made my peace about losing Travis, but somehow, seeing these people, all close and happy, played with the strings of my heart. My vision blurred for a second, and I blinked, chasing my emotions away.

Handsome turned his head as if he sensed my gaze on him, and his eyes found mine. He stared at me for a second too long, his gaze glued to my face. My mouth went dry. Feeling like a stalker, I moved to the side, away from the window, but the towel around my body caught on the window handle and puddled at my feet, exposing my bare chest for everyone outside to see.

"Fuck." I swore and folded my arms over me to hide my nakedness. Handsome's eyes flared, and the corner of his lips curled into a lazy smile. Exposed, I dropped to my knees on the floor, hoping he saw nothing from where he stood.

I snorted. Men had a sixth sense for naked chicks. No way had he missed my breasts.

When I raised my head a little to see if he still stood there after a long minute that dragged infinitely, Handsome and his perfect family had disappeared inside their cabin.

Heat flared in my cheeks. *I'd flashed a stranger.* Not just any stranger, but my neighbor. I crossed my fingers, hoping I wouldn't run into him or his family again in the next month, or I'd die of shame.

Me and my clumsy self.

4

CARTER

Filling my lungs with the distinctive and addictive mountain air, I was rummaging through the trunk of my SUV when I noticed Dahlia and Jack returning from a walk, sauntering my way. We exchanged grins before I turned to lift Jack into my arms, his laughter, as I spun him around, lighting me up inside.

With one arm, I pulled Dahlia closer and planted a kiss on her temple.

I could feel eyes on me. Jerking my head, I took a look around.

If paparazzi had found a way inside the gate, I would never feel at ease here ever again. Not as long as Dahlia and Jack were with me. When my best friend suggested I install a fence when I bought the lot, at first, I brushed it off as unimportant. With everything that had happened in the last two years and the woman I grew to hate probably perfecting a revenge plan, I had never been so relieved that I'd listened to Dahlia.

A group of businessmen occupied the cabin down the road, meeting once a year for a retreat. They'd been here in the past and had never troubled the peace. Or *my* peace. My sixth sense told me they were not the ones spying on me.

With another scan, I perused my surroundings. Nothing. Still, I could feel the presence of someone close by.

When I spotted no one, I was about to retreat inside when, as if pulled by a magnet, my gaze landed on the second-story window of the cabin next door. I knew a woman had moved there, but I had yet to meet her.

Fervor spread through me.

My heart rate accelerated.

We fixated our gazes on each other for longer than required. For some reason, I couldn't avert mine. She sported faded pink hair and had the bluest eyes I'd ever seen. Azurite embedded in her porcelain visage. Her lips formed a heart, and her cheeks flushed as I took her in.

I stood there, frozen, oxygen barely making it to my lungs as she stood still, and my gaze roamed over her delicate features.

My throat rippled, and electricity traveled through me as neither of us broke eye contact.

Whoever this woman was, she had a pull on me that I couldn't explain or escape from. My body ignited under the weight of her gaze. I felt like we already knew each other. Yet I was sure if we had ever crossed paths, I would remember. She possessed one of those angelic faces that once you saw them, you could never forget.

A buzz tingled my spine. A sensation I'd never experienced before while facing a woman.

My heart flipped in my chest, and I wondered if it was a knee-jerk reaction to the lust swirling between us or something else that I had no idea how to define.

My neighbor parted her cherry-pink lips, and the trance we were under dissolved.

A cold wave replaced the warmth that had infiltrated my chest seconds ago.

When she retreated to the side, the towel wrapped around her caught onto something and fell, exposing her bare chest through the glass. To me.

My jaw slackened. I blinked, making sure this wasn't a dream.

A dark-red hue crept up her cheeks, and she met my eyes for half a second before dropping down and hiding from my sight.

Amusement pulled at my lips, and I stifled a laugh.

"Everything all right?" Dahlia asked.

"Yes. Everything is perfectly fine. I think my stay here will be good for me. Yes, I feel it in my bones."

I cocked my head, trying to catch one more glance of the woman, but all I could see was the pink top of her head.

Reality kicked in, and I wondered if she recognized me and her motives for spying on me were less than honorable or if she was embarrassed.

I hoped it was the latter. A diversion appeared to be what I yearned for these days, and I might have found the perfect woman to keep my mind occupied.

Yes, in that instant, I decided this would be my mission. Find out what her deal was.

Because as it turned out I was in Green Mountain for a while, vacationing, away from the limelight, and except for working on my new album and spending time with my family, I had nothing more important to do than to spy on her too.

With determined steps, I followed Dahlia and Jack inside for our cartoon marathon.

———

The three of us sat by the fireplace, and armed with blankets, pillows, and popcorn, we spent the next hour and a half watching Jack's favorite movie, a story about an orphan dinosaur searching for a new family that would take him in as theirs. In a lot of ways, the storyline fit mine. Sure, I wasn't an orphan, not in the theoretical sense at least, but I was on my own, searching for a place where I belonged. I hoped, someday soon, I'd find my place in this world. For now, I was good by myself. Never again would I put my happiness in the hands of someone else. I had learned my lesson the hard way. As my therapist explained, my living-in-hell years should be classified under life experience. A bump in my journey, not my destination.

Earlier, when I woke up and realized Dahlia and Jack had gone for a walk, I missed the cacophony of having them around. The house sounded too quiet without their chatter between these walls.

When she stayed over, Dahlia often went down the road to call her husband. My cabin had poor cell reception, and by the gate, we always got a better signal. Nick and Dahlia lived a few miles from here, in a farmhouse they bought and renovated after Nick moved to Green Mountain and they got together.

The idea Jack and Dahlia would soon go back home had my heart sinking.

Thanks to their contagious happiness, my family's presence healed every piece of my broken heart. When they were around, everything seemed better in my life. Lighter. Brighter. My anxiety levels dropped, my priorities changed, and all the complicated stuff vanished. Even my smile returned.

Since Dahlia met Nick, they hadn't needed me as much as they used to. The four of us formed this unconventional family. It wasn't always easy, but we made it work. And so far, we were happy.

As Jack settled in my arms under the blanket, a hollow sensation lodged in my chest when my eyes landed on his mama. My thoughts drifted to the baby on the way. Dahlia smiled at me, and it quieted the doubts swirling in my head. Then my mind drifted to the new neighbor I couldn't wait to catch sight of again.

<hr>

After his nap, Jack ran toward me. I picked him up and pulled him close to my chest, the beat of our hearts merging together. Jack had grown so much since the last time I saw him. With his dark hair, square jaw, and melted-steel irises, he was the spitting image of me at his age. Talented, he fed his creativity through music the same way I'd always done. However, the kid also had wit, a focused intelligence I envied, just like my brother Jeff.

His presence brought back all the mixed feelings I'd experienced years ago. The tightness in my chest and throat increased, and I pushed away the memories trying to make a return. No need to dig out the past. It wouldn't do us any good. A few years back, Jeff, Dahlia, and I had messed up. We all did. For a while, it divided us. Pulled us apart. Nowadays, that mistake—with a capital M—had turned out to be a blessing in disguise. If we had a do-over, I wasn't sure any of us would change how it unfolded because if we did, life wouldn't be the same. Still, all the unanswered questions haunted my nights sometimes. One day, I'd be brave enough to deal with the lingering mystery once and for all. Yeah, one day. Not today, though.

At the thought, my airways constricted, making my breaths shallow and difficult.

Calm down, Carter.

Tugging at the flimsy threads of my self-control, I kept my discomfort under wraps and faked a smile, searching for an out. A diversion from my troubling thoughts.

"Hey bud, I have an idea. You know the song we've been working on over video chat? Let's record it," I suggested. Jack's tiny fingers squeezed mine in delight, the slight gesture lighting my heart up like a Christmas tree. Moments like this one kept me going; they kept me alive. Thanks to them, I breathed easier.

Together, we made our way to the home studio, a room I had gotten built by some of the best professionals in the industry. With perfect soundproofing, it had two sections. The first one consisted of a navy-blue couch, two upholstered, matching tan chairs, a small end table, and a console, opening to the recording studio through a glass wall. The smaller room contained two stools and a microphone and a designated area for a drum kit and a keyboard. The walls were pale and the ceiling dark, the hardwood floor the same shade as the rest of the house.

"Ready?" I asked him as we positioned ourselves on the stools, holding our instruments, after I turned the console on.

Jack bobbed his head fast, his smile unfaltering. "Yes. Let's do this."

5

APRIL

"You flashed your tits to some stranger?" Saunders laughed so much it turned into a train of hiccups. "April, you'll never cease to impress me. I'm so incredibly proud of you, girl."

"Stop making fun of me. It was humiliating enough. He was with his wife and child. Can you imagine this? I hope to never come face to face with him again, or I'll die of shame." My cheeks flushed, burning at the thought of meeting my neighbor up close.

"Is he hot? Please tell me he's a fit bloke. I have nothing against nerdy men or average-looking guys, but for your sake, I hope he's smokin' hot."

Sometimes I forgot Saunders came from the UK and moved to the States to attend college. Then she reminded me with her choice of words.

"You don't understand. Hot is too weak an adjective to describe him. I swear I could've gotten pregnant just from looking at him. He eye-fucked me while my breasts hung there, in all their gloriousness. Seriously, this guy is the most handsome male specimen I've ever seen. Pure spank bank material, I'm telling you. He's what fantasies are made of." I fanned myself with my hand as I recalled his gaze on me, heat stirring low in my belly.

"Now I wish I'd come with you to the cabin. Girl, you need to meet him again. It's an order. Take pictures this time. I want to see if your hormones are messing with your head or if he's that good-looking. Besides, it wouldn't hurt to build yourself a glorious male portfolio. Something to indulge in when you feel lonely at night."

"You're impossible." I sighed at the recollection of the man who saw me topless. "He's *that* hot. I'm telling you, Saund, I didn't dream it. You have to see one of these special creatures to believe in them. I thought they only existed in movies. Put him on a motorcycle or in a cowboy hat, and someone will have to sweep my jaw from the floor. Tall. Dark. All testosterone-y. So damn sexy." I gulped the rest of my wine, clenching my thighs together. "Why are the handsome ones always taken?"

"C'mon, because they're hot. Even if they're psycho crazy, women love them because they're a better accessory than any purse or pair of posh shoes."

"In addition to the hotness factor, he's a family man. No woman can resist a man like that. I'll dream about him for the next month, I'm telling you." For a second, I got lost in a daydream. "I bet there was a set of killer abs underneath his shirt. He's the whole package deal. With one glance, he woke up my hibernating hormones. Now I'm all tingly. And giddy. Oh God." Laughter left my mouth. "Damn, I'm objectifying my sexy neighbor. We shouldn't talk about him this way—"

"Don't shut me out, girl. It's good for you to open up. I think you're ready to get back out there. Don't forget to send me a visual. Some pick-me-up fantasy for the dark days. My vibrator and I could really use it the nights Reed pisses me off. By the way, we're not objectifying him. We're only assessing his exceptional features." My friend burst into a fit of giggles, and I joined in, both of us sounding like schoolgirls obsessing over their first crush.

"What about Reed? I know you two were having a fuck marathon the other night when I called you on my way here."

"He wants me to move in with him." Saunders let out a long huff.

"What's wrong? You love him, right?"

"I do. His house is nice and closer to your place, which is a plus."

"Then what is it?"

"The idea of having one penis for the rest of my life scares the shit out of me."

"Reed isn't asking you to marry him, at least not yet, only to move in with him. Believe me, if he's the one, you won't even care he's the last penis you ride."

"You're probably right. I told him I'd think about it." She drummed her fingernails on something, probably her desk. "Anyway, I gotta go. I have a meeting in five. A new client looking for an Amazonian retreat. Keep me posted about your hot next-door neighbor ."

I shook my head in disbelief, unable to stop smiling.

We promised to call each other the next day before hanging up.

Hours later, and with endless energy to burn, I ran to my bedroom and got dressed. "I need some fresh air," I told Bernice when we crossed paths on the staircase. Saunders told me a fence surrounded the lot, and there was no risk of facing a bear if I wandered around.

Dressed in a sleeveless peacock-blue puffer vest over a golden turtleneck sweater and black leggings, I slid my feet into my favorite sheepskin boots.

Once outside, I welcomed the crisp January air into my lungs.

The late afternoon sun's rays cast a glow around me.

My feet orgasmed at the sound of fallen leaves and pine needles crunching under my steps.

I never got to enjoy the full extent of all four seasons in Georgia. This, right here, felt amazing.

Oak and pine trees surrounded the property. The cold breeze wavered their tops and sent a tingle to my cheeks. Whoever said the mountain air was addictive didn't lie.

I rubbed my palms against my leggings, warming them up to avoid the slight tremors before I settled to take a panoramic shot with my phone.

Moving slowly slowly in a full sweep, I captured the beauty surrounding me, the view—mountain peaks covered in snow in the distance—taking my breath away.

"Hey. What do you think you're doing?"

A powerful masculine voice startled me from my left. I turned my head and came face to face with Handsome. Damn it. Up close, wearing a pair of washed-out jeans and a tan corduroy jacket over a plaid shirt, he looked even more gorgeous. In a devastating way. My shaky heart free-fell to my knotted stomach, and my breaths quickened.

My nostrils wriggled at the faint scent of pine, cedarwood, and soap wafting from him. My neighbor even smelled delicious.

I swallowed hard and found my voice. "Are you talking to me?" With a cocked brow, I pointed at my chest with a thumb.

This man meant business, with no trace of friendliness on his face. Attractive and symmetric. Full lips. Straight nose. Melted-steel irises that could swallow me whole. He frowned, the worry lines deepening the storm in his eyes.

"Yeah, I'm talking to you. There's no one else around. Were you taking a picture of me?"

His clipped tone aggravated me. I folded my arms over my chest. "Excuse me?"

"You heard me. Now answer the question. Were you—yes or no—snapping a picture of me with your phone? That's a simple question. You should be able to give me a straight answer."

"I should've figured you'd be a prick. You can't look this good and not be a dickhead."

He squinted before his eyes flared and threw daggers at me. "Why can't you just answer the damn question?"

"Wow, that's an enormous ego you have, mister. No wonder you need a house this big to contain it all."

"You still haven't answered the question."

Why wouldn't he let it go?

The wrinkles around his eyes deepened.

"Why would I want a picture of you?"

"Do you always answer a question with a question?" He huffed his aggravation.

I shrugged. "Are you always this nice to people you meet for the first time?"

My neighbor balled his hands at his sides.

Yeah, I noticed.

"We met earlier. Don't you remember?" His full lips tilted at the corner.

I couldn't believe he went there. I prayed my cheeks wouldn't flush under his scrutinizing gaze. "Nah. You must be mistaking me for someone else. I would remember meeting you if I already had. It's not every day I get the chance to run into a jerk in the woods."

His focus descended to my chest

"By the way, my eyes are up here."

"You think you're a smart ass, don't you?"

I pinched my lips together. This was the most fun I'd had in a long time. "Maybe." I offered him my cheekiest smile.

"Stop wasting my time. Did you or didn't you take my picture?" His words now spewed venom.

I sighed. This man had no right to talk to me like that. "I'm glad we've decided you're an ass. It'll be easier not to talk to you ever again."

Handsome's eyes bulged out, and he gave his forehead a scratch with the side of his thumb. "I'll ask you one last time. Did you or didn't you take a picture of me?"

"No. I didn't. Happy now? I took a panoramic picture of this beautiful view." I motioned my hand all around me. "Being handsome doesn't give you the right to be an insensitive jerk and talk to me like I'm worth less than you."

Did I just call him handsome? *Abort, abort. April, retreat. Don't show him any weakness.* I tipped my chin up, turned on my heel, and didn't spare my hot neighbor another glance.

"You think I'm handsome?" Gone was his annoyance. Amusement now filled his tone.

I stormed away from him. Every word he spoke infuriated me, and I wasn't about to indulge him or inflate his ego any further.

"Just so you know, I'm not an insensitive jerk." The irritation in his voice had dropped a notch.

I glanced at him over my shoulder while I swaggered further away. "You've done nothing to prove otherwise. Sorry, but I'll file you under the asshole category. That's where you belong with your over-dimensioned ego and wrongly aimed anger."

"You have categories for men?" Genuine surprise lit up his gorgeous face. His stare drew me in. He smirked, never breaking eye contact.

My knees buckled under the intensity of his gaze.

"Why not? I think you deserve—" *Bam*. I bumped headfirst into a large, obviously misplaced, oak tree as I turned my head around. I shut my eyes for a second, trying to regain my balance and shake off the dizziness that made my legs feel weak.

"Are you all right, miss?" a small voice asked me in a strong Southern accent.

Blood rushed into my ears and I looked down, blinking. Handsome Neighbor's son was tugging at my sweater sleeve, worry filling his eyes. Where had he come from?

"Yeah, I-I'm good…huh…I think. I hope I gave this tree a big pounding headache. It shouldn't stand in my way." I winked at him, and he giggled.

Handsome Neighbor hurried to join us. "Are you sure you're okay? You seem a little pale. Do you want to sit down for a minute?" He had switched to a softer tone while addressing me this time.

I saw concern swimming in his gray eyes, the shade reminding me of agitated ocean water minutes before a storm. When I stared into them, I drifted away, lost in their depths. Why did everything about my neighbor have to be so damn hot and enticing?

I wobbled on my legs, and he caught me before I humiliated myself further, his strong arms holding me upright. Heat developed where his palms rested on my waist, a sensation foreign to me. Not sure how to interpret it, I pushed away from him and adjusted my sweater, avoiding his eyes. "Huh, I'll be all right. And…and I should go. Sorry for the a-hole comment." I rubbed my forehead with a hand, trying to dissipate the soreness thumping in my skull.

I sidestepped, and dizziness made my head spin. Handsome Neighbor clutched my elbow from behind, and I leaned into him for a quick second. The same warmth I felt seconds ago returned. His touch erased all traces of the uneasiness we shared. Something passed between us, fiery and potent, that sent a discharge through me, but I chose to ignore it.

His hand lingered on the small of my back, and I breathed him in. His smell was addictive—and manly. A part of me wished I could bury myself in his chest and stay there, just to feel his arms wrapped around me once more and the security they provided.

"Miss, why is your hair pink?" the little voice next to me asked, clueless to my inner thoughts. "Is it real? Because my friend Beatrix wants pink hair too. She thinks that it will make her a fairy. If you have pink hair, it means you're a fairy. Beatrix was right. Fairies exist. This is *soooo* cool."

Aware of his eyes on me, I ignored HN's amused gaze. In my head, I renamed him HN. A simpler and shorter version of Handsome Neighbor. Or Hot Neighbor. Or Highly (Annoying) Neighbor. Yeah, HN fit him fine.

I squatted a little to level my eyes with the boy who still watched me with interest and awe, ignoring the throbbing in my head. "What's your name?"

"Jack," he quipped, a genuine smile stretching his lips. He held out his tiny hand, and I shook it, his striking resemblance to HN impossible to ignore.

"I'll tell you a secret, Jack. Beatrix is right to believe in fairies. Life is full of magic. Most people choose to ignore it, but if you look close enough, you'll see magic every-where. My hair turns pink whenever I focus on everything amazing in my life. It makes my days much more exciting. When my hair is blonde, I feel like a grown-up, and my life isn't as much fun. If you believe in magic, it will find you."

His eyes sparkled, and HN mouthed a silent *Thank you* in my direction.

Without another word, HN reached for the boy's hand. My ovaries did a happy dance. "Come on, buddy, I'm sure dinner is ready by now."

"Bye," the boy said with a wave. "Beatrix will not believe me when I tell her I met a real fairy."

I waved back, and as they walked away, I stood there, watching father and son waltz to their cabin, hand in hand, confused and amazed, all at the same time.

At least, from what I saw, HN seemed like a hands-on dad. I had yet to meet the wife. I winced at the thought. She had to be an angel to deal with his huge ego and attitude problem.

I shot Saunders a few quick texts, hoping the reception was better out here.

ME

Met HN face to face.

HN = Hot Neighbor

Wet my panties. Much better than from afar.

Kind of a jerk, though.

Met his son. Sweetest boy ever. Has a thing for pink hair.

Won't be able to send you a visual, though. He got angry when he thought I snapped a picture of him.

Long story. He's not friendly. Just mouth-watering hot.

Come visit if you wanna see for yourself.

I roamed around with the phone in my hand above my head until the chimes announced the messages had gone through.

As I walked back to my cabin, I wondered what my neighbor's panic was all about. With one last glance over my shoulder, I tried to catch a glimpse of him.

In vain.

Once inside, with my back pressed against the closed door, I cupped my heart. I wasn't allowed to fantasize about him. This was wrong. So very wrong.

And yet, even his broodiness ignited my hormones.

Saunders was right. It was about time I got back on the dating scene because having filthy thoughts about my married neighbor was so not the way to go.

The next day, I was sipping tea on the back deck, wrapped in a fluffy blanket, my feet propped on the small wooden table by the jacuzzi when I heard voices next door. I couldn't make out what they were saying, but I swore there was another man in the driveway. Curious about the commotion, I stretched my neck to see what was going on. And who knew, maybe HN had an equally attractive single brother, and fantasizing about him wouldn't be a sin. I slapped myself mentally. Since when did I become a nosy neighbor? Could I blame being isolated here as the cause? Deep down, I knew what the source of my nosiness was. Since the first time I caught sight of him, HN had been on my mind all the time. *He's married, for God's sake.* How many times would I have to repeat that before my mind got the memo? What was worse than dreaming about him was that I didn't even like the guy. I found him attractive, yes. And he ignited something deep inside me, yes again. But then I recalled his erroneous accusations and *assholeness,* and it killed the fantasy.

My neighbor and the stranger hugged and laughed at something. His wife joined them, but instead of cuddling with him, she went to the other man and kissed him.

Wait…what did I just witness? Three of them? I

blinked, not sure what was going on. Were my neighbors…
in some kind of polyamorous relationship? Even though I
begged myself to mind my own business, I couldn't look
elsewhere, waiting to see how the scene would unfold.

Was that why I was asked to sign a non-disclosure
agreement before I came here? Because the sexual activi-
ties of my neighbors were controversial?

Many questions swirled in my head as I watched their
interaction.

The two men exchanged a few words, but I was too far
away to hear anything they said. And I wasn't good at
reading lips.

Jack disappeared into the idling car, then the wife
dropped a kiss on HN's cheek before following the other
man to the vehicle.

Straight back and chin high, my neighbor stood there
as they trailed away, not moving. What did I just witness?
Polygamy wasn't allowed in the United States.

This whole situation was becoming all the more
interesting.

My nose tickled, and before I could hold it in, I
sneezed.

No, no, no. I shut my eyelids, wishing I wasn't about to
get caught spying.

Was my life so not entertaining these days that now I
had to live vicariously through other people's?

When HN's eyes snapped in my direction, I retreated
inside, hiding behind the curtains in the living room.

He cocked his head toward me like he knew I'd be
standing there, and I begged the ground to open up and
swallow me whole when our eyes met.

6

CARTER

Three days into my stay in Green Mountain, Nick picked up Dahlia and Jack. I offered to drive them home, but he was already on his way. "Hey, Carter," he said, giving me a side hug when we met him outside. "You don't look so bad."

I scrunched up my nose. "Well, it's a"—I held in the curse about to leave my mouth—"nightmare I'm trying to navigate out of. I still can't believe I put up with her for two years." I shook my head and shoved my hands into my pockets. My pulse raced just at the thought of the Evil Queen.

"Don't be too hard on yourself. This stuff can happen to the best of us. Listen, if you need someone other than Dah to talk to, I'm here. Whenever. Call me."

"Thanks, man. Shit, I forgot. Congrats on the baby."

A smile lit up Nick's face. One radiating with pride. He had a gleam in his eyes. The last time I saw something similar was on his wedding day. Their baby would be beautiful. I had no doubts. Nick reached the six-foot mark and had tanned skin and broad shoulders from years of working as a carpenter. He had a chin dimple, which I knew Dahlia found cute as hell, and golden-brown eyes. I could already imagine a toddler with his blond hair and Dahlia's green eyes running around.

"Thanks. We're thrilled."

Dahlia inched closer and wound her arms around her husband's midsection. He kissed her, and when they looked at each other, something passed between them.

Love.

My heart sank in my chest. I wanted that. Someone to share my life with. Hopefully, one day, I'd find it. Or it would find me.

To avoid staring at them, I lifted Jack in my arms and nuzzled his neck. "I'll see you soon, buddy. I love you." I kissed his cheek, and he tightened his grip around me.

"I *looooove* you too."

I lowered him to his feet, and he hurried toward the car.

"See you, Carter." Nick clapped my shoulder before following Jack and helping him into his car seat.

"Call me anytime," Dahlia said. Rising on her tiptoes, she dropped a kiss on my cheek and squeezed my arm before following in her man's footsteps.

A sound from next door caught my attention. When I turned, I spotted my nosy neighbor standing on her back deck. Without acknowledging me, she disappeared inside. Was she spying on me?

"Bye." Jack's small voice pulled me out of my thoughts. I spun in his direction and waved back when I noticed his tiny hand through the open window.

In the driveway, standing next to my SUV, I watched them retreating, holding my breath, a piece of me leaving with them.

Even after the taillights disappeared, I stood there, my

hands stuffed in my pockets, a million thoughts circling through my mind. From the corner of my eye, I caught a glimpse of my neighbor through her living room window. Her hair was tied in some sort of a half-do on the top of her head. She averted her eyes and scurried away, leaving me to my own devices.

The next morning, I woke up early, oversleeping not an option with the never-ending night I had. The entire time, my brain raced with *what-ifs*. After breakfast, I locked myself in my music studio, only to emerge thirty minutes later, my brain a blank slate. Restlessness had invaded me after my family left yesterday. I missed them. And I missed the noise. The one preventing my mind from going haywire.

To keep myself busy, I cooked, ran fifteen miles on the small country roads, took a nap, lifted weights.

Nothing distracted me long enough.

Hours ticked by.

The sun disappeared beyond the tree line.

Slouched on the couch in the media room, I ate left-overs for dinner while watching a hockey game, the TV on mute, and dumb scrolling on my phone. What a waste of time. When I stretched my legs, the clicker fell on the floor and changed the channel by accident. It stopped on a late-night gossip show. I leaned forward to grab the remote but stopped halfway when my face filled the screen. Minus the beard and the untrimmed, disheveled hair. *Goddammit.* With the clicker now in hand, I unmuted the TV. Savannah Prince's diabolical eyes stared back at me. I swallowed the pool of acid filling my mouth.

"There are rumors that longtime lovers, Savannah Prince and Carter Hills, have broken up for good. Everyone thought there'd be wedding bells in the next year. Insiders believed Carter Hills proposed during the holidays. A source reported an unexpected pregnancy. Miss Prince, who said in a statement she's still in love with Carter Hills and that he broke her heart, has resumed her activities in Hollywood, while Mr. Hills is nowhere to be found. Another source told us the country music star dumped the actress for a famous model. Sadly, it seems like sex rehab might not have worked for Mr. Hills. We'll keep you updated. In other entertainment news, Pierce Callaway…"

I hit the remote and turned the TV off.

Fucking fame.

I loved the music, hated the spotlight.

Lies, lies, and more lies. Wedding. A baby. Mistresses. A model. Sex rehab. Nothing they reported other than the breakup being final was even close to the truth.

When had my personal life become more important than my musical talent? I loathed scandals. I should've thought about that before linking my name to Savannah Fucking Prince.

By tomorrow, our faces would be plastered on the front pages of every trash magazine around the world. I threw the clicker across the couch.

Breathe in. Breathe out.

Those tabloids spread lies, the same way Savannah Prince spread her thighs to get what she wanted, and people bought that shit without second-guessing anything.

When I dumped her ass, I knew she'd paint me as the bad guy despite all the watertight precautions. Although, with Dahlia and Jack around for a few days, I kinda forgot about all of the shit show.

My eyes shifted to the cabin next door, and I wondered what my neighbor was up to. For reasons I refused to analyze, she kept me on edge. Yep, if I was being honest with myself, this blunt piece of a woman with pink hair intrigued me. There was something about her that appealed to me. It wasn't just the vibrant blue of her eyes that captured my attention and jumbled my heart, her angelic face, or her pink hair. No, it was something more. Her energy. That one time in the woods, we pushed each other's buttons, and it left me with a hard-on. I could've found a smarter way to engage with her than to pick a fight. Juvenile, right? But it worked. I got her attention. Under all the fieriness that infuriated me like nothing else ever did before, she fascinated the hell out of me. She held her head high and didn't refrain from arguing with me. I enjoyed that she was her own person and had enough confidence in herself not to shy away from her opinions. Self-confidence was sexy on a woman. Most women crossing my path tried to seduce me, to take advantage of me. Pixie didn't. She couldn't care less about my name or what I did for a living.

When I caught her after she bumped her head and her knees buckled, I could swear our bodies reacted to each other. A surge of heat had traveled through me, and for an instant, I had found it disorienting because I had no clue where it came from and why it would arise with my neighbor in my arms.

When she confided in Jack about fairies, the sparks dancing in her eyes, the way she spoke to him like his questions mattered, it unleashed emotions inside me. This woman wasn't just fun to banter with, she cared. That made a big difference in the grand scheme of things. I was more used to people demanding than people caring, and the latter weighed more in the balance of my heart.

Fairy hadn't taken my picture that day. I was well aware. For a short instant, I just enjoyed riling her up and having her attention on me. Now that Jack was gone, I couldn't use him as an excuse to meet her anymore. I'd need to resort to new tactics.

I switched positions on the couch, praying I'd see some movements next door so that I could go for a walk and pretend to bump into her. Even though I refused to acknowledge it, I wanted to test a theory. See if the pull I felt for her the two times we faced each other was a product of my imagination or something tangible.

And also, there was a story here. One I couldn't wait to uncover. The reason she had rented a cabin on a mountaintop by herself for a month. Was she running away from something like I was—an ex-boyfriend, a divorce, or her life—or did she need some time off far from the rest of the world? A breather in the hustle and bustle of her everyday life?

If she was hiding, it raised a bunch of new questions in my mind. From what? From who? Did someone hurt or fail her? Did she leave someone or something behind?

When the agency informed me about the last-minute change of tenant a few days ago, I thought this April Simmons would be much older. Never had I anticipated my neighbor would be an attractive woman about my age. I hadn't planned for this, but now that she was here, I was curious. Most people renting my cabins were either older folks or businessmen, not attractive single women under thirties.

Right now, my life was a clusterfuck, and focusing on something, or rather someone else, would be a more than welcome distraction. The moment I caught sight of her bare tits through her bedroom window, I knew she'd be trouble. And yet, considering my rap sheet, it seemed that lately I was seduced by it.

As if someone had heard my prayers, I spotted my neighbor through the living room window. She was struggling to carry a pile of wood to her cabin and looked like she'd crumple under its weight. I rushed out of the media room and crossed the house. In the entryway, I slid my arms into my lined-denim jacket and exited into the night. Humming a song, I ambled her way, my hands stuffed in my pockets, projecting as much nonchalance as I could muster.

"Hey, Neighbor. What a great night, huh? Need a hand?"

If only looks could kill. "Hmm, no. I'm fine." Feisty and proud. I liked that. A lot.

I circled her until we faced each other. "Come on, let me help you." I leaned forward and grabbed the firewood from her arms, which were shaking from the effort. Our fingers brushed, and a zing worked through me, strong enough that it took me by surprise, and I almost dropped the logs in my grip.

Arms crossed and chin lifted, she held her ground with unwavering confidence. "I was fine, just so you know."

I pinched my lips together to avoid smiling and pushed her a little more. "Keep telling yourself that. Someday you might believe it. Don't overestimate yourself. You're drenched from your exertion."

She snorted.

"Thank you would have sufficed. It was my pleasure to come to your rescue. Good neighborhood manners and all that."

"My rescue? I can see your ego is still a problem. Don't hide your superiority complex under the pretense you're here to help me. I won't fall for your schemes. Sorry. Better try something else if you wanna impress me. Because, so far, your attempts are pretty lame. And those big guns of yours aren't cutting it."

My eyebrows shot up. "Lame? I'm the one helping you

out, and you decide it makes me lame? What kind of jackasses do you hang out with? Please enlighten me."

"You know exactly what you did. Don't play innocent. I'm not some damsel in distress." She tipped her chin up, looking defiant. But she couldn't trick me. This woman couldn't hurt a fly. Even when she spewed insults at me.

"Okay, now you've got me confused. Don't mock me with your words. I've met angry women before. Take a number."

A shadow crossed her gaze, so fast I wondered if I dreamed it.

"Anyway, being thankful isn't a weakness. It's just basic civility. You should try it sometimes, I'm sure you'd like it." I smirked. Because I knew it would rile her up even more.

Her eyes rounded for a fraction of a second before she regained her composure—and her angry frown. My words had rattled her. She pointed an accusing finger at me.

"Are you, out of all people, trying to teach me to be civilized? Funny how some people are clueless about what's right in front of their eyes." She eyed me with disdain. "Since the moment we met, you've been insufferable. Nothing but obnoxious. And you think I'm the one with the attitude problem. Enlightening."

My head fell back, and a loud laugh escaped my lips. It released the pressure building up inside me.

She blinked, looking confused. "Why are you laughing? I just told you how I feel about you, and you think it's funny? Something is definitely wrong with you."

"You're cute when you're angry. I didn't know fairies had it in them to be hostile. I'm impressed. You're not as innocent as you look."

"Innocent? You have no idea who I am and what I'm made of." A loud growl left her mouth, and I was pretty sure smoke came out of her nostrils.

"Calm down, dragon, it was a compliment," I teased, trying to ease the tension between us. "Am I not allowed to say nice things to you? Is this some rule I'm not aware of, or are you allergic to niceties?"

Her brows furrowed. Okay, my attempt at being nice had failed.

Without thinking, I inched closer to her and touched her elbow with my free hand, trying to show her I wasn't the bad guy she portrayed me to be.

Our gazes locked. The deep pool of her eyes swallowed me in. Her lips parted, but no sound came out. I noticed the pulse point in her throat pounding, and I wondered if she felt the pull as much as I did. Her tongue swept over her lips, and I followed the movement, unable to look away.

She tipped her face up, and for a quick instant, I wondered how it would feel to kiss her. It was stupid. We didn't know each other, and I'd been burned in the past. I was in no hurry to play with fire again. And yet, every bit of me was attracted to this woman. As if a force greater than us was pushing us together. I couldn't explain it, and it scared the shit out of me. But still, I was too weak to walk away.

A cocktail of emotions filled her baby blues, and as if injected by a truth serum, I babbled like an idiot. "You're beautiful. And I-I'm...sorry." I closed my eyes and reopened them, chastising myself for my bluntness. I cleared my throat and tried a new approach. "I think we should start over." Releasing her, I extended my arm. "Hi, my name is—"

My neighbor's eyes widened, and she snorted before I could finish my sentence. "Sorry? You are sorry?" The short-lived truce between us vanished as an expression of incredulity entered her eyes. And just like that, the spell we had both fallen under shattered. She jumped back, putting distance between us.

I scratched the side of my head. "That's all you heard from what I just said?"

She raised a hand between us. "Stop. Don't try to seduce me. It's too late for you to kiss my ass and pretend you're this white knight in shining armor. You've ruined our neighborly relationship. Don't come knocking if you're out of sugar. I won't have any left for you."

Wow. She had really decided I deserved no second chance. Did I imagine the last minute we shared? I flashed her my best smirk, wrapping my hurt under a layer of humor. "I love it when you're being sweet. Keep going, Bubble Gum. If you're ever out of sugar, I'll keep a cup just for you."

"Argghhhh… I'm not sweet, and I'm no candy. That little thing you're doing, it's not working."

"What little thing? I complimented you, again, and you acted out, again."

"Flirting. And faking being nice. I'm not interested in anything you gotta offer. Here, you can go now."

"Tell me, do you hate men in general or just me?" I asked, now curious.

"I don't… I don't hate men." She dropped her shoulders, looking vulnerable for half a second. "I don't like people in general—not just men—who think they're better than others. I never asked for your help, and yet, you believed I wasn't able to deal with a pile of wood on my own. Assumptions. Those make me upset."

"Glad to know it's a *me* problem, then. Want me to give these logs back to you if it helps preserve your ego? Maybe if I do, we can start over."

"You're so infuriating, you know that? Why would you give them back to me? It makes no sense because you didn't want me to carry them in the first place. Whatever. Go play your mind games elsewhere. I prefer quiet to the sound of your voice. And my cat's company to your face."

"Ouch. You're wounding me."

She averted her eyes. "I didn't mean… It's not… Your face is kinda nice to look at." As if she'd heard her own words, she slapped a hand over her mouth, and her cheeks turned an adorable shade of pink.

"Glad to know my face makes up for my full-of-assumption character. Too bad each time we meet, you read me wrong."

"So far, all you've done is prove to me you are, in fact, an ass. Stop pretending otherwise, and maybe there's hope left for you." A tiny curl of her lips made me believe she wasn't that indifferent to our banter after all. Or I hoped that was what it meant.

"Are you succumbing to my charm?" I asked, unable not to engage with her once again.

"Oh gosh. You're the worst. I said your face was nice, not that you were charming. Big difference."

"But the other day you said I was handsome too. Did you forget about saying that after you bumped your head?"

"It just means I need to stop saying what's on my mind out loud." After a moment, she shook her head, her aggravation back and straining her features. "Just drop the wood on the porch."

With a look her way, I noticed how my neighbor's hands were now balled into fists. I bowed my head and nodded.

·Okay, this was not going as I expected. I thought our banter the other day was hot. And I believed she felt the connection too. Had I been wrong all along?

Sure, our first encounter had been surprising, to say the least, but I hadn't dreamed of the electricity I experienced when our skin connected minutes ago and the way we eye-fucked each other right before I had the audacity to say I was sorry.

A big part of me enjoyed her fieriness and the fact she wasn't making it easy on me to gain her trust. It was a nice change. Too often, in my life, people gave in easily when they realized who I was. I loved how my neighbor wasn't impressed with me by any means. It was oddly refreshing.

With my back to her, I sensed her eyes drilling holes through my clothes. The heat of her gaze sent shivers down my spine—the good kind—and my dick jerked up in my pants. *Easy, boy.*

With her in such proximity, something in my chest snapped. A restraint? A chain? I ignored what it was, but I knew my heart had changed its tune. My body tensed for a quick second before it adjusted to the new rhythm. I watched my neighbor over my shoulder. With her arms folded over her chest, she stepped back, forcing me out of her personal space. I grinned. She frowned. This woman was a ball of attitude. In many ways, she reminded me of June. Except, I wasn't attracted to my personal assistant.

I placed the wood in a neat pile on the porch and turned around, not knowing how to navigate the hate slash attraction vibe simmering between us.

I stuffed my hands in my pockets, not sure what to do with them.

"So." I pointed with a thumb behind me. "You're all set. Want me to bring more in case you go through those by the morning."

Without saying a word, she shook her head.

Her throat worked, and it captured my gaze before I brought my eyes back to her face.

The ire I'd seen on her features since I came over faded away.

Like a magnet pulling me in, I inched closer to her, hoping for one of her feisty comebacks. She turned her head to the side and breathed out, her eyes locked on mine. Baby-blue laser beams. I shivered under their intensity.

"Well…I should go now," I said.

Her attention moved back and forth between my eyes and my mouth.

Before I had time to analyze the meaning, the wind picked up and sent the stray strands of her hair flying.

My mind didn't catch up with my action when I padded forward and brushed the tendrils back. My fingertips skimmed the side of her face as I did, and electric bolts traveled throughout my body. Pixie's scent, a mix of lavender perfume and lemon shampoo, swirled around us and filled my nostrils. She watched me, remaining mute while we faced each other.

As if I'd been tased, I jerked my arm back and let it hang at my side. "I'll return to my place. I know you need no help, so I won't offer anymore." What was I saying? It made no sense. I sounded ridiculous. I should shut up now.

"I'm all good on my own." Her tone was definitive and left no place for argument.

"O-kay."

With her arms still wrapped around her body, she walked me down the steps of the front porch, avoiding my eyes. The tight-lipped smile that grazed her lips displayed the lingering specks of her annoyance toward me. My chest puffed out in response.

"Thank you for this," she whispered, the words tumbling out her mouth like they were scorching her tongue.

My eyebrows bunched together in a silent question.

"For your…huh…unsolicited help."

A grin formed on my face. "You're welcome." I shook my head and waltzed back home. Feeling her eyes still on me, I looked over my shoulder, only to catch sight of her, in full spy mode, peeking in my direction from behind the curtains of her living room now that she had retreated inside. Again.

Okay, this had to be one of the most awkward, yet confusing encounters of my life.

"Guess I'm not the only one who's curious now," I said to myself. She could pretend as much as she wanted, but I'd spotted my neighbor spying on me more than once. She said things, but her actions spoke louder. Perhaps I intrigued her as much as she intrigued me.

From her expressions to her actions, I was certain the lust I felt wasn't just one-sided.

Every time we butted heads, my attraction toward her increased.

I doubted this woman could hold a grudge. From what I'd seen, she lacked a sense of wickedness. Her act didn't fool me, though. Her fake fury only made her more adorable. More alluring. More interesting. It tripled her sexiness. Everything about her captivated me, and I prayed she would crack at some point and reveal her true self. And let me in. For a reason hard to explain, everything about her mesmerized me. From her brightly colored hair to her sass. She held her own, not having a care in the world who I might be. That impressed me, and even at just twenty-six years old, I was hard to impress. Unbeknownst to her, cracking my neighbor's armor had become my newfound mission.

7

APRIL

I woke up and lay in bed for a little while, feeling fresh and well-rested, which hadn't happened in a long time. Bernice padded on the mattress, and getting closer, butted my chin, ready to be fed. "Can you just oversleep for once, sweet girl?"

She let out a loud meow as I patted her furry head. She had no intention of going back to sleep. Traitor.

"Okay, fine. Give me a minute." I stretched my arms above my head, my body swallowed by the fluffy bedding. My smile faltered as I swung my legs over the edge of the bed, disappointed to leave the comfort and warmth of my cozy nest.

While brushing my teeth in the bathroom and glancing through the window, I looked over at my neighbor's cabin. I rolled my eyes, thinking about how we bantered every time we met. Three days ago, he took it upon himself to help me carry wood to keep my fireplace running, and that was kinda nice of him. Until I realized his intentions weren't noble and he opened his stupid—but kissable—mouth. Nobody in their right state of mind could stay indifferent to his full lips. No matter what, HN infuriated me like no one else. Both times we met in person, he pushed my buttons as if he knew exactly what would make me tick. I hated the idea he possessed that piece of information about me. Since that night, I'd been asking myself the same question. Did we really share a moment, or did I dream the entire interaction? The latter made more sense since we had proven so far that we couldn't stand each other. The most infuriating part was that he left afterward as if nothing happened. *Ass.* Still, I had no idea what his deal was. Since they left the other day, I hadn't seen the woman or the child around, which intrigued me more than it should, feeding the mystery surrounding him.

Slipping into an oversized knitted sweater, I was fixing my hair when movements outside caught my eye. Talking on the phone while pacing the driveway, HN appeared like he was about to blow a gasket. Taut features, ramrod straight back, tensed shoulders, his entire being screamed infuriation. Still, my skin tingled as I drank him in. Even angry, he projected confidence. And appealed to the woman in me.

I promised myself I would stop spying on him, but for a reason I couldn't explain, I stayed in the same spot, unable to avert my eyes. HN dropped his head and shook it, then ran a palm over his face, looking dejected. His entire demeanor changed, and he appeared younger. Less cocky. In that instant, I wished I could go to him and give him a hug because it seemed like he needed a friend.

Soon enough, his head jerked back as if he'd been stung by a bee, and his mask of displeasure returned, erasing the vulnerability that had flashed across his face seconds ago.

He kicked the tires of his SUV multiple times, fisting his hair with one hand, his aggravation on full display.

Whoever was on the phone with him was at the receiving end of his wrath. Anger darkened all his features, and I felt even more attracted to him. He was this mysterious, hot-as-hell male and the first one in the last couple of years to get my hormones into overdrive.

HN paced across the pavement, his fury unmistakable, even from a distance.

Without thinking any further, I rushed downstairs, filled Bernice's bowl with kibbles—because by now, her meowing had turned into uninterrupted background noise —and went outside, aiming for my car.

Looking for the novel I remembered leaving there the night I arrived, I rummaged through the console between the front seats. When did I become so lame? Was I really snooping on my neighbor again? I wanted to slap myself. The guy wasn't available, but I yearned to find out why he got so angry when he thought I was snapping his picture the other day. Or why he couldn't seem to stay away three nights ago when he carried my firewood or brushed my hair back. Without trying to eavesdrop on what he was saying, I still heard fragments of his conversations.

He flexed his jaw. His eyes had become a sea of gray lava. He changed direction mid-stride, all his movements jerky and stiff. His magnetism pulled my gaze in.

"…she won't get away with it that easily…"

"…no, I won't do it. Forget it…"

"…and you think I'm not aware this is manip-ulation…"

"…no fucking way. That's not up for discussion…"

"…Never mind. I'm over this craziness. For good…"

I held my breath, trying to make myself as invisible as possible, not wanting my neighbor to think I was listening to his phone call, even though I was kind of doing that. *A little.* I winced. *Not really. Totally.*

He hung up, shook his head, and took two deep breaths, erasing all traces of anger from his model-like face. His eyes dropped to the screen of his phone, and he laughed at something he saw. Or read.

My hope deflated inside me. HN didn't need me as a friend or anything else.

Entertaining thoughts about hugging a perfect stranger, because he looked conflicted, wasn't smart either. It had to stop. No more eavesdropping or trying to catch sight of the man next door.

There. I had a new resolution.

Before he could acknowledge my presence and realize I was a desperate cause, I rushed back inside, holding up a tire pressure gauge instead of the book in my hand. *Real smooth, April.* I dropped my head, twisted my mouth, and creased my eyebrows, feeling so dumb. Why was I acting like a child? I ignored the reason why my neighbor's mood mattered to me. Not wanting to give my erratic behavior too much thought, I made tea, and with my laptop perched on my knees, I settled into the hanging chair, intending to write and forget all about the sexy slash obnoxious, probably married, man next door. After what I witnessed the other day, I now had some doubts about his marital status, which didn't concern me, no matter how tempting snooping around sounded.

"Get a grip," I said aloud. Bernice, who was stretched on her side in front of the window, soaking up the warm rays of the sun, purred. "I'm glad you agree, girl."

Focused on my work, the hours slipped by without me realizing. I emerged from my writing bubble at dinnertime. I patted myself on the back mentally when I realized that in my trancelike state, I had written over thirty pages. I stood to fix myself a snack, and sitting at the dining table, I reread everything. I fought the urge to cry my relief and fist-bumped my cat when I grasped how good this first draft was.

Have I been cured of my writer's block once and for all?

I flopped back into my chair and sighed, a grin pasted on my face. I emailed the pages to my agent and decided to treat myself tonight. I deserved a little fun. I cooked chicken fajitas and opened a bottle of wine. Then I snapped a photo of me with my wineglass in hand and sent it to my best friend.

ME

Getting my groove back (I hope). Cheers

It took almost a minute for the message to go through. The internet connection here was all or nothing. Then, when I didn't expect it, I received a text from Saunders.

SAUNDERS

You rock. Glad the mountain air is helping.
Love you xx

After dinner, still feeling festive, I aimed for the jacuzzi on the back deck. The darkness and absolute silence surrounding me made this night perfect. A bit cold, but nothing the heated water of the hot tub wouldn't fix.

With the bottle of white wine resting on the little wooden table and my glass in hand, I sank my white-string-bikini-clad self in the bubbling water.

A whimper escaped my mouth when my cold skin met the hot water. All my muscles relaxed, and I slipped in deeper.

Mellow country music played on my phone, and I sipped on my wine, gazing at the open sky. I'd never seen so many stars in my entire life. The night swallowed me, and I became one with the starry display. Nothing else around me existed, except me atop a mountain in the middle of nowhere.

I thanked Saunders in my head.

She couldn't have come up with a better spot for a month-long writing retreat slash vacation.

My thoughts wandered from my new book that finally got me excited to my best friend afraid to take the next step with her longtime boyfriend, then to the little boy next door who asked me about fairies, and finally, to Travis, who, I imagined, was staring down at me from a shiny star above.

Raising my glass, I cheered at the sky. "I hope you're happy and safe over there. I miss you."

A star twinkled, and I imagined it was his way of telling me not to worry about him. Travis loved stars. "We're just dust particles, part of a bigger plan. Life doesn't end with death," he'd once said. I loved believing he was right. More than ever, I loved the idea that he lived somewhere out there, watching over me. It somehow lessened the void left inside me that his departure had caused.

A shooting star, bright and glittery, crossed the sky.

Closing my eyes, I made a wish that everything would fall into place in my life.

I had many things to hope for, and they all fit under this big umbrella wish.

Completing my book.

Finding my true purpose in life.

Getting out of my comfort zone.

Falling in love again. True, head-over-heels, *I am yours, you are mine* kind of love.

Health, adventure, fun, friendship, and family.

My ultimate goals.

I'd work hard until I had checked them all.

I yawned. The late hour combined with the hot water had melted away the remnants of my energy reserve.

Craving my bed, I staggered out of the hot tub. My feet slipped on the cold deck, and I held myself steady, thanks to the small table.

The high temperature of the water had magnified the effect of the alcohol in my blood. I was tipsier than I thought I'd be. Off-balance, it took all my might to put the lid back on the jacuzzi. Soon enough, the warmth from the water dissipated. Looking around, the realization hit me. I'd forgotten a towel. *Great.* The winter night was freezing my bones under my soaked skin.

In four strides, I reached the door. Whatever I did— push, pull, turn—it didn't budge. My frozen fingers fought with the doorknob. In vain. *Did I lock myself out?* Bernice appeared on the other side, stretching her body against the glass. "Bernice, let me in. Please. I'm freezing." She purred and sauntered away. "Come on, girl, help me here." My chest deflated.

My fingers shook, turning into popsicles. With my phone in hand, I staggered down the deck and circled the cabin to unlock the front door. Dying from frostbite would be a lame way to go.

The crunchy leaves littering the ground felt like thorns under my bare feet.

As it did on my first night here, the indicator light on the super-sophisticated electronic latch refused to turn green. I placed my hands under my armpits, longing for some warmth. Shaking from head to toe, I tried to focus on my task and the fireplace awaiting me inside. With trembling fingers, I rebooted my phone and tried positioning the device a dozen different ways over the latch. Nothing.

Panic swirled through me. The cold air I breathed hurt

on its way in, and I couldn't stop the tremors shaking my limbs.

As I stood there, half-naked, wet, and freezing cold in the night, with no idea how to improve my fate, I felt minuscule. Thanks to the frigid air, even my thoughts were sluggish now. When I blinked, my eyelashes weighed heavy. With a numb hand, I pushed my damp hair away from my face. Icicles had formed at the tips of my locks. My feet burned from the contact with the frosty wooden porch.

What should I do? I had nowhere to go, no one to call to help me out. Even if I wanted to, I wasn't sure I'd be able to dial my phone, my fingers unresponsive.

Out of options, I staggered to HN's cabin.

Misty clouds exited my mouth with each breath I blew out.

Uncontrollable shivers ran through me.

Each step was a struggle.

My teeth chattered, the sound reminding me of Morse code telegraph machines used in old movies.

My skin was turning blue from the biting cold.

My lungs idled.

I tried to wiggle my toes, but they felt like concrete. Stiff and leaden.

Perhaps I should go back into the hot tub. My energy levels were empty. Even if I wanted to, I couldn't get there. Anyway, it wouldn't help anything but my shivering.

A translucent version of Travis appeared in front of me. He nodded his head. Like he was delivering a message from wherever he was. That I could do this. And survive. And fight.

With one last strained effort and a leap of faith, I lifted my balled fist to knock on the door. Frozen, I'd lost all my strength. The muffled sound of my fist on the wood panel disappeared under my jagged breath.

Hugging myself to stop the shivers, I dropped my forehead on the doorbell button.

Now HN or his family would hear me. *Please, please, rescue me.* My eyelids grew heavier, and I resisted the urge to curl up into a ball on the porch.

Did HN have a spare key to my place? Would he help me out with the stupid lock once my body temperature reached a decent-enough degree?

The door opened. I almost fainted. Black spots danced before my eyes. My vision blurred.

A wall of muscles greeted me. It towered above me by almost a foot.

HN's eyes flared when he noticed me. A worried expression colored his face. "What the fuck. Have you lost your mind?"

I shook my head. "Stupid lock—" I mumbled the words as loud as I could muster.

My neighbor pulled me into his arms, and his heat spread through me. He kicked the door shut and walked me to the living room, positioning me in front of the fireplace. In seconds, I had two blankets wrapped around me. When he sat on the floor behind me, he pulled me into his lap, his whole masculine and intoxicating body circling mine.

Exhaustion spread through me, and I fought to keep my eyes open.

April, you're safe now. My thoughts were still languishing.

In an attempt to send hot blood to my extremities, I wiggled my fingers and toes. I could barely feel my body.

Survive. That was the only word popping up in my head on a loop.

My neighbor fastened his arms around me. *I'm safe.*

The more I warmed up, the more tired I felt.

My blood burned like lava in my veins as it flowed through me.

I buried my face in HN's chest, and the sound of his strong and steady heartbeat rocked me to sleep.

8

CARTER

I sat in the middle of the living room with my neighbor nestled in my arms, the heat emanating from the fireplace radiating over us. Listening to the steady sound of her breathing, the night replayed in my head. How did I end up here?

Before Fairy barged into my house—and my arms—minutes ago, I had spent the evening locked in my home studio, strumming my guitar. The peace music brought me, which had been missing in the last year, had finally found me. For once, I succeeded at shutting out all the noises in my life. The pollution that grabbed hold of my mind way too often these days. Surrounded by soundproof walls, it took me a minute to register the faint sound of the door-bell. Since I was alone in here, I didn't bother closing the door after me when I settled in. I did a double-check when I fished my phone out of my back pocket. *Ten seventeen.* Except for Dahlia, nobody ever visited me this late. Anyway, they had to go through the gate first, which clearly didn't happen just now because only Dahlia, the rental company, and my handyman had the code. The people renting my cabins used an electronic key fob to come and go, and any visitor had to be announced a day in advance to go through the background check. I hadn't received any such notice. Whoever stood on my front porch had no reason to be here and hadn't been invited.

I rubbed my eyes with the heels of my hands. With long strides, I padded through the house, my hands clenched into fists, ready to punch the fucker standing on the other side of the door. I prayed gossip hunters hadn't climbed over the fence to find me. Ready to give shit to whoever stood on my front porch, I stopped myself when my hand clamped around the doorknob. *Don't get into trouble, Carter. It's not worth it.* I swallowed my anger and looked through the peephole. My eyes widened at the sight of my neighbor wearing nothing but a white string bikini, soaked, her hair frosted, and her lips blue.

Seriously? How could she forget to put on winter clothes?

"What the fuck. Have you lost your mind?" I screeched, opening the door, ready to send her back where she came from. I sighed. I didn't feel like dealing with her right now. She'd just interrupted my creative process. I narrowed my eyes and steeled my back, hoping she'd get the message loud and clear.

Her eyes flared, and her lips quivered. No words came out. Her eyes pleaded with me to let her in.

Her teeth chattered, and she shook her head. "Stupid lock—"

All the color drained from her face, and she faltered.

My blind impulse took over, and I wrapped my arms around her. Her small body sank into mine, and the smell of chlorine and lavender filled my nose. The wetness of her frigid body made it through my own clothes.

I held on to her, trying to stop her from shivering.

Without even thinking, I wrapped her in blankets and curled my body around hers, hoping my body temperature would be enough to spread warmth through her so she wouldn't get hypothermia.

Except for Dahlia the other night, I hadn't held a woman in my arms in months.

I had a few rules in my life, but the ones I had, I never backed down from.

Stay healthy. Whatever it meant.

Be there for Dahlia and Jack. No matter what.

And lately, I added, stay the fuck away from Savannah Prince. Or any woman gunning for me.

As much as my neighbor intrigued me and I liked getting a rise out of her, I knew I should keep her at a distance. After the mess I'd just gotten out of, even though I was still set on finding love one day, I wasn't ready for another relationship. Much less with a woman who was just passing through my life. And certainly not one who had all my instincts kick in every time I was in her vicinity.

Fairy, with her pale-pink hair framing her face, big eyes, and luscious mouth, had shattered my walls with one look. When she flashed her tits at me in her bedroom, I believed she might have been after my fame.

After the way she bantered with me in the woods, challenging me, I concluded she was clueless about my identity.

Our argument over firewood the other night confirmed my beliefs.

My face was plastered all over the Internet, magazines, and TV. My neighbor either lived under a rock, or she hadn't been paying attention to the world around her. Either way, I enjoyed being a regular Joe around her. Her spirit and the memory of the way she confided in Jack played with my heartstrings.

Tendrils of her hair tickled my nose.

Buried in my chest, her body grew heavier and her breathing, steadier.

Did she fall asleep in my arms? *Who does that?* I blinked. How could she trust me? We didn't even know each other. And so far, she had proven not to be my biggest fan.

I twisted to look at her face. Yup, she was out of it.

I hesitated to wake her up. Maybe the warmth after freezing so much had messed with her body thermostat or something and she needed to sleep it off to reset it? Or regain her strength?

I was no doctor or hypothermia expert, but I decided letting her sleep could do no harm. I tightened my arms around her, shifting her so that her side pressed against my chest, and I could watch her face for any sign of discomfort.

Entangled together, we sat there for a long time. I was in no hurry to move, in case it woke her up, because I was enjoying this moment of peace between us. Even though I doubted she would remember it once the morning came.

My heart frisked in my chest with Pixie in my arms. Like she belonged there. Like a long-lost puzzle piece, now recovered.

I brushed the crown of her head with my lips as I debated my options. What should I do?

Not ready to wake her up, but needing reassurance her body had thawed enough, I slid my hand under the blankets until my fingers grazed the softness of her creamy skin. A shiver ran through me, and my dick swelled in my pants. I shut my eyes and inhaled. *One, two, three, four.* I exhaled.

Why was my body so reactive to her all the time?

My hand found the curve of her waist and lingered

there for a moment. The contact of our flesh toyed with all my willpower. With a tight grip around her body, I let my frozen neighbor sleep in my arms for the next hour, captivated by the sound of her breathing.

I tucked the wild strands away from her angelic face with my fingertips, unveiling her delicate features. Plump lips, button nose, soft-angled dark-blonde brows—probably her natural hair color—thick eyelashes.

Out cold, she looked serene and didn't budge when I tried to wake her up. With a gentle movement, I lowered my hand down to her throat. Her pulse beat at a regular pace. Our heartbeats synched, and a deep sigh escaped my lips.

I should send her back to her place. Or ask for explanations.

Instead, I tightened my grip around her, refusing to let go of her.

I tried to convince myself that keeping her here was a bad idea. I didn't need the complication the morning would bring, and still, my gut won the tug-of-war against my reason.

Ready to go to bed and clueless about the right course of action, I shifted to my feet, and with my neighbor still asleep in my arms—the woman was a lightweight—I climbed the stairs to my bedroom. I laid her on my king-size mattress, wanting to look after her in case she struggled in the middle of the night. One by one, I examined her every finger and toe. None of them was still cold or blueish. The only thing I knew about hypothermia was that it affected the extremities first. My current assessment confirmed she should be okay.

Relieved, I tucked the blankets around the woman in my bed, undressed to my boxer briefs, and slid under the sheets on the opposite side. No woman had ever slept in this bed with me, but somehow, the idea of her sleeping here didn't freak me out like it should have. Lying on my side, I propped myself up on my elbow, the heat of my body rising and making my breathing harsh, at a loss, unsure how to act. Should I pull my neighbor in my arms or were the blankets enough to keep her warm? A part of me, the one that made no sense, itched to hold on to her like my life depended on it. To be her knight in shining armor as she once accused me of. The other half knew it was a bad idea.

Unable to make up my mind, I scanned the room, but soon my eyes returned to her silhouette. My neighbor stirred in her sleep, and I waited, all my senses on high alert. Her eyelids fluttered, and she stretched her body, but never woke up. I let go of the breath I was holding and relaxed. Extending my arm, I turned off the bedside lamp and fell onto my back, still wondering how I ended up sharing my bed with a stranger.

I grimaced, ran my hands over my face, and finally gave up the idea of pulling her to me. Flipping over to my other side, after making sure she was still out of it, I closed my eyes and chased sleep.

———

The next morning, I woke up with my neighbor's body entangled in mine. Tendrils of her pink hair spread on my skin. Her soft breasts, under her white bikini top, pressed against the side of my torso. With my eyes closed, I breathed her in.

Fuck. How did this happen?

My thoughts froze in my head at the idea I would have to explain our predicament to her as soon as she woke up.

I held my breath and wiggled to get out of bed, but Pixie's arms tightened around my midriff, and she moaned. *Kill. Me. Now.* Her breaths tickled my skin. I exhaled through clenched teeth, enjoying the feeling, but fearing her reaction. If it turned out to be anything like our previous interactions, no doubt it'd be explosive.

Why did I strip down to my boxer briefs last night? I should've slept in pajama pants with a T-shirt on. Or on the couch.

My neighbor's eyelids fluttered open, and her baby-blue doe eyes locked on mine. I offered her a tight-lipped smile and a small shrug. Like a sixteen-year-old caught staring at a girl he had a massive crush on.

Half-awake, she let out a loud shriek, and cold sweat pearled on my nape.

Stay calm. Explain everything. You cared for her. She can't get mad at you. You did nothing wrong.

"What did you do to me?" she asked point-blank, propping herself up.

I hopped to my feet, anger building up inside me.

What happened to keeping my calm? Breathe in, Carter.

"Relax, Pixie." I held my stance, unyielding. "Why would you assume I did anything to you? I saved your ass last night. You came to me, remember? I watched over you the entire night to make sure you wouldn't lose your fingers or toes after your spectacular hypothermia scare, which you still need to explain to me."

A dark blush colored her cheeks when her gaze scanned my body. I rubbed my jaw with my hand before pulling a pair of gray sweatpants on. No doubt my neighbor had a full-frontal view of the outline of my morning wood, my boxer briefs doing nothing to hide my erection.

She surveyed the bedroom, looking anywhere but at

me. Until a deep frown creased her forehead and her cheeks turned a shade darker when she realized she was only wearing that ridiculous tiny bikini. Guess we made a great pair. In one swift movement, she pulled a blanket and fastened it around her half-naked self.

With bed hair and a sleepy face, she looked younger in the morning light.

"Why am I in your bed, hooked onto you?" The muscle in her jaw flexed, and she folded her arms over her chest, mirroring my stance, her eyes flashing with challenge, her face set in stone—a look she had mastered perfectly as if she'd been roughened up by life before and had to learn to stand up for herself.

My breath sounded like a whistle when it caught in my lungs. "Christ, did you hit your head last night? Would you have preferred I let you sleep on the couch in a house you might not even remember coming to? Maybe I should've let your toes and fingers fall off—"

Pixie's gaze dropped to her hands. My eyes flared when, one by one, she counted her digits. And then her toes from where her feet peeked out from under the blanket. I bit my lips to avoid laughing. After a deep sigh, she brought her attention back to me.

"Listen, I'm sorry for snapping at you. I don't know you. I don't even know your name, and I woke up in your arms, in your bed. Put yourself in my shoes for a minute. That's awkward." She tucked her hair behind her ear, and her features softened, chasing her troubled expression away.

I resumed my normal breathing. Desperate to cover up, I snagged a dark hooded flannel shirt from my closet and buttoned the front. "I'm just the guy next door. I'll fetch you something to wear and help you get back inside your cabin."

On the second floor, I rummaged through Dahlia's stuff and came up with a cream sweater and a pair of gray yoga pants, before rushing back upstairs.

"Is your wife going to be okay with my sleeping in your bed and wearing her clothes?"

A laugh, loud and harsh, escaped my mouth. "Wife?"

"You know, the person you share your life with, the mother of your child, the pretty redhead I saw you with."

"Did you spy on me, sweetheart?"

"Don't ever call me *Sweetheart*." Her eyes threw bullets at me, and I lifted my hands in surrender before me.

"What's up your britches, lady?" I asked.

Her eyes rounded. "Who says that?"

"You're unbelievable. Let me say it again. Don't get your panties in a twist, lady. There. Better?"

"Don't patronize me."

"Geez, relax already. It's not even nine o'clock yet."

Her tone hardened. "Where's your wife? Or maybe she's your mistress and the boy, your love child? You guys look like you have one of those open relationships. Not that I'm judging. I'm only stating the facts."

Fury boiled in my veins. Whoever Dahlia and Jack were to me didn't concern her. I tugged at the roots of my hair and paced the room to calm the fuck down before I blew a fuse. I had endured another woman talking shit about my family for two years. I wasn't about to let anyone else express their nasty opinion about them. Much less a woman I'd just met.

"Stop talking. You have no right to say anything bad about my family. They're all I have. I don't need to explain them to you. Don't disrespect them ever again." The words bruised my tongue on their way out. "Did I make myself clear?" I dragged my hands down my face, unable to settle the wrath bubbling inside me.

My neighbor neared me and placed a hand over my forearm. The tension building in my shoulders evaporated under her touch. "I...I'm sorry. I didn't mean to upset you. They're obviously important to you. By the way, your son is adorable. He has your eyes."

Her words pierced my heart like swords, making me bleed inside. How could she have read the situation and concluded they were mine? *My* wife. *My* son. *My* eyes. She couldn't know what kept me up at night sometimes. All those secrets hovering over me I had yet to address. A surge of unwelcome heat rooted in my stomach, and I placed my hand over my chest to quiet my throbbing heart.

The woman, standing inches away from me, infuriated me, and I should get her back to her place and keep my distance from her for the rest of her stay. We were done playing games. She wasn't worth the trouble.

Every time she opened her mouth, it stirred up all the things I worked hard to keep settled inside me.

Fifteen minutes later, armed with her cell phone, I fumbled with the digital lock on her front door. When it refused to unlock, a few curses left my mouth before I could reel them in. "This thing is useless."

Now dressed in Dahlia's clothes, Fairy stood beside me, arms crossed over her chest, lips pinched together, a frown creasing her forehead. I wondered whether her annoyed demeanor was her usual stance or if it was reserved just for me. "I told you it's not working. I'm not tech-savvy, but I can tell when something is broken." She lifted her chin, her defiant expression unwavering as we locked eyes.

"Yeah. No kidding." I returned to the latch and grumbled as I fought the urge to tell her to shut up. She could keep her sassy attitude and her *I told you so* to herself right now.

After a few attempts, the stubborn lock gave up the fight, and the light flashed green. I blinked. *Finally.* I studied it for a minute, as if the reason it'd been difficult would appear by magic. *I should get it looked at.* I made a mental note to reach out to my handyman later.

"Don't worry. I'll get someone to fix it. I know a guy… Hopefully, today." I couldn't risk a repeat of last night. Fuck that. Without asking, I entered the cabin and pounded across the first floor toward the rear door. It was locked from the inside. Fairy didn't lie to me last night. I silenced a sigh of relief. She'd genuinely locked herself out of her cabin. "I'll ask my guy to change the back door deadbolt. Just in case," I informed her when I returned to the living room.

The cabin smelled like her. Lavender. Soft music played on a wireless speaker on the kitchen counter. A sweater and two pairs of socks lay forgotten on the couch, while five empty mugs cluttered the coffee table. Without being a slob, my neighbor had made the cabin hers. It pleased me that she felt at home here, probably more than it should. Instead, I should call her on that. Surveying her mess once more, I decided it was better and safer to think of her as untidy. Yeah, untidiness grated on my nerves, just like her. Couldn't a grown-up woman pick up after herself? If I noticed all the things that annoyed me, I wouldn't be tempted to get to know her better. It sounded logical. At least in my mind.

When I turned around, I took in the sight of my neighbor bent over a few feet away, stacking wood in the fireplace. My gaze lingered on her backside before I caught myself and stepped closer. "Let me help you with that."

She turned around as if she'd been burned and crossed her arms over her chest. Again. That had to be her signature move. Guess I wasn't special after all. "Who do you think you are?"

I blinked twice, her cockiness making her irresistible. "The guy helping you out. Now move, I'll start the fire."

"I thought we already concluded I *don't* need your help."

"So how do you explain last night? You knocking on my door and needing my warmth? Me saving you? What would you have done If I hadn't been home?"

She growled.

"Yeah. You would have been screwed. I fucking saved your life, Fairy. Kill that pride of yours and admit it."

She shot to her feet, planting her heels with the kind of defiance that needed no words. "Ohmygod, are you one of those sexist males who think women are idiots and that we require you, Neanderthal specimens, to save the day? Please, tell me you're not that dumb."

"What? I never said that."

She murdered me with her blue laser beams and harrumphed. "You implied that since you're a *man*, you're better at dealing with the fire than *I* am. And the last time I checked, I'm a woman. Which means you think men are superior."

"Are you high? I only offered because I was being a nice neighbor and was happy to help you out. Jesus, woman, sheathe your claws. It's too early for your little tantrums." There, I said my piece.

Red clung to her cheeks. "For your information, I'm a very capable woman, *HN*, and I can start a fire by myself. We're not in the fifties anymore, in case you didn't get the memo. And by the way, last night was a one-time thing. I didn't plan on having to warm up at your place. Don't get used to my asking anything from you."

"Go on, play your own hero. Why would it be so bad if

you needed someone else's help for a change? I understand you have one of those egos, but don't you think you're overreacting?"

"Easy for you to say. You don't know me. Stop judging."

"I'm not. I'm trying to understand." I angled my body to face her and crossed my arms over my chest, mirroring her stance. Why was everything with this woman a confrontation? Couldn't she let go for once, or did she have to always have the last word? Lifting one eyebrow, I asked, "HN? What does that even mean?"

"Whatever." She stamped her foot like she was defending something. "It's none of your business."

"I wanna know. Spill it."

"I won't. See yourself out." She pointed in the direction of the front door with her chin.

I huffed. This woman enraged me to no extent. "Tell me, and I'm out of here."

"No way. I'm not telling you." *Really mature.*

With a step forward, I shrunk the gap between us. "You know you're infuriating, aren't you?"

"Not my problem, *HN.* You're the one acting like an ass."

"No, you're the one implying I am." I paused for a second before using her own words against her when I added, "You think I'm handsome, that I have a nice face to look at, and that I'm an ass. You think you've got me all figured out, huh?" I let the words sink in. "You're wrong. I'm not an ass."

The woman clenched her teeth, fury radiating from every pore of her petite frame. "Then stop acting like one, *HN.*"

"I swear I am not."

A grunt slipped from her sassy lips, the words garbled.

"What?"

"You're also a jerk, you are obnoxious, and you think too much of yourself."

"Do I?" The air between us frizzled.

With a pout, she nodded, conviction never leaving her face.

"You were quick to run to me last night, though. I bet you didn't think I was an ass when you jumped into my arms, did you?"

Those blue laser beams closed in on my face, and an audible groan escaped her mouth.

The sound reverberated deep inside me. "So, now you're speechless. After insulting me, of all things."

"Don't take my silence for weakness. I'm just not sure if you're worth my anger…and my words. Still debating here." She tapped the side of her head with a finger. "One moment, you're nice and the next, you're a prick. Decide. Here and now. Which one are you?"

I tipped one eyebrow, giving her my most charming, panties-melting smirk—the one I knew women couldn't resist. "Why can't I be both?"

The woman facing me clenched her hands and groaned once more. "Ohmygod, you're impossible. Why can't you act like a grown-up and stop messing with me? And you just said you weren't an ass. Wow, impressive," she shouted before turning on her feet, about to stomp away.

Not ready to end our banter, I added, "Yeah, leave. You're the one acting like a petulant child."

She halted, and from where I stood, I noticed how her fingernails dug into her palms.

She sighed. "I'm not a child. I'm just trying to be the better woman here and walking away." When she spun around to face me, her eyes glistened. Not with tears, but with something much more intense.

"Okay. Prove it. Only a child would bolt in the middle of a conversation."

Her nostrils flared. Her eyes got so big I thought she'd popped an eyeball. "This is no conversation. It's just that your thinking you're smarter than me." She relaxed her hands. "Anyway, I've got nothing to prove to you. I'm not the one playing stupid games."

"You sure about that?" I asked, eyeing her. "There's no shame in admitting defeat or asking a man for help. Isn't that what you did last night? God, I thought you were a wise woman."

She brought her fists to her hips. "Ugh. And I thought you said I'd figured you all wrong." She cocked a brow, and I sucked in a long breath, trying to cool down, every inch of my body sizzling under the intensity of her gaze. We were now facing each other, both panting, neither of us bold enough to break the silence.

My gaze traveled from Pixie's blue eyes to her pink mouth and lingered on her breasts, focused on the movement of her chest with each intake of air. My entire body stiffened. Yeah, every part of it. I felt lightheaded. Was oxygen even reaching my brain anymore? Everything about this girl sent my body into a blazing mess. I wanted to hold all her attention and have my name lingering on her lips. She tsk-tsked, and I brought my attention back to her face.

Her cheeks had turned a dark shade of red.

Cast under her spell, my eyes locked on hers.

Holding her stance, unflinching, she blinked but never looked away.

A fat minute passed.

Her gaze turned to heat—scorching heat. Hot enough to melt all my defenses, and any retort hanging on the tip of my tongue.

Her breathing accelerated.

She parted her lips, and her tongue grazed the rim of her mouth.

The fury that had colored her face until now faded.

Her eyes roamed over my features, gave me a slow once-over, then locked back on mine.

Particles of electricity swirled around us. Time stopped as we faced each other without another word.

I was transfixed, nailed to the floor. Air barely reached my lungs. Even swallowing turned out to be a challenge. My mouth was dry. My wild heartbeat was all I could hear.

Frustration and lust mixed together.

"I can't stand you," I said, my voice lacking conviction.

"You are the most infuriating human being I've ever met." Her pupils dilated, and for once, her words didn't sound like an insult.

My throat worked, and her stare dropped there.

From where I stood, I noticed the pulse point in her neck quickening.

Neither of us motioned to leave.

Fairy's eyes darkened until they were almost midnight blue. If I were scared easily, I'd run for my life, her hold on me growing by the second.

Awareness bloomed on my skin, and I shivered under the weight of her dedicated attention.

Without another word, I stepped forward and erased the distance between us. Pixie gasped when my hands connected with her hips, and I lifted her up in my arms. Her legs wrapped around my waist holding me against her at the same time I crashed my mouth on hers.

I devoured her lips like I depended on them to stay alive. I took a handful of her firm ass cheeks as she moaned against my mouth. She played with the hair at the back of my head, and a croaky groan passed my lips.

Unapologetic, I cupped one of her breasts over her sweater, and she melted under my touch, her body fusing with mine. The image of her bare chest the other day flashed through my mind. Her tits felt fuller in my hands than how they'd appeared from a distance. I'd been obsessed with feeling them from the moment I got a peek of them almost a week ago.

She nipped my bottom lip and my earlobe. I curled my hand around the back of her neck, angled her head, and ate her mouth like it could satisfy my hunger. The tips of her fingers dug into the skin of my shoulders.

In one swift movement, she peeled the sweater off. I caught it and tossed it on the floor. I tugged at the loose string of her bikini top with my teeth and untied it, leaving a trail of kisses on her chlorine-scented flesh. The tiny piece of fabric joined the sweater at my feet.

I tightened my hands around her waist, and I feared it'd leave bruises on her pale skin.

I flicked my tongue over her hard nipples, one at a time, and feasted on them, tasting, licking, and biting her flesh. Pixie arched her back, begging for more.

"Fine, you're not a child," I whispered, breathless.

She moaned in response, shattering every restraint I had left.

My dick pulsated in my pants. A surge of warmth coursed through me.

The image of her body clenching around my shaft increased my arousal. My mouth watered at the thought of her sweetness lingering on my lips while I ate her up.

Our tongues entangled together, and Fairy sucked on mine. For a half second, I watched her. Her eyes rolled back in her head before they captured mine. Enough to confirm she needed this as much as I did. I plunged my hand into her bikini bottom and swept my fingers over her wet center, so ready for me. I slipped one digit inside her tight channel, her flesh feeling like velvet around mine, and her inner walls tightened. I licked the corner of her lips, swallowing all her whimpers. I spread her wetness over her folds, and rubbed her clit with my thumb as I entered a second finger inside her, gliding them in and out, helping her ride the orgasm building deep in her core.

Pixie's body clenched over my digits as I bit on her lower lip, her lids fluttering close. Her ecstasy coated my fingers. Not wanting to jizz in my pants, I focused on my breathing. *God, it's been too long.*

The woman dissolved in my arms, and I drew her into me as pleasure rippled through her in soft waves.

Her big blue eyes, with flecks of green, drew me in when they opened, taking me hostage. I panted, at a loss for words, admiring all her beauty. Plump lips. Flushed cheeks. Swollen breasts.

Smart. Sexy. Sassy.

My neighbor checked every box on my *Ideal Woman* list.

For a minute, nothing else existed but us.

All the tension in her body faded, and she turned into a puddle in my embrace.

She blinked when she came back to her senses, and it broke the daze we had fallen into.

She pushed my shoulders with both hands. "Put me down."

I complied.

She stepped back.

"What the fuck, Fairy?" I asked, my cock throbbing inside my pants, my control hanging by a thread, in desperate need of a release. "We're just starting." My eyes zoomed in on her reddened lips, and I wondered how they'd feel wrapped around my dick, licking and sucking me until I saw stars.

She raised her hands in the air, annoyed, ready to murder my aroused self. "Don't touch me. You might have a wife and a kid. I won't be the girl you cheat with. No way. You may be hot, but you're not worth it."

Yeah, I thought the same thing about you ten minutes ago.

I would've thought the mention of Dahlia and Jack would get my dick to surrender. But no. The storm in my neighbor only made it harder.

She pulled at my sanity every time she opened her damn mouth, but it made me crave her even more. Damn, she looked fucking adorable when pissed at me.

"I thought we'd already ruled this out. Listen to me. I don't have a wife. And I don't have a kid."

"You're impossible. God, you're such an ass. I hate liars."

I stepped forward. Pixie stepped backward. Two could do this dance. I had all day—and nowhere else to be—except buried balls-deep inside her.

"I'm not lying." And now I had to justify myself.

"Huh, I saw you with them. You know, while you ogled me. You're a pig, HN. I can't believe I allowed you to touch me. Must be the aftermath of my hypothermia. My brain hasn't thawed yet."

I neared her, invading her personal space, forcing my eyes to stay on hers, while they kept wanting to drift to her full lips and naked chest. "I want to fuck your dirty mouth right now and fill it so tight you won't be able to say another word. I want to be deep inside you until you forget your own name and only remember mine."

Her eyes widened, and for a second, I thought she'd slap me.

"I made you come. You make me come. It seems like a fair deal, don't you think?" I raised my brows at her.

I extended a hand in her direction, my palm upward, a

gesture meant to settle the peace between us. Now a cock-block, my neighbor balled her tiny hands on her hips, a superior air etched on her flawless face.

At six feet five inches, I was at least a foot taller than this woman.

"Come on, Pixie, don't be a prude. You know you want me as much as I want you. My dick here is tired of waiting for you to give up your protest."

She gasped before flipping me the middle finger and spinning around on her heels.

"Tell your dick it won't happen. Not in this lifetime. You're such an ass," she growled, and I rolled my lips over my teeth to avoid smiling.

Hiding her bare tits with the sweater she picked up from the floor, she left me in the middle of the living room, speechless and with my lower self hard and pulsing, and darted away.

Angry Woman, that's what she should be called right now, slammed a door behind her.

"You keep saying that. Believe whatever you want."

No reply.

"I'm not done with you, woman," I said mostly to myself. "No. I am not."

I stood in the middle of the room, hoping she'd come back. In vain. A yellow cat neared me and arched its back. I squatted to pat its head. "Hey you. What are you doing here?" The feline purred in response and butted my leg, pushing me. "Okay, fine, I'll go."

The cat and I ended up in a staring duel. After a minute, it turned its back on me and followed the direction to where my upset neighbor had disappeared. I clenched my teeth and pounded through the cabin, my cock still hoping she would change her mind and give it a chance to prove itself.

What's wrong with these people?

Wait, did I just consider a cat a person? Fuck. I was more screwed than I thought. With fury boiling in my veins, I let myself out and slammed the door behind me, ready to take my dick out of his misery myself. *Yeah, right now, I considered it a person too.*

9

APRIL

"Who does he think he is? He toyed with me, then thought I'd suck his dick like a perfect housewife? He might be married, though the jury is still up on this one. Ugh, he's such an ass. I was right. I don't care how hot he is. He keeps arguing he's not a jerk, but he's never proved me wrong."

Saunders snickered. "I can't believe you let your hunk of a neighbor finger you. Girl, you should've told me all you needed was a change of air. It's about time you come out of your shell. I'm so proud of you, Bubble Head. My girl has finally graduated from Slutty School. You're getting your groove back."

Wrath sliced my words. "After everything I told you, that's all you have to say, that you're proud I almost let a complete stranger, one who drives me nuts, by the way, fuck me." I huffed a loud sigh. "Did you forget he could be married?"

"Gosh, he told you he wasn't. So, I don't see a problem."

"Listen to you. You're ridiculous. HN acted like a

prick. He thinks he can do whatever he wants." I paused, my body so tense it could rip at the seams. "Not with me. He'll never get his dick in my precious mouth. Fuck him."

My friend giggled, and my anger left me. I slouched my shoulders forward and buried my face in my hand.

"Does he kiss like a god?"

"Better. I've never been kissed like that in my entire life. It was animalistic. He possessed me with every flick of his tongue. I swear I could've come only from his lips on mine. And from what I felt, he's huge down there."

Saunders whimpered. "Oh yes, that's exactly what you need. A big dick to get back in the game. I think your HN is the perfect specimen to help you reach that goal. You've been alone for far too long. A real man's touch will do you good. You need some human connection. Some flesh on flesh. If he fucks like he fingers, you're in excellent hands, girl. Hang up. Put on something sexy and a thick coat of red lipstick. Go ring his doorbell. And suck his dick. He's worth it. You'll thank me tomorrow."

"He's *maybe* married, for God's sake. He looked cozy with that woman. And stop saying I'll thank you for everything good happening in my life, Saund."

"You should. Your publishing contract, the cabin, your hot neighbor. When was I ever wrong? I'm your voice of reason. Your guardian angel. You need me to push you to do things you're too afraid to do on your own."

"Okay, fine. Send yourself flowers. Put the same effort you put in my love life into your own relationship. Stop screwing around with your man. If you love him, move in with him, and stop avoiding any kind of commitment. You're better than this. Take the next step."

"I know Reed is perfect for me."

I grinned, glad the focus had shifted away from me. "He is. And he loves you. Always has."

Saunders and Reed met the same night I went on a horrible blind date two years ago. They actually met because of my disastrous date. Their love story made this night one to remember.

———

"Saunders, I don't do blind dates. And I'm not looking for a boyfriend."

"Bubble Head, go on this one date. Do it for me. Just put your-self out there for once. I know you're not ready to date, but meeting new people won't kill you. And who knows? Maybe you'll get a new friendship out of this. You've been pretty lonely since Travis. If you promise to give this guy a chance, I promise to save you if he's an arsehole. Deal?"

I forced a breath out through gritted teeth. "Okay. Fine. I can't believe I'm doing it. This is crazy. I'm so not ready."

"I know, but you need a first time. The next will be easier."

I closed my eyes and mouthed to myself, Sorry, Travis. You know Saunders, she won't give up. I love you. *I kissed my fingers and directed them toward the ceiling. Then I brought my atten-tion back to my best friend. "Let me get the details, and I'll let you know. Not sure I still love you, though."*

"I know. Trust me. You need this." We hung up, and I threw a pillow across my bedroom.

Why did I agree to have dinner with——? Wait, what's his name again? Oh yes, Paul. The first time I texted him, tears streamed down my face. Somehow, I felt like I was betraying Travis.

I sat across from Paul in the restaurant, a glass of Chardonnay in hand. Everything about this night felt forced. Even my smile. Paul wore a light-blue sweater and beige pleated pants. He parted his light brown hair to the side. Why did Mrs. Mayers, the old lady living down the street, match me with her nephew? We had nothing in common. He sat there with a stick in his ass and a cocksure grin. The pants alone should've been a hint to run away.

Before I even finished my appetizer, I texted my girlfriend.

ME

9-1-1. It's HORRIBLE. Please, please, please get me out of this.

SAUNDERS

Coming. Hold on. You got yourself a blighter?

ME

YES. Hurry. Dying here.

My best friend entered the restaurant less than five minutes later and strode into the upper-end Italian bistro, ready to create a diversion.

How? Had she been waiting in her car all this time?

In perfect Saunders fashion, she caused a scene to remember. Our gazes met for half a second, the fire already burning in her hazel eyes. The one telling me my date was in big trouble. My best friend put her best game face on, grabbed a glass of red wine from an adjacent table, walked toward us, and started yelling at my date.

"Paul, are you kidding me right now?" My date's eyes widened, and his forehead wrinkled. "You're cheating on me with this"—Saunders turned her head toward me—"this skank. I hate you." In one epic motion, burned into my memory forever, my best friend hurled the drink in the guy's face.

"Miss, I think you've got me mistaken for someone else," Paul protested, wiping the dripping red liquid from his chin with a cloth napkin.

"No. You're a bugger. A cheater. A womanizer. Get out of here." My friend took a step back and pointed at the entrance. My date wasn't brave enough to argue with a crazy-acting Saunders. He lacked not only balls but decency too. He tossed his napkin on the table, and

without even excusing himself, he pussyfooted away with his head hanging low, under the stares of the entire restaurant.

I felt bad for the guy, but not really.

Paul kept disparaging women like we were still living in the nineteenth century. "Women shouldn't work." "Women shouldn't vote." "Women are only good for raising children."

I tried to express my point of view, but he cut me off every time with a flick of his wrist, his opinions ingrained in his fundamental values. Jerk. I could've picked up my purse and left, but I preferred to let my best friend give this guy a run for his money. He deserved a lesson in humility.

Saunders dropped into the seat facing mine and smirked my way. "So, what are we having for dinner, girl?"

I pursed my lips to avoid chuckling.

Soon after, things took an unexpected turn.

The man Saunders stole the wineglass from neared our table, sat next to my friend, and offered her a fresh glass of wine. He had light-brown, almost gold, hair, and bright blue-green eyes. He must have been a little over six feet and was lean, his shoulders not wider than his hips. He looked handsome in his black slacks and silver-gray button-up shirt, rolled to his elbows, with the top three buttons undone. A silver watch with a thick black leather bracelet adorned his left wrist. The guy had a smart, successful, no-nonsense look in his eyes.

"Here. You deserve this. I think I'm in love. Do you believe in love at first sight?" He cocked an eyebrow at Saunders. "You were amazing. A superhero, sexy and badass, coming to your friend's rescue. That guy was a dickhead. No offense. He deserved each drop of the wine—my wine—you threw at him. I forgive you."

They clinked their glasses and forgot all about me. The guy held out his hand. "I'm Reed, by the way."

"Saunders," my friend said with an enormous grin, almost Joker big.

"Wow, you can throw your wine at me any day if you let me take

you out on a proper date. I promise your friend will never have to barge in and save you."

The rest was history.

———

When I hung up the phone, my head and heart had reached a new level of insecurity. Saunders was wrong. I wouldn't make a move on HN.

For the rest of the day, I immersed myself in my writing, and in just a few hours, I'd written four more chapters. Being angry and sexually frustrated helped my focus, and it made creativity bubble up inside my head. Who would have thought? My fingers typed on their own, and I got lost in the words popping up on my laptop screen. No time to reread anything, too busy trying not to miss a scene, an expression, or a line of dialogue.

After dinner, afraid to lock myself out again—the locksmith guy HN called hadn't come yet—I ended up in the giant, freestanding bathtub instead of the hot tub.

Small candles flickered around the room, plunging the bathroom into semi-darkness. The moon, half-full, shone through the window. The trees danced under the winter breeze.

I added some bubble bath and two drops of blood orange essential oil to the hot water and soaked my body.

With all my attention centered on my breathing and my eyes closed, I tried to put my mind to rest.

My lips mouthed the lyrics of the song playing on my phone.

My mind swam between Saunders back home and HN next door. I wondered what his deal was. The other day, he barked at me in the woods because of a stupid picture, then helped me out when I struggled to stack the firewood, and last night, he cared for me like I belonged to him. This morning, he did everything to push my buttons, then he ate me up as if he'd die without a taste of me.

Like I was the oxygen he needed to breathe. Even his broodiness when he argued with me or was riled up played with my hormones. Was I that sex deprived? *Maybe. Yeah, no doubt I was.*

I contoured the rim of my mouth with the tip of my index finger, reminding myself how HN's touch felt on my flesh. How intoxicating his kisses were. I parted my lips and licked my finger, my tongue circling the tip slowly, making me ache in all the right places. I sucked on my digit while my other hand traveled down my body. Stopping at my breasts, I rubbed a stiff nipple between my fingers, fancying his hands playing with my skin. My hand lowered further down, and I spread my thighs to make room for it.

The climax built inside me, ripping at my core as I dipped one finger into my moist center, smearing my wetness all over my aching self. My sensitive bundle of nerves throbbed under my soft touch.

I dived a second finger inside me and thrust them in and out at a slow dizzying pace—the same way HN did earlier—the heel of my palm grazing my clit with each movement.

I hiked one leg over the edge of the bathtub, giving me more space to pleasure myself.

My spine arched, shivers tracing each vertebra, electrifying my every cell, rivers of ecstasy furrowing inside me.

My swollen clit vibrated, and a jolt of pleasure, raw and powerful, tore through me.

I removed the finger from my mouth and brought my hand to my swollen breasts instead, kneading and pinching, seeking a second release.

My hips moved in sync with my fingers as they hit the sweet spot inside me, over and over, consuming me.

As a loud moan escaped my lips, I threw my head back, and the orgasm shook my entire body. It took me a few minutes to regain complete consciousness.

The whole time, I pictured Hot Neighbor in my head.

Damn it, how could I be so screwed up?

———

The next morning, HN still haunted my thoughts. I'd been flipping over the entire night in my bed, unable not to think of him. I cursed at myself. When I accepted the offer to come to Green Mountain, it was to clear my head. To get my creativity into high gear and pen the first draft of my new novel. Not fantasize about some unavailable man living next door.

I grimaced because I was really doing good…great even…

Until him.

Now I feared my creative mind had left me once again.

Only HN occupied the corners of my brain. And my dreams.

My hormones took over. The bathroom mirror, when I showered earlier, reflected the image of a sex-deprived horny teenager back at me.

Dilated pupils.

Rosy cheeks.

Plump lips.

Swollen breasts.

And it didn't even take into account my state of arousal and my need to rub myself with anything at any time. When did I get so horny?

Last night's pleasure session in the bathtub didn't cut it.

I needed a penis. Flesh. The real thing. Stamina. Warmth. Thickness. Arms around me. Fingers tangled in my hair. Lips to kiss. Eyes to drown myself in.

The guys renting the cabin facing mine were all business-type people over fifty. They wouldn't do it. I double-checked them, just to be sure. No, none of them would cure me of my constant state of arousal.

Pacing the living room, restless and unable to stay still for a full minute, I slipped my feet into my sheepskin boots, wrapped a blanket around my shoulders, and stood on the front porch, relishing the mix of cold winter air and hot sun's rays caressing my skin. With my eyes closed, I took a full breath in. Exhaled. And started over again. There. I could feel the peace and quiet spreading through me and erasing the throb that was wreaking havoc on my body. Another inhale and I blew out the remaining of my angst.

I enjoyed the sunshine on my face a bit longer before opening my lids.

All my zenitude dissipated when I locked eyes with my broody neighbor standing a few yards away from me, his hands shoved in the pockets of his denim jacket. The deep frown wrinkling his forehead made him look lethal. But the intensity in his gaze could set the house on fire. The mix of the two sides of him played with my hormonal state and sent packing my newfound calmness.

Leaning my head backward, I shut my eyes and prayed my mind had conjured him and he wasn't really there, watching me. I craved space away from him—for my sanity—and every cell in me he troubled with his presence. In vain. When I brought my gaze forward again, he hadn't moved.

I sighed and fastened the blanket around me. "Why are you here?" Could he sense the disdain in my voice? "I was having a great day. Why did you have to spoil it? I'm not in the mood to engage in a battle of wills with you. Scram. Go back to whatever it is you do, and let me be. Not interested in taking part in your childish games today."

"Oh, you're sassy even at an early hour. Shame on me. After the rant yesterday morning, I should've guessed. My bad."

I killed him with my eyes. "Are you done? I have a big day in front of me, and you are disturbing my energy… and my peace. Again, leave me alone. Want me to spell it out for you? Go bother someone else." I flicked my wrist toward his cabin. "Go. Now."

He stayed put, not moving a limb.

I growled my dissatisfaction. "Ohmygod, you're so annoying. What do you want from me?"

He shrugged. "I was coming back from running errands and saw you there. I thought you had locked yourself out once again."

"Oh." I relaxed a bit. "I..huh…I have not. I just needed some fresh air. You know, I-I was suffocating inside."

"Ok, then. Thanks for letting me know. Being friendly and welcoming in the morning isn't a skill you have mastered very well. I'll be aware from now on."

He turned to leave, and somehow, for reasons I failed to understand myself, it upset me.

"That's it? You came over here to check on me. Instead, you spied on my little calm-myself-down routine, then you throw an insult my way, and you leave? Don't you have anything better to do with your time? Where's the fight in you?"

He halted and spun around so fast I was startled, then padded in my direction. He climbed the two stairs leading to the front porch and stopped, bringing his eyes level with mine. A smirk curled the side of his lips, a contrast to the menacing image he projected otherwise. "Tell me, Fairy, you want us to fight?"

His proximity sent a wave of neediness through me. Why couldn't I stay indifferent to this man? I squirmed at his closeness and tried to hide it under a shiver. Being that close to him did nothing to quell the arousal that had been plaguing me since our kiss.

He gave me a slow once-over, as if he was aware of the effect he had on me. His smirk widened, and I screamed inside. I refused to let him see through me.

"You didn't answer the question. It's really something you should work on because you're failing at the basics of a conversation."

Anger radiated through my being. "You're condescending. Take a good look in the mirror before accusing me of lacking communication skills."

His deep baritone laugh worked through me.

"What's so funny?"

He shook his head. "You. You let yourself believe you're all rough and tough when you're fairy tall. It's cute. Really."

I stepped forward, eating every inch of distance between our bodies. "Don't talk about me like you know me. You have no idea what I can and cannot do."

HN's face neared mine, and I held my breath. "I love it when you get angry. It's kinda hot." Before I could add anything, he leaned forward and spoke into my ear. "Bet you touched yourself replaying our encounters, right? Tell me I'm wrong." He angled his head, watching me, waiting for me to say something.

Instead, I stayed mute. What else could my neighbor read on my face? Was I so predictable even a stranger could perceive my inner thoughts?

"See? You can't deny it." His mouth returned to my ear. "I'll see you later then." Before he stepped back, his nose traced the side of my face, leaving goose bumps behind.

Tremors invaded me. I closed my eyes, trying my best to maintain my composure. Biting my lower lip to stifle a moan, I said nothing, unable to form coherent thoughts. Until his small action registered and I pushed away from him, my eyes fully open now. "Did you just sniff me? What kind of a sick psycho are you?"

HN climbed down a step, a red hue coloring his cheeks. "Stop mixing your fantasies with reality, Pixie."

I growled under my breath. "Stop pretending you know better." Without another word, I twirled around and returned to the safety of my cabin, deciding to put him in my rearview mirror once and for all.

———

Curled in the hammock chair, a cup of hot chocolate in my hand, and Bernice dozing in my lap, I prayed this would heal me from my horniness.

"Hot chocolate is supposed to heal everything," I said out loud, mostly because I needed to believe it. Badly.

My mind wandered, needing a distraction. Unable to sit still, I got up and went for a walk. I trapped my cat in the first-floor bedroom and jammed the back door with a rock, to prevent it from shutting completely. The fresh air stung my cheeks, and the tip of my nose tingled under the crisp breeze.

Bathing in the cold late January sunshine, I did a few yoga poses. Warrior one, warrior two, triangle pose. I welcomed the flow of energy coursing through me.

Energized, I jumped, stretched my legs, raised my arms

over my head—my fingertips tickling the clouds—bent over, rotated my hips.

Warmer and calmer, I roamed down the path leading to the gate, the fallen leaves and pine needles crunching under the soles of my boots, twirling on myself with open arms, letting the mountain air flush all my fears, uncertainties, and dirty thoughts away.

Upright, standing a dozen feet away from the cliff, I closed my eyes and let the sounds of nature rock me to peace.

When I came back, the front door of the cabin was wide open. What the—I'd locked it when I left.

Panic knotted my stomach.

I skulked toward the door, my hands clenched in fists, ready to defend my five-foot-three self against an intruder. Or a bear. Could a bear break in? *No, silly.* In elementary school, Nana used to tell me I should project assurance even if I lacked self-confidence when I doubted myself . "Fake it until you make it," she used to say. Now I'd be strong and fearless. I put my Mighty April suit on and padded toward my cabin.

My hand relaxed, and I blew out a sigh of relief when I noticed HN, kneeling, stacking wood in the fireplace. My eyes took in his firm ass through his low-cut jeans, the ridges of his back muscles underneath the light fabric of his long-sleeved black cotton shirt, his muscular hand holding the poker. He looked younger with his dark hair untamed and messy, like he'd run his fingers through it multiple times. His focus stayed on the burning wood, and I studied his square jaw, still cloaked in the same dark stubble from yesterday. It seemed he hadn't shaved in quite a few days.

My hormones kicked in, and I felt like eating him for lunch.

HN whirled around, and I snapped out of my daze.

Our eyes met, and I swallowed hard, at a loss for words, my mouth hanging open.

His stare burned holes in me, and I steadied myself against the wall. His Adam's apple bobbed, and I blinked, wanting to avert my gaze. Impossible. My lips pursed, but nothing came out. Handsome Neighbor stepped forward, and I sucked in a ragged breath.

His own breathing quickened. His pupils dilated, and for a second, I thought he'd make me come just by the way he eye-fucked me.

With his single gaze in my direction, I soaked my panties. It should be illegal to be that hot. That male. That enticing. *Take me. Play with me. Fuck me.* I blinked my dirty mind to silence.

His stormy-gray irises, now a shade darker, liquified me. I became a puddle at his feet, burning for him to touch me, to fuse my skin with his, to eat me alive.

I blinked again.

Smitten, with his glazed eyes full of need, I took a step in his direction. I lost all control over my body. Like a magnet, HN's was my lodestone, the one with whom I'd readily clash. The sexual tension between us had grown tenfold since yesterday. The air around us was electrified. We risked catching fire with every breath.

He prowled forward, eating up the space between us.

He grazed his bottom lip with his tongue.

My eyes flared.

We got lost in our own world.

He was about to swallow me whole, and I had no intention to put a stop to it.

On their own, my feet carried me forward, but I halted when someone cleared their throat behind me.

"Hey, how is it going? It's been a long time." A small,

chubby man stomped in our direction, his face flushed and a wolfish grin playing on his lips. "Sorry to interrupt. The door was open, and since you said I could come by anytime this morning, I didn't ring the bell. I hope it's all right."

HN approached him, and they exchanged a handshake. My neighbor found his composure in a heartbeat, like we weren't about to rip each other's clothes off ten seconds ago.

"Your timing is perfect, Desmond." HN coughed. "The wireless lock is giving the lady here some trouble, and the knob on the back door needs to be checked. The other night she got locked out of the cabin in the cold."

"How are things back home?" Desmond asked, opening a red toolbox.

HN shrugged and stuffed his hands into his pockets, raising a wall around him, clearly not in the mood to discuss his personal life with the man.

Desmond bent down and peered at the back door lock. "Let's not take any chances and just change the deadbolt. I might even have a spare one in my truck. Can you check for it? Back shelf. Third row on the left."

HN disappeared outside, and I forced a smile at the man eyeing me a bit too closely. I hugged myself and offered him my best fake smile.

Soon enough, HN came back empty-handed. "Desmond, you're out of luck, man. No spare lock in your truck."

"I'll come back another day to fix it then. Let me just look at the front door first. These high-tech latches are fickle sometimes."

"You don't mind if I stay here while Desmond does his thing?" HN asked me in a low voice, his warm breath tickling the shell of my ear.

I shook my head. No way would I stay in here alone with this Desmond guy. I hated when some men stared at women for no apparent reason. It made me feel self-conscious. So, not a fan of people staring at me. Neither did I enjoy engaging with unknown people or starting a conversation with them. Except for my neighbor. I couldn't seem to resist bantering with him. He, too, seemed to have no problem breaching the walls I'd erected around myself. In all honesty, if the attraction wasn't mutual and parts of him didn't appeal to the woman in me, I wouldn't let him get close to me either. For some reason, though, I enjoyed his attention and our face-offs, so I let it slide.

But the handyman wouldn't get a free pass. Glints shone in his eyes when his gaze collided with mine, but I wasn't interested in him. Nope, there was no lost lust there.

Keeping a neutral expression, I spun around and aimed for the kitchen. Nothing like putting as much distance as possible between two people and not carrying on small talk to show your nonexistent interest.

With my back to the guys, I busied myself making tea. HN joined me, and his hands brushed my hips from behind for a nanosecond. The simple touch made my heart bounce in my chest and ignited my skin. I sucked in a shaky breath and swallowed a gasp, keeping my gaze down, not wanting my neighbor to witness the effect his closeness had on me.

10

CARTER

Desmond stared at my sexy neighbor like he craved a piece of her. I noticed. Fuck him. Not under my watch. She was destined to be mine. Our mutual attraction had reached new heights, and suppressing the sexual tension between us now seemed impossible. Every fiber of my being crackled around her. Not touching her became less bearable each time we were near each other.

Now that I knew how she tasted and felt, I was hooked. I needed more. A lot more. Her scent was my drug, her lips my kryptonite.

If I didn't stake a claim, Desmond would try to get into her pants. That I knew. I was a man too, and I'd known Desmond for years. The guy was a player.

He'd been my on-call handyman since the day I bought my first cabin in the area. With the small resort I'd created here, I needed someone I could trust to do all the small work and make sure everything stayed in order.

Desmond proved himself to be that guy.

The man didn't care about my celebrity status or the

money in my bank account. For all the work he did around here, he charged me next to nothing. Each year, I thanked him with an expensive bottle of scotch on Christmas Day.

His wife died a couple of years back, and I'd seen him in action multiple times, trying to charm the ladies down at the dive bar on the outskirts of town where I hung out from time to time.

My sassy neighbor had everything he had a boner for.

Petite and delicate, with curves to fill a man's hands.

Enough edge to banter with me endlessly and indisputable sex appeal to bring any man down to his knees.

Big, bright blue eyes and a gorgeous smile that could melt Antarctica.

Pixie was dynamite in our little town.

Dangerous and mesmerizing.

Even Jack fell under her charm the other day. And he was five, for God's sake.

Fairy busied herself in the kitchen, and my hands met with her hips before I could think about what I was doing. A sense of calm washed over me like a wave on the shore. It felt like the natural thing to do, as if we'd rehearsed this dance before.

My hands brushed her hip bones, and I wasn't even sure she noticed. I pulled myself together before she could say anything. She avoided my eyes, keeping herself busy, but I caught the faint blush coloring her cheeks.

I had this urge to be close to her but feared scaring her away, not in the mood for another one of her angry ramblings.

Go slow, Carter. Baby steps.

My lips itched to kiss hers. There was no way she would agree if I simply asked. I'd learn my lesson. It was better to let our sizzling attraction do the work for me. That, she seemed to have no problem resisting.

"Okay, here's the thing," Desmond explained, disrupting my daydream. "I'll be able to fix the back door, but there's something wrong with the front electronic latch. Unfortunately, I don't keep any in stock. I can order a replacement, but it'll take a few days. Those things are tricky."

"Can we still use the front door in the meantime?" Did I say *we*? Fuck. I slapped myself mentally.

Baby steps, Carter. Focus.

"Sure, but I can't guarantee it won't act out again."

Pixie stood beside me, her arms folded. "I'll stay in. I have nowhere else to go anyway." She shrugged. "I'll jam the back door with a rock just in case if I go outside." She swiveled on the balls of her feet and walked back into the kitchen. My eyes widened in awe. Nothing ever seemed to bother her. Except for my attitude.

I bet something, or someone, had hardened her up. Made her tough. I saw it in her eyes. A few times already. A dark shadow. Sadness. Or fear. And resolve. I couldn't decide.

"Okay, I'll come back in a day or two. Will call you beforehand." Desmond let himself out after waving at me over his shoulder.

An idea flashed through my mind.

A perfect way to break the extra layer of ice that had settled between Fairy and me after we made out yesterday.

Getting her doors fixed would probably earn me some brownie points—important, sure—but I needed something more immediate for now.

I excused myself and went back to my place to get everything ready.

Later, I rang her doorbell, my hands full. A lopsided smirk stretched my lips. My neighbor greeted me wearing skinny jeans so tight it looked like someone painted them on her, making her curves even more delicious than I remembered, along with a black metallic top. Her feet were bare, her toenails painted in a golden hue.

My jaw popped open at the sight, and I asked, spellbound, "Are you going somewhere?"

A hint of a smile bent her lips as she twirled a strand of pink hair around her forefinger. I grinned. Like a fool.

"No. Remember, I'm stuck here. I felt like dressing nice for a change, that's all. I've been wearing my share of sweats and leggings since I arrived in Green Mountain."

"You look beautiful."

With her chin, she pointed at my overflowing arms, choosing to ignore the compliment. "What's all that?"

"Huh, I forgot. How do you feel about the real estate market?"

"Wait. What?" Her brows knitted together, confusion spreading over her face. Her blue eyes glistened, the sparks emphasized, thanks to the shimmery gray eyeshadow and her thick, mascara-coated lashes.

"Since you're stuck here, I thought keeping you company tonight was the least I could do. I brought dinner and Monopoly. Hence the real estate market interest." I quirked one brow, waiting for her to invite me in.

Her soft laughter rippled through me. "I'm here every night, HN. Being stuck at home doesn't faze me." She crossed her arms over her chest, tipping her hip forward, unimpressed. Her eyes remained on me, giving me a slow once-over, a tiny smile curving her lips.

Okay, she liked what she saw. I could work with that.

She searched my gaze when she asked, "Unless it's you

who can't fathom the idea of spending a night on your own?"

I loved the challenge in her defiant tone. Fucking turn-on. I repositioned my stance to ease the tension in my groin.

"Yeah. You caught me. I need a five-foot-tall, pink-haired woman to look out for me in case a broad-shoul-dered, three-headed, six-eyed alien lands here tonight. Or a grizzly bear."

Fairy chuckled, and I joined in.

"I'm here. Ready to defend you with my five-foot-*three* height, by the way, against hardcore criminals who may want to attack your weak ass." She straightened her back. "I'll let you in on one condition."

"Name it," I agreed, ready to dye my hair blue and howl at the moon if she asked me to.

Her shoulders tensed, and she narrowed her eyes. "And this is the moment you tell me the truth. No bullshit."

I nodded, a million thoughts running through my head, splinters of ice lining my spine. Did she know about me? Was she about to expose my lie by omission and confront me about not being honest about my identity? Adrenaline shot through my system, and my blood pressure soared. I rolled my shoulders back and held my breath, ready for her to deliver the punch.

"Is the redhead your wife?"

What? I stumbled back a step. The tension in my back vanished. *That* was her question? Okay…I was safe.

"Why does it matter? You're interested?"

"Answer the question. I won't have dinner with some-one's husband."

"I'm not married. Never have been. She's my family, but I won't explain her to you. Not yet at least." My grip tightened around the pot in my hands. Telling her about

Dahlia would put my anonymity in jeopardy, and I wasn't ready to throw myself under the bus just yet.

"And this is the truth, the whole truth, you swear?"

"I promise you she's not my wife or my girlfriend."

She studied me for a minute, her lips pinched in a thin line, her jaw set, and her brows wrinkled, looking like one of those tiny Angry Birds. With a sigh, she moved to the side and opened her arms to invite me in. "Then come on in, big guy, make yourself at home. I'm starving, and you mentioned you brought dinner."

In my head, I high-fived myself as I kicked the door shut.

One point for me.

I breathed easier, and my body warmed up at the thought.

"Wine?" my neighbor asked as I dropped everything on the kitchen counter once she lifted the board game out of my arms.

A wireless speaker set beside a small essential oil diffuser played soft music, giving the space a cozy, homey vibe. The fresh scent of lavender filled my nose, and I relished the atmosphere the setup created.

"No, thanks." I shimmied out of my jacket and adjusted my navy-blue plaid shirt I'd rolled at the elbows. "I'll stick to water." A song of mine, "Forever," started playing, and she hummed the first notes. My body tensed, and my back stiffened. "Country music fan?" I asked, doing my best to busy myself in the kitchen and avoid staring at her.

"I love just about any music. But country soothes me. There's something about it." She shrugged. "I must sound silly." She swayed her hips. "I love this song."

A tight feeling gripped my chest, and I forced out a breath.

"Why don't you relax while I set the table? Everything should be ready in ten minutes."

She neared me. "Oh, this smells good. And it looks divine. Gnocchi?"

"Yeah. With tomato pesto. Here," I said, bringing a piece to her mouth with a fork. "Taste it."

She pursed her lips, blew on it, and took a bite.

Fucking hot. Not the food. This woman was a vision.

Fairy licked her lips but forgot a little drop at the corner. With a sharp intake, I wiped the smear of red sauce with the pad of my thumb and brought it to my mouth. She bit her bottom lip, and I thought I'd die of a heart attack. Lust clung to us, making us its prisoners. Before I did something my whole body was burning to do, I stepped back. The knuckle of my thumb found my forehead. My pulse quickened.

I was dying to finish what we started earlier, but I refused to make a move and spoil the evening.

My neighbor lowered her gaze. "Thanks. This is delicious. I'll set the table while you finish up here." She poured herself a glass of Chardonnay and chugged half of it in one mouthful. Soon color crept up her cheeks.

Why did I think coming here tonight was a good idea?

I plated our food and added fresh herbs from the container set on the windowsill to give it a chef's treatment. With a step back, I admired my work and smiled. Yeah, that looked good.

When Jeff turned eighteen—I was fifteen—Mom gave us cooking lessons for months. She feared he would only eat takeout in college. She told us people ate with their eyes, so my brother and I learned how to present our food in a tasty way. Now I'd mastered the skill. It was useful when I wanted to impress a girl. Yep, it worked every time. It didn't hurt that I liked to cook either.

I placed both plates on the wooden table, along with the bottle of wine, where Pixie had already set two glasses of water. She lit up a white candle centerpiece while whistling a song I didn't recognize.

"What are you singing?" I asked as we sat on either side of the table, the candle projecting shadows on the wall behind us.

"Oh, that? An old jingle from a cereal ad I watched too many times when I was a kid. Every now and then, it pops up into my mind, and I can't get rid of it for days."

She grinned. I grinned back. Tonight, it looked like someone had tattooed a permanent smile on her face. All the restraints I saw every other time we crossed paths had melted away. I loved every second of it.

I lifted my glass. "To our first dinner."

Fairy clinked her glass with mine. "And to greater—"

"Company?" I asked, hoping she would agree.

"That's what I was about to say."

"Oh, I can read your mind." I took a sip of iced water.

With her elbows propped up on the table, she studied my expression. "Let's see if you're a mind-reader." She drummed her fingers on the wooden surface. "My favorite color."

I snorted. "Pink. Duh."

She cast a glance up. "Duh. Really? What are you? Ten?"

I laughed along with her. "Sometimes I wish."

"Let's try again. I have a tricky one."

"Bring it on." I clasped my hands together.

"What's my favorite perfume?"

My lips stretched into an easy grin. "Come on, you can do better than that. Lavender."

Fairy watched me with a surprised expression. "Why? How? You noticed?"

I shrugged. "Did you forget you slept in my arms for hours the other night?"

She hid her face in her palms.

I extended an arm and pushed her hands away. "Don't."

"It's embarrassing." She shivered at the reminder. "Gosh, I was so cold. I thought my toes would fall off."

I took a gulp of water and leaned back in my seat. "Well, it could have been worse. I'm glad you're okay."

We exchanged timid, tight-lipped smiles.

"And you got mad when you thought I sniffed you earlier? Don't forget that." I winked, and she shook her head, laughing. The sound clear and contagious. "I guess I'm forgiven?"

"So, you are admitting you took a whiff of me this morning."

I lifted both hands between us. "I'll never admit nor deny it."

"And yet, here I was thinking you were a reformed ass."

"Stop trying to pretend I'm not charming."

She flushed.

"I think it's a good thing you love pink so much."

"Why?"

"Because. It looks good on you."

Her lips separated, but no sound came out.

I extended my arm to rest my hand on her forearm. "Let's eat."

Fairy spread her napkin over her lap. We studied each other for a beat, exchanging smiles and something more potent I couldn't define. Whatever lies she tried to feed herself, our relationship wasn't neighbor-like anymore. Had it ever been? If the charged air surrounding us was any indication, we'd burst into flames by the end of the night.

As the first bite crossed her lips, a sound that I could only define as a deep-throat cry of pleasure left her mouth. It sent a signal right to my groin. I coughed, trying to keep my composure. "Having an orgasm?" I covered the lust I could barely contain with a tease.

"*Mouthgasm*," Pixie replied with a huge smile. "It's creamy and tasty, what's not to like, right?" She dipped a fingertip into the sauce and brought it to her mouth before sucking her digit clean. Another whimper filled the silence.

I blinked multiple times, still unsure if I heard her right. When I parted my lips to speak, she winked. She fucking winked as if it was all a game to her. Right then, I almost shot my load in my pants. Was this woman for real? I hadn't had sex in a very long time, and her dirty little games were screwing with my sanity.

"Keep doing what you're doing. Don't stop on my account." I brought a forkful to my mouth, trying to busy myself—and my mind—to avoid thinking about other creamy and tasty things I could provide her with.

The sound of my neighbor's voice brought me out of my filthy fantasy. "Tell me the truth. Are you a chef? Because you cock like one."

She pinched her lips together, and her eyes grew big. Mine did too. Did I hear her right, or was my mind so screwed I was imagining words she didn't speak out loud?

She sipped her wine, avoiding my gaze for a second, then corrected herself. "No, what I meant was *cook*. C-O-O-K. You *cook* like a chef. Gosh. Sorry for the slip-up."

"Don't be," I mumbled.

"What?" She dropped her fork, staring at me.

"Nothing. I'm happy you like it and enjoy the creamy texture."

She blushed darker, and her hotness multiplied. Did she look this irresistible on purpose?

I smirked, then lifted my water to my lips. "No, I'm not a chef. Maybe I should rethink my career choice."

Fairy regained her composure. "Please. If you do, let me invest in your business."

A loud laugh escaped my lips. "You can't stand me, but you wanna invest in my business?"

"I'm not kidding. This tastes amazing," she said, pointing to her food. "And I have to admit, you're not always being an ass."

A broad smile lit up her face, and my knees weakened under the table. "If only I'd known the way to a compliment was through your stomach, I would've cooked for you days ago."

She scrunched up her nose, and I freed the laughter bubbling inside me.

The rest of the dinner went down smoothly. I was in no rush for it to end, and by the look of it, Pixie mirrored my thoughts. The entire time, I fell under her charm a little more. I pushed back my chair and started clearing the table. When she motioned to follow, I stopped her with a raised hand. "Let me. What about some Monopoly now and some dessert later?" I quirked a brow.

"You brought dessert?"

"Sure did. I told you, I'm not just a handsome ass. I can also be a gentleman." I watched her from the kitchen. "Unless you want me to feed you a treat right now?"

She coughed her wine but regained her composure quickly, the tilt of her lips matching mine. "All good. I'm full. And we, women, prefer when the pleasure lasts. Sure, a quick fix is satisfying…on occasion. But enjoying what's good for a little longer is usually worth the wait." As if she just didn't fuck with my mind—and my throbbing dick—she moved to her feet and offered me a blinding smile.

What did happen here? Was I dreaming the entire night?

How could all the words she spoke sound so dirty to me?

We set up the game on the coffee table in the living room and sat on pillows. My neighbor placed the half-drunk bottle of wine beside her on the floor after refilling her glass.

Her eyes sparkled in the dim light. Keeping my hands —and my mouth—to myself was sweet torture. How could the connection between us be so effortless? Like we'd known each other inside out. Like we'd been friends for years.

"Okay, HN. I hope you're not a sore loser because I thrive at Monopoly. And I'm heartless."

"I'd expect nothing less from you. But never underestimate me. I was a real estate shark in another life."

I winked.

She gasped.

I threw the dice.

Pixie switched the playlist for a jazzy one. Everything about her oozed sex. She was so easy to get addicted to. Her laughter rippled through me, and her scent left me dizzy. A mixture of lavender, fruity shampoo, and happiness. Something exclusively hers.

From the fleeting glances she cast my way to the shimmer in her eyes, I noticed everything about her. The woman loved the game. She was fierce and unapologetic.

"Eight hundred dollars, HN. You'll see, I'll wreck you." She held out her hand.

"Please do," I whispered under my breath. "I'll give you everything."

She ignored my innuendo, but her face flushed, proof she'd caught every word that left my mouth.

Her features told me everything I needed to know. A twitch of her eyebrows meant she was about to pay me a large sum of money. The gleam in her eyes appeared each time she had the upper hand. Her lips curved whenever she cashed in on her properties. We weren't playing Monopoly anymore. We were playing self-restraint—at least I was.

I bet she knew the effect she had on me, even without catching sight of my erection under the coffee table. A fever stirred beneath my skin, and every inch of me felt it. In my mind, I pictured myself laying her on the kitchen table and cherishing every inch of her flesh with my tongue. She would ride me to oblivion, and I'd pound into her with purpose, shattering both our worlds. Or maybe she'd wrap her lips around my shaft, and I'd forget everything, my only goal to coat the back of her throat with my cream. Fuck. I swallowed, hopped to my feet, and made it to the kitchen. I refilled my glass of water, taking care to keep my back to the woman who was killing me softly.

"Dessert?" I asked once I regained some of my weak self-control.

I brought the plate of fresh fruit dipped in dark chocolate that I'd prepared earlier to the living room. Sitting back beside her on the floor, I fed her a strawberry. All my blood rushed to my groin. I was playing with fire but didn't care if I got burned doing so. Pixie closed her mouth over the juicy fruit and moaned, and for a second, I imagined it was my cock she was feeding on. My throat worked as I tried to put to sleep the storm raging inside me. I inhaled through my mouth. Once. Twice. Three times. I was hard as a flagpole.

As if she sensed my growing uneasiness, she rose to her

feet and lit a few candles all around the room. She beamed in the flickering light. How could she waltz through the sexual tension like it meant nothing? She bent over to pick up the matchbox she'd dropped on the floor, giving me a front seat view of her perfect heart-shaped bottom. Was she tempting me on purpose? Testing my self-control? She put the matchbox back on the fireplace mantle and sat down on the opposite side of the coffee table.

"Get ready, HN. I'm going to end you."

Yeah, I know you will.

11

APRIL

Ohmyfuckinggod. We were playing Monopoly, and it felt as if I was being fucked senseless. My body vibrated the entire time. Could someone die from horniness? At that moment, I wondered. For real. When I opened the door and saw HN, all man and gorgeous on the doorstep, I feared my jaw would hit the floor. For a second, I was tempted to pinch myself to see if I was dreaming. No. I wasn't. I was wide awake. His navy-blue plaid shirt looked good on him. It fit snug to his chest in all the right places. I stuffed my hands in my pockets, resisting the impulse to touch him.

Okay, I had to be honest. HN was not only good for the eyes, but he was also an impressive cook.

All night, his presence ignited every one of my senses. Like fireworks on a summer night.

We were halfway through our game of Monopoly when he got personal. "Tell me why you're here, in Green Mountain."

I hesitated a moment before answering. "I needed a place to unwind. To get a fresh start." Why did being honest feel like laying my inner secrets on the table? "What about you? You're here for pleasure or work?"

"You want the truth?"

"Always."

A dark shadow passed over his smoky irises. "I needed an escape. A moment to stop and breathe. To reassess my life."

His throat rippled, and I feared our night would turn sour, so I changed the subject. "Okay. Let's raise the stakes here."

His full lips curled upward. "What do you propose?"

I tapped my chin with a finger as I thought about what we could do. "The winner will cook breakfast tomorrow morning. People always assume the losers must pay some price, so why don't we change things up? Make it more interesting."

HN leaned forward and held out his hand. "Fine with me. You'll be lucky to taste my vegan sausage if I win."

His words sucked all the air from my lungs. I shifted in my seat, my body an aching mess. When I regained some sort of self-control, we shook on it. He winked, and if I weren't sitting on the floor, I would've fallen off my chair. HN exuded confidence and sex appeal like they were tailor-made for him. My body was hot and bothered, and I wondered when someone had cranked up the thermostat in here.

A ball of lust settled down my throat. I coughed and found my voice. Two could play this little game. "Well, I'm not sure I'll let you enjoy my buns, but how do pancakes sound?"

For the first time tonight, I noticed a slight pink flush rising up his face under his dark stubble. My eyes lingered on his throat, where I witnessed his pulse spiking. I clenched my thighs when our gazes met. HN swallowed hard, and the movement sent jitters between my thighs and down to my toes. My skin burned, and my heart quivered. Ohmygod, his grin could, without exaggerating, liquify me on this floor.

"Show me what you've got."

All my inhibitions died right there. His eyes ate me up like I was some sort of candy melting on his tongue. He grazed the side of my face with his knuckles, and I shivered. With a glint in his eye, he leaned back and settled onto his side of the coffee table.

His intoxicating presence sucked every molecule of the air from the room, leaving me breathless, and all my senses heightened.

His genuine laughter and soft chuckles made me dizzy. With desire. And need.

When I won the game after he went bankrupt, HN cupped his heart. "You own me, Fairy." The way he'd faked I bruised his strong male ego made me shiver. I tried to ignore the game we were playing, but I couldn't stop. Every time I bent over, pushed my boobs up whenever I folded my arms over my chest, or wet my lips with my tongue, he missed nothing. And the more his eyes darkened, the more my inner thighs pulsed. Monopoly was just an excuse to test each other's restraints. No matter what, I wouldn't give in to temptation. HN would crack first.

———

The next morning, after just mere hours of sleep, I woke up with a purpose. Since I won last night's game, according to our terms, I was on breakfast duty. Armed with freshly mixed pancake batter and chocolate-dipped fruit leftovers, I paced the kitchen for long minutes before mustering the courage to go next door. On my way over there, my heartbeat was louder and more out of tune than a little kid's orchestra. I slid my hands into my sweater sleeves and stretched my neck muscles in all directions, trying to calm the flock of birds taking flight in my chest.

Last night had been amazing, but what if, in the morning light, things felt awkward between us? My neighbor had occupied too many of my thoughts since he had walked away the night before.

Whenever we were together, the world around us stopped existing. Nothing could happen between us, and yet, I kept going back to him as if I had become a glutton for punishment.

No matter how many times I told myself I should stay away since I woke up, my feet couldn't care less and brought me next door of their own volition. Now that even my legs were on his team, my body had been forever categorized as a traitor.

Standing on the front porch, I tried to collect myself and act cool, but inside, I was all but calm.

When I heard HN's hurried footsteps on the other side of the door, I held my breath, not sure I was ready to see him again, fearing the emotions it would stir in me.

Nothing had prepared me for the sight of my just-woken-up neighbor, standing bare-chested mere inches in front of me, with unruly bed hair, an unconcealed erection, and an adorable sleepy smirk grazing his lips. His abs. Gosh. They looked as if they had been sculpted on him. They had haunted my dreams since the morning I woke up in his bed, entangled in his warm, toned body, after my hypothermia scare. My mouth watered as I stood there like an idiot, picturing him wearing only boxer briefs in my head, his tanned, rock-hard chest on full display.

No amount of blinking could coax my voice back to life.

Travis was handsome, but my neighbor was out of this world. Had I become so rusty with men that just being this close to one was enough to send my hormones into a frenzy? Last night, in a moment of weakness, drunk on more than the wine in my glass, I had feared my ovaries would take over and beg him to ram into me, on repeat, till next year. Because I missed sex. And until I moved to Green Mountain and met him, I had forgotten just how much.

All evening, I caught him checking out my butt—more than once. And each time he got busted, he didn't shy away or offer any excuses. Instead, he offered me a shrug and a smirk that sent surges of heat through my being. Loving the effect I had on him, I took pleasure in swaying my hips a little more whenever I got the chance.

From the doorway, HN studied me without a word, his head tilted to one side. For an instant, I feared he had forgotten I was coming over and felt my blood rising in my cheeks. I was ready to bolt and lock myself in my cabin when he snapped out of it and ushered me inside, killing some of my will to flee. His warmth bled through me as I passed him in the entryway, and right there, I knew I was completely in over my head with my neighbor.

12

CARTER

ing. Dong.
I woke up to the sound of the doorbell.

I pried my eyes open and rubbed them with my fists, my eyelids still half-closed from sleep. Squinting, I unplugged my phone from the charger on the nightstand. *Eight o'clock.* I exhaled in one big huff knowing I hadn't slept more than a few hours.

Ding. Dong.

I blinked. "Go away," I whisper-yelled. Who could it be? No one had announced themselves from the gate.

I slipped my naked self into a pair of dark-blue cotton pants and tucked my morning wood in, to prevent flashing a tent at whoever stood on my front porch.

My hand raked through my hair, trying to comb the tousled dark strands I knew were pointing in all directions.

Two at a time, I ran down the stairs, not bothering to put on a shirt. I stretched and scrunched up my facial muscles to remove all traces of sleep and unlocked the door.

Fairy.

She stood there, a soft smile drawn on her lips, dressed in a sleeveless puffer vest over a black sweater, silver leggings, and sheepskin boots, looking freaking gorgeous.

Her night had been as short as mine—four hours at most—but unlike me, she was every shade of radiant.

Holding a plate wrapped in aluminum foil in her hands, she singsonged, "Morning, HN."

I cleared my throat, my larynx clamped from sleep. "Morning to you."

Was her presence here a dream? I shook my head as my mind drifted to last night.

Dinner. Monopoly. The best night of my life in a fucking long time.

Around three a.m., she had ended me for real. I had no money left and went bankrupt.

I had even raised my hands in surrender. She owned me. Yep. I was ruined in all the ways that counted. Her incredible smile told me she knew it.

Later, we had both yawned, then stood to put the board game back into the box.

Even now, I remembered my attention zeroing in on her lips. All night, I'd resisted kissing every smile, every pout, every word that fell from them. *You just landed in the friend zone, Carter.* We'd reached a truce, and I wasn't about to screw up everything. Not yet at least.

Desperate not to let her know how affected I was last night, I'd shoved my hands into my pockets. Rocking on my heels, I'd hesitated for a moment before bidding my farewell.

She had nodded and walked me to the door. Then she did something that stunned me. Without a word, she wrapped her arms around me and gave me a hug. One that lasted longer than required. It was awkward and magnificent at the same time. I felt tipsy as I breathed her in. My heart had leapt to my throat the entire walk home, and my mind kept asking the same question throughout the night.

What the fuck just happened?

Facing me in the morning light, my neighbor cleared her throat. The memories of the previous night faded away, and my attention returned to her.

She flashed me a ten-thousand-dollar grin. "Made pancakes. Hope you're hungry." She handed me the plate. "Wait? Did I wake you up?"

I grabbed the dish she offered me and nodded with a lopsided smile.

"I'm sorry. It's a beautiful day, though, and I intend to make the most of it. Time to get moving, neighbor."

I turned my head to the side, my eyes fixed on her. "Are you for real?"

She raised her gaze to meet mine, and a slight flush tinted her cheeks. Her lips parted, but she stayed silent, her blue irises swallowing me in. "You forgot?" A frown marred her forehead.

"No, I didn't…huh…yeah…well, I kind of did," I said, rubbing the back of my neck.

She pivoted on her heels. "It's okay. I can go."

My heart thundered in my chest, and I held out a hand to grab her elbow. Tingles tickled the pads of my fingers. She turned her head toward me, her molten irises burning with lust. Did she feel it too? My throat tightened, and I cleared it before speaking again.

"Don't go. You're already here. Come on in." She followed me to the kitchen where I set up plates and silverware on the island, before offering her a stool and taking the one next to hers.

Just like the night before, the conversation flowed naturally between us. None of the silences were uncomfortable.

My neighbor's blinding smile reached her eyes and her face became a ray of light in my darkness.

Before we knew it, it was past noon.

"I need to go. I have work to do," she said.

"Sure. I'll hit the gym." I needed to release the exponential tension growing in me with every passing minute in her company.

As soon as she left, that was what I did.

I sweated on the treadmill until my clothes were drenched. I lifted weights until my muscles trembled. And then I locked myself in my music studio, doing what I did best in life.

Write music.

13

APRIL

Hours later, as I sat in front of my laptop, the memory of all the moments HN and I shared since last night still got me all tingly and giddy. The stolen glances. Long stares. Barely-concealed lust.

When I left his cabin around noon, I believed I'd get some writing done. Who was I kidding? I shifted in my seat. Fidgeted with my digits. Chewed on my purple pen. Not even the fantastic hammock chair with the perfect view of the mountains was appealing enough today. Like a caged lioness, I roamed around the cabin, not knowing what to do with myself. My fingers itched to do something but refused to comply on the keyboard. I fanned myself with a hand, a wave of fire rippling through me. I rolled a bottle of cold water down my nape, between my breasts, over my forehead. Carved into my nose, HN's manly cedarwood and pine scent was all I could smell.

The sound of my own fingertips tapping on the pad of my laptop drove me nuts, and I aborted the idea of writing for now. Instead, I layered a soft blanket over my lined jacket. Slouched in an Adirondack chair on the back deck with a fantasy novel in hand, I welcomed the winter sun above, hoping it would clear my mind and make me forget about HN's hotness.

The story, dark and exciting, kept me on the edge of my seat for hours as I immersed myself in the pages. My heart did a little dance. Mission accomplished.

I fixed myself a quick dinner, sprawled on the couch, and dozed off. Bernice curled up beside me, her furry body resting against my belly, my dreams spiced up with everything I wished my hot neighbor would do to me.

Some time later, a loud thud woke me up. I flinched and leaped to my feet, wondering whether it was part of a dream or not. My heart scrambled in its cage and felt heavier in my chest. The sun had settled down hours ago. I scuffed to the far corner of the living room and flicked on the light. The room swam in a warm, golden glow.

Another loud bang thundered outside, startling me. I held my breath, all my senses waking up.

Was it a raccoon going through the trash can? A skunk? Or a bear?

No. The fence. Saunders told me it prevented bears from getting too close to the property.

While my heart tumbled down to my stomach, I padded across the room and grabbed the TV remote on my way to the front door, ready to hit anyone standing in the dark.

I caught a glimpse of myself in the reflection of a window. Armed with only a remote, I wouldn't even scare a baby. I sighed.

For a second, the idea of calling my hunk of a neighbor to my rescue flashed through my mind, but I shook my head and pushed the thought to the back of my mind.

We never exchanged numbers, or even names. Our nickname game sounded silly and juvenile right now.

Anyway, I could take care of myself on my own. *You can do this, April. Be fearless.*

I didn't need some tall, handsome, obviously fit guy with corded back muscles and a six-pack to save me from whatever wandered around my cabin. Nah…I was fine on my own. Another thud. I jumped three feet up. Seriously?

On my tiptoes, to avoid making noise, I flung the front door wide and growled, the guttural sound piercing the now quiet night, ready to chase the intruder away, a death grip on the TV remote in my hand. My options to protect myself were limited, and I couldn't think clearly, my brain still foggy from my nap.

A loud chuckle resonated in the dark.

A familiar figure appeared under the porch light, flashing an amused, wary eye. "Who do you think you're scaring away?" my neighbor asked, his arms overflowing with a pile of wood. "Wait, is that a TV clicker in your hand?" HN shook his head, and his smile reached his eyes.

I stuck my tongue out, annoyed at the way he teased my attempt at self-defense. I loved his smile, though. It lit up his features even more than usual, giving him a boyish look. A grown-up boy with stubble. "What are you doing here? It's late."

"It's cold outside, and the weather forecast said it'd snow tonight or tomorrow morning. I'm making sure you've got enough wood to keep the fireplace running." He shrugged like it wasn't a big deal.

I blinked.

It'd been a long time since a man cared enough about me and my well-being to make sure I had everything I might need at hand. I relished the idea. A bit too much.

Flutters danced in my stomach. The small gesture meant a lot to me.

"Wow, that's nice of you. Really."

HN flashed a small smile my way and dropped the wood under the covered porch where we stood.

Another loud thud echoed in the night.

I'd barely ever seen any snow in my life. The thought of being stuck in a snowstorm or buried under truckloads of white frozen flurries got me on edge. In my head, snow was a threat. Yeah, I was that girl.

My gaze traveled to the pile of wood my hot neighbor already brought over.

I'd be fine. This time my own lips stretched into a grin. "Thanks."

"Glad I could help." He stuffed his hands in his pockets and ambled away.

My eyes stayed fixed on his firm ass as he disappeared into the night.

"Good night, neighbor," HN yelled over his shoulder, waving at me.

Uneasiness sprawled inside me as I watched his back as he retreated. I had no clue what the right thing to do was. Should I have invited him in?

For a fat minute, my feet remained glued to the wooden porch as I stood there, swept by the chilly breeze, wondering what to make of him. I glanced at his cabin, where he had already vanished, unable to make up my mind about his confusing personality.

My attention zoomed in on the pile of logs by the door. Peace settled over me.

He cared.

Electric happiness prickled along my skin at the thought he really did.

The next morning, a thin blanket of snow covered the ground and the treetops. Not feet high like I feared, but about an inch. Breathtaking. With a mug of hot tea in my hand, I watched, from the hammock chair in the living room, the perfectly defined snowflakes falling. With the sun already shining, I knew this white wonder wouldn't last long. Still, the snow filled me with a rush of giddy energy.

I changed into warmer clothes, put on my jacket and a black beanie and my sheepskin boots, and ventured outside. With my arms stretched wide on either side, I spun around, my eyes fixed on the sky, a giant smile splitting my face in two. Unable to resist, I hummed a Christmas song. A fervor radiated through my body, pooling in my heart.

"The kid in you happy this morning, Fairy Girl?"

I was so mesmerized by the winter display that I hadn't seen my neighbor standing nearby. My chest flipped when I noticed his smirk as he caught me spinning around. Flutters, akin to butterfly wings, invaded my stomach.

I halted and, without thinking, hugged the man standing beside me, wrapped up in my own little world. Nothing could temper this moment.

His scent made my head spin as I buried my face in his chest.

HN stiffened under my touch, and I stepped back. "Sorry. Huh…got a bit swept away by all this beauty."

He tucked a loose strand of my hair behind my ear, and shivers raced inside me.

I sucked in a breath and met his eyes for a nanosecond before averting my gaze. I hoped he couldn't hear the hammering of my heart from where he stood. His attention stayed locked on my face, shifting between my eyes and my mouth. Just to tempt him and see what he would do, I bit my bottom lip in a way I knew was both sensual and sexy. His Adam's apple bobbed. This game of seduction we were both fully engaged in was getting more fun each day. I'd never indulged in foreplay like this before—not one to attract much attention from guys in general—but I was sure I could master the art perfectly by the end of my stay. As long as all we did was flirt with each other, there was no harm done, right?

After a moment, HN broke the silence that had settled between us. "Desmond will be here after lunch to change the back door lock. I'll come over to deal with him."

I nodded, staring at his mouth. "Great," I mumbled with a shuddering breath.

He kept talking, but I didn't process anything he spoke.

"Hey, did you hear a word I said?"

My eyes landed on his. I pursed my lips, having no clue what HN just told me. "Mm-hmm. Sure."

He touched my forearm, and I snapped out of my daze. I shook my head, blinking, rebooting my confused brain.

"Hello?" he asked again.

"Sorry. Got lost for a moment. What did you say?" I straightened my back, projecting fake confidence.

"I said I'm going into town this afternoon. You need something? Groceries? A pair of boots? Anything?"

He fixed me with a heavy stare, waiting for me to say something.

Instead, my organs failed, and my breath caught in my lungs. I opened my mouth to speak, but no sound passed my lips, so I closed it a second later.

"Did you hear me? Pixie?"

Liquid lust stirred low in my belly at the sound of my neighbor's deep, husky voice. With a step forward, he closed the distance between us, his body now grazing mine.

When he spoke close to my ear, I stopped breathing for a beat. "So, do you need anything?"

"I-I'll go later…by myself," I stuttered, my voice shaky and low.

"No offense, but the roads are icy, and your car will never make it up here on the way back. We'll take my truck."

The spell I was under broke. "Excuse me, are you making fun of Miss Dolly?"

"Miss who—? Oh crap, did you give your car a name?" He raked his fingers through his already tousled hair sprinkled with snowflakes.

"Don't look so surprised. Lots of people do." I gave a single nod, hoping it would lend weight to my argument. "Anyway, I bet your dick has a name too. Not judging." Why was I fixated on his penis? Damn it. *Keep your thoughts to yourself, April.*

"I…never mind," he said before his eyes drifted down my body. His voice lowered, and when our gazes collided, I found myself under a familiar trance. "What if my dick has a name? You—"

I swept my tongue over my lips, breath catching in my throat. I had no oxygen left in my brain to argue. His palm brushed my shoulder, and I closed my eyes, inhaling his masculine scent, the addictive mix of pine and cedarwood. Everything inside me screamed to kiss him again. His warmth reached my core. I leaned into his touch, butting his palm the same way Bernice always did when I petted her.

"I… What?"

HN's sudden intake of breath sent shivers down my body. His focus descended to my mouth before climbing back up to my eyes.

I squeezed my thighs together, my already flimsy composure slipping away.

My neighbor, without a doubt, the most handsome male specimen I'd ever laid eyes on—according to my sex-crazed hormones—seized my forearms with both hands and flashed me a grin. My chest rose and fell in quick succession. I was panting like I'd just run a marathon, even though my feet were glued to the snowy ground. I stepped forward, the gap between us shrinking. My breasts swelled. My lips tingled. And my lungs idled.

Without saying anything, he released his grip on me, pivoted on his heels, and walked away.

Frozen in place, I stood there, thoughts tangled and the snow forgotten. What had just happened?

"See you later, Pixie." His voice pulled me out of my stunned daze. With long strides, he reached his cabin in no time, leaving me speechless and spellbound, aching and needy before I could even form a reply.

The heat radiating from me could melt the freshly fallen snow blanketing the entire town. I had to regain some control around my neighbor before this thing between us ignited and consumed us both.

14

CARTER

Did only my presence steal away my neighbor's ability to speak? I closed the door behind me, shrugging off the snowflakes clinging to my hair. Even in the comfort of my house, I could still feel the heat of Pixie's big doe eyes as they licked me up from head to toe, only to linger over my mouth for a beat longer.

Earlier, when I had noticed her from my kitchen window, twirling around in the snow, I found her so irresistible that I had to come up with an excuse to go to her under any pretense.

Desmond had called me at the same time, giving me the perfect reason to talk to her. She never saw me coming, and the surprise on her face when I appeared before her doubled her adorableness.

I could tell she'd barely ever encountered snow before. Her astounded eyes had given her away. Anyone accustomed to winter's sparkling dust wouldn't be this smitten by a few snowflakes. But Fairy totally was. She looked like a little kid enjoying the tiny crystals falling from the sky as if they were the most precious and rare diamonds she'd ever seen.

Then her gaze had landed on me, capturing me and making my body acutely aware of her proximity. The more she stared at me, the deeper and darker her vibrant blue eyes had become.

My lungs constricted, and my mouth went dry at the memory. The entire time I had stared at her, my heart had hammered against my ribs. Even now, I could still feel the lingering echoes of the last few minutes.

For some reason, I always felt like a stupid, starstruck teenager around her. Never before had a woman had this much effect on me. This was all new to me and a bit confusing to navigate.

When she had wrapped her arms around me, I had stood frozen, torn between hugging her back and stepping away. My dick, already semi-hard, had enjoyed the contact. All the air had left my lungs when she had leaned back, and I had to take a few deep breaths to calm the zing coursing through me.

Until she admitted she had fucking named her car *Miss Dolly*. I shouldn't be surprised. But somehow, I was. She always found new ways to astound me. But out of nowhere, she'd started talking about my dick, and the attraction brewing between us had returned. The sucker loved hearing its name. Its throbbing against the zipper of my denims had been a telltale sign. And now, in the privacy of my own home, it was still standing tall, ready for some playtime of its own.

Was Fairy aware of her dirty mouth, or was she innocent enough that she didn't think before uttering those words?

In the heat of the moment, I had been tempted to kiss

her. To shut her up once and for all, instead of engaging in one of our face-offs.

The words had frozen on the tip of my tongue, and instead of revealing the dirty thoughts swimming in my head, I had walked away while I still had some self-control left.

My neighbor had woken up something in me that I thought had died a long time ago. Feelings. Addictiveness. The need to connect. I had no idea how to resist her charm anymore. The worst was that she had no clue how sexy she was or how enticing I found her. Entering my kitchen, I readjusted the crotch of my pants and sighed. The last thing I needed was to be pussy-whipped by another woman who'd walk away from my life in just a few weeks after destroying me.

Easier said than done.

No matter how many times I tried to erase the image of Pixie from my head, it stayed front and center in my mind.

A scary-large grin appeared on my face as my thoughts swam back to last night when she had tried to scare me away with a growl and a TV clicker. The picture had stayed with me for hours afterward. That was funny as hell. And stupid. But damn hot. My body temperature had shot up at the sight of her. My neighbor was fascinating. A breath of freshness in my life. A vision to lose myself in. All I could think about was her lips on mine, her tight and curvy body clenching around my fingers as she orgasmed in my arms. The memory filled all my thoughts, all my dreams.

I raked my hands through my hair, a tightness squeezing my insides. She was just passing through my life. I shouldn't get attached or become bewildered by her. Maybe fucking her for real just once would erase the tension between us and free me from my blue-balls syndrome. That was it. A case of unrequited lust. Nothing more. She was the only woman in my life right now. She wasn't special. I had an itch to scratch, and Pixie was here. I'd fill two needs with one deed if only I could get into her pants. Damn. New goal. Yeah, I needed to set goals.

First one. Fuck my neighbor until I got her out of my system.

Second one. Keep her at a distance afterward. For my own good.

I squeezed in an hour of training before lunch, yearning to expend all my excess energy, bury my unsatisfied needs, and clear my head. After a much-needed jerk-off session in my shower with images of the woman with cotton-candy hair dancing in my mind, which left me raw and sore, I toweled down and got dressed into a pair of denims and a beige hoodie to meet the girl haunting me at her place to wait for the handyman to show up.

"The back door is all fixed," Desmond said matter-of-factly, fifteen minutes later.

"Great. Thanks, man. We can still use the front door, right?"

"Yeah. But you won't be able to lock it, though. I dismantled the whole thing. I thought I might be able to fix it until I get the new one. I watched a tutorial last night and believed I'd give it a try. Now it's not working at all. It got stuck, and when I pried it apart, it broke. I'm sorry. I'm not a tech-savvy guy, and I don't know how to put the remaining pieces back together the right way." He gave me an embarrassed smile and lowered his voice. "With your status, I wouldn't risk leaving this woman here alone without a fully working lock on the door."

I blinked. My neighbor had no idea who I was, and I intended to keep it that way. She frowned as her eyes traveled between me and the handyman. Not wanting him to spoil my anonymity or say something he shouldn't, I urged him outside, my hand between his shoulder blades, blocking Fairy from eavesdropping on our conversation.

"Don't say a word around her. Please."

Desmond clapped my shoulder. "You're a lucky man, Carter. She seems like a keeper." He winked and stored his toolbox in the back of his van. *If only.* With one hand in the pocket of my denims, I waved at him before his truck pulled away.

Back inside, I accepted the cup of tea my neighbor offered me, hoping she wouldn't get mad as a new idea formed in my head.

———

"Move your piece of garbage, asshole," I said, my anger directed at the car blocking the narrow mountain road. It'd been obstructing the only way down for the last five minutes. Outside, most traces of the morning snow were gone, leaving us with a brownish-gray scenery.

"You sure know how to keep your calm around the ladies," my neighbor teased, a glint in her eye.

I chuckled. "Yeah, well…sorry?" It sounded more like a question. "I'd like to be able to go to town and come back before next year."

A ghost of a smile appeared on her pink-painted lips. Pixie had put on a little makeup after Desmond left. Combined with her loose turtleneck cream sweater, black faux-leather leggings, and pink hair, she made winter look sexy.

The bald man wearing a plaid flannel jacket, who blocked the road, got out of his car and rummaged through his trunk. His eyes lit up when he found a pack of cookies. *Really?* A car honked behind us, and more cars lined up on the opposite side of the road.

Fairy rolled down her window and propped her head out. "Hey you, dear gentleman. Yes, you who's stalling everyone. Do you need help?"

The man swiveled to look at her.

Before he could say anything, a man in his late forties, with a salt and pepper goatee, wearing a brown trucker hat and corduroy jacket, jumped out of his old pickup truck and swaggered, spitting anger toward Cookie-Eater. "You better move your car, bald man, or I'll move it myself."

Cookie-Eater turned his head to face him but said nothing, his chubby cheeks now a dark shade of red.

Without a warning, Fairy climbed out of my truck and bounced in Cookie-Eater's direction. I rolled down my window, a mix of surprise and wariness simmering inside me, ready to intervene if I needed to. Adrenaline coursed through my bloodstream, all my senses on high alert. I hated the idea of her inserting herself in an about-to-explode face-off. However, I also knew my neighbor could take care of herself. Words were her weapon of choice. I held my breath, not wanting to miss anything they said.

Trucker-Hat continued, ire coloring his words. "I know you're hungry and can't wait to fill this belly of yours with empty calories, refined sugar treats that look oh so yummy, but I'm sure you can manage to shut your stomach for a mile or two and do all of us a favor. Stop being a jerk and move your *not of this decade* piece of junk out of the way."

My hot as fuck and fearless neighbor neared the older man and placed her hand over his shoulder in a protective gesture. Round at the waist and short on legs, Cookie-Eater was only an inch—or two—taller than her. "Sir, do you need help?" she repeated in the sweetest possible voice, concern clear in her tone.

"That's it, sweetheart, ask him to move his woody wagon off the middle of the road," Trucker-Hat said.

I gulped down a breath. Poor guy. He had no idea what he just did. Fairy's little hands clenched at her sides, and a blood-red flush crept along her neck and cheeks. She pivoted on her heels to face the cocky bastard who'd just called her *Sweetheart*. I cringed, my eyes glued to the scene unfolding before me. My stomach filled with a handful of pebbles. Would they merge into a big giant rock, or would they turn into proud fireworks?

"Don't ever call me *Sweetheart*, you jerk. You better shut your dirty mouth, or my boyfriend over there will shut it for you. If you want a lady's help to control your temper, all you need to do is ask. But don't get on my last nerve because I'm in labor right now, and you're about to assist in delivering this nine-pound bundle of joy. I'm sure you'd like to be on the receiving end of my placenta. Hope you played football in college. Could end up being useful. By the look of it, you probably won't be a big help. Unless you have something smart to say to this man, I suggest you go back to your dump and mind your own business." She rested her fists on her hips and glared at Trucker-Hat.

"Don't be a smart-ass, lady. You can't be pregnant. You're like child-size. What are you, twelve?" Underneath her loose sweater, Fairy could be hiding a pregnant belly, and nobody would know.

"Are you willing to bet on it?" Fury crossed her usually peaceful face.

Trucker-Hat eyed her for a moment. Part-spooked and part-confused, he rubbed his bearded jaw before climbing back behind his wheel, giving my neighbor a long stare.

Fireworks. Yeah, the whole show.

Once Trucker-Hat was out of the way, she turned her attention back to Cookie-Eater and whispered something that made him smile. They exchanged a few words, and she hugged him before he hauled himself back into his car and resumed his drive.

Pixie flashed me a proud smile as she opened the door. "That's how it's done, HN. You're welcome."

I clamped my mouth shut, my eyes wide and unblinking.

Who was this girl, and where did she come from?

When I finally found my words again, I side-eyed her. "Impressive. But not very ladylike. You called Trucker-Hat a jerk." I winked as my passenger punched my upper arm and stuck her tongue out at me with a wrinkled nose. The air thickened in the car. "Boyfriend, huh? Something I should be aware of?"

"Don't flatter yourself. Would you have preferred husband?" She cocked an eyebrow, challenge dancing in her blue eyes—bluer with the mascara coating her long lashes. Yeah, I noticed.

I shrugged, trying to look unaffected. "Maybe."

The girl snorted, and we stayed silent for the rest of the drive while she fidgeted with the ring on her right hand, looking through the window, her face unreadable as I parked on Main Street.

"Is the baby mine?" I asked.

"Why? Do you want it to be yours?" She studied me with her ocean-deep gaze, and after a minute, I shrugged.

I swallowed, my throat working a double shift, all my hair standing on end at the way her stare burned a tunnel straight into my soul.

Parked in the lot next to the grocery store, I turned the upper half of my body and stretched my arm to grab a cap from the back seat. I placed it on my head, and without removing my shades, I made my way inside the building.

"Wait for me." Pixie jumped out of the truck, and in small strides, she followed me. "Stop acting like you're being chased by paparazzi, HN. Oh, dear God, you look ridiculous with your sunglasses indoors."

If only she knew.

June had texted me this morning that she'd received over fifty phone calls, offering her a lot of money if she revealed where I was hiding. She'd never betray me. At least, that I knew for sure.

"The fluorescent lights. My eyes are sensitive." Lame. I'd lied better in the past.

"Do you want me to unfold the red carpet for you? Perhaps you'll feel more in your element."

I poked her arm, and her giggle went straight to my dick.

"Hollywood is this way." She pointed toward the front of the store with her thumb and grabbed a bottle of barbecue sauce from a shelf on her right. "I can even present you with an Oscar if you like and give an emotional feel-good speech, complimenting you on your tear-jerking performance."

I bit the inside of my cheek, refraining from unmasking my identity by revealing I'd much prefer a country music award.

"Come on, woman, let's do this." My fingers knitted with hers, and I led her toward the back of the supermarket, not wanting to draw anyone's attention to us. Locals knew I owned a house around here. They rarely cared. However, tourists were unpredictable for the most part. I couldn't risk their recognizing me.

A little girl, with white-blonde hair and big, doll-like honey-brown eyes, stopped us in our tracks. "Hi, my name is Alicia. Can I take a picture with you?" My heart jackhammered in my chest. The air froze in my lungs. *Fuck.*

Here I was, fearing tourists, when I should have been wary around kids. Were they the new weapon used by paparazzi to get closer to their victims? I swallowed the rock in my throat. *Relax, man. It's just a kid.*

"With me?" I faked being surprised. Perhaps this girl would think she'd mistaken me for someone else. A little prayer never hurt anyone.

"No, silly. Her," she said, pointing her finger in my neighbor's direction. "I love your hair."

Fairy placed a hand over her heart. Her priceless reaction got me tongue-tied. "Awww. You're so cute. Sure. I've never done this before."

The child walked over and handed me a phone—probably her mom's—using a bossy tone to address me. "Here, mister. Take the shot but not before I tell you to."

Enjoying the dynamic a little too much of not being the one chased around, I snapped half a dozen pictures when the kid ordered me to.

My neighbor was flustered. Beautiful, shy, and radiant all at once. "This is weird. It has never happened before. Next thing I know, I'll be signing autographs."

I bit my lips to avoid laughing. Pixie made it almost impossible not to want to kiss her. Her eyes glistened with happiness. I wondered how her pink lips would feel around my shaft. *Stop.* Feeling involved in the conversation, my dick swelled in my pants, and I forced my mind to wander elsewhere. The old lady on our left. Desmond. Savannah. I swallowed and filled my lungs with much-needed air. That did the trick. Kinda. A little. And I huffed in relief.

"Believe me, you're a natural. You should wear your shades inside too."

She poked her tongue out at me once more, and I resisted the urge to kiss the life out of her, right here in the middle of the deli section.

My fingers itched to brush the soft flesh hidden under her sweater and to get her hands all over me. I wanted to taste every inch of her skin. To finish what we'd started the other day. I had no idea for how long I'd be able to resist her. My body shook with all the dirty thoughts that crossed my mind. I was *so* doomed.

Together, we sauntered down the aisles, and Pixie added chicken breasts to our buggy when we reached the meat section. I turned around and put them back on the shelf.

"Hey. Give it back."

"No meat for me, Fairy. You should try it."

She laughed, and I cracked a grin.

"It doesn't matter. We're not sharing a fridge, Big Guy."

"Big Guy, huh? I think I prefer HN. Whatever it means. Sorry to tell you, but you're not going back to your cabin. Starting tonight, you're staying with me."

With a scowl, she planted her hands on her hips and stopped, daring me despite her petite frame. The sparks in her eyes faded. "Excuse me, who are you to decide where I should live? I'm a grown woman, and I'm not gonna do whatever you say because you feel entitled. Don't assume I'm some weak girl who believes you're the one who'll save the day. When we get back, I'm going to *my own* cabin. Thank you for the offer, but I'll pass."

"Don't be difficult. Geez. I'm helping you right now. There's no way you're sleeping in your cabin if you can't lock the front door properly. The latch is broken."

"Don't be a chicken, Hotshot. No pun intended. There's a gate. Nothing can happen to me. I'm a big girl. I can take care of myself. Thank you for your concern, but no thanks."

"Yeah, right. You're fully capable of defending yourself, I forgot. Armed with a TV clicker? Yep, you're invincible."

She threw daggers at me with her eyes, but it rather felt as if she were throwing kittens my way. She stayed silent, her arms folded and her stance rigid. She studied me, as if trying to read something in my offer I hadn't spoken out loud.

"Why do you even care? I'm not a child, and I'm not your responsibility."

"You'd be surprised the freaks you can come face-to-face with when you're least expecting it."

"Okay. First, there's a gate around the lot. So, your 'freaks' argument isn't good enough. And second, I love my cabin. I don't want to move. Considering we both know you can be an ass, I prefer avoiding being around you for too long. I wouldn't want to risk your cynicism rubbing off on me."

"I'm not cynical. And I already proved to you I am not an ass. You don't have any logical reason to refuse. You're not my responsibility, but gate or not, your safety matters to me."

She eyed me. How long would she fight me over this?

"Where will I sleep? No way are we sharing a bed…or a room. The last time we did, it didn't end well."

"Yeah, my dick still remembers."

Pixie nudged my arm. "You know what I mean. Don't be an ass."

Amusement bubbled inside me, and I bit my inner cheek, silencing the wheezy snicker threatening to escape my mouth. "You'll never let it go, will you? Anyway, I bet I can find a guest room for you to sleep in. We won't even be on the same floor. I'll be a happy camper, I promise. And a very discreet roommate."

"No funny business?"

I raised my hands in surrender. "Not unless you want it too." I winked.

Her face turned crimson.

"Okay, fine, no funny business." *We'll see about that.*

Since my stubborn neighbor ogled me every chance she got—yeah, I had noticed—this roommate situation should be fun.

My full attention returned to her when she harrumphed. "I have conditions."

"Yeah, I assumed nothing less from you. We'll discuss them in the car. Now let's decide on something for dinner."

We roamed through the aisles.

"Cheese?" she asked

"Nope."

"Cream?"

"No."

Pixie gave me a puzzled look and sighed. "You're impossible."

"No. It's called being healthy."

"Whatever, take the lead, I wanna see what you get."

Just like that, we bought groceries together, and it felt like the most natural thing in the world. Again.

When we neared the cashier's, I stopped in my tracks. My own face looked back at me. Multiple times. On the covers of four different magazines. Each in dozens of copies. My airways tightened, and my legs weighed a ton.

"Where's Carter Hills?" one title said. *Fuck.*

"Carter Hills dumped Savannah Prince for one of his mistresses," said another.

The muscle in my jaw ticked, and I clenched my teeth.

Seconds later, my legs regained their function, and I slid my body between the buggy and the magazine stand to block my neighbor's view. I crossed my fingers, hoping she had no interest in flicking through gossip rags while waiting in line at the grocery store.

Probably not.

If she did, she'd know who I was. I had appeared on so many front pages in the last two years that I lost count. Not giving her time to think about anything else, I kept the conversation going.

"Should I be worried about that cat of yours moving in? It doesn't seem to like me very much."

She chuckled, the sound fucking delicious. "C'mon, HN. Bernice is harmless. She won't attack you in your sleep. Ohmygod, are you scared of a fifteen-pound feline?"

"Don't be ridiculous. Just trying to get to know my new roommate, that's all. I'm sure we'll be best friends in no time." I smirked. "What's not to like? I'm irresistible."

She snorted. "Yeah, well, we'll see about that."

A mass lodged in my throat. I hated lying to her. I should come clean before she learned about me from another source, but a big part of me liked our relationship as it was. Telling her the truth might destroy what we were building. I clenched and unclenched my fists at my sides again and again, battling with my conscience. I faked a smile when my future roommate said something I didn't quite catch. *Relax, Carter. Breathe in. Breathe out.*

When we reached my truck, a guy pointed his phone at us. With my hand on the small of Fairy's back, I rushed her into the passenger seat, after dropping the grocery bags on the backseat, and closed the door after her. I cursed under my breath as I rounded the vehicle to slide behind the wheel, my insides sizzling with anger. I ignored the guy on the opposite sidewalk, keeping my head down.

Shit.

I prayed in silence he hadn't gotten any significant pictures of us. Fucking fame.

My neighbor didn't need to have her face plastered on the covers of tabloids all around the world because she bought groceries with me this one time.

I had no idea how to explain my celebrity status to her. She seemed so clueless about me and my life, and I'd love to keep it that way as long as possible. Maybe I was being egoistical about it, but I'd been burned in the past, and the last thing I wanted was a repeat of the tragedy my life had been.

One day, I'd tell her. Not today, though. Today, I'd keep my anonymity.

I peeled the cap off my head and ran my fingers through my hair before pulling it back down. All my insides were knotted together. The selfish part of me wasn't ready to let the woman occupying the passenger seat walk away from my life. I wanted to keep her all to myself for as long as I could. From experience, I knew that the truth—and who I was—would mess everything up. Why couldn't it be simple for once?

Not willing to let the press drag my clueless neighbor into the dirt, I sent June a quick text message while waiting at a red light, keeping my best poker face on. I prayed Fairy couldn't read me. She didn't know me well enough, and all my friends agreed my poker face was shit. They always made fun of me for not being able to hide my emotions. Just this once, I hoped I could pull it off.

"Are you okay?" she asked, her fingers grazing the skin of my forearm.

"Yep. All good." I tried to inject cheerfulness into my words, but it fell flat. Inside, I was coiled tight and ready to burst.

"Tell it to that frown of yours," she teased.

"It's nothing. Just something I have to deal with. Don't worry."

"If you say so." A tiny smile formed on her lips, and the sight of it chased my grumpiness away.

"I do."

"Then let's get rolling because I'm starving. Never keep a pregnant woman waiting when it comes to food."

Peals of laughter left my mouth. I couldn't resist her humor. "Fine. I hope this imaginary baby loves my cooking too."

"He sure will." She winked, and I shook my head.

My attempt to stop smiling failed. "By the way, I can catch a football. In case it ends up being useful," I said, using her earlier words about delivering that fake baby.

We exchanged a grin and this time, she was the one who burst into laughter. God, I freaking loved making her laugh.

How could Fairy's bubbly personality always have a way of adding colors to my toneless existence? Even though I couldn't explain it, it grew on me. And I relished every second.

———

While Fairy went next door to pack some of her stuff, I attacked dinner. Tingles of excitement swirled in the depths of me and lifted up my mood. No woman, except for Dahlia, had ever stayed over with me before. Not even Savannah. I thought the idea of having someone else living with me would freak me out. Truth was, I loved the thought of sharing my personal space with the woman living next door.

Fairy kept a low profile as she settled in, not asking for a house tour or to repaint the bedroom walls. I appreciated her even more for this because the last time I let a woman in, she made everything about her and turned my life upside down in the worst possible way. Even though I wanted my neighbor to feel at home, I wasn't ready to let her all in. My defense mechanisms wouldn't let me lower my walls. Not all of them, anyway.

After freeing Bernice from her carrier, she disappeared upstairs to unpack her suitcase in the guest room. I showered real fast and dressed in a pair of dark sweatpants and a white T-shirt. When my guest returned to the kitchen, now wearing a pair of pearl-gray lounge pants and a black fleece, looking at home in my space, I offered her a glass of white wine from the bottle I uncorked for the risotto.

"You want me to pour you a glass?" she asked.

"No, I'll pass."

Keeping my back to her, I added another cup of vegetable broth to the rice simmering on the stove. This way she couldn't read my expression. Or distract me. My new roommate seemed to have a special key to my soul when her eyes locked on mine.

Tilting my head, I watched her over my shoulder as she chopped mushrooms and shallots on a cutting board, her hips swaying to the rhythm of the music playing low in the background. Some country ballad she said she adored. For an instant, I imagined her moving her hips and humming the melody of one of my songs, like she did the night I invited myself over to her place and we played the hottest game of Monopoly known to humankind. My lips curled up at the memory. A *but* lingered, though. Would she even be here with me if she knew the truth?

Glass shards crept along my spine, and not being ready to assess the *what-ifs*, I pushed the thought away.

I returned my focus to the dish simmering in front of me, knowing I would have a hard time resisting this woman if I looked at her, and let the sweet aroma of dinner envelop my senses instead.

Every time we faced each other, her baby-blue eyes acted like magnets to my steel-gray irises. They called to something inside me, and I felt naked as she assessed me. This was something I never experienced in my life before. A connection I lacked words to describe.

"No alcohol, no meat, no dairy? Something else I should know? Are you a sugar freak too?"

Not looking away from the pot on the stove, I chewed on my lips and rubbed the back of my neck. "Well, I started eating clean six years ago. My brother…he was in the army…huh…died of sudden cardiac arrest. He had completed a tour overseas a couple of months earlier. You would've thought that would've killed him. Nope. He died on his way back home from the gym one night. I-I used to love my Tennessee Whiskey, but after his death, I promised to take care of his wife and unborn child. Somehow, I always believed if I took extra good care of my health, I wouldn't abandon them too. After my brother passed away, I hired a fitness coach, and he changed my entire philosophy about food and health. I cut off all animal products from my diet, and it impacted more than just my overall health. It increased my energy levels, my stamina, my creativity. I'd never go back."

I had never confided in anyone about my family like this. About Jeff's passing.

The air thickened in the room, but then something in me shifted. A weight I'd been carrying around for years lifted from my shoulders. My back straightened. I inhaled, and some of the knots in my stomach slackened. The lump in my throat melted, and I breathed easier. My fists unwound.

Why did I feel safe telling a woman I barely knew the story of my life? Why did I feel like my heart could beat again when she was around? That her presence only could heal the scars of my heart?

Her soft voice brought me back to reality. "Are they the ones who stayed with you the other week?"

I blew out a long breath. Legitimate question. Jitters tickled my stomach.

She's not snooping. She's genuinely interested. She's just making conversation.

Relax, Carter. Breathe in. Breathe out.

I pushed strands of my hair away from my forehead with the back of my hand. I was in dire need of a haircut.

"Yeah. Dahlia and Jack. Their names." A small smile lit up my face at their mention. "Dahlia and I, we kinda grew up together. She was my first love. When I mustered the courage to tell her I loved her, at fifteen, it was too late because she had fallen for my brother…Jeff. His name was Jeff. He…he died when she was four months pregnant. They'd just gotten married." My throat bobbed. I closed my eyes and inhaled through my mouth to keep my emotions at bay. "After his death, I took over. They're family. They are my entire world."

Back when Dahlia and I were members of Carter Hills Band, we made the covers of magazines countless times. People's interest in us escalated once they found out about the pregnancy. Every time we ventured outside of Nashville, fame-sucker enthusiasts tried to snap pictures of us. We had to lie low to escape the hell our lives had become.

One day, Dahlia cracked, packed her stuff, and kissed me goodbye. She moved here and never looked back.

Three years ago, she opened a bridal shop on Main Street. She had this new life and was happy. That was what I'd always wished for her. For the last six years, I'd been devoting all my free time to Jack and her. Nobody else in this world meant as much to me as they did. Whatever I did in my career, wherever I was in the world, they remained my top priority.

Fairy brought the mushrooms and shallots over. Our hands brushed. I sucked in a breath. Her other hand lingered between my shoulder blades. Through her touch, she healed a broken part of my heart. A tiny piece that went missing years ago. I took a deep breath to stop the tears threatening to fill my eyes. When was the last time I felt alive? And hopeful? Emotions blocked my airways. I forced my shoulders to relax and cleared my throat, chasing the surge of emotions inside me.

Change the subject. Quick.

"You play any instrument? Musical instrument, I mean."

"Nah. I tried piano when I was like ten, but I had no talent. I sang a duet in the garage band of this guy I had a crush on in high school, once or twice to impress him. Didn't work. I had no singing talent either. Anyway, I'm pretty much a music-playing virgin."

I whirled around and brushed her shoulders, the need to touch her so strong, my heart throbbed in my chest. "Wait here. We'll change that."

"Now?" Panic filled her blue irises.

I snickered and hurried to my studio to pick up my Taylor, one of my acoustic guitars. I put the risotto on the back burner and led her to a chair. She wasn't just my neighbor anymore. She was becoming so much more. I ignored what exactly that was, but I was thankful we had crossed paths. That life placed her on my journey.

Inhaling a cleansing breath, I forced myself to let go of the tension straining my body and prayed the music would ease the tightness spreading through me. It always soothed my nerves. My roommate stared at me, her eyes wide and filled with questions. The heaviness of our earlier conversation had spread goose bumps all over my skin. Time to lighten the atmosphere and present her with a happier side of me. Her tongue darted out, wetting her lower lip, as she watched the guitar in my hands, a deep frown etched across her forehead.

Oh, did I make her nervous?

A smile broke free on my lips.

Fairy scrunched up her nose. "Don't get your hopes up, HN."

I gripped her hand in mine, and the pounding of my heart decreased at the touch of her skin. The now familiar sensation of her palm in mine. The softness of her fingers. "Don't be too harsh on yourself. Everyone must start somewhere."

She hissed a low laugh, and it quieted my mind.

I forgot all about the world outside my cabin.

Her eyes rounded and darted between the guitar and me, and I battled with myself not to drop a kiss on her forehead. To pull her to my chest and promise everything would be all right. All colors drained from her face, and she appeared scared as if I had told her we were going bungee jumping over a river filled with crocodiles.

"You'll be fine. I swear." Oxygen came in and out of my lungs easier around her, the sensation of my chest being crushed under piles of rocks dissipating. "Come on. Let me give you your first lesson."

15

APRIL

As I sat on the kitchen chair, I sucked in a breath and dug up some courage from deep inside me. Maybe I could do this. How hard could it be, right? HN squatted in front of me and placed the guitar in my hands. A drift of his scent washed through me, and for a fleeting instant, I wondered if he tasted as good as he smelled. The temptation to find out grew stronger every time we were together. *Shut down your crazy, needy hormones, girl.* I closed my eyes and evened out my breathing. There. Better.

"Place your fingers right here." I did as he instructed. "No, this one needs to be higher. Yes. Perfect."

Our eyes met, and all the air in my lungs left me. I could do this. All I needed was to focus. HN's fingers brushed mine, and I combusted from my core to my skin.

"Ready for your first chord? I'll show you an Em." He positioned my digits. "Try this."

I glided my thumb against the strings.

"Not bad," he said, grinning. He looked so handsome when he let go of whatever walls he kept high around him.

Carefree. And happy. "See? I knew you were better than what you credited yourself for."

Pride shot through my bloodstream.

"Now let's try a C." Once again, he repositioned my fingers, and I strummed the guitar chords the same way he showed me.

In the next fifteen minutes, he taught me three more chords before we started from the beginning as I tried to remember all five of them. I wasn't the most promising student, but he didn't seem fazed by my lack of musical talent. My fingers tingled each time he moved them, and on a few occasions, I faked not remembering a chord so he'd touch my hands again. My eyes traveled all too often to his lips. I wanted to feel them on mine once more. To savor their addictive fullness. The only time we kissed, I was so hungry for him that I didn't take the time to brand the feel of it into my memory.

When I stopped obsessing over his mouth, I listened to him—for real this time—and enjoyed his teaching. The best part? HN's smile lighting up his face throughout the hour-long private guitar lesson. At some point, he placed himself behind me and leaned forward, pressing his chest to my back. My breaths caught in my lungs, and my entire body pulsed in his presence. I coughed and shifted in my seat. His steady fingers blanketed mine, and his soft breath fanned over my nape, catapulting my heartbeat into a wild, new tempo.

During dinner, the tension between us faded a little.

"Are you living here full-time?" I asked.

"No. Sometimes I think I should move here for good, though."

"You own the cabin?"

HN nodded. "And yours. I own a few more in town. My dad always told me real estate was a good investment, so—" He shrugged and took a sip of his sparkling water.

"Now I get why you acted like you owned the place every time you came over. It makes more sense. It wasn't an act."

My neighbor smirked at me from behind his glass.

Later, I went to bed with a fluttering heart and a grin that lingered well into the night.

When we prepped dinner and he opened up about his brother's story earlier, with each word he spoke, his pain tore at my heart. It rang too close to home and sent sharp, painful chills up and down my spine. I didn't open up about Travis. I couldn't. Sorrow and pain swam in HN's stormy irises, and I fought the urge to hug him and tell him everything would be fine. He was still struggling with his grief, and I could relate to it in ways he'd never know. Not trusting myself to resist the urge to kiss him to soothe his pain, I kept a safe distance between us, only allowing myself to press my palm to his back to let him know I was there.

Dahlia and Jack were his brother's family—not his. I had misread the entire situation from the start. A sigh of relief escaped me even though I already knew the red-haired woman wasn't his wife. It shouldn't matter to me who they were, but in a lot of ways, it did.

His caring for them was such a selfless and loving act. New sensations ran through me. Tonight, every time he said their names, his eyes glowed, and a smile tugged at the corner of his lips, making him look way younger, giving me an insight into the boy he must have been years ago. No wonder I thought the redhead was his wife that day through my bedroom window. They had this strong bond that couldn't be faked. It showed even from a distance. He admitted she was his first love. But after everything they'd been through, was he still in love with her? After all this time? What was their relationship like nowadays? Plenty of questions swam in my head for which I had not enough answers. The only thing I knew for sure was that Jack was his mini lookalike. A tight knot formed in my stomach. So much mystery surrounded my neighbor, and for some reason, it made me feel queasy. It didn't make sense, yet somehow, it did. I felt like a complete nutcase.

Under the covers, in a bedroom I didn't recognize—hardwood floor, white walls, steel-blue accents—I closed my eyes, images of him filling the darkness.

Our night and the closeness we shared replayed in my head. Tonight, HN's confessions, the vulnerability in his eyes and in his words made him even more attractive than usual. Like he had stripped a part of himself bare before me, and now I had no idea what to do with it. One thing was certain. I needed to move back to my cabin. For my mental health. And my sanity. This roommate thing would be too hard on me. I could sense the chaos coming our way. My neighbor was trouble, and I should stay away.

The next morning, I woke up and stretched before grabbing my phone to look at the clock. *Eight fifty-eight.* Another night of uninterrupted sleep. I wished I could have high-fived myself. My eyes adjusted to the morning light peeking through the curtains, and I swallowed hard as I scrolled through my notifications and saw that i had two missed calls and four text messages from Saunders. I frowned. What did she get herself into this time?

SAUNDERS

OMG April, WTF?

Call me. NOW.

Blimey! Call me already, girl.

CALL. ME. BACK. ASAP *9-1-1*

Saunders and I only ever used the 9-1-1 code in case of extreme emergencies. Breakups, Travis's death, walk of shame, broken condoms, or dates gone wrong. Those types of situations.

I dressed in a pair of leggings and a fluffy sweater and hurried downstairs. HN had left a note on the kitchen counter next to a cup of tea. I lifted it and realized it was still warm.

Good morning, Bubble Gum.

I laughed at the term of endearment.

Went to town for a meeting.
I'll be back for dinner.
HN – Heavenly Nice? Hot and Natty? Or Handsome and Neat? Pick one.

I cupped my mouth and snickered. *Hot and Natty.* I loved it.

So far, living with him hadn't been that bad. Anyway, he left me no choice. He'd moved furniture around yesterday to create a writing nook in the den for me and filled the kitchen with the widest range of tea I'd ever seen because I mentioned I was a fan. He even let Bernice venture all around his place. *Sweet.* It was just one of his many layers. Spending my day alone in his place made me a bit uncomfortable. In all honesty, the grandeur of the place intimidated me a little. It wasn't decorated like a mansion—nothing too grandiose or overly expensive—but still, I was used to much smaller spaces. Here, the windows were so large, I felt like I was living outside while still being inside. At least he trusted me to be on my own, and the realization sent a flutter to my chest. In the den, I sipped the mug of tea he had left behind, basking in the sun's warm rays streaming through the floor-to-ceiling windows.

This room had stolen my heart the first time I'd stepped in. Not that I'd seen every room, but there was a warmth between these walls that made me feel at home.

The cell phone reception wasn't any better here than at my cabin, so after walking around with my phone held above my head for a few minutes without getting a good-enough signal, I shrugged it off, put on my puffer jacket, and strolled toward the gate with a pep in my step. I hummed a song, trying to guess why Saunders would use the 9-1-1 emergency code. Was she freaking out about moving in with Reed? The Saunders life crisis. Typical. I grinned, putting my best friend suit on.

I neared the gate and dialed my friend, who answered on the first ring.

"What took you so long? Why are there pictures of you and Carter Hills all over the web?"

My eyes widened at her inquisitiveness.

"Hello to you too. Sorry, who?"

"Carter Hills. The country music legend. The sexiest singer on the planet. Also known as the fit bloke who makes an entire stadium wet their panties when he plays his guitar and sings love songs."

"Carter Hills?"

"Yes, Bubble Head. C-A-R-T-E-R-H-I-L-L-S. The one and only."

"It must be a mistake. I've never even met him. Are you sure it's me in the pictures?"

"Sexy, pink-haired girl with sparkling blue eyes. Who else could it be?"

I sighed loudly, grinding my teeth. "I don't know. Maybe we were at the same place at the same time once, and I ended up in the pictures somehow. Who cares, right? Anyway, what's the emergency?"

"Okay, you know I love you, but get real here. April, your Handsome Neighbor *is* Carter Hills." Saunders paused to let the words sink in.

I laughed so hard I thought I'd choke. My eyes watered, and a fit of hiccups exited my mouth.

My friend sighed. I imagined her rolling her eyes. "April. Stop."

Why couldn't she let it go?

"This isn't a joke. The pictures were taken in Green Mountain. Yesterday."

I sucked in some air. Carter Hills? *No.*

HN looked nothing like the country singer. Did he? *Okay, maybe a little.*

Although, it couldn't be him. If so, he would've told me. *Wouldn't he?*

My neighbor, a big country music star? No way. This made no sense. Wait… Unless he shaved off the stubble on his jaw and cut his hair shorter. *Fuck. No, no, no.*

Was it really him? Had he been playing me all along?

The air sliced through me, making me dizzy.

My hand shot to my chest, pressing against my pounding heart as it skipped a beat.

Anger surged through my veins.

Did HN lie to me? *No. Not really.* Unless a lie by omission still counted as a lie. *Did it?*

This was a nightmare. He was the first man I'd trusted in years, the first one I'd let get too close, and it turned out he was a liar. Gosh, my asshole radar was spot on at first… Except he wasn't an asshole. Not really. My liar radar, though? Defective, kaput, broken. How did I not see it sooner? How much more of an idiot could I have been?

How much fun did he have messing around with my ignorance?

But, on the other hand, we never even exchanged names... Did that count as a lie? It had to, right? Or was it fair game, and I shouldn't hold it against him?

My thoughts spun in dizzying circles, racing through my mind.

Ohmygod, how could I have been so blind? The guitar lesson, the shades he kept on at the grocery store, the note I found on my countertop the day I got here. *Your host, C.H.* A tightness spread deep in my stomach, like a knot that wouldn't untangle. I'd been living with Carter Hills. *The* Carter Hills. And he kissed me. We laughed together. We bantered. Oh God, he put his hand in my panties, his fingers inside… Dry heaves rattled my body.

I scratched at my throat, my airways tightening as a cold feeling crept up my spine.

Saunders spoke, but my brain locked her out. I dropped my phone on the ground and placed my hands over my ears, silencing the buzzing sound reverberating in my head. A chime caught my attention, and I lowered my arms. I picked up my device, brushing off the dead pine needles from the case as I skimmed over the screen with shaky fingers. I held my breath and opened the message Saunders just sent me. A picture. No. Not a picture. Pictures. Like lots of them.

The first one showed me and HN, or should I say Carter Hills, buying groceries together yesterday.

The second one was a shot of us in his truck the same day, exchanging smiles.

A third one captured his hand on the small of my back, talking close to my ear.

I felt as if someone had violated my privacy. This was worse than a nightmare. It was a goddamn clusterfuck of epic proportions that I'd gotten entangled in without even knowing it. I bent at the knees, gut-punched, desperate for air.

The fourth picture, a cover of *Star News Magazine*, displayed a close-up shot of Carter Hills—yes, that was definitely him—and a photo montage of us together with the title *Carter Hills has moved on. Who's the new girl?*

Another cover claimed he left Savannah Prince for one of his many mistresses. A.k.a. me.

My knees buckled, and I almost collapsed on the ground.

I kept scrolling. More pictures. More shots of us looking awfully close, sharing smiles and touching.

More gossip magazine covers.

More exposure.

More invasion of my privacy.

More lies for everyone to see.

"April, are you still there?" Saunders asked, worry lacing her voice.

"Y-yeah." I stuttered the word, my eyes clouded with unshed tears. My chest hurt. I placed my hand back over my aching heart. My lungs seized. I coughed, trying to ease the discomfort creeping inside me. More dry heaves.

My world crumbled beneath my feet. I was the butt of the joke. I thought HN and I were friends and that he trusted me… After all, he told me about Dahlia…and his brother. I thought we shared something real. How naïve.

Fuck.

"I gotta go, Saund."

"No, April. Don't hang up on me. You're not in a great state of mind right now. You need your best friend."

I snorted. Tears pricked the back of my eyes.

"Let me in, girl. I'm worried about you."

A sarcastic laugh left my mouth.

"April, I'm coming to you. I'll spend a few days in Green Mountain and help cheer you up."

"Don't. I'll be fine."

"No games. I know what the word *fine* means, pal. I'm a girl. Give me a day or two to sort out my schedule, and I'll ring your doorbell." My friend paused for a few beats. "Did you really have no idea who he was?"

I shook my head, feeling so dumb. "No… Yes… He's not the same guy you see on TV, in magazines, or all over the internet. Around me, he's relaxed. His scruff's longer, his hair too, and his smile is genuine. And he looks much younger." My entire body shook, the truth slicing my heart open. HN was Carter Hills. *HN was Carter Hills.* "It's like all his guards are down and he's himself. He doesn't have a mask on. HN looks nothing like Carter Hills." Tears streamed down my face, and I let them flow.

"April, you're falling for him." She said it in the sweetest possible way, trying to protect my heart and my feelings.

"No, I'm not. I just thought we were friends. Friends don't lie to each other." Anger replaced my sadness. I wiped my soaked cheeks with the sleeve of my sweater. "You don't have to come here. I'm a grown woman, and I'll deal with this on my own."

"Whatever. I'm still coming. It might be my only chance to meet him. Call me a groupie, but you know how I've always thought he's one of the finest male specimens on the planet."

A high-pitched laugh came out. "You're being ridiculous, Saund, but that's why I love you. He's human. No need to start fangirling over him."

"I love you too. Talk to him. Listen to what he has to

say before running away. I know you. You guys are really friends now?"

I shrugged. "Yeah. Or I thought so." I withheld the fun fact that we were now sharing a house together.

"In that case, let him explain. He may surprise you."

"No promises. If I go to jail after killing him, will you bail me out?"

"Always. And April, I don't want you to end up with another broken heart. Be careful."

After we hung up, more tears streaked down my face, a storm of mixed emotions raging inside me.

With a constricting throat and a hitching breath, I dragged my feet back toward Carter's cabin. *HN is Carter Hills.* How many times should I say it to start believing it?

The tears I couldn't stop blurred my vision.

In that instant, I hated myself. How could I have been so clueless?

Once inside, I climbed the stairs to the guest room, where Bernice lay on my bed, stretching. I collapsed on the mattress, face first, and she inched closer, purring into my ear. She'd witnessed my crying so many times over the years this new surge of sadness wouldn't surprise her. She slid her head under my chin, her way of comforting me, and I patted her soft fur.

"I hadn't seen this one coming. I...I feel cheated." My voice cracked on the last word. "I'm such a fool. Never trust people, Bern. They all...they all leave at some point. Now I'll be the one leaving first. Remind me to never get attached to anyone else, okay? Not that I'm attached to him...it's just...I-I could feel some sparks between us. They mean nothing, though... How could they? We're from two different universes. He's a freaking rock star. And I'm...I'm just plain me. A regular girl. Not that it's bad. It's just... I'm just not cut out for a guy like Carter Hills. God,

I still can't believe this is his house and I'm living here *with* him. That he touched… Damn, I've been so stupid."

I snuggled up against my cat, holding on to her like a lifeline, and closed my eyes. Using my sleeve, I wiped away more tears from my cheeks.

For the next hour, I dozed on and off. When sleep evaded me, a new resolve steeled my back and firmed my shoulders. Moving to my feet, I emptied the closet and the dresser, dropping all my belongings on the bed, and started packing.

Amidst everything, I had forgotten why I agreed to move in with HN. Oh, yes, the lock. Now I understood his panic when he thought I snapped a picture of him in the woods and why he refused to let me sleep in a cabin with a broken latch, even though we were surrounded by a fence. Carter Hills probably had tons of crazy fans out there. The mere thought of them gave me the creeps.

I dried a new batch of tears with my fingertips. My vision clouded once more, and I dropped to the floor, my head between my folded knees. *Don't cry over a liar. Someone who played you. He's not worth it.*

A woman's voice drifted up from downstairs—clear and soft. "Cart, are you here? Your door is unlocked. That's very unlike you."

I closed the bedroom door, deciding hiding was my best option. No more humiliation for the day. *But what if the woman calls the cops or thinks I'm a crazy stalker?* I should show my face…just in case.

From the bedroom, I called out, "Carter's not here. He's gone into town"—my voice sounded croaky, and I coughed to clear my throat—"and should be back in a few hours."

Unsteady on my feet, I stepped down the stairs.

"And who are you?" the voice asked.

"A...a friend. The neighbor. I-I'm not sure anymore. Anyway, I'm supposed to stay here until my cabin gets fixed." In my rambling, I came face-to-face with Dahlia. I stopped in my tracks. Up close, she appeared even more beautiful than I remembered. She was this gorgeous redhead with pale freckles sprinkled over her straight nose and high cheeks, wearing minimal makeup. There was an unmistakable calmness about her, and sparks danced in her moss-green eyes.

Dressed in black jeans and a simple gray, off-shoulder knitted sweater, she beamed. Her gaze swept over the length of me. "Oh, it's you." She didn't seem surprised to see me here.

I frowned, unsure about what I should say.

Her smile acted like a soothing blanket.

"You know who I am?" I asked, my eyes widening.

"Carter and I have been friends for many years. We can read each other like an open book. I heard the smile in his voice when I talked to him yesterday. In fact, he called to talk to Jack, my son, but we ended up having a long chat."

"He did? Wait. He...huh...he talked about me?" My eyebrows bunched together as I was having a hard time believing Carter Hills had anything to say about me to his dearest friend.

"You're kidding? He talked about you nonstop. He told me he met this amazing woman. Carter has never said stuff like that about any other woman in the past."

"Oh." *Did he?* Lava pooled in my cheeks.

She stepped forward and held my forearms in a comforting gesture, like a big sister would do. "I can see what he sees in you. Your heart is pure." *Or that I'm stupid because I had no idea who he was.*

Flustered, I had nothing to add. She dropped her

hands and took a step back, probably noticing my uneasiness.

"I'm sorry. I'm really protective of him. Carter is family."

I nodded. My lips parted like a fish, trying to suck in some air. Dahlia said nothing about my glossy, red-rimmed eyes, and I thanked her in my head. Before coming downstairs, I'd grimaced at my reflection in the bedroom mirror, but had no time to do anything about it.

"Are you leaving?" Her eyes traveled to the suitcase in my hand, a confused expression drawn on her face. I kind of forgot about it.

I cast a glance down and shrugged. "It's, huh, complicated. I-I've learned some things today, and I… Let's just say that I can't stay here. Carter… He lied to me." My voice wavered. I hated showing weakness. Taking a deep breath, I shoved my emotions down and squared my shoulders. "Anyway, I shouldn't stay here. It's not right." I sighed and placed my piece of luggage on the floor.

Dahlia grabbed my hands in hers. "You're not going anywhere before you and I have a girl talk. You'll tell me what Carter lied about, and we'll go from there. Then if you decide to leave, I'll know I did everything I could to convince you to give him another chance." She snaked her arm through mine and led me to the kitchen.

Was she for real? Why would she want me to give Carter Hills, the country superstar, another chance? My curiosity got the better of me, and I followed her.

"Tea?"

I nodded.

"Carter doesn't drink coffee, so I hope you're not a caffeine junkie because I'm sure we won't find any in here."

"No, I'm more of a tea, hot chocolate type of girl, actually."

"Perfect," she said, clasping her hands in front of her. "You and I will get along just fine."

I watched as she filled the kettle and placed tea bags in two mugs. She was a natural in HN's kitchen. No doubt she came here a lot. I reached for the plate of chocolate chip cookies I baked yesterday and slid it between us.

"Hungry?"

Her eyes rounded. "You baked those?"

I nodded with a tight-lipped smile.

"Sorry, I didn't introduce myself. I'm Dahlia Ellis, Carter's oldest friend." She held out a hand for me to shake.

I slipped my palm into hers. "I'm April. April Simmons. I live in the cabin next door. Or at least, that's where I'm supposed to be staying."

The woman leaned her back against the kitchen counter, bringing the cookie to her mouth. "These are amazing. It's nice to finally meet you, April. Oh, and I love your name by the way. What brings you to Green Mountain?"

"It's a long story. I'm an author, and I was having writer's block. Or rather a creative outage. My friend Saunders, who owns a luxury vacation rental company, had rented the cabin next door for one of her clients, and he had a change of plan at the last minute. She offered it to me, hoping it'd unblock my creative flow." I shrugged. "I guess you could say life brought me here."

"That's amazing. Living here is like an addiction. When you've breathed the mountain air once, you always need more."

We both exchanged a smile.

"How long have you been here? In Green Mountain, I mean."

"Well, I moved here while pregnant with Jack. You've met him, right?"

"Yes, and he's adorable. He looks a lot like Carter."

"He does." Something dark passed in her eyes. A memory. "Enough talk about me. I want to know why you want to leave and what Carter lied about. Men… They can be idiots sometimes." Dahlia filled our mugs with boiling water and took a seat facing me. "Carter is a complicated man. However, once you get to know him, there's not a more passionate and selfless man in the world." A soft smile spread across her face.

I fidgeted with the handle of the mug, hesitant to confide in her. I knew nothing about this woman, except that Carter had been loving her forever. Dahlia offered me a hearty smile. I tucked strands of my pink hair behind my ear and fished my phone out of my back pocket.

After unlocking it, I slid the device toward her across the counter. On the screen were the pictures Saunders had sent me earlier. Dahlia swiped them, one by one, a deep frown marking her porcelain face.

"I see. And you were clueless about who he was. Am I right?"

I buried my face in my hands. "Yeah. It sounds so stupid, but I really had no idea… I swear. For me, he was just this half-annoying, half-sweet neighbor." I lifted my head to meet her gaze.

Dahlia rested her chin on her open palm, her elbow propped up on the counter.

"April, I'll tell you something. That's what makes you even more special in his eyes. The truth is that you don't care about who he is outside these walls. You treat him like a man. Not a country star or a celebrity. You see the real

Carter Hills, not the image he creates for the media. Only a handful of people have access to this version of him, and you're lucky to be one of them."

"It doesn't change the fact that he lied to me," I said, my heart pounding in my chest.

"Carter loves how normal his life is around you. He should've told you. You're right about that. But he also did it to protect you. April, you don't need this circus in your life, believe me. It's not good for anyone. Not many people are built for this kind of attention. I walked away from the music industry and fame because I refused to let my baby be a part of this." She blew out a long sigh. "Carter must be with June as we speak, trying to find ways to keep you away from the press." She brought her mug to her lips but didn't take a sip.

"June?"

"Juniper. His assistant manager. The media will create any story they see fit if it helps them sell copies and captivate their audience. Carter despises everything about this side of the business. He loves the music. He's the best songwriter I know. I don't say it because we're friends. It's the truth. But he struggles with fame…daily. That's why he comes here every chance he gets. To escape. To ground himself. To clear his mind and just be."

I pondered her words for a moment as we basked in the confidences she just shared.

After I promised her I'd talk to Carter before deciding on anything, Dahlia left. She hugged me on her way out, and I realized I'd just met my first woman crush. Right then, I understood why HN loved her so much.

I was sitting at the kitchen island, writing with Bernice curled up at my feet, snoozing, when Carter walked in three hours later. With dark circles under his eyes and worry lines etched into his face, he looked ten years older than he did last night.

He erased the distance between us, caged me between his arms, and kissed me on the cheek.

He hadn't shown me any sign of affection since the day we practically devoured each other's faces in my cabin when I first arrived. Yet somehow, my heart fluttered at the simple gesture. It felt like something normal between us... As if he'd done it a hundred times before. Like I belonged here. With him.

I shivered at the thought. A big part of me loved how I felt around him—like everything finally made sense when we were together, and I didn't have to overthink every little thing. Like I could just be myself.

After my talk with Dahlia earlier, my anger toward him had subsided. The voices in my head telling me to run away had quieted.

I loved her honesty, and our girl talk helped me see the situation from another perspective. His.

"How was your day?" I asked, swiveling on my stool and resting my hand gently on his forearm, the cord of his muscles flexing under my touch.

Carter sighed, bent over, and scooped Bernice up, petting her head and nuzzling her fur. "Painful. What about yours?"

"Eventful."

He furrowed his eyebrows.

"Dahlia came by earlier."

His frown deepened. "She did?"

He had no idea? My girl crush intensified. I appreciated her discretion. "Yeah. She's nice. We...huh...we talked. She's really a fan of yours."

"What did you two talk about?"

"You." I averted my gaze, scared he would be mad I talked to his best friend about him behind his back.

"Cool. I hope you said wonderful things." He leaned forward and laid a kiss on my lips, again, as if it were the most natural thing in the world.

My eyes flared, but I said nothing. Butterflies danced in my belly when he pressed his mouth to mine. It awakened all my senses and filled me with renewed energy.

"Glad to be home. I'll change and cook dinner." He turned around to walk away, but I caught his wrist. I felt his pulse, strong and steady, beating under the pads of my fingers.

"No offense, but you look like shit. I can prep dinner."

He grazed my shoulders with his fingers, and his voice softened. "I want to. I insist. Give me ten minutes. I'll be right back." His lips connected to my forehead before he disappeared upstairs.

What the hell's going on?

Carter Hills was acting like we were dating. What did I miss?

Now, I refused to spoil the night by venting my frustration. Deep down, I wasn't even sure I was still angry. Hurt, maybe, but my anger had faded hours ago. I cringed inside. Gosh, I was so screwed.

———

We finished our dinner, and I sat back in my chair, my half-empty wineglass in hand, looking at Carter over the rim. His dark hair was disheveled, the way I liked, and the sleeves of his Henley black shirt were pushed up, revealing his corded forearms and the leather cuff around his left wrist. Even dressed in a casual outfit, he looked handsome. I should've picked up on the signs about his identity sooner.

Now that I knew who he was, I couldn't unsee it. He stabbed the last piece of food on his plate, his face strained and eyes unsettled, something that had been there since the moment he walked in earlier. He didn't look upset, but rather dejected. With a roll of my wrist, I spun the clear liquid around in my glass, thinking about my next course of action. I loathed secrets. Bringing the glass under my nose, I took a whiff of the alcohol, the gears in my head spinning to find the right words as my heartbeat sped up.

You can do this, April. You have to.

My gaze wandered all around me, avoiding my host's, and I cleared my throat. "I know about you." Clear and concise. Straight to the point. I struggled to keep my voice low and even, too many emotions bubbling up inside me.

His eyes locked on mine for a split second, and his lips tightened in thin line.

Something passed between us.

Carter pressed the heels of his hands over his eyes and leaned forward, resting his elbows on his knees. "You do?"

I nodded, keeping my gaze down.

"Fuck, this wasn't supposed to happen. I'm sorry. I never meant for you to learn it this way. How did you—?" His voice cracked, and it drowned his last few words.

The same way I did with Dahlia today, I pushed my phone across the table, a picture of us visible on the screen. "My friend Saunders sent me those. Thought I knew about you and kept it a secret."

Carter raised his head, grabbed my phone, and swiped through the pictures with devoted focus.

His Adam's apple bobbed with an audible swallow, and he breathed out. "Listen, I-I'm sorry. I messed up. Shit. I'll understand if you want nothing to do with me anymore."

I extended my hand to grab his, but he leaned back and punched the table. "Stupid press." He stood up and dragged a hand over his face, smoothing the worry lines, and started pacing across the kitchen.

I watched him for a minute, his expression morphing from anger to a painful one. For the longest time, I stayed silent, not sure what to say.

"I fucking despise this side of my life. I hate that you found out like this. It's not fair to you. I should've...I should've thought it through."

Curiosity won the battle inside me, and I finally asked the question I'd been holding onto all evening. "Wh-why didn't you tell me?"

Carter stopped pacing and faced me. "I love how I'm just HN around you. You expect nothing from Carter Hills. You're yourself, standing your ground, not afraid to call me out on my bullshit. People always treat me differently when they know who I am."

I failed to hold in the smile stretching my lips. Rising to my feet, I joined him in the kitchen. He slid an arm around my shoulders, and when he pulled me close, I buried my face in his chest.

"I was mad earlier. Super mad. Extra mad. You lied to me, and I wanted to leave before you came back home. But then Dahlia stopped by, and she explained stuff to me. About fame and how you hate it. She told me you left this morning to take care of that," I said, pointing to my phone on the table with a grimace.

"Yeah, I did. Wait. You wanted to leave? Without saying goodbye?"

He was so much taller than me that I had to crank my neck back to meet his eyes. Carter did a poor job of hiding the hurt shadowing his face.

I nodded and swallowed through the shards lining my throat.

"That's why your suitcase was in the foyer, isn't it?"

I bowed my head, and he grabbed my hands in his muscular ones.

"Honestly, I didn't know what to think of all this, and I still don't. I felt betrayed because I thought you and I were friends. You…you hurt me."

He brushed his thumb across my cheek. "I took your luggage back to your room earlier. That's where it belongs."

"Thanks," I said, avoiding his heavy gaze, my head still hanging low.

He extended his hand to shake mine, and I blinked before lifting my gaze to meet his. "April Simmons, I'm Carter Hills. Nice to finally introduce myself."

I gasped. "You knew my name all along?"

He lowered his eyes, a pink flush coloring his cheeks, and winced. "I know the names of all my guests. Wasn't fair to call you by yours while withholding mine. Sorry about that."

I blinked again. "If it means anything," I said, "I loved the nickname game we were playing. I enjoy a bit of mystery now and then. It keeps things interesting."

His intense stare liquified me. I kept my eyes locked on his. Heat flooded my cheeks, and a flurry of emotions swirled in my chest.

Carter pulled me back to him, and I breathed him in. A shiver traversed my body, and he wound his arms around me, bringing me much-needed warmth and shelter. The emotions of the day seeped through me, and my eyes burned as I fought back tears. The reality of my neighbor's identity still sounded unbelievable to me. Right now, I, April Simmons, was nestled in *the* Carter Hills's embrace, and it didn't even feel weird.

Not knowing what to do with my hands, I fisted his shirt, not ready for him to release me. His lips rested at the crown of my head, and after a beat, he planted a soft, lingering kiss. I swore I saw stars.

Carter Hills and HN were the same person. I felt silly for never catching onto the truth. Somehow, a part of me was relieved I hadn't, because I couldn't help but wonder how different our relationship—or whatever it was—would have been if I had known.

"I flashed you. That first day…I…huh…flashed you. Oh, this is mortifying. You must have thought I was some sort of crazy groupie chasing after you."

He snickered, his chin resting on top of my head. "It wasn't even the first thought that popped into my head. I wondered if we had ever met before… I got entranced by the blue of your eyes. Even from a distance, they fascinated me and took me hostage. Sure, I appreciated the view, but your eyes were to blame for my growing interest in you."

Our laughter died down, and we remained silent for a long while, both of us unable to break apart.

"I'm glad you didn't run away earlier." Carter's deep voice vibrated through me.

"Well, for what it's worth, I'm glad I stayed."

One arm released me, and seconds later, low music played on his phone. "April, dance with me."

I leaned back and lost myself in the gray of his irises. My own personal storm. The one that could be the death of me if I wasn't careful.

I bobbed my head, and Carter repositioned his arms around me. With my eyes closed, I followed his movements, losing myself in the slow melody and the sensation of his body pressed against mine. In his masculine scent. In the safety his arms provided.

Our feet fell in time, and our hearts followed. Soon, our breaths matched in perfect rhythm.

Time stopped.

The man holding me right now wasn't a famous country music star. He was the one who cared for me. The one who kissed me earlier when he arrived like we were a couple. He was the one who enraged me but also fascinated me. Who rearranged his furniture around to create a writing space for me when I moved in and taught me how to play the guitar.

He was just that. A man. No matter what I tried to let myself believe at first, he was an incredible one.

And I was a woman who was trying to keep her heart under lock and key to make sure that man wouldn't shatter it to pieces.

When did we become more…so much more?

The song ended, but Carter didn't release me.

The first notes of a song about love and forever started, the heartfelt lyrics enveloping us.

"This is yours, right? The song? Isn't it?" I asked, my voice barely above a whisper.

"Yep." He grazed the length of my back with his fingertips, eliciting shivers in their wake.

We slow danced in silence, melting into each other, for a full minute.

"Thanks for dancing to my words with me, April."

"Anytime." I pressed my cheek against his beating heart, loving how both our bodies fit against each other. How his enveloped mine and I felt safe in his embrace. "Your songs are inspiring. Filled with love and so many emotions, I feel them all. It's a rare gift you possess."

After the third song, I risked a gaze up. Carter's eyes captured mine. I swallowed, not prepared for the heat I saw on his face. Every particle aimed at me.

"I trust you." I felt the need to reiterate the fact in case there were still doubts lingering between us.

"Thanks." He nodded, never breaking eye contact.

At the same time I moved to my tiptoes, he leaned in. Our lips brushed together as if it was the first time. A zing tingled the tip of my spine. The tentative kiss evolved into a languorous one, and my entire being got electrified when our mouths danced together like a perfectly rehearsed choreography.

Carter's hold on me tightened.

Swaying to the music, we kissed some more.

It was nothing like our first kiss. We were in no rush this time. No desperation. It wasn't about sating a thirst, but more like a promise. Filled with trust, respect, and something I couldn't quite name.

We were equal.

No celebrity status or exes stood between us.

We were Carter and April, two people who had no idea how to navigate the connection they shared and the reality they both stepped in when they met.

Our lips moved together, and soon we were devouring each other's mouths without restraint, the heat enveloping us palpable. We were both starving, kissing as if the world would end any second.

Carter's palms moved up and down my back, and I twisted his shirt in my fist, craving a physical connection other than him to keep me grounded in the moment.

Heat shot through me, ribbons of lust coiling around me and making me their prisoner.

Light-headed, I wasn't sure how I ended up here but wished to be nowhere else.

The proof of his desire pressed against my lower belly, and I rubbed myself against him, searching for some much-needed friction that would tame the flames licking my skin and turning my insides into molten lava.

One large hand cupped my cheek, angling my face so

Carter could deepen the kiss. The one that had my toes curling.

I lost contact with everything around me.

I looped my arms around his neck and pulled him down, relishing how his teeth toyed with my lower lip. Moans I couldn't keep inside for another second escaped, burying the sound of our combined frantic breaths.

Carter lowered his hands to my ass, grabbing a handful before lifting me onto the kitchen counter, leveling our faces. Even through layers of clothes, his touch felt like a burning caress. My legs wrapped around his, keeping him close to me, trying to erase any space left between us.

With his lips, he cherished the corners of my mouth, traced my jawline, and kissed the column of my throat. He sucked on my pulse point before licking his way down to my collarbone and returning to my lips.

My head swam in a blissful haze of pleasure, and I couldn't tell who broke the kiss first. With our faces about three inches apart, we stared at the other, breathless, neither of us saying anything.

Carter's chest rose and fell in quick succession. A glint shone in his eyes, and his lips curled into a lazy smile.

I grinned, never letting go of him, feeling vulnerable when he watched me like I mattered to him and I belonged in his arms.

A new song began playing, and until that moment, I had forgotten all about the music. The only sound I could hear was the drumming of my own heart.

Carter lowered me to my feet, and his arms pulled me back to his chest. Tangled together, we danced some more. Each time our gazes fixated on each other, there was a sense of peace settling between us that wasn't there before. Some sort of silent agreement.

Whatever happened, Carter had my back. And I had his.

"Listen, I'm giving a show next Saturday in Nashville. June, my assistant manager, convinced me it'd calm the storm surrounding us. Some sort of gift to my fans. I'd like for you to come along, but it's up to you. If you refuse, I'll understand."

Carter Hills said *us*. I wanted to fan myself but refrained. After a rock and roll morning, my day had taken a wild, unexpected turn. "I'm not sure I'm cut out for all this attention."

He shook his head. "It won't be like this. I promise. You'll stay with June the entire time. She's part of my team. I trust her. You'll be backstage. It's gonna be an acoustic show, not a big concert. Me and my guitar. Nothing too glamorous. You know, a few hundred fans, maybe even less. My team is setting it up as we speak. I don't have all the details yet."

Since when did HN ramble around me? He slouched, releasing a heavy breath through his nose.

After a beat, he gently tipped my chin up with a curled finger, and we gazed into each other's eyes. I saw the plea in his melted-steel irises.

"I'll think about it."

He curved a hand around the back of my head, pulling me closer, and pressed a kiss to my forehead. "Thanks."

My frantic heart rate dropped a notch.

And time stopped.

16

CARTER

"Okay, there are quite a few things I enjoy. Let's see. What I like the most about Green Mountain are the feet orgasms I get while walking on crunchy leaves covering the ground and the sunsets."

Feet orgasms? I mirrored April's grin. Even her words sounded like poetry.

"I also shed tears every time I see old people kissing. The ocean breeze gives me goose bumps, and fireflies on summer days entice me."

"Anything else?"

"I adore candy apples because they remind me of my childhood, and I believe wishing upon a star makes dreams come true." She took a sip from her mug.

I leaned in to wipe the hot chocolate off the corner of her lips with my thumb. Our gazes locked, and for a minute, I forgot how my lungs worked.

Fairy averted her eyes. "Where was I? Oh yes. Hot chocolate heals everything…"—her voice dropped to a lower and huskier tone—"or it should."

My entire body pulsed with need. Sitting on the couch,

next to the chair I was in, with her legs tucked under her, she tightened the white fluffy blanket around her shoulders. After we slow danced and kissed earlier, keeping a safe distance between us seemed imperative. Until we figured out the specifics of our blossoming relationship—and what it all meant. The fire crackling in the fireplace and the cat's slow, steady snoring were the only sounds in the house.

"What about you? What do you like, Carter?" April's words had turned into a guttural whisper...or was that just my imagination?

My heart shuddered each time my name—my real name—fell from her lips. *You*, I wanted to scream. I swallowed hard, doing my best not rip her clothes off and ravage her with my mouth like I did mere hours ago. "I love music. It's an addiction, a drug. Without it, I'm lost. It keeps me sane. Don't tell anybody, but I also enjoy watching rom-coms." I scratched my jaw. "I already told you about Jack and Dahlia, so… Oh, and I like sledding. It's something I do with Jack. A tradition. We should do it together. You and me."

"Huh, you're sure it's a good idea? I'm not even sure I like winter yet."

"How about we go tomorrow? Everything about flying down a snowy slope feels like magic." I didn't exaggerate. "For a minute, you're back to being a kid again. You don't have to like winter to enjoy this."

"Okay, you make it sound fun. I can do this."

"Now that you know all about me, tell me why you're staying in Green Mountain for a month by yourself. And what are you writing all the time on your laptop? You spend hours a day glued to that screen."

She sighed and rolled her jaw back and forth. Did she not trust me? I didn't have too much time to ponder this possibility when she started talking. "I'm writing a book. A novel. I'm an author…huh…for now."

My eyes widened. "Nice. You said, *for now?* Why?"

She shrugged. "I don't know. It just kind of happened, but this wasn't a dream of mine. I love it, believe me. I'm good at it when I put my mind to it, but I'm not sure it's what I'm supposed to do. Sometimes I feel like I'm missing something. My true purpose. I haven't figured out what it is, though."

"You published anything yet?"

Fairy nodded. "Two books. And they're doing quite well."

"Anything I might have read?"

Her laugh rang out, sending a zing through my entire being. "No. Unless you're into magic and fantasy worlds kind of literature."

I shook my head. "Nah. I don't think so. Perhaps I should try it. Do you think it would suit me?"

Her sweet laughter doubled in intensity. "Please don't. I refuse to picture you as my typical reader."

I puckered my face and pretended to stab my chest. "Ouch, that hurts. Anyway, I think it's great. Might explain why we're so good at bantering. I found my word-lover soul mate." I winked, and April shook her head, her smile not faltering.

"Well. Anyway, even if you tried searching for me online, you wouldn't find a thing. I'm using a pen name, and my picture isn't out there. I relish my privacy too much."

My interest grew even more. "What is it? Your pen name, I mean."

"If I tell you, I'll have to kill you afterward because only a few people know. Not sure it's worth the risk. I'll keep it a secret, so your life is safe."

She winked, and I almost melted in my seat when I realized she wouldn't tell me, for real. Should I be impressed or run for my life? April Simmons was dangerous around me. She was both a drug and a mystery, all wrapped up in one bubbly and sexy woman. I fixed her with a stare, speechless—and spellbound. Had I finally met my match?

The crackling of the fire filled the silence, and both our gazes drifted toward the burning logs. The rich smell of the brownies April had baked after dinner clung to every particle of air around us.

Here and now, I felt content. And relaxed. It'd been an eternity since I last felt fully at ease around anyone who hadn't been part of my entourage for what felt like forever.

After a long moment, she fought a yawn. "Well, I'm going to bed. I have no idea what time it is, but I'm exhausted. Today was an emotional ride."

"About that, I'm...I'm sorry. I never meant for you to find out this way. I was afraid you'd run away if you knew who I was. In the past, I've been... Let's just say I've been burned and learned my lesson, and now I'm more careful."

"Don't sweat it. It's fine. Maybe if I had known early on, it would have freaked me out. You're kind of a big deal out there. Some part of me relishes the fact we got to know each other beforehand. Still, gimme some time to get used to it, though."

We eyed each other for a few beats. April hugged herself with her arms, and I cleared my throat. "Okay. I can do that. Thanks for giving me another chance to make things right. I'll let you go to bed now. Good night, Fairy." There was so much more I wanted to tell her, but I couldn't find the words. "I'll see you in the morning."

"Yeah. Night, HN." She waved at me and walked away,

leaving me all alone with my thoughts. And a massive hard-on.

I raked my fingers through my hair, leaned back, and breathed out, the pressure of the day melting away.

Once I was sure April wouldn't come back downstairs, I turned off all the lights and made my way to my bedroom. I undressed, and butt-naked, I collapsed, face first, on the mattress and fell asleep in no time. Images of my roommate filled every one of my dreams.

The next day, April and I spent the morning working. She was writing in the den while I was locked in my music studio, sitting on the couch, trying to come up with a melody for a song I wrote. After lunch, we drove to Dahlia's.

"*Carrrter*," Jack shouted, running into my arms as we climbed out of my SUV. He lowered his voice. "Is the fairy your friend?" A loud chuckle left me as he looked at me with wide eyes.

"Yes, she is." I extended my arm to grab April's hand in mine and pulled her forward. "April, you remember Jack?"

Letting go of my hand, she dropped to her knees, bringing herself to his eye level. "Hey, Jack. It's nice to see you again. How is your friend Beatrix doing?"

The boy's eyes flared. "You remember her name?"

"Yes. How could I forget the name of the biggest fairies fan?"

"You want to meet her?" His voice was full of hope. And excitement.

April grinned. "Sure. I'd love to."

Jack lifted a finger to stop her from moving or talking.

"Okay. Wait here. I'll be right back." He hurried inside, leaving us in the driveway.

"Guess we should go inside," I said, pushing her forward after I helped her up. Some sort of electricity passed between us from where my hand rested on her lower back., and my heart jolted. I swallowed hard and kept walking.

Dahlia appeared in the doorway before I had time to knock. "Hey guys." She rose on her tiptoes to kiss my cheek and greeted April with a genuine smile and a hug. "Nice to see you again, April. Glad you two made up."

April offered her a small, lopsided smile. "Nice to see you too."

"Carter told me you need winter clothes. I'm taller than you, but we're about the same size. Follow me. We'll find you something." Dahlia grabbed April's hand and led her away. "Give us a few minutes, Cart."

"Where's Nick?"

"Working," my friend said from a distance. "Some emergency."

In the kitchen, I was pouring myself a glass of water when Jack came running. "Is April still here?" he asked, breathless.

"Yes, why?"

He bent forward to catch his breath. "Bea will be here in five minutes. Her mama is dropping her off for the afternoon. We're having a playdate."

"Does your mama know?"

He bobbed his head quickly. "Yes. She told me I could invite her over."

When the doorbell rang, I greeted Mrs. Foster and Beatrix, just as April and Dahlia came back, my roommate dressed in navy-blue snow pants and a bright pink jacket. My lips curled at the sight. "For someone who's not a winter fan, you pull those off pretty well," I teased, throwing in a wink.

A rosy hue spread across her cheeks.

Jack disrupted the moment when he tugged at her sleeve. "This is my best friend, Bea. Bea, this is April, Carter's fairy friend I told you about."

Just like she did earlier, April squatted and held out her hand to shake Beatrix's little one.

The girl's hazel eyes grew big as she offered April her best smile.

"Hi, Bea. I'm happy to meet you. Jack told me all about you."

The questions spilled from Beatrix's mouth in rapid-fire succession. She barely had time to catch her breath before launching into another one. Beatrix didn't even notice her mom slipping away, her face lit up with a giant grin as she watched her daughter in full awe mode.

I snickered behind my hand, watching the two five-year-olds embroiled in a serious debate about hair color.

"Well, if you wanna go, I guess I need to break this party up," Dahlia whispered in my ear. "Either that or April will faint from heat stroke underneath all these clothes." Her hand found mine, and she gave it a strong squeeze. No words were needed.

"You've made quite an impression," I told April as we climbed back into the truck a few minutes later. "You're lucky those kids let you go."

She laughed—a clear and happy sound that went straight to my heart. For a long time, I had to deal with Savannah Prince's pretenses, and right now, it felt good to witness a woman being herself fully, not playing a role or wearing a mask.

"I'm not joking. Ever heard of being abducted by kids so they could experiment with strands of your hair and steal your magic? It's some serious shit. Being a fairy, you should know all about it. For your safety."

She laughed some more, and I joined in.

Ten minutes later, we arrived at my special spot, the one I'd been bringing Jack to since he was old enough to stand on his feet by himself. My heart beat a little faster, knowing I brought someone else here. April was the first woman I allowed around him without a second thought. For a reason I ignored, it felt right. A rock grew in my stomach. Her time in Green Mountain had an expiration date, and I needed to remember that. My heart had been broken too many times already, and I wasn't interested in putting it through the wringer again.

"I'm surprised there's snow here." Her eyes traveled all around us. "Everywhere else, it has melted."

I snapped out of my daze and cleared my throat. "The valley is always feet deep covered in snow. This and the ski resort. Everywhere else in town, it comes and goes. Ready?"

She followed me close, glee radiating from her. We'd parked at the top of the hill, and the view from there was breathtaking. Snowy mountaintops. Valleys. A glimpse of Main Street below. The slope was a fraction of a mile long and not too steep.

"It's peaceful here. I understand why it's your special spot." Fairy's eyes were wide as she took in her surroundings, and a piece of my heart expanded.

We settled ourselves on the sled, way too small for two grown-ups. With my height, it was a bit of a challenge to fit both of us on the wooden sleigh, but April was so small that we made it work. She positioned herself in front of me, and I wrapped my legs around her.

"Zip up. You don't want to turn into a snowman."

"All done," she said, excitement clear in her voice. "I can't believe we're doing this."

"Hold on tight," I warned her as we launched ourselves down the snowy hill. With a push of my hands, I propelled us down the slope before wrapping my arms around her waist. It satisfied some of my urges to touch her. Whenever April was nearby, my hands itched to brush her skin.

The sled hopped. She yelped. My heart swelled in my rib cage.

This girl lit up like a Christmas tree for things most people would consider boring. Snowflakes. The crisp crunch of fallen leaves beneath her feet. Hot chocolate. Her cat snoring. Sunsets. Winning a game of Monopoly. Buying groceries.

The sled tipped over at the bottom of the slope, enveloping us in white flurries. April's contagious laughter resonated around us in the valley. We were in our own world when we tumbled in the snow together. The kid in me was having a blast.

"Oh. My. God. That was insane. I can't believe I've never done this before."

We were both lying on our backs on the ground. I turned to my side, removed one of my gloves, and using my fingertips, dusted off snowflakes from April's nose and cheeks. The air in my lungs turned to ice. Her bottom lip shuddered when the pad of my thumb smoothed the contours of it. She closed her eyes. This was it. The moment when I abandoned all my restraints. Our lips were a hair's breadth apart, breath mingling, hearts racing, the world narrowing to just the space between us.

April cocked her head and sneezed, breaking the moment. "Sorry," she said as she sneezed again and sat upright. I rose to my feet, grabbed her hand to pull her up, put my glove back on, and dusted off the snow covering her hat and coat.

"Can we go again?" She looked at me with her best puppy dog eyes.

"Come on." I turned around, adjusted the erection in my pants, and squatted low. "Hop on." She locked her thighs around my waist and her arms around my neck, and I carried her on my back the entire way up. Even from under all our winter clothes, her heartbeat, strong and fast, thudded against my back and vibrated through me.

At the top of the hill, April fixed her hat, her smile never faltering. "Thank you, Carter. I'm glad you insisted I wear proper winter clothes. This is so much fun."

Yeah. One hypothermia scare was more than enough.

———

"Today, I'm giving you a snowboarding lesson. I bet you've never tried it before."

April shook her head. "Isn't it dangerous? Can we break our backs or something?"

I dropped a kiss on her wrinkled forehead. Pixie was clueless about everything related to winter. "You're cute. I'll never let anything bad happen to you. I promise. You're safe with me."

"Okay, then. Let's gear up."

I burst out laughing. "It's a bit more complicated than that. We gotta rent you a board and boots first. Get changed, and meet me in the truck. I'll gather my gear."

The lesson lasted half a day, and the entire time, every cell in my body ached to touch her. I locked my hands around her waist, helping her with her balance too many times to keep count. It wasn't much, but it fulfilled some of my touch-April needs. With a reluctant smile and a high dose of trust in me, she held on to me with a death grip. We exchanged heated stares, and I forced myself to think about olives, a fruit I hated, and gooey snails, a mollusk that grossed me out. Focused, she worried her bottom lip between her teeth, and it almost pushed me over the edge. *Relax, Carter.* My roommate had a way of enchanting every parcel of me. I jumped up and down, faking I was cold and trying to shake off the tightness in my pants, the fabric suddenly feeling a little too snug.

"I did it. Carter, I did it." April carved a few turns without falling and jumped into my arms when I finally came to a stop next to her, ecstatic, her feet still strapped to the board.

My level of pride skyrocketed to outer space.

We hugged for a bit too long, unable to break apart.

I breathed her in. Lavender. And mint lip gloss.

Another wall around my heart crumbled, leaving it exposed.

"I'm fucking proud of you, Fairy." I held on to her before lowering her back down. My thumb brushed her lips when I cupped her cheek and she shivered under my feather-soft touch. With a step back, I released her and broke the spell. "Let's go again."

———

"Tomorrow, we're leaving for Nashville, but what about ice skating this afternoon? You can get some writing done before we go. Anyway, I have a song to finish. Work in the morning, fun later. How does it sound?" I asked April as we finished breakfast, sitting side by side at the kitchen island, both in sweats and bare feet. Half of her hair was tied in some sort of knot on the top of her head, and with flushed cheeks and her lids still heavy from sleep, she looked adorable.

"I'm not a very athletic person, HN. Don't be too optimistic here. Also, all my muscles are still aching from snowboarding and sledding."

"You'll be fine. I'll be right beside you the entire time, holding your hand."

Ice skating was another one of April's first times. From now on, I wanted them all—all her first times.

And her lasts.

During the entire ride to the ice rink, she kept her hand firmly lodged in mine.

Once we arrived, we sat on a bench and removed our boots. I put my skates on in less than a minute and kneeled in front of April once she slid her feet into the pair we rented for her, eyeing them as if she had no idea where to start.

I curled my fingers around her shin and positioned her foot between my knees to keep it in place.

"What are you doing?" she asked, watching me with a curious gaze.

"Tying these. Let me know if it's too tight."

"Oh. You don't have to do this. I-I probably can do it myself."

"Let me do it. If they're too loose, your ankle will roll. They gotta be tight, but just enough. You'll understand what I mean." I laced the first skate, enjoying being able to do this for her.

April snickered, studying each of my movements. "But you're kneeling in front of me."

I winked. She blushed.

On unsteady feet, April glided forward, her hand never leaving mine. We took a few tentative steps on the ice, so she could get the hang of balancing on blades. With a soft pull, I guided her closer to me, turning my back to the other skaters so we were facing each other.

"See? One foot, then the other. You can do this."

With panic flashing in her eyes, she tightened her grip on my hand, draining it of blood, but she did as I said.

She looked out of her element on the ice at first, but after half an hour, she found her footing. I missed her touch the moment she let go of me. April glided on the surface on her own, feet apart from me, sparks of pride shining in her eyes. I got drunk on her laughter and light-headed on her lavender perfume.

"Hot chocolate?" She jumped to her feet, her rental skates removed and hanging from her fingers.

"Sure, I'll—"

"You stay here, and get those off your feet," she said, pointing to my still-laced skates. "I'll be right back. My treat." She waltzed away, and my eyes stayed glued to her retreating figure. Was that drool that pooled on the ground? My drool? I pinched my lips together, gave my head a small shake, and finally freed my feet from the skates.

Later, we sat on a wooden bench, watching a teen hockey game on the second rink, a big icy rectangle. A light breeze swept across our faces. I pushed strands of April's hair behind her ear and smoothed her beanie into place over her head. Families surrounded us. The ice rinks were in the middle of River Park, the largest park here in Green Mountain. Behind us, two little boys ran around, chasing each other. A husky puppy neared us, and April gaped at his sight. Both of us leaned forward to pet its head before its owner pulled on the leash. My eyes traveled back to the two boys, now laughing their hearts out, sitting on the ground.

"My dad played hockey all his life and would've made

it to the pros if he hadn't messed up his knee in college. He taught Jeff and me how to skate when we were still in diapers. We spent most of our Sunday mornings on the ice growing up. Neither Jeff nor I shared a passion for hockey like our dad did, though. We loved the game, but I've always preferred music and words, while Jeff enjoyed building stuff. He'd never really been into sports either." A low laugh escaped my mouth.

"Did your dad encourage you to follow your dreams, or was he the kind of dad who only wanted you guys to follow his own?"

A small smile tugged at the corner of my lips. "One winter day, when I was maybe seven or eight, our dad woke Jeff and me up early to go to the rink first thing in the morning. Both of us begged our mom to let us go to the winter fair instead. There was a band playing and some sort of *build a mailbox for Santa* workshop for kids. You should have seen my dad's face. He tried everything to discourage us. In vain. We ended up spending the day at the fair." Nearly twenty years later, that day remained vivid in my memory. "He let us follow our own path. I think the idea we'd never play hockey was a gut punch at first." I shrugged. I hadn't thought about my parents in quite some time. "What about your parents? Did they encourage you to follow your dreams?"

April's smile faded. She rolled her shoulders back and inhaled. "I don't know my parents. Never met them."

I angled my body to face her, keeping my face neutral. "You were in foster care?" Not that it mattered.

"No. My mom's aunt raised me. It forced me to grow up faster than any kid should. My mother got pregnant at sixteen. After she gave birth, she panicked and left me on Nana's doorstep one morning and disappeared. Nana was already over fifty-five when my mom left me. If it hadn't been for her, I would've ended up in the system. Nana lost touch with her after I turned six. The last letter she sent to my mother bounced back. Over the years, I never tried to reach out to find her. I have nothing to say to her. And my sperm donor? Nobody even knew who he was. I've forgiven my mother a long time ago and always refused to live with the ghosts of my past. In my head, and in my heart, Nana is forever going to be my mom. Biological or not, she'd been my only parent growing up.

"Saunders, my best friend, the one who sent me here, is my only family now. We met in college, and it was love at first sight. We shared a dorm room freshman year and haven't been apart since. After Nana passed away, Saunders became the only person I could count on." April gazed at me, a tinge of pink coloring her cheeks. "We had little money growing up. Over the years, I've been knocked down more times than I can count. I learned to be independent and resourceful early in life. And resilient."

I draped my arm around her shoulders and cradled her close. "I'm sorry. I didn't know."

"It's okay. I struggled for a long time, scared to let people in. Nana died during my freshman year of college. At eighteen, I was all alone in this world. Saunders and Travis, my college boyfriend, showed me I mattered to some people and that I wasn't as lonely as I thought. It took me a while to accept their unconditional love—" She averted her gaze and toyed with the lid of her hot chocolate to-go cup. "I'm a better person because of them. They showed me every day I was worthy of love."

I kissed her temple, and April relaxed in my embrace. We exchanged a ghost of a smile and watched the rest of the game in silence, her head resting against my shoulder the entire time. Something shifted inside me, and an urge to protect her, no matter what, grew inside me. Unlike the last time when I dated the Evil Queen, this time there were no voices in my head pleading with me to run for my life.

———

How come the trip from Green Mountain to Nashville seemed shorter this time? As if more than a hundred miles had vanished. April had this way of making even the most boring things in life colorful. Forget Nashville, we should've aimed for a thousand-mile road trip instead. Vanish into the sunset. Fuck under a palm tree. Never come back.

We grabbed green tea to go and settled in my SUV, playing each other's music playlists on our phones.

"Okay, I have to tell you something. It might hurt your feelings, and I'm sorry about that." I sucked in a breath and put my best poker face on. "This song sucks. Big time. I can't understand why sane people would listen to this. There's nothing good about it. Sure, the chorus is catchy, but other than that, it's punishment to endure the"—I looked at the in-dash entertainment slash navigation screen—"entire three minutes fifty-seven seconds of it. There's no vocal technique and too much Auto-Tune, it's distracting. Nails on a chalkboard would sound less painful."

"Shut up, HN. What do you know about pop music?" April cocked a brow, and I burst out laughing like a kid, choking on a sip of scorching hot tea.

"Did you forget I'm the professional here, Pixie?"

She made a funny pout. The kind I'd die to kiss. Ignoring the rise in my body temperature and my permanent hard-on, I nudged her arm. April played another song on her playlist.

"Whoa, that is even worse. Where's your taste in music, woman? My ears are bleeding right now. I thought I could trust you as the honorary DJ on the road. Kill me already. I was wrong. You're fired."

Her laughter—a sound I had come to associate with her—was clear and genuine, and I couldn't help but laugh along with her.

"Please stop this massacre you call music. New rule. My truck, my music."

Her eyes glistened every time I teased her, and I suffered from not kissing her a little more each time. She wiped off the tears welling up in the corners of her eyes with her fingertips before regaining her composure, a long-lasting grin imprinted on her pink lips.

Eyes shut, she sighed, her palms touching as if in prayer. "Okay," she said once her fit of laughter had subsided. "I'm really disappointed in your lack of open-mindedness about other music genres. You get one free pass. Let's settle on classic rock and country. Truce?"

"Yeah, better. There's this guy, Carter Hills…huh…I think. Don't know if you've ever heard of him. He has had a few hits. You should give his music a try. I heard it's amazing. Just sayin'." I shrugged, and April kept her face emotionless.

"I've heard about this guy. Such an ass. I hope his music is better than his attitude."

We drove a few miles, the silence comfortable between us.

"This pen name of yours, are you going to tell me what it is?"

She tapped her chest with her open palm. "You sure you want to risk your life for this?" She arched a brow, challenging me with her gaze.

I dropped my shoulders, trying my best puppy-dog eyes, hoping she'd crack. I was certain I could master it too if I gave it a try.

"You're not fooling me, Big Guy. Nice try."

We arrived in Music City mid-morning, and after a quick late breakfast, I walked April to her suite. My team had booked each of us a suite at City Garden, Nashville's finest hotel. There would be a small after-show party in mine later. I had hesitated between staying at my penthouse overlooking the city skyline or the hotel. Somehow, I feared inviting April to stay with me at my place would scare her away, which sounded ridiculous. After all, we'd already been living together for almost a week now. Had we stayed in town for more than a night, I might have offered her the choice. Not this time, though. I preferred to play it safe.

Deep down, a selfish part of me hoped she'd stick around long enough for us to come back here. Together.

I had no idea why I kept referring to an *us* when I thought about her, but somehow, I couldn't help it.

To avoid any weirdness between us but also not wanting her to feel all alone, here I was, staying at City Garden too for the night.

Since it was April's first time in Nashville and her first time in this world of mine, I wanted her night to be ultra special. I loved this city so much that I couldn't wait to give her a taste of it.

The fun part, at least.

Never in my life had I invited a woman to join me backstage at one of my concerts. Savannah didn't care about my music, and except for movie premieres or galas, she barely ever left LA, her only interest being my fame—and my money.

This, having April here with me, was a huge deal for me, and I intended on making every second of our time in Nashville count.

17

APRIL

Carter walked me to my suite right before leaving for sound check and whatever else he had to do hours before a gig.

I gasped when I entered the room. The entryway with its white walls and eight-foot-tall paintings framed in gold reminded me of a museum.

Down three steps, it opened to a living room area worthy of a multi-million dollar house. High ceiling, panoramic windows, thick dark velvet curtains, a matching set of couches, and a plush carpet. This was the fanciest hotel room I'd ever stayed in.

A long dining table big enough to seat ten people separated the living room section from the state-of-the-art kitchen. On my left, a hallway led to what I assumed was the bathroom and bedroom.

"This is our suite?" I asked, still surveying the space, slack-jawed.

"No. This is *your* suite, Fairy. I'm staying down the hall."

"I-I... This is all for me?"

He shrugged like it was no big deal. "Yes. All yours."

"O…huh…okay. Wow. I'm—"

He swiveled to face me and grabbed my upper arms. "You okay?"

"Yes. It's a bit much. Didn't they have like regular-size rooms with a queen bed and a balcony?"

Carter tossed his head back and laughed before planting a kiss on my forehead. "No idea. I told you I would make it up to you. Enjoy." He checked the time on his phone. "June will be here in one hour to take you shopping."

"Shopping?"

"For a dress. For tonight. Let me spoil you. Just this time."

I froze there, mute.

"Anyway, before she gets here, you can either go to the spa on the second floor or take a nap or plunge into a bubble bath. Anything that helps you relax." His hands moved to my shoulders, and he massaged the tension away. "Are you gonna be okay on your own?"

I found my voice. "You're kidding, right? I'm still not sure I'm not dreaming."

He lowered his lips to mine, grazing them in a soft, fleeting kiss. "Enjoy, okay? I'll see you later."

I bobbed my head. "Yeah. Sure. Don't worry about me."

He turned to leave but stopped midway. His eyes captured mine over his shoulder. "And June barks but doesn't bite. Unless she has to. Don't let her scare you, okay? She's very protective of me."

"Huh… What do you mean?"

"Stand your ground. You two will get along just fine, I swear." His lips curled up, and he shook his head as if thinking about something funny. "Yep. You two will hit it off."

As if Carter had predicted our first encounter, June wasn't exactly thrilled at the idea of me attending his concert tonight. This became clear when she came to pick me up to go shopping. She didn't offer to take me as an act of grace but only to assess me and my intentions toward him. She didn't trust me. It was written all over her face, from her tightly pinched lips to her defiant glare. She acted all friendly and shit at first, but once we sat side-by-side in the backseat of the SUV, she went straight for the jugular without flinching, her mama tiger suit on.

June studied me with a frown, her arms crossed over her chest. "What do you want from Carter?" The words sliced the already thick air in the car as one of the security guys drove us around. "And don't fuck with me. I won't let another crazy bitch profit from him. Not happening again. Not under my watch." Disdain had dripped from her words. She never broke eye contact. Though she was shorter than me, I didn't doubt she'd kick my ass if she ever had to.

Carter had warned me she was protective of him, but I didn't think I gave her any ammunition to doubt my character. I wouldn't let her intimidate me. If he thought June and I would hit it off, I trusted him enough to believe it was true. Even though, at first, I couldn't see it happening in the near future.

"Okay, I think you sized me up wrong. I'm no crazy bitch." I raised my hands between us. "I'm here because he invited me. Nothing more, nothing less." My cheeks flared in anger.

"I'm sure you're after something he has. They all are."

I harrumphed, balling my hands under my thighs. "I

really do not care about anything else but him. None of this matters," I explained, motioning one hand around us. "Carter and I are friends, and none of it is your business. Maybe I should go back to the hotel since you clearly don't want me around. I didn't even want to come, but he insisted. It was *his* idea. But now that I'm here, you gotta deal with it." I folded my arms over my chest, mimicking her pose.

June opened her mouth, but nothing came out. She clamped it back shut, her gaze never leaving mine. "I think you and I will become friends. Welcome to Nashville, April."

And just like that, we reached a truce, and her guard-dog attitude vanished. The wrinkles around her mouth softened. "Let's find something incredible for you to wear tonight." She snaked her arm through mine like we'd been best friends for years, and I blew out a cleansing breath, shifting in my seat, the weight on my shoulders fifty pounds lighter.

My skin itched at the idea of spending Carter's money, but when I turned down the sixth dress after a quick glance at the price tag, June took matters into her own hands. She grasped my upper arms and forced me to look at her. "April, pick anything you like. It's Carter's treat. Ignore the price tag. Just this once, okay?"

I nodded, my head hanging low.

"I stopped arguing with most of his orders long ago. Don't worry. I have your back. Also, he gave me specific instructions, so you don't really have a choice." June shrugged, no doubt used to this.

Once she drove me back to the hotel one hour later, I locked myself in my suite and lay down on the expensive couch, thinking about how my life had changed since moving to Green Mountain. I could hardly believe I had been that lonely woman unable to put the pieces of her life back together for so long. This new life was temporary, but it had given me a taste of what I could accomplish, what I could aim to be. My stay in Green Mountain had transformed me, and the month wasn't even over yet. I was happy again. Smiling didn't feel like an effort anymore. And my insomnia was a thing of the past. Even Bernice appeared happier since we arrived.

For an instant, I wondered if it was the result of the mountains or the man who played a huge part in getting my groove back and stealing bits of my heart with every smile.

My phone chimed with an incoming text notification from Carter, and I held my breath as I unlocked my device. I hadn't been in Nashville one day, and already I had been swept off my feet multiple times, living the princess dream. The suite, the dress, the concert tonight. It all felt surreal.

I read his words, and despite myself, my heart banged in my chest.

Carter Hills was messaging me.

My lips tipped into an oversized grin.

The guy had a way of making me feel weak in the knees without even trying.

I controlled the tremors in my fingers as I texted him back, trying to act like I was not freaking out about this entire weekend, when in reality, I was nothing close to chill inside.

Unable to erase my grin, I wrote a simple reply, pressed *send*, and exhaled.

I downed a bottle of water to ease my nerves, waiting for him to text back.

18

CARTER

After I left the hotel, I used my free time to check on the venue and decide on the playlist for tonight.

Acoustic shows with only a small crowd had always been my favorite. Sure, the rush I got from playing sold-out stadiums compared to nothing else, but I always preferred the intimacy of small venues.

At that moment, I wondered why I hadn't thought to focus my energy on smaller gigs before, since they brought me more joy and serenity. The idea of scheduling a string of unplugged concerts instead of a worldwide tour next year began to grow on me.

Me. My guitar. My music. My rules.

Riley, my long-term manager, greeted me. He'd organized this last-minute show using all his contacts after our emergency meeting days ago.

Alone in a room with my phone on speaker set on the table in front of me, I got connected to my favorite radio station. The one we teamed up with to announce my show.

"Carter Hills will do a surprise performance tonight,

folks. We'll draw tickets throughout the day. We'll reveal the location at the last minute. Stay tuned for more details."

Then the host, Mark, a decent guy I went to high school with, took my call. I wouldn't have done an interview with anyone else. I thought it'd be nice to chat with him on-air since we hadn't seen each other in person in quite some time.

"Hey, Carter. Thanks for talking to us today. How are you doing?"

"Good, Mark. Excited about tonight. Thanks for having me."

"I and everyone else in Nashville are glad you're doing okay, Carter. With all the fake news out there about you, you had us worried for a moment."

I laughed and shook my head, even though nobody could see me. "You're a smart guy, Mark. Don't believe everything you hear or see. In all honesty, I'm better than I've been in a long time. It's good to be back, even if it's just for a night."

"Do you have any scoop about tonight's show? It's the talk of the town right now."

"All I can say is that it's going to be unplugged, and I may have a surprise up my sleeve. I guess we'll see how it goes."

"That sounds amazing. I'll let you get ready for tonight then. Always a pleasure to talk to you, Carter. Have a great show."

"Thanks, Mark. Have a good one."

"That was Carter Hills, folks. All y'all, ready for tickets? I—"

I tuned out and hung up. I sighed, a small smile grazing my lips.

My entire team believed getting back on a stage with a

pop-up concert would help deflect the attention my love life had gained lately, and that fans would love the intimate setting.

I trusted my team. And my gut.

Apart from the Savannah Prince fiasco and some stupid suggestions from Carla, my ex-PR person who had since been fired, I never had any major reason to battle with my management team or my label in the past. Sure, we'd had our share of disagreements over the years, but nothing of importance. The biggest mistake of my life had been the clusterfuck I had brought upon myself by dating Hollywood's Evil Queen. Probably the lowest point of my existence.

Tightness lodged in my chest every time the memories resurfaced. I could write a book about all the craziness our relationship brought into my life. I was sure it'd be a best-seller. People would definitely wonder if I made it all up. Yeah, it was that much nonsense.

For the longest time, my personal life had lacked direction. While my career had its ups and downs over the years, it remained the one constant—the one thing I could always count on when everything else seemed to burn to ashes. For years, I felt stuck, unable to commit to anything worthwhile outside of my music. But after everything I went through, I could see the clouds parting. Perhaps I would finally get the new beginning I'd been craving for so long.

Lately, things had turned around, and in a short span of time, the positives had begun to outweigh the negatives. As this sank in, my thoughts wandered far from here.

Dahlia and Jack. Who were happy and living fulfilled lives.

The future. Which appeared much more encouraging than I would have thought a few months ago.

Fame. Which had its perks, but oh so many downsides. I was still debating sometimes if it was all worth it.

April. How, with her pink hair and quick wit, she had brought a wave of fresh air into my life in the short time we'd known each other.

How she infuriated me but also mesmerized me.

Her freedom. Her sass. Her magnetism. Her childlike ways of being amazed by small everyday things.

At the mere thought of her, my body relaxed. My thoughts got sorted out. Never before had I expected another person to have this much effect on me one day.

And truth be told, I needed her energy in my life.

She possessed some special powers strong enough to soothe all my inner demons. My doubts. My insecurities.

Amid everything I put her through, photos leaked to the press, becoming fodder for the gossip mags, she deserved to have some fun tonight.

And I planned on making her night one to remember.

I high-fived my musicians and turned toward my manager. "Did I lose my magic touch?" I asked in a teasing tone.

Riley neared me and pulled me into a one-arm hug. "You? Losing your magic touch? Nah, never. I'm glad you're getting back out there. It was about time you walked on a stage." He let go of me and stepped back, grinning.

"Well, I missed it. A whole lot. We should talk about booking a few shows in the next few months. I have new stuff I wanna try, and at this rhythm, I may have enough material for a new album soon."

"That's what I'm talking about. The Carter Hills standing in front of me is the star I recognize. Green Mountain is good for you, man. Your smile is back. And you seem happier. Dahlia always says the mountain air is addictive. I guess it's time I believe her."

I scratched my neck, glancing down as I debated my next words. "The mountain air is great, Ry. Fantastic even. I love it. But…huh, there's also that girl."

"I thought you said she was just a neighbor living in one of your cabins?" He quirked a knowing eyebrow, taking a sip from the to-go cup in his hand.

"Yeah… well, about that… We kinda live together now?"

He choked on his coffee, studying me for what felt like an eternity. "Is that a question?"

"Huh, no."

"You said, *We kinda live together now?* As if you were asking me."

"The electronic lock at her place broke. I didn't like the idea of her living on her own in the cabin until it got fixed, so I moved her into mine."

My manager stared at me, his lips forming a line, and his eyes assessing my level of stupidity—or that was what it looked like.

"You moved a woman you barely know in with you. Okay… And when we met to talk about this gig after pictures of you two leaked, you didn't think to share this piece of information because?"

"It is new. I didn't know how long she would stay. It's… huh…complicated." He parted his lips, but I kept going to avoid him bursting my bubble. "She's here. In Nashville. With me. June took her shopping." He raised a hand to shush me, but I kept talking. "You'll meet her later. Don't make up your mind before you do., okay? Please. Do it for me. You gotta trust me on this. You said I look happy. Well, April is the reason."

Riley slapped my shoulder. "I won't. Not my style,

man. All I want is for you to be thriving, you know that. I'm just careful this time around. We've all been burned by your previous relationship, and I don't want a do-over."

"I'm not in the same state of mind that I was in the last time. And did you once tell me during the length of my relationship with you-know-who that I looked happy?"

He shook his head. "Nah. You looked every shade of miserable." He paused, and we exited the venue after he gave all of us instructions for tonight. "Tell me more about April then. I wanna know why she's so special."

For the next ten minutes, we talked about the woman I couldn't get enough of.

"I can't wait to meet her." He turned to haul himself into his car when he halted and turned around. "And for what it's worth, I trust you, Carter. I've always done so, even though, sometimes, you let your emotions run the game and get the better of you. You always find your way back when the clouds part. Remember, I'll always have your back. See you later."

I nodded. His words pleased me, a lot.

Riley was like my true north in the chaotic whirlwind of my professional and personal life. He helped me stay on track, even when I derailed or whenever we didn't see eye to eye on something about my career. I respected him enough, both as a human being and as a manager, to never go behind his back. In the end, we always found common ground that worked for both of us. Over all these years, he knew me so well yet never tried to impose his vision on me. Riley respected me too—as a man and also as an artist.

When I messed up, he always offered me a hand to help me get back on my feet. I understood his reservations about April, but deep down, I knew he would change his mind once he met her. This woman left no one indifferent. Me included.

On the drive back to the hotel, I called June. "Hey, how is it going with April?"

"Drove her to the hotel half an hour ago. We had a great time. My bitch radar didn't detect anything suspicious. Still, be careful. You don't need a repeat of Savannah Prince's story."

"I'm not asking your permission." I clenched and unclenched my fists. I knew June meant well. As did Riley. "All I'm asking is for you to treat her with respect."

"Will do, Carter. No worries. We hit it off."

Stopped at a red light, I texted April next.

ME

Late lunch in my suite? I'm on my way to the hotel.

I would've made a reservation at one of my favorite restaurants in town—the barbecue shack on Broadway or the southern bistro in East Nashville—but people were looking for me, so I preferred lying low.

For her sake.

And my own sanity.

APRIL

Sure. Text me when you want me to come over.

In Nashville, most people let us *celebrities*—God, I hated this word—be. They didn't care to share their everyday life with famous athletes, Hollywood stars, or country singers. It didn't impress them. It was just the way things were. A far cry from Hollywood. Things would be different now that the press was hunting for juicy pictures of me and "my new lady." Anyone with a cell phone became a threat. A hunter ready to make a few bucks selling pictures of me as I bought toilet paper or drove around town with a woman.

I cringed at the idea they'd sell shots of April without her knowledge or consent.

Over the years, I'd grown a thick skin to protect myself from these vultures. She hadn't. She had no idea how careless these fame-seekers could be or the extent they'd go to get a great shot of my taking the garbage out or eating a burger. Fury boiled in my veins as it did every time those thoughts consumed me. Desperate to keep my calm, I forced myself to relax my white-knuckled grip around the steering wheel. I pictured April's smile in my head, and a wave of calm washed over me, leaving me with a stupid grin tattooed on my face instead.

———

I walked April back to her suite so she could get some rest before tonight's show. Sitting on the couch with my guitar, I played for a little while before giving Riley a call because I had made some last-minute changes to my set that I wanted to go through with him. Once we both agreed, I dialed June. She met me, holding her tablet in one hand and her phone in the other, ready for whatever I asked of her.

"Hey," I said when she crossed the threshold of my room. "It won't take long."

She brushed past me and took a seat by the kitchen counter. "I ordered tea. It should get here soon. I also sent bubbled water, an assortment of juice and chocolate, and a basket of fruits to April's room. I thought she might need a snack before the show." She scrolled through her notes. "The hotel will see to it. Food will be delivered to your suite around eleven tonight. I asked for the usual. They'll set it in here, on this counter, so when we have that little gathering later, we won't have to go out to eat or order in."

I stood in front of her, my palms pressed on the counter, waiting for her to finish her spiel.

"Anything else I missed?" She was almost out of breath.

I flashed her a smile. "Nope. All fine." I peered down at her, before asking the question burning the tip of my tongue. "You and April, you're good?"

A wrinkle etched across her forehead. "Yeah. I told you earlier. Why? Did she tell you she hated me when you two had lunch together?"

I stepped back and hooked my thumbs into my pockets. "She only had wonderful things to say about you. I wanted to thank you. For having her back and giving her a chance."

"Cart—"

"I'm not gonna go all sentimental on you, June. I just appreciated it. That's all."

"Carter, I'm just doing my job." She shrugged as if it was no big deal.

"We both know you do much more than what's on your job description. You're not just my assistant or Ry's assistant, you're my friend. And I wanted to thank you, for always having my back but also doing the right thing. I know I've pushed you away in the last two years, and I wasn't very open-minded when you tried to tell me I was making huge mistakes, but I never stopped looking up to you. Sometimes, I need to fuck it all up to understand the lesson. I'm just happy you never held it against me." I paused, looking down for a second before bringing my attention back to her. "I talked to Ry earlier. I'm doing better, and I'm feeling better. I'm not sure I'm ready to headline a world tour just yet, but I do want to get back out there. A few shows. Test some new material. Write new music. Record an album."

By the door, we hugged for a minute.

"Carter, I've missed you. I'm relieved the real you didn't get buried under all that shit. Take as long as you need to unwind and get back on your feet. And don't worry about April. I'll take care of her."

"Thanks." It was about time I made amends with the people who had stood by my side when the storm rocked the boat. In the grand scheme of things, the people who stayed in your corner when your life fell apart were the only ones who ever really mattered…the true friends you'd fight for anytime, without hesitation.

Jack called the moment my assistant walked out. That kid had a sick sense of timing.

We had this tradition going where we'd call each other before all my concerts. Jack would tell me about his day, and hearing his voice always helped with my mindset and defused the before-show jitters bomb inside me.

We talked for a little, but then I could sense his restlessness on the other end of the line. "What is it, buddy? Something you wanna talk about?"

"Can Bea and I come over soon?" he finally asked in one breath. "We want to spend a day with April."

"Let me check with her, but I'm sure it can be arranged. My fairy hunch tells me she'd like to see you both again."

"Cool. Thanks, *Carrrter*. Bye."

"We'll talk later, buddy."

"Wait. Mama wants to talk to you. She keeps asking me to give her the phone when we're done." He lowered his voice. "She has this weird look on her face. You know. *The* look." He snickered. "Good luck with that."

A soft chuckle bubbled out. I knew the look. Dahlia's *I mean business* frown.

"Thanks, buddy. I'll take all the luck I can get. Be nice to your mama."

"Hey, Carter," Dahlia said in greeting.

"Dah, everything all right?"

"Yeah. What's going on?"

I dragged my hands over my face. "Not much other than trying to get the press off my back, I reckon. I'm doing a pop-up show tonight. Something to ease everybody and make everyone forget about Fairy."

"Fairy? You mean April?"

I closed my eyes and nodded, even though Dahlia couldn't see me through the phone. "Yes…huh…April."

"She's one of the good ones. I can tell."

My thumb found my forehead and grazed it. "I know." I stayed silent. In my head, I counted to three.

Dahlia finally spoke up like I knew she would. "It's none of my business, but you're family, Carter, and I love you too much not to say anything. You're falling for her… more than you realize yourself. And I can tell she's falling for you too. Call it feminine intuition or whatever you want. I saw the glint in her eye when you two came over. And when you lied to her, she was devastated. This whole fame thing you've got going on is scary. I've been there…" She paused. "What I'm trying to say is, if you like her as much as I think you do, don't rush things with her. If what you two could have is worth it, give her some time to ease into the idea this is your life. If you move too fast, she'll run away. She…she almost did once. It's intimidating to date someone in the limelight, Carter. Think about it. You know I love you."

I closed my eyes, taking deep breaths in to ease the knots strangling my heart. Love. Falling. The idea sent waves of dread through me. I'd been to war, and I still bore the scars. Over the years, my relationship rap sheet had been less than glorious. While my best friend spoke to me, one thing became perfectly clear: like clouds parting after a storm to let the sun shine, I deserved love—and everything it entailed. Her words didn't rattle my soul but filled me with courage instead, and something resembling determination. It took me a long time to understand Dahlia and I were better as friends, but right now I was quietly grateful our relationship had never become something more— because when I thought of April, she was the one woman who could slip under my skin and stir something deep in me. The one I couldn't get out of my mind. No one else.

"I don't want you to end up with another broken heart. That's all," she added. "Last time, it really took a toll on you."

Riley, June, Dahlia. They all worried about me, and it broke my heart knowing I was the reason. Like I had already done with my manager and his assistant, I tried to reassure my best friend.

"You're right, Dah. I love you too. You and Jack will always be my family. And I'll be careful with April... There's something there. I can't quite name it, but it's powerful. Exciting and frightening all at once. I need to explore what it means and see where it can go."

"You're allowed to thrive, Carter. You're allowed to find happiness. To love and to be loved. For what it's worth, I'm glad you're putting yourself out there again. I can tell April is the one who's putting that smile back on your face, and it pleases me a lot."

After she sent me positive vibes for tonight's show, we hung up.

———

At six, I knocked on April's door, rocking on my heels. I breathed in and rubbed my hands over my denims. A sense of peace filled me.

My heart rate slowed to a steady rhythm as I waited for her to open the door to her suite.

When she did, my jaw hit the floor, and my breath stuck in my lungs. A tidal wave of heat rippled through me, and no words came out. I stood there like an idiot, unable to avert my eyes, tongue-tied.

Hot as fuck in her short ombre sequin dress, I stared at her without blinking. A wide smile brightened her face as she twirled around. My dick throbbed when I noticed the low-cut back, the V of the dress ending just above the swell of her ass. April had curled her jaw-length pink hair in soft waves and wore cowboy boots on her feet instead of heels. I closed my eyes and evened my breathing. My tongue darted across my lips. She did this thing where she swayed her hips, which drove me crazy.

She had to be aware of how the simple movement sent my body into overdrive and my libido skyrocketing.

I rubbed the heels of my hands over my eyes, desperate to calm the desire awakening in me. I tried to push away all the dirty thoughts racing through my mind. *Olives, gooey snails, Riley, Savannah Prince.*

My sight clouded, and my heart soared into my throat.

Air whistled through my lungs.

The vision of April in her dress—too short for anyone's eyes but mine—jolted my heart back to life. It resuscitated my dormant state, shattered my walls, and the last threads of self-control left in me. Her legs appeared longer, her skin creamier, her hips fuller.

"Fuck." The low curse passed my lips, and I scratched my jaw, my gaze laser-focused on the sequin number she was wearing, unable to look away.

"Something wrong?" Her grin vanished. "Oh, you don't like it? I should've picked out the black halter dress. I knew this one was too short. I can go and change." She mumbled, doubt flickering across her face, cheeks flushed, her features strained.

I harrumphed and adjusted the crotch of my pants. They had tightened so much that I feared my dick would die of asphyxiation. April's eyes widened and followed my hand. "Babe, I love it so much that all I want to do is watch you all night and forgo the show." My voice cracked. "We should go. Now. I cannot come inside your suite, or neither of us will ever get out." My sinful mind was in high gear. I clenched my teeth, fearing all the dirty thoughts would spill out of my mouth without permission.

She flashed me a shy smile, and I turned around to lock away what was left of my willpower.

My wild heart banged inside its cage. I pressed one hand over my chest. *Is this what a heart attack feels like?* I paced the hallways, trying to will the blood that had pooled in my groin back up to my brain. How could I ever focus on my set tonight, knowing she'd be watching me from the wings, looking so sinful?

Drawing a shaky breath, I slid my thumbs into the belt loops of my dark denims and exhaled. *There. Better.*

After a few deep breaths and some quiet self-talk, I pivoted and held out my hand for her. Shivers raced up my arms where our skin touched. It was as addictive and thrilling as it was disconcerting.

"Fairy, you look amazing. I wouldn't want anybody else by my side tonight."

A genuine grin spread across her face, and all traces of hesitation vanished. To ease any lingering doubt, I leaned forward and pressed my lips to her forehead.

Dahlia's words replayed in my head.

If what you two could have is worth it, give her some time to ease into the idea this is your life. If you move too fast, she'll run away. She…she almost did once. It's intimidating to date someone in the limelight, Carter.

Out of the corner of my eye, I glanced down at my date, hoping she'd give me a chance to show her how good we could be together. That we could make this thing between us work. *Small steps, Carter. Be yourself. That's all April will ever need.*

The venue looked amazing. About two hundred fans screamed my name when I walked onstage of the old barn turned into an auditorium. I'd missed this. The energy from a crowd. The feeling I was where I belonged. I'd never performed here before. On the outskirts of town, it gave this private, exclusive concert a more intimate and meaningful atmosphere. The owner of the barn had kept the original wooden plank floor and walls and beamed ceilings but had added acoustic panels and other decorative elements to achieve the best possible sound and eliminate any reverberation. I wasn't convinced it would work at first, but he proved me wrong. I loved everything about this place. The cachet. The history. The ambiance. But tonight, I couldn't seem to enjoy any of it. For the entire set, my eyes kept drifting to my girl offstage, in that sexy dress. *My girl.* It made no sense to think of her as mine, and yet, it made perfect sense.

Without even trying, she occupied each corner of my mind. All the time.

Every song I sang, I sang for her.

After finishing the last one, "Someday You'll Fly," one of my greatest hits, I bent down from my stool to take a sip from the water bottle at my feet, my thoughts spinning faster than ever. With newfound confidence, I gave in to my inner will.

"Hey guys, thanks for coming tonight. It means the world to me." I loved small, intimate concerts because they gave me time to talk to the crowd and soak in their energy. "I have a special gift for you. Please don't tell anybody; they'll be jealous." Laughter rippled through the audience. "I have this new song I've been working on, and I want to share it with you tonight."

The small venue buzzed with cheers. People whistles and howls.

My pulse spiked, and I breathed in and out at a steady pace, trying to ease the bundle of nerves knotting my stomach.

My eyes drifted to April, a goddess in her sequin dress.

My fingers strummed the first chords of "Pink and Country."

> **I couldn't see the light**
> **I thought I had it all**
> **figured out**
> **But I didn't, I had no clue**
> **And then you came my way**
> **You disrupted everything I've**
> **always known...**

I kept my eyes closed, letting my voice and my guitar do the talking.

> **... Girl, I just want you**
> **to know**
> **I want my life to be pink like**
> **yours**
> **Babe, I'll never let you go**
> **You're my absolute favorite**
> **color.**

On the last words, I blew out a nervous breath. My voice and fingers, steady and self-assured, were a far cry from the way I felt inside. My stomach was a puddle of jelly, and my heart a mushy ball.

The applause from the crowd filled the space, and it tugged at my heartstrings. I cocked my head, and April captured all my attention. She wiped the tears rolling down her cheeks with the tips of her fingers and shot me the most dazzling smile.

There was no going back now. I had laid my heart on the line.

The only way I knew how.

19

APRIL

Carter sang the last verse of *my* song. *My* song. Carter Hills, the one and only, wrote me a song. My heels were glued to the floor, my fingers laced, palms pressed together in prayer, resting under my chin. I stood tall, my body rock-solid, a stark contrast to the jittery chaos roiling inside me. A flow of tears streamed down my face, and my heart danced around in my chest. A tingling sensation traveled throughout my body, leaving a trail of goose bumps behind, like raindrops on cobblestones. Carter couldn't feel this way about me. We barely knew each other. However, the idea that I inspired him to write a song made me all kinds of emotional.

I, April Simmons, the girl who always ended up alone, had inspired the lyrics of a song written by a famous country music star. Speechless, I pinched myself—three times, just in case. The pain didn't wash the dream away. Euphoria took roots inside me, and all my thoughts dissolved, my eyes and ears consuming the emotionally charged, *it won't happen twice*, best four minutes of my life.

Carter wrapped up his show, and I heard the applause

and cheers, but my feet refused to move. People talked to me—June, Riley, and a bunch of other people—but I didn't register anything they said. The idea Carter Hills saw me, really saw me, shattered a boulder the size of Australia that had been buried deep inside me for as long as I could remember.

The one I pushed aside years ago after I met Saunders and Travis. The one that made me believe, for a long time, I wasn't worthy of anybody's time and affection, thanks to my biological parents. Now it was gone, for good. From offstage, I let my eyes linger on Carter.

With purpose in his stride, he waltzed toward me backstage. My body shut down. I couldn't breathe, my heart frozen, and my limbs numb. When his hands circled my waist, I snapped out of my daze. I cupped his cheeks, my eyes wet with a mix of confusion and amazement. I brushed my thumbs over his short stubble and crashed my lips against his, forgetting about June beside me and ignoring everyone else around us.

Excitement tickled my spine.

My emotions trapped the words, so instead of speaking, I allowed my lips to express the vortex of feelings trampling my heart, leaving it raw and unguarded. Our mouths feasted on each other. My knees buckled, and I tightened my grip around his neck. *Carter Hills wrote me a song.* His mouth tasted like mint and sweat, a deadly combination wreaking havoc on my hormones. With a swirl of his tongue around mine, he ignited me and turned me to ashes in his arms. Our friendship—I cringed, lacking a better word to describe what we were—made no sense, yet our lips fusing together felt as natural as breathing. He leaned back, one large hand cradling my nape, the other hooked on my hip, keeping me upright. The raw desire in his eyes scorched me, and the smug grin on his face glistened, giving him a devilish edge.

Hours later, in his suite, sitting amongst some of his closest friends, his musicians, and his managing team, I still couldn't believe this night wasn't a dream. A fantasy world. A parallel universe.

Carter introduced me to the people he cared about as if I'd always been part of his life. As if I belonged there, with him.

I took a sip of my champagne, the aftermath of the concert sinking in.

In the folder of *Crazy things that had happened in my life*, tonight stole the top spot, by far.

A foreign thrill blistered inside me, and I rubbed my throat to ease the air coming in and out of my lungs. I closed my eyes and inhaled through my mouth, hoping to erase the crippling sensation knotting my stomach. My memory would fade over time, and I wished I had the first time Carter Hills played my song captured on video. One I could replay over and over every time I had a bad day or the urge to listen to it, the exact way he sang it tonight, not the one he'd record or the tenth time he'd sing it, but *this* one time. The very first time. I wanted to bathe in his words and drown in his melody.

All my senses heightened as I listened to his friends tell stories about the good old days, as they called them. When the world wasn't ruled by social media and cell phones were a shit substitute for cameras. His pine and cedarwood scent, now that he'd showered and changed into a clean pair of jeans and a plaid shirt, filled my nostrils and made me lightheaded. His calloused fingers, roughened due to years of playing the guitar, sent tingles straight to my core as they skimmed my skin, making me wish we were alone.

The essence of him lingered on my tongue, hours after we kissed, and I wished it'd never fade away.

Carter Hills possessed me in a way I never thought possible. Tonight, he rocked my world with a song and a kiss. A pretty memorable kiss, though. The reminder of it made my toes curl, and a twitch rumbled deep inside me. *Ohmygod.*

My heart cartwheeled in my chest every time my brain wandered back to the song. *My* song. He sang for me and made me his with only his words. I pressed my thighs together, heat pooling low in my pelvis.

Saunders. I needed to reach out to her and tell her about my night. And the song. Mostly the song. She'd go batshit crazy over this.

As if she'd read my mind, my phone vibrated inside my little golden clutch, and my best friend's face lit up the screen.

SAUNDERS

Bloody girl, are you kidding me right now?
Tell me I dreamt the whole thing. I'm arse
over tit over this.

With my lips pinched together to avoid smiling too big, I typed a reply.

ME

Have no idea what you're talking about.

SAUNDERS

Stop playing dumb. He wrote YOU a
freaking song. It's all over the web.

ME

Kidding, right?

Shit. You're not. How would you know?

SAUNDERS

Girl, get real, Carter Hills professed his
feelings for you, and now the entire world
can see it. Or hear it, I guess.

ME

STOP.

It's nothing like that.

SAUNDERS

You're living under a rock. Or in a cave. Not
in the mountains. There's a mix-up. You're
lacking oxygen in your brain. Altitude can
do that to you.

ME

We're friends. Who care about each other.
That's all.

SAUNDERS

April, your song is Carter Hills's new hit. It
has over six million views already.

I reread the last message a dozen times. Still, it didn't register.

ME

Can't be. Are you sure?

So, a video existed somewhere of my song being sung for the first time. My body temperature flared. I wanted to fan myself with my hand. To jump to my feet. To scream. To laugh. Just the thought people could watch Carter perform it sent shivers through me. Why did I want to keep it under wraps? Somehow, I felt possessive of my song, and I wished it was only meant for me. I sucked in a breath. I was being silly. I swallowed, hard. The entire night was a whirlwind I wasn't prepared for. I liked it as much as I feared it. The vibration of my phone stopped my racing mind and my galloping heart from bouncing out of my chest.

SAUNDERS

If you two wanted to hide your little country fling, you failed. BIG TIME.

ME

No relationship here, Saund. Don't get ahead of yourself. Carter and I are friends.

SAUNDERS

[Link to video]

Check it for yourself.

My fingers itched to click the link. Right now. I closed my eyes and exhaled. This could wait. It had to. I was surrounded by people, and now wasn't the time.

SAUNDERS

Believe what you want. Reed's jaw is still somewhere on the floor. He watched the video ten times already. Your man got himself a new fan. April, you're in denial.

Reed wants me to tell you you're getting banged tonight if you haven't already figured it out or haven't already been fucked many times *winking emoji* And also to get stocked on condoms 'cause you'll need a whole king-size box.

I placed my hand over my mouth to silence the chuckle threatening to escape.

ME

No comment.

SAUNDERS

Enjoy your night with your there's-no-
romance-between-us hot piece of country
ass. We'll talk later. I need to glue Reed's
jaw back to his face. I'm happy for you.
Love you x

A little smile tugged at my lips, and my heartbeat quickened. The charged air in the room soared and suffocated me. I fidgeted with the gold band around my right ring finger. Was I blind or stupid or were my friends right about Carter's feelings?

Carter arched a brow and stretched his arm, his hand finding the small of my back. "Everything okay?"

I nodded. My pulse skyrocketed at the sound of his hoarse, low voice.

"Everything's perfect." I mirrored his grin, zooming in on his lips for a fraction of a second.

Saunders's words replayed in my head. *If you two wanted to hide your little country fling, you failed.* Carter and I were just friends, right? My head said yes, but my heart vetoed it since there was a big flashing, warning neon sign stating we were so much more.

Maybe I was really fucked after all.

With an appreciative smile aimed at me, June refilled my champagne glass for the fourth time. The bubbly alcohol helped dissipate part of my discomfort, and I felt more at ease amongst Carter's entourage.

I forced an upward curl back to my lips as my heart continued to thunder inside my rib cage.

As more alcohol was consumed and the hours ticked by, the chatter in the suite grew louder—and so did my heartbeat.

Carter placed his hand on my thigh, and I gasped, sucking in a breath. Dizziness blurred my senses, and flutters danced in my belly. I squeezed my legs together, trying to ease the ache building up inside me.

Deep in conversation with Tim, his tour manager, about a show scheduled in Berlin next summer, Carter looked handsome with his closely shaven jaw—leaving only stubble—shorter hair, a relaxed stance, a look I'd only seen on him for the first time this afternoon. He turned and flashed me a grin. A panty-melting grin. One no girl in her right mind could ever resist. His eyes burned holes into my skin, and his fingers dug deeper into my flesh.

I grinned back, and some of the tension in my back left me.

He traced lazy circles on my bare flesh with his thumb, just above my knee, and I scooted closer, his touch intoxicating.

My insides melted. I drew in a deep breath, stifling the soft moan rising in my throat.

The pulse in his neck throbbed. Carter tried to act nonchalant, but his body's responses gave him away. His palm, the one still attached to my thigh, got clammy. He scraped the other through his hair every few minutes, and a tightness appeared around his eyes. The air in the room heated another few degrees. I wasn't sure how to act with all these people around. His hand moved higher. I chewed on my lower lip to distract myself from writhing under his hold. Whatever game he was playing, he made me feel like the ultimate goal, the endgame, the coveted prize. I struggled to stay put, wanting more. More of this…more of him.

June sat beside me, and I welcomed the distraction. We chatted about her last trip to Europe and exchanged numbers. Around midnight, she rose to her feet and picked up her things. "I need to go, y'all. My munchkin, tomorrow morning, won't care if her mama got less than five hours of sleep." She hugged everyone in the room. When she reached Carter, she whispered something to him that brought an upward curve to his lips. I stood as she inched closer and hugged me. "April, I hope to see more of you soon. I don't know what you've done to this grumpy fellow," she pointed her thumb at Carter, "but I haven't seen him smile like this in a very long time. Whatever your secret power is, please don't stop. He's usually much more withdrawn after a show. I'm glad we're good." She winked, and her words touched my heart.

First Dahlia. Now her.

Truth be told, I had no clue what they both meant. Carter and I weren't even dating. For all I knew, I left him with a serious case of blue balls after our make-out session that morning in my cabin when I locked myself out after the hot tub incident.

We were friends with *no* benefits. Two people enjoying each other's company without the complications of sex or a relationship.

Around one-thirty in the morning, everybody left the suite, and Carter and I ended up alone in the dimly lit room.

His face turned serious after his last guests walked out. The lightness in his features faded, and his lips pressed into a thin line.

Did I piss him off somehow? Was I clingy or awkward tonight? No. I got along with everyone, and he seemed to like having me around. Chasing away the crippling thought, I waited for him to say something. A second later, his melted-steel irises darkened, and his heated gaze took me hostage. A chill ran through me under the intensity of his stare.

I held my breath. The air between us crackled with sexual tension.

A few feet separated us, yet I stood frozen, fingers twisted together, unsure what to do

In four strides, Carter closed the distance between us and crashed his mouth on mine, his lips soft and demanding. Startled, I almost lost my balance. His strong arms wound around me, holding me against his firm chest. No matter how much I wanted to resist him, I failed. Instead, I indulged in his kiss, parting my lips to welcome him, forgetting everything. Where I stood. What day it was. What decade we lived in. I combusted inside out, dissolving under his touch. He cupped a breast over my dress with his hand, and I almost lost it. My nipples hardened into stiff peaks, begging to be taken care of. His tongue tangoed with mine, stealing my breath away. My entire body tingled. With a hand around his nape, I pulled him to me, wishing no more space existed between us.

Could I catch fire from just a kiss?

The moans that left my mouth sounded foreign. This time I didn't silence them.

A force stronger than me had taken over my whole being. At this moment, he could consume me, and I wouldn't put up a fight.

I yelped when he grabbed my ass cheeks and lifted me until my legs could circle his waist. My dress bunched up around my hips, and Carter ground against me, leaving me panting and aching, needy and lusty. The outline of his manhood sent thunderbolts throughout me. I raked his muscular back over his shirt with my fingernails, and shivers woke up in their wake.

He ran his tongue along my collarbone and bit the skin of my neck softly.

Whimpers passed my lips, and I arched my back, about to ignite from too much sensory overload.

I rubbed myself against him, needing friction to tame the fire burning inside me.

My panties, already soaked, stuck to my flesh. I shivered under the pads of Carter's fingers, arching my back to allow him more space to devour my skin.

Desire throbbed deep in my core, and a throaty moan escaped my mouth. My dress slid down my arms and exposed my bare chest. It had a low-cut back, and wearing a bra hadn't been an option. His primal growl pulsed through me and confirmed I had made the right choice when I chose this outfit earlier. Scorching heat emanated from the man facing me. He licked one of my hardened nipples, rolling and sucking the dark-pink tip with tenderness and hunger. He assaulted the second nipple with his mouth, giving it the same delicate yet greedy attention.

Breathless and never letting go of me, Carter stepped further into the room until he landed on the loveseat by the window with my legs still wound around him. Our mouths reconnected, our tongues restless and our lips starving.

His short stubble rubbed against the sensitive flesh of my cheeks, no doubt marking me.

He drew a line with his finger over the crotch of my black lace panties, tracing the seam between my thighs. "God, you're so wet."

I swallowed hard, torn between crying from pleasure and turning into a puddle in his hands. I let my head fall back, drawing his attention to my neck once again.

With his other hand, he cradled my face, fingers tracing my jaw, his kisses a mix of intensity and tenderness. He took his time to cherish my mouth with his, tasting every corner. My toes curled, and my body hummed under the devoted attention.

"All night, the sight of you in this dress was fucking torture. I can't wait to taste all of you, Fairy." He pushed my drenched panties to the side and grazed my clit with his thumb. I quivered, using his shoulders to ground me.

"Please...I—" I couldn't even form a coherent sentence anymore. "Don't stop."

My hips rolled in sync with his hand, desperate for his fingers to dive inside me and put out the fire burning me alive.

"Fuck, you're gorgeous." He tugged at my lower lip with his teeth, then licked the sting with his tongue.

I purred, unable to contain the sounds spilling from my lips as sensations swirled inside me.

Yearning to feel him too, I shifted one hand downward and rubbed him over the fabric of his pants. His hard-on throbbed under my touch, begging to be freed. I accelerated the up-and-down motion, relishing each jolt of his thick erection against my palm.

His breathing caught, and the playfulness vanished from his face. He increased the pace of his fingers, rubbing my clit in delicious circles.

Desperate to feel his skin on mine and unable to wait any longer, I peeled his shirt off over his head, not bothering with the buttons. I traced the ripped muscles of his chest and abs with my hands. I didn't have enough fingers to explore each inch of his tanned skin the way I wanted to.

In one swift movement, Carter lifted me from him and laid me on my back. I gasped before framing his face with my hands and pulling him down on me. Our tongues battled for the upper hand. He positioned himself on top of me, supporting his weight with his stretched arms.

We were both panting, breathing hard, and hungry for each other.

Carter lowered himself, his hard chest pressing against my soft breasts.

Every cell in me shuddered with an ache only he could quench.

He entangled one of his hands in my hair, and I tilted my head up when he sucked on the flesh of my neck.

Lifting myself up on my elbows, I pushed him back just enough to be able to unbuckle his belt. We both couldn't take our eyes off my fingers as the strap glided through the loops when I tugged on the other end.

Carter kneaded one naked breast, his mouth returning to mine.

I licked the length of his jaw, nipping his earlobe and reaching for the button of his dark jeans.

A low, guttural growl rumbled in his throat, drowning out the sound of our harsh breathing.

I pushed a hand inside his boxer briefs, the warmth of his length seeping into my palm.

Before I could stroke him the way I had been dreaming of, he leaned back and stopped me with a hand. His thickness quivered under my fingers.

"April. Stop." He sounded breathless. "I-I don't want us to rush this. Whatever this…us…is, I don't want to ruin it."

Wait. What? I released him and blinked, unsure if I heard him right. Was he pushing me away? My cheeks burned, and my breath hitched.

The expression on his face, something that said *I can't believe I'm doing this, but I have to*, told me this was indeed not a joke.

I had no idea how to react. Part of me wanted to laugh, thinking he was messing with me, while another part wanted to cry, feeling humiliation creeping in.

I couldn't tell whether I should be pissed or proud that Carter was acting like a decent guy. Right now, I didn't want a decent guy, though—I wanted a man. Hard and powerful. Passionate and insatiable. Wild and unstoppable. And I wanted the sex. Dirty and animalistic with a side of tenderness.

"Ruin it?" Trying to catch my breath, I could barely utter the words. Carter's index finger traveled the length of my lips, and I sucked on the tip, my vision already blurry from the building desire. "Tell me you're kidding," I said through the whimper I couldn't keep inside. Gosh, I wanted him to take me in every possible way, right now, until I was completely satiated.

In the last few hours, my desire for him had reached new heights. That was saying a lot, considering I'd been yearning for him since the first time our eyes met. Each day, my need for him grew stronger. Every time our skin touched, my longing became harder to conceal. Inside, I was a ticking time bomb.

Right now, it was a miracle I still had any restraint left after ceding control to the rock star who had been moments away from ravaging me.

My pulse throbbed between my legs, the ache refusing to be put out.

Every inch of me trembled at the thought that I might not come undone tonight. I was wound so tightly that I could detonate at any second.

Every bit of me craved Carter's intimate touch—his caresses, his love—but the resolve I could read on his face acted like a cold shower.

He isn't kidding when he said we should stop. This wasn't a joke.

With a strong grip around my body, he lifted me to straddle him once more, the feel of his big, calloused hands on my soft skin almost enough to bring me over the edge. His hooded eyes sucked me in.

I wanted to beg him to keep going, to continue what we were doing, but I knew it would be futile.

He released me and raked his fingers through his disheveled hair.

Still aroused, I blew out a shuddering breath at the sexiness of his gesture.

"Don't be upset. Fuck, I can't believe I'm doing this. I…I must be crazy. No one has ever affected me the way you do, April. I can't…I can't just fuck you and forget all about it. Please. End me already." He closed his eyes again and breathed through his mouth as if his body and mind were at odds with each other.

He dragged a hand over his face and with a shake of his head, opened his eyes. We stared at each other for a moment.

"April, this…you…me…us… You must be certain this is what you want. Because once you're in, we won't be able to hide forever, and you must agree to all that it means to be with me. I know it's unfair to both of us, but it's my reality. If we do this, it won't be a one-time thing because I'll never be able to stop. I'm fucking sorry. I want you so bad right now…all of you. Everything you're willing to give me. You could never be just a fuck. Not to me. This would be wrong, and I would never go through with it if that was what you wanted." He dropped his head in the crook of my neck. "Not sure my dick will ever forgive me for this. I hope your pussy will."

When his attention returned to my face, his lips quivered, and he claimed my mouth. In slow motion, he curled his hands around my nape, and he kissed me as if it could somehow soothe him, but also his fears and his doubts.

I rested my forehead against his, panting.

"Pixie, I want to bury my face between your thighs so

bad. The taste of you is all I'll ever need to stay alive. I'm starving."

How could his words hit me right where they felt good? Where I longed for him?

"Don't shut me out." I nipped his lower lip. "We both need this. Let's be bad tonight. We'll talk tomorrow. We don't have to decide everything right now."

Carter leaned further back, putting more distance between us, stealing the heat that had been swirling between us, and shook his head. "Can't. It's all or nothing."

A lump dissolved down my throat. "You serious?"

He nodded and offered me a tiny shrug. "I'm not playing the field. Not interested."

"Wow. And some people think you're a womanizer who only cares about getting laid, whatever be the consequences."

A soft grin grazed his lips, and he moved closer, winding his arms around me. With the gentleness I had come to associate with him, he peppered kisses on my eyelids, his lips warm and soft.

When we stared at each other, he combed my hair back with his fingers, the small gesture sending a flock of butterflies to my stomach. With his free hand, he adjusted the crotch of his jeans, a painful glaze shining in his eyes, his erection straining at the seams.

I sighed. *What a waste.* With a tentative gesture forward, I caressed the bare skin of his torso, the need to touch him still running high inside me, and met his eyes. "Thank you…for tonight. And for the song. *My* song. I still can't believe it."

"April, you inspire me in so many ways. If only you knew…"

We sat there for a moment, breathing each other in,

my head pressing against his bare chest, his hands playing with the waves of my hair.

After a while, I inhaled some courage. "I should go."

He nodded, and we both moved to our feet, fixing our clothes. After putting his shirt back on and tucking his erection back into his pants, Carter escorted me to my suite. An air of sweet torture settled over us. I ached to slide my palm into his, yet I had no idea how to navigate this new status of our relationship—or lack thereof.

I unlocked the door to my suite, but before I could hide inside my room and freak out with no witnesses around, his mouth found mine, and his teeth toyed with my bottom lip for a second, making me tingly and horny for him all over again. I pushed him back with both hands. "Go. Now." My tone betrayed the smile in my voice.

Carter walked backward, a huge grin plastered on his face, his eyes capturing mine, refusing to let me go. I cupped my chest with both hands, calming the pounding of my overexcited heart.

Once in my suite, I pressed my back against the door and let go of the air I'd been holding in my lungs for far too long.

I smiled at the realization.

Tonight, Carter Hills had rocked my world...several times. My night had been nothing like I imagined it would be. Exceptional in so many ways, I didn't have enough words to describe it

With resolve in my steps, I walked to the bedroom, needing a release more than ever. Where was my vibrator when I needed it? Without a care in the world about how late it was, I filled the giant bathtub, too big for just one person, and sank my pulsing body into the warm water. I itched to invite Carter over, but he made it clear. This wouldn't happen tonight. Once again, I was condemned to pleasuring myself without any outside help. I closed my eyes, and the images of his lips on mine took over. I felt his hands on my breasts and sucked in a breath. A tidal wave of pleasure rocked my body. The temperature of the water rose. My fingers found my tight channel and slid in and out of me with ease. My skin vibrated with need. Damp heat filled my lower belly. I out soft, breathy cries, unable to keep all my arousal locked inside.

Less than a minute later, I was panting, recovering from the climax that had reduced my body to jelly. This— bringing myself to orgasm—wasn't enough anymore. I craved the real thing. The flesh. The shivers. The kisses. The man. "Carter Hills, put me out of my misery already," I whispered, my pulse deafening me as a new wave of desire crashed over me.

I woke up with an untamable grin on my face. Whatever I did, shower, make tea, or meditate, that grin refused to wash away.

My song.

From the moment I pried my eyes open, I tried to sing it from memory, but I failed. I could only hum the melody. Sort of.

With one goal in mind, to listen to it again, I clicked the link my best friend had sent me last night, surprised at myself for having resisted watching it for so long.

Goose bumps blossomed all over my skin when the first words left Carter's mouth. This time, I listened to each verse. Butterflies took off in my stomach. Nobody had ever done something as huge as writing a song for me before. A song about *me*. The chorus started, and it took all my inner strength not to cry right there.

Girl, I just want you to know
There's no one else like you
You are the sunshine in my
    storms
You color my night sky
You are the star I wish upon
    every night
You hold my heart, I'll never
    let you go
Babe, I'm blind without you.

Flashes of last night surged through my mind.

How devilishly delicious HN looked on that stage with his guitar.

How his voice soothed every fiber of me, down to the dark corner of my soul.

How every chord he played made my heart vibrate.

How his lips tasted.

The sequin dress, folded on a chair, reminded me the night hadn't been a dream after all. I held both hands to my heart, still overwhelmed with emotions.

A soft knock on my door disturbed my daydream.

I pressed pause on my phone and tripped over my feet, trying to get to the door. Frozen for a second, I broke out into a loud laugh when my eyes locked on Carter standing in the hallway. The sight of him rendered me speechless.

He stood there with two disposable teacups in his hands, wearing baggy cargo pants in a questionable shade of beige, a puffer lime-green jacket, a mustard-yellow beanie, and some oversized shades. My eyes overflowed with tears, and I patted the moisture under my eyes with my fingertips. "Ohmygod, HN, Halloween was months ago. What is this?"

His gaze licked me from head to toe, lingering on my

breasts, showcased in my tight white shirt. My laughter died in my throat. Did I forget to put on a bra? I cupped my chest, just to make sure. No. I didn't. No clothing mishap. Carter swallowed before meeting my eyes again. I clamped my legs shut and exhaled. His heady gaze ignited flames that ran the length of my spine.

I blinked, tongue-tied.

I stopped fondling myself, dropped my hands, and took a calming breath.

"Good morning to you too, Fairy. Today, I'm giving you a tour of my city. I don't want us to be chased down, so I decided we'd get creative and dress up for the occasion." Carter walked in with resolute steps and handed me a bag full of equally mismatched clothes.

"You can keep your jeans and shoes on, but you must hide your pink hair. I'm sorry. I love it. Very much. But if we don't want to be recognized, we must play the part. Today we'll be tourists. It's a shame to hide this shirt, though. Perhaps we should stay in."

His gaze lowered to my breasts again, and I snapped my fingers. "Eyes up here, Country Boy."

He shrugged, and his lips curved into an irresistible boyish grin as he raised his eyes.

"Not a chance. I've been dying to discover the city. Stop ogling me."

Carter pushed his bottom lip out, pouting, but it didn't last. "Go get ready. I'll wait in the living room." He closed the door after him with a kick. His security details, two men I saw for the first time yesterday, stayed behind in the hallway, dressed in street clothes.

Astonished and unable to utter any coherent words, I disappeared down the hallway into the bathroom.

"Usually, we don't have to hide in Nashville. People let us be. But after last night's show, my team thinks I made the matter worse instead of helping it." Carter was talking about my song, his voice echoing through the hotel suite. He continued, his tone changing to a more serious one. "I'm sorry you were brought into this. Again. I never meant for you to be drawn into this mess. The song meant a lot to me, and I thought you'd like it too. It was an *in the heat of the moment* thing, and I didn't think it through."

I came out of the bathroom, dressed in my new clothes, only to be met with the sad expression on his face when I stepped into the living room. His hands were stuffed in his jacket pockets—a gesture he did when he was either uncomfortable or trying to act detached—and his head hung low. My pulse rattled at this sight. I treaded through the room and placed a hand on his forearm.

"I know you didn't mean to. It's okay. We'll deal with it. I'm sure some young actress will forget to put panties on or a wannabe rock star will trash a hotel room or burn down a house. Soon enough, we'll be old news." I offered him a reassuring smile. "And the song means everything to me. Never apologize for it, okay? This is the best gift I've ever received." I rose on my tiptoes and dropped a kiss on his cheek.

The worry lines around his eyes smoothed. "Are you sure? People will make up all kinds of stories about us… About you…"

"How bad can it be?"

His face darkened, and he opened his mouth to say something, but I silenced him with a finger pressed against his lips. "We'll deal with it later. Now tell me who picked up these horrible outfits."

Genuine amusement lit up his face, replacing the somber expression. "June. She said she had a blast selecting each piece for us. She knew your size and let her imagination run wild. I bet her daughter is to blame. That kid has the weirdest taste. She's heartless, I'm telling you. She has something against me and made it personal." He flashed his pearly whites. "Anyway, June said she got inspired."

His manager or personal assistant, or whatever she was, chose a large purple knitted sweater for me, white aviator shades, a matching purple beanie to hide my pink strands, a long mustard-yellow scarf, the same shade as Carter's hat, and a sleeveless royal-blue puffer vest.

Carter gave me a slow once-over, and holding the lapel of my vest, he smirked—a giant, wild smirk. "Even when it looks like you got dressed in the dark, you still look beautiful, Fairy."

I curtsied, and admiring ourselves in the full-length mirror, we chuckled together. Each expression of joy I drew from him felt like a small victory.

Still giggling and looking ridiculous, I followed HN to the elevator. Feeling brave, I inhaled and slid my hand into his. He intertwined our fingers and looked at me. No, looked into me. In that small gesture, he said much more than his words ever could. My heart doubled in size, and prickles woke up inside me. I stopped breathing as the elevator doors closed, and my pulse spiked with a mix of anticipation and excitement.

20

CARTER

April and I played tourists for the rest of the day. We ate sweet potato pancakes at this little place mostly visited by locals, far from the tourist hot spots, where I knew we wouldn't be disturbed, and strolled through Centennial Park.

After lunch, we sauntered across Music Row. "I recorded my very first album here," I said, pointing to a little craftsman powder-blue house with white columns.

"With your band?"

"Yeah, before we all went our separate ways." I stifled a laugh as memories flooded my mind. "God, we were just kids… It seems like a lifetime ago."

Later, we hopped into one of those golf carts that transport tourists all over the city.

"Broadway and Fifth, please," I asked the elderly man who took it upon himself to give us a tour. April listened to everything he said, asking questions. The next thing I knew, they were talking about the man's grandchildren, and he was showing her pictures on his phone. April gave him her full attention, and I watched the exchange in silence, a wide smile stretching my lips.

"So, where are y'all from?" he asked.

"Georgia," April answered without missing a beat. "We're in town for the weekend. Huge fans of country music here." She elbowed me in the ribs.

"Sure," I said, scratching the side of my head. "The biggest fans."

She smirked and brought her attention back to our tour guide, squeezing my arm with her small hand.

The man dropped us in front of the Ryman Auditorium. "Y'all enjoy your trip."

"Frank, tell Rosa to try frankincense essential oil for her arthritis. It should help. She can contact me if she has questions. You have my contact info in your phone."

Who was Rosa? His wife? If so, when did April have the time to learn about our tour guide's spouse and her health? Lost in my daydream, I hadn't paid attention to much they said.

"Will do." Frank turned around to face me. "Take good care of your wife, sir, she's a keeper." He winked, and I stopped in my tracks. *Wife?* How much did I miss?

At lunchtime, we grabbed vegan tacos from a food truck on Second and traipsed down Broadway. The entire time, April's face sparkled.

"All the bars are already open." This was more an affirmation than a question. Even at this time of the day, bands were playing live music. "Did you ever play here?" she asked me, pivoting on her heels until we faced each other. I nodded. April watched me, and I had a hard time reading her eyes through those shades.

My mouth went dry as echoes of the past consumed me.

"I wish I'd heard you play back then." She rose on her

tiptoes and brushed her lips over mine, not quite kissing me. We breathed the same air, and I got dizzy.

I locked my arms around her waist, and I drew her toward me. "Let's hang out here for a while."

She turned and pressed her back to my front. I gripped her waist, and she swayed her hips to an old Garth Brooks hit as we listened to the cover band through a large, garage-door–style window from the sidewalk. Pixie couldn't miss how much I loved having her in my arms. My appreciation pressed firmly against her lower back.

I'd spent years shielding my heart, keeping it unreachable. Why was it so different with her? Why did I feel like opening up to her, spilling all my secrets, including the one that had been eating me alive for a long time?

"Riley and my friend Tucker own this place." I pointed to the bar across the street. "It's the hottest spot in town. And Jeff used to work there." I motioned to the establishment right next to it.

"I thought he was in the army."

"Yeah. But he moved here after high school. He dropped out of college after a few months and started working there instead. He's the reason we got signed at eighteen to a big label. He made some contacts, and one day, Riley came to see us play. The rest is history."

"Wow. Were you guys close? I've always wondered what it'd be like to have siblings."

Growing up, my brother and I got ourselves into impossible situations more times than I could recount. Up until his death, Dahlia and he were my two best friends.

"There was this time. When I was about nine years old…I think. We built a soapbox out of the junk we found in our neighbor's backyard. We used the little money we had, the money we earned mostly from doing chores, to buy paint because we wanted our cart to look fierce. For two months, we hid our secret project under a tarp in the back of the garage. Our parents were clueless about it…or rather, we thought they were. Anyway, we worked on it for weeks. It helped that Jeff was good with tools. Proud, we took our soapbox out for a road test, wearing helmets and elbow pads. To this day, I'm still grateful we did.

"I remember that day perfectly. The sun was shining high and glowing in the blue sky. Jeff sat in the front, both hands on the old, rusty trash can lid serving as a steering wheel. He told me to hold on tight as I sat behind him, my little arms wrapped around his waist. *Don't be nervous, Carter,* he said, trying to reassure me in his big brother way. We wheeled down the hill at high speed. I remember how I felt. Free. Invincible. Excited. I remember the breeze on my skin and messing up my hair. We laughed the whole time. Until we realized, too late, we forgot to install some sort of brake on our little cart. One wheel broke, and the soapbox tipped over, ejecting us. Jeff ended up with a broken arm, and I broke two ribs and chafed the skin of my back on the pavement." I smiled. "That minute of freedom was worth every broken bone and every burn."

April's grip tightened on my forearm. "Ohmygod. Did you get grounded? What happened afterward?"

"Wait, that's the best part. Once we both fully recovered from our injuries, our dad surprised us with an improved version of our soapbox. He'd fixed it and added two sets of brakes, just in case. Jeff and I entered the town's annual derby competition at the end of the summer, and we finished in second place."

"That's amazing. I would've loved to witness the troublesome Hills brothers at that age. I missed the action growing up. Nana wasn't much of an adrenaline junkie or a prankster."

"Ask Dahlia. I'm surprised our parents didn't die from children-induced stress."

"Carter, I'm sorry Jeff is gone."

I inhaled a shaky breath. "Me too."

She pivoted and planted a kiss on my lips, so soft it freed me from years of pain. The twinkle in her eyes glued back together more pieces of my heart that'd been hanging around in my chest for years. Pieces I thought were lost forever. April had this way of making everything in my life better. Even my sorrows.

In Centennial Park earlier, I'd kissed her under a tree. I couldn't resist. She made all these cute sounds whenever I showed her something new, and it turned me on. Big time. When her eyes flared, I knew she saw something exciting. When she scrunched up her nose, something was bothering her. A lopsided smile meant she wasn't sure. Without a word, I could read her like an open book. I'd pushed her against the trunk of a willow tree, caging her with my arms, and the hunter side of me had taken control, craving to claim her as mine. Our mouths fused. Hungry. Yearning. Desperate. She whispered my name, and my chest cavity expanded to make room for my swollen heart. Her lips on mine deprived my brain of oxygen. Every lap of her tongue against mine reminded me how stupid I had been last night to push her away instead of holding on to her like I should have. Time stopped. April liquified in my arms, and I never wanted to let her go.

We continued our stroll down Broadway, heading toward the Cumberland River.

"The other day, you said you didn't know if you were supposed to be an author. When you were little, what was your dream job?"

She lifted our joined hands and brushed my knuckles with the pad of her thumb. "It's silly. I always knew I wanted to be a writer. When I was little, I was obsessed with poetry. Not sure I could've made a living out of it, though, so I picked journalism as a major in college. Seemed like a smarter choice at the time." She shrugged.

"Do you want to be a journalist? Right here, right now, tell me the truth."

"Hell, no. I prefer writing fun things. Creating worlds…from scratch."

"Ever wrote song lyrics?"

She stopped in her tracks and stared at me, her lips parted and her eyes big.

"It's a bit like writing poetry. You should give it a try. Just a thought."

She stayed silent as if what I'd asked required some in-depth analysis. As if I'd spoken a different language. Or I'd opened a door she never knew existed before.

"If you're interested, I know a person who does that for a living. He's an ass but a charming one. Think about it." I kissed her still-open mouth and winked.

April didn't say anything. I could probably see the gears working in her head if I looked close enough. Her eyes were focused. Her lips slightly twisted. Her nose wrinkled. She was processing my words and looked fucking adorable.

Halfway down the pedestrian bridge, Fairy fished her phone out of her purse and stepped on a concrete bench, now standing as tall as me. "Scoot closer, HN, I want a picture. This is one of those days I want to remember forever." She snapped pictures of us, our back to the Cumberland River, her lips on my cheek, her eyes as bright as fireworks on the Fourth of July.

My gaze landed on her face as she scrolled through the photos she'd just taken. My clothes felt too tight and itchy. I removed my beanie and ran a hand through my hair. *Breathe in. Breathe out.*

April jumped into my arms to kiss me just as we were about to climb into my truck and drive back home. *Home.* Green Mountain. The cabin. Anywhere with her felt like home.

"Thanks for everything, HN. It's like we spent the last two days in a snow globe where everything is magical."

I dipped my head, and our foreheads met. The air us seemed charged with a million tiny sparks. I said nothing, struggling to keep my hands to myself—and other parts of my body too. At the moment, I wished I could bend her over the hood and thrust into her until neither of us could stand upright.

On the ride back, we entwined our fingers, and I traced circles on her palm with my thumb, fully aware of each movement.

"Tell me. Any crazy fan stories?" Her eyes flashed with interest. "Any women who threw their panties at you mid-show?"

I mirrored her grin. "Let's see… Where should I begin…? There was this one guy who bypassed the security, way back when I bought my first house, and ended up naked in my bed. Somehow, he knew when I'd be back from tour and wanted to surprise me."

April's hand flew to her mouth as she tried to suppress a laugh. "Ugh, I would have freaked out."

"It's was pretty memorable. Another time, a guy convinced everyone he was my half-brother and landed a backstage pass, giving him access to places he shouldn't have. He followed me into the green room and threatened me with a blade."

Her eyes nearly popped out of her head. "You're not joking?"

"Nah. I wish. I have funny stories too." I told her all about the girl who got my face tattooed on her chest and the one who wore no panties when she interviewed me on live TV, flashing me her hairy pussy the entire time.

"It's kinda gross. How did you keep a straight face?"

"No idea. I was young, and let's just say it took a long time for my brain to erase the images of that day."

We stopped for gas, and April bought the biggest assortment of snacks I'd ever indulged in. And slushies.

For the next hundred miles, we talked about everything and nothing, our conversation flowing effortlessly. Even the silences felt comfortable. I had no idea what to make of the familiarity settling between us.

Two hours in, she fell asleep, slumped against my side. The corner of my lips lifted as I pressed a gentle kiss to the crown of her head. If only I could drive all night and never have to wake her, knowing we shared this moment of peace together, I'd be a content man. Left alone with nothing but my thoughts and the soft sound of her breathing, my mind wandered into uncharted territories. Places I tended to avoid. Doubts crept in slowly, occupying the corners of my mind where the past still lingered. My throat tightened as memories swept by, and each breath became heavier. Deep inside, fear bubbled, threatening to surface and suffocate me. Reservations about my burgeoning emotions teetered on the edge, threatening to derail the fragile connection simmering between us. Lust. Desire. Trust. Happiness.

I didn't know if I could trust what I was feeling at the moment. Pixie was creating chaos in my life, upsetting the twisted balance I had set for myself a few months ago. Looking at her, I knew she wasn't the typical woman you banged on the side and left behind with the bedsheets still covered in hot sweat. She was a girl you planned a future with. A keeper—like our tour guide had said. A girl you introduced to your parents. The kind of woman you'd see yourself married to. The one you'd never forget or get over when she stepped out of your life.

The one you'd give forever to.

This relationship needed time to blossom and lots of patience. Did I have that in me? Besides, the attraction between us was an inferno, threatening to leave only ashes behind. Such an attraction could be a dangerous game. How hadn't I realized it sooner? I was sinking in too deep, my thoughts consumed by her. After my last experience, how had I removed the icy walls around my heart so easily? Now my organ longed to beat only to her rhythm. Even the idea of not being able to spend days without feeling her skin on mine or getting a whiff of her lavender perfume had become unbearable. She was seizing my control, and I was willing to give up my freedom for her. How did that happen? When did I drop my guard down long enough to let a woman get close to me all over again?

I strangled the steering wheel, my knuckles turning white and my palms clammy. No, I shouldn't bear feelings for the woman sitting next to me. Not only did it not make sense, but it was too much too fast. I had escaped my last relationship not so long ago. Was I ready to dive right back into another one? With no safety net? And with a trusting heart?

Just the thought of everything that could go wrong sent my heart into a chaotic tempo. The cab of my truck grew smaller, stealing all the viable oxygen and suffocating me. I was insane. How could I risk another heartbreak? Didn't I learn my lesson the last time? Didn't I suffer enough already?

A little voice in my head kept telling me to give it a

shot. To have faith that this could lead to something amazing.

April stirred in her sleep, forcing my attention back to her. Her relaxed features made her look younger. When we first met, I had noticed the shadow lingering in her eyes. After she told me about her past, her family, I could tell that was what had toughened her up. Right now, the lines around her eyes were invisible, and she looked at peace. If only I could swallow her worries with one kiss. And then fill her with unfaltering happiness with every other one. I'd kiss her every day to make that happen.

I parked my truck in the driveway and turned the engine off but made no move to get out as I watched her sleep a bit longer.

Her eyes fluttered open and landed on me. "Hey," she said.

"Hey."

"How long was I out?"

I shrugged. "An hour maybe."

Her face wrinkled as she studied me. "Are you okay?"

I swallowed my discomfort and nodded. "Yeah. Sure." Before she could gauge the uneasiness troubling me, I leaned over and kissed the back of her hand still connected to mine. "Come on, let's go inside."

———

The next morning, I woke up early. A train of yawns left my mouth. I grabbed the torn envelope I kept under my pillow. This was my demise. It used to be immaculate and white. Not anymore. It'd followed me all around the globe for years. I traced the faded black ink letters scribbled on the front. *Carter.* Dahlia's handwriting. And the answer to the one secret I'd been holding on to for years. The one neither of us had any certainty about. I turned it around between my fingers, took one last look at the sealed flap, and slid it back where it belonged.

Would I ever be able to open it? I blew out a shuddering breath. Not today. Over the years, I'd asked myself the exact same thing more times than I could remember.

After tossing and turning most of the night, unable to shush the voices in my head or go back to sleep, I got up. As much as I'd miss spending my day with April, I knew a day spent on my own would be a smarter choice. The intensity of my attraction for her had been troubling me all night, and it still did, even hours later. It played with all my insecurities. And scared the hell out of me. Fairy appeared in my life when I least expected it—when I had no plans to let anyone in again, not so soon after the disaster of my last relationship.

The idea she was sleeping a flight of stairs below me topped my anxiety. One side of me wanted her to move back to her place, while the other hoped she'd hang around and become mine. That she'd welcome me into her bed and never let me go. That she could be the long-lost piece of my heart I'd been looking for all my life.

I raked my fingers through my hair, and my pulse spiked dangerously.

Dressed in faded black sweatpants and a brown hoodie, I tiptoed downstairs and grabbed my car keys. With every step toward my truck, I prayed April stayed in bed, not feeling strong enough to face her right now. What would I even say to her? *Leave, but don't go? Stay, but I'm not ready for you? I want you, but I'm too scared?* My insides and my head were a scrambled mess. What I wished for and what I was ready for didn't seem to fit together anymore. Last night, on the drive back from Nashville, as I watched her sleep, a chain had grown around my heart, squeezing it, each pull and twist more painful than the other. How could I feel something for a woman I had met just a few weeks ago? How had she slipped under my skin and into my heart so easily? The other day, Dahlia said I was falling for her, and at the time, I brushed it off. But what if her words spoke the truth?

April wasn't my ex. The two of them had nothing in common. The time spent together wasn't a game she played. A role she was auditioning for. She didn't make me feel like I owed her something…everything. A meal ticket to a scripted end. We were equals. Friends first.

Still, doubts lingered. Big, fat, persistent ones.

Was I so infatuated with her that I imagined things the way I hoped they'd be? I did that once, and it cost me my soul.

Panic froze my blood. Breathing became harder with each gulp of air.

Outside, the early morning was still bathed in darkness. Riled up, I didn't feel the cold winter breeze across my face.

Breathe in. Breathe out.

I bent in two, trying to quiet the voices in my head. The hand of steel crushing my heart. The rocks sitting on my chest and messing with my breathing.

My own doubts trapped me in. I'd loosened up for a few days, and now my closeness with April was tampering with all the rules I'd set for myself. And the fears of another failed relationship. One that was destined to crash once she went back to her life. And leave me behind.

The aftermath of our weekend in Nashville acted as a cold shower. Where was my self-control when I needed it?

As much as I was attracted to my smart and gorgeous guest and wanted to see where this thing between us could go, I also feared it would end badly.

Every relationship in my life always does.

The only thing I had, for sure, was my career, even though Savannah tried to wreck it with all her fucking lies. Why did I tell April I wanted us to be serious the other night? Committed to each other? What was wrong with me? Seriously. Was I ready to be consumed by another human being? Again? April's heart was pure. Fame and money meant nothing to her. But would she ever be cut out to be part of a life like mine? Fucking fame. Always in the way.

Last night, on our way back here, she asked me, "Are you sure your people packed my dress? It's the nicest piece of clothing I've ever owned."

"You're attached to a dress?" I raised a brow, not sure I heard her right.

She offered me a timid smile. "Think what you want, Country Boy, but that dress is amazing. I love it."

That girl fell in love with a dress. A *dress*. A fucking piece of fabric with glitter.

My lips curled up at the memory. I'd never met anyone like her before.

How could a grown-up woman be in love with sequins and silk, no matter how amazing and tempting they looked on her?

She even insisted on paying for lunch yesterday. Except for Dahlia and my mother, no woman had ever offered to pay a bill in my company. Nope. Not once. Never happened.

People knew I had more money than I could spend in this lifetime. I never bragged about my wealth, but it was common knowledge. And they always took advantage.

Yesterday, even dressed in her ugly outfit as we played tourists, I couldn't look away from the woman holding my dreams captive.

I hit the steering wheel with all my strength. *Fuck.*

This wasn't supposed to happen. In the short time we'd known each other, April had taken a front row seat in my life. She'd not only stolen my heart, but also my soul.

The realization hit me hard. My thoughts spiraled in my head. A new surge of panic spread through my being. Oxygen felt scarce when I took a big inhale that didn't fully reach my lungs.

With a hollowed-out chest, I drove to a house on the other side of town that I'd transformed into my escape place three years ago. Nobody knew about my secret hiding spot. Not even Dahlia.

It had an attached garage, making it easy for me to come and go without anyone getting a glimpse of me. The place consisted of a gym, a giant TV hanging on the wall, a small kitchen, an old and ugly, but comfortable, couch, a bathroom tinier than a closet, and a few guitars. No bedroom or fancy things. Basic necessities. A place to unwind. To let go of the things haunting me. It looked more like a teenager's basement than a grown man's hangout spot. Nobody would bother me here.

I parked my truck but didn't get out.

I wrote Desmond a quick text message.

ME

Hey, it's me. When do you think you'll be able to fix the lock?

But then I stabbed the backspace button many times with my finger. What was I doing?

Did I really want April to go back to her own cabin? No. I wanted her in mine. With me.

Shit. I had no clue what to do. Spots appeared in my vision. I knew the signs. Seconds later, I was hyperventilating, moving my head back and forth, massaging my temples with my fingertips to calm my overwhelmed mind. A cloud of darkness blanketed me. My blood turned to ice. My body craved to move, but I was frozen. *Breathe in. Breathe out.* My throat tightened. I choked, my eyes filling with tears.

After gathering my thoughts, I stumbled out of the SUV and changed into the workout clothes I kept in the trunk. The back of my eyes blazed with unshed tears as I hit the treadmill. My feet stomped on the running belt with a soft thump. I ran away from my life. And away from my fears. Until all my muscles burned and twitched from exhaustion. My legs weakened by the twelfth mile. My chest heaved. My breathing scorched my lungs. Drained out, I steadied myself against the wall to stretch my calves, quads, and hamstrings. Bent over at the knees, afraid I'd hurl even on an empty stomach, I inhaled slowly. The gears in my head sprinted. What was going on with me? Once the storm in me lessened, I chugged a purple sports drink I fetched from the refrigerator. The drenched fabric of my shirt stuck to my skin, and every inch of my flesh itched. With shaky hands, I peeled it off as if it were on fire.

I was trying hard not to lose it, but the more time passed, the more restless I felt.

My vision blurred.

My stomach grumbled, begging to be fed.

Sports drinks couldn't be considered food.

Desperate to silence my stomach and get over with it, I mixed a protein shake and gulped half in one gulp. I heaved as it went down. I paced the main floor, trying to do those stupid breathing exercises that were supposed to help me calm the fuck down. *Breathe in. Hold. Breathe out. Repeat.* Doing my best Clayton Kershaw impression, I threw my half-drunk shake into the kitchen sink. The thick, dark-green liquid splattered the backsplash. I shrugged, turned around, and reached the two-car garage. My house-cleaning obsession just went out the window. My episode was worse than I first thought. Darkness thickened around me. It made me a prisoner of my own mind. Of my inner demons. I rubbed my eyes with the heels of my hands. The giant ball of knots filling my stomach made my breaths shorter. This was a fucking nightmare.

"Let go, Carter," I screamed at no one. "You can't embark on another relationship. Anyway, women always fail you." Why would April be different? My therapist would disagree with my assessment. We went over it multiple times in the past. I really believed I was over my mother's abandonment issues, but right now, blaming her was all I could do to soothe the pain surging inside me. After all, she was the first woman I loved unconditionally who'd turned her back on me. She was supposed to be in my corner, to cheer on me, but she quit. The wounds she sliced in my heart ran deeper than anyone could imagine. Myself included.

With a kick, I opened the door leading to the garage. Not risking any injuries, I wrapped my hands and slid them into the worn-out black boxing gloves I kept on a shelf. My muscles were still warm from the running, so without losing a second, I assaulted the heavily taped red punching bag hanging from a beam in the ceiling. I punched the motherfucker like I wanted to end its life. Like it had wronged me.

"Fuck you, Savannah Prince. For trying to ruin me." I punched the bag with a succession of uppercuts. "Take this, Mom. Take this, Dad." I punched harder. "You left me when I needed you the most." I dried off my tears, hot as flames, with my upper arm. "Jeff, take this because you abandoned me too. You were my best friend, and you left me all alone to fend for myself. And Dah. Take this. I loved you, and you always picked other guys over me. I never stood a chance because you never gave me one. All of you, go fuck yourself."

My chest and back dripped sweat. My body trembled from exhaustion.

It wasn't enough. It never was.

It did nothing to keep my mind from wandering back to my roommate. To erase my mixed feelings toward her.

An hour later, on the back deck, I stripped down and welcomed the cold air on my body. The icy breeze tingled my skin. I buried myself, bare-assed, in the hot tub and closed my eyes, stretching my arms on either side.

In the past, I drank my weight in whiskey whenever I needed to evade my mind. Now, except for exercising like a person on the edge of a mental breakdown, I didn't know what else to do.

I pictured April in my head. These days, I always fucking pictured her. Awake. Asleep. Laughing. Smiling. She occupied every free corner of my mind.

All the memories of her resurfaced.

My tongue tasting her flesh.

Her lips locked on mine.

The sultry dress she wore.

Her swaying hips when she listened to music.

Her tits bouncing when she jumped into my arms.

Her ass in those skinny jeans she loved so much.

The memory of her, nestled in my arms that morning in her cabin after we met, her body clenching around my fingers, haunted me even after all this time.

My cock sprang hard, and I pumped it in fast strokes, trying to get rid of the discomfort crippling me.

Yet, jerking off thinking about her was never enough. I tried. Countless times.

My entire body ached whenever I pictured her in my head.

I should've fucked her out of my system in Nashville when she begged me to. Perhaps that would've helped keep her off my mind. To keep me from craving her. April had crept under my skin the day we bantered in the woods and became much more than an itch to scratch.

She had become the center of my world. Fuck. *Fuck, fuck, fuck.*

I had no idea how to do this—how to be with her. That was what had thrown me into this anxiety-driven episode to begin with. I wasn't prone to anxiety when I was younger, but Jeff's death triggered something in me. After he passed away, the attacks began.

April. Why was just the thought of her powerful enough to send me spiraling down?

My head spun. I climbed out of the hot tub, the breeze too cold against my junk, reminding me I was naked. A shiver started in my toes and made its way to the back of my neck. My body shook, and I hurried back inside.

Showered and dressed, I jumped behind the wheel of my SUV and drove without purpose for hours, music blasting through the sound system, deafening my brain, preventing it from going to places I refused to venture.

Why couldn't I have a normal life?

April refused to reveal her identity as an author. If we were to be together, how would she deal with being recognized? Because no matter how hard I tried, people would know we were a couple. How much would she hate me after being exposed by the press vultures? Her face would be on magazine covers, her name whispered on gossip shows. Strangers would criticize her and everything she did, as if it were their birthright—like they were entitled to it because their own lives sucked and they were miserable.

A sour taste filled my mouth.

In a short amount of time, she had become precious to me. A true friend. And a woman I yearned to call my lover. That connection we shared, it couldn't be faked. Like we'd known each other forever, and we were just finally meeting again. Being offered a second chance at love.

My head swirled with unanswered questions.

Could I ever make both sides of my life fit together? The personal and the professional one. I wasn't willing to give up my music, but I wasn't ready to lose April either. Not before we explored what we could be.

My body hurt as if thousands of needles pricked my skin. The fog surrounding me wouldn't disappear. It enfolded me tighter. My lungs were compressed. I fought the urge to get to her. To explain where I stood and pray the celebrity side of my persona wouldn't scare her away. That it wouldn't stand between us once the novelty of a new relationship wore off.

What would happen when her stay in Green Mountain was over? Would she walk away like I never mattered to her and turn out to be a mirage in my life? Or would she be willing to put in the work—and sacrifice her anonymity —so we could be together in the long run?

Would she be a constant in my life or become someone I longed to hold on to, but essentially inaccessible?

Once again, Dahlia's words replayed in my head. *If what you two could have is worth it, give her some time to ease into the idea this is your life. If you move too fast, she'll run away.* My gut told me to move in, to seize my chance. I was tired of listening to everybody else's opinion about my own life. Dahlia. June. Riley. Carla. Savannah. Why couldn't *I* decide once and for all what was good for me? Sure, I had misjudged Savannah's motives, but I was already in a dark place back then—a far cry from the life I was leading these days.

All the scenarios my mind conjured left me dizzy and more confused than ever.

"I'm fucking tired of chasing happiness. Why can't it be simple?" I asked no one but myself.

More crippling thoughts paralyzed my brain.

What if April didn't want me as much as I wanted her? Chills worked through me at the idea.

Abandoned in the cup holder, my phone buzzed with a call. Followed by another one. My focus moved to the road in front of me, and I chose to ignore June's and Riley's attempts to reach out. Anyway, the race in my mind would prevent me from having a normal conversation with anyone.

It had been a long time since I'd had an episode that overwhelmed me so much, and once again, it involved my fear of losing someone I cared about. I itched to call Dr. Diaz, my therapist, but I wasn't in the mood to be asked existential questions I should have answers to but would take me forever to figure out. He would nod, waiting for me to fish out the truth from inside me. Probably something I subconsciously had decided to bury deep down. Then I'd cry, get angry, and cry again. Finally, he would say, "I'm proud of you, Carter. Now how can we fix this?" Yeah, been there, done that. No thanks. Not today.

The chime of an incoming text message grabbed my attention. Just the sight of April's name on my phone screen was enough to twist my troubled heart into another knot. In a swift gesture, I threw my device on the backseat. There, I could breathe easier and swallow the bubbling sobs down my throat. Turning up the volume of the radio, I sang along to the tune playing until my voice became hoarse.

Around midnight, struggling to keep my eyes open and not ready to face April yet, I drove back to my secret spot and slouched down on the couch. I kicked my shoes off and shifted position, the tightness around my heart not releasing its deadly grip. Panic attacks had been my hell for years. For the longest time, I almost forgot they existed. Until they came back with a vengeance last year.

With shaky fingers, unable to leave her in the dark and not wanting her to worry about me, I shot April a text.

ME

Won't make it home tonight. Have some things to deal with.

Reclining back, I stretched my legs, crossed them at the ankles, and propped my head up on a pillow. With my eyes closed, I did some breathing exercises to silence the voices in my head. The ones that usually helped when nothing else did. My limbs grew heavier. The air in the room trapped me, making it hard to draw a full breath. With a flick of my wrist, I sent my phone sliding across the floor to resist glancing at it all night. A strangled cry of despair lodged in my throat as I fell into an agitated slumber, my body and mind restless.

Vivid dreams and nightmares disturbed my rest.

21

APRIL

Carter had disappeared at least twelve hours ago. Nobody had heard from him all day. My gaze drifted outside, the pink and orange stripes of sunset having long faded away.

When I had woken up this morning, I had been optimistic about the day. Even though the moment my lids opened, I made the decision not to push him into something we both might regret. I would draw the line at friendship. Maybe I'd agree to add some groping and kisses to the mix, but that would be it. I wasn't cut out for one-nighters. And sooner or later, it would haunt me if I dropped my guard and gave in to whatever my body vibrated for.

My heart felt lighter.

Yep, limits. They would help our situation stay in the friendship zone. With a new resolve to enjoy my time left here as much as possible, I had extracted myself from the comfort and warmth of my bed, ready to jumpstart my day.

After I had showered and dressed, I added makeup to

my eyes and lips, putting a little effort into my appearance, aware HN and I would spend the day together.

Downstairs, there had been no trace of him. Cold had seeped through the cabin's walls, and a shiver ran through me. The fireplace hadn't been lit since we left for Nashville two days ago. Whenever Carter woke up first, he always made sure to start a fire to warm up the place.

When I couldn't find him anywhere, I had concluded that my housemate was still asleep.

Not wanting to wake him up, I had tiptoed around the place. In the kitchen, I had fed Bernice before filling the kettle with water to make some tea.

Once I had lit up a fire, I sat in front of it, hugging myself, until my body reached a comfortable temperature and the chills running through me dissolved.

It was around noon, when I went out for a short walk to clear my head, that I realized Carter's truck wasn't parked in the driveway. The massive black SUV was indeed missing from its usual spot. Carter had left. When? Why? I had no recollection of his telling me about a meeting or some other place he had to be first thing in the morning after we had returned from Nashville last night. Anyway, his whereabouts were none of my business. Carter owed me nothing. Yet, something felt off.

For the rest of the day, I had kept myself busy. The more I had focused on my work, the less Carter had infiltrated my thoughts and the less I had worried about his absence.

Eight-twenty-six.

It'd been a whole day since I heard from him, and here I was now, switching between worrying about him and working on my manuscript, moving chapters around. My mind wasn't into it. I looked at the time on my phone screen again in case I missed his call. In the last hour, I must have done that at least a dozen times.

Unable to focus anymore, I kept myself busy in the kitchen prepping dinner, praying that by the time I was done, he would show up. Wherever he was, I was sure Carter would like a home-cooked meal after his long day. I decided on broccoli and cashew pasta, a vegan recipe I found in one of his cookbooks. I rummaged through the pantry for cashews, but came up short. Maybe if I asked, he would stop by the grocery store on his way back, so I sent him a text.

He never replied.

I ended up making pasta with basil and tomatoes instead. For half an hour, I picked at my food before throwing it away, and I put the plate I fixed for him in the refrigerator and stuck a note on the plastic wrapper.

If you're hungry.
April

Exhausted from the weekend, I sat in the living room in front of the fireplace, with a glass of white wine and a novel. Time ticked, but Carter never made it home.

Around eleven, I climbed the stairs to my room. With one last glance at the driveway through the second-floor window, I concluded he wouldn't be coming home tonight.

After my nightly routine and from the comfort of my bed, I shot him one last message. My heart deflated in my chest when once again, he didn't reply. Whatever happened, I just prayed he was safe and sound. Lying on my back for the longest time, I replayed our weekend in my head, wondering what had changed since we came back. The whole day, no matter what I did, all my thoughts narrowed down to him and our amazing time in Nashville. Gone was the broody man I had met in the woods when I first got here. From what he confided in me, Carter had a complicated life, and he hid behind this angry version of himself when, in reality, there was nothing dark about him. He was not only genuinely nice and caring, but he also possessed a huge heart and could light up an entire town when he smiled. Something I could never get tired of being on the receiving end of.

With a hand, I pressed my chest over my heart, calming its tremors. I was not ready to go back to the real world once this vacation was over.

Even though I enjoyed how Carter made me feel and the undeniable hot and sizzling chemistry we shared, I couldn't envisage a future with him. We were much more alike than I could have ever imagined, but we belonged to two different worlds. He, the famous rock star recognized worldwide. I, the author hiding behind a pen name and refusing to let people in and have access to the real version of me.

The night of his concert, when we kissed, it felt as if the stars were realigning themselves for us. But after much consideration, indulging in the lust simmering between us would have been the wrong move. A bad decision. If we got attached to each other, how would I ever be able to walk away when my time in Green Mountain was up? I knew my heart—and all its weaknesses. Without hesitation, I could already tell Carter Hills was one of them.

When he said if we ever had sex, it wouldn't be a fling, I agreed. What he forgot to mention was what would happen if we ever gave in to the attraction we couldn't deny. I lived in Southern Georgia. He lived in Tennessee. Our statuses weren't the only thing that would keep us apart. Distance would too.

Bernice came to snuggle in bed with me, her purr lulling me toward sleep. Soon sleep claimed me, and I wished Carter would come back to me in my dreams.

———

I woke up feeling like someone had sat on my chest all night. My shoulders and neck were strained. Wrapped in the white duvet, I stretched my arms and legs. On the nightstand, I grabbed my phone. Carter had sent me a cryptic text message around two in the morning.

CARTER

Won't make it home tonight. Have some
things to deal with.

My insides constricted. Something was wrong. Anger surged through me. Was I stupid for being mad at him?

We were nothing more than friends, and I was acting silly. He had engagements and a rock star like him probably had tons of meetings every week. He was a grown-ass man and didn't require my permission to do anything. I knew I shouldn't worry about his whereabouts, but a little voice in my head insisted he wasn't being himself. After breakfast, I went for a walk to clear my head. Last night, for the first time since I came to Green Mountain, I had insomnia. Entangled in my bed sheets from tossing and turning for hours, I often woke with a start, convinced I heard him coming in. How I didn't even notice my phone chime in the middle of the night when he texted me remained a mystery.

Bernice bunted my leg as soon as my feet touched the hardwood floor, begging me for food. "Girl, is that all you ever think about?" I lifted her into my arms, nuzzling her fur.

I was filling her bowl with kibbles when the sudden chime of the doorbell made me jump. Wondering who it could be, I rushed to the front door.

"Hi, April," Dahlia said once I cracked the door open. "Where's Carter?"

"Huh…not sure."

Jack glided through the open door. "Mama, look. Carter has a cat," he said, kicking off his boots.

I turned my head to face the boy and caught his jacket when he threw it off. "Her name is Bernice. I think she'd like to have a friend." The boy flashed me a two-thousand-dollar grin—reminding me of the man I was, despite myself, obsessed with—and ran after Bernice. I brought my attention back to Dahlia. "Sorry, you were saying?"

"Carter's not here. His truck is gone."

I peeked through the doorway to look past her even though, deep down, I knew that once again the black SUV wouldn't be parked in the driveway.

"I haven't seen him since the night we drove back from Nashville two days ago. He's been missing all day yesterday too."

"Did he say anything to you?"

I shook my head. "No. For all I know, it's not like him to leave without a word…or is it?"

Compassion filled her eyes. "It depends. Sometimes, Cart longs for some space from everything and everyone. Usually when he has to think or breathe alone. If I were you, I wouldn't worry. Unless he had stuff to deal with in Nashville. If that's the case, it would make sense he slept there."

"But we just came back from Nashville. Why would he have returned here only to go back?"

"You're right. I'm sure he'll turn up later and explain everything. Guess we'll come back some other time then."

"Can I help you with something?"

She shook her head. "No. Not really. Jack wanted to say hello."

"Huh, I—"

The little boy traipsed in our direction, Bernice in tow. "Look, April. We're best friends."

"I think Bernice loves you very much."

"Jack, we're leaving," Dahlia said. "Carter isn't here. We'll come back another day."

The boy crouched down and patted the cat's head. "Bye, Bernice." Without a warning, he hugged me next. "Thanks, April, for letting me play with your cat." He grinned, and I ruffled his hair.

Dahlia must have seen the puzzled look on my face because she angled her body until our faces met and whispered, "Don't worry, okay? He'll be back."

I nodded, unsure of what to say.

They both waved me goodbye as they drove away.

Standing on the front porch, I watched their taillights until they disappeared, wondering where Carter could have gone. It wasn't his style to leave without a note. Something felt off, now I was certain of it, and yet, I couldn't pinpoint what exactly.

Had I done something to scare him away? Had the whole Nashville thing confused him?

Fear prickled at my spine. The breath I was holding escaped me, and every piece of me prayed he was okay.

Still, I had a hunch something was wrong.

After forcing myself to eat a few bites of oatmeal, my appetite gone with the man I lived with, I got dressed and ventured outside. Close to the gate, I returned Saunders's call.

"Hey, Bubble Head. How is it going with your man?"

I sighed. "He's not my man."

"Did you guys have dirty sex the other night?"

I sighed. Again. "If you mean in Nashville, no, we didn't." I braced myself for the questions that would come.

"Did you panic?"

"Why do you think I'm the one to blame?"

"Well, are you? Tell me the truth." She lowered her voice in the caring tone she often used with me. "It's okay if you're scared. But it's also okay to let go."

"Saund. Stop. Carter was the one who stopped our make-out session. He said he didn't want us to be a fling and walked me back to my room."

"Blimey. You're kidding, right? You snogged, and he turned you away?"

I buried my face in my hand. "It wasn't—"

"He's a wanker. Anyway, I'm coming to Green Mountain on Friday night. I'll assess the situation with my own eyes. Your life is so entertaining."

"You're coming? For real?"

"Yep. Oh, crap. Can we talk later? I have an important call coming in. I'll text you. Bye." My best friend hung up before I could add another word.

I danced in place. Saunders would be here. On Friday. I squealed, unable to contain my joy.

My cabin's lock should be fixed by then, and I'd be out of Carter's way. A girls' weekend was everything I needed.

After lunch, Jill, my agent, called me back, and we went over the first half of my manuscript to discuss my work. Over the years, Jill and I had become friends. We chatted for a bit and brainstormed ideas. Once we hung up, I got back to work and rewrote some pages like we discussed and sent her two more chapters. With a mug of hot chocolate, I settled in the den, my fingers unstoppable on the keyboard. HN's disappearance wouldn't mess with my brain. I wouldn't let him. If he chose to leave, vanish, or ignore me, that was on him. I poured all my restlessness into my work. April Simmons, the author, was in full creative mode. Finally. A wide smile spread across my face. I hadn't felt this hopeful about writing in a long time.

Orange and purplish brush strokes filled the sky as the sun settled down for the night. Done for the day, I found myself alone in this *too big for one human being* cabin, with more knots tying my stomach. I put music on, songs whose lyrics I knew by heart, to keep my mind busy, and cleaned up the place, hoping Carter would come back tonight. Somehow, I missed him and the way he stared at me with interest—and lust. Like he cared. I missed the bantering, the nights by the fireplace sharing pieces of our past, his plant-based cooking, and how he asked my opinion whatever the subject. I even missed his grumbling over my music choices.

My phone chimed on the kitchen counter.

JUNE

April, any news from Carter?

I wrinkled my nose. What should I tell her? The truth sounded better than a blatant lie. I sighed, trying to put to sleep the flock of hyperactive butterflies in my belly.

ME

Not since late last night. Still not home. Sorry.

She replied almost instantly.

JUNE

Keep me updated. Please.

ME

I will.

You think he's all right?

JUNE

I hope so. Sometimes he disappears for
days. Don't worry, he'll come back. It's his
way to unwind when he's overwhelmed. I'll
text you if I hear from him first.

ME

Okay. I'll keep you updated too.

JUNE

Thanks, April.

Our weekend in Nashville played back in my mind once again. Where did it all go wrong? Even though both Dahlia and June told me not to, Carter's vanishing act worried me. Was he really that overwhelmed? Did it have something to do with me?

The first stars appeared in the inky sky, and I double-checked the doors to make sure they were all locked, knowing how he hated the idea of me being in a cabin by myself with no lock. I wouldn't neglect my security now that I knew why he insisted I move in with him.

Over the weekend, Carter had confided a lot about personal stuff. Why would he open up to me if he wanted nothing to do with me anymore?

What changed between us after we got back to Green Mountain?

No matter how hard I tried to convince myself I wasn't responsible for his disappearing act, my instincts kept insisting I was the cause.

All weekend, Carter acted like my boyfriend. He made me feel special.

A headache took root at the front of my skull. I closed my eyes and massaged my temples.

Bernice purred, and I leaned forward to lift her up. "Hey girl. Ready to go back home?" She arched her back and mewed. "I know it wasn't the plan. But how can I stay here? If Carter doesn't come back, I…I can't stay here by myself. It feels wrong. And if he does come back, things may be awkward between us. Don't be sorry. We had a great time." She stared into my eyes for a long minute. "Don't worry, we'll be fine." I put her back down, and she traipsed toward the music studio. "Yeah, just leave me alone too. Nice job, Bern."

Around midnight, lying in my bed, I felt lonelier than I'd felt in a long time. After Travis's death, I had learned to be on my own. To count only on myself. Since moving in with Carter, I had rediscovered the joy of sharing my time with another human being—with a man. Now I realized how much I'd missed it over the years. I loved the company. Sharing meals and talking about anything and everything. Stealing glances and catching smiles. No more insomnia. No more procrastination.

With Carter, I was back to being alive.

Too bad it was over so soon.

22

CARTER

I woke up before dawn with a pounding headache. In the mirror, I caught my reflection when I took a leak. Bloodshot eyes with dark shadows underneath, disheveled hair, a few days' long beard. I looked like shit. I rubbed my fists over my eyes and swallowed two painkillers with a tall glass of water. After I forced a protein shake down my throat, and not feeling like spending myself physically for a third day in a row, I opted for the thing I did best in my life. Writing music. The mere thought of it soothed something inside me. I poured all my restless energy into my art, diving into the sound of the guitar.

My whole being ached from what I put myself through over the last two days. Punishing workouts. Hot baths. Falling asleep, exhausted.

Worried my body would give up, I curled up on the couch and napped for an hour. When I woke up, the storm inside me had lessened. I blew out a long breath. By the end of the morning, I had written three new songs, including a guaranteed top charter. Putting my heart on paper eased my mind and shot me with pride.

Even if I tried to deny it, April had inspired most of the lyrics. There was just something about her that roused my creative side and made the melodies flow and the words poured out of me.

As I strummed the last chord of a song I just wrote, my heartbeat slowed, and my mind took a break. I slouched back on the couch, a pillow underneath my head, and exhaled all the lingering anxiety and anger inside me. Music was my drug of choice. No matter what I tried to tell myself, whatever happened in my life, I could never give it up. It answered the question that had been nagging me since yesterday.

I had become a greedy bastard because, this time, I wanted it all. The music, the career, the girl, and I wasn't willing to sacrifice any. I did it once. Never again.

With steady fingers, I turned my phone back on. Notifications of messages and calls I'd missed during the last forty-eight hours popped up on the screen. I winced at the high number.

Dahlia's name flashed on the screen while I scrolled through my messages. For as long as I'd known her, I'd never ignored her calls. But for a second, this time, I debated shutting her out too. She was my best friend but also the first woman who made me believe I wasn't good enough to be loved. Both times we could've been together, she chose the other man. She never chose me. Not once. I rubbed my thumb over the screen of my device, wondering what to do.

What if she needed me to be there for her and I was too busy fucking my entire life up?

What if Jack had had an accident…or…or something was wrong with the baby?

I cursed under my breath. The caring side of me won the battle, and I accepted the call.

"Dear God, Carter. Finally. Where are you?"

I sighed. "Are you and Jack okay?" Nothing else mattered.

"Yes. It's you I'm worried about."

Some tension left my back. They were both fine.

"You're in one of your episodes, aren't you?"

I glanced around, trying to gather my thoughts.

"Carter, talk to me. Where are you? I'll come to meet you." She kept her voice even and low, knowing I needed her calm. She was used to dealing with my racing thoughts and my anxiety attacks.

"I'll be fine, Dah. I'm messed up. It all… Everything was spinning too fast in my mind, and I panicked."

"Hey, it's okay. I'm here. What do you need?"

"Don't hang up. Talk to me. I need to hear your voice. In my head, it's all fucked up. I'm…I'm sore. I'm tired." My voice cracked, and hot tears pooled in my eyes. "I'm so tired, Dah. Like I wanna sleep forever."

She sucked in a low breath. "Don't say that, Carter. You don't want to sleep forever. If you do, I'd haunt you in your grave. You know I would."

I snickered through my tears. Dahlia knew I didn't want to sleep my life off. And she also knew how to lift my spirits.

"What happened? Was it Nashville?"

"Yes. No. I don't know. I'm restless."

She hesitated for a few beats. "It's April, isn't it?"

I stayed silent. How could she always tell what was troubling me?

She sighed and raised her voice a tad. "Carter, is it about her? Talk to me. Are you afraid to trust someone else with your heart?"

I cleared my throat. "I'm scared….and I-I'm never scared of anything. I'm Carter Hills, for fuck's sake. I'm supposed to be in control all the fucking time. I'm never supposed to mess up because the entire world will judge me afterward. I did something stupid once, and the planet spread nasty rumors about me. In the last two years, my personal life has been reduced to gossip. It's exhausting… I'm exhausted. How can I hide my feelings, my insecurities, and my stupid fears so people won't take advantage of me? I'm supposed to piss gold and shit diamonds." A sarcastic laugh escaped my mouth. "I'm not sure I can even be in a relationship. Last time, it almost killed me. What if once again it becomes a clusterfuck? What if the reality of my life is a turn-off for any sane woman? I can't lose the music again. Where does this leave me?" I fought with my inner demons with all my might. "Tell me how am I supposed to do this? And why would April want to be with someone like me? I'm damaged goods, Dah. Whenever I put my heart on the line, it always gets crushed."

A long silence stretched between us. Neither one of us dared to comment on the confidences I just threw on the table.

"Carter—" Dahlia's voice, familiar and comforting, sounded like music to my ears. "Nothing is damaged about you. Savannah was just a bump in the road. Or what if she was a means to an end? A stepping stone in order for you to follow the right path. Have you ever thought about it this way? Like if you hadn't survived hell, you might have never ended up where you were supposed to be because it wouldn't have given you the opportunity to get stronger and aim for what you really wished all along. All those years you thought you were in love with me…a part of you was…but you were also in love with the image of us you'd created in your mind when we were kids. Together, we wouldn't have been good. We're too emotional around each other. And it took you a long time to arrive at the same conclusion I reached a decade ago. Nothing that happens is in vain, Cart. There's always a reason behind everything... I truly believe that. Sometimes though, it takes longer for the explanation to reveal itself."

We both said nothing for an infinite minute.

"I'll tell you something I never told you before. Because you weren't ready to hear me out. Jeff always envied your talent. He asked me multiple times why he hadn't inherited those music genes too. He never told you because he felt insecure about it. Searching for his place in this world... He found it hard to be in your shadow sometimes." Dahlia's words pierced my heart. I never knew my brother felt this way about me. Most of the time, he was a happy guy, joking around and gripping me into headlocks until we both ended up laughing out loud, whatever bothering us long forgotten. "But one thing was clear. He wanted you to succeed. He would have done about anything to help you get there. No matter what, he always wanted what was best for you... Always. Even when you guys wouldn't talk."

The last memory of us hit me like a freight train. The moment I told my brother I didn't want anything to do with him anymore...or asking him to leave me the fuck alone. A long-buried sob bubbled out. "I did something horrible to him, Dah. If he had known, he would have never forgiven me. Jeff trusted me, and I...and I let him down. And then I shut him out. I. SHUT. HIM. OUT. I'm sure I'm the reason he dropped dead. Me."

"Shhh, Carter. Don't blame yourself. Never. Please, don't say that. Jeff was aware... He...he knew everything. I told him."

"You did?" I blinked, my jaw hanging open.

"Yeah. I was always honest with him. I'm not certain he knew what hate was anyway. All along, he could tell there was a strong bond that needed to be settled...a story he wasn't part of. I…I dropped the bomb after we returned from Australia, right after he asked me to marry him. I had to tell him the truth. He wasn't happy about it, to say the least. Believe me. He got mad and everything, but he didn't push me away or end our engagement. It took him a while to come to terms with what had happened, but in the end, forgiveness and moving forward were all that truly mattered to him. That's how amazing he was. See? You didn't kill him. None of us could have prevented his heart from stopping when it did. Never blame yourself."

My hands shook. A strange, foreign sensation coursed through me, and I could barely draw a full breath.

Flashbacks that had haunted me for so long, memories I'd carried around for all these years, lifted from my shoulders.

"Don't be hard on April because your mama is gone and your crazy ex-girlfriend hurt you, okay? I met April three times. She really cares about you. Your ex had problems you couldn't fix. And your mother, well, there's nothing you can do about it either. You tried. We all know you tried. She's heartbroken and has no idea how to overcome her grief. Same for your dad. They love you, Cart. They're just failing at dealing with their own broken hearts."

"It doesn't change the fact that they left me, Dah. Even after hours of therapy, when I stop and think about it, it's still a hard pill to swallow. They fucked me good." My throat worked. Could my body shut down from too much pain?

"You're not alone. And you never were. I'm here. We're here. Everyone who loves you. About April… I think you should talk to her. She's a smart girl. You two should figure out what you want…together. Listen to what she has to say. It's not just up to you this time. If you believe she's worth it, don't push her away because you think it's the right thing to do."

A long moment passed before Dahlia spoke again.

"And Carter, no matter what you think, you *are* boyfriend material. You don't give yourself enough credit. All these years, you've only been distracting yourself. Maybe it's time you stop finding excuses, let go of the past, and act like a man. Any woman would be lucky to be loved by you."

Her last words simmered for a moment. "I love you, Dah."

"I love you too, Cart. I always will. Now call back your people because they're worried sick about you. Nobody has heard from you in the past few days. They think you got into an accident or something. About everything else you said, we'll talk about it later. Talk to April. Please. Don't shut her out. She's good for you. I can tell. You need someone like her in your life. Who is grounded and level-headed. Someone who is real and not easily impressed by your career choice. And Carter, remember. It's okay to be scared. Just don't be scared alone."

After promising Dahlia to clean up the mess in my head, I hung up and scrolled through the five text messages April had sent me since I disappeared without a word.

Monday morning:

APRIL

June called and said you're not answering your phone. I told her you were busy. She said you need to call her back ASAP.

Monday night:

APRIL

HN, I'm sorry to bother you. I was
wondering if you could stop at the grocery
store on your way back. Call me if you have
a minute.

Monday late at night:

APRIL

Okay, no news for an entire day. Should I
worry? Call me when you get my text. Or
text me if you're alive. Kidding. Not kidding.

Yesterday evening:

APRIL

I'm sorry if I did something to upset you. I
should've never tried to have sex with you
the other night. It was dumb. I acted like a
groupie, which I'm not, I promise. I got
carried away in the heat of the moment.
Hope we can still be friends.

Earlier today:

APRIL

Carter, I'm packing my stuff. You don't want
to be around me for whatever reason. Your
team keeps calling my phone. They're
worried. At least let them know you're okay.
It's fine if you don't want to see me
anymore. Your silence speaks louder than
your words. Thanks for last weekend and
for the song. I'll cherish it forever. Maybe
someday we'll cross paths again. Goodbye,
HN. By the way, it might or might not be
Hot and Natty... Who knows? The mystery
adds a little fun to our short-lived
friendship. I wish you the best. You deserve
it. You're pretty amazing when you're not
being an ass. Never let anyone tell you the
opposite. Keep shining xx

By the last one, my heart had plummeted down to my toes. April blamed herself. She was so damn wrong. My only wish was to be around her. Not to push her away.

Last Sunday, on the drive back from Nashville, I had realized being around her was much more effective in calming my mind than any therapy. Her presence alone eased everything inside me. It silenced the nagging voices in my head. That wasn't supposed to happen. Now I was not only mesmerized by the woman, but I needed her too. My throat tightened, and I rubbed my hand over my face. How could I even fathom letting her go? Was I more insane than I thought?

Deep down, I knew I had to be honest with her. About everything. Even the doubts crippling me and my episodes. One day, I would have to tell her about the thoughts keeping me awake some nights and how they affected me. How could I expect a relationship based on communication and honesty if I hid facts from her? And didn't tell her how I felt? Sharing about my inner struggles wasn't something I excelled in, not when it included the fuck-ups of my past, but here I was, alone, exhausted, and miserable without her. I needed her light and optimism in my life, like I needed oxygen to breathe.

If I pulled my head out of my own ass, maybe I could salvage what we had before it was too late. Maybe I could redeem myself...explain stuff. Starting with how my brain worked sometimes or how my fears took full control of my mind and body and asphyxiated me. I could do this. Open up and trust another person with my life and my secrets. I didn't wanna live in uncertainty forever. I owed it to myself to face my worst fears and free myself of the *what-ifs* once and for all. To move forward and not be tied to a past that no longer suited me. To chase my own happiness. And true love. For real this time.

April sent the last message over an hour ago.

If I didn't act—and fast—she'd go back home early to avoid me. *Breathe in. Breathe out.* She would leave. Our cabin. Green Mountain. Me. Forever. I scratched my forehead with the side of my thumb and shot her a text. If I hurried, maybe I could catch her. My heart raced into a frantic rhythm. I had only one thing left to do.

ME

April, don't go. Please. I'm sorry. We need to talk.

I didn't wait for her to reply. Instead, I showered, changed, and drove back home.

When I pulled in, some of the tension in my upper back eased at the sight of her car still parked in the driveway. She hadn't left. She was still here. I pressed my hand against my chest, resuming my breathing. Would she give me a chance to explain? Would she let me in, or had I lost her trust? I swallowed hard. The knots in my stomach multiplied.

Once I regained some composure, I squared my shoulders, straightened my back, and climbed out of my truck.

Pixie and I weren't done yet. I hadn't said my last word.

23

APRIL

I blinked a few times and took calming breaths to keep the tears burning the back of my eyes at bay. Carter didn't come home last night. Again. No message this time. He'd chosen to end our story—or whatever we had—on his own terms. Fine. Screw him. I wouldn't define myself through a man.

As soon as I was out of bed, I sent a message to my best friend back home.

ME

Don't bother driving up here. I'm leaving early to come back home.

SAUNDERS

Is everything okay?

ME

Yes. No. Not discussing it.

SAUNDERS

You're sure you're not running away in typical April Simmons fashion?

ME

Maybe. Not sure. It's complicated. I'll talk to you later.

SAUNDERS

Everything fine between you and (OMG!!!!!) Carter Hills?

ME

I'll call you once on the road.

I wasn't in the mood to explain to her that if I stayed here, as soon as Carter came back, my stupid heart would break, and it'd hurt too much to be around him, knowing I had scared him away.

SAUNDERS

April, do I need to worry?

ME

Please don't. I'll explain everything. Later.

I would. Once I'd put enough distance between me and this place and when the memories of the precious stolen moments we shared didn't feel like a stabbing pain anymore.

SAUNDERS

Reed wants me to tell you to be careful.
The roads are icy.

I really wanted to visit you.

ME

I know. Raincheck, okay?

SAUNDERS

Call me when you can. Be careful xx

Then, after some hesitation—and four drafts later—I

sent Carter a text message to inform him I was leaving. For the second time in a week, I packed my stuff. My heart quivered, and my eyes overflowed with tears. Not rushing it, I filled my suitcase, hoping Carter would show up in the meantime. But he didn't. *Get real, April. Stop wishing for a happy ending.*

With all my feelings in the pit of my stomach, I zipped up my suitcase and placed it in one corner of the bedroom. Squatting, I lifted Bernice from the bed and cuddled her against my chest. She purred in the crook of my neck, and I felt better. Sort of.

My phone went off, and thinking it was Saunders, I looked at the message. My heart skipped a beat when his name and the picture we took on that bridge in Nashville filled the screen.

CARTER

April, don't go. Please. I'm sorry. We need to talk.

I should've left at that moment, but my curiosity got the better of me. And maybe I wanted to see him one last time. For closure. Yeah, closure was necessary. To move on.

I reread the message for the third time. What did Carter want to talk about? His actions were clear enough. No need to hear him say he regretted befriending me or that kissing me was a mistake. Or that I was just a fling, after all, and what we shared meant nothing. Or that my actions, when we almost had sex, were inappropriate or whatever. My ego didn't need to be kicked to the curb face-to-face. Not by the first man I let in after Travis. Not the first time I dared to be vulnerable with someone other than my best friend.

Carter disappeared three days ago after we spent an amazing weekend together. After we spent a day flirting and kissing as we strolled around his city, as he called it. Was our time together all a joke to him? Did he play me for his own sake? Slouching forward, I buried my face in the bent of my elbow, my arms resting on my pillow, and let out a shaky breath.

How did I end up in this mess? Why did HN have to be so sexy and such an amazing person? And why were my hormones so horny?

I couldn't leave without hearing what he had to say. Even if the truth scared me, it was better than coming up with scenarios in my head for the foreseeable future about why even our friendship didn't work out. I needed closure, otherwise I'd be miserable.

Like the masochist I'd become lately, I sat on my bed and played "Pink and Country" on a loop. By now, I knew all the words. Each time I pressed play, my heart did somersaults, and tears welled up in my eyes. Listening to Carter's raw masculine voice, his heartfelt words, and his rich and bittersweet melody made me feel closer to him. Like he was talking to me. As if our souls were connected in the most primitive way, bare and uncensored.

Last night, Saunders sent me a link to an interview Savannah Prince had given over the weekend.

With a warning.

SAUNDERS

This bitch is crazy. Don't listen past forty-eight seconds. It's best if you hear it from me instead of some low-key gossiper.

Saunders was right. I preferred it when my best friend was the one delivering the news. However awful it was. Until now, I'd done my best to avoid watching the interview. Without overthinking everything, I clicked the link, and the actress appeared on the screen. Flawless makeup, dressed to impress, and shiny hair that appeared silky even through a screen.

"How are you feeling about Carter moving on so quickly after your very public breakup?" the interviewer, a tall brunette with injected lips and perfectly shaped eyebrows, asked.

"Carter is a hard man to tame. Women are his ultimate weaknesses. I'll never stop loving him. I hope he remembers how good we are together and stops fighting what we have. I'll stay by his side to help him overcome his challenges. We'll figure it out together as a couple." Savannah flashed a pearly-white smile to the camera.

"So, you've seen Carter lately? We're all wondering where he's been. Can you tell us more?" the interviewer continued with a cheesy smile and wide eyes, fangirling over the movie star.

"All I can say is that you'll see more of us together soon."

"And what about the song he wrote for the mystery woman he's currently seeing?"

The actress rolled her eyes at the camera. "Come on, Cindy, you can't be serious. Carter wrote that song a long time ago. It has nothing to do with this—" I held my breath and closed the browser tab, ending the video. Enough. *Forty-nine seconds.* My stomach churned, and I inhaled deeply to calm the emotions storming inside me. Savannah Prince had nailed the act of the manipulative bitch to perfection. For a second, she even almost got me convinced Carter was the bad guy. That was why I never watched entertainment news or read gossip magazines. People vomited words to sound interesting and sympathetic when, in fact, they had nothing meaningful to say. How could Carter ever fall for her and then be interested in someone like me? His ex-girlfriend oozed confidence and sexuality—the exact opposite of me. I sighed, feeling completely out of my league.

The day I found out who he was, Carter had straightened out some facts about their relationship before I heard things and panicked. Everything he'd said that night kept running through my mind, and I couldn't seem to stop thinking about it.

"We're both to blame for this mess," he had told me. "I agreed to this relationship when everything in me screamed I shouldn't. I didn't get out when I should've. At first, we seemed like a good fit. It changed once we moved in together. She became some sort of evil, and I stayed because I wanted to make it work. To prove to myself I could be in a long-lasting relationship. And do things differently, I guess. I was lost."

"Did you love her?" I had to ask, but regretted it the moment his eyes had met mine—wide and startled, as if I'd said something terrible. I had lowered my head, feeling like I was intruding on his personal life. "Sorry…it's none of my business."

"It's okay. No, I didn't love her. I wanted to, but I couldn't. Maybe that's why I endured this nightmare longer than I should have. Because I wished, one day, I'd feel something. Anything. In the end, I learned facts I'd been blind to. Lots of them. A part of me still thinks it's surreal. But then I remember I lived through this and it's nothing but the truth. Everything about that woman is fake. Her laughter. Her orgasms. Not just her tits or her lips. She told every one I was a sex addict to portray me like a cheater. I wasn't sick. I was sexually frustrated, and she had been the one playing me… Let's just say she reached new lows to secure a role. Not long after I moved to Los Angeles to be with her, I began a dry-spell diet. She always had a far-fetched reason to keep me at a distance.

Too tired or too stressed. Too everything. Her nails got done, or she refused to mess up her styled hair. One time, she even told me she'd cleaned her aura and that close contact with me would misalign her chakras or some shit. And then she became someone else entirely. No kidding. I was literally living in hell. She thought she was being sexy when the truth is that she was scary as fuck. At some point, I was afraid for my sanity."

"You're joking, right?"

"I wish. The day I left, I wanted to rip my eyeballs out. Still, months later, she's telling the media we'll get back together. Our relationship was one big clusterfuck. A gigantic mistake. She hated me. So go figure." He had then risen to his feet and disappeared into his music studio while I had attacked the dishes, fiddling with the dishcloth in my hands, wondering why I had opened that can of worms.

Carter had joined me in front of the fireplace an hour later, his smile back, our conversation about his ex-girl-friend forgotten.

The Carter Hills I'd gotten to know had nothing in common with the one the actress described in interviews.

Now, with my eyes closed, his song did all the talking, and I wondered how long it'd take for him to come back home. When did I start considering Green Mountain and Carter's cabin as *home*? Not ready for an internal freakout, I pushed the thought away. None of this mattered anymore since I was leaving today. Ginger Creek was my home. Green Mountain was more like a fairy tale. No matter how exciting they seemed in books or on TV, fairy tales didn't exist in real life. As long as I remembered that piece of information, I would be all right. Adjusting my position on the bed, I relaxed my shoulders, my brain half-awake, and got lost in Carter's voice. To hell with what his ex-girlfriend had said. This song was mine.

Every word he sang. Every single note of it.

Lost in my head—and my song—I didn't hear him coming in. He pulled the earbuds from my ears, and I jumped. My eyes sprang open, and my breathing hitched. It took a second for my brain to reboot.

Carter's eyes locked on mine. Dark and penetrating. Lustful. With him so close, I struggled to remember why I had been mad at him in the first place, or why I had wanted to flee his house just hours ago. He looked tired and stressed, yet still handsome, with his unshaven jaw and untamed hair. The time we spent apart didn't mean anything anymore. His metal irises swallowed me whole, and I lost myself in them, swimming in their depths.

And right now, I had a hard time remembering why fairy tales didn't exist in real life.

24

CARTER

I strode inside my cabin and kicked the door shut after me. Like a wild animal, I went from room to room in search of April. Living room? Nope. Kitchen? Nope. Media room? Not there either. Where the hell was she? The den. Sure. Why didn't I check it first? Fairy loved that room. I strode into the vast space lined by panoramic windows, scanned around me, and turned on my heel once I realized she wasn't there either. The pounding of my heart deafened me. She was here somewhere. She had to be. Her car was outside.

I laced my fingers together, rested my joined hands on the top of my head, and blew out a breath. Seconds later, I whirled around and sprinted up the stairs to the second floor. I found her in the guest bedroom—her room. Lying on the bed, her back propped up against the headboard and her eyes closed, she was listening to music with earbuds in, Bernice curled up in a ball next to her. The sight of them sent a bolt of warmth through me. This was what coming home should always look like. Feel like. Be like. Except April shouldn't be lying on the bed in the guest room. She should be lying in mine. Fuck.

Her fingers drummed a beat on her folded legs. I resisted the temptation to kiss her pink lips as she mouthed the lyrics of a song.

She wore heather gray sweatpants and a white cotton V-neck, long-sleeved shirt. Her face was bare, and her pink hair was tied in some complicated knot on the top of her head. She looked every shade of beautiful.

With my hands stuffed in my denim pockets and my shoulder resting against the doorframe, I watched her for a long moment, holding my breath, unable to tear my eyes away from her figure. Lost in her own world, April hadn't heard me coming in and had no clue she was being observed.

I studied the pattern of her breathing, the soft rise of her chest with every intake. My mouth watered when I laid eyes on the swell of her breasts visible from the neckline of her low-cut shirt. I felt like a hunter about to attack his prey.

I zoomed in on the pulse beating beside the column of her throat, and a small reddened area on the left side below her ear caught my attention. Did I mark her the other night when I feasted on her in my hotel suite?

I smiled at the idea.

On my tiptoes, I neared the bed and sat on the edge of the mattress, leaning forward to remove her earbuds. As I did, her eyes shot open in surprise. I brought the buds to my ears and recognized the music, confirming my suspicion. A wide grin spread across my face, mirroring hers, and the pounding of my heart intensified.

"Hey, I didn't hear you come in." She gave me a slow once-over, and a frown replaced her smile. She straightened her back and sat cross-legged. "Are you okay?"

Was that worry I could see in her eyes?

"You were listening to your song?" I asked.

She got flustered and gave me a shy glance, but didn't confirm or deny it.

"You know this is fucking hot, right?"

She gave me a half-shrug. I leaned in, but she pushed me back, both hands splayed across my chest. There was no way she could miss the throbbing of my heart beneath her palm. Yet, she kept me at arm's length.

"No kissing. You disappeared on me…without a word. I was worried. And hurt. You also said earlier we needed to talk. Go ahead, I'm all ears." She folded her arms over her chest, pushing her tits up, her shirt barely able to contain them.

My dick saluted the gesture, pushing against the zipper of my faded denims. If I were being honest, I kind of deserved her rejection, and the walls she had erected between us. I ran away like a coward after we spent an incredible weekend together—one of the best weekends of my life—and cut off all communications with her without an explanation. If I had been treated this way, I'd be upset too.

I messed up—big time—but I came back. I was here to make things right. To fix us.

In my defense, I had to walk away to assess everything. To calm the panic that had taken root deep inside me. April deserved the best version of me. If I hadn't left, I wouldn't have been able to see straight, and one day, it would've blown up in our faces. Now that I was calmer, more level-headed, I could open up to her. I didn't want any secrets standing between us. And I was done keeping her at arm's length. If what we had was real, we both deserved the chance to see where this relationship would take us.

April pressed her lips together and arched a brow, giving me the *talk to me, I'm listening* look.

"I know I said we needed to talk, but there's something I gotta do first. Come with me." I reached for her hand and tugged gently until she got up. April dug her heels into the floor as I led her toward the staircase leading to the third floor. For the first time since I'd returned, I noticed the deep lines around her eyes, and hated myself for it, seeing the insecurity tightening her features. I cupped her face in both hands, tilting her head so she could see the truth in my eyes as I spoke. "Listen to me. I'm sorry for worrying you. My head was a mess, and I went away to clear my mind. It wasn't your fault. Please, never blame yourself, okay?" I swallowed hard, unable to break eye contact. "But my going M.I.A. had nothing and everything to do with you."

"Me?" She pointed her thumb at her chest, looking at me with puzzled, baby-blue eyes.

"Yeah, Fairy Girl. I don't possess the strength in me to resist you. I tried—I fucking did—but you cast a spell on me. I'm under your charm, and it's messing with my mind."

"I…you… Wait. What?"

I nodded, unable to look away, drunk on her lavender scent, her energy, her beauty, everything that made her *her*. "Listen, Nashville was a mistake."

As if I had just stabbed her, she flinched and stepped back, shrugging off my grip, her face a roadmap of pain and confusion.

My words replayed in my head, and I wanted to slap myself for being such an idiot. "Shit. I didn't mean it like that. April, what I meant is that I regret pushing you away. That's the mistake I'm talking about."

"You do? You are?"

I bobbed my head multiple times. "I am. I acted stupid and I'm sorry."

"And now?" she asked in a low voice, her cheeks flushed and her eyes fixed on mine, glistening and a shade darker.

"I ran away because I was scared…but I-I failed at staying away. There's no way I'll ever be able to resist you. Just the thought of your leaving and I became a nutcase."

Her bottom lip shuddered, and I smoothed its length with my thumb. Her eyes drew me in, pleading with me to kiss her. My dick hardened, begging to be freed.

This time, I wouldn't fight the attraction. I'd dive in headfirst—or rather dick first. My ache for the girl standing before me drowned out any rational thought, and I knew I wouldn't stop cherishing her until we were both breathless and satisfied.

Until I made up for pushing her away and disappearing without an explanation.

Until everything between us made sense again.

Until I branded myself on her skin and sunk so deep inside her that no one would ever be able to tell us apart.

I brought my hands to her hips and lifted her into my arms. On instinct, she wrapped her legs around my waist. Our gazes fused, and we exchanged so much without speaking a single word. With my palms molded to her ass cheeks and April attached to me monkey-style, I climbed the stairs, my mouth glued to hers, our tongues dancing together.

A fervor rolled down my spine. Blood left my brain and pooled in my groin.

This was us, catching fire together and not taming the flames anymore.

With her back pressed against my bedroom wall, I sucked on her tongue like a madman. She tasted the same way I remembered, mint and summer. She stole my breath away as I ground my hips against hers through the fabric of our pants, letting her know how turned-on she made me. Pixie writhed under my touch, her hands traveling all over the planes of my abs, my chest, my arms, and my face. She devoured me like she couldn't get enough of me. Her hard nipples pushed against her bra and the thin fabric of her shirt, asking to be cherished too.

We kissed as if we had only one chance to mend the emotional distance I had created when I vanished. My spine buzzed with arousal, and I lost contact with reality, my entire self consumed by her.

I slid my hands under her shirt, her skin soft as velvet beneath my fingers.

A shiver worked through her as I caressed her ribcage, pushing her shirt over her head.

I growled when my eyes drifted to the fullness of her breasts, a heavenly sight, thanks to the white lacy bra she was wearing.

"Fuck, I missed those." I leaned forward, tracing the contour with my tongue. "I've missed you."

Leaning back, I pinched the collar of my shirt at the nape, peeled it off, and tossed it over my shoulder.

"I've missed you too," April whispered between kisses. "What took you so long?"

I groaned in response. Both my hands weren't enough to touch her everywhere I craved. Holding her body against mine, I stepped back until the back of my legs crashed into the bed frame. I curled a hand around her neck and tangled my fingers in her hair, guiding her mouth back to mine. "I acted like a fool. I'm sorry." I sounded breathless even though we had done nothing but kiss so far.

She hummed something , her mouth gliding over mine and her tongue sweet torturing me.

In a swift motion, I flipped her over, and her back landed on the mattress with a soft thump. April gasped, and I almost lost control right there. I hovered over her, feasting on her jaw and the flesh of her neck. At that moment, I knew for sure I would die without a taste of her. Our bodies moved in sync. April writhed under me some more, every one of her movements tugging at my willpower and the remaining strings of my composure, the back-and-forth motion of her pelvis against the bulge in my pants about to make me lose my mind.

"Pixie… Geez… Keep doing that, and soon I'll be fucking your brains out."

"Why don't you already?"

I pushed up on my arms to watch her, drowning in the ocean of her eyes, the glints shining in her irises becoming the stars of my dark nights.

That was all the encouragement I needed.

Her eyes glazed over as she nibbled her bottom lip, her teeth grazing it lightly.

I leaned forward, tracing the length of her jaw with my tongue. Her hands traveled to my waistband, and she unbuttoned my denims, freeing my cock. I growled. I would fucking humiliate myself in no time if I ceded all control to my dick right now.

April's eyes flared when they landed on my erection, and when she licked her lips in a slow, mesmerizing motion, I prayed for some of my self-control to return. Everything inside me shattered. My fears, my sanity, the knots holding my heart hostage. My chest lightened. Oxygen reached my lungs.

April curled her fingers around me and stroked my cock painfully slow, teasing me and increasing my arousal.

Pre-cum leaked from the slit, and she rubbed her thumb over it, my body shaking with tremors under her mesmerizing touch. My breath caught in my lungs, and I tried to swallow, my mouth as dry as sand.

With an urgency I couldn't subdue, I ripped the rest of her clothes off her body, throwing the pieces all over the room, until only a set of matching white lace remained. My eyes trailed over her figure, admiring every one of her curves and the lusciousness of her creamy skin. Her cheeks turned pink under the heat of my devoted attention.

I leaned forward, using the tip of my finger to trace a line from the hollow of her neck to the waistband of her panties, relishing each shiver working through her.

April panted, watching me with something akin to worship, and I couldn't detach my eyes from her figure, captivated by every curve. I brushed my mouth over hers in the slowest torture, biting and sucking on her tongue, eliciting more breathless whispers from her.

Every cell in my body vibrated with need, and I moved back to stand in front of her.

She splayed a hand across her abdomen, her fingers drifting dangerously close to the scrap of lace I was dying to tear off her. She eye-fucked me, the desire I could read on her face enough to make me lose the remnants of my self-control.

Unable to wait anymore, I kicked off my shoes and stripped out of my denims and boxer briefs.

For a few seconds, we both stayed immobile. I, standing at the end of the bed, and she, lying on her back, admiring each other's bodies for the very first time. Our chests rose in quick succession as we panted with unconcealed desire, cast under some invisible magnetism.

April arched her back, pushing her chest forward, offering me her swollen breasts.

Aching for this woman and unable to deny myself even a taste of her, I dived forward and pushed the cups of her bra down, my lips closing around one stiff nipple as I kneaded her other breast.

I slipped one hand underneath her back, freeing her from her bra, and tossed the piece of clothing behind me, ready to have her fully naked and at the mercy of my tongue.

Leaning back, I hooked my thumbs into her panties, sliding them off in the slowest motion, exposing every part of her to my sight.

A new surge of warmth spread through me as I appreciated the view I was too stubborn and scared to enjoy that night in Nashville.

April looked beautiful. Every inch of her was.

I glided back over her, bracing myself on my arms, and captured her mouth in a bruising kiss. One of my hands traveled down to the apex of her thighs, and I dipped one finger into her warmth, sliding it in and out, the wet heat coating it in the most delicious way. Her moans mixed with my harsh breathing. A perfect symphony. I spread her arousal all over her folds with a soaked finger, loving how she arched her back, begging for more.

I closed my teeth around one hard nipple, toying with the tip, and she sucked in a breath that vibrated through me.

My spine tingled, my arousal soaring, and I could hardly keep myself together anymore. "How did I fight this for so long? Why did I deprive myself the other night?" I hastened the movements of my finger, helping her chase her climax. Kissing her, I swallowed her low whimpers, the sweet sound sending a signal to my dick.

April watched me with hooded eyes, her head jerking back as desire built in her core. She looked so fucking hot right now, at my mercy and about to explode in bliss. My balls grew heavy, and my vision blurred, undeniable signs I would come if I didn't slow down. It'd been too fucking long since the last time I had sex. Yes, I was a time ticking bomb, ready to detonate at any moment. Trying to lengthen the pleasure, not ready for it to end too soon, I grabbed a handful of her pink locks and kissed her, her gasps becoming my new addiction and her touch, my new obsession.

"Fairy, I'd record an entire album of every single whimper coming out of your mouth if you let me. This is my new favorite melody." I kissed her again. "Fuck. You'll be the end of me."

She squeezed my arm with her thighs, taking my hand hostage. With a roll of her hips, April chased her own pleasure, digging her nails into the flesh of my biceps. She rode my fingers, crying my name over and over as she thrashed with abandon.

This woman. She was my muse, my haven, and my demise all at once.

"Carter," she murmured.

I rubbed her bundle of nerves with the heel of my hand, making her cry in ecstasy. I played her body slow and gentle, rough and with precision. She rocked her hips faster, meeting me touch for touch, and I got intoxicated watching her. Nothing stood between us anymore. I locked my other hand around my throbbing dick, pumping it in long strokes to relieve some of the tension straining every inch of my body.

"I can't... It's... Don't ever stop. Don't even think about walking out on me this—"

"Never. Never again will I leave you behind or deny you the pleasure you deserve."

I feasted on her mouth, licking a trail down the column of her throat and kissing her bare shoulder. I only had threads of composure left. I focused my attention on her neck, the lobe of her ear, the angle of her chin, keeping my own release at bay as much as I could.

"You're gorgeous, Fairy. Go ahead. Fuck my hand."

She did as instructed, our eyes meeting for a fleeting second.

I drew circles over her clit with my thumb, applying just enough pressure, as she rolled her hips once more before a loud cry broke the silence.

She fixed her glossy eyes on me, a bliss I'd never seen before painting her features.

I returned my mouth to hers in a dirty kiss that left us both breathless.

"Spread your legs. I gotta taste you now."

I molded my hand to her cheek, and we watched each other for a beat, April more beautiful than ever with her blushing cheeks and the friction burns from my stubble standing out in stark relief against her fair complexion.

I lowered my hands to her thighs and opened her legs wider until she dropped her folded knees on either side of me.

Kissing my way down from her chin to her navel, I cherished her skin with my lips. I wandered lower, skimming her clit with the tip of my tongue, tasting her essence for the first time, already drunk after just one lick. Her body quivered, and her hips bucked off the mattress for a second, pushing against my mouth, increasing the friction between us, begging me to relieve her. I laved her center with my tongue, addicted to her taste as a new wave of desire built deep inside me. A cry parted her lips, and I ventured lower, sucking and teasing the soft flesh of her inner thighs. April tasted like summer rain. Musky and sweet. With a jerk of her pelvis, she lifted her hips from the mattress, her hands going to my hair, fisting and tugging so I'd bring my mouth where she craved it the most. Instead of ceding to her silent demand, I homed in on her thighs, leaving kissing trails down to her knees.

Even though I was burning to be buried balls deep inside her, I didn't want to rush this. I wanted to commit everything to memory so I could replay our first time later. The time when we relinquished all sense of control and let pleasure rule the game.

I brought my tongue back to her clit, sucking and kissing her throbbing flesh while I clamped her thighs with both hands, keeping her still, as I tongue-fucked her to oblivion.

Her fingers entangled in my hair, and she pulled me forward. Instead of complying, I stood my ground, not ready to forfeit my feast.

She threw her head back, the pillows swallowing her as I kept eating her up like a starved man until she shuddered against my mouth. I stopped just before she could come.

"Carter, I need more. Fill me. Please—"

Bracing myself on my hands, I moved upward and silenced her with a hungry kiss, letting her savor the taste of herself on my lips. "If you pressure me, I'll torture you even more." I tangled my tongue with hers. The slow fore-play was as excruciating for me as it was for her. My cock was pulsing with need, ready to get in the game. Our tongues moved in a dirty tango, and April squirmed under me when I pinched a nipple. We admired each other for a second, and the pleasure radiating from her broke me apart. She flicked her other nipple between her own fingers, and mesmerized, I couldn't avert my gaze. "Please keep touching yourself. You're a fucking vision right now."

Her other hand replaced mine as I lowered it to her waist, holding her in place while I returned to the apex of her thighs, still hungry for her.

April yelped when I pushed two fingers inside her and ravished her sweet spot with my mouth, taking my fill. I increased the rhythm of my fingers, and she matched the pace with her hips until she convulsed under me, squirming from pleasure.

"Oh God—"

I wasn't God, but at that moment, I felt like one as her toes curled and her body stiffened under my touch. I swept my tongue over her pulsing clit once more, and she came undone, surrendering herself to my greedy mouth.

While Pixie surfed the waves of ecstasy, I grabbed a condom and rubbed my sheathed hard-on along her wet center, giving her no time to regain full consciousness. The urge to be inside her was greater than anything I'd ever felt before.

A cry parted her lips when I pushed the tip inside her tight channel. "Oh yes." She looked gorgeous, shiny eyes and reddened cheeks, waiting for me to give it to her, propping herself up on her elbows as she watched my length disappear inside her in awe. "Keep going."

I spread her sex with my thumbs, and she engulfed all of me, inch by inch, her body warm and soft. Mine. This feeling. It was where I belonged. Like coming home after a tour. Our souls blended, and I knew, at this instant, that whatever I did or said in the future, April would always own a part of me—or every piece of me. Nobody would ever be able to erase her imprint off me. Exhaling a jagged breath, I paused, needing a second—or two—to regain some self-control. I could easily come only with the knowledge of how perfectly our bodies fit together. How perfect I felt inside her. The corner of my lips tugged up into a smile as I savored the moment I'd been dreaming about for weeks. Me. Her. Both of us giving in to our most primitive instincts. Being one. Indulging in the sexual tension simmering between us since the day we met. The hard inches of me fit inside her as if she'd been carved for me. As if someone had tailored her body to house mine.

"Feels so good…yes…more…" she gasped, and I searched her face—her eyes, sparkling and half-closed, and her lips, pink and trembling—as I stretched her to fit all of me.

She pushed herself further upright and curled her fingers around my neck, pulling my face down to hers. She devoured my mouth in a sensuous kiss that had my head turning.

"Are you okay?"

She nodded before lifting her hips, so I could fill her deeper. The way her body clenched around mine shattered any lingering doubts I had. And my restraints. Dear God. We hadn't even started, and I was already a goner.

"Don't hold back," she murmured in a husky voice. "Give me everything you've got. I need you. I need this… I need…us."

My hands found her breasts, and I gave them the attention they deserved, sucking and biting the hard pebbles. Her heat coated my dick, and I could barely stay still. I refused to move to avoid coming too soon, overwhelmed by sensations, like a teenager having sex for the first time.

I trailed kisses in the dip between her perky breasts and along her collarbone. I sucked on her neck, wanting to leave imprints all over her. Like an animal, I wanted to make her mine. To mark her.

"Please," April begged, writhing under me. "Fuck me already."

She wouldn't have to beg me anymore. I parted my

legs, dug my knees into the mattress, raised her ass from the bed with both hands gripping her hipbones, and speared into her. With restraint at first. April purred, and I increased the tempo, thrusting into her faster and harder. She fisted the sheet, her mouth open, her eyes full of stars, offering me a vision. The one I'd dreamed of so many times.

Our hips rolled together. My mind shut off, her whimpers the only sounds making their way to my brain. The only sounds I needed to hear for the rest of my life.

My grip on her tightened as I pounded into her harder.

April moved under me, begging me for more. She flexed her back, looking delicious and gorgeous as my over-enthusiastic dick rammed into her.

She wet her index finger, lowered her hand between us, and started rubbing her swollen mound.

Ohmyfuckinggod.

Her eyes snapped to mine.

Did I say that out loud?

Her eyelids fluttered, and pearls of sweat bloomed across her chest.

I leaned down and licked them all, enjoying the saltiness on my tongue.

"Carter… Carter…" The way she said my name affected me in the most primitive way.

I hammered into her fiercely, and a low guttural groan formed in my throat.

Her eyes sprang open, and she fisted my damp hair to bring my mouth to hers, her tongue sweeping in with lust. And hunger.

"Ohmygod, woman, you're wrecking me. You're fucking killing me."

With both palms, she pushed at my chest and motioned me to flip to my back. She positioned herself over me, riding me, her chest bouncing with each movement of her body. I was her stallion, and we were winning the race. My hands molded to her thighs, at the knees. The view from here was breathtaking. Fairy glued her eyes to mine, drawing me in. My breath caught in my lungs as she leaned forward and peppered kisses all across my chest, tracing a line from my navel to my chin. She rolled her hips over mine, bringing me to the verge of insanity. When she flicked her tongue over my jaw and nibbled at my earlobe, I grunted. She sucked on my lower lip, and my balls tightened. Yes, she was waking up the devil inside me. When she pushed back, I lifted my ass from the mattress and rammed into her, unable to go slow. She wound her hand around my neck and pulled me toward her. Her mouth attacked mine, and she raked her fingers through my hair, tugging at it. Pain, lust, pleasure, desire. It was a deadly combination.

With a shift of my hips, I flipped her beneath me. Her head fell back, and I lunged at her neck first as her muscles clenched around me, making my length vibrate in her depths. My muscles tensed, and we climaxed together, her body shuddering as violently as mine.

For a moment, I worried she was having a seizure. I lowered myself, bracing most of my weight on my arms, careful not to collapse onto her as I pressed my forehead to hers. Our hearts thrummed together. I sprinkled kisses across her collarbone and her chin, brushing her hair away from her face with my fingertips.

Once the tremors in me lessened, I slid out of her, already missing her warmth, and rushed to the bathroom to discard the condom.

Back in the bedroom, still needy for her, I blanketed April in my arms and kissed her. We took our time, our carnal needs satisfied for now. I grazed the skin of her bare stomach with my fingertips, and goose bumps blossomed in their wake.

A shiver ran through me, ripping my body and my soul into a million pieces.

I'd slept with half a dozen women in my life, and none of them had ever broken me and built me back again the way April just did.

Not even the one woman I thought I belonged with for the longest time.

Nothing made sense anymore, including the beliefs I took for granted most of my life.

April opened her eyes and looked at me with something close to awe. Combined with the sweet whimpers leaving her mouth, it made me hard for her all over again.

We stared at each other for a while, unable to break apart, breathing hard and fast. Her heart drummed in her chest, and I felt every jolt under my fingertips.

I pulled away from my girl's embrace. My girl? I was in more trouble than I thought. We hadn't known each other long enough for me to go full alpha on her. And yet, she made everything tick inside me.

I was protective of her. Possessive. I wanted her all to myself and to ruin her for other men so they'd never be good enough for her. I rubbed the back of my neck, my heart and head at war, struggling to understand how I could be so consumed by this woman.

My gaze lingered on her naked flesh, taking in every inch of her, with thoughts of all the dirty little things I'd still like to do to her. I traced the faint scar on her hip with the tip of my finger, and she shivered when I leaned forward and kissed the length of it.

With a grin, I jumped to my feet and stuck a hand out, palm up, inviting her to follow me. She slid her hand into mine, placing all her trust in me.

Utterly and completely.

"Where are we——?"

I cut her off, swallowing the last of her words as my lips claimed hers, craving her taste and touch. "You haven't seen anything yet. Right now, I'm famished. So, come on, let's get dressed and grab a bite in town."

25

CARTER

After we both got dressed, I treated April to a late lunch. Hand in hand, we strolled down the sidewalk after I parked my SUV by the library. I took the time to point out all the buildings on Main Street, giving her a quick tour.

"Town Square is the place to be in the summer. All the town festivities are held here. There are kids' workshops on the weekends and yoga classes by the gazebo. As soon as spring arrives and the weather warms, all the restaurant terraces fill with people enjoying great food."

April gestured to our left. "Dahlia's Bridal Shop. Is it—?"

"Yes. It's Dah's business. She really turned her life around when it all went to hell. She worked hard to pick up all the pieces and make a life of her own here in town. One day, we'll go together. I'm warning you, though, it's full of glitter and shiny fabrics."

"What's not to like, right?"

"Yeah. I thought you would approve." I planted a kiss on the top of her head.

A minute later, we reached Ivy's Café. It was one of Dahlia's and my favorite eateries in town since our Carter Hills Band days when we were still teenagers with big dreams and the ambition to make it to the top.

"Hey, Carter. Long time no see," Ivy, the owner, greeted us when we walked in.

I shrugged. "Been busy."

She nodded. "Yeah, I heard. I'm glad you're back." She motioned us with a hand. "Come. Your table is free." We sat down in a little corner at the back. "It's funny you're here because I've been working on a menu I'm sure you'll approve."

"Can't wait to be your taster."

She smiled before bringing her focus to April. "Hi. I'm Ivy."

"Nice to meet you. I'm April." Her eyes surveyed the whitewashed walls filled with pictures of people who had eaten here over the years. There was a dozen of Dahlia, Stud, and I, and some with Jeff too. The place had a country farmhouse decor with its white walls and black accents. It was one of the few places that made Green Mountain feel like home when I was in town. "You have a lovely restaurant."

"Thank you, and welcome to town, April. Let me know if you need anything."

Ivy turned around, leaving us to ourselves.

"You have your own table? Pretty impressive." April's eyes shone at the teasing.

"Yeah, well, every time I'm in town, I try to come to eat here at least once. Ivy makes the best vegan sand-wiches, and she always has a new creation she wants to run by me. From time to time, she sends me a box with samples just to get my opinion. It's our thing. To be honest, it was Dahlia's table too back in the day. We would eat here whenever we played at Green Mountain Fest. For a long time, we were the opening act until we finally headlined the festival a few years later. When it happened, it felt as if we won the lottery."

"I'm kinda sad I didn't have posters of you on my bedroom walls when I was sixteen. You would have been my celebrity crush for sure."

I shook my head with a chuckle. "Well, I can still be. Your crush, I mean. Want me to sign you a poster and pin it to the wall behind your bed so you can wet your panties while looking at me when you go to bed?"

"Ohmygod." April joined in on the laughter and tossed her napkin at me. "Lucky for you, I'm aware you're not an ass. Else your ego wouldn't get through doorways." She smirked. "The poster offer is tempting, though. Better late than never."

"I agree. Let me see what I can do." I reached for her hand and knitted our fingers over the table. "I know I said it already, but I'm sorry I left. Sometimes, my thoughts are chaotic, and I need time and distance to sort through them. It's like it just becomes too much in my mind, and I can't deal with them. My therapist says they're anxiety attacks. They started after my brother died and Dahlia left town soon after. For a while, I was doing better, but my last relationship was a trigger, and they kinda returned. I'm trying hard to deal with them, but some-times, I panic and just disappear for a few days. Don't worry, okay?"

"Are you fine right now?"

"Yeah. After what we did, I'm more than fine."

She twisted her lips. "It-it's not what I meant…"

My smile faded. "I know. The truth is… I'm exhausted, but I'll survive."

We ordered, and Ivy brought us our food minutes later.

"Just to make it clear, this is not a date," I said after we were done.

"No?"

"Nah. Gimme a few days, and I'll take you on a proper date and treat you to a nice dinner."

"You think I'll let you wine and dine me, HN?"

"Yes, and afterward, I'll undress you and kiss you everywhere."

April scanned the space around us as if to make sure nobody heard us. "I love the sound of it."

"Me too. If it weren't clear earlier, I'm kicking you out of the guest room."

She blinked. "You want me to go back to my cabin? It…huh… It may be a good idea to avoid blurring the lines."

I leaned over the table and stared into her eyes. "Fuck your cabin. I want you in mine, in my bed, and this isn't up for debate."

April parted her lips. "You sure?"

"Never been surer of anything in my life. You and me, we're just getting started, and I have no intention to stop."

———

With her hand nestled in mine, once we were back to my place, I led April to the bathroom, toward the shower, large enough to be a small room on its own. Her eyes widened in awe. A floor-to-ceiling window occupied the whole wall behind the bathtub, giving the impression we were floating over the valley. The shower stood on the right, enclosed by three glass walls. The fourth wall, tiled in light gray, featured a handheld showerhead and ten body jets, while two rain showerheads hung from the ceiling.

"What are we doing?" April asked.

"I thought we could pick up where we left off earlier." I waggled my eyebrows, waiting for her to agree.

"You want to get into my pants again, Country Boy?" Her voice sounded lower than usual, and it affected every part of my body.

"All the fucking time. So?"

She raised her arms, and I slowly glided her shirt over her head. "Let's test run that shower then."

My heart swelled in my chest.

In slow motion, taking my time, I undressed her, exposing her bare skin to my eager eyes. When I unclasped her bra, April gasped and shivered against me. "Be ready. I'll never be done with you, Fairy."

We undressed each other without a word until the beating of our hearts and our hastened breaths were the only things filling the silence. April tugged at my shirt until I stood bare chest before her, before plunging her hands inside the waistband of my denims and freeing my throbbing erection.

"Fuck, I'm about to ruin you for other men out there."

"Stop talking and show me just how much."

While the water heated up, our mouths stayed fused together. Once inside the glass box, I turned her around until she faced one of the glass walls.

"Keep your hands beside your head."

April complied, and standing behind her, I spread her legs wide with one knee.

She turned her neck, gazing at me with questions. "What—?"

I silenced her with a swipe of my tongue and positioned one of the rain showerheads over her to keep her warm. The water rolled down her perfect figure. Long legs —for her height—firm and the same creamy shade as the rest of her skin, ass cheeks I longed to dig my fingers in, and a back I couldn't wait to massage and worship.

"Close your eyes," I said in a husky voice, my lips an inch from her ear.

Her eyes flared, and with a ragged breath, she did as I said.

Taking the soap in my hand, I lathered every inch of her, my fingers lingering on her neck, her pulse racing under my tips. My breathing quickened, and my tongue darted out of my mouth, watering at the idea of tasting all of her again.

I lowered my hands to her shoulders, leaving a trail of shivers under my touch. Dipping my head, I ran my scruff across her cheek, along the back of her neck, and down her upper arms. April quivered and gasped, but never moved. With my tongue, I flicked her earlobe and rested one hand against her throat as I whispered, "Be nice, and I'll make it up to you."

Her lips trembled, and her chest rose and fell at breakneck speed. Her throat worked under my soft touch, and I took a deep breath in to keep my composure intact. I smoothed the skin of her back with my hand, gliding it along her spine before skimming it across the velvety flesh between her legs.

April shuddered, and her cry vibrated through me.

My cock pulsed, and I pumped it a couple of times to lessen the tension.

The tip glistened, and I stroked it some more, not ready to thrust into her just yet.

I traced her legs with my palms, lathering them one at a time until her knees buckled. Clamping her hips to keep her still, I inserted my thumb inside her, circling and pumping, her wetness enveloping my digit. Her center throbbed, and every inch of me tensed.

I pressed my hard body against hers. Her breasts were flattened against the cold glass of the shower, stiffening her already diamond-hard nipples, and I wished I could see our reflection in the fogged mirror.

I peppered kisses across her nape, molding my body to hers. With April caged between my arms, I circled her wrists with my fingers, her hands still splayed on the wall beside her head.

In slow motion, I ran my erection up and down her ass cheeks.

The air between us, wet and electric, thickened.

Picking up the handheld showerhead, I aimed the water jet between her thighs. She yelped and rose to her tiptoes. I slithered my arm around her waist to keep her pinned to me. After I hung the showerhead back, I slid my hand between her and the glass wall and brushed the skin between her breasts with the tips of my fingers down to her belly before entering her throbbing center.

My grip on her waist loosened. I fisted her hair and pulled her head back, searching for her lips until we collided. April's tongue dived into my mouth, consuming me. Her hips moved against my hand, but I cut the rhythm once her body stiffened, ready to climax.

Inch by inch, I lowered myself to the floor and kneeled between her spread legs.

"Keep your hands on the wall and bend down," I said. "And keep your eyes shut."

She agreed with a small nod, and I let my tongue traveled along the seam of her legs.

I flicked her clit, sucked on it, and devoured her, slow and desperate at once. My hands found her bottom, and my fingers dug into the smooth flesh, holding her up.

I tongue-fucked her hard, her wetness dripping into my mouth. Her knees shook, and I tightened my grip on her ass, helping her keep her balance. I slid my lips down her legs, kissing her thighs, the back of her knees, and her ankles. April shuddered from head to toe. She yelped, and it gave me the strength to keep torturing her. In a slow, painful, and delicious way.

She peeled away from the wall and turned around, her eyes now midnight blue. Something fierce shone in them. She leaned down, her fingers digging into my shoulders, and gave me a dirty kiss.

Once she spun around and returned to her position of facing the glass wall, I brought my mouth back to her center, stroking her folds with my tongue. She rocked her hips as I glided my fingers in and out of her, matching my pace.

Her body contracted around my digits as I gripped her swollen bud between my lips.

She clawed the shower wall, waves of ecstasy rippling through her, her body swaying back and forth, lost in the pleasure. My pulsing cock refused to be on the sidelines any longer.

Back on my feet, I grabbed the condom from the bathroom floor and tore the package open before burying myself into her wetness from behind, not giving her time to finish riding her orgasm.

She clenched around my aching manhood when I entered her, firm and swollen from desire. All the hair on the back of my neck stood on end.

I laced my fingers through hers. April lifted herself on her toes, giving me better access to enter her. I bit on the flesh of her neck, pressing kisses all over her spine. She moaned and cried out my name at the top of her lungs. She sucked in a breath and exploded in bliss for the second time in my arms.

My legs wobbled, and I came right after, tremors shaking my body.

With my arms wrapped around her waist, we both crumpled to the floor, spent, lost in a rapture that left us breathless.

"Now you're the one who wrecked me," she whispered, her face buried in my chest.

I dropped a kiss on the top of her head, and we stayed on the tiled floor, our bodies entangled, in silence, until she grew heavy against me, her breathing slow and even, the water raining down on us.

Fifteen minutes or maybe an hour later, I had no idea, I carried her back to my bed.

"Fairy, I'm doomed. I'm spellbound by you, and I never want the spell to break," I whispered, breathless. "I'll never be able to stay away from you."

Without knowing it, in her own way, April was repairing every crack in my heart. The pieces that had been running around loose for years in my chest. In perfect April fashion, she knew how to join them back together. One fragment at a time.

With all her naked glory wrapped in my embrace, I dozed off, my heart lighter than it'd been in years.

26

APRIL

Okay, so that was how being thoroughly fucked felt. Who knew sex could be this life-shattering?

Travis and I had great sex. Fun sex. But we were young and lacked experience. Nothing compared to what Carter and I did together. What we shared was out of this world. It left my body sore in all the right places, making it impossible to forget his body cherishing and ravaging every inch of me. In the best possible way. It was like Carter knew exactly what my body craved. He fucked me hard and soft, deep and slow, igniting my flesh with every touch.

I had no idea when we fell asleep, but when I woke up sometime later, I was hungry and confused. The intimate moments we shared replayed in my mind.

As much as I longed for a do-over, it felt like a mountain of rocks was pressing down on my chest. What did I get myself into? After our time in Nashville, I knew not ceding to the smoldering passion between us was the right thing to do, and yet, it all went to hell the moment he came back home and kissed me.

This was not closure but added complications in our short-lived relationship.

And then it hit me. I had sex with Carter Hills. The country music god. The man who wrote me a song. I had sex with him twice.

Holding a sheet around my naked self, not sure how to act, I scanned the space around me. My eyes lingered on the sleepy silhouette of the man who had rocked my world, deep asleep beside me. He looked at peace now, the worry lines that once creased his forehead gone. I fought the urge to kiss him and slide my body between his arms. If I did, he would wake up, and he really needed his sleep. I could see the turbulence in him at a glance when he came home. Carter looked like he'd traveled to hell and back in the last three days.

I watched him a bit longer, unable to tear my eyes away from his perfect figure. I itched to trace the contour of his jawline with my fingertips.

It'd been so long since the last time I let a man care for me—and kiss me. Whatever lies I fed myself, I knew sex changed things. I'd never been a casual-sex kind of girl, and I had no clue if I could become one just for a chance to explore what Carter and I could be.

Emotions I had buried long ago simmered inside me. I'd allowed myself to be vulnerable with someone again— a feeling I hadn't experienced in so long. Since Travis, I'd locked my feelings away, but now, it was liberating to feel alive once more.

Rolling to my side, I slid away from Carter's large hand that was hooked onto my waist. He stirred in his sleep, and his eyelids fluttered. I held my breath while he muttered a few inaudible words and buried his head in the pillow. I watched him, praying he wouldn't wake up. I needed some time alone. Rising from the bed, I let the sheet slip away and spun, hunting for my clothes strewn across the en-suite. My bra hung from the vanity mirror—classy. Once I gathered every piece, I tiptoed butt naked down the stairs to my bedroom. Flutters danced in my lower belly as I relived the afternoon in my head. I trailed my hand down from my neck to my navel as heat pooled in my cheeks. A storm raged inside me. A million questions popped into my mind. Would sex ruin our friendship? Was it a one-time thing? Did we make a mistake? The last few hours had been a whirlwind, and I was now landing back on Earth and realizing what had happened and how crazy it had been. It was like I had been living in a dream and was just waking up from it. I had no idea what I'd gotten myself into and couldn't tell if it would come with regrets later. Not wanting to overthink everything, I immersed myself in a hot bubble bath with a few drops of lavender essential oil and shut my eyes.

There. A sense of peace invaded me, and I relaxed.

My mind wandered back to the man deep asleep upstairs.

When Carter came home earlier, the dark circles under his eyes and his wild hair made it look like he'd spent time in a crack house.

Since he refused to drink alcohol, I doubted he used crack or any other drug. Still, it appeared as if he had put his body through the wringer.

Despite what he'd said, we never had that talk—the one Carter insisted on having. Sure he had opened a little about his anxiety and struggles when we took an hour off our sex marathon to grab some food, but I needed more. His confession didn't answer all my questions about his disappearing act. Instead of talking, we both had indulged in each other once again when we came back here, unable to resist the lust sizzling between us any longer. Hours later, I now feared whatever it was that HN wanted to discuss.

In the pit of my stomach, I kept wondering if sex would ruin everything we had ever shared.

I had no idea what to think of any of this because the other day, in Nashville, Carter had said he didn't want us to be a fling. No matter how I spun the facts around in my head, I arrived at the same conclusion. How could we be anything else but a fling? I was leaving soon, and what we had just done could mess everything up. My heart included.

I refused to give my mind free rein to ponder the meaning of our actions or how Carter felt. If I did, it would only end one way: with my heart in fragments. And my spirit crushed.

I grimaced at the thought and decided to push it away as far as possible…for now.

Flashbacks of our afternoon together replayed in my head for the umpteenth time, and a grin stretched my lips.

Was I that weak when it concerned him? I sighed. I was. When he returned after his absence, Carter's heated gaze unraveled my every thought. With just one look, my anger and sadness evaporated, replaced by an over-whelming desire, my conscience slipping away.

It was a wonder I could keep him at arm's length for the last three weeks. Seriously, I couldn't even explain how I had resisted the tension between us for so long.

I was so screwed.

My stay in Green Mountain had an expiration date, and the mere thought of leaving unsettled my stomach. Now that Carter Hills had touched me, I couldn't imagine not having his hands on me ever again or feeling the warmth of his gaze whenever he looked at me.

I rubbed my hands over my face, and it did nothing to erase how torn apart I felt inside.

Our story wouldn't end happily. For me. Carter and I lived in different states, and our lifestyles didn't match. We both had a lot of baggage from past relationships. It didn't matter if our bodies fit together like yin and yang and we understood each other without words. HN and I weren't meant to be together in the long run, whatever he said that night when he sang my song. I couldn't shake the feeling that it wouldn't work. How could it, really?

A lone tear glided down my cheek. Another relationship would crash and burn. Perhaps I was destined to end up alone after all. Yep, by now, I should have gotten the memo.

I slouched lower in the tub, the hot water helping to untie some of the knots straining my shoulders.

Keeping my lids closed, I breathed in and out, desperate for my mind to take a break and my body to relax.

In vain. Images of us, pleasuring each other, flooded my brain.

My body combusted at the memory of his voice, asking me to spread my legs in the shower.

A rush of heat washed through me.

Never before had I experienced so much physical pleasure. And the *keeping my eyes closed* part added some sort of intangible excitement to the already mind-blowing experience.

I was certain now. This couldn't be just a one-time thing, no matter how hard my conscience tried to convince me otherwise. I, April Simmons, was claiming back my womanhood and indulging in my hot neighbor for as long as I was in town. If said neighbor agreed with the plan too. If I had only one chance to feel this beautiful and desired,

I would enjoy every second of it, consequences be damned.

———

Carter never woke up after part two of our intense sex-fest. I checked on him before dinner, and he was still sleeping like a baby and snoring like an old man. It did nothing to alter his hotness, though. The sheet barely covered his naked ass. One peek at his muscled bottom and my insides melted all over again.

Whatever Carter did while he was away had exhausted him.

His actions had taken their toll on him. He had lost weight and looked older, unsure, and somewhat scared.

While snacking on pasta leftovers and chocolate chip cookies, I called June to let her know Carter had returned.

"Thank God. I'll come to see him," she said with a heavy sigh. "If I leave Nashville now, I should be there in three hours."

"He's sleeping right now. Don't worry. I'll tell him to call you tomorrow. Don't drive here tonight."

"I don't know, April. Riley will ask to see him too."

"Please, June. Let me do this. If there's something wrong, I promise to tell you, and you can make the drive tomorrow."

She remained silent for a long beat. "Okay, fine. I trust you, April. Keep our boy safe," she said before hanging up.

I knew nothing about their dynamics, but I could tell June and Riley loved Carter very much and respected him a lot. A big sturdy knot in my stomach loosened. Carter wouldn't be alone once I left Green Mountain. He had people in his corner. People who genuinely loved and cared about him.

Carter Hills, the country star, was a mystery to me. From what I'd seen the night of his surprise gig in Nashville, he shone onstage. Carter Hills, the man, was addictive, and his smile alone could shatter a glass house.

Sitting cross-legged on the sectional sofa, my laptop perched on my lap, I spent the evening in the media room, watching a movie while working on my novel. Bernice slept beside me, her head resting on my thigh.

Saunders called me at eight, the sound of the ringtone startling Bernice who padded away, tail high and loud purr vibrating through the air.

"Hey girl, are you on your way? I'm sad I had to cancel my trip to see you next weekend." Saunders pouted. I could hear it in her voice, even over the phone.

I huffed and shook my head. My heart trembled in my chest. I'd never be able to lie to my best friend. A huge grin split my face in two. I took a deep breath in, trying to conceal the euphoria in my tone. "Huh…about that. There's been a change of plan… I-I'm still in Green Mountain."

"You are?"

"Yeah. It's a long story."

"Shoot. I have all night, girl. My man is out with friends tonight, and I'm not even a bit tired. Tell me everything."

I closed my eyes, staying silent for a few seconds. "Okay, let's see." I might withhold information and torture my best friend as well. "I finished packing when Carter—"

"You're on a first-name basis now? No more Handsome Neighbor, huh?"

"Saund, let me finish."

"Okay, I'll zip my lips now."

I imagined her sliding her fingers over her lips, sealing her words in a playful gesture.

"Where was I? Oh, yes, Carter. He disappeared three days ago after we returned from Nashville. No news, nothing. Radio silence. This morning I texted him I was leaving, and he wrote back, asking me to wait for him to come home because we needed to talk. Anyway, I pushed my ego aside because I got curious and waited. I wanted to know why he ghosted me after we spent an amazing weekend together."

"Oh, April, I'm sorry. I had no idea."

"I know… Don't be. I didn't feel like talking about it. I was upset he had left without a word after he wrote me a song and said we couldn't have sex because he didn't want us to be a fling. Anyway, he came back today after lunch, looking like hell, but also with a fire in his eyes."

"And? What did he do? What did he say? Don't leave me hanging. Talk, Bubble Head."

I exhaled and blurted, "Then he told me he'd left to stay away from me."

"He said that? Girl, are you all right? What a jerk. I'm coming to get you. If he messes with you, he'll hear from me."

"Saund, you're supposed to zip it, remember?"

"Yes. Sorry."

I snorted. "When he came back, well…we never talked." More images of our afternoon together passed through my mind. My breath caught in my lungs as I remembered his hands on me, his mouth eating me up, and how we became one person. My tongue ran over my lips as I relived all we had done in the shower. My body tingled, and I fought the urge to run upstairs and wake him up so we could do it all over again. Sore but energized, my body yearned to be cherished by him again. Blood warmed my cheeks. I shut my eyes, my heart wild inside my chest.

"April?" Saunders's voice snapped me out of my daydream.

"Sorry. Got lost for a moment." I composed myself, a grin forming at the edges of my lips. "After he came home, Carter kissed me like a madman and fucked me like an animal. Twice. We had dirty shower sex, and I can't stop thinking about how hot it was." I blew out a long breath. There, I said it. I needed a repeat performance to wipe the first one from my memory, to stop it from running in endless loops through my mind.

My friend gasped but said nothing.

Where was her usual smart-ass retort?

"Saund? Are you still there?"

"Oh my freaking God, April," she shrieked, and I pulled my phone away, my eardrums crying in pain. "Carter Hills fucked you. You saw him naked. He touched you. Ohmygod. Ohmygod. I can't believe it. Dammit, girl, I'm so proud of you. I feel like a mama bird whose chick has flown out of the nest for the first time. I thought you'd never live again. That you've forsaken the idea of love and sex forever." Saunders's humor died down, and her voice got serious. "What now? Did you finally have that talk? Is this a one-night kind of thing or will you two be at it like rabbits until you leave next weekend? Does Carter hope to see you afterward? Do you want to see him again? I'm dizzy. I have too many questions. So?"

I gulped down the lump forming down my throat before it choked me. "That's where it gets tricky. We haven't really talked since we did it. He-he's still asleep, and I'm like a caged bear pacing his house, doing everything I can not to think about it. I have no clue what it means. Even if it's a one-time occurrence, I'm okay with it. Or I have to be." Placing my friend on speaker, I slouched down into the sofa with a heavy sigh. Could it ever be just sex? I buried my face in my hands, a tightness developing in my chest.

"You want to do it again, girl. I know you do. I can tell. There's happiness in your voice. Something I haven't heard in a long time."

Tears prickled the back of my eyes.

"Don't be sad, hon, you deserve to be happy. Travis left you. It wasn't his choice, well…not entirely. You deserve love, even though you doubt it. Don't push Carter away just yet. Wait and see. He might surprise you."

I sniffed, unable to speak, as tears streamed down my cheeks—no doubt messing up my face and reddening my eyes.

Coiled in a ball beneath a blanket, I lay on my side, my best friend's voice soothing me through my sobs, her soft words erasing some of my doubts and my fears.

———

With a jolt, I shot up into a sitting position, wide awake.

I had no memory of falling asleep. The last thing I remembered was Saunders telling me over and over that everything would work out. That I had to trust the universe for once. Did she hang up on me when she realized I'd dozed off? I scratched the side of my head, the last few hours blurry in my mind.

In the dark, I patted the area around me, searching for my phone.

I found it between two cushions.

Three thirteen a.m.

Was my insomnia coming back? *Please, no*, I prayed to whoever was listening to me. Just thinking about it, a sense of panic filled me.

The notification told me I had one unread text message

my best friend had sent at ten o'clock last night. With my thumb, I unlocked the screen and opened the app.

SAUNDERS

Sleep it off. We'll talk in the morning. Love you xx

My lips curled into a tiny smile. "I love you too," I whispered.

I scanned the room. Someone had turned the TV and the lights off. *Carter.* He must've woken up after I'd passed out.

I stood, draped in the blanket, still needing its warmth. And Carter's. I shuffled to the kitchen in search of water and a *middle of the night* snack. With my head in the refrigerator, I picked up a faint sound coming from the northern side of the house. I'd never ventured there. Carter had his home office, his music studio, and a gym in that part of the cabin.

I ambled toward the sound. Music. Guitar. Carter's voice.

Tiny prickles blossomed all over my skin.

Even from a distance, his singing soothed me.

My entire body woke up at the sound of his voice, hoarse and raw.

I found him in his studio, in sweatpants, bare-chested, lost in his own world, strumming his guitar.

Through the ajar door, I stared at his fingers. Skillful and strong. He handled the strings with so much gentleness.

My mouth watered, thirsty for this man. All I wanted to do was lick him, taste him, turn him into a blaze with one sweep of my tongue all over his sensitive flesh. He shouldn't be allowed to wear a shirt ever again. This should be a rule. A tingling sensation ran along my spine, and I squeezed my thighs together.

Carter raised his eyes to me, the gray of his irises darkening and capturing me, and smiled. The blanket around me trailed on the floor like a sophisticated gown as I entered the studio.

The upward curl of his lips sent jolts to my heart, and my heartbeat picked up.

His throat worked, and he shifted in his seat, inviting me to sit between his legs.

I unhooked the blanket from around me, and it pooled on the floor as I shuffled toward him in a trance.

His arms wrapped around me from behind as I sat onto his lap, and he dropped a kiss in the crook of my neck. His lips rested there, and he breathed me in.

Tremors shook my core. He placed the guitar in my hands, locking our fingers together, and strummed the instrument with our hands intertwined.

He played a few chords, singing to me.

My heart leaped in my chest.

Butterflies danced low in my belly.

I leaned my head back against his hard chest and lost myself in his voice, his manly scent enveloping me.

> **Hold my hand**
> **Hold on tight**
> **It's just the beginning**
> **I'll teach you everything**
> **I know**
> **You'll show me the world**
> **through your eyes**
> **You and me, we're cut from the**
> **same tree**

You and me, we're a forever love story.

I mouthed the lyrics to his greatest hit.

My body sank deeper into his. I felt his heart banging between my shoulder blades.

Carter put the guitar on its stand and turned me around until I straddled him. He tucked my hair behind my ears and tipped my chin up with a curled finger. As we faced each other, I drowned in the ocean of his eyes.

"Why didn't you wake me up?" His husky tone shot untamed desire between my legs, and I shivered. A grin painted his full lips.

"You looked like you needed your sleep."

"I don't wanna sleep if you're not in my arms, April." The way my name slipped from his lips sent a jolt of electricity straight to the apex of my thighs. "And babe, I think your cat is a voyeur."

"What? Why?" I cocked my head to follow his gaze. Bernice sat, straight-backed, in the doorway, her eyes fixed on us. I pinched my lips together to silence a giggle. With my hand, I forced Carter to refocus his attention on me. "Forget the cat," I said, my voice gravelly. I wet my lips and devoured his bare chest with my eyes.

I swallowed as he watched me, not missing anything I did. The intensity of the desire tightening his features messed up my self-control. Carter outlined my lips with his finger before tasting them with a sweet stroke of his tongue, and my breasts swelled. All hints of playfulness vanished from his face. My blood heated in my veins.

"What…" He lifted my shirt over my head, his fingers leaving shivers in their wake as they trailed over my skin. "If…" He reached for my bra. "We…" And unclasped it. "Do…" His tongue found my erect nipples, ready to be consumed. "It…" He pushed my breasts up with both hands, rubbing my aching tips with his thumbs. "All…" He claimed my mouth with fierceness. "Over…" He raked his fingers through my hair, massaging my scalp and holding me still. "Again…?" His mouth traveled down my throat, his tongue licking, his lips sucking, and his teeth biting my flesh in the most delicious way.

A low whimper broke free. My bundle of nerves required his undivided attention as my body vibrated with desire.

As if he'd read my mind, Carter lifted me up and lowered me to my feet, hooked his fingers into the waistband of my pants, and slid them down my legs until they puddled on the floor. A devilish smirk broke free on his face when he noticed my black lace panties. I circled his neck with my hands, and he raised his eyes to meet mine. The intensity glowing in his irises spread all over my flesh like a burning caress.

Releasing him, I started to slide the scrap of lace down my hips, but he stopped me, his hands cupping mine.

"Keep them on." His groan pierced the silence, and I almost came undone right there.

Carter gripped my waist, and he pulled me until I straddled him again. He positioned me right above his hard-on, clamping my thighs with both hands as he rolled his hips, the friction relieving some of the tension between my legs. I ground my sex against his, but he leaned back a little.

My eyes widened, and I begged him in silence.

"No fucking tonight, Fairy. We'll go slow. I want every cell of yours desperate for a release. When I'm done with you, you'll feel me everywhere. Every. Where." He attacked my mouth, and I was a goner. I was pretty sure I blacked out right then.

Carter didn't lie to me. And he didn't disappoint either.

He did exactly what he promised to do.

His tongue and hands touched every inch of me.

With my legs wrapped around his waist and my back arched, he laid me down on the table next to his recording console as his mouth played with my throbbing bud over the thin fabric of my panties.

My arms stretched on each side of me as the pleasure built in my core.

Just when I was about to go over the edge, he stopped.

His eyes met mine with the same evil grin as before.

His thumb and index fingers pinched my puckered nipples, and more waves of pleasure washed over me.

Carter ignited my entire body.

He played me like he played the guitar.

Exceptionally.

Skillfully.

And easily.

My wet center ached, desperate for him to put out the fire raging inside me.

Angling myself to the side, I stretched one arm toward him. I pulled at the drawstring of his pants, and Carter stepped forward. I dived my hand under the waistband, but before I could get a grip of his warm flesh, he took a step back.

"Carter… Please…"

He circled my navel with his tongue and brushed the side of my legs with his hands. Warmth radiated through me. I gasped. He groaned. We were past the point of no return. My body and my soul were consumed by this man. I was wet clay in his expert hands, and he molded me as he wished. Even though I wanted to take the lead, I couldn't. At that moment, I was at the mercy of his touch. Of his kisses. Of his entire being. How could someone I'd known for less than a month possess me like this? When did Carter Hills become my home?

Tingles danced all over my naked flesh. They cavorted at the sight of him.

Each word escaping my lips sounded like a plea. Like a whimper. My blood simmered in my veins. My mouth watered. My chest rose and fell painfully with each breath. All my senses were attuned to him.

I could feel him in every cell of my body. In every breath I took. He was under my skin, over my skin, inside and outside of me all at the same time. A yelp exited my mouth. My need for him was greater than anything I'd ever experienced in my life. When did my hot neighbor become my drug? When did he get me so hooked on him that I couldn't think clearly in his presence? I writhed under him. Carter wasn't even doing anything to me, and I was turning into putty in his hands.

"Carter…"

"Mm-hmm."

"Carter," I said, firmer and louder.

"Beg for it, April. Beg me to finish you."

"Please…"

"Beg me for real, or I'll never relieve you of your misery. I could eat you up all night."

He swept his tongue over my wet folds, his teeth teasing my clit.

"Carter…I…I… Fuck. Please." Dear God. Could someone die from an unattained orgasm? "Put me out of my misery."

With dark eyes and purpose straining his features, he lifted me up in his arms again, like I weighed nothing, and sat back into the chair. I wound my legs around him, and he freed his manhood. I could barely tear my eyes away, practically salivating. He pulled a condom from his pocket, and after pushing my soaked panties to the side, he sheathed himself inside me.

I welcomed all of him in one thrust, so wet I needed no more foreplay.

My body clenched around his length. My toes curled, and I stiffened before convulsing as he pounded into me over and over until my tight walls milked his erection. Breathless, I collapsed in his embrace, and he tightened his grip around me, his head dropping to the crook of my neck. I breathed him in. Cedarwood and pine. My chest expanded to make room for my bursting heart, and the years of grief it had carried melted away as his hungry lips claimed the sensitive flesh of my neck.

"What have you done to me, Sweet Fairy?"

Addictive shivers skated up and down my back.

If only I knew. This thing between us wasn't just about sex anymore. My heart was being ripped apart. Torn open. Shred into slivers of glitter. I kept quiet and closed my eyes, chasing the hot-as-fire tears away, aware that what we shared would end.

Too soon.

Going back home was the only way to salvage my heart and prevent it from being broken all over again before I was in too deep with the man sweeping me off my feet.

27

CARTER

In the kitchen, standing between her legs, I fed strawberries to a half-naked April perched on the counter, wearing only pink lace panties and an unbuttoned shirt of mine, giving me the perfect view of the fullness of her breasts. I massaged her thigh with one hand, drawing circles with my thumb on her bare creamy skin. Little yelps tumbled out of her mouth each time my finger neared the sensitive flesh of her inner thighs.

April caressed the muscles of my chest with the pads of her fingers, sending shivers down to my toes. Her presence cursed me with a permanent erection. Pixie knew the effect she had on me because she never missed toying with my hard-on, sending torturous waves of lust through me. This time wasn't different. She rubbed me over my denims, my dick standing up, ready to be her playground.

"Desmond will change the stupid lock on your cabin this afternoon. Will you stay here, though? With me? Like I already told you, I want you in my bed at night, not next door or a floor below."

She lifted her gaze to mine, the vibrant baby-blue

shade sparkling in the natural light coming from the giant window. She bit into the juicy fruit, her lips now a darker shade of pink. "Carter, I… Huh, I'm leaving on Sunday. Don't get too attached." She huffed, hanging her head low, looking sad.

"Yeah…speaking of your leaving… How do you feel about extending your stay?" I tipped her chin up, forcing her to look at me, then framed her face with both hands. "I mean it. It'll give us more time together. And to figure this out."

She kissed the palm of my hand. In my world, I wasn't used to asking for whatever I wanted. People usually begged to give me everything I wished for.

"I-I don't know. I haven't been home in a month, and I'm tired of living out of a suitcase."

"But I thought you could work from anywhere…" Now I was the one begging. "We could go shopping or ask June to get clothes delivered to you here." I shrugged, trying to act casual, the opposite of how I felt inside. "Or we could spend our days naked. Yep. All day. Every day. Clothes optional. It would solve the problem."

April brought her lips to mine and smiled against my mouth. "That naked offer is very tempting. However, even if I can work from anywhere, living together complicates things. I hate labels, but we haven't talked about what we are yet. Don't you think we're skipping steps here?"

I dragged my hand down her bare front and stopped at her waist, leaving a trail of goose bumps behind. "Can we figure this out together? Along the way. The last thing I want is to put pressure on you. On us. I don't know anything except I'm not ready to let you go, and I love having you here." I raised an eyebrow, challenging her.

April snorted a laugh.

I erased the little distance between us and pulled her to

me, melding her body with mine. Her soft chest pressed against my hard one, and all hell broke loose within me. Every one of my cells vibrated with renewed energy. My heart merged with hers.

With her arms around my neck, April's big doe eyes glistened as she stared at me.

"You're so sexy. I could eat up you right now." My eyes lowered to hers, drawing her in, and my mind went wild at the idea of what I could do to her on this surface.

As if she could read my dirty thoughts, she nudged my arm. "Stop. Be serious for once. Can I think about this?"

I bowed my head and dropped my shoulders. "Yeah… Sure."

Not giving me time to be disappointed, she whispered against my lips, "Catch me if you can, Country Boy." She escaped my grip, jumped off the counter, and ran upstairs, laughing.

I shouted after her, "Run, Fairy. Run. I'm going to catch you, so you better hide because I'm ravenous, and if I catch you, I'll torture you with my tongue."

It'd been two days since our sex-fest, as she called it. Days of pure bliss. Days where we barely kept our hands to ourselves. Days where mornings and nights blurred together and nothing else existed except the two of us.

Before I could run after her, my phone went off. "Howdy, Ry. How is it going?" I was sure my manager could hear the happiness in my tone even over the phone.

"Hi, Carter. Glad to see you're doing better. Listen. Sam Stevens dropped out of this fundraiser event tonight. I need you to cover for him. His wife had a miscarriage."

"Shit."

"Yeah, well, he wants to keep the news under wraps for now. I'll send the private jet to pick you up in two hours."

"Tonight? Your timing sucks, Ry. Big time." I rubbed

my chin with my hand, rolling my jaw back and forth. "Christ. Where's this thing?"

"New York. I'll fly you back first thing tomorrow morning. I need you for the entire event."

I ran my hand over my face and closed my eyes, taking a minute to think it over.

"Who's hosting?"

"The Bensons. They asked for you personally. Stevens was their second choice…after you. You were supposed to be in Europe this week before we canceled most of your engagements. That's why they picked Stevens instead of you. Now you're free. The timing is perfect."

I cursed under my breath.

"You know they love you, man. And it'll be good for you to get out there."

I sighed and kicked the stool behind me. "Okay, fine. I have one request, though."

"Anything."

"I want to bring a plus one. That's my only condition."

Riley harrumphed. "Carter, Savannah will be there. Not sure if it's smart of you to bring someone else. You know firsthand how unpredictable she can be. Remember That Talent's afterparty when she took the pill…?"

I didn't need a reminder of that episode of my life.

"Fuck, Ry. April is leaving on Sunday. I won't go if she can't come along. My crazy ex is not my problem anymore. You witnessed it firsthand. I'm done with her, and I couldn't care less about her presence or her whereabouts."

"Carter, is this serious? You and April, I mean. Are you in a relationship? I'm not risking another fiasco. Haven't you suffered enough in the last year?"

"Screw you, Ry. Since when do I have to justify my actions to you?"

"Relax, man. I witnessed your hitting rock bottom not

so long ago. Your happiness means a fucking lot to me. I'm not asking because I wanna insert myself into your love life. I'm asking because I care. And I don't want you to go back to that dark place, seeing you're standing on your two feet once again."

"Fine. Don't worry about me. I've learned my lesson. Can we just see where this is going first before making an official statement? For tonight, she'll be my date. That's it."

"The new song, the pictures in the press, and now this. Carter, your actions are not helping. It's hard for us to do our job and keep the press off your back when you act like this. Where were you a few days ago? I tried to reach out. Multiple times. We all did. You were MIA, and I'm aware, by now, of how it goes when you disappear. No matter what shit you spin on me, I'm worried about you, man."

"I know you are. And thank you for having my back all the time. It's just… The truth is…I needed time on my own. To think. I like her, Ry. I really do. And I never expected to. I'm aware it's new, and we haven't known each other for long, but April is good for me. I swear it's not a repeat of the last time. I'm not trying to prove something to myself with her. Or to overcompensate for my shitty parents. We're taking it one day at a time. Anyway, you've met her. Don't tell me you think April is like Savannah. They are nothing alike."

"You're right, and I understand what you're saying. I just don't wanna see you hurting, man. Promise me you won't move too fast, and you'll take the time to consider everything. Bringing April tonight sends a statement. The media won't stay quiet about it. You know the drill by now. I'm trying to protect you."

"Thank you. Even though I sound irascible, I want her there. She makes me better. I feel whole with her by my side. Grounded and calm. Can you pull some strings and make it work?"

"All right. Let me see what I can do. I'll reach out again in thirty minutes."

"Fine. Do whatever you gotta do to make it happen." I hung up before he could say anything else. I loved my manager, but he wasn't the one calling the shots here.

In April's room, sitting on the edge of her bed with my hands clasped between my knees, I waited for her to exit the bathroom. I repeated in my head everything I wanted to tell her and held my breath when she opened the door.

Her smile stole all the oxygen from my lungs. "Hey, I waited for you to join me in the shower." She pouted, pursing those lips of hers, and my heart ached. All I craved was to put smiles on her face. Nothing else. She studied my expression, and a worry line appeared on her forehead. "What's wrong?"

"April, listen. We gotta talk."

She frowned and tightened the towel wrapped around her. "Is everything okay? Why are you dead serious right now?" I pulled her onto my lap, and her arms wound around my neck. "Did something happen?"

I rubbed my brows, hoping she wouldn't overreact. "No. But promise me you won't freak out, okay?"

She nodded.

Stop being a chicken, Carter.

"Riley called. He booked me for a fundraiser…huh, tonight. Without giving me a heads-up. It's a last-minute gig. I-I'm covering for someone."

"Oh." Her hold on me slackened.

"I'm aware I promised you a date night. What if you came with me?" I quirked an eyebrow, fidgeting with the hem of her towel to keep my fingers busy. "You could join me…as my date. What do you think?"

Her eyes flared. "Won't there be media and all those people we're trying to hide from?"

I nodded. "Yeah. And actors and professional athletes. And Savannah Prince too." I wouldn't hide anything from her. "We won't say anything about the status of our relationship. I'll stay by your side the whole time and be a perfect gentleman."

She eyed me sideways. "Carter, I'm not sure I can do this. Look at me. I'm not cut out for your world. I'll never fit in, and I don't even have something chic enough to wear. I'm a simple small-town girl, Carter, not a model." She looked adorable with her unjustified self-doubts.

"Babe, do you trust me?"

She looked at me and nodded, her teeth worrying her bottom lip.

"Then believe me when I say I'll take care of everything. I don't give a damn about anybody else. I want you. If you're not sure, I'll opt out. You're the most amazing woman I know. Don't ever sell yourself short. We either go together or we stay home."

She blinked. "You'd opt out for me?"

"Yeah. Anytime."

She pondered the idea for a moment, her bottom lip still caught between her teeth. "You're sure I'll fit in?"

"Pixie, you'll be perfect. Every guy will envy me. I'm telling you." My lips found hers, and she dissolved against my mouth. I grabbed a fistful of her hair and deepened the kiss. "I would never lie to you or lead you on. Does this mean you're in?"

"I'd be a fool to refuse the opportunity to show up on Carter Hills's arm," she said against my mouth.

I leaned back to make sure I heard her right, and she winked. I cupped her cheeks with both hands and swallowed her laughter as I kissed her.

"What's the fundraiser about?" she asked.

"Some disease. The organizers throw it once a year. It's kind of personal to them."

"It's for a good cause. One more reason to go then." She dropped a chaste kiss on my lips, and heat rippled through me.

"Let's get ready then." We sprang to our feet, and my hand connected with her ass. "Pack a bag, and meet me downstairs in fifteen minutes. I'll get Dahlia to meet us at the shop. She'll find the perfect gown for you to wear." I exited the room to run upstairs to grab my own things and send a quick message to Riley to arrange all the details about the flight but stopped halfway there. "April, bring the Nashville dress while you're at it." My grin threatened to tear my face in two.

28

APRIL

When did I become a princess in a fairytale?

Dahlia opened her store early for us after Carter asked her to help me find a gown for tonight's fundraiser. A gown. I'd never worn one of those. This would be the fanciest night of my life. How would I ever fit in? *Me.* April Simmons. The girl who rarely spent over fifty bucks on a piece of clothing and had owned the same pairs of shoes for years. *Me.* The girl who dyed her own hair and spent her Friday nights at home instead of barhopping with her friends. Saunders was right. I'd be a full-time cat-lady before turning thirty. Perhaps twenty-four was the new fifty. I sighed. There was no denying it. Travis's death had changed me. Deeply. I was aware now I should have gone out more and met new people. Only it had seemed meaningless back then because I enjoyed my quiet life. Away from any potential heartache.

Until Carter.

In a matter of weeks, he'd disrupted everything I'd spent years perfecting.

He came into my life like a tsunami and took over my heart and soul with a single glance at me.

Deep down, I loved how he challenged me. How alive I felt beside him.

We entered Dahlia's Bridal Shop together, our fingers intertwined. My heart fluttered in my chest, and my jaw went slack. It was as if I didn't have enough eyes to drink it all in. Silk. Rhinestones. Shoes. Tulle. Mannequins wearing designer wedding dresses. The bridal-and-evening-gowns paradise was everything I'd dreamed about as a little girl.

Carter's grip on my hand tightened. "Have fun, okay?" he whispered in my ear before dropping a kiss on my cheek. I nodded, my mouth open, fish-style, the words stuck in my throat. He stared at me, amusement dancing in his eyes, and snickered. "Hey buddy, ready to go?" he asked Jack. They looked ever more alike this morning, both of them wearing similar washed-out jeans and black sweaters and sporting tousled messes of hair.

"Yes," the little boy said, jumping in our direction. "Is April okay?"

Carter let out a loud chuckle. "Sure. All this glitter. She's like in fairies' heaven right now."

"What's heaven?"

Carter grabbed Jack's hand. "Come on, I'll explain. Time for our boys' hour." Secret code for eating an endless supply of pancakes at the restaurant next door. He winked at him, and my heart turned to mush in my chest.

"Bye, Mama. Bye, April," Jack singsonged.

Carter leaned in to kiss me. The last drop of my melted heart pooled on the floor.

Dahlia neared us and ruffled her son's hair before kissing him goodbye. "Have fun, you two. And please behave." She turned to face me and shrugged. "Carter transforms into a man-child when he hangs out with Jack."

Once again, I found myself alone with the only woman Carter had ever loved. I shouldn't feel at ease around her, but somehow, I did. Carter didn't look at Dahlia the same way he looked at me. He had this hungry stare when our eyes met. With Dahlia, it was more of an affectionate look.

I offered her a small smile, and she returned it.

"Okay, I have to tell you this. Carter looks ten years younger since he met you." She squeezed my forearm. "Whatever you're doing, please don't stop."

Tingles moved up and down my spine. Saunders would probably say the same thing about me if she were here. My zombie days were behind me. My after-Travis-induced insomnia had retreated. I hoped for good, this time. I wasn't sure if Carter, Green Mountain, or a mix of both were the cures I needed. Whatever it was, I never wanted to return to my previous state of mind.

"April, do you have any idea what you're looking for?"

Dahlia wore royal-blue yoga pants and an off-shoulder black Sherpa sweater, her red hair tied in a single braid over her shoulder. She was beautiful. Each time we met, I noticed she possessed a gleam in her eyes and a way of making other people feel important. Like she genuinely cared about them.

I blew out a breath and tucked loose strands of my hair behind my ears. "No idea. To be honest, I'm nervous. Carter insisted I come with him, but I'm not even sure I'll fit amongst all these rich and famous people." I could feel blood pooling in my cheeks as they warmed up.

Dahlia clutched my trembling shoulders. "Listen to me, April. I know Carter's world is scary. It can be overwhelming and destructive if you don't grow a thick skin. But if he is by your side, you have nothing to worry about. He'll never let you down."

"Huh…You think so?"

"I know so."

"Can I ask you a question?"

"Sure." The smile she aimed at me was both warm and comforting. "What is it?"

"If I'm overstepping here, please tell me. Call it curiosity, but why did you leave the band? Why did you leave that life?"

She rubbed the back of her neck. "Well, I found out I was pregnant, and I got tired of this glamorous life. I also did it to protect my baby because I refused to raise him in the limelight. You know, traveling the world and living in hotel rooms got to be tiresome. After some time, globetrotting wasn't my thing. Sure, I loved the music, but not enough to sacrifice my life for it. All I wanted was a low-key existence with the man I loved." Her gaze dropped to the ground. "I'm glad I left the scene when I did. It was my choice. After Jeff's death—he was Carter's older brother and my husband—it confirmed I'd made the right choice. In the end, I would've been forced to give it up anyway." Dahlia cradled her belly. "Enough of this. I'm happily married, and I love my life the way it is." She smiled, but a prickle of sadness remained in her eyes.

"I'm sorry. I didn't mean to be insensitive."

Dahlia held my hands in hers. "Don't be sorry, April. It was a long time ago. And I would be curious too if I were you. This lifestyle is probably a far cry from life as you know it. To tell you the truth, I never regretted leaving the band. Carter has always been the star. He deserves everything he worked so hard for." She paused and searched my eyes. "Don't break his heart, though. Please be gentle with it—it's delicate, okay? Be honest with him. He cares about you. A lot. I can tell. He appears strong and fearless, but underneath his tough exterior, he's hurting." I nodded, and her lips curled into a soft smile. The trace of sadness in her eyes evaporated. "Carter deserves to be loved. He doesn't think he does, and it breaks my heart. He'd catch a bullet for anyone he cares about. I'm sad he doesn't know how truly special he is."

I mirrored her smile. The last thing I wanted was to break Carter's heart. Or for him to break mine. I shifted the conversation, my pulse spiking at the thought of the man I was getting far too attached to, against my better instincts. "About this dress, can you help me choose something because I have no idea what I should wear? I'm more used to comfy clothes than gowns." I gestured to my skinny black jeans, ankle boots, and cream turtleneck sweater with one hand.

"Don't worry, gowns aren't part of my everyday wardrobe anymore. I much prefer comfort these days." Dahlia clapped her hands, her smile blinding and her excitement effervescent. "I have exactly what you need. Follow me. Once we're done, Carter will have to duct-tape his jaw if he doesn't want to drag it across the floor, catching dust."

She selected a few pieces while I drew the dressing room curtain and undressed.

The first gown I tried on was an asymmetric black number. It had a crystal strap on one shoulder and a long sleeve along the other arm. A string belt made of tiny crystals, like the ones sewn on the shoulder strap, circled the waist.

I exited the dressing room and parked myself in front of the three-panel, full-length mirror, admiring my reflection as I twirled around. "Wow, it is beautiful. I like it," I said, smoothing the soft fabric with my hand.

"It looks wonderful on you. Elegant and classy." Dahlia handed me a second gown. "Now try this one."

Strapless, it had a long slit on the side, showing a significant amount of leg. An embroidered gold pattern embell-ished the navy-blue bodice. Paired with gold loop earrings and a large golden bracelet, I resembled a Greek goddess.

"Do you love it?" Dahlia asked as I looked at my back-side through the mirror.

"Yes. I can't decide which one I love the most." I spun around, unable to resist the urge when wearing such a beautiful dress. "They're both gorgeous."

"Try this one," Dahlia said, handing me a third gown.

It was a silver mermaid-cut gown with a plunging neckline, a low-cut back, and a short train, embroidered from the bodice to the skirt with cascades of sparkly beads and feathers.

I parted my lips, but only a low "Oh" left my mouth when I caught my reflection in the mirror outside the dressing room.

Unable to look away, I pressed my hands over my heart, blinking back emotions.

"You are very pretty. Carter is very lucky to go on a date with you." I turned around at the sound of the little voice speaking highly of me. Jack stood a few feet away from me, stars in his eyes. "Can I take you out on a date too?"

A sweet, uncontrollable laugh escaped my lips. "I'd love to go on a date with you, Jack. But I promised Carter I'd go with him to this one, though. It's a big deal for him." I furrowed my eyebrows and lowered my voice. "I think he's scared to go alone. Don't tell him I said that, but he needs me to hold his hand."

The little boy chuckled. "I won't tell him anything," he said with a wink.

Carter walked in. "Are you two talking behind my back?" He stopped in his tracks when his eyes took me in. His lips parted, but no words eased out.

Dahlia backhanded him in the chest. "Close your mouth, Cart. You'll catch flies." Her eyes drifted toward me. "I think this is the dress, April. The guys are right. This was made for you. Follow me. We'll pick up shoes, then we'll see if I gotta do some quick adjustments."

Carter's hand closed around my forearm as I passed by him, pausing me mid-step. My eyes raised to his, and his lips found mine. "April Simmons, you look amazing. You'll be the most beautiful woman tonight. I can already tell." His melted-steel irises darkened, and for a moment, the world around us disappeared. My mouth went dry, and I could barely draw a full breath in. His stare held me prisoner. I couldn't move. Couldn't talk. A mischievous glint, tinged with lust, danced in his eyes. I wet my lips with my tongue. Carter brushed his knuckles along the length of my face, and I closed my eyes, breathing him in, addicted to his manly scent. Cedarwood and pine. I kissed the tip of his thumb when it skimmed my bottom lip. He leaned forward and pressed his forehead to mine. We were both panting, lost in our little bubble.

After what felt like seconds, Dahlia's voice broke the moment and the spell that had settled between us. "Carter, keep your hands to yourself," she commented, laughing, as she neared us. "We're not done. April, I think I found the perfect heels. Try these on."

Carter let go of my arm.

My heart rate picked up.

I refused to fall for Carter Hills, but each time his stare burned me alive, I couldn't keep lying to myself. I was freefalling a little more.

Carter and I both cleared our throats, and I followed Dahlia to the back of the store for a few adjustments after I put the heels on, living the princess dream, wearing the silver mermaid gown. Were my cheeks bright red? I pressed my hands to my face, calming all traces of Carter's effect on me.

"All done," Dahlia said after she put away her sewing kit and moved to her feet to admire her work. "It's perfect. And you look absolutely beautiful."

"Thanks. For your help. And for opening the shop for me."

"It was my pleasure."

In the dressing room, I slipped the gown off and handed it to her through the curtain opening. When I returned to the front of the store minutes later, Dahlia was handing Carter the garment bag. I grabbed the shoe box and stowed the jewelry pouch inside my purse.

"You're all set, guys. Hope you have a wonderful time in New York."

"New York?" I choked as I blurted out the words.

Carter angled his body to face me. "I wanted it to be a surprise. We're boarding a private jet in half an hour." A giant grin spread all over his face. "April Simmons, will you come to New York with me and be my date tonight?"

I placed my free hand over my mouth. "Ohmygod. New York? This is surreal."

He watched me, a glazed look in his eyes, his eyebrows raising just slightly. "So?"

"There's nothing I'd like more than to be your date."

Carter pulled me in for a kiss. "I can't wait."

"I'm sorry I spoiled the surprise, Cart," Dahlia said with a grimace.

"Nah, it's fine. I needed to come clean eventually. I just didn't want to scare her away too soon." He laced his fingers through mine, and my heart overflowed with emotion, throbbing so hard I feared they could all hear it.

Jack inched closer and pulled at my sleeve. "April? Do you remember Beatrix, my friend who loves fairies?"

"Yes."

"She wants to meet you again. Can we come over? Or you can come to my house and drink tea with my mama."

"Oh, Jack. I'd like to spend time with you two, but I'm leaving on Sunday. I'll try to find a moment to meet with you guys before I go."

"You're leaving? Forever?" The sad expression on his face tugged at my heartstrings. Jack was the spitting image of Carter. Same hypnotic gray eyes and thick dark hair. A grin to die for. And undeniable charm. Carter Hills must've been handsome even at a young age.

I squatted to level my eyes with his. "I hope it won't be forever, but I need to go back home at some point. But I'll always be your special fairy friend. This will never change, okay?"

The boy looped his small arms around my neck, and we hugged for a brief moment. "Can I come to visit you sometime? And Bernice?"

"Sure. I'd like that." I blinked, trying to prevent tears from flowing down my cheeks. Reality burst the bubble I'd been living in for the last few weeks. "You know what? If it's all right with your mama, you should go see if Bernice is okay later today. I'm sure she'd like some company."

His eyes lit up.

"I think it's a great idea. Let's do that when we're done here," Dahlia agreed. When my eyes found her, she mouthed a silent *Thank you.*

Something in me ruptured, and the ache radiated throughout my entire body. The thought of walking away from Carter when my month was up tore at my chest.

That small pinch in my heart was all the confirmation I needed.

Carter grabbed my hand when we boarded the private jet. I stopped halfway up the airstairs, but he pulled me forward.

"C'mon, Fairy. Let's get seated." He bowed his head, brushing his lips against the shell of my ear. "Just so you know, we'll be all alone in there. No team member. No security. No flight attendant. Only us and the pilot."

I swallowed hard. His heated stare started a kindle between my thighs.

A fuzzy feeling swirled inside me as I followed him.

As soon as we were at cruising altitude and the seat belt sign switched off, Carter approached me like a predator. My breath caught in my lungs, and I coughed to open my airways.

He leaned forward, his hands resting on the armrests of my seat, his face an inch from mine. So close I could see every detail of his gray irises. "Have you ever been fucked in an airplane, April?"

My self-control left me when my name escaped from his kissable lips. We eye-fucked each other, neither of us breaking the trance we always fell into so easily.

"So?"

I shook my head, not breaking eye contact. My body tingled, and I became a pile of molten flesh under the weight of his stare.

"Perfect. We'll rectify this situation." He traced the length of my jaw with his lips, and a load moan passed my lips. Carter growled, the sound vibrating through me. A devilish smirk brightened his model-like face.

Walking backward, he returned to his seat and beckoned to me with a finger. My body obeyed before I could think this through.

I sat onto this lap, then turned and straddled him.

Everything in me quivered at the proximity. "Are we supposed to do this up here?"

Carter traced a line from my lips to the delicate skin between my breasts with his calloused fingers. Goose bumps bloomed on my skin. His mouth sampled the flesh of my neck. "Stop overthinking everything, Pixie. Relax and enjoy the ride." His tongue followed the seam of my lips, and I surrendered every thread of control I still possessed to him. His hand found its way inside my panties, and when he coated his fingers with my wetness and thrust them inside me, I lost touch with reality. I writhed under his touch, relishing the first ripples of pleasure washing through me as my eyelids whispered against my lashes. I arched my back, unable to silence the sounds of arousal bubbling in the depths of me. "You want it, babe? You want me to ease all the tension in you?" His gruff whisper acted like an orgasm detonator.

My vision blurred as heat shot through me in addictive waves while he rubbed my clit in slow strokes.

"Fine. Please. Fuck the tension out of me, HN. Just do it." My lips parted on an exhale, and I lost it.

Carter's free hand kneaded one of my breasts.

Our mouths sampled each other's skin. Our hands explored every inch of our flesh. Carter pounded into me until I saw stars. My body clenched around him, and I milked his erection. His tongue flicked my nipples, one at a time. A bolt of electricity singed through my body from head to toe, leaving me trembling. I fisted his hair, bringing his face to mine until our mouths fused. Carter clamped my waist, and with my front molded to his chest, we cuddled for the rest of the flight.

We landed and climbed into the car waiting for us on the tarmac—a black luxury sedan with tinted windows—

after the driver put our bags in the trunk and held the door open for us to get in.

I hadn't even put on my gown yet, and already I felt like Cinderella.

The last time I visited New York City, I was nineteen and had come with Travis. We'd spent a week at his parent's place, strolling all over the city and visiting every tourist hotspot. This time, though, I wasn't here to roam around the city but to attend an event. I felt a rush of excitement in my stomach at the idea of spending the evening mingling with people I never once thought I'd meet in real life. In a matter of hours, once again, my life had become surreal.

"Thanks," I said. The driver, in his late fifties, with salt and pepper hair, bowed like I was some sort of royalty before closing the door softly behind us.

Like in the movies, an opaque window divided the front of the car from the back, adding to the dreamlike experience.

Carter pulled me onto his lap, and all the tension left me. His hands traveled under my loose sweater. I indulged in our kiss, and a flush of heat spread through me.

"What's the smile for?" he asked, leaning back against the seat of the car when we broke apart, breathless.

"You. You make me smile. Like a fool. I was thinking about what we did up there." I pointed my finger at the sky. "It was kinda hot. Very hot," I said in a husky whisper, not sure if the driver could hear us through the partition.

"I'm glad you liked it. We'll have a do-over tomorrow."

With a sweep of his tongue, he licked the length of my neck, and I pushed him away, giggling. "Not here."

For the rest of the drive, Carter gave me a rundown of how the evening would play, and excitement bloomed inside me.

My courage tumbled down to my toes when the driver parked in front of Sky High Hotel. Two beefy men, looking like oversized football players, wearing black suits and dark shades—the same guys who hovered around us in Nashville—waited for us. At their sight, the ability to speak words left me.

How did I become part of this? When did I become friends with someone so famous that there was security waiting for us at a hotel where I probably couldn't even afford the cheapest room?

Carter grabbed my hand and squeezed it tight, injecting me with much-needed moxie.

The beauty team—something June had arranged for me as a surprise—knocked at five thirty sharp. Wearing a wrap dress in an electric shade of green and knee-high black boots, Betty, the makeup artist, applied a range of powders and creams to my face. Her purple-framed glasses and her short dark curls gave her a boho-chic look. Rob, the hairdresser, wearing a three-piece sparkling black suit with a crisp white button-up shirt and a purple bow, curled my locks in waves. Thirty at the most, his bleached blond hair was coiffed into a Viking-style mohawk. I congratulated myself for retouching my pink hue last night. Rob fixed a few strands of my hair with a silver barrette and sprayed some glitter. "Girl, you'll look fabulous in pictures." He clapped his hands before him, looking satisfied.

Rob handed me a mirror, and Carter grinned as I gasped in surprise when I saw my reflection for the first time.

"It's beautiful. Wow. Thank you so much." I fanned myself with a hand, in awe over my hairstyle.

Betty covered my eyelids with a shimmery powder and contoured my face with different shades of bronzer and highlighter. "Stop smiling for a minute. I can't do your lips," she said with a wink. "Take this lipstick, and please retouch it a few times tonight. The trick is to never let it fade away. You're such a sweetheart, April." She smacked her lips together, motioning me to do the same. "Perfect." She offered me a little pouch. "Keep it in your purse. I hope you two have a wonderful night."

On their way out, I hugged Rob and Betty, ignoring the etiquette, after being pampered like a princess. "Thank you so much," I said, rapidly blinking away my tears.

"Oh dear, don't you cry. You'll ruin your makeup," Rob said with an air kiss. "Mr. Hills, this girl is a keeper." He exited the suite, his arm linked with Betty's, and waved at us. "Drinks?" I heard him ask the makeup artist as I closed the door behind them.

I turned around, Carter's approval illuminating his features and making me feel like a queen.

———

The driver, dressed in a black suit, opened the car door, and Carter got out. My heart drummed so fast in its cage that I thought I'd die of a heart attack. Or throw up and pass out. *Breathe, April.* My date held out his hand, inviting me to join him. I took a deep breath in, trying to kill the jitters whipping inside me. I slid my palm into his and melted, his warmth my safe harbor. I plastered a smile on my face, lifted my chin, and climbed out of the car, praying I wouldn't trip over my own feet—or my gown—and project as much confidence as I could muster.

The heels Dahlia found for me weren't too high. "One less thing to worry about," she'd said. Right now, I thanked her in my head.

Carter's eyes glistened as they landed on me, and his smile broke all my reservations.

I snaked my hand around his arm and dug my shaky fingers into the sleeve of his slim-fit charcoal tuxedo. Dressed to impress, he looked like a movie star. A wet dream. He'd shaved, and Rob had cut his hair earlier, styling it into a sexy *just got out of bed and looking fabulous* kind of way.

I kept my stare on him.

Steadying my breaths, I fought the urge to bite my lips, afraid to ruin my lipstick.

"Relax, April," Carter said in a voice so low I barely heard him. He brushed my temple with his lips, and I shivered from lust.

His mouth stretched into a large smile, putting to rest the last threads of my reservation. Yes, I could do this.

The camera flashes blinded me as soon as my feet hit the pavement, and I tried my best to block them out.

"Keep walking, and soon we'll be inside," he said, not losing his composure, his free hand enveloping mine as if to make sure I wouldn't run away. "You're beautiful. Don't let them intimidate you."

I raised my eyes to meet his, and Carter's confidence rubbed off on me.

When I agreed to walk the short distance between the car to the entrance of the museum where the fundraiser was being hosted, I never thought that it'd be this unnerving. All my cells trembled with agitation. The good and the bad kinds.

A tall man sporting gelled-back blond hair stopped before us and thrust a microphone at Carter's face. My date's smile never faltered. A short woman sporting a pixie cut, dressed in a strapless blue dress and black stilettos, neared us next, invading our personal space.

A few seconds later, a hurdle of cameramen and reporters circled us and fired questions our way while Taylor and Ed, Carter's personal security, pushed them back, keeping them at a safe distance from us. I took a calming breath. My eyes stung from the lights aimed at us and the camera flashes. My attention remained on the man standing tall beside me, and I smiled because I had no clue what else to do. And I was pretty certain it would look better in pictures than a frown. I hated all the attention. If only I could crawl into Carter's arms and disappear. My heart leaped into my throat. Could I throw up my own heart?

I kept my smile firmly in place, counting the seconds in my head. Each one felt like hours.

As if he could sense my discomfort, Carter detached his arm from my grip, and his strong hand found my moist one. He laced his fingers through mine, seeding more courage into me.

"Carter, can you tell us who's your date tonight?"

"Is she the woman you were pictured with a few weeks back?"

"Is your new song about her?"

Camera flashes.

"Carter, did you cheat on Savannah with this woman? What's her name?"

"Are you still in love with Savannah Prince?"

"Carter, are the rumors true? Have you—?"

More camera flashes.

My stomach churned, and I inhaled slowly as I blocked them out. This circus made me lightheaded, and I tightened my grip on Carter's hand, digging my fingernails into his flesh, certain I would draw blood. He didn't pull away and returned my squeeze.

He gazed at me, his eyes literally fucking me, as he

answered some of their questions. "She's my muse. She appeared in my life at the exact moment I needed to believe in magic again." The words flew naturally out of his mouth. They reminded me of the ones I'd spoken to Jack the first time we met. My heart did a cartwheel in my chest. The air came in and out of my lungs easier. Carter had my back. We were in this together, just like he promised.

"Let's focus on what really matters tonight. This foundation and how meaningful it is," he said, addressing the press. "Now, if you'll excuse us. I have a fundraiser to attend and a performance to prep for. All y'all have a great night." He dropped a soft kiss on my forehead, and Taylor cleared the way until we finally entered the venue, freed from the press attention, Ed tailing us from behind.

"Thanks," I whispered, rising on my tiptoes so Carter could hear me. He circled my waist with one hand, bringing me comfort. I came to a sudden stop, taking in the space around me. We were in the contemporary art museum hall, surrounded by gigantic pieces, framed on twenty-foot-tall walls. The room had been decorated with touches of black and gold. Fancy and chic. Servers passed appetizers and glasses of champagne around. Everybody was so elegant. I recognized Bradley Stevenson—the football player—two actors, and a rock star amongst the crowd. Tiny thrills pirouetted through my chest. This night already felt surreal, and we hadn't been here ten minutes.

People—lots of them—came to greet Carter. Hands were shaken. Smiles were offered. Air kisses were thrown. The room felt a hundred degrees warmer as more guests introduced themselves, and I resisted the urge to fan myself. An older woman wearing a faux-fur—or I hoped it was—silver shrug over a long lilac silk gown sauntered our way.

"Dear, your gown is exquisite," she said.

I thanked her with a heartfelt smile.

With his arm still around my waist and a soft curl on his lips, Carter handed me a glass of champagne. Our eyes fused for a few beats. "April, this is Judith Grayson. A music producer. Judith, this is April." A tall man with a beard tapped Carter on the shoulder, seeking his attention. I followed their interaction, but soon my gaze landed back on Mrs. Grayson.

"You two look absolutely ravishing together, my dear," the woman said in her strong English accent. "It's lovely to see Mr. Hills beaming tonight." She rested her frail hand on my forearm. "He's usually moody at these events and doesn't mingle." Closing the distance between us, she added, "Mr. Hills never smiles in public. Tonight, he's radiant—more like the Mr. Hills he is in private. Don't lose your magic touch, dear, it's precious."

Whoever this woman was, she seemed to know Carter well. Though I doubted I had anything to do with the change of attitude everyone kept talking about.

The woman patted my arm and left. Carter was still deep in conversation with the man. Taking a sip of my champagne, I surveyed my surroundings. A woman I vaguely recognized but couldn't put a name to the face was talking to a couple in their fifties. The man turned to address someone, and a loud gasp left my mouth. I strangled the glass in my hand, almost crushing it.

Too eager to fit in, I'd ignored the actual event tonight.

His wife's eyes snapped to mine.

Our gazes collided, and I stopped breathing.

My skin burned.

My stomach churned.

The column of my throat filled with acid.

This couldn't be happening. Was fate that cruel? From

across the room, we engaged in what I could only describe as a staring contest. I chugged half of my champagne in one gulp, hoping it'd dissolve the acerbic taste in my mouth. Feeling brave—or crazy—I forced a smile. They didn't return it. My chest tightened, my airways constricting, and my knees nearly gave out.

Since Travis's death, things had never been the same between us. They blamed me for how their son's life ended, never taking the time to understand his last wishes or to hear my side of the story.

In their state of grief, Travis's parents had preferred to alienate me than to be mad at their own blood. I got it. But it didn't hurt any less. Once upon a time, I had considered them family.

We used to have a great relationship. Not anymore. Travis pushed them away at the end. They never forgave him and shifted their wrath on me since I was the one still alive.

The Bensons and I hadn't talked since the funeral. Three years ago. Every detail was dealt with by our lawyers after that day.

I took no penny from Travis's family. Not a dime. After his death, once my relationship with his parents shattered, I sold our house and distanced myself from everything related to them. I moved to Ginger Creek with my best friend and never looked back.

"What's wrong, April?" Lost in the moment, I'd failed to notice Carter had come back to me. He gave me a quizzical stare.

I swallowed the lump in my throat. "Huh... I-I saw people I haven't seen in a long time. Never thought I'd ever see them again. Not...not here. Not now. They... huh... They belong to my past." A thread of air made its way to my lungs. I knitted my fingers through Carter's, using his hand as my anchor. "I-I'm fine." I blinked, not sure I believed my own words.

Carter dipped his head and skimmed his lips over mine, light as feathers. "You're pale. Are you sure you're all right?"

I nodded, managing a smile.

"I need to get ready. Will you be okay by yourself for a moment?"

I nodded again.

"Taylor will stay close if you need him."

Ice filled my veins. I wasn't okay, but how could I tell him? Carter brushed his knuckles along my jaw, and I shivered. We stared at each other for a beat before he followed Ed backstage.

For a second, I closed my eyes and took a cleansing breath before downing what was left of my champagne. Accepting a fresh glass from the server, I took in the crowd of rich and famous people surrounding me.

The space around me was vast with high ceilings, but right now it felt like I was a prisoner in a small box.

A tall brunette neared me. "Oh, it's you. I've been dying to meet you," she said, closing in from my right. I swiveled my head, and my eyes clashed with the onyx-brown irises of a siren—Savannah Prince.

Unlike Carter Hills, I would recognize her anywhere.

Probably around five feet ten, with long dark-brown hair, onyx-brown irises, and high cheekbones, she looked nothing less than fabulous.

We eyed each other for an endless minute. Beside her, I felt small. Not in personality, but in size. This woman had legs for days and generous curves in all the right places.

She pouted, her plump lips giving her a sexy and irresistible appearance, clearly not impressed or intimidated by my presence.

Savannah Prince crossed her arms beneath her large breasts, lifting them slightly, as if threatening to free them from the plunging V-neckline of her red gown. A fake smile was plastered on her full lips, and she studied me, disdain twisting across her face. "When I heard Carter was filling in for Sam Stevens tonight, I truly hoped he'd be stupid enough to bring you along. Guess he didn't grow brain cells lately, but it all plays in my favor since I get the opportunity to size you up myself."

Her gaze darkened, and she towered over me, leaning forward to whisper in my ear so no one around us could catch a word.

I tried to keep my face neutral. A foreign sensation tightened my insides so much that I wanted to curl up in a ball on the floor to ease the pain. I dug my fingernails into my thigh to avoid shaking. While keeping my smile intact, I savored the champagne, letting its bubbles dance on my tongue before slowly swallowing, acting as if Savannah's proximity wasn't affecting me. After everything Carter had confessed about their relationship, I knew I couldn't trust her. Anyway, she had evil written all over her plastic face. How could anybody be so blind to her manipulative ways? Tonight, she went straight for the jugular. She didn't lead me on. Savannah showed me her true colors right from the start.

There must have been a sweet side to her, hidden somewhere deep within. After all, Carter had liked her at some point.

The thought of them together burned through my chest, choking me with pain.

Her high-pitched voice stopped the panic unfurling inside me. "Carter will never be yours. Soon, he'll get tired of this little game you're both playing, and he'll come running back to me."

She gave me a slow once-over, her face scrunching up in disgust. I looked around, trying to catch Taylor's attention. In vain.

"Don't expect him to stick around, girl. You're so not his type. And you're too childish for him. Why are you even pretending to play grown-up for a night? Get real. You know you don't belong on the arm of a man like Carter Hills. He's like a rock star God, and you're just a… a…a horrible elf." Her shriek-like laughter resonated between us. "Carter found a distraction. Very soon, he'll get over it. Were you a cartoon character in a previous life? You're worth nothing in his world. Don't overestimate yourself, girl." She took a long sip of her champagne and offered me a smile that didn't reach her eyes. Looking satisfied. As if she'd complimented me instead of tearing me apart.

I snorted. "I'm not sure you should waste your precious time talking to me then. I bet there are more important people you gotta meet tonight. Don't you?"

"Oh, so you think you are a smart one. Duly noted."

Her fake laughter reminded me of a hyena and sent chills down my back, echoing the words Carter had spoken to me one night. *Everything about this woman is fake. Her laughter. Her orgasms. Not just her tits or her lips.*

Savannah sighed, examining her manicured nails as if I was boring her, before bringing her threatening gaze back to me. "The truth is, you are nothing. You are a worthless woman who tries to profit off a star like Carter to improve your social status. It's pathetic. Really. Look at you. Playing dress-up at an event you don't even belong to. All these celebrities around, they've been mocking you from the moment you walked you. They pity you. You're playing on the wrong field. I'm sure if you ask nicely, they can set a kiddo table for you in the corner. Where you won't be a nuisance. Maybe they can even scoop ice cream for your dessert if you eat all your veggies or you bat those unimpressive eyelashes."

Was she for real?

"Oh, nobody taught you how to speak when you were little? Poor little elf, pretending to belong to a crowd who couldn't care less about her pathetic existence."

My lips parted, but no words slipped out. I blinked instead, not sure whether Savannah Prince was kidding or not right now. Her words sounded like a rehearsed joke, and I couldn't form a reply in my head, too stunned by her accusations.

Did Savannah possess a sixth sense? I had to wonder. Even though I knew she couldn't possibly know about my childhood and my parents, her hurtful words had hit close to home.

Usually, I would've had a retort ready and would defend my honor and my character. But this wasn't my world, and I had no intention of creating a scene here.

"Want a free advice? Close your mouth. You look like a stupid fish when you move your lips but don't say anything. It's disturbing. Yep. The more I look at you, the more I feel sorry for you." She huffed. "There's a burger place down the street if you're hungry later and you want to stuff your face. Since you're not a size zero, you must often eat your weight in junk food, right? I sympathize with you. Being the outcast must not be fun. I'll make sure to tell Carter it wasn't cool to lead you on." Her lips swelled into an exaggerated pout. "I'm sure he didn't mean to, but still, the guy can be heartless sometimes. It's best you're aware now rather than later. If you want to make a quick escape, I'll cover for you and inform him you bailed. Girls sticking together and shit."

"Sorry to disappoint you, but I'm not going anywhere."

I inhaled and prayed my voice wouldn't shake when I asked, "Are you done?"

Savannah admired her manicure for a long moment. "Yeah. I think I said it all. I hate being direct and saying things as they are. Sometimes, the truth is better left unsaid. But you? You deserve a reality check. You're honestly pathetic—it's almost embarrassing. Someone has to to tell you the truth, because otherwise, you'll keep pretending your existence actually matters. You are being played, girlie. Once you calm down, you'll thank me for saving you from a very hurtful relationship and preserving your reputation." She turned to leave but seemed to think better. "One last advice. Whatever you do, don't mess with *my* man, or you'll be sorry," she warned between clenched teeth. "Carter and I, we're the real deal. Never forget that. He's mine."

I lifted my chin up and stared into her eyes. "Savannah, I'm sorry you're so insecure around me that you feel threatened by my presence. I hope you're having a great night, nonetheless. Now, excuse me. I won't stay here and give you the chance to insult me further. I heard you loud and clear, but it doesn't mean I have to agree and let you give me shit for another second. Girls sticking together and shit? In your dreams." *Take that, bitch.* I sidestepped on wobbly legs, spun on my heel, and sashayed away, my heart jackhammering in my chest and my breath idling in my lungs. The back of my eyes burned from unshed tears threatening to spill out and ruin my makeup.

...I still feel your lips on mine
Even after all this time
Babe, you're it, yes, you're it
Now all I want is to make you
mine...

Amid my confrontation with Savannah Prince, I hadn't noticed Carter taking the stage.

And he was singing *my* song.

I cupped my pounding heart with a hand. *My* song. Not Savannah's.

I'd missed his performance because his ex-girlfriend chose this time to stalk me.

Fisting my silver feather dress to lift it off the floor, I ran away, all my insecurities taking center stage in my mind.

And tears spilling down my face.

29

CARTER

I walked onstage with my guitar in hand and took a seat on the lone stool in the middle. I adjusted the height of the microphone and cleared my throat.

The presenter spoke a few words to the crowd, then slipped away as cheers and applause erupted around me. I barely registered any of them.

My eyes searched for the woman wearing the feathery silver dress. My eyes worked hard to spot her, as all the people in front of the stage were blanketed in shadows due to the lighting. I chose to sing her song tonight, and I hadn't told her, wanting to surprise her.

After the show in Nashville last weekend, someone posted a video of it online, and it became so viral that I planned to record an acoustic version of it and make it my new single. Would April agree to be on the cover with me? I was imagining something simple and romantic, where our faces weren't even in the frame.

As if I was wired to find her amongst a group of people, my gaze finally landed on her. Discussing something with—wait, what the fuck—Savannah Prince.

All the air left my lungs, and I coughed. Some guy, dressed in a black tuxedo and sporting stretched earlobes, brought me a bottle of water."Thanks," I said, my voice croaky, before taking a sip.

My gaze returned to the nightmare playing in front of me. Why didn't I bring April backstage? Oh yeah, I wanted to surprise her. Damn it. How could I forget about Savannah being here tonight? The sight of her sent a wave of nausea up my throat. It burned like fire. Blazing-hot red fire. The devil always left a path of destruction in her wake. Savannah would do anything to destroy April if she put her mind to it. Shaming people was second nature to her. Another thing I'd learned the hard way. She fought with no rules, bullied with no shame, and manipulated with no conscience. One day, she told a pregnant assistant on a photoshoot to lose a dozen pounds because, according to her standards, she "looked fat." Yeah. Total shaming bitch.

Her toxic energy was palpable, reaching me even from where I sat on the stage. Pearls of sweat bloomed on my nape. April's eyes darted around the room, looking for a way out. *Where was Taylor?* He was supposed to watch over her. All. The. Fucking. Time. The room closed in on me. *Breathe in. Breathe out.* I couldn't risk a panic attack here. My racing thoughts swirled around in my head at a dizzying pace.

I hadn't prepared April enough for a face-off with Satan and her weapon of choice—poison and hatred. I scratched my forehead with my thumb.

My fingers strummed the first chords of "Pink and Country," but I sang with no conviction, my eyes glued to the two women facing each other. At this rate, my heart would stop by the end of the song, and they'd have to take me out on a stretcher.

April's face flushed, and Savannah's eyes bulged out of their sockets as she let what looked like venom—and probably tasted like venom too—out of her mouth. I'd been subjected to her spite too many times to keep count. The gleam in her eye didn't lie. I'd recognize the devilish spark anywhere. The pressure in my larynx strangled me.

Savannah had said the most awful things to me during our time together. The small scar on the side of my skull, a reminder of our time together, tingled.

> **... You are the sunshine in my**
> **storms**
> **You color my night sky**
> **You are the star I wish upon**
> **every night...**

The verses flew out of my mouth, and I closed my eyes, trying to calm the agitation raging inside me and the shakiness of my fingers. My only wish was to scrape the lining of my throat. It was itchy and dry, as arid as the desert.

"Pink and Country" was one of the most emotional songs I'd written in a long time. April had inspired every word of it. In a cruel twist of fate, she was the one not paying me any attention as I was singing her song. Tonight, the words tasted sour on my tongue.

A turmoil arose inside me as my gaze stayed fixed on my woman facing the female version of Lucifer.

Two years ago, the damaged side of me believed Savannah Prince was the best I could do. My eyes burned, tears blurring my vision. Icicles lodged in my lungs. I shuddered a breath out. I feared April's encounter with my ex would dampen the fire burning strong inside her. She was my strength. Each time she smiled at me, it kept erasing fragments of the hell I'd been living in for the last six years.

...You're my compass
My muse and my other half
Babe, I'll never let you go
This is my promise to you...

I strummed the final chords and exhaled a shaky breath. "Thank you, all y'all. Be generous tonight." I sprang to my feet and scurried offstage, a bad feeling crippling me. The applause rang around me, but I didn't hear it.

April had stormed away a minute ago.

I saw her leaving, desperation etched in her stride. I had witnessed the entire altercation. The tightness around my heart grew, splinters of wrath and guilt piercing through it.

April's leaving was a punch in the gut. If I hurried, I'd catch up with her and maybe save the night.

Were Riley and June right about April not being ready yet to enter my world? Would tonight leave her with such a bitter aftertaste that she'd run away on Sunday without looking back? Unable to process the possibility, I buried my face in my hands and inhaled deeply.

The thought of her leaving was enough to shatter my heart into a million pieces. I doubted meeting someone who felt like the extension of yourself occurred twice in a lifetime.

Something powerful brewed between us. Something unique and exciting. And I really wanted to see where it would take us.

Ed pressed his big hand to my shoulder when I passed him backstage. The guy with the stretched earlobes grabbed my guitar, and my bodyguard leaned closer.

"Taylor is watching her, Carter. She's fine. Come with me."

Ed parted the crowd, and I followed in his six-foot-seven-giant-self footsteps. Taylor and Ed had been my security detail for the last five years, and I considered them my friends. They'd traveled the globe multiple times by my side. They'd witnessed my best moments and also my worst.

I trusted them with my life. And trusted them to take care of April too. But tonight, Taylor had failed. Anger carved my chest, but I managed to keep it under control. Now wasn't the time to let my fury slip out.

My chief of security neared me as I entered a small room adjacent to the staff's break room. Self-loathing swam in his dark eyes. "I'm sorry, Carter. I was helping with a situation back there. I was only gone for two minutes. This won't happen again." His throat bobbed.

I breathed out and calmed down.

When I spoke, I weighed each word. "Never let her out of your sight ever again." My tone was sharper than I intended. I unclenched my fists. "It's okay, man. I'll deal with this. Just make sure the Queen Bitch stays away from us." Taylor nodded and stepped back next to Ed, giving April and me a little privacy.

My girl sat on a wooden crate, her dress meticulously splayed out around her. She treated everything in her life with so much love and care. Me included.

I gripped my pant legs, loosening them over my thighs, allowing me to kneel beside her. April lifted her chin, and I lowered myself to align our gazes.

"Hey."

She blinked, fighting to hold back the unshed tears, her eyes red and glossy. "I…I missed my song."

I curled a hand around her neck and pulled her to my chest. To my heart. "I'll sing it a thousand times more just for you. Don't believe a word Savannah said.

She's an envious woman. An opportunist. She dated me for fame. Behind closed doors, she wanted nothing to do with me. She thought I'd be her puppet. Her ticket to stardom or something. I despise everything about her. I want to be with you, April. No one else. I wish you could see yourself through my eyes and realize how wonderful you are." I tipped her chin up with my forefinger. "You're the only woman I want to spend my nights with. You're the only woman I want to hold in my arms all the time. You're the only woman who challenges me, who makes me want to be better, who makes my heart beat faster. You're the only woman I've ever cuddled with for hours."

She closed her eyes and hung her head low.

"April, you're incredible. Do you know how lucky I am? We're good together. Fuck this circus. If you want to leave, just say the word. I'll follow you to the end of the world if I have to. We can go and have dinner somewhere else. Or go on a proper date. Or order room service."

She stayed silent for a minute. A long, never-ending, fat minute. "Carter, do you mean everything you just said?"

I inhaled, and all my doubts left me. "All of it. And more."

She sighed, and a shy smile peeked through her tears. "You were right. Savannah Prince is evil."

"She used to say awful things to me. She's psycho. I'm sorry Taylor wasn't around like he was supposed to be. I don't want anything to do with her. Never again. I want *you.*"

"I want you too." Her voice sounded like a low whisper.

"Does that mean you'll stay in Green Mountain with me?"

"I'm not sure if I should…" New tears filled her eyes.

"What's wrong?" My heart floundered in my chest, and a quiver shook me from head to toe.

She patted the skin around her eyes with her fingers, then looked at her fingertips. "Oh no. My makeup," she exclaimed, her laughter a high-pitched sound beneath her sobs.

"Talk to me."

Her lower lip quivered. "I'm damaged, Carter. You shouldn't want to be with me." I cradled her face, leveling our eyes, as she continued speaking. "You should push me away now before we get too deep into this."

"What are you talking about?" I sat down next to her, my legs stretched in front of me. I loosened the bowtie around my neck and lifted April up and pulled her onto my lap, the need to comfort her stronger than ever. "I see you, Fairy. All of you. There's nothing broken about you."

She's perfect the way she is. Why would she want me to push her away?

"Except for my friend Saunders, everybody I've ever cared for in my life has always ditched me…"

I raised a brow, waiting for her to explain further.

"I'm alone in this world, Carter. I have no family. People always leave me. There's something wrong about me, but I haven't figured out what it is yet." She shrugged. "I've learned to accept it. It's like I was born with this curse, and I'm clueless about how to break it." She fidgeted with the gold band on her right ring finger.

"You're not cursed. Don't push me away because you're afraid I'll leave you too. It's not going to happen. Don't let whatever Savannah said fuck with your mind. I'm not going away. Give us a chance." I cleared my throat, swallowing my emotions down. "Think about it. Please."

April nodded, her gaze still fixed downward.

I brushed her tears away with my thumbs. Her eyes

found mine, and I saw fear and doubts swimming in them. I also saw strength and hope. I pressed a gentle kiss to her pink-painted lips.

"We'll work through this together, okay? I'm damaged too." I shrugged. "Maybe we can be damaged together."

"I'd like that." Her voice sounded so small.

"Do you want to leave?"

She shook her head, drying off the last of her tears.

"Then let's freshen up. You have mascara smudges under your eyes."

She laughed, and I joined in. Her laughter, the most marvelous sound I'd ever heard, fixed another piece of my broken heart.

"There are a few more people I want you to meet." I stood and stretched out my hand, inviting her to take it. *I'll never let her go.* I knew nothing about love, but this I was sure of. April Simmons belonged with me.

Flutters invaded my stomach at the possibility she'd stay in Green Mountain with me. For weeks. Months. Or maybe forever.

When we argued in the woods a month ago, April woke up something in me that I thought was dead. She breathed life back into the part of me that had lost hope. She colored my heart and freed it of the shackles I'd put around it many years ago. It was in the way she looked at me. Proud, fierce, and fearless. In the way she smiled. Or was it in the way she kissed me?

When she befriended Jack, it looked like it was the most natural thing for her to do, and the simple action appealed to every part of me. She took the time to answer his questions and engage with him. The fact that she cared meant a lot to me.

Without even trying, April was giving my existence a breath of fresh air. A new start. A meaning.

She had pulled me out of the dark cave I'd spent years buried in.

I never wanted to go back down there. I hated the darkness, and I feared a world she wouldn't be part of.

Stay with me, please. Don't ever leave me.

I intertwined my fingers with hers and led her away.

30

APRIL

S avannah Prince exited the stall just as I finished
retouching my makeup in the restroom of the
museum. Betty was an angel sent on Earth when
she gifted me this little makeup case for tonight. "Just in
case," she had said. Well, she was my hero right now. I
smiled at my reflection as I smacked my freshly painted lips
together. All traces of the mess on my face had been
erased. Savannah neared me and gave me one of her
poisonous smirks. I kept my gaze on the mirror and rolled
my eyes, making no effort to hide my annoyance at her. I
wouldn't storm out and give her the satisfaction she was
looking for. Savannah had nothing on me. I wasn't afraid
of her. No. I'd never give her any power over me. She
didn't have to know my heart was racing in my chest. She
didn't have to know my hands were clammy, or that it took
all my self-control to keep my breathing steady. I knew
she'd lash out—that was what she did best. This time, I'd
just ignore whatever she did or said.

"Poor little elf. You're still here? I thought you left a
long time ago. Well, I guess you couldn't pass up a two-

thousand-dollar meal, could you?" She whistled. "You're a pathetic woman. You're Carter Hills's charity case."

Was the shrill sound coming from her mouth a laugh? Chills ran through me. Was this poor insult her only weapon? I could work with that. My entire body relaxed, and I tipped my chin up. Forcing a fake smile and wrinkling my nose, I gave her my best resting-bitch face as Saunders called it.

"Don't waste your breath on me, Savannah. I'm sorry for you because you feel threatened by an elf. Who's pathetic now?" I smiled—an extra-large one for good measure—and exited the room without another glance her way. If only I could high-five myself. No way would Savannah Prince get the last word in. *Take that, Miss Hollywood.*

With his back pressed against the wall, Carter was waiting for me. He looked good enough to eat, and my ovaries practically danced with joy when he grinned and slung his arm around my waist as I joined him. His warmth shot right through me. Our eyes locked, and he cocked a brow. "What's this smile about?"

"I'm happy to see you."

His eyebrows drew together, and I rose onto my tiptoes to brush my lips against his. "Okay then."

Savannah walked out of the ladies' room at the same time. Carter's eyes ping-ponged between the two of us. His shoulders tensed, and he clenched his jaw, his hands balled into fists at his sides.

I put a hand on his forearm. "Don't sweat it. She's not worth our time."

His eyes followed his ex-girlfriend as she disappeared around the corner.

"We exchanged a few words," I said. "She'll stay away."

Carter's eyes cleared, and he laced his fingers through mine. Every bit of tension in me evaporated. His shoulders sagged with relief. "We'll talk about it later."

I nodded. Everything was good. A sense of peace flowed in my veins. Carter was right. We could work through our heartbreaks. Together. He led the way, never releasing my hand. Heat bloomed in my stomach. Carter Hills owned the secret code to the door of my soul, and right now, I thanked the universe for putting him on my path.

After an exquisite five-course dinner—I never knew a salad could be that fancy—Carter and I were standing by the stage, chatting with a sports agent who'd just signed the latest basketball superstar when Mr. and Mrs. Benson neared us. I sucked in a shaky breath, my chest aching as if it would split apart. Every ounce of tension returned to my back. As if dealing with Savannah Prince—twice—wasn't enough for one night. The Bensons exchanged a few polite words with Carter. Wait. They knew one another? How much smaller could the world get? My throat closed, and I swallowed the bile back down.

I busied myself with the wineglass in my hand, twirling the liquid around. However, the heat of Mr. and Mrs. Benson's stares made it impossible for me to ignore them. It burned holes in my skin.

The Bensons attended so many fundraisers I should have considered they might be here. Was I so consumed by this relationship that I had missed all the signs? Inside, I cringed, not sure how to act. All of us being here was a nightmare.

"April dear, how are you doing?" Mrs. Benson asked, breaking the awkward silence thickening the air, inching closer to me.

My mouth twitched into a tight-lipped smile, a mass

now blocking my airways. I dug my fingernails into Carter's arm through the fabric of his tuxedo.

Mrs. Benson leaned in, and we air-kissed. She squeezed my forearm with her pale hand. Wearing a long champagne silk gown, with her sandy-blonde hair tied in a low bun, she looked as beautiful as I remembered.

"You all know one another?" Carter asked, rubbing the back of his neck, confusion swirling in his gaze. His eyes captured mine, waiting for me to explain.

"How do you know Mr. and Mrs. Benson?" I asked, trying to move the conversation away from me. I drank my wine, pretending as if nothing was bothering me. In vain. Inside, I was coiled tight, and cold sweat beaded on my nape.

"I've performed at their fundraisers before. Didn't you know they were the hosts tonight?"

I placed my hand over my mouth to avoid spitting my drink.

Ice replaced the blood in my veins. How much worse could it get? Was tonight's fundraiser part of the foundation they'd started after Travis got sick? Ohmygod, I felt stupid for being so clueless.

Carter grazed the side of my face with his knuckles, expecting me to speak. I sucked in a shaky breath. I could feel the weight of his gaze all over my face. When I met his eyes, something resembling worry passed through his irises. "April?"

Mr. Benson jumped in. "We've known April for a long time, Mr. Hills. April is…was…" Even he had a hard time defining what we had been to one another.

"Right. I…I dated their son back in college." I hoped my simple explanation would help put all of us at ease. No need to get into the details of our complicated relationship tonight. My thundering heartbeat echoed in my head. I rubbed my chest with the heel of my hand, trying to ease the ache lodged there. Could this conversation be over already?

Mrs. Benson mouthed a *Thank you* my way, and I nodded. There wasn't a single good reason to dig up the past here and now. Tonight was about the charity, not our personal disagreement.

"How do you know Mr. Hills, dear?" Mrs. Benson asked.

My cheeks heated up, the question putting us on the spot.

The Bensons must have noticed my queasiness because Travis's dad added, "April, it happened a long time ago. We were wrong to blame it all on you. We're sorry it took us so many years to come to terms with the reality of everything."

Tears stung the back of my eyes. I drew in a shaky breath, determined not to cry. I'd already shed enough tears tonight. For years, I had waited to hear those words come from their lips. To ease the pang of guilt I still felt sometimes. It was too little, too late. But maybe accepting his words—the closure I had prayed for on countless sleepless nights, when I felt trapped by a crime I had no part in —would help put the aftermath of the whole tragedy behind us.

As if he could sense my distress, Carter wound an arm around me, tugging me just a little closer—enough to bolster my fading strength. I relaxed against him. He had my back. He had promised he would and had already proven so tonight after the Savannah episode.

Travis's parents exchanged a subtle glance. Yeah, I noticed the silent question that passed between them.

With deep wrinkles around her mouth and a permanent sadness etched in her eyes, Mrs. Benson had aged two decades in the last couple of years. She stepped forward and grabbed my hands, and I felt the tremor in hers.

"April, I know it's a long shot, but we'd really like you to come over for dinner sometime. Donald and I have been wanting to reach out to you for quite some time, but we weren't sure how. Or if you would hear us out. Maybe, tonight, fate is giving us a chance to make things right again."

I blinked, unsure if I'd heard her right. A protest formed in my mind, but she went on before I could say anything.

"Don't answer now. Think about it. That day, we lost both of you. You were our family too. We've never forgiven ourselves for how we treated you. We hope one day you'll give us a chance to make amends."

I pinched my lips together in an attempt to keep my emotions in check.

Mrs. Benson squeezed my hands between hers and led her husband away. I clamped my jaw shut, unable to form words.

I needed a replay. *What the hell just happened?*

Carter swiveled to face me. "You all right?"

Speechless, I nodded, my mind racing.

"What was that about? What did they do to you?" he asked, a worrisome expression flashing in his gray irises.

I blinked, still trying to calm the emotional cataclysm raging within me. "Huh…long story. I-I'm not sure reconnecting with them is a good idea. Don't worry. I'll…I'll tell you all about it some other time." I gave his hand a small squeeze. "Let's put our pasts behind us for a couple of hours and enjoy tonight. Besides, I have the most handsome date, and I want to savor every second by his side. If I'm granted only one Cinderella night, I want to make the most of it."

"Then follow me, Fairy, you're about to meet Ron Presley."

My eyes flared, and Carter stifled an amused chuckle as I blurted, "The producer?"

"The one and only. We're friends. Come on." He knitted our fingers together and led the way. Despite trying to keep that part of my life under lock and key, my mind wandered to my past. The one I'd been wishing so hard to put behind me once and for all when I moved to Green Mountain.

———

Stuart University - Junior year

"We should cancel. Or fly far away from here. What do you think? You and me. All alone for a week. Hawaii? Could be fun. Bora Bora? Fiji? Whichever. As long as you're with me." Travis tickled me. "C'mon, April, pick a destination. Somewhere warm and sunny so I can ogle you in a tiny bikini."

"We're not running away. Not during the holidays. Your mom has been calling me nonstop for the last month to make sure we'd show up. I promised her we'd even sleep over. You should've heard her, Travis. She sounded excited."

"My mother, excited? You talked to the wrong lady, baby. My mother doesn't do excited. She doesn't show emotions. A refrigerator is more expressive than her. Are you sure we're talking about the same woman?"

I elbowed him. Travis raised my tank top to expose my midsection, kissing and teasing the flesh of my stomach with his mouth while lying beside me on our bed. I combed his blond hair with my fingers.

"I'm telling you. After we missed Thanksgiving, she fears we won't show up at all for Christmas. I missed all the family traditions

growing up. This year, I even bought matching pajamas for us. It'll be fun."

He sighed.

"Where's your Christmas spirit?"

Travis pressed a trail of kisses on my bare skin. "I know how much it means to you. The thing is, I want you all to myself. Sharing is not my thing. I'm a selfish prick when it comes to you."

With a firm grip, I pulled at his shirt until he leaned closer and our lips met. "I'm here, and I won't go anywhere because I can't imagine my life without you."

He peeled my top over my head and brushed my skin, his hands sending shivers all along my spine. "April, we're destined to be together. There's no one else for me out there. I wish we could stop time and stay in this moment forever. I love you."

My eyes glazed over at his words. My boyfriend wiped the tears off my cheeks with his thumb. Our mouths fused, and I forgot everything else. Only he existed in this instant. Only us.

"I love you too, Travis. You're the other shoe I didn't realize I was missing until I found it. Or rather until you found me."

"How romantic of you, baby." He snickered.

I pushed his chest back with both hands in a teasing manner. "You know what I mean. Growing up, I pictured the man of my dreams a million times but never thought I'd meet him someday. It all seems like a dream." I ran my fingertips over his back muscles.

He gripped the hem of his shirt and raised it over his head before throwing it on the floor. He deepened our kiss and rolled me over him. With my hand holding my long blonde hair over one shoulder, I peppered kisses all over his tanned skin.

"You know that house we put an offer on last week?"

I nodded, never lifting my mouth from his chest.

"We got it. They called this morning while you were in class. We'll be able to move in by the end of next semester."

My head sprang upward. "You're kidding?"

The grin he flashed my way lit up his entire face. Stars shone in his eyes. "No, baby. We're officially homeowners."

I crashed my mouth on his, and we kissed until my lips felt sore and he stole every molecule of air from me, burying himself inside me as we screamed each other's names when we came undone together.

Once we landed back on Earth, excitement bubbled up inside me. "I can't wait to tear down the wall between the kitchen and the living room." Nana would be proud I'd put some of the life insurance money I inherited to good use.

"I can't wait to fill all the bedrooms with little blonde babies running around."

I shoved him in the chest, laughing. "Don't get in over your head, Travis Benson. We're twenty. Give us a couple of years."

"The more we wait, the more babies we'll have."

"Is this a threat?"

"No. A promise." His hands found my waist again, and he dug his fingers into my flesh, tickling me until I surrendered.

"Okay, fine. Let's fix the house first, then we'll talk about this plan of yours. Can we at least wait until we both have jobs? Like real jobs?"

"Oh. That means you won't work as a clerk at the library forever? I kind of dig the whole sexy librarian look."

"No, sorry to ruin your fantasy."

"Fine, we'll get grown-up jobs. In the meantime, let's practice some more. To be ready when the day to have babies comes."

We spent the rest of the afternoon in bed. One orgasm turning into many. Later, Travis stepped out of the shower of our small apartment with a towel wrapped around his waist.

I tugged at the corner of the fabric and exposed him. "Oops." I put my hand over my mouth and widened my eyes, feigning surprise. "I think I might need another lesson. I forgot what we did last. You know that new trick we tried."

My boyfriend quirked an eyebrow, but his body betrayed how much he loved the idea of giving me another private session, the hard part of him pushing against my thigh. "You forgot? Really?"

"Mm-hmm. You wouldn't want me to be redshirted, would you?"

"Not if we want this plan of ours to unfold perfectly. I'll be the bigger man here and make sure you remember every single detail of this lesson. I'll even give you a free pass. You may try it some other time at no charge if, for whatever reason, you need to perfect those skills some more after today."

Dressed in a pair of skinny jeans and a baby-pink top with ruffles, I applied gold eyeshadow as I waited for Travis to get dressed. Drenched in sweat after our little rematch, we ended up taking another shower. My boyfriend walked into the room, his hair disheveled and a smirk plastered on his face.

"We're meeting Saunders and company tonight at the karaoke bar near campus. Let's have dinner somewhere before. To celebrate."

"I'd go anywhere with you, April. Hawaii. Bora Bora—"

I shut him up with a kiss. "You're impossible."

Our gazes met, and all the love pouring out from his eyes filled my heart.

Travis brushed strands of my hair off my forehead. I shivered at the slight gesture. "Fine. We'll go on this trip on our honeymoon instead."

"Honeymoon?"

"I'll want to marry you before having a bunch of babies with you, my love," he said matter-of-factly.

I burst out laughing. "You'd better." With my arms looped around his neck, we kissed some more.

Travis leaned back, and all traces of playfulness in his eyes disappeared. "I have a feeling our time together has an expiration date. I don't know. It has been nagging me for a few weeks."

"What do you mean?"

"I'm not sure. Like somehow, it's too incredible to last."

"Don't be silly. You said it yourself—we're it. We're just lucky we found each other early in life. I'm all in."

He sighed. "I hope you're right. I love you. I can't wait for the house to be ours. And the babies to pop out." He was half-joking. Maybe. Or not. "The guys keep telling me we're too young to commit, but it feels right."

His lips found mine again, and I forgot all about the rest of the world as he took me to heaven.

We never thought that Christmas would be the last one we'd celebrate together.

Nine months later

In our room, our bodies entwined, I rested my head on my boyfriend's chest, listening to his labored breathing.

"Travis, I want to get pregnant. I thought about it." His energy levels had dropped significantly in the last month. He turned his head to look at me, the twinkle in his eyes reminding me he was still in there. The disease hadn't taken him away from me just yet. He'd lost weight, and his previously muscular body was now thinner and paler, his cheeks hollow and his arms skinny.

"No. I can't stand the idea of your having to raise a child on your own. It wouldn't be fair."

"None of this is fair," I said, motioning around us with my hand. I struggled to keep the tears at bay. "I want your child growing inside me to remind me of you. Of our love. Knowing we made this tiny human being together. That our bond is stronger than this disease drawing us apart forever. I can't fathom the idea of your disappearing forever without leaving some sort of legacy behind."

"I'm not leaving you desolated. You'll always have me, April. In your heart. I'll forever be there. It doesn't sound like much right now, but someday you'll understand we were only meant to pass through each other's lives. I'm not your happily-ever-after…but you are mine."

Tears prickled at the corners of my eyes.

"You're young, baby. You'll meet somebody. Someday. Someone

who will love you as much as I do. And you'll have a family of your own. Don't add extra challenges to your life because you're sad."

"What if I can't live on my own?"

Travis's arms squeezed me harder.

"Don't abandon me. I can't live knowing everyone I care about leaves me. My parents, Nana…you. What's the point if I always end up alone and miserable?" I asked, the stream down my face unstoppable.

"You have your entire life to live, baby. It's not your time. Mine has come to an end. The ride has been shorter than I expected." His chapped lips met with my forehead. "Please live your life to the fullest. Enjoy the sunrise in the morning. Go to the beach. Dance in the rain. Smile at strangers. Be fearless. You deserve to be happy. Because you've made me a lucky man."

I sniffled. I often refrained from crying in front of him.

"We should get married, though. I want to leave this world knowing you have been mine up to the end."

"For real?"

My boyfriend nodded, and his body trembled as he exhaled.

"I'd like that. Very much. I do want to be your wife." My sad tears transformed into happy ones.

Travis propped himself up on his elbows, and with a trembling hand, he grabbed something from the nightstand of the bedroom we never got to repaint or update. Then he rose to his feet slowly as if his body could shatter any second, dropped to one knee, and opened a velvet box, presenting me with two gold wedding bands. "April Simmons, would you do me the honor of becoming my wife, to have and to hold, until death do us part?"

I cupped my mouth with both hands. "I will."

Our lips fused together.

"I want us to elope. Vegas. You and me."

"What about your parents?"

"They won't understand. I've made my peace with it. I want it to be just the two of us." He wiped off the tears streaming down my

cheeks with his thumbs. "And let's get one of those hotel rooms with a garden view or something. Not the Strip. It might not be Fiji or Hawaii, but that's the best I can do right now."

I nodded with a smile. "Let's do this. It's more than enough for me. It'll be perfect. I love you so much." We kissed, and for a moment, I forgot this was the beginning of the end for us.

———

As memories of Travis and me faded away, I made up my mind. I would stay with Carter in Green Mountain for a little longer. Travis's last words replayed in my head. *Promise me you'll never stop chasing love.* I owed it to myself to give my relationship with HN a try. Never would I have thought caring about two men just as much was possible, but here was life, proving me all wrong.

Carter Hills had stolen my heart, making it whole again. He had filled it with passion and hope.

As if it was being summoned, my heart quivered. The realization that I loved him, no matter how crazy it sounded, left me breathless. And both excited and scared. Yes, I was in love with Carter Hills, even though I had a hard time wrapping my head around the fact.

A small smile tugged at my lips. Maybe Travis had been right, and life was offering me a second chance at love after all.

31

CARTER

After the episode with Savannah, April and I avoided my ex for the rest of the night, enjoying the moment instead of worrying about the past and her actions.

"It's nice seeing you here tonight," Charles Woolsey, a music producer I had worked with in the past and a friend of Riley, told me when I went to the bar to grab some water for April. "I'm happy you found great company in Ms. Simmons, Carter. She's smart and funny, and from the conversation we've had, she can hold her own in any situation."

My lips twitched at his words. "Yes, that's a pretty accurate observation. She's one of a kind."

He clinked his glass to mine. "I'm happy for you, Carter. You deserve it. I can tell she's good for you."

I nodded. "Thanks, Chuck."

He left, and my attention zoned in on the woman in the pearl-gray gown, talking with an Olympic gold-medalist snowboarder, Taylor standing close and watching over her. Yes, Chuck was right, I deserved the happiness her presence brought into my life.

She threw her head back, laughing at something the guy said, and I became a predator at the glimpse of her long, exposed neck.

With her drink in hand, I weaved through the dissipating crowd, exchanging smiles and nods with people I'd met before, the need to be with her growing inside me. "Ready to get out of here?" I asked her after the guy, whose face I recognized but not the name, excused himself.

"Yes. If you are too."

I ran a hand through my hair. "I'm done. Enough mingling for a night. I wanna be with you now. Just us."

"I love this plan."

I threaded my fingers through hers. "Come on then. I have an idea. Something I like to do whenever I'm in town at night and need both a dose of energy and a way to relax after a long day."

With our bodies entwined in the backseat of the rental, we admired the city for the next hour, soaking in downtown Manhattan's energy while Taylor drove around aimlessly. All those lights, the people roaming on the sidewalks, the traffic, no other place vibrated like New York City at this time of the day. I combed my fingers through April's hair as her cheek rested against my chest, her hand tucked in mine. Even something as simple as a car ride felt right with her.

"Carter?" Her low voice pulled me from my contemplations.

"Yeah."

"I've been thinking… What if I stayed in Green Mountain for another two weeks?" She shifted so we could face each other.

"Two weeks? You serious?"

"Yes. I'm not ready to go home, but I'm afraid the longer I stay in Green Mountain, the harder it will be for me to walk away afterward." She remained silent for a minute. "I'm not looking to get my heart broken, but I hate the idea of our relationship having an expiration date." Something dark passed through her eyes. Hurt? Sadness? Fear? I couldn't tell. "I'd like for us to have more time to see where this could go. To know if we're compatible long-term or if it's just the honeymoon phase and it'll implode eventually because it's too good to be true."

I brushed her cheek with my thumb. "There's no expiration date, April. And it's real. We are real and what we share is real too. Stay forever if you want to. I told you a while back I don't want us to be a fling. I want us to be together. To call you my girl, to hold your hand, and kiss you whenever and wherever I feel like it. I want to have you in my bed every night and wrap my arms around you until the morning. And I want to come home to you at the end of each day. Let's see where this thing between us goes." I inhaled until my lungs twitched. "I want us to give it a real chance. Believe me. For the longest time, I thought I should forfeit the idea of love...or a relationship. I never thought I'd say these words to someone someday. You're the first, April."

"Let's start with two weeks because, at some point, I will have to go back to Georgia and deal with stuff. But after that, perhaps we could find a way to work things out and extend my stay if you're not tired of me by then." She offered me a timid smile, but her irises betrayed the lust banking low in her eyes.

"Never. I'll never grow tired of us. Of you."

My lips found hers, and I lost myself in the kiss. I leaned back with a sigh, knowing I had fourteen more days to help her get used to my world. It wasn't only defined by gossip and a crazy ex-girlfriend. It had a lot of perks too. She needed to realize that.

"Thank you. For giving us a chance."

"I'm glad we're doing this." She resumed her previous position, her cheek pressed against my chest, and my fingers returned to her hair. "Thanks for inviting me tonight. I wouldn't want to be in New York City with anyone else."

Exhausted and surfing some sort of high at the idea we had more time together, we asked Taylor to drive us back to our hotel room. After we showered, April and I slipped under the covers, cuddling until we both fell asleep. I relished the feeling of her heartbeat against mine. With her in my arms, my life finally made sense again, and I prayed it would never end.

———

On my back with an arm folded under my head and my gaze focused on the ceiling of our suite, my heart burst with millions of emotions. April was snoring lightly, her body sprawled over mine. Pink strands of hair tickled my nostrils every time I inhaled, but I stayed still, afraid to wake her up if I moved.

I had pushed our flight back to Green Mountain for the following morning and asked June to make a reservation for dinner in one of Manhattan's best upper-class restaurants for tonight.

The waiting list was months long, but when your name was Carter Hills, you could ask for favors about anywhere without having to wait for it. I rarely used my name to obtain privileges, but this time was different. I was in New York City with the woman I could imagine a future with.

The morning light filtered through the crack in the

curtains. Fairy shifted in my arms and popped open her eyes, one at a time. Her tousled hair looked like a bird's nest on the side of her head, and she had mascara stains under her eyes. My lips curled up, and I pressed a kiss to her mouth. "Good morning." My body reacted to her closeness like it always did. I held her close, letting her feel how bad I was gone for her.

Her loud moan resonated through the bedroom. "Shower sex?"

My entire self vibrated at the sound of her husky morning voice. Without a word, I nodded, scooped her into my arms, and rushed us to the bathroom. April wrapped her legs around me, laughing. Soon we lost ourselves in each other under the hot stream, making the most of our shower.

After a quick breakfast, we bundled up and strolled through Central Park, enjoying the crisp air and the anonymity wearing winter clothes gave us. Nothing like a puffer jacket, a beanie, and a scarf to mix with the masses without being pointed at.

April watched me with expectant eyes. She looked adorable with reddened cheeks and the endearing smile that had taken up permanent residence on her beautiful face. "Want to play tourist for the rest of the day?"

"What do you have in mind?" I asked.

"Normal stuff tourists do. Buy something in China-town, cross the Brooklyn Bridge, and eat a giant pretzel. Get hot chocolate in a coffee shop, and take a picture at the top of the Empire State Building. That sort of thing."

Her wide grin was contagious, and I caught myself returning it. How could I resist her when she looked so happy and adorable all at once?

"Anything else on your list?"

She tapped a gloved finger against her chin. "Yes. Ride

the subway. We already did the Times Square thing last night."

"Let's go then."

We boarded a taxi down to Greenwich Village and ambled through Washington Square Park. A little girl, about Jack's age, ran after a flock of pigeons, catching my eye.

April snuggled against me, and her voice directed my attention back to her. "Carter... I'm sorry about the Bensons last night. I would've told you about them if I'd known beforehand which fundraiser we were attending."

I skimmed the skin of her cheek with a finger and halted there. "You don't have to explain anything if you don't want to. I trust you." I leaned down to kiss her but stopped. "I just hope they were good to you."

She bowed her head. "It's a long story. And it didn't end well. I'll tell you some other time. It's hard to talk about that period of my life." Her lips trembled, and her breath picked up. "But, trust me, you've got nothing to worry about. It's in the past, and I intend to keep it there."

My lips found hers, soothing them. "No pressure, okay?"

She nodded again, her eyes closed this time.

"You tell me when you're ready. I'll never push you for anything. For the record, I have met the Bensons a few times over the years. They've always been nice to me. A bit stuck up, but nice. They often want me to perform at their fundraisers. Our relationship is strictly business."

"They're good people, but they have a hard time dealing with emotions. They keep a stiff upper lip, no matter what, and refuse to show any weaknesses. For a while, they'd been the parents I never had. My found family. I spent my holidays at their house. We talked on the phone, made plans, had game nights. When Travis left, they blamed me and pushed me away like I'd never meant anything to them. Like I was a stranger. They resented me for things out of my control. I guess their pain was so intense that they got lost for a moment. In the end, even though I knew they were hurting, they hurt me too. When I needed them the most, they didn't want anything to do with me anymore." She paused. "Now they want to make up for lost time…three years too late. Like I said, it's complicated."

I cupped her cheeks. "Let's enjoy ourselves and forget about everyone else for the rest of the day."

Her smile blinded me. "I'd like that." Her lips searched mine, and when she kissed me, my entire world lit up, putting an end to our discussion. The pain I'd noticed in her eyes a few times faded away as she leaned against my shoulder.

With our hands linked, we reached the southern end of the island. April jumped onto my back, and I carried her, piggyback style, across the Brooklyn Bridge, her breath tickling my nape. Every now and then, she leaned closer to drop a kiss on my cheek.

Ed and Taylor trailed after us. Up until now, they had done a great job at being invisible. Well…almost…considering they were both taller than me. Still, they were used to staying in the shadows, offering us some space and a false sense of freedom.

We were halfway through the landmark bridge when April started firing questions at them.

"Taylor, what's your last name?"

"Ed, is your name Edward or Edison?"

"Have you ever seen a show on Broadway?"

"Has any of you ever played football or hockey?"

She tried to include the two professional-football-player lookalikes in our conversation. Not breaking character, my bodyguards kept a straight face. Out and about, they always acted all business. Off the clock, they were both two of my best friends.

"I'll pierce their armor, you'll see," April whispered in my ear, a whiff of her lavender perfume going straight to my brain—she even smelled amazing. She loved the challenge, and I loved how much she hated the idea of my security guys being left out while tailing us.

I'd seen her interact with many of my favorite people since she landed in my life, and she always made sure everyone felt important and heard. This woman had the hugest heart I'd ever encountered.

A giant grin shaped my lips, and I shook my head as she kept asking questions that lay abandoned, without answers. "Good luck with that, Fairy. You'll need it if you wanna crack them."

"Watch and learn," she said. "I'll get through them. Give it some time."

Once we reached the other shore, we decided to cross the bridge again. The sun was bright today, and I relished its warmth on my face. April was still perched on my back. "I want to do dirty things to you," I whispered. "Again. Can we go now?"

She nibbled at my earlobe. "Not yet. Our tourist day isn't over. Patience is a virtue, Carter."

I let out a growl and felt the vibration of Pixie's laughter through my back.

"Okay, guys, I bought each of you a classic *I love NY* shirt," April said as she exited a store on Canal Street a while later. "It's our first trip together, and you all need to put it on. It's tradition."

"Says who?" I asked.

"Me."

The guys and I exchanged a glance, and I shrugged.

Ed winced. And Taylor shook his head, part-amused and part-scared. I burst out laughing as my bodyguards put on their shirts over their jackets. Just to witness the smile on April's face was worth indulging in her game.

"Ed, can you please take our picture?" I asked, lifting my girl in my arms, honeymoon-style.

"I want one with the four of us too," April said, stopping a jogger, a brunette in neon-pink spandex. "Would you be nice enough to take a picture of us, please?"

"Wow, I can't believe you got the guys to agree to all of this."

She flashed me a proud grin. "See? I can be pretty convincing when I need to be. Don't forget I'm a woman."

I snickered. How could I forget?

"You're all guys. It gives me some advantage when it's time to negotiate. You get the point. Anyway, it's just a picture. And a few silly shirts."

We walked to Ground Zero, then rode the subway back to upper Manhattan. At the corner of Madison Avenue and East 59th Street, we entered a coffee shop and grabbed hot beverages. As we crossed Central Park back toward our hotel, I ordered four giant pretzels from a street cart.

One at a time, I checked every box of April's perfect tourist day in my head.

Back at the hotel, we lay down for a nap that involved no sleeping at all. Entangled in the bedsheets, fully clothed and panting, April and I stared at each other—lips swollen, eyes glazed, cheeks warm. Even though we were both combusting with desire, we kept our makeout session PG-13. I couldn't tell if it was exciting, frustrating, or just plain hot. Every nerve in my body was ablaze. Only a small push and we'd burst into flames.

Pixie's eyes glimmered as they met mine.

A soft hue colored the places where my day-old stubble had grazed her skin.

Her full lips trembled, an unspoken plea for attention.

I let my fingertip follow their curve, pausing over the delicate dip in the center.

Her baby-blue irises turned midnight blue and sucked me in. My body defied gravity, and she caught me in her embrace as I levitated toward her. We kissed some more, our hands traveling all over our still-clothed bodies.

"Tonight, wear the Nashville dress. We could buy you something new, but I didn't enjoy that dress as much as I wanted to the last time, and it's been haunting me ever since. You have no idea how hard I struggled not to rip it off you that night. If your goal had been to torture me all along during my set in Nashville, well, it worked. My dick had a zipper imprint for two days afterward."

April offered me a sexy grin, and I was a goner. She grabbed the hem of my T-shirt, but before she could lift it up, I stopped her.

"No. We'll wait until tonight. I'll take you in ten different ways until you cry my name so loud the entire hotel hears it rolling off your tongue."

Pushing away from me, she untangled herself from my embrace and leaped to her feet, breathless and flustered. "You wanna play dirty? I can play too. Don't follow me in the shower then, HN. I need to get ready. No distractions. And right now, you're a big one."

I laughed because I fucking loved being her personal distraction.

Her clear laughter vibrated inside me, making me hard for her all over again.

With April, I felt like I got my twenty-year-old stamina back. One bat of her eyelashes, one curl of her lips, or one look my way and my cock pulsed, ready to ravage her in the most animalistic ways.

"I'll ask Ed to drive me to the gym. Taylor will stay here if you need him, and I'll be back in two hours."

"You're going to the gym now?" She stripped before me, taking her sweet time, and I bet it was part of her *let's torture Carter* mission.

It reminded me of the day when her towel had come off, and I'd caught her in all her naked glory through the cabin window. That day I hadn't averted my gaze. My eyes had lingered on her figure, enjoying every curve, every inch of her creamy flesh, and the look of embarrassment turning her cheeks a crimson shade of red for the few seconds she had been exposed.

Over the past month, April had become *my* greatest distraction, and I couldn't get enough of the way she toyed with me so deliciously.

Her shirt pooled on the floor. Next, she shimmied out of her skinny jeans, wiggling her ass. She pivoted on her heels until her back was to my front and unclasped her bra. The white piece of fabric joined her shirt and pants at her feet. Dressed in only a pair of white cotton panties, she twirled back until she faced me. Her unfettered breasts drew me in. She hooked her thumbs into the waistband of her underwear and, without breaking eye contact, dragged them down her legs. My mouth went dry. I stilled on the bed, unable to move, my jaw hanging open. All my blood rushed to my groin, and my pants felt too tight.

Her stomach teased me, and my mouth watered at the thought of trailing my tongue upward from her toes.

April said something, but I couldn't register a word she spoke.

"Stop eyeing me like I'm a prey you wanna chase,

Carter. Perhaps the gym is a good idea. Leave. Get that tension out of you. Bench it out of your system."

"Mm-hmm."

"Carter, you're not listening to me. You're drooling. Get some control over yourself, big guy." She whirled around, swaying her hips, and giving me the perfect view of her firm ass and smooth skin.

My feet carried me toward her of their own accord, but she slammed the bathroom door in my face, the click of the lock stopping me mid-stride.

I rapped softly on the door and cleared my throat. "April, open up. Let me in. I've changed my mind. I would prefer to relieve my tension with you…in you. Let's take a shower together and do that thing you love so much. Don't push me away. Please." I begged her using my most gentle tone. "Come on, don't leave me hanging. I promise I'll keep my hands to myself…if that's what you prefer. I'm a very lonely man when you lock me out."

A stifled chuckle resonated from the other side of the door.

I knocked again.

She hummed a song over the sound of the running water.

Fairy had turned her back on me, leaving me with an aching erection.

I blinked. She had cock-blocked me. Fuck, she really had. A large smile crept across my face.

April was playing a dangerous game. I could play too. And I just happened to know the best revenge.

I swung my gym bag over my shoulder and gave Taylor my instructions.

Still bewildered, I shook my head in disbelief as I headed toward the elevator.

Cock-blocked. Never saw that one coming.

32

APRIL

With my back pressed against the bathroom door, I couldn't erase the expression on Carter's face from my mind. For a moment, I thought he might force his way in.

By now, I knew that look—the one that screamed how badly he craved me.

Parted lips, dark irises, a straight back, every step loaded with intent.

Carter Hills was dangerous for my body and my sanity. He could shatter me with only a glance my way.

His stamina in the bedroom was out of this world. His sexual endurance rivaled that of a college frat boy, and he had more moves than an entire cheerleader squad in bed.

He never seemed satisfied—and I couldn't get enough of it...or of him, myself.

I wondered if he was always this good with every woman he'd slept with, or if the blazing chemistry between us made him insatiable. I prayed it was a me-thing.

After losing Travis, I'd become a nun in the sex department, something Saunders reminded me of many times, and no other guy had touched me for over a year.

Then I gave dating a try. Big fail.

I wasn't cut out for one-nighters. I'd learned that the hard way after letting an egotistical jerk into my pants. He came before I even got in the mood. The kind of guy who only cared about his own pleasure and had no clue clits even existed.

"I hope it was as good for you as it was for me," he had said with a smug expression. My hair stood on end over my arms at the memory. What a douchebag.

The moment he went into the bathroom to clean up, I bolted—and blocked his number. Even the reminder of him, years later, engaged my gag reflex.

Sex with Carter was everything I'd dreamed of after such a long dry spell.

A strong male who liked to take control and flip me around to satisfy both our needs, with a dose of playfulness and a side of tenderness.

He understood my body's needs without a single word.

It scared me how I always hungered for more, yet soothed me to know he hungered for me just the same. I didn't if he took the lead as long as we both surrendered to our most primal instincts.

The mere thought of him ignited my flesh once again. I fanned myself with my hand and clamped my legs together, calming the ache building deep inside me.

No. I wouldn't touch myself. This was Carter's job now to get me undone. I would have to get used to this new reality. Anyway, the wait made sex even more incredible.

Dressed in a plush robe, I sucked in a calming breath, unlocked the bathroom door, and peeked into the bedroom once I drained the water from the tub, looking for the man who could put a stop to my horny state.

"Carter? Are you back?"

I ventured into the bedroom. No sign of him anywhere. I sighed, reminding myself I was the one who chased him away. If he were half as horny and needy as I was right now, he'd spend the entire evening at the gym. The thought of him, burning with desire yet channeling it into sweat, brought a smile to my lips. New fantasies fueled my imagination.

Our hot late-afternoon makeout session had left me craving a release…or two. My bath hadn't been as relaxing as I'd hoped, and I wondered why I played his little game instead of giving in the way he begged me to.

Desperate for a distraction to occupy both my mind and body, I got ready for our date. The same way Betty had done last night, I applied golden eyeshadow and black eyeliner, giving my lids a smoky look, then added a touch of bronzer to my cheeks, trying to perfect the contour thing like she'd explained. The image the mirror reflected satisfied me. Two coats of mascara and a single swipe of natural pink lip gloss, and I was done with my makeup. I smacked my lips together and straightened my hair with a flat iron, ditching the wavy look I'd planned.

I felt ready for whatever tonight would bring my way. Carter hadn't revealed any of his plans to me, but the unknown added a layer of excitement and magic to our night.

In the bedroom walk-in closet, I slid into the ombre sequin dress. Just like the first time I wore it, I felt beautiful as it hugged my curves. Memories of that night in Nashville replayed in my mind. So many things had happened since then. Wonderful things I could have never imagined even in my craziest dreams. I spun around, admiring myself in the full-length mirror, silently praying I'd succeed in driving Carter crazy again tonight in this dress.

My heart leaped in my chest, thrilled and feverish, when the door to our suite opened. Carter was back. I blew out a jagged breath. Yes. I was ready for the night to come. And all it entailed.

Carter wolf whistled as his eyes traveled the length of my body. Shivers ran through me. He erased the distance between us and brushed my lips with his. "I won't be long. Stay out of the bedroom if you don't want to forfeit dinner and spend the night here because I have all I need in this room to keep me fed for hours." He winked, and my knees buckled.

Each time his eyes landed on me, he pulled me into a trance. I swallowed hard, my gaze locked on his back while he retreated into the bathroom.

Ten minutes later, dressed in dark jeans and a snug navy-blue dress shirt, sleeves rolled up to his elbows and his hair gelled in that just-got-fucked kind of way, he joined me in the living room. He looked every shade of handsome. I bit my lower lip and clenched my thighs together while I drank in the sight of him.

We stood by the window, which offered a panoramic view of the city skyline below. "Where are we going?" I asked, my voice throaty and low, when his hands circled my waist.

He leaned forward and whispered in my ear, his warm breath sending electric bolts down to my toes, "Nathaniel's. June got us a table there."

I cocked my head to meet his eyes. "Nathaniel's as in Drew Zerlinger's restaurant? The celebrity chef?"

A large grin spread across Carter's face. "Yeah. That's the one."

"I heard the waitlist is like five months long."

"More like four months. June can be persuasive. Our reservation is at seven thirty."

"They bumped the waitlist for us?"

He shrugged, never letting go of me. "Kinda. It's no big deal, they do it all the time. They always have tables left for last-minute reservations when…" *Celebrities. Famous or rich people.* He didn't have to say the words out loud for me to connect the dots. "For…special circumstances."

I pushed away from him and shook my head. "Nope. It won't do."

"What do you mean?"

"It's nice that you want us to have dinner there, and I've heard great reviews about the place, but we're not going." I turned away, putting distance between us, before he batted his eyelashes, clearly trying to change my mind.

"Why? I want us to go. Let me treat you to a fancy dinner, Pixie. It's the least I can do. We're in New York, and I want us to have the best time ever. And we've never been on a date, somewhere, just the two of us."

I pivoted to face him and pressed my palm to his cheek, smoothing his frown with my fingers. "As much as I'd like to go, this isn't happening. I'd prefer a low-key evening with you at some unassuming three-star restaurant over taking someone else's reservation. Let's go somewhere nobody's ever heard of, where we can just be ourselves, instead of spending hundreds of dollars on a fancy meal I won't enjoy because everyone will be staring and I'll feel like we've stolen someone else's chance to eat there."

Carter inclined his head, staring at me. "You serious?"

"Totally. We'll still be in New York, and we'll still have an amazing night. I would just feel more in my element if we did normal-people stuff after last night's extravaganza."

He said nothing, studying me as if to make sure I wasn't bullshitting him or something.

"I swear it will be fun. Let's ask the front desk for some recommendations instead, okay?"

Carter dropped his shoulders, eyes locked on mine, amusement and confusion warring in his expression. "Fine." He tugged at my hand, his smile widening. "You pick the place, then."

"You agree?" I would have thought he'd put up more of a fight about it.

"Yeah. Sure. Seriously, we could grab hot-dogs from a street cart right now and I would be happy. Because I'm with you."

"But you don't eat meat."

"Well, I could possibly make an exception if it's for you —and only if it's the *only* food you'd agree to eat. Or I could have a bun with mustard and onion and still be happy about it." He claimed my lips, as if to underline his words. The kiss turned heated, our hands frantic and our mouths hungry. Carter leaned back as a moan left my mouth. "I have no clue how you appeared in my life, April Simmons, but fuck, you're hot. You'll never cease to amaze me. Now lead the way. Let's get out of here before I rip this dress off you."

"You think June will be mad?" I asked when we entered the elevator car.

"Nah. She's pretty down to earth herself. I think she'll be impressed we turned it down."

Overdressed for the small Italian eatery, we didn't have a care in the world. Nothing other than this time together mattered. We sat in a half-circle, crimson leather booth, the dim lights casting a warm glow over our table. An older man wearing a black suit played jazz music on a grand piano in the back corner. The smell of garlic, fresh bread, and tomatoes filled the air. My mouth watered. Fuzzy feelings danced in my chest. I loved everything about this place. It was both rustic and homey, and exactly how I imagined our first real dinner date would be.

The romantic vibe of the restaurant rubbed off on us, and neither Carter nor I could stop smiling like fools.

"April, this is the date I owed you." Carter's hand wandered to my lap, and I stifled a gasp.

"No touching, Mr. Hills. This is not how a gentleman would act on a first date with a lady." I used my most sensual voice, rubbing my toes against his shin under the table.

"It's not the girl, it's the dress. It's killing me." He winked, and I fell a little bit harder for him. A flock of butterflies danced in my stomach, multiplying with each passing day. I had no idea how I could have fallen for him in just a few weeks—but I had. Not wanting to spoil the night, I forced my mind to stay in the present, shutting out thoughts of the future and all the questions I couldn't answer. I wasn't ready to either assess my feelings or come clean about them. For now, I would enjoy the moment. Carter scooted closer to me. His hand traveled to the apex of my thighs, and I choked on my breath when he brushed my clit with a finger.

"Don't make me wish this night was already over," I said, my voice a pleading murmur.

"You haven't seen anything yet, Fairy." He flashed me a devilish smile, and I turned into a molten pile of burning flesh under his touch, unable to resist him any longer.

———

Carter hit the stop button of the elevator, and the car halted midway between the twentieth and the twenty-first floor. My heart leaped in my chest at the sudden movement.

I gasped, and my eyes found his. This was the end of me.

A darker shade of gray lit up his irises. His hands balled into fists at his sides.

His gaze zeroed in on me, freezing me on the spot.

An animal grunt escaped his mouth.

For a second, I watched the bobbing of his Adam's apple. My throat worked overtime to swallow. On trembling legs, I took a step back—slowly. Carefully.

I leaned back against the rail rounding the inside of the elevator car, struggling to keep my balance on those three-inch heels that killed my feet a little more with each step after I spent hours walking in them.

Carter prowled toward me, and I sucked in a breath.

I had no way to escape. Nowhere to go.

I was completely at his mercy.

With another step forward, he trapped me between his strong, defined arms against the mirrored wall.

My breath hitched in my chest.

I heard a buzz, probably the lobby trying to reach us, but the deafening thumps of my racing heart buried its sound.

Carter's eyes captured mine and sucked me into their depths as turmoil overtook all my senses. He made me his prey, cornering me in a mirrored box with no escape. Towering over me by nearly a foot, I knew I was no match for him. The desire in his gaze held me hostage.

I couldn't talk. I couldn't think. I couldn't move.

Watching him closely, I held my breath, waiting for his next move.

His hand ventured between my legs, and he ripped my black panties with a twist of his wrist, before placing the ruined fabric in his back pocket. My heart hammered, and my whole body quaked.

My dress being dangerously short, I felt the cold air

from the ventilation shaft against my soaked center, making me shiver with lust.

Before he could make another move, I dropped down to my knees and unbuttoned his pants with unsteady fingers, craving the taste of him.

His length greeted me with a salute, and I teased the tip with my thumb, and ran my tongue along the length of it, leaving a trail of moisture all over his firm flesh. Silk over iron. A shiver traveled through him. I smiled as a groan left his mouth. I had all the control and relished every second of it. My mouth watered as I engulfed most of him, taking my time to rob Carter of any self-restraint, pumping his velvety shaft with a hand. I released him with a pop and licked the sensitive tip.

He pulsed between my lips, and a triumphant smile curved my mouth.

I quickened the pace of my hand, growing hotter with every muffled curse that escaped his lips. I tilted my head, and the sight of his hooded eyes was all the encouragement I needed.

Leaning forward, I teased him with flicks of my tongue, making him beg for more.

Carter's fingers fisted my hair and guided the rhythm of my mouth.

He cursed my name under his breath, and I sucked him deeper.

Buried inside my mouth, he tensed, growing harder.

A primal heat built deep within me. Before I met Carter, I never though giving head could fill me with such an addictive buzz. But seeing him ceding every thread of his control to me was a powerful aphrodisiac.

When I caught his eye, they glittered, now almost black from where I kneeled, filled with wicked lust. They seared into me, so hot I feared my dress might catch fire.

In the slowest motion, he wet his lips and grunted, as if he could barely hold it together.

I didn't lose a second, stroking, licking, and teasing his hard flesh until his head fell back.

"Oh fucking God, April."

His erection vibrated inside my fist, and I worried he would come too soon.

I rose to my feet, and Carter caught me before I lost my footing, my legs weak and shaky. Two strong hands lifted me until my ass rested on the railing of the car and our faces were aligned. He clutched my hipbones, pinning me against the wall. His face twisted as if in pain, a stark contrast to the fire burning in his eyes.

I tried to speak, but no words escaped.

He positioned himself between my legs, and with one jerk of his hips, he entered me. A cry parted my lips, and my head hit the wall behind me at the same time my chest arched into him. I trembled at the intrusion, and the man about to ravage me halted his momentum, giving me time to adjust to his girth.

My entire body lit up when he moved inside me. Slowly at first, prolonging the pleasure, all my nerve endings tingling each time he rubbed against my sensitive spots.

Desperately seeking to anchor myself in the moment and steady my body, I lifted an arm over my head, letting my open palm glide slowly across the mirrored wall as Carter pounded into me with abandon.

I kicked his ass cheeks with my heels as he rode me faster, my body responding with urgent need to each of his motions. With rolls of my hips, I deepened our physical connection, hungry for the delicious friction only our connected bodies could provide.

Waves of pleasure built inside me and threatened to

shatter me to pieces. I cried out and felt myself clenching around his shaft, surges of ecstasy washing over me.

He leaned in, his teeth teasing the soft flesh of my neck, and his tongue licking a line down to my collarbone.

Right now, he could devour me alive, and every part of me would welcome it.

He squeezed one of my breasts over my dress, and shivers rippled through my core.

Carter thrust into me until I could barely keep my eyes open, blinded by all the sensations rushing though me.

The nails of my other hand dug into his biceps.

My toes curled. I teetered on the edge of ecstasy, ready to explode.

Before either of us could come, he stopped and slid out of me. I blinked, not sure what was happening. My body shuddered at the withdrawal.

Carter backed away, the heat in his eyes still burning hot, and his dress shirt all wrinkled. He said nothing as he watched me, stealing my ability to speak. My heart hammered in my chest cavity, and I could barely suck a full breath in. Confusion took over, and I studied him, wondering why he stilled when I was this close to erupting into an earth-shattering orgasm.

Keeping a straight face, he pressed the elevator button, and the car resumed its ascent to the forty-eighth floor, giving me a moment to adjust my dress and smooth my hair in the mirrored wall.

My lipstick was smudged, and my lips were swollen. Mascara streaked under my eyes, and my hair was a tangled mess. I blinked, uncertain I recognized the woman staring back at me.

I caught Carter's gaze in the mirror, and I shook under the intensity of his eyes, two dark and lustful abysses.

Taylor and Ed waited for us in the hallway when the

doors opened. With blank faces, they nodded at us. There was no way our flushed cheeks, dark eyes, and disheveled appearance could hide what had just happened in the elevator.

The men moved forward with resolute steps, and Ed swept the small space we just exited before leading us to our suite. Carter kept his hand on my behind the entire time, shielding me from his security and prying eyes. I moved cautiously, careful not to let my dress ride up.

When I stumbled on my heels, his hand snapped to my waist, holding me close enough that I could feel his warmth steadying me. Our gazes, still dripping with lust, collided, and I looked away to prevent myself from eating him right here in the hallway of one of the poshest hotels in New York City in front of an audience.

I tried to act cool and unaffected, as if my world hadn't been completely shaken just minutes ago, but I doubted I succeeded. My tongue grazed my lips, remembering him in my mouth, the way he kissed me, and the imprint of his hands on my skin.

"We made sure the elevator cameras were off and all footage erased," I heard Ed whispering in Carter's ear.

Carter nodded his appreciation and slapped him on the back.

A bucket of ice with a bottle of pink champagne awaited us in our suite. After Taylor rounded the place to make sure everything was fine, Ed and he left us to our own devices. Alone. Horny. Needy. I leaned against the closed door, my breathing shallow. Carter handed me a glass of the pink bubbles, before walking further inside the room and turning around to watch me. Facing me with his arms folded over his chest, he looked lethal. He eye-fucked me without blinking as I sipped on the alcohol, relishing the freshness as it slid down my throat.

With a shuddering breath, I held his gaze, every cell in me aroused and ready to detonate in bliss.

The champagne helped me relax. I had no idea what Carter intended to do with me next, but I couldn't wait to find out. Still, I needed a moment to myself.

My chest rose in a rapid succession of inhales and exhales, the air so hot it set my lungs on fire.

If my panties had been still on, they'd have combusted under the searing intensity of his attention.

Carter stood there, not saying anything, ogling the length of my body in a way that sent a buzz to my blood and ignited my flesh even from a distance.

I rubbed my thighs together, not sure how long I could resist before indulging in the attraction I couldn't escape from.

He didn't budge. His pulse, visible at the base of his throat, betrayed his false sense of calm.

I felt weak under his unwavering stare. His eyes undressed me, searing through my skin, each blaze igniting something deep inside me.

He stood there, and I couldn't help but let my mouth water as I drank him in from head to toe—tall, hot as fuck, and lusting for me.

I gasped, pleading for attention. "Carter—"

Unable to stay still, I ran a finger between my thighs, wiping off the moisture. I brought my glistening digit up before pushing it back down. A shiver crossed my body when I touched myself, so turned on. A low, needy purr escaped me.

Shivers raced down my spine, and I quickened the movement of my finger.

Carter stepped toward me, and the moment he faced me, reality slipped away—hunger radiating from every inch of him, his heat wrapping me completely.

The next thing I knew, my dress was bunched at my waist and my naked breasts were pressed against the floor-to-ceiling window of our hotel suite. I had the most exquisite view of the Manhattan skyline while Carter thrust into me from behind, not giving me any time to catch my breath, one hand threaded through my hair, and the other one holding my hips, preventing me from moving.

"I have wanted to fuck you in this dress for as long as I can remember. It's fucking indecent. You can't wear it in public for anyone else, April. Ever. It's meant for me. You're mine, Fairy. All mine."

He pulled my head back to connect our mouths, like we both needed each other's oxygen to stay alive.

"Then show me. Fuck me harder, HN."

He flipped me around, and my dress crumpled to the floor in a puddle of glitter. I kicked off my heels just before he lifted me, one arm wrapped around my middle while the other caged me in place, my back now hitting the cool glass overlooking the city below each time he rammed into me.

My fingernails left marks on his toned chest.

He bit my neck, and I died in his embrace.

Then he revived me. Every cell of me. One at a time.

Flames of pleasure licked my insides, burning me alive.

My bare back enjoyed the coldness of the glass, a contrast to Carter's heat. It highlighted all my senses. I ignored the soreness between my legs, the tender flesh throbbing. In just one week, Carter Hills had made up for all the years I'd gone without intimacy—more than I'd ever imagined. He made me forget my loneliness, the challenges I'd faced, and the lingering sadness in my heart. He brought light back into my life. He brought hope. With him, I felt passion, and it was exhilarating to feel alive again.

He drove his hips into mine with punishing strokes, and I hung on to him, spent but euphoric. He feasted on my neck, but I grabbed his hair and brought his mouth back to mine. Our tongues danced a well-choreographed tango. I bit his lower lip as I moaned his name. His grip on my hips tightened, and he pounded into me one more time, his lips brushing mine slowly. We breathed the same air, and a jolt of electricity ran through me.

All my muscles clenched, trembling with intensity.

We both climaxed in a loud howl, our bodies fused together.

Euphoria ripped through me as wave after wave of pleasure consumed me, and in that instant, I knew my heart had been claimed.

The car turned left instead of right, away from the airport.

"Where are you taking me?" I asked Carter the next morning after we left the hotel.

"Trust me, Fairy."

I laced my fingers through his and rested my head against the window, taking in the sight of New York City one more time.

Last night still felt like a dream. One I would eventually need to wake up from. For the time being, I let myself surf the moments we'd shared a little longer. Reality would crash my fantasies soon enough.

After we fucked like animals the night before, Carter and I spent an hour in the bathtub, soaking together in comfortable silence, low music doing all the talking.

Later, we woke up, aroused and needy. We didn't fuck

this time. The way we kissed and convulsed in each other's arms felt more like making love than succumbing to the lust simmering between us. Once again, I refused to analyze what it meant, scared that if I did, my heart would break in the process.

The driver parked the car and opened the back door, and I snapped out of my daydream. It wasn't until both my feet were planted on the sidewalk that I noticed the Empire State Building standing tall before me, and I stopped breathing. He remembered.

"There's one last thing to do on your perfect-day list," Carter said, pulling me in for a kiss. Warm flutters spread through me. "Come on, they're waiting for us."

At the top, Carter snapped pictures of us from every angle. The view all around us was beautiful, but I saw nothing except my man. Being together up here, alone and so high above the world, felt like we were flying and nothing could ever temper our happiness.

We were allowed only a few minutes of privacy, and I cherished every second of it.

"Thank you." I wrapped my arms around his waist as I took one last mental picture of us with the city skyline in the background. I closed my eyes and breathed him in. Every day, he made it harder for me to keep my feelings for him locked in. I exhaled.

Carter gripped my hand in his, and together, we made our way back to the waiting car.

We landed in Green Mountain by the end of the afternoon.

Exhausted from the last forty-eight hours, I dozed off for the entire plane ride. This time, Ed and Taylor flew with us. Carter wrapped me in a blanket, keeping me close to him while he spent his time working on his new music and chatting with his bodyguards slash friends.

Hours later, the memories of our time together in New York City kept playing in my mind, making me breathless and nostalgic all at once.

Our day stroll around the city, the amazing dinner Carter treated me to, and our sleepless night worshipping each other for countless hours. Those were memories I would cherish for the rest of my life. Our expiration date was approaching, and the life that would come after Green Mountain scared me. It made me emotional.

When we talked to June over the phone on our way home, she couldn't believe we had forfeited our upscale restaurant reservation. She agreed with me nobody needed a four-course dinner or an overpriced glass of wine to have a great time.

I loved doing normal stuff with Carter since I'd never get used to the rich and famous lifestyle he could provide. It still didn't compute in my mind why people couldn't enjoy the simple things in life when given a choice.

The cabin appeared at the end of the road, and a sense of peace filled me.

Home. I was referring to Carter's cabin and Green Mountain as home more and more every day. Carter and I both remained silent as we fixed ourselves dinner and ate in the media room while we screened a movie. Once we were done, we slouched on the sofa, and he played with the strands of my hair while I rested my head on his lap. Yes, this was what being home should feel like.

How could I ever leave Green Mountain?

How could I ever leave him?

My head and my heart were fighting a battle of wills that neither could win.

My whole life had been turned upside down in just a month, and I had no idea how to go back to my lonely and colorless existence once this chapter was over.

How was I supposed to go on with my days as if nothing had happened, knowing I'd be leaving a big part of myself behind the day I returned to Ginger Creek?

Using a pillow to hide my trembling hands, I kept my focus on the screen, having no clue what the movie was about.

Carter's arms tightened around me, and I wondered if he felt as torn apart as I did. In case he did too, I reached for his hand and squeezed it, craving his inner strength to find mine.

With my eyes shut, I held back the tears building up in my eyes. A fragment of my heart cracked, and it hurt more than any physical pain.

When the credits rolled on the screen, Carter lifted me in his arms and took me to his room. To his bed.

The simple gesture set a quiet fire in my chest. I had no idea how to admit to him the intensity of my feelings because they scared me as much as they excited me.

He molded his body to mine, his front pressed against my back, lulling me into sleep with gentle caresses and soft kisses on the side of my head, just behind my ear. A second piece of my heart fractured, and it hurt as much as the first time.

33

CARTER

I woke up from my slumber with my dick ready for war. Was I dreaming? Everything around me seemed blurry. Warmth enveloped my lower body. A soft caress shooting stars behind my eyelids. My eyes popped open, and my brain finally took over. April was kneeling between my legs and had my cock deep in her mouth. One hand was pumping me, and the other was gripping my ass cheek.

"Babe. Oh God—" I couldn't speak. She stole the ability to form words from me. This was the second time in as many nights that I woke up with Pixie all over me. Yesterday, I woke up to her riding me. *Middle of the night* sex was the greatest. She'd learned from the best. How many times had I woken her up to satisfy my own urges?

Once the sleepy numbness left my body, I tugged April by the shoulders until she lay over me. "I need to be inside you. Now," I said in a husky voice as I buried myself in the depths of her.

We both climaxed and went back to sleep in no time.

Since we returned from New York two weeks ago, April

had been withdrawn and lost in her thoughts—a lot. Sex was still off the charts, though. Our connection was stronger by the minute, and my case of blue balls had been switched to a case of chafed balls.

When I re-opened my eyes sometime later, my girl was already all dressed up and ready to go.

I propped myself up on my elbows and asked the same question I'd been asking for days. "How can I convince you to come with me?"

Same answer as always. "You can't. Carter, I need to go home. There're things I gotta do."

I had a three-concert run scheduled this week: Portland, Seattle, and then across the border to Vancouver.

"If you need space, tell me. I'll give it to you."

From the moment I got a taste of her—every inch of her—April and I had spent all our free time together.

She neared the bed and hovered over me, her lips a hair's breadth from mine. "We're fine." That stupid word again. "I'll come back next week. We already talked about this." Same answer. Every fucking time. She brushed her lips over mine.

I relaxed under her touch. As always. Like she possessed some special power over me and my body. "What's bothering you then?" I could tell something was off.

Over the last two weeks, I'd caught her staring off into the distance or sitting in front of her shut-down laptop for long stretches of time. Other times, she'd flash me that smile—the one that made me as utterly whipped as a teenager in love—and I'd forget what we'd been talking about just seconds ago.

"Got a lot on my plate. That's all."

Was she doubting our relationship?

I checked the time. "Taylor will be here in fifteen

minutes. Why didn't you wake me up sooner?" At my request, my chief of security had agreed to drive April to Ginger Creek and promised to keep me updated. I thought she could use the company and protection in case someone recognized her. For once, she didn't argue with me, offering me some peace of mind.

"Do you know how sexy you are when you're drooling on your pillow?" She winked, and just like that, all my worries vanished. If only April knew how she had me wrapped around her finger. I sighed. When she was near, everything inside me softened. Jeff would have had a great time teasing me if he were here.

I wrapped my arms around her and drew her close. April looked her usual sexy self in silver leggings and a V-neck pink sweater. I tugged at her lips with my teeth. She melted in my embrace and covered my naked body with hers, my erection pressing against her lower belly.

I begged her with my eyes. I needed her one more time before we parted ways for a whole week.

"We can't, Country Boy. I'm already late. I'm not sure Taylor would like our chorus anyway. It was humiliating enough that he caught us in New York after we exited the elevator."

"Nah. It was fucking hot. Don't worry about him. And the thing is…I kinda like it when you sing my name. Taylor will wait outside." I cupped her breasts over her sweater, and she whimpered, my favorite sound in the world.

"Carter…"

"Yeah, like that." My hard-on bobbed between our bodies. "You can't leave me like this. It would be very inconvenient to walk around with an erection all day."

She broke free from my arms and jumped to her feet. "Let's turn it into a challenge. You're not allowed to take care of yourself while I'm gone. See how long you last without me." She winked, and I was a goner.

Tempted to toy with her restraints, I stroked myself a few times, desperate to release some tension.

April stood by the bed and waggled her finger. "I said no touching."

I let out a shaky breath and pressed my palms in some sort of prayer. "Then kill me already."

"One last time. Because I can't let you walk around with a tent in your pants. That would be really uncomfortable, and I'm not heartless. One rule, though. You can't undress me. Hands to yourself. And no cheating."

I nodded.

She joined me back on the bed, and I took a handful of her ass. She writhed beside me and pumped me, hard and fast. A couple of minutes later, stars exploded before my eyes. The whole fucking galaxy.

April walked away a little while later, her pink hair tied in a messy bun, followed by Taylor. A bad hunch crippled me as I stood on the front porch. With my hands stuffed into the pockets of my faded denims and the winter breeze freezing my bones through the thin fabric of my long-sleeved cotton shirt, I felt helpless. My feet itched to run after her. To hold her one more time. To gather doses of strength from the simple touch of her lips. Instead, I stayed there, immobile, trying to chase away the horrendous feeling of losing her, repeating in my head that we'd be okay—that she would come back to me. April glanced in my direction and waved her hand, holding Bernice's carrier in the other one, before hauling herself into the car.

I mouthed *Don't go* when the vehicle disappeared from my sight. My throat tightened at the thought of us apart, on opposite sides of the country.

In many ways, it felt like goodbye. No part of me

would ever be ready for a finality when it concerned that woman, and somehow, it felt like my heart was being driven away from me.

———

I grabbed my phone from my back pocket to shoot April a text message. I clicked her contact details and smiled at the picture of us where both of us were lying in bed with sleepy—happy—grins with Bernice curled around the top of April's head.

ME

Boarding the plane in 5 minutes.

I sent another one after the first one remained unanswered.

ME

Please stay in touch. Thinking of you.

All my insecurities resurfaced when she left yesterday morning. A part of me feared she wouldn't come back in a week. She'd left some of her belongings behind to soothe my anxiety, but it still made me queasy. We talked about it, and yet I still didn't understand why she was in a hurry to go back to Ginger Creek…to leave. The taste of her last kiss still lingered on my lips. Mint and strawberry.

April had lost some of her spark after she ran into the Bensons at the fundraiser, and I worried about her.

Most nights, a cocktail of conflicted emotions passed through her baby-blue irises, clouding them. But with every kiss, every touch, and every smile, her eyes cleared a little more each day. A part of me believed I was the reason.

A load of questions had been nagging me since then, for which I possessed no answers.

Did her ex-boyfriend cheat on her? Did he hurt her? Chills ran through me, and my stomach tightened at the idea.

What happened with Mr. and Mrs. Benson? Why had they turned their backs on her and said they regretted pushing her away? Each attempt to bring their names up had ended in a "Not now, Carter." So, I stopped trying to push it. April promised she'd open up about them. Soon. It didn't prevent my imagination from creating scenarios in the meantime, though.

I rubbed a hand over my face. Even though April had said she would explain their relationship, everything inside me screamed at me to do something. To search for the truth. But I had to respect her wishes and be patient. One call to Taylor and I could easily obtain the information I was looking for. My chief of security had connections, which had been useful when I was still linked to Savannah Fucking Prince.

In the last week, I'd spent a lot of time in my music studio and in the gym to silence my screaming thoughts and prevent myself from crossing boundaries I had no right to. No matter what, my inner voices just wouldn't shut up.

June nudged my side, saving me from my overzealous ruminations. She and Ed were boarding the plane with me while Riley had agreed to meet us in Portland later. He barely traveled with me nowadays but sometimes, he liked to make an appearance.

"Where's April?" my assistant asked. "Is she coming? I was looking forward to having a girl friend on board for once."

My shoulders sagged. "No. She's back in Georgia… I wish she were here, though."

June flashed me a concerned look. "Oh. Did she move back home for good? Are you guys over?"

"No and no. She was not supposed to return home just yet. She had some stuff to do. At least, that's what she told me before she left." I sighed. No doubt my despair couldn't escape my assistant's sharp eyes.

She angled herself until she faced me, her eyebrows bunched together. "When will she be back then?"

"A week. I hope. Fuck, I can't believe she's gone."

June squeezed my forearm. "I'm sure the two of you will figure this out. Is she the real deal?"

"You have no idea—" My throat clenched from the emotions lodged there. "I think she could be."

"Sorry, Carter. I know she means a lot to you. I'm sure she'll be back in no time. And in case it wasn't obvious before, I really like her. She's good for you. She's funny and smart, and you two make a great couple."

I glanced around, avoiding her penetrating gaze. The thought April could decide to stay in Georgia unnerved me. "Yeah, well…let's just focus on something else."

We spent the first half of the flight going over some business, and after a quick nap, I worked on a new song while June dealt with whatever she had to do, and Ed read a graphic novel he'd brought along.

Stud Burgess greeted me once I touched base in Portland, his signature smirk firmly in place. He hugged me and tapped my back before I climbed into his old red pickup truck while Ed and June drove away in a rental toward their hotel.

After Dahlia left the band six years ago, Stud retired too, and Carter Hills Band became Carter Hills, solo artist. My ex-bandmate longed for a slower pace of life. He'd made enough money with his musical career to start afresh. And he deserved his happily-ever-after.

While I was busy drinking my sorrows away, he moved to the West Coast, bought a piece of land, and built his dream house on the outskirts of Portland. Married to his former personal assistant, he had two kids, owned a woodworking shop, and he and his wife managed a small inn they'd built on their property. He said he didn't miss the fame and all its perks and downfalls. Sometimes I envied him. I wished I could get off the bandwagon and build a farmhouse in the middle of nowhere and just be. No one to impress, no one to report to, no one expecting anything from me.

Each time I came to Oregon, Stud and his wife Belinda insisted I stay with their family, and I never missed a chance.

Stud merged onto the freeway, his eyes seeking mine. "How are things back home?"

"Calmer," I said with half a smile. "How's the family?"

"Good. The kids are growing up. Tristan is now playing the guitar. You're going to be proud."

The moment I stepped foot inside the house, Tristan and Kimberly ran into my arms. I dropped my bags on the floor and ruffled the little boy's blond hair before picking his pigtailed sister up. The child wound her two-year-old arms around me and rested her head in the crook of my neck. Stud didn't lie. They'd grown up a lot since the last time I visited, only a few months back.

Kimberly chattered in my ear with her contagious cheerfulness, "Uncle *Catttter*, Uncle *Catttter*, I missed you."

My arms fastened around her tiny body. "I've missed you too, Kimmie." I kissed her forehead.

"Come upstairs. I want to show you the train I built in

my room with Daddy," Tristan said, tugging at my sleeve. "Follow me, Uncle Carter."

Belinda shook her head. "Kids, give Uncle Carter a minute."

I leaned forward to place a kiss on her cheek. "It's okay, Belle. I owe these guys some quality time. I missed them while I was busy straightening out my life." I squatted and picked Tristan up under my arm, tickling him with my fingers.

His infectious laughter wrapped my heart in layers of happiness.

With the two children in my arms, and doing my best impression of Papa Bear, I disappeared upstairs to their bedroom, stomping up the stairs and growling. The farmhouse was just how I remembered it. Whitewashed recycled barn wood walls, dark wood sliding doors the same shade as the plank floors, and mint-green kitchen cabinets. The scent of dried eucalyptus branches titillated my nostrils. Their house was a home. Warm and welcoming. I took a big gulp of air. Peacefulness washed over me, and the tension in my back loosened.

"He's so good with children," I heard Belinda whisper to Stud downstairs. "I wish he finds someone nice who makes him happy. Enough with the Hollywood divas or superficial models."

Stud replied something I didn't quite catch from where I stood at the top of the staircase.

A hint of a smile stretched my lips, and my pulse picked up. If only they knew.

My mind drifted back to April. For the first time in my life, maybe I could be happy and a long-term relationship was something I could envision. Tingles of excitement bloomed all over my skin.

A family. Was it even something April wanted?

I put the kids down and fished my phone out of the back pocket of my denims as they ran to their bedroom.

My smile faltered when I realized she never replied to the messages I sent earlier. Why was it bothering me so much? She was probably just busy. After all, she'd said she had things to take care of back home.

How could I envision a future with a woman I barely knew? But mostly, why wasn't I freaked out by the thought?

I shot her another text. In case she missed the other two or for whatever reason they didn't get delivered.

ME

Landed. Safe and sound. At Stud's. Call me when you can.

I shoved my phone back into my pocket and entered the kids' room, but then I changed my mind and picked it up again.

ME

Miss you xx

There. I said it. I really missed her.

I just hoped April missed me too.

"Okay, guys, show me this train," I said, sitting cross-legged on the floor.

"You're telling me the great Carter Hills might be in love?" Stud teased, a twinkle in his eyes.

Belinda gasped, studying me without a word.

We sat at the dining room table, a wooden piece of art Stud himself had created from an old Sequoia tree on his land. The kids had gone to bed over an hour ago, and the three of us were catching up over dessert. With my fork, I stabbed the fresh blueberries rolling around on my plate, toying with the last bite of my apple crumble.

I cleared my throat, unable to wash the stupid grin from my face. "Well…not in love, but yes, I've met someone. This time, I can picture myself going the distance with her. She's incredible and generous. Smart and fearless. She's…huh…different and doesn't care about fame or money. She prefers burgers and tacos to five-star restaurants." I shrugged. "She's amazing, really. And she gets me."

"Ohmygod, Carter, your eyes light up and glisten at the mention of her," Belinda squeaked. "What's her name?"

"April." My pulse soared when her name left my mouth. "We've spent the last six weeks together in Green Mountain. I kinda forced her to move in with me. Long story… It was for her safety, but afterward, I was hoping it could become permanent. To this day, she still hasn't moved out."

"The girl from the song?"

I nodded.

"You're screwed, man. I'd recognize the look of love anywhere. This girl got through your stone heart. Big time. She must be quite a catch. Are you finally turning into a grown-up?" Stud asked.

My throat worked double time trying to swallow everything my friends were throwing my way. It was a lot to take in.

"Have you finally decided you deserve the best?"

Could what April and I shared be love? *No. Yes.* Was it?

I had loved once. Dahlia…or I had thought I did.

What April and I had was so different.

Could I be *in love* with her? Was I?

A warmth rolled down my spine, and a strange sensation worked its way through me. I dropped my gaze, tongue-tied. Mixed emotions clashed inside me.

Stud inched closer and tapped my back. "You're lovesick, man. It's finally happening." He raised his hands toward the sky as if he were thanking the gods above. Soon, his tone softened, and his smile dimmed a little. "I know it must be nerve-racking, but it's okay, Carter. You deserve to be happy. You're my brother from another mother, and you know I love you like family." I raised my eyes to meet his. "Does she love you back?"

My heart pounded in my chest, desperate to be freed. I rubbed my throat, trying to ease the tightness constricting my airways.

Did April love me? I had no fucking clue.

"How would I know? No one's ever loved me for…me. They all had an endgame." I struggled with my breathing. "And Dahlia never loved me back the way I loved her. Fuck… See? I don't even know what true love is." The reality of my life tasted sour as I spoke the truth loud.

"Do you trust her?" Belinda asked with a seriousness in her eyes that I hadn't noticed until now.

I nodded. "Like I haven't trusted anyone in a long time. April fits right into my life and with Dah and Jack. And the sex is phenomenal. Like we connect on a deeper level." A hint of a smile curled the corner of my lips at the thought of how insatiable we were for each other.

We'd fucked nonstop in the last two weeks.

In my truck.

In the hot tub on my deck under a starry sky.

On the kitchen table.

In front of the fireplace.

Against the glass wall in the den.

Two nights before she left, April surprised me, showing up in nothing but her cowboy boots and one of my ties around her neck in my home gym, and I almost dropped the casting iron kettlebell on my foot as my eyes roamed over her.

We ended up pleasuring each other against the mirrored wall, on the bench, against the padded floor, in the sauna.

I breathed out. "I think she could be it." Images of her filled my mind. Her smile. Her vulnerability. Her optimism.

"Does she trust you?" Belinda's voice snapped me back to reality. She searched my eyes, studying my reaction.

"I think she does. No. Scratch that. I *know* she does."

The first time we had sex, she put all her trust in me.

That night in the elevator in New York. And also, against the window of the hotel later.

The fundraiser she agreed to attend on a whim, as my date.

The day we strolled in Nashville dressed like colorblind hillbillies.

The meals I cooked for her, different from everything she was used to.

The pillow talks we shared. Like the time she confessed she only became an author because her best friend sent her manuscript to a publisher friend, and things got out of hand from there.

"You guys might be right." I inhaled. "I think I'm in love. Fuck. What do I do now? She's not even replying to my texts. I have no experience in relationships. You saw how the last one unfolded." I scratched my temple, my heart a messed-up jumble. "Damn it. I need a plan. This wasn't supposed to happen." I shook my head, dragging my hands up and down my face. "You're right. I'm screwed. She's been gone for two days, and I'm struggling. I miss her. Like a fucking lot."

Stud burst into a fit of laughter. Yeah, he knew me too well.

He clamped my shoulder. "You, my friend, are in big trouble."

I elbowed him. "Yeah, no kidding."

"Man, you have the next week to figure out what you want with this April girl. Then you man up and do what you gotta do. Just be honest with her and tell her how you feel."

"She's all I can think about. I'm obsessed, man. Except for Dah, I've never been obsessed over a woman before… Is this normal? Is there something wrong with me? Time away from her feels like an eternity. I'm not sure I can wait that long. What if…?"

Belinda touched my hand. "Carter, what do *you* want?"

The words tumbled out of my mouth before I could think them over. "I want her. All of her. I want her by my side days and nights. I want what you guys have. She's not here right now, and I'm a mess. I want to hold her hand, kiss her all the time. Make her bad days better. Is this normal, or am I going nuts?"

I retreated to my room after ten. With my eyes glued to my phone screen, I considered calling April but then realized it was after one in the morning her time. I paced the room, tugging at the roots of my hair. Why wasn't she texting me back?

Unable to stay put, I sent her another text, trying not to sound desperate.

ME

Hey, Fairy. Everything okay? Call me whenever you wake up, forget the time difference.

An episode was coming my way, and right now, only

April held the power to calm me down. I had to talk to her to reassure myself we were good.

For the longest time, I tossed and turned, my mind racing ten thousand miles per hour. The show in two days would be a clusterfuck if I didn't get any sleep and shut my mind off.

Around three in the morning, I got up. With the heels of my hands, I erased the sleep—or rather, the lack of it— from my face. Dressed in workout gear, I plugged my earbuds in, cranked up the volume of the music on my phone, and went for a run around Stud and Belinda's property. The crisp air burned the lining of my lungs, and I coughed a little before finding my pace, matching the rhythm of my pounding heart.

The fog clouding my mind cleared up, and I realized I'd been running for hours when the sun rose behind the tree line.

Drenched in sweat, my body aching and my stomach grumbling, I made my way back to the house, breathing in the Pacific morning air.

Tristan and Kimberly greeted me in their one-piece matching pajamas when I let myself in.

"Good morning, guys." I kissed both their heads and rushed upstairs. "Wait for me. I'll shower and be right back."

Twenty minutes later, I entered the kitchen and sat at the table. Belinda placed a cup of tea in front of me.

"You didn't sleep?" she asked with a cocked eyebrow, a worried expression wrinkling her face. She was dressed in black pants and a long-sleeved, nugget-yellow sweater, her long black hair braided loosely down her back.

I rubbed my freshly shaved jaw with a hand. "Nah. Not really."

"This woman is on your mind?"

"All the fuc…freaking time." I huffed, bracing my elbows on the table and resting my chin over my joined fists. "She's the one person I wanna confide in. I pushed women away for years, and now I can't fuck—" I dropped my voice, remembering the children close by. "Sorry. I can't function when she's not around. I can't think. I can't sleep. My bed is empty and cold without her."

Belinda neared me and wrapped her arms around me. I smelled the lilac perfume of her shampoo.

"Carter, you need to tell her how you feel, and you owe it to yourself to figure out if she feels the same."

I nodded, at a loss for words, my throat thick with emotions, and my heart throbbing.

My morning run had helped push some of my uneasiness away, but it still lingered deep in my bones, underneath the calm surface. The threat of an episode still hovered over me.

"What should I do, Belle? She's not answering any of my text messages right now. Taylor, my chief of security, is with her, and he tells me she's okay. I need to hear it from her, though." To hear her voice.

Belinda placed her hand on my arm, in a way only mothers did, and gave me a tight smile. "Carter, you'll figure it out. You always do."

Silence stretched between us for a fat minute.

"You know what? You're right." I stood up and grabbed my phone from the countertop to call June. "Good morning. Listen, I need a plane for a round trip to the East Coast. Private jet, coach, or first-class, I don't care. I want to leave in less than two hours."

Belinda's eyes grew wide, and she rose to her feet, shaking her head. She failed at hiding her smile.

"Carter, you have a show tomorrow night. You need to

get ready. Riley scheduled a meeting this afternoon. They're expecting you," June reminded me.

"Make something up or cancel it. Better yet, tell them I've got a stomach bug. I don't care. I'll be back tonight. There's something I need to do, and it can't wait. Either that or I'm going AWOL."

"Carter, I love April, but can this wait?"

"No. April means more to me than you'll ever know, June. She's everything. I can either go alone, or you send Ed with me, but I'm not asking for your permission."

We hung up, and Belinda wrapped me into another hug. "Do what you have to do, Carter. You only live once. You better make the most of it."

That was all the encouragement I needed. "Thanks, Belle. You're the best." I planted a kiss on her forehead.

I ran upstairs, packed a light bag, and waited for Ed to pick me up from their driveway after a copious breakfast with my friends.

"Bye, Uncle Carter," Tristan yelled my way as I tossed my bag on the backseat of the rental.

"I love you, Uncle *Catttter*," Kimberly echoed with a tiny wave of her hand.

I ran from the car, back to the house, kissed both their heads, and jumped back into the black SUV.

"Wish me luck, guys."

34

CARTER

I spent half the flight writing everything I wanted to tell April when I saw her again. And the other half making up for my lack of sleep.

The words *I love you* didn't come out easily from my mouth. I hadn't spoken them out loud in years, except to Dahlia and Jack.

When we finally touched down in Georgia, I had a severe case of restless leg syndrome.

Breathing heavily, I messaged Taylor, my fingers shaking.

ME

> Hey man, it's me. I'm in town. Please tell me where I can find you guys.

Then, while Ed drove the blue sedan we rented at the airport, I returned Riley's urgent message that he left on my voice mail and found myself in a conference call with June and my new publicist.

The car screeched to a stop, and I jumped out, my heart pounding, flutters in my stomach, and my throat dry.

I rang the bell and waited, my clammy hands shoved in my pockets, rocking back and forth on my heels.

A young woman, about April's age, with dirty-blonde tresses and hazel eyes, opened the door. Her eyes widened when they locked on me. She gave me a slow once-over and slammed the door in my face before I could even speak a word.

I stood there, frozen, and then scratched the side of my head. What the hell. I glanced over my shoulder at Ed, and he shrugged. I stepped back, and my eyes traveled between the screen of my phone and the golden numbers on the wooden plate by the door. This was the right address.

A loud shriek echoed from the other side of the door. I frowned. Was I supposed to run or stay here?

I took a deep breath, lifting my knuckles to knock again, but before I could, the door swung open, and the same woman appeared, this time offering me a grin.

"Fucking kill me already. Carter Hills is standing on my front porch." She spoke in a mixed accent, part American and part English.

My eyes flared, and I pinched my lips to avoid smiling, nodding at Taylor, who stood a few feet behind her.

I cleared my throat, angst crawling inside me. "Hi… huh…is April here?"

"Where are my manners? Come on in, Mr. Hills." The woman moved aside to invite me in.

"You can call me Carter," I offered with a tight-lipped smile. This was awkward.

"I'm Saunders." She held out a hand for me to shake. "April," the woman yelled, "there's someone here to see you."

Fairy muttered something but stopped in her tracks when her eyes landed on me. She looked even more petite than I remembered, her complexion paler, and her pink hair a shade darker.

"Carter? Wait… What are you doing here?" Her eyes lacked their usual glow.

My heartbeat doubled its frenzied rhythm.

Did I make a mistake? I closed my eyes, scared that she didn't share my feelings. Did I overstep by coming here? Why did I believe I was meant for love? When my best friend chose my brother over me, I should've gotten the message loud and clear. Now I got it. Fucking joke. Fury boiled in my veins.

Find a way out, Carter. Save the last bit of pride you have left.

Why did I lower the walls around my heart?

April didn't miss me. She was gazing at me as if I'd intruded into her life. She hadn't even replied to any of my messages. What did I expect?

I slapped myself mentally, cursing for letting my guard down and thinking this time it would be different. That April Simmons could ever love me, Carter Hills, the man —not the famous country music singer—for who I was.

Her doll-like baby-blue eyes focused on me, her painted lips parted. "Aren't you supposed to be in Portland right now?"

I nodded, hanging my head low, avoiding her gaze. "Yeah…I-I thought… I'm sorry. This was a mistake… I shouldn't have come here… This…this was stupid. I-I don't want to bother you…you're…huh…busy." All the words rushed out of my mouth. "I should've called first. I-I'll go now."

Slivers of glass scraped the back of my throat raw.

I was such a fool.

I spun round, ready to bolt out the door.

April gripped my hand, pulling me toward her before I

could slip away. "Carter, don't go." Her words sounded more like a plea than a demand.

I kept my emotions buried deep inside as my eyes flicked back to her, stunning in the purple sweater June had bought her in Nashville. *She had kept it.* The realization hit me like a ton of bricks. Paired with skinny dark jeans and a black scarf, it wasn't half-awful as I remembered. April looked gorgeous. She could wear a paper bag, and I'd still find her irresistible. Love was a joke.

"Why are you here?"

My inside vibrated at the sound of her low voice. Ed, Taylor, and April's friend vanished from my field of vision. Nobody else existed besides us. "You didn't answer any of my messages. I got worried."

"My phone must be off. You could've called Taylor—"

"I did."

Even Taylor had no idea why she was ignoring me.

April closed the distance between us, and I leaned in, tracing the length of her jaw with a feather-light touch. "God, I've missed you."

My stare lingered on her small button nose, her thick lashes coated in black mascara, her heart-shaped mouth, her earlobes that I liked to nibble on.

I'd missed all of her.

I inhaled the scent of her, gathering every particle of courage within me. Time to man up and deliver the truth lying in my heart. "Can we talk? In private?"

"Sure. Follow me." April knitted her fingers through mine, and the gesture calmed my agonized self. Her hand in mine felt like home. She led the way to a small bedroom upstairs and closed the door after us.

"Carter, why are you here? Tell me the truth." She faced me and splayed her small hands across my chest as my heart banged in its cage.

Breathe in. Breathe out.

I tugged her closer, erasing the space between us.

We breathed the same air.

Holding her gaze was hard. My eyes kept wandering to her lips. I wanted them over me, taking all of me in. Kissing me until she was all I could taste.

I raked my fingers through my hair.

Time to be real. I wouldn't chicken out of this.

"Listen… There's something I need to tell you. I don't know where you stand, but I cannot not say it for another minute, even if it makes me sound crazy." I steeled my back.

She watched me, her expression unreadable.

Come on, get it out.

"April, I love you." There. I said it. My heart leaped in my throat, pounding so hard I thought it might choke me. "In the last few days, I've missed everything about you. I want you in my life full-time. Days and nights. I want you to join me when I'm on the road. I want to wake up next to you every morning and make love to you in the middle of the night." I let out a breath that felt too tight, grabbing her hands with a desperate need. "I know it's sudden, that we haven't known each other for a long time, that neither of us expected this…huh, connection we share, but I've spent my entire life thinking love wasn't in the cards for me. That the women in my life had a tendency to ruin my heart. I didn't… I-I can't explain how we happened or how right it feels, but I know I love you, and this is the rawest and scariest feeling in the world. One I'm so not used to. I'm ready to take a leap of faith with you if you're ready to be with me because when you're with me, I don't feel so scared anymore."

I blinked. Never before had I opened up my heart like this to another person. A woman. It felt oddly liberating to put my feelings out there instead of keeping them locked inside or turning them into lyrics.

April's watery eyes met my hopeful ones. "Carter…Oh wow. Okay, I wasn't expecting this."

This was the moment when she would tell me I was being ridiculous or that she didn't share my feelings.

"The thing is… I-I love you too. So, so much."

"You do?"

"Madly. But this is huge for me. My heart has been broken once, and it's a big step for me to trust someone else with it. I've been on my own for so long… My last relationship has left me scarred."

I grazed her face with a finger. "I've said those words to only one woman in the past, and she didn't reciprocate my feelings… This is huge for me too. I can't sleep when you're not around. My mind wanders to you all the fucking time. It's driving me insane." I leaned in to capture her lips in a slow kiss. "April Simmons, I want to be with you. Only you. I want to give us a try, to see where it goes. I'm willing to do anything to make our relationship work. Ask it and I'll do my best to provide it…huh…to meet you halfway because I know how much you cherish your independence, so I won't get all cocky." My humor died down, and I spoke the next words slowly, hoping she could see the sincerity shining in my eyes. "Fairy, I want this with you. Love. A future. Us."

Her eyes brimmed with tears, and she rose on her tiptoes. A tiny bob of her head informed me she yearned for the same thing I did.

"For real?" My voice sounded croaky, my throat tight with emotions.

"Yes. I want an *us* too. Even if it sounds crazy and rushed. Even if it makes no sense. Like it's surreal."

Our mouths crashed together, hungry and frantic.

Three days without kissing this woman had seemed like a lifetime. Our tongues tangled with each other, our breaths harsh, and our hands impatient.

A renewed energy spread though me.

This. Us. It felt right. Like I was whole for the very first time in my life.

I lifted April into my arms, my hands steady under her butt, holding her as though I never wanted to let go as I deepened the kiss and consumed her mouth with long strokes of my tongue. I was desperate for her and yearned for more. For all of her.

Her smile imprinted on my lips. "Carter, I've never met someone like you. It's like you came straight from my perfect guy fantasy. You rocked my world when you accused me of taking your picture in the woods when I moved next door. You woke up something in me that day. You made me feel alive. For the longest time, I convinced myself we wouldn't work. But I was so wrong, because I love you so much, I can't imagine how I ever spent years without you by my side. Being here, by myself, has made me realize how much I've missed you. How much I need you in my life…in my heart."

I pulled back, breaking the kiss to look at her. "Does that mean you're flying back to Oregon with me?" A tingle of hope prickled my heart.

Her shoulders slouched forward, and she pressed her forehead to the crook of my neck for a second before staring at me again. "I wish. Just the thought you're leaving soon is unbearable. It's like I've been waiting for you for so long and now that I have you for *real* real, I gotta say good-bye. It hurts even though it's only for a week. I know I sound stupid, but who cares, right? I hate wasting precious time together. Waking up and falling asleep in your arms is the highlight of my days."

I hugged her tighter. "Me too."

"I can't believe you came all this way just to tell me you love me. Now I'll have to pinch my arm every hour until we're together again to remind myself it's not a dream. That I didn't imagine today."

"I'll text it to you so you don't have to harm yourself."

Her soft laughter filled the space around us. "I actually love this idea. Since you're a songwriter, I expect a different love declaration each time."

"Don't tempt me. I might write you a song instead."

"I already know the power of those songs of yours. I might fall for you harder if you do."

I brushed her hair and leaned back in to rub my nose against hers, skimming her cheek with my lips. "Fall as hard as you wish, Fairy. I'll always catch you when you do. And then we'll fall again. Together."

She twisted a strand of my hair around her finger. "How did I end up moving next door to you at the exact same time you decided to spend time in Green Mountain? I don't believe in coincidences. Do you think it's possible we were destined to fall in love?"

"Yeah." I pressed a kiss on the corner of her mouth. "Maybe we should thank that stupid lock of yours. It kinda set everything into motion."

"Oh yes, the hot tub incident. Don't remind me." Her mouth searched mine, soft and demanding. April kissed me with a newfound passion. She took the lead, sampling my lips, her tongue seeking mine. Her hands traveled over the expanse of my chest before she circled my neck with her arms, yanking me to her, our bodies pressed together. "I love you, Carter Hills." Her voice was a throaty whisper. "Thank you for being here. And being honest with me."

I molded my palm to the back of her head to deepen the kiss, craving the taste of her mouth. "Come with me.

Just this time. I want you by my side. We can come back here next week."

"I wish, but I can't. There are things I gotta deal with here. Important stuff. I can't go with you. Not this time. If I don't handle it now, I'll never be free of my past."

"The Bensons?" I asked, my eyebrows bunching together.

She sighed. "Yes. They reached out and asked me to come over since I'm in town. Even though I'm not excited by the idea of spending time together, I think it could be the closure I need. To put our history behind me for good and be able to move forward with you without ghosts standing in the way." She buried her face in my chest and sighed. "The timing is bad."

I breathed her in, her lavender perfume wrapping around me, holding onto it for the long days ahead without her.

For the longest time, we stayed like that, neither of us in a rush to break apart.

"Carter, I still can't believe you are here. With me."

"It's real. I've missed you so much. So fucking much."

"How long do I have you?"

I shrugged. "I'm missing rehearsal and soundcheck right now. My show is tomorrow night. I need to be back by tonight. I can't stay for long. It's gonna be pure torture to walk away."

I repositioned her in my arms, and April locked her legs around my midsection, the exact way I liked it. She ground her hips against mine, and my dick sprang wood when I rubbed it against her center. A soft moan escaped her reddened lips. Fully clothed, we dry-humped each other like horny teenagers.

"I want to be inside you." Lust filled my voice and every cell of my body. Before she could reply, I dived my tongue into her needy mouth, showing her just how much I was aroused. Our lips did the talking, and our souls fused together.

Pixie raked my nape with her fingernails, and I was at risk of exploding inside my denims, tension running high inside me.

"Carter?" she purred in a husky voice that she used only when she wanted to be boned hard and fast. "Love me."

Fisting the collar of my shirt, I lifted it over my head and dropped it at my feet. With one hand, I removed her purple sweater, which joined mine on the hardwood floor. I lowered the cups of her bra, exposing her naked breasts to my starving mouth. April gasped and pushed her chest forward, increasing the connection between our bodies when I inclined my head forward and captured a puckered nipple between my teeth. A loud growl exited my mouth at the taste of her. I teased the tip with my tongue, sucking on her hard flesh, eliciting a train of whimpers from her.

After a three-day withdrawal, she felt like putty in my hands.

"April, I love you," I repeated, the desire so strong I wanted to rip all her clothes off. "I'll love you every day if you let me because I'm so fucking gone for you."

"Good. Because I'm so fucking gone for you too."

Unable to wait a second longer, I lowered her to her feet and undressed her with frantic movements. When my forefinger traced the shape of her lips, she sucked the digit in her mouth, bringing me to my knees. She shimmied out of her panties while I peeled off all my clothes. The moment my fingers grazed the softness between her thighs, I lost touch with everything else except for the woman who told me she loved me. *Me*. The man, not the rock star.

She loved me.

Without expecting it, I had found love. With the only woman who could drive me crazy in the best ways.

Love was the one thing I spent my whole life running after, and it happened the moment I stopped looking for it.

As April lay on her back and I pushed inside her, I felt the stars realigning themselves. And for once, it made perfect sense.

35

APRIL

"Carter Hills knocked on my door and proclaimed his love to you. He told you he freaking loves you, Bubble Head." Saunders had been screaming the same thing nonstop since Carter flew into and left Ginger Creek two days ago. "Again, why did you refuse to go with him? Are you sick? *Ohmygod*. He made the quickest roundabout trip known to mankind to see you and tell you how he feels. If he had crossed the country back and forth to ask me to go on a plane with him to the end of the world, I would've accepted, and I'm not even in love with the guy." She leaned forward to place her hand on my forehead. "You're not burning up. What's wrong with you? Talk to me. Maybe you require some kind of intervention."

Taylor shook his head. His upper lip twitched, his amusement obvious. He peered up at me, and I shrugged. By the end of the week, we were going to be friends. I had a newfound mission: break the bodyguard's serious stance and transform him into a human being. Something to focus on instead of the man I loved who was still on the West coast of the country.

When Carter flew back to Portland, he left with a huge chunk of my heart. Its rhythm now felt offbeat without him around to take care of it.

A wide smile crept on my lips. Something that had been happening a lot in the last few days every time his words played back in my head. Carter told me he loved me. He did.

I love you, April.

I could still taste the words on my lips. The imprint of his hands on my waist. The caresses of his breath as he murmured sweet nothings into my ear. Carter wore his love for me on every inch of his body.

My heart did somersaults in my chest at the reminder, and it doubled in size. His words. They were much more than just a love declaration. Food, air, and water weren't necessities anymore. I could surf and live on love forever. Carter Hills's love.

Feathers of excitement took up permanent residence in my lower belly.

When I drove away from Green Mountain, a part of me had hoped it would clear my thoughts and I would realize our relationship had just been a vacation fling, that there could be no future possible for us. But coming back here proved to me how wrong I had been. The more miles and hours I put between us, the more I concluded I had fallen for him. Big time. And yet, I hadn't been courageous enough to proclaim my love for him this early in the relationship. I needed more time. To accept how I felt. And to see if I would snap out of the love bubble surrounding me by coming back home. Because if I was falling in love with Carter, it changed things. It complicated stuff. It meant we would have to find a way to make it work, whether it was long-distance or something else. And if we failed, my heart and I would be shattered forever. I wasn't looking for heartbreak, and I wasn't even sure I could survive another one so soon. I was just starting to get control of my life back, to live and get out there. Risking this new freedom was a scary thought.

My phone hadn't died down like I'd told him. Not returning his calls and messages had been my ridiculous attempt to put more space between us. To see how much I would miss him if we had no contact whatsoever. And I had failed. I missed him like crazy the entire time we'd been apart.

Carter beat me at my own game, though. He flew here on a whim, spending over ten hours on an airplane, just to check up on me. Amongst the most insane things that had ever happened to me in my life, this topped the list. If that fact didn't by itself scream *love*, then nothing ever would. He loved me. He was willing to make it work. The simple realization sent all my inner insecurities flying out the window. I loved him. I had a chance to be happy again. I would be stupid not to dive all in and believe the universe would have our backs—my back.

"Bubble Head, are you even listening to me?"

I escaped my mind feed and brought my attention back to my best friend. "Saunders, you gotta get over it. You've been repeating the same thing over and over since I got here." I had come over for breakfast at her house—or rather, hers and Reed's. Yeah, they had finally moved in together. We used to do that every weekend on the mornings Reed had to go to work early before I moved to Green Mountain. I was proud of my friend. She had stopped being afraid, and I knew I could follow her example. She and I were becoming brave, stepping into the unknown with a bucket of optimism and love and trusting our hearts to lead the way.

"It's still big news. Sorry if I need a little more time to freak out. Girl, I can't believe I actually met Carter Hills. Why aren't you more stunned?" She batted her eyelashes at me. "Oh, I forgot the guy is giving you daily orgasms."

"You are terrible. You knew we were together."

She bobbed her head. "Yep. But knowing and witnessing are two very different things."

"Are they?"

"Absolutely. Also, I slammed the door in his face. Me. I did that. He must have thought I was a lunatic. For my defense, he was standing there, looking all hot and normal, and I panicked. Do you think he will ever forgive me? I'm sure he's seen worse, no?" My best friend jumped to her feet and paced the living room while I sat on a chair, Taylor facing us from the entryway. "Tell me he won't hold it against me. Bloody, girl. He can totally do that, right? Sure, he can. He's Carter Hills. Country music god."

"Saund, stop acting like a crazy fangirl. You look insane. Relax already. Taylor will start keeping you at a distance if you don't calm the fuck down and stop rambling." Her eyes found the bodyguard's, and he nodded in silence, never breaking his stoic expression. I rolled my lips over my teeth, a laugh bubbling inside me. "Carter is my boyfriend, Saund. He's human like the rest of us. Sure, he's hot, but he's also sweet and takes good care of me. I love him. No need to make such a big deal out of this." Inside me, a rush of excitement flooded my veins. Nothing felt regular about dating a music superstar. Or the last six weeks of my life.

My best friend pondered what I said for a few beats. "Listen. I'll act cool around him. I promise I'll do my best. I swear."

I grinned, and she mirrored it. A swell of emotion filled me from the inside out. Nothing would mean more to me than my best friend and my boyfriend getting along. After all, they were the only family I had.

Family.

Was it something Carter could envision with me some-day? Was it too soon to think about the future? We hadn't discussed anything yet, but from what I'd witnessed, we shared the same core values.

"Girl, stop making that face." Saunders's voice broke my train of thought once again. "Every time you think about your hunk of a boyfriend, there's a lustful glaze in your eyes and you blush. It's cute, really, but I feel like I'm witnessing your getting aroused right in front of me, and that is disturbing."

I slapped her arm. "Oh, shut up. I got distracted for a moment. I wasn't thinking about him *that* way. And if I recall correctly, you were the one telling me to put red lipstick on and suc—" I remembered Taylor's presence just in time and swallowed my next few words. "You were the one to tell me to get back out there, that it would be good for me. Now let's go shopping." I lowered my voice to a whisper. "At the rate he rips my panties off me, I'll have to walk around town commando if I don't refill my stock soon."

Saunders stifled a chuckle. "Oh, naughty girl, I knew I was right. You *were* fantasizing about your man. Not that I blame you, though." I felt my cheeks warming up as she added. "Seriously, I'm glad you're finally having some fun. You deserve it all."

36

CARTER

"Uncle Carter, why are you smiling so much?" Tristan asked. He tugged at my shirt, and I was jolted back to reality.

"Sorry, buddy. You were saying…?"

"I said. Why. Are. You. Smiling. So. Much? You look like a crazy person. You never smile like this. Are you sick? Did you tell Mommy? She cares for me when I'm sick."

I shook my head and laughed my heart out. "It's okay. I'm just very, very happy. That's all. I haven't been happy in a long time." I shrugged. "Now I feel like smiling all the time. Even if I do end up looking like a lunatic."

"What's a lunatic?"

My jaw worked back and forth. I repeated his own words. "A crazy person."

The image of April's friend rolling her lips over her teeth when we came back downstairs after we had our "talk" two days ago flashed through my mind. No doubt she had heard us professing our love to each other. Taylor and Ed too. I offered Saunders a lopsided smile, the gleam in my eye probably visible from space, when I left her house, April in tow, walking me to the car, flustered and light on her feet. We both sported sex hair and matching glows.

With April, I was back to being a teenager all over again.

I couldn't help texting her dirty promises and humming the new songs forming in my head, all inspired by her. After everything I'd been through, I still couldn't believe I was in love. Like the real thing. A new grin split my face in two at the thought. Yes, I was a desperate cause, but for once, I couldn't care less.

Last night, I gave a concert to a sold-out stadium, and I barely remembered singing a verse. My head and heart had stayed on the East Coast. Only my body had made it back here.

"Don't leave, Uncle *Cattter*," Kimberly said, sitting on the mattress next to my duffle bag. "I *loooove* you. Don't leave me."

I spun the little girl around, dropping a kiss on her forehead when I lowered her back on the bed. "Guys, I have a show tomorrow night. I promise I'll come back soon because I miss you guys too much." Tristan jumped on the bed next to his sister, and I unleashed Tickle Monster on both their bellies. With a deep voice, I added, "You better be good to your mama, you clever little bunnies. Uncle Carter will know if you two have been naughty." The sound of their laughter filled me with warmth. These kids owned my heart. Tristan clung to my back as soon as I leashed the monster back. I lifted Kimberly in my arms, wading around like a robot.

From the second-floor window, I spotted the shiny black SUV we rented for the week down the driveway.

Ed parked in front of the house and honked twice before getting out.

I clasped my hands together in front of me. "Time for me to go, guys. I'll call your mama to set up another trip. Next time, I'll try to spend an entire week with you two. If it's warm enough, we could make a bonfire outside, roast marshmallows, and ask your daddy to play some music on his guitar."

"Yay," Kimberly exclaimed.

"You promise?" Tristan asked.

I nodded. "Absolutely." They both knew I always delivered on my promises. "For now, though, I must go."

The three of us climbed down the stairs, Kimberly still perched on my back, and Tristan's free hand nestled in mine.

The little boy carried one of my bags to Ed, who was waiting by the front door, and Kimberly snaked her arms tighter around my neck, like she wasn't ready to let go of me. I shifted her until she was positioned in my arms instead. "I'll miss you, baby girl." I planted a kiss on her cheek, and she did the same. Maybe, one day, a little blue-eyed girl would do the same. A mini version of April. The idea jumpstarted my heart, but I refused to let my mind drift there right now. April and I had a lot to discuss. Arrangements to make. Now that I was aware she loved me too, I couldn't wait for both of us to be back in Green Mountain next week so we could make plans. Together. Like couples did. I lowered Kimberly to her feet and hugged both children goodbye once more before meeting Belinda on the front porch.

"I'm proud of you, Carter," she said as I opened my arms to hug her too. "I have a good feeling about all this. Keep me updated, will you?" She stepped back and cradled my face with both hands. If Stud was a brother to me, his wife was a sister, an old soul, who always tried to impart her wisdom to me. She took her role seriously.

"Carter, now you listen to me. You can have it all. Never sell yourself short. This April woman is lucky to be loved by a man like you. I hope she knows it. You are one of a kind, and I'm happy you're following your heart this time."

I felt my cheeks warming up. "Thanks, Belle. I'm the lucky one to have you and Stud as my family and for you to give me that kick in the ass when I need the push. Thanks for having me over, even though it was a short stay. We should visit more often. I told the kids we would plan something soon. And there's a special someone I want you to meet."

"Sounds good. I would really love that. You two are welcome here any time."

I kissed her cheeks and met with her husband standing by the SUV, chatting with my bodyguard.

"Thanks, man. For always being there for me."

Stud smiled. "It goes both ways. Go rock that stage for old times' sake and give those fans the show of their lives."

"Do you miss it?" I asked. I knew my friend loved his life here, but from what he'd said over the years, I also knew he missed the rock star life at times.

He shrugged. "Only a few times a year. I'm happy here, and I wanna offer my kids the chance I never got growing up. Unconditional love. And a stable and safe environment to flourish."

"For what it's worth, you're succeeding. They are thriving, man. Kimmie and Tristan...they are great kids. You and Belle did right. If you ever wanna do a surprise appearance one of these days, let me know. We could set it up. It would be fun to share a stage with you again even if it's just for a night. I'd love to revisit those years with you."

His lips curled up at the offer. "I'll think about it. Belle has been talking about it too the other night. I think a part of her misses those days too...in her own way. Not now, okay? When the kids are older, maybe we could talk about it then. Let's see what the future has in store for us both first."

"Noted. We'll revisit the idea in a few years. I gotta go. Thanks again for everything and for helping me realize what I was too blind to see in my relationship."

"My pleasure, Cart. You're always welcome here. And please let me know how it goes with April. I'll be rooting for you two. I can't wait to meet the woman who shattered the walls of your heart."

I nodded and clapped his shoulder before climbing into the idling vehicle while my security detail slipped behind the wheel.

Twenty minutes later, we picked June and Riley up at their hotel, and the four of us got going.

June sat in the front seat, next to Ed, handling last-minute details about Seattle, her tablet resting on her lap. Riley sat behind her in the second-row seat, already absorbed in his phone, exchanging a few words with all of us and giving us instructions for the day between calls. My manager didn't join me on the road often, but he said tagging along this time would do him some good. According to him, he needed a change of air. I didn't question him. He would open up when the time was right. Anyway, I loved having him around. So here he was, riding with us. We could've afforded better transportation to Seattle, but somehow, for a reason I never put too much thought into, we loved traveling all cramped up in an SUV. It felt like old times.

Carter Hills Band times.

I sat in the third-row seat, the space too small for my size, but loving the privacy it offered. I planned on calling April as soon as we hit the interstate, and I didn't wanna be stuck up front in case our conversation got heated.

June twisted in her seat to face us. "Okay. Listen, people. Carter, I scheduled three radio interviews for tomorrow morning and a quick appearance on a podcast at noon. There's this promoter who has a bunch of merch he needs you to sign. The boxes have already been sent to the hotel. All items will be auctioned to benefit Drew McAllister Children's Hospital in Seattle. Riley, you have a dinner with that investor scheduled for tonight at eight. I booked you a table at Les Deux Fondues downtown. You'll go for drinks at six thirty with Don Delucas, a rep for REV, the sneakers company. They want Carter to be the face of their new worldwide campaign. I also received another call from Napoleon, the Canadian men's underwear brand who reached out last month. They're launching a new line and want to invite us to the headquarters when we are in Vancouver later this week. I'll schedule an appointment as soon as you two look through their portfolio and business and give me the green light to go ahead. You should have both received their catalog in your inbox as we speak. They're expanding their reach to the US market and are convinced you"—she pointed at me—"would fit their vision. They are putting together a Times Square launch next July. From what they've shared with me so far, it's gonna be big. Anyway, look into it and tell me what you think by tomorrow night so I can tell them whether or not we're interested. I know it's last minute, but I still think it could be great exposure. *Positive* exposure."

Riley and I both nodded.

For twenty minutes, June updated us on all our other engagements for the next few days and other business details we had to tackle as a team. The entire time, I flipped my phone between my hands, the device feeling like hot coal in my grip. I nodded to every statement, wanting to be left alone and for everyone else to return to their own businesses.

As if she could sense my restlessness, my assistant wrapped up the discussion. "Good, now that it's all settled, I'm going to block you out while I reply to my emails. You guys behave while I'm busy." She winked and turned around, exchanging a few words with my bodyguard before pushing earbuds into her ears.

"You good?" my manager asked.

"Yep. When you check that Napoleon email, let me know so we can discuss it further."

His phone vibrated in his hand. He stared at the screen with a frown. Riley looked concerned these days. Through the years, we'd learned to read each other's moods pretty accurately. Surfing my love bubble, I hadn't noticed the deep lines around his eyes, nor the tight line of his lips. Before I could ask him how *he* was doing, he spoke. "Sorry, gotta take this."

I nodded. "Sure. Go ahead. I have a call to make too." I gestured to my own phone. "We'll talk later."

"Good." He shifted position until his focus was back on his screen and accept the call.

Pushing all thoughts of my manager's troubles away, I dialed the woman whose voice I couldn't wait another minute to hear.

37

APRIL

Carter was on his way from Portland to Seattle when he called me. It was almost noon my time.

My entire self lit up at the sound of his voice, and it woke up an ache between my thighs he had yet to put out.

Lying on my bed, my head propped against a pillow, I answered, feeling my cheeks turning dark-pink when his handsome face filled the screen. I was back to being a teenager with a crush every time we spent hours on the phone. "Hey you." Why did I sound breathless? I cleared my throat and took a big inhale. Captured by the intensity swirling in his eyes, I forgot my next words.

"Fairy, is it a bad time? You sound out of breath?" Oh, he noticed. Heat waves spread through my being at the idea he could tell even from a distance how bad he affected me.

"All good. I'm all yours until you gotta go."

"Is it normal I already miss you?"

My spine tingled at the sound of his admission. "Yeah,

because I miss you too. I can't believe you're gonna be gone for an entire week. How was your show last night?"

"Great…I think. I landed in a parallel universe and only sang my heart to you. You know those out-of-body experiences…? Anyway, it was your face I imagined the entire time."

"In a way, you sang to me. I played your songs in the order of your set list." I paused for a long minute. When I spoke again, emotions were lodged in my throat. "I'm sorry I couldn't join you. I hate the fact I'm missing out on this."

"Me too. Next time, I'll bring the handcuffs on the road to keep you close to me."

"Oh, I've never tried handcuffs. Do you think I'd like that?" I was teasing. Sorta.

We fixed our gazes on each other, the temperature soaring between us even though there was a whole country in the middle.

"Fuck. You can't tease me like that. Not fair."

"Oops. I thought you liked my dirty mouth."

"Not the point." He growled. "Last warning. The last thing I need right now is a boner. I'm already suffocating back here."

"Okay, fine. I'll take pity on you." I changed the topic before the conversation made us both achy with need and we wouldn't be able to do anything about it. "Back here? Are you in the car?"

"Yes. I'm in the third row, and the space is way too small for my frame. But I'd endure about anything to have a little privacy."

I blinked my surprise. "Is your entire team riding with you?"

"Yep." He popped the *P*.

"Ohmygod, they're gonna hear our conversation." I lowered my tone as if I was the one with an audience. "It's weird. And…huh…we talked about handcuffs…"

"Don't worry, they're all busy. Riley is on the phone and will be for the entire trip, Ed is driving, lost in his own world, listing to an audiobook, and June is sitting beside him, sending emails and doing whatever she does. She has earbuds in, and I know for a fact she's either listening to a podcast or some music to block out the chatter of everyone else. We're safe."

He flipped the phone around, angling it to show me the car through the screen, as if to prove his point, before bringing his face back into the frame.

"How will you survive three hours on that seat? You look like you've been folded in two." The image of Carter trying to fit in the third row of the SUV pulled a chuckle out of me. Yes, I could picture him clearly in my head.

"Stop laughing. I'll be all right. I've been in worst positions before…" A memory passed through his eyes, but he blinked it away. "For once, I wish I had requested my own car… I kinda wanna be alone with you. Even if it's over the phone."

"Me too. How did you end up all cramped up in an SUV anyway? I presumed rock stars always traveled in those big-ass tour buses or private jets."

"When I go on tour, yes. But since it's just three shows, it's fun to go back to our roots sometimes."

"I wish I had been there in your early days. Think we would have fallen in love if we had met back then?"

"April, I would have noticed you for sure. There's just something about you that appeals to me. Like we're linked in some invisible way. We were destined to meet. That's the truth, and I strongly believe it. But I also think we both had to go through stuff so we were ready for each other. Even if that stuff almost ruined us in the process and broke our hearts."

I mulled over his words for a moment. "Makes sense. Even if parts of my past are painful, I wouldn't be me without them. It's kinda crazy to think about it like that…"

"I agree." We remained silent for a long beat. "What are you doing?"

"I'm spread on my bed, maybe naked…or not…fantasizing about this hot guy I met in Tennessee. He's been living under my skin, and I love to imagine his hands on me when I talk to him on the phone. If you could hear him. Even his voice is sexy as hell."

"Christ, Fairy, don't say things like this when you're over two thousand miles away. You know I can't resist you. I'll do another round trip just to fuck the fantasy out of you. I thought we agreed on no more teasing."

I trembled with laughter. By now, I knew Carter was crazy enough to fly across the country and back just for a chance to be with me.

Images of him, butt naked, flashed through my mind. I breathed through my nose to calm the surge of hormones making me hungry for him.

"Seriously, are you naked?"

"Sorry, Country Boy, my lips are sealed." I had positioned the phone at an angle where all he could see was my face just for the fun of sweet torturing him. My new favorite hobby.

"Well, I know a trick or two that would help unseal them."

"Who's doing the teasing now?"

"Well," he said. "You make it hard to resist. You don't wanna be in my head right now."

"Or maybe I wish I could be…"

"Babe, I have to hang up," he said after a while.

I huffed, barely able to contain my deception. "I know. I kinda wish you were here, though. So far, we're not good at the long-distance stuff."

A loud chuckle parted his lips. "Yep. We're going to have to figure out how to make it easier on us. Singing for two hours with a case of blue balls isn't my definition of fun either. I'd rather sing all my songs to you and be able to make sweet love to you afterward."

"Me too. If all your gigs are like that one time in Nashville, I'm sure I'll be wet every time you sing an entire set."

"Fuck, don't say that out loud. I'm getting hard just picturing your aroused face in the crowd."

"I'm glad I can provide some visuals for you to work around later." I blushed thinking about my next words. "We could try phone sex tonight."

"Yeah, but with the time difference, my midnight will be middle of the night for you."

"I…huh… Okay, maybe tonight isn't the best time. We could try tomorrow instead. Also, don't worry about time zones. There are worse things than being woken up in the middle of the night because your boyfriend wants to give you an orgasm, no? Even if it's done virtually."

"Well, I can't say. Never had a boyfriend before." His warm laughter felt like ribbons around my heart.

"Super funny. Ha. Ha. Ha." Despite me, I joined in on the humor. "Fine, boyfriend, girlfriend, your special someone. I won't deny myself the chance to hear you grunting on the other end of the line as I speak dirty things to you and send you some visuals."

"Please stop using your sex voice. I get hard every time. Again, not helping while I'm stuck in a car amongst other people."

"Stop complaining. You usually love my sex voice."

"Touché." He paused. "What did you mean earlier

when you said tonight isn't the best time? Do you have plans with Saunders? I'm happy you two are spending time together. She really likes you. I could tell the other day. And I'm aware you've missed her during your stay in Green Mountain."

"Yeah, well…I'm not seeing her. No…" I hadn't told Carter about my plans. "It's just that tonight I'm having dinner at the Bensons. I might not be in the best emotional state for phone sex afterward."

"Oh. Are you sure that's a good idea? I don't wanna get in the middle of this, and I have no idea what happened between you guys. I won't intervene unless you ask me to. But seeing them in New York upset you. I just don't want this reunion to affect you more than it already did. I won't be there to hold your hand or dry your tears if it does."

Carter deserved the truth. "I don't want to hide anything from you. I swear. When you're back, I'll tell you everything. I promise. Don't worry about me. I'll be okay. I love you. The Bensons and I have… Let's just say our reunion is long overdue. I think it'll be good for me."

"You're not saying that to ease my mind, right?"

"Nah. I wouldn't have agreed to it if I believed it would destroy me. Sure, I might be sad right after… There's a lot of history between us. And hurt too. We all went through something traumatic together, and we didn't all react the same way. I understand that piece of information now. Back then, I was so shattered, we… I… Let's just say I think the ordeal we survived changed us all, and it took us the longest time to pick up the pieces of our broken selves. Sorry if I don't make sense. Maybe it will be good to put our past behind us once and for all. Or I hope it will. Just don't worry, okay?"

"Yeah. I trust you. Let me know how it goes. Please

keep me updated afterward. No matter the time, I'll call you if you need me."

"I will. And I'll reach out tomorrow if you have some free time."

"For you? Always. Love you, Pixie."

38

CARTER

The almost three-hour drive to Seattle flew by. April kept me fully busy as we talked about handcuffs and phone sex amongst other things.

I unfolded my body from the backseat into the parking garage of our hotel. Riley left as soon as we were parked, stating he had stuff to deal with. June updated us on the evening's schedule before following in my manager's footsteps.

After the call with April, uneasiness had taken over me, and now I felt restless, the nagging voices in my head adding to the discomfort.

Tonight, she was having dinner at the Bensons', and the idea didn't sit well with me. No matter how much she said it was fine and that she needed the reunion. In New York, they'd hinted at a long history between them. And hurtful memories. I still had to learn all about it. Tonight, she would be at their house, talking about a story I wasn't part of. One I wasn't privy to. To compensate for the lack of information, I conjured all sorts of scenarios in my head. I knew the Bensons hurt her, and just the thought of it got me unhinged. I loathed the feeling of powerlessness I faced, knowing I was too far away in case she required moral support. Or a shoulder to cry on. Or an ally to pick up the pieces afterward if their meeting broke her. I had witnessed firsthand how seeing them had affected her the last time, and I despised the idea she was going to their house all by herself with no one in her corner.

No matter how much I tried to push the idea of April and her ex-in-laws away, my thoughts always circled back to them. A bad feeling twisted my guts. One I would only be able to put to rest when I heard back from her.

Lost in my mind, I scratched my forehead, trying to recall everything April had ever said about their relationship.

Except mentioning she dated their son in college and they pushed her out of their lives when tragedy hit them, I couldn't think of anything else. There was more to the story. I could tell. Would her ex-boyfriend be there tonight? Were the Bensons playing matchmakers, hoping April and their son got back together? A tightness grew around my heart, and my skin itched at the *what-ifs* that invaded my mind. I shut my eyes, begging my brain not to go there, the idea it could all be a setup making me jittery.

I trusted April, and she could look after herself. If she believed their motives were less than honorable, she would have told me, right?

Even though I tried to block my train of thought, my brain kept conjuring all these possibilities.

What was April and—what was his name? Tim? Trevor? No, Travis. Yeah, that was it. What was their relationship like nowadays? Did they still talk? Did they meet to catch up every now and then, or were they strangers to each other? More unwelcome questions popped up in my head. I had to shut down the voices telling me to worry or else I'd have one of my episodes, and I really didn't need to plunge into darkness right now.

April loved me. She told me so herself.

This had to be enough. We loved each other. We were good together.

But my dating rap sheet was a clusterfuck, and so my doubts resurfaced.

Did she still love Travis too? The same way she loved me? Did she miss him sometimes?

My lungs idled.

My mind started racing, and I suffocated.

Breathe in. Breathe out.

I had to regain control of my mind, or I would lose the battle inside me.

April was mine. All mine.

I trusted her.

She told me earlier she was sad she couldn't come with me this week.

Like she said, she needed to close this chapter of her past to move forward with her life. With me. Us. This was a good thing. It meant she was serious about us. I should hang on to that fact.

What we had couldn't be faked. I'd witnessed fake in the past. Our relationship looked nothing like it. It was genuine. Based on trust and respect. I blew out a scraggy breath, my nerves settling down.

"Let's take our luggage to our rooms because I'm going for a walk," I informed Ed as he opened the trunk to retrieve our bags. "I'm suffocating, and I need some air."

"You okay?" He knew me enough to understand my mental state without my admitting it out loud.

I nodded. "Just some pent-up energy to get rid of. Nothing a little exercise won't relieve."

He studied me with a concerned expression.

"I have it under control. Come on, let's go."

Ten minutes later, with a gray beanie and a pair of shades on, I ambled through downtown Seattle, Ed flanking me, dressed in street clothes. I let the vibes from the city uplift all my senses, silencing my overactive imagination.

Suffusing myself with the energy of the city I performed in was vital. Some sort of ritual I did whenever I had the chance.

The show tomorrow would be electric. I could feel it in my bones. It tickled my core. I loved the thrill it always brought me. I scanned my surroundings, the excitement palpable in the air. My hair stood on end on my arms. The humidity in the air sent shivers through me. For a fraction of a second, I stared at the Space Needle in the distance. Everything around me seemed so familiar and yet, so foreign.

The stroll helped me clear my head. It brought me a sense of peace. Usually, I preferred to go on a run when my racing thoughts didn't shut up, but today, I decided to let the warm rays of the sun and fresh air soothe my agitated self.

On our way back to the hotel, I halted before the window of a jewelry store on Pine Street.

Through the glass, the display embedded in a bed of baby-pink and cream rose petals caught my eye. With my hands shoved in my jacket pockets, I stood there for a long moment, staring at a piece of jewelry. Simple, yet sophisticated. Rose gold. Perfect.

My feet entered the store of their own accord. Every piece of pink jewelry reminded me of April. Ed stood by the front door, his hands linked in front of him, giving me a puzzled stare. With a shrug, I ignored him and ventured further into the store.

"Oh dear God." The woman behind the counter gasped upon seeing me. "Are you who I think you are?"

I bobbed my head once, my lips tight, a warning in my gaze, asking her to be quiet, hoping her whisper-yell didn't turn into a full-blown shriek that would attract any attention to me.

"I'm Ruth, the owner. Please follow me, Mr. Hills. We'll provide you with the privacy you need."

I cocked my head in Ed's direction, and without a word, he followed me into a small room on the far left, behind an impressive watch display.

Ruth dropped the fangirl act and switched to business-woman mode.

Thirty minutes later, I exited the store with a box I stuffed into the inner chest pocket of my jacket, my thoughts anchored to the woman I loved. "Wanna grab a bite?" I asked Ed as we passed rows of food trucks.

"Starving."

We checked our options. Once we decided, he followed me as we parted the crowd. I stayed on the side while he ordered, trying not to bring attention to myself.

Back at the hotel, I paced the suite. My earlier panic about April and her ex had diminished, but there was still something about April meeting the Bensons tonight that unnerved me. She said she would keep me updated, but hours later, I still hadn't received any news. No matter what I told myself, their reunion still got me antsy. I raked my fingers through my hair, buttoned my shirt, and once again, tried to push the damning thoughts away.

June knocked on my door. "Carter, are you ready to go?" she asked as she peered into my hotel suite and let herself in.

"Yeah. Coming." I picked up my keys, phone, and wallet and followed her out the door to the idling car parked in the indoor garage, that would drive us to the restaurant she picked for tonight.

From the backseat, as I watched the city lights through the window, my mind wandered to one of the first shows I gave in Seattle, many years ago. Carter Hills Band's first sold-out concert.

I could still feel the excitement of that night deep in my bones. Stud, Dahlia, and I were surfing a high. It was also the first tour that Riley was managing. All of us were in for the ride of our lives. That show was everything we'd always dreamed of and so much more. It was our big shot. The beginning of what later made history as we sold more tickets that year than any other bands in the previous decade.

I wore my hair longer back then. We were still experimenting with our style.

I remembered the electricity in the air, the energy of the crowd, the cheers and wolf-whistles when we walked offstage after singing our hearts out for two hours straight.

It felt like a lifetime ago, but also like it had been last night. Time was a weird concept sometimes.

My heart rate accelerated, and a renewed fervor swirled inside me.

Something in me, *call it a hunch*, told me the show tomorrow would be as special, if not even more.

As long as I locked my worries away, I'd be fine.

Breathe in. Breathe out.

39

APRIL

I smoothed my hair back with shaky fingers and evened my breathing as I stood on the Bensons' front porch, my stomach in knots. I hadn't been here in over three years, but it appeared the same, except for the rosebushes Mrs. Benson had planted after Travis's death. A large brownstone with a copper-colored roof, front door, and shutters, a half-circle driveway, and a black iron gate.

I pushed a rebel strand of hair behind my ear, rubbed my clammy hands over my cream turtleneck sweater dress that I accessorized with taupe ankle suede boots, and knocked on the door. As I waited, I wondered if throwing up my own heart was possible. A little voice in my head pleaded with me to run away. The logical part of me knew I had to do this. Close this door once and for all. My chest rose and fell in quick succession as I wondered why I was putting myself in a situation I was aware would make me feel vulnerable.

Standing on the doorstep of Travis's parents' house, I was hit with a rush of memories I'd buried long ago. No matter how bad I wanted to disappear right now, it was time to deal with my past. To heal. To put my wounds to rest if I wanted a future with the man I loved. I sucked in a jagged breath, rolled my shoulders back, and emptied my lungs in one big huff. I could do this.

Memories I hadn't rehashed in a long time resurfaced.

A ball of emotions lodged in my chest. This moment felt like déjà-vu.

———

Stuart University - Freshman year

Winter semester

"I can't believe I'm so clumsy," I said out loud, mostly to myself. A series of curses followed my words.

Nana, my late grandmother's sister, the one who had raised me, wouldn't be proud of me if she heard my choice of vocabulary.

"Stupid phone. Why don't you have some battery left? You're a pain in my ass. Digging through this pile of trash has to be one of the most disgusting things I've ever done."

I sighed, angry at the electronic device that had ruined my morning. Set in the middle of the campus, The Hut, the most popular coffee shop, bustled with college students and professors desperate for a shot of caffeine at this early hour. When I explained my situation, the manager pointed me toward last night's pile of trash bags the cleaning crew had put in one corner. My stomach churned at the idea of rummaging through those. There were six bags, most of them full. The putrid smell of used coffee grounds and day-old remnants filled my nostrils.

Using the elastic band I kept around my wrist, I tied my blonde hair into a knot at the top of my head, removed my hoodie and stowed it in my bag, and then rolled the sleeves of my shirt up to my elbows, ready to get my hands dirty.

I sidestepped to the left, trying not to ruin the mid-calf high heel boots I'd gifted myself for Christmas, as I closed in on the stack of trash bags.

I began rummaging through the rubbish, breathing through my mouth in case the smell engaged my gag reflex. "C'mon, phone of hell, show yourself. I need to get to class, you asshole. Way to begin a new semester."

"I'm sorry to bother you, but are you picking apart those poor garbage bags? What have they ever done to anger you?" A male voice questioned my senses from behind me.

I blew loose tendrils of my hair off my face, not willing to touch it with my filthy hands, and turned around, recalling not to wipe my hands on my favorite pair of jeans.

"You would too if this pile of shit had engulfed your pricey electronic gadget last night."

"Last night? I'm confused." The guy scratched the side of his gorgeous face. Unruly blond hair, symmetrical face, straight nose, athletic shape. He wore his washed-out jeans low on his hips and a snug white T-shirt that showcased his toned body. Not that I noticed, but I totally did. "Have you been headfirst into these trash piles all night?" His words cut short my ogling of him.

"Why do you care? You're not the one with the lost phone." Smoke exited my nose. And my ears. Or at least I imagined it did. I was losing valuable time here.

"You're feisty. I like that." The guy fished his own device out of his messenger bag. "Give me your number. I'll call this phone of yours. That way you'll be able to go on with your day." He shrugged and flashed me a lopsided smile.

I folded my arms over my chest, avoiding touching anything with my soiled hands. "You think I hadn't thought of that?" I arched an eyebrow. "I may look every shade of stupid right now, but I can assure you I'm not. My phone is dead, Mr. Smarty-Pants. That's why I'm tearing apart these disgusting trash bags with my bare hands, hoping it will show up."

"Did you really spend your entire night looking for it?" He frowned, and I found him even more irresistible. At least six feet tall, broad shoulders, dimples, and a smile to die for. My eyes traveled from his head to his toes, taking him all in once more.

Why did I have to meet the only cute guy who made my heart bounce when it seemed I hadn't showered in weeks and smelled like a waste dump?

I let out the longest and deepest sigh ever. "I came here last evening to study with my friends. It was late when we left, and I must have dropped my dead phone in one of those," I pointed to the trash bags circling me, "and only realized it too late. The place was closed when I came back, so I returned early this morning to search for it. Why am I even telling you all this?" I shook my head and tore open another bag of junk, ignoring Mr. Know-It-All.

He stood there, with his arms folded, staring at me. Silver-blonde strands of hair fell over my face, and he pushed the locks back with the tips of his fingers. A shiver ran along my spine at the contact of his skin on mine. My cheeks warmed, and I forgot to breathe for a minute. I tried to thank him, but no words came out.

I smacked myself mentally.

Nana would tell me to woman up.

Saunders would tell me to seize the chance.

I did nothing.

I half-smiled and turned around, with a mushy heart, to plunge my hands in yet another heap of junk.

"Let me help you."

My eyes flared. Why would a stranger want to help me out? Under these circumstances? What was wrong with this guy?

"You don't have to. I mean, they are my trash bags to deal with. I'm the one who threw my phone away. It was in my tray with my burger wrapper and an empty can of soda," I said, flashing a shy smile his way.

The blond guy's eyes—which I hadn't taken the time to study— were gold with flecks of green around the pupils, sucked me in.

"I insist." He shrugged. "I wanna help you."

"You're strange. That suits you." I chuckled and pondered a thought for a few seconds. "If you find my phone, I'll buy you dinner tonight. Pizza sounds good?"

The guy nodded, a glimmer of amusement in his gaze. "Pizza is perfect. What if you're the one who finds your phone?"

I giggled. "It would be weird to treat myself to dinner. That's what I do every night."

"What if I was the one to invite you to dinner then?" He tipped his eyebrows up, and a weird chuckle escaped my lips.

I clamped my mouth shut. The amusement painted on his face made me giddy.

"You want to buy me dinner if I find my own phone that I dropped in the trash can in a moment of inattention last night? This is what you're saying?"

He shook his head. "No. I want to cook dinner for you if you find your own phone, that you dropped in a garbage can last night, after an entire evening of studying, by mistake. You were exhausted. These things happen."

My heart throbbed in my chest. Had I asked a guy out without intending to? His friendliness puzzled me.

"So, do we have a deal?" He raised an eyebrow in question.

I inhaled deeply and stared at his boyish smile longer than I intended to. Time to act upon it, April. Make Nana proud. *"Okay. We have a deal." I held out my hand to shake his, but he scowled at it.*

"Usually, I would shake on that, but right now your hand is kind of disgusting, so I'll pass."

My eyes dropped to my mustard-stained palm, and we both burst out laughing. "Huh…then let's feet bump."

We both shifted our weight to one leg and raised the other one to kick each other's foot.

"Let's dig in." A huge grin brightened his handsome face. How could he turn this mishap into an exciting challenge? "It looks abso-

lutely yummy in there. Maybe I could put together a healthy breakfast right here. Hungry?"

A wide smile spread across his lips, and I forced myself to avert my gaze, the temptation to crash my mouth on his growing with every passing second.

"By the way, I'm Travis."

"April. Thanks for helping me out, Travis." My entire body tingled with heat.

"The pleasure is all mine."

———

I used my fingertip to wipe a tear, waiting for the Bensons to open the door, not sure how to act.

My eyes watered at the memory of how Travis and I first met.

Love at first sight. The moment our eyes locked, I knew deep in my heart I'd love him forever.

That morning at The Hut, he ended up finding my phone but placed it—not so subtly—into the trash bag in my hands, so he'd be able to cook me dinner. Tacos. I'd never forget.

We shared our first kiss on the second date. It seemed like a lifetime ago but also as if it had happened last week.

On our sixth date, Travis brought me here for the first time, and I met his parents that night.

We had sex on the ninth one and moved in together after six months. In his shoebox-size apartment.

He died a little over three years later.

I heard footsteps inside and braced myself for the reunion I was so not ready for while remembering my first time here.

Travis had promised his parents would love me. At first, I had doubted it. Why would they love a girl like me?

An orphan who didn't know her own parents because they'd left her before even giving her a chance to be loved.

Wearing a pastel-green dress with a bouquet of white lilies clutched tightly in my hands, I had prayed the Bensons would welcome me into their family. Travis had reached out for my other hand, and my fears had vanished.

I was invited to their weekly Sunday night dinner after two months. In no time, they became the parental figures I never had growing up.

We spent vacations together. Travis and I came over for game nights. Movie nights. Mrs. Benson treated me to the spa a few times and shopped with me when I needed a new dress or had a hard time picking out a comforter for our bedroom.

Our relationship changed when Travis got sick, and they ordered him to move back home. It came from a heartfelt place…or I hoped it did. They wanted to take care of their only son when his health declined faster than any doctor could've predicted. Travis refused. He wanted to stay with me. In our own house.

My relationship with his parents unraveled from that moment. They loathed me. They saw me as their rival. For a while, they forgot we all played for the same team and wanted what was best for Travis.

My boyfriend pushed them away, and they never forgave either of us. They blamed me for all his choices.

The door opened, and I sucked in a breath, the memories dissolving in front of my eyes. Mrs. Benson greeted me herself, and I hesitated a second. Usually, Louise, the housekeeper, welcomed all the guests. Her arms wrapped around me in an awkward hug that I returned with a rigid stance. She released me and invited me inside. I clenched and unclenched my hands at my sides, not knowing what to do with them, and inhaled a shaky breath as I entered the house I'd never thought I'd set foot in ever again.

I followed Mrs. Benson but stopped in my tracks once I entered the foyer. A montage of black and white pictures of Travis through the years covered the wall on my left. I recognized at least two of them, that I had snapped myself. There was also one of all of us on Christmas morning, sporting matching PJs and giant grins. A fog clouded my vision, and I looked away.

I surveyed the mansion from where I stood. Everything else in the foyer was the same as I remembered, and a wave of nostalgia hit me. The Bensons were wealthy. I kind of forgot about it.

Travis didn't want the same lifestyle as his parents. He wanted to earn his own money—he had two jobs while studying computer science and engineering full-time in college—and always refused to let his parents pay for anything. I never complained. I loved that about him. His independence. His strong will. We put the deposit on our house using a portion of his grandparents' inheritance and most of the little life insurance money I inherited after Nana passed away.

I lacked nothing growing up. Nana always made sure I had all my basic needs covered. But we weren't rich, and I learned early on to fend for myself.

Mrs. Benson erased the gap between us and wrapped her arms around me once again, hugging me against her soft chest and not letting go of me this time.

She'd never been affectionate toward me before, rarely showing any emotions. She always kept everything locked in. Two hugs in as many minutes were a first.

Tears rolled down my face, and sobs rocked my body.

"Shhh, dear. Let it all out. It's okay. I'm here now. I'll never push you away ever again."

All my bottled-up feelings toward the Bensons and the tragedy that struck us years ago burst free.

Travis's mom traced small, soothing circles with her hand on my back, and it helped calm me down. At that moment, I missed having a mother in my life. A maternal figure to support me through hardships.

To regain some of my composure, I firmed my shoulders and lifted my chin up. "I'm sorry for breaking down, Mrs. Benson." She used to hate any show of weakness.

"Don't apologize, April. Never. You can break down anytime you want around us. It's okay. We know how much you must miss him, because we do too. Every day. And we miss you too. A lot."

I blinked, stunned.

Mrs. Benson led me to the living room, where her husband offered me a glass of wine, and we all sat down. I perused the room, my eyes lingering on mementos honoring Travis's life spread around the space. A painting he did in art class when he was a teen. A signed football from his favorite professional team. A trophy from his T-ball team days. More pictures of him from his early age up to his last days. Everything about being in Travis's childhood home and facing his parents felt both familiar and unusual. I smoothed my dress with trembling fingers, doing my best to avoid their stares. The wine flowed down my throat, dousing the blaze in my mouth. Being here awoke loads of memories I'd tucked away years ago. My lips quivered. I had no clue how to act. For a split second, I wondered why I accepted their invitation to come here tonight. It was a bad idea. I should excuse myself and leave. And yet, here I was, glued to my seat and unable to move. The spiral of emotions inside me made me dizzy, and I feared I wouldn't be able to contain the new batch of tears I was trying so hard to keep inside.

Mr. Benson cleared his throat. "April, we're grateful you came here tonight. There's so much we need to apologize for."

I eased a little at his words, and my blood warmed so much I could feel it running inside my veins.

I ran my tongue along my lower lip to bring moisture back to my mouth.

"We're sorry, dear. We were wrong. You stayed by his side right up until the end, and for this, we'll always be thankful. You were Travis's angel, and when he chose to leave this world, we should've been there for you. You needed us, and we failed you. We needed you too, but our pride took over, and we missed the chance. You were the love of his life, and we should have respected the fact he wanted to spend his last days on this Earth by your side. Even if it hurt us. We know it wasn't his intention. Our grief blinded us. Travis would be ashamed of how we reacted. He would hate us for pushing you away and making your life a living hell because we were heartbroken."

I wiped off the lone tear rolling down my cheek with the pad of my forefinger. I swallowed around the rock-hard lump in my throat, and my shoulders relaxed. It took Mr. and Mrs. Benson three years to say these words to me. The agitated part of my heart simmered down. The voice in my head urging me to leave quietened. With the last hurtful memories linking us all together and the aftermath of our epic fallout following Travis's death not sucking all the oxygen molecules away, the air inside the room lightened.

For the next hour, we talked about Travis. A lot. I cried. They cried. I laughed at some of the stories about his life, and so did they. With care and gentleness, I removed the padlock from the door of the memories I'd carefully stowed in my heart. At some point, the acidic taste in my mouth—the one that had been there for so long I thought I was born with it—dissipated, and I breathed easier.

"How is the foundation doing?" I asked when we moved to the dining room.

Mrs. Benson's lips curled up, her face a poster of all the pride filling her. "Oh, it's doing great. Better than we ever expected." She reached across the table and gave my hand a squeeze. Never before had I seen Mrs. Benson breaking etiquette. Tonight, up until now, she'd broken at least four of her own rules. "April, have you known Mr. Hills for a long time?"

My face warmed up, and I glanced down for a moment, trying to calm the rush of heat surging through me.

Mrs. Benson offered a shy smile my way and spoke before I could say anything. "April, you and Mr. Hills make a great couple. Travis would approve. I know the look of love when I see it. Carter Hills is madly in love with you, in case you didn't know. He's lucky he found you, dear. You're a rare gem."

A soft laugh left my mouth as flutters danced under my skin. Never would I have imagined sitting in the dining room of my late boyfriend's childhood home, discussing my new love life with his parents over a glass of wine and cheesecake.

Mr. Benson weighed in. "Mr. Hills has a good head over his shoulders, and he seemed to care a lot about you the other night. We want you to be happy. You deserve another chance at love."

My heart tightened. My breathing hitched. With a few blinks, I prevented another flood down my face.

"In case we weren't clear enough earlier, we're sorry, April. We knew how stubborn and proud Travis was. We should've never blamed anything on you. We were upset… It doesn't make it right, though. Life stole our only child from us, and you paid the price. You were a daughter to us. We had no right to reject you. You found yourself all alone with no family once again because of our selfishness. We overreacted, letting our sadness take over our better judgment. You don't have to see us again after tonight if you choose not to, but we'd like for you to call us from time to time. Keep us updated. We're not your family anymore, we understand that, but we'd love to be your…friends? If that's something you're open to consider." Mr. Benson's confessions made my eyes watery again. He wasn't a man of many words. The ones he spoke beelined straight to my heart and jolted it hard.

Tears welled up in the corners of my eyes. I wiped them off with a napkin. "I'd like that. When Travis died, I- I lost the only family I'd ever known."

Mr. and Mrs. Bensons got up and enveloped me in their arms.

Like loving parents did.

"I'm sorry I didn't tell you about what Travis was up to. He asked me not to say anything. He…he feared you would interfere and stop him. I shouldn't have kept it to myself." I sniffled. This guilt had weighed on me for so long.

"It was his wish, dear. We've learned to accept it. It took us a long time. Don't blame yourself anymore. We've made our peace with it. You should too." Mrs. Benson took my hand in hers, and somehow, I felt the tension melt away, replaced by a quiet sense of belonging.

Later, when we parted ways, my heart felt lighter.

I wheeled out of the driveway, wishing I could go home to Carter and bury myself in his arms. To let his strength wash over me. To feel his love, and to love him back.

What was I doing here, in Ginger Creek, Georgia, when he was on the West Coast about to rock a stage in less than twenty-four hours?

I missed him.

Since I had made my peace with my ex-in-laws, I was ready to move on. The first step was to cheer my man on and stand by his side.

Taylor had taken the night off after I insisted he take some time for himself. At first, he declined when I offered, but I wouldn't take *No* for an answer. I promised to call him after dinner to ease his worries. I didn't need a security detail following me around twenty-four seven. Also, I yearned for some alone time to think as I drove myself. It took a bit of convincing, but he finally agreed when I told him Reed had the night off too and they could have dinner or do some guys' stuff. We'd spent a lot of time with Saunders and Reed since we arrived in town, and the guys got along pretty great. I was glad Taylor had someone to hang out with since he was away from his wife, who lived in Nashville, and had to put his life on the back burner to babysit me.

Carter's bodyguard answered on the first ring.

"Hey, it's me. I just left. I should be home in forty minutes." The Bensons lived just outside Clementine, a short drive from Stuart University where I went to college.

When I parked in my driveway, Taylor was waiting for me, his back pressed against the front door, hands linked in front of him, seriousness in his gaze. I fought a smile at the sight of him—standing there like some kind of Secret Service agent—on my front porch.

"Never thought I'd have 007 waiting for me at home," I joked the moment I eased out of my car.

He kept his composure, but I noticed a small twitch of his lips and a twinkle in his eye. Whether he wanted it or not, we'd be good friends soon. I could tell. Taylor opened the door and stepped aside so I'd get in first. I turned around to face him as soon as he shut the door behind him, craning my neck back to meet his eyes. Beside him, I looked like a child as he towered over me by more than a foot and was about twice my width.

"Listen, I've got a plan, and I gotta know if you're on board. I'll make us a late snack and tell you all about it."

Sitting side by side in the kitchen, we indulged in chocolate chip cookies over tea as I browsed the internet.

"Okay," I said. "The first flight to Seattle tomorrow morning is at seven. You're in?"

"Absolutely."

With my credit card in hand, I purchased two tickets. I was done waiting for my life to happen. Time to woman up. Nana would approve. Tonight, something had shifted inside me. In some twisted way, Mr. and Mrs. Benson had granted me permission to start living again. Their approval of my falling in love again had set me free. Nothing could hold me back anymore.

"I'll text Ed and inform him about our arrival tomorrow."

I nodded. "Please ask him to keep it to himself. I want it to be a surprise. Since we need an insider for it to unfold as I have imagined, he'll be our guy." I chuckled. "It sounds as if we're planning a heist."

Taylor shook his head, chewing on a cookie. This time, he didn't even try to hide the amusement playing on his face.

"I know you're not used to flying coach, but I don't own a private jet," I teased with a wink. "So, those tickets will have to do. You have long legs. I hope you won't be too uncomfortable."

"You know I could've chartered you a private plane or gotten first-class tickets, right?"

"No, I want to do this on my own."

"April, I gotta say, you're a special one. Carter is lucky to have you in his life. You're good for him. Also, don't worry about me. I love remembering where I come from. I always choose to fly economy when I travel on my own."

His words made their way to my heart and brought a smile to my lips. "Thank you."

"I mean every word."

I reached for his hand over the counter and squeezed. He didn't yank it away, and it made me happy. I had an ally in my go-to-Carter mission, and right now, I couldn't wait for the morning to come.

We were at the gate, waiting to board our flight. I fidgeted with the hem of my sweater and pushed my hair behind my ears for the tenth time in as many minutes. Taylor read a book on his tablet, but I was unable to sit still. I paced the airport floor. Dizzy and filled with angst, I called my best friend who answered on the third ring.

Before she'd even spoken a word, I facepalmed. "Oh, sorry, Saund. I forgot how early it is. Did I wake you up? I can call you back later if you prefer."

"Hello to you too. Don't. I was up. My bladder was about to explode. Your timing is perfect. What's going on? Insomnia again?" Saunders did a poor job of hiding her worries about me, fighting a yawn. I couldn't blame her. Over the last few years, my hitting rock bottom and losing myself more than once had given her enough ammunition to be concerned about my mental state when I was acting out of character.

"Not quite. Going to Seattle on a secret mission." I blew out a breath. "I wanna surprise my boyfriend in Seattle and woo him before his big show tonight."

"Wait. What? You are?"

I bobbed my head even though she couldn't see it through the phone. "At the airport right now. With Taylor."

"Go, get that hot piece of ass, girl. Find that man of yours and make sweet love to him." She cleared her throat. "How did it go with monster-in-law and her husband last night?"

I sighed. "The evil in-laws episode in my life is over. We're good. I can move forward. They even claimed HN and I look great together. And said he was madly in love with me." I twisted the ring on my right finger. It felt weird to admit it out loud. "Anyway, they gave me their blessing, not that I needed it, but still, it felt great to have them in my corner again. Who would have thought?"

"Whoa. I'm speechless. They did? April, this is huge. Keep me updated, okay?" Saunders's voice was low and croaky. "I want all the details."

"Is everything all right?"

"Yeah, no worries. Just the lack of sleep. With the moving and my assistant being away on maternity leave, I'm knackered. Going back to Bedfordshire again. Be safe, and don't do anything I wouldn't do."

"I have to go anyway. We're about to board the plane. Will you or Reed be able to feed Bernice for a few days?"

"Yes. I'd watch your ugly ball of fur anytime if it means you're getting laid. Have a nice flight." She paused. "And, April, I'm proud of you. Happiness suits you. I love you."

"Love you too."

Another piece of my heart fell into place.

We landed in Seattle early in the afternoon. Ed had arranged for a car to pick us up. My plan was to wait inside Carter's dressing room before his show and surprise him. Nothing excessive. I didn't do complicated. My mind surfed back to last night. Through his parents, Travis too gave me his blessing to be happy again. It made me yearn to scream "I'm free" at the top of my lungs. Something I didn't know I craved until I got it.

New day.

New me.

New goal.

———

Dressed in a sexy black lace dress with a plunging neckline, that ended mid-thigh, and golden pumps I found in a store in downtown Seattle when Taylor and I went shopping earlier, I sat in the green room. Waiting.

The dress wasn't as sophisticated as the gown I wore at the fundraiser or the sequin designer number from Nashville, but it fitted in my budget and looked great on me. It showed just enough skin to drive Carter crazy. By now, I knew the man's weaknesses. And tonight, I was playing with them on purpose, and I enjoyed every second of it. I relished the fact I was the one who planned a surprise this time around. The idea only spread shivers of lust through me.

In the mirror, I checked my reflection one last time, adjusting my décolletage and fluffing my hair.

Yes, I looked hot and couldn't wait to see Carter's expression once he saw me.

My phone chimed, breaking the silence. Excitement filled me when I read the message on the screen.

ED

Carter is on his way.

I held my breath. The hammering of my heart deafened me, and no matter how much I told myself to keep calm, I was a ball of nerves as I waited for my man to join me. Needing to keep my hands busy, I fidgeted with the gold band on my right ring finger—the wedding band Travis gave me that I wore as a good-luck charm—and took a seat. Even after all this time, I never could convince myself to take the band off. Instead, I just switched hands a few months after he passed. Through the years, it had become a piece of me. A little reminder life could be fleeting and that we had to seize opportunities when they presented themselves. Something I had a hard time doing before I moved to Green Mountain, but that I was now fully embracing.

On the white leather chair, sitting with my legs crossed at the ankles, I waited, my back straight, my hands entwined between my knees, trying to project the confidence I lacked.

My pulse escalated. I loved the badass idea of being here without Carter's knowledge. It'd been a long time since I did something impulsive, but this felt right.

Minutes ticked by.

Where was he? Carter should be here by now. Time had slowed since I received Ed's text almost ten minutes ago.

My leg bounced, anticipation running high inside me.

I was about to shoot Ed a message when I heard muted voices on the other side of the door. My heart heaved, and I smoothed my hair with my fingers one last time.

The door opened, and Ed peeked inside, scanning the room. He gave me a small nod and moved aside to let Carter in. I held my breath, taking the time to admire him. Right now, he looked every bit of the star he was. Watching him, I had to remind myself he was mine. Engrossed in his phone, his thumb flicking across the screen, he didn't notice my presence. His fingers tapped the screen in quick motions. The chime of my phone cut through the silence, startling us both.

His head jerked up. An expression of confusion followed by blossoming happiness spread across his face. Pure lust replaced his shock as his gaze took me in from head to toe. Until it returned to my face.

We watched each other.

A buzz developed at the tip of my spine.

Excitement bubbled up in my bloodstream.

His gorgeous face. His stunned expression. The blaze in his eyes. They all rendered me speechless.

Without breaking eye contact, I sucked in a silent breath and fished my phone out of my purse with shaky fingers and read the message my boyfriend had sent me mere seconds ago.

CARTER

Wish you were here.

My fingers moved across the keypad, and I fought to control the tremors and my shallow breaths as I typed back.

ME

Wish you could see your face right now.

His gaze returned to me. With enough heat to melt the stadium. I rubbed my thighs together, trying to diffuse the ache building in my core.

CARTER

My eyes are playing tricks on me. I see you everywhere.

I bit my tongue to avoid smiling and took a big inhale as I typed the next words, knowing his answer would set the room on fire.

ME

What would you do to me if I were there?

Desire darkened his eyes, making my pulse thrum in response.

The game between us was the best kind of foreplay.

CARTER

Dirty things. Real dirty.

My fingers swiped the screen on their own. I could barely suck a full breath in as scenarios filled my mind.

ME

Show me. I'm all yours.

I kept a poker face, not an easy feat when Carter cocked his head and studied me, seriousness dripping from his features.

He returned his attention to his phone, but not before hesitating, making me squirm in my seat, the heat building inside me.

CARTER

We only have thirty minutes. I'm not sure it's
enough.

I let out a soft whimper, licking my lips as my mouth watered at the promises his words carried.

ME

I'll take whatever you give me.

I was tempted to add *Please*.

A sly smile broke through his intensity, and a spark ignited in his irises.

Carter stepped back to lock the door of the dressing room. I blew out the breath I'd been holding. He spun to face me, and I swore that even at a distance, he could control my body without laying a finger on me.

CARTER

Take off your dress and sit on the counter,
legs spread.

Turning around slowly and with my back to him, I undressed, swaying my hips to tease him. I took my time, enjoying the burn his gaze left on the skin of my back as I titillated him with a striptease. My dress pooled at my feet. Bending over, I picked it up, giving him the perfect view of my ass, and placed it on the chair.

Spying on Carter over my shoulder, I relished the expression on his face. From the slack jaw to the dilated pupils as he took in the black tulle and lace corset and garter set I wore underneath my dress that I bought with him in mind.

His throat bobbed, and his eyes followed my movements when I sat on the counter used as a makeup station, legs spread, my hands on each side of me as instructed.

Carter ripped his long-sleeved charcoal shirt open, and the buttons flew away as he prowled in my direction.

His hands, big and strong, clutched my bare thighs, and his fingers dug into my flesh. A soft gasp escaped my mouth. His dark irises burned holes into my flesh, and the sound of my pants echoed through the room. I extended my neck enough to brush my lips over his, but he leaned back.

"You don't get to make the moves, Pixie. You came into *my* dressing room, and that means I'm in charge. Now spread wider."

I did as I was told. Oxygen couldn't reach my lungs anymore.

My body shuddered with desire.

With a twist of his wrist, Carter ripped my panties and tucked them into his back pocket. "Don't look for them later. They're coming onstage with me."

I had no idea, when I came here, that the little game I had planned would turn me on so bad. I nibbled my bottom lip, sure my teeth would leave an imprint on my flesh, waiting for the next command.

"God, April, stop doing this. It's killing me." His husky voice sent a bolt of electricity between my thighs.

All my cells trembled in anticipation. My hormones were having a blast messing with my body.

Carter circled my naked thighs with his hands and pulled me closer to the edge of the counter. He kneeled in front of me and kissed my center before running his tongue along my wet folds.

"Fuck, you taste like heaven." I almost came at his words and the soft contact of his greedy mouth. He leaned back for a brief second, and our eyes met. He flashed me a victorious grin and dropped between my legs, his ravenous tongue stealing my ability to think or speak.

My head fell against the wall, and I moaned so loud the air vibrated around us. He dived two fingers into my soaked center, and another whimper tumbled out of my mouth. His tongue circled my bundle of nerves, and I writhed, unable to stay still, my body coiled tight with all the sensations swirling through me. Carter's curled fingers slid in and out of me at a steady rhythm, each stroke taking me toward my climax. His other hand clamped my hipbone, holding me in place as if he feared I would disappear.

He sucked and rolled my clit between his lips. I dug my teeth into my bottom lip again, silencing the cries building up in my throat. Unable to sit straight, I reclined and braced my weight on my straight arms, surfing the first rush of ecstasy forming in my core.

"Oh God, keep going," I blurted out the words, breathless, my body aching, overwhelmed by too many sensations.

"You can call me Carter, you know," he smirked against my flesh. Devilish glints flashed in his gaze when he looked at me.

The pleasure inside me rose past the trigger point.

His fingers increased their pace. He assaulted my throbbing flesh with purpose. My entire body quaked, and my walls tightened around him. Before I could drag another breath in, I came all over him when he tongue-fucked me to oblivion. My body tenses, and tremors shook my body. How could he always transform me into an achy mess every time he touched me?

My man brought his fingers to his mouth and licked them clean. His eyes remained fixed on me, never blinking. The temperature in the room skyrocketed.

My mouth watered at this sight.

My inner thighs ached for more. A lot more.

By surprising him here, I had woken up a beast, and I relished the animalistic side of him.

Carter's hands found my chest, and I gasped when he lowered the garter cups, revealing my full breasts. He kissed its way up to my rock-hard nipples. I stifled a cry, and he slid his fingers into my mouth, silencing me, while his lips played with my tender flesh, licking and teasing me in the most delicious manner. I tasted myself on his wet digits, and the thought he'd been savoring me seconds ago and getting high while doing so increased my arousal.

Just when I believed I couldn't take it anymore, he flipped me on my stomach and laid my upper body over the counter, my feet still in my golden heels, glued to the floor. My naked breasts pressed against the cold surface, my nipples now stiff peaks.

He grabbed a fistful my hair, holding me still. This version of him was highly addictive. I loved it when Carter made love to me, but when he was demanding, it always woke up the part of me I never knew existed before him.

The sound of the zipper being lowered sent tingles in my lower belly. A second later, he freed himself and speared into me in one slow and alluring motion, not even taking the time to undress completely, his jeans and boxer briefs bunched around his knees.

All my cells quivered at the intrusion.

I bit on my fist, swallowing every whimper coming from my mouth.

With one hand on my hip and the other still fisting my hair, he rammed into me. "Come for me, April. Come hard."

I lifted my ass higher, deepening our connection, his balls hitting my clit every time he thrust into me, sending high voltage to my core.

"That's it, Fairy. Get yourself off. Use me."

He pushed into me with punishing strokes. My legs weakened. The familiar zing of an orgasm built inside me. I got dizzy.

Balling my hands with nothing to anchor me, I let go.

I stifled a scream when I came undone, my eyelids fluttering as surges of pleasure filled me. Before I could realize what he was doing, Carter slid out of me, flipped me to my back, and pumped himself until he jerked off, splashing my bare chest. Our lips met in a frenzied kiss that stole the remnants of my breath away. My head spun as he devoured my mouth hard and soft. Hungrily and with love. Taking everything from me. And giving me everything he possessed.

Before our trip to New York, we had ditched the condoms—we were both clean, and I had confirmed I was on birth control. I thanked the universe we did because having all of him, raw, hot, and swollen inside me, equaled nothing I'd ever felt before.

With a tissue, he wiped me clean and helped me up to my feet once the tremors subsided. My knees wobbled, and he kept a hand on my waist until I steadied myself.

In the sweetest gesture, he lowered his head, and his lips connected with my chest, where he'd just erased all traces of him, marking me with his love this time. "Babe, I'm gonna give the best show tonight. You being here is all I've ever wanted. How did you make this happen?"

I winked. "A girl doesn't tell all her secrets."

"Fuck, I love you."

I grinned and got dressed. Minus the panties. "I guess I'm not getting my underwear back?" I asked with a tip of my brow.

"Forget it. They're mine now."

Carter picked another shirt from the rack on the back

wall, put it on, and laced our fingers together as I followed him backstage.

From backstage, I watched the man I loved give the performance of his life.

Twenty minutes through his set, he sang my song, and I almost liquefied on the side of the stage, each of his words vibrating deep inside me.

Savannah Prince had stolen this moment from me the night of the fundraiser. Nobody would take it away from me tonight. Carter stared at me the whole time he sang the lyrics, shooting an arrow straight to my heart. The first time I heard my song, I thought I'd only inspired some lyrics. Now that I knew Carter loved me for real, it changed the way I listened to his words. They now held so much more meaning.

Each line made my heart jump in my chest. I resisted the urge to run into his arms and kiss him on this stage in front of tens of thousands of people. Instead, I stood there, singeing this moment into my memory as I watched him with tears of elation in my eyes, swallowing each of his words, my love for him running high.

Life had a funny way of placing people on your road sometimes.

After Travis's death, I was convinced my heart had been ruined forever. That I would never get over the grief that had paralyzed me for so long. I concluded no one else could ever resuscitate my bleeding heart, and losing him had condemned me to be single and miserable for the rest of my life. In some ways, I felt like I had used up my one chance at love and that no matter what the future held, nothing would ever compare to our love story. Epic and powerful.

Little did I know that strong and earth-shattering love could hit twice and that I could be consumed by my love for another human as much as I had been with my first truelove. Never in my wildest dreams had I imagined my heart could heal and learn to love again.

Saunders sending me to Green Mountain was the wakeup call I needed. She put me on the path I was destined to travel on. Now I had the certitude.

Falling for Carter had changed everything I believed I knew about love.

He came into my life when I least expected it and swept me off my feet.

All those times I wished upon a star for a new beginning, I never thought the universe had been listening to me. But it had. It just made my wishes come true when the timing was right and I was ready. I tilted my head back and winked at the ceiling, imagining it was the sky. A silent *Thank you* parted my lips. Perhaps it was Travis's doing or my destiny, but I was thankful all the same for how my life had turned out lately and the second chance I had been offered.

Carter strummed his guitar, capturing my eyes.

Goose bumps spread all over me as the man I loved sang for no one else but me. In a sold-out stadium, he made me feel as if we were alone.

Mid-show, he roamed backstage to lock his lips to mine. He kissed me like he hadn't had a chance in weeks. His shirt stuck to his skin, drenched in sweat. Mixed with his pine and cedarwood scent, it woke up my entire body. Again. My desire for him soared. He stared at me with unconcealed heat, and for the second time tonight, I feared my desire for him would drip all over the floor.

After claiming my mouth one last time, he ran back onstage, giving his all to his screaming fans, leaving me panting on the sidelines.

Riley neared me. "April, you woke up something in

him. You brought him back to life and dusted years of pain off his heart. The Carter Hills we used to know is back… I don't know how, and I had to see it to believe it, but girl, you did it." He squeezed my elbow and offered me a tight-lipped smile. "I'll forever be grateful. I'm happy you could make it tonight and witness it with your own eyes."

A shot of happiness traveled straight to my heart.

Did Carter know he'd brought me back to life too?

40

CARTER

People clapped my back as I exited the stage. Someone gave me a thumbs-up. Another bumped my fist.

"Nice show, Carter."

"You rocked tonight."

"You were on fire."

"Freaking incredible."

They all spoke to me, but I heard nothing. My eyes remained glued to the pink-haired girl waiting for me, her arms hugging herself in the sexy-as-fuck black dress, backstage. My throat worked. With tunnel vision, I swaggered in her direction, reminding myself of the black tulle and lace set she wore underneath her dress. My jaw tightened at the idea of ripping the fabric to shreds with my teeth. My imagination spun out of control, and I adjusted the crotch of my pants to conceal my erection. I handed my guitar to a technician and lifted my girl into my arms, twirling her around.

Our mouths fused.

My hands found her waist, resting in the dip of her hipbones.

She combed the hair on the back of my head with her fingers, eliciting shivers in their wake.

Nothing came close to having April by my side after a show. She'd traveled across the country to join me. I had no idea if it was all her doing or if my team was behind it, but right now, I didn't care. Having her here made me fucking happy.

I rubbed my hard-on against her, letting her know how horny her presence made me.

"Carter, my ass. I'm flashing everyone," she whispered in my ear, laughing.

In the heat of the moment, I had forgotten I'd confiscated her panties before going onstage. I lowered my hand, pressing the lace fabric of her dress against her bare skin.

"You're the best. I'm so proud of you." She rammed her tongue into my mouth, oblivious to everyone watching us.

"You're my muse, Fairy. Nothing can go wrong when you're beside me." I lowered her to her feet and led the way to the green room, flanked by Ed and Taylor on each side. "We've been invited to a VIP party downtown. I'll shower and change, then we'll get going."

———

We found ourselves in a dark room overlooking the dance floor below. Purple and green light beams swept the crowd and the DJ booth on the first floor. A set of remixed pop songs blasted throughout the club.

"I've never pictured this being your scene," my girl whispered, leaning closer, grazing the firm muscles of my stomach over my designer T-shirt, ripped at just the right spots, with her fingers. My groin throbbed, and I suppressed a growl, trying to keep myself under absolute control. I eyed April sideways, her irises darkening the more her gaze rested on me. The pulse in her neck made me wish I could devour her right here in the nightclub.

When my life crashed and burned months ago, I never imagined I would rise from the ashes and find happiness again. Little did I know I would also find love with a capital *L*. And here I was, pussy-whipped by the fairy tornado who had entered my life and colored every bit of it in pink and hope.

I curled my hand around the back of her neck and held her at a hair's breadth distance from me. "Anything can be my scene. It all depends on the company." I crashed my mouth on hers, plunging my tongue inside with possessive strokes, making us forget what we were talking about seconds ago.

She sank her body into mine, clasping my upper arm with her fingers as if she required my strength. My biceps flexed under her gentle touch. I struggled to keep my breathing even. Once we broke apart, I noticed how she captured her bottom lip between her teeth, the undeniable sign she was horny. I rubbed the back of my neck to avoid unleashing myself onto her, laying her on the floor and eating her up in the middle of the VIP room.

Fuck, I always turned into an animal around her. And when had I become so tempted to piss all over my territory? Hungry to let everyone know she belonged to me, I clamped my right hand on her thigh—higher than I should in public. Her skin warmed up, the gesture igniting her entire body. Pixie shifted in her seat, forcing her legs closed, blocking the view of her bare self from any curious gaze.

Her underwear was still in my pocket. I refused to give

it back to her when she asked earlier, and her eyes had lit up at the challenge.

I loved the game we'd been playing all night.

I, the hunter, and she, the prey, luring me to my dressing room with her sweet scent and that sexy mouth of hers. Once more, my body overheated as I recalled she'd flown across the country to be with me tonight. That little fact put a smug smirk on my face.

I slid my hand a little higher up her thigh, and April yelped, the sound vibrating through my body. Pretending to be unaffected, I crossed one leg, my ankle resting on my knee, acting casual when everything squirmed inside me. My pinky grazed her moist, naked flesh, and we both sucked in harsh breaths. Oxygen stopped reaching my brain.

Craving a diversion, I dropped my head and ate up the soft flesh of her neck, getting high on the lavender scent that I now associated with her.

Each of my gestures had a purpose. An endgame. I loved how April writhed, fighting between indulging in my little game and keeping a straight face around everyone else. Patrons in the bar didn't glance at us, but the forbidden aspect of my hands roaming over her body sent tingles of excitement through me. I hid my lopsided smirk by sipping the water I held in my hand. For anyone watching us, the champagne and cocktails she kept indulging in could be blamed for the glaze in her eyes. But I knew better. The drinks helped cover up her state of arousal from the people surrounding us, though it didn't fool me. I dug my finger into her wetness, and all hell broke loose. A low whimper parted her lips. Her chest inflated and deflated at a fast pace. Her eyes darkened to a midnight hue. I lowered my hand, but she squeezed her thighs, keeping me prisoner and buckling her hips, searching for the delicious friction that I knew would drive her nuts. April was longing for my touch as much as I was longing to touch her.

We went at it for a few seconds until we broke apart, both of us aware we were heading toward dangerous territory if we kept going.

She widened her thighs, releasing my hand, and I leaned back, breathing hard as if we had just completed a run.

"That was fucking hot," I whispered as my lips connected to the side of her face.

"Now I'm horny," she murmured, her eyes trained in front of her, taking a sip from her cocktail like nothing happened.

I returned my hand to her leg, not wanting to be tempted from wandering over her body further. Clamping her thigh above the knee, I shifted in my seat and eased back a little, using the contact to smother the hunger coiling me tight and regain some of my self-control. And maybe hide the erection straining my denims.

My head of security joined us, placing a fresh glass of water on the table next to me and sat on my other side.

The DJ played a mix, the first notes of the bass pounding through my skull. Beside me, April swayed to the rhythm of the deafening music. Fingers drumming to the beat on her thigh, I struck up a conversation with Taylor, while Ed watched over the room from the top of the stairs.

April and I stayed like this for a while, keeping each other on the brink of heightened awareness, playing with the flimsy restraints we still possessed. This constant urge to touch her was overwhelming. Never before in my life had I felt a desire to be close to somebody all the freaking time.

Since the day I flew to Georgia and back to declare my

love to her, I had come to the conclusion that April possessed some power over me. I had no idea how to explain it, but all I knew was that her presence alone affected me. Even when we were not touching or kissing, it soothed me. My uneasiness vanished when she stood in my vicinity. My brain stopped working overtime when she smiled my way.

I felt at peace around her. This, even though I lacked logical reasons to explain it, confirmed my earlier assessment that she and I could never be just a fling.

Flashbacks from the show tonight drew a smile on my face.

Her song. "Pink and Country." Every time I sang it, it brought tears to her eyes and a pinch in my chest. Now that we were together for real, the lyrics bore a truth my heart knew before I had even realized I was head over heels in love with her.

Lost in my mind, I didn't notice June taking the seat beside April after Taylor resumed his place next to Ed. The music was so loud I couldn't catch a word the girls said. April had the ability to make people feel comfortable around her in no time. June played guard dog around me, even though she had fallen under April's charm the moment she met her too, after the initial resistance. April hadn't said anything about it, but my assistant had admitted they had a face-off the first day they went shopping together.

April looked at me with her best puppy dog eyes, stealing my attention, and I snapped out of my daze.

"What?"

"June and I want to dance."

"Go ahead," I said, pointing to the empty space next to the bar where three girls and a couple were drinking and dancing.

She shook her head, and I lifted one brow. "There," she said, pointing to the lower-level dance floor with a finger.

I cringed, not thrilled about the idea. What if people recognized her? What if a fight erupted and she was on the receiving end of an angry fist? I inhaled, trying to let go of the control.

She didn't miss the hesitation on my face because she leaned closer, cupping my cheek with a palm. "Carter, I'm a big girl. I can take care of myself."

It was true, at least, with her words. She was a tough opponent whenever she ran her mouth after someone pissed her off. Or armed with a clicker.

I fought a smile at the images of that night when she believed I was an intruder and threatened me with the TV remote as her weapon of choice. Back then, desperate for her attention, I had found a million different ways to be close to her and to engage with her. It felt like a lifetime ago. Like we'd been together for years.

Every day spent with April erased the memory of one without her in my life. I barely remembered how my existence had been before her. Somehow, I liked to pretend she'd been around forever.

"Okay, but Taylor will go with you." My security detail nodded and followed the women down the stairs. In the week they'd spent together, April and Taylor had grown closer. I caught them, a few times tonight, exchanging knowing glances and laughter. She even rested her hand on his arm twice without his putting distance between them like he would with anyone else touching him when he was on the clock.

I sighed. Another one who couldn't resist her charm. I was glad she got along with my team and my entourage, though. It was important to me that April felt comfortable around the people I worked with, my friends, and my family. After the disaster my last relationship had been, it was about time the tables turned.

Taylor had cornered me after my show. "April is a good person, Carter," he'd said, raving about her. "We're what you could call friends. I wanted to tell you first. I hope you don't mind. She's pretty persuasive when she puts her mind to something. Her home-baked cookies are a convincing weapon."

I had clapped his back, grinning. "Tell me about it. It's fine, man. I'm happy you two hit it off. Keep her safe. That's all I'm asking. As long as she's safe, you can be friends with her as much as you want."

Taylor had lowered his voice. "You know she booked our flights herself, paid for my tickets too. She refused my help or my asking June for a favor."

I'd let out a loud chuckle. "April is her own woman." She never ceased to amaze me, and her generosity knew no bounds. She had not a care for the money in my bank account or the privileges my name or notoriety could bring her. The opposite of every other woman I'd ever known or dated, except Dahlia. For this reason, I felt an urge to take care of her because even though she cherished her independence, she deserved someone in her corner doing the heavy lifting on the days she didn't have the strength to do it herself. And I yearned to be that person. *Her person.*

My lifestyle could be extravagant, and April wasn't used to it. Soon enough, she'd realize there were certain events and other engagements I couldn't escape. No matter what, never would I let her squander her savings to follow my sometimes exuberant lifestyle.

The reality of our lives hit me. I'd talk to her about it. Set some ground rules, without suppressing her sense of independence.

April and June made their way toward the middle of the dance floor, and my gaze followed every one of my girl's movements like a predator lurking in the dark. June gripped April's hips while my girl looped her arms around my assistant's neck. They exchanged a few words, and April threw her head back, laughing. I zoomed in on her throat, desperate for a taste of her flesh.

I watched the two of them, resting my hands against the banister overlooking the dance floor below. The alcohol they drank had lowered some of their inhibitions. The girls moved to the rhythm of the music. April raised her arms above her head, mussing her hair with her fingers as she did.

I bet she had no clue how sexy she looked right now.

They ground against each other, their smiles anchored to their faces, shooting a jolt of happiness through my system.

As if she sensed I'd been watching her this entire time, she lifted her head, her eyes seeking mine. She licked her lips in slow motion, aware of all the power she possessed over me in that instant, and I almost threw my load in my denims at the sight of her.

Two guys, one tall with sandy-blond hair, and the other, smaller with a dark crew cut, both dressed in black suits, prowled their way.

A dark shadow clouded my gaze, and I clenched my teeth, my back now as tense as a ramrod.

The blond guy clamped my girl's hips from behind and flashed her a grim smirk when she cocked her head to check who stood behind her. He murmured something in her ear. April's smile faded, and she stepped sideways with a don't-touch-me glare. The guy shook his head, and with one jerk of his arm, he pulled her to him, his slimy fingers digging into her waist. April said something to him and yanked free from his filthy paws, but he kept pursuing her. They argued about something, the fire in Fairy's gaze unmistakable even from where I stood. My body grew rigid upon seeing how he manhandled her, but I trusted her. She had enough spine to deal with him on her own. If I intervened now, she would tell me she had the situation under control. The jerk closed in on her once again, and she pushed him back with both hands. He stood almost a foot taller and didn't budge at the impact. His sleazy smirk only stretched wider as he kept harassing her. Sick fucker. Was he getting hard by messing with my woman? April started to turn to leave when he grabbed her forearm and spun her around. This was it. The moment I was ready to blow a gasket. I knew she was used to caring for herself, but she was my woman, and no jerk messed with what was mine. Not fucking happening.

From the corner of my eye, I spotted Taylor pushing the other handsy guy away from June when he tried to force a kiss on her, holding her by the shoulders, as my assistant squirmed with rage.

April's frantic gaze searched the mezzanine. This was my cue I could rip that asshole away from her on my own terms.

My feet carried me to the staircase, and I pounded down, keeping my head low to avoid being recognized, then stomped across the dance floor. Everything went black in my mind. Ed followed me, stretching his arms to keep people at a distance while making sure not to draw attention to who I was. With his buzzed, ash blond hair, dark denims, and a black blazer over a simple white T-shirt, he looked like a regular Joe instead of a bodyguard.

Ed took the lead, and by now I knew it meant he did not want me to cause a scene.

Too late.

My body vibrated with wrath.

When we reached the girls, Taylor had already brushed both jerks aside. I clenched and unclenched my fists. My hands itched to punch the two assholes, no matter how far they stood now from what was mine. "Don't you ever lay a hand on my girl again, you dickhead. Get the fuck away before I make you." The words passed my lips before I could leash them in. I knitted my fingers with April's and placed my other hand on June's back, leading them away. "We're leaving," I said, my tone urgent. I sent a warning glare to the two dickheads.

The blond guy stared at me, his cocky attitude not faltering. "Don't let your girl act all slutty if you don't want any trouble, man. She was asking for it. It won't be your name she moans when I get her on her knees and fuck her mouth senseless later."

I blinked, hot fury blinding me. "What did you just say?"

I balled my hands, ready to throw the first punch if I needed to. We exchanged a few heated words, and I was about to retreat when the short guy put in his two cents.

He stepped forward. Sporting broader shoulders, he had bad news written all over his features. He neared me, his stance set for a fight. Unlike his dumb friend, he could be a problem. He just had no chance with Ed and Taylor by my side if things went sour. "Dude, you have no right to tell her shit. She's not your girl. Which means she's free to suck any dick or dance with whoever she wants. A hot piece of ass like her shouldn't be left all by herself shaking that sweet booty, *dude*. Your loss, my win. Duh."

Did he just "dude" me? Twice? My eyes grew wide, and my nostrils flared.

The guy pivoted to face April, who stood a foot behind

me. "Tell him you're not his, *sweetheart.*" His smirk reached his ears.

That was her trigger word.

My self-control crashed at high speed. I tightened my fists, so close to letting them do the talking. I shut my eyes for a split second, trying to dissipate the anger rising inside me, and took a deep inhale.

Ed and Taylor moved closer, flanking me on both sides, ready to intervene at my request and take the heat off me. It wasn't our first rodeo. We'd encountered our share of fuckers over the years. They knew when to defuse the spat.

April clamped my elbow and tugged at it. She pressed her front to my back. The feeling of her was enough to tame some of the rage about to consume me. "Don't get yourself into trouble for someone who's not worth it, HN. Let it go." I silently thanked her for calling me HN instead of Carter in front of these jerks. "Let's go back upstairs and forget all about them."

Taylor and Ed positioned themselves on both sides of us and led us away, keeping an eye on the two guys who yelled in our direction, their voices now drowned by the loud beat.

We stopped by the staircase. "Are you okay?" I asked April. All my muscles were still taut from the altercation. Before she could answer, I pulled her towards me, one arm circling her waist while I scanned her face for any damage I might have missed.

She nodded, burying herself in my chest. I relaxed at the contact."I'm okay. Thanks for saving me and preventing me from causing a scene."

I pressed a kiss on the crown of her head as a reply.

Without releasing her, I turned my head to speak to Ed. "Get those punks thrown out of here."

He nodded and disappeared into the crowd.

I hated fights and couldn't risk getting dragged into one or being caught on camera punching some douchebag who thought women were just toys to play with. I inhaled and exhaled through my nose, my annoyance rippling through every cell of my body.

Don't get yourself into trouble for someone who's not worth it.

I repeated the words in my head. The ones April spoke to me mere minutes ago.

The angst in me decreased.

The tension in my shoulders evaporated.

With her hands secure in mine and June next to me, we returned to the mezzanine, Taylor hot on our heels.

"Drinks?" April asked my assistant.

"Yes. Please. Let me order shots. I'll be right back." June left us, sauntering toward the bar.

"You sure you're okay?" I asked April, tucking strands of her hair behind her ears.

"Yes."

"You would tell me if you weren't?"

"Yes. Now you owe me a dance."

I quirked a brow and pointed to my chest with my thumb. "I do?"

"Yep. You've been keeping my panties from me all night and since I can't dance with anyone else while I walk around commando, it means you gotta step up and sweep me off my feet."

My grin split my face in two. "I thought we already agreed it was a done deal?"

"The dance or the falling in love with you because I want both."

"Whatever you want, it's all yours, Fairy. I'm all yours."

She steered me toward the dance floor, and we lost ourselves in each other, swaying our hips to the rhythm of the music.

41

APRIL

I woke up thirsty, with a pounding headache and a full bladder. Battling a series of yawns, I stretched and sat on the edge of the bed. A cup of peppermint tea waited for me on the nightstand. *Carter.* I scanned the room. No sign of him. On unsteady feet, I made my way to the bathroom, keeping the lights off and breathing through my mouth to steady the churn in my stomach.

Feeling a bit better after the shower, I slipped into one of my boyfriend's hoodies—so big it could almost pass for a dress—rolled up the sleeves, and slid my legs into a pair of knitted black leggings.

I looked at my reflection through the full-length mirror. Disheveled but comfy. I could live with that. Enveloped in Carter's scent, some of my hangover dissipated.

Clutching the warm cup with both hands, I wandered into the living room section of our lavish hotel suite. Never would I get used to this way of living. I took a little sip, testing how my stomach processed the tepid liquid. So far, so good.

A note stuck to the hallway mirror caught my eye. I lurched closer on wobbly legs.

Gone to the gym and a meeting.
Order what you want.
Taylor is on call if you need him.
Love you, Hot and Natty xx

A smile broke free.

I had a hard time figuring out how Carter could be so focused on his career, so sweet around me, and so dominating in bed. Using his instincts, he could always tell what I liked and how I liked it, in every aspect of my life.

All the time.

His entire person amazed me, and I felt whole around him—and so damn happy.

The loving side of him also appealed to me. It felt freeing not to have to hold the entire burden of life on my shoulders anymore and to be able to rely on someone when it got too heavy for me to carry. Like that night in New York when I got into a verbal fight with his ex. Carter was there to pick up the pieces of me after I fell. I'd been on my own for so long that sometimes I forgot how good it felt to have a lover who cared, someone ready to fight for your happiness and safety.

After ordering too much food to my room, unsure of what I could stomach, I invited Taylor over. Over the past week, I'd gotten used to sharing my meals with him. I enjoyed his company. I'd been eating alone for so long, and his presence always cheered me up, even though he wasn't the talkative type. I could talk for two, so it sorta balanced out. Without having to insist too much, he joined me minutes later, and we shared croissants, eggs, and blue-berry pancakes while talking about trivial things.

Around me, the bodyguard appeared relaxed. He told me on the flight the other day that I reminded him of his little sister, and that they used to be close growing up.

Carter came back and raised an eyebrow as he caught us deep in a debate about chocolate versus red velvet cakes.

Taylor sat on the couch, his long legs spread on the coffee table while I faced him, sitting sideways with my legs crossed.

"So, you two have this friendship thing going strong as I can see," my boyfriend teased, a grin on his face.

Taylor sprang to his feet, regaining his steeled compo-sure, looking ready to go to war for his boss slash friend.

"I'm sorry," he apologized in a professional tone he no longer used around me.

Carter motioned for him to sit back down. "As long as you protect my girl, you two can be friends all you want. I already told you. And I love the idea you can chill too and that you're human."

Taylor's lips curled up. "April keeps luring me with food. I'll have to run five extra miles to burn all the calories she made me eat this morning alone."

A chuckle parted my lips. I was that girl, the one baking every time she was nervous or had a bad day. During our stay in Ginger Creek, I was obsessing over my relationship with my rock star boyfriend and might have subjected his bodyguard to a bunch of unsolicited baked goods.

Carter shook his head, unable to hide his amusement. He neared me and leaned over to kiss me, and I melted. His gaze perused the table filled with leftovers. "Anything left for me?"

I cringed. "No. Sorry? I think everything contained

either bacon, eggs, or some meat by-products. I didn't think you would arrive so soon."

"No worries. I'll order something for myself."

Taylor left minutes later, and I followed my boyfriend into the bedroom.

He halted in his tracks, right in the middle, and swiveled to look at me. "I love you in my clothes, Fairy. A whole fucking lot."

Heat bloomed across my cheeks. "I love me in your clothes too."

"The food will be here in ten minutes. I'll shower and change, and then we can do something together. Want to join me?"

"I think I'll have a teeny tiny power nap while you get ready." I pointed to the bed behind me.

"You look like you're about to pass out. Go ahead. I'll wake you up when I'm done."

I slumped on the bed, eyes closed, and fell asleep before the bathroom door even clicked behind him.

When I cracked my eyes open two hours later, feeling rested and my headache a memory of the past, I met Carter in the kitchen and sat on the counter. He stood between my legs, a tall glass of orange juice in one hand, the other clamped firmly around my knee.

"How are you feeling?"

"Better. Much better. Thanks for letting me sleep this long. I'm sorry we didn't get a chance to go out or stroll around the city together."

"It's fine. I had stuff to do that I'd been putting aside, and I also used the time to call Jack. I'm glad you're feeling better." He paused, searching my gaze. "Listen, we're having dinner downtown tonight. The entire team will be there. June, Riley, my musicians, the techs. We planned it before you showed up. We always try to dine together at least once when we're on the road. Some sort of tradition. Will you come with us? The reservation is at eight. We'll have a private room, and nobody will bother us."

After last night's clubbing, a night in with takeout and a movie sounded heavenly, but joining Carter on the road meant mingling with his world, something being in a committed relationship required. I loved that he asked instead of imposing this dinner on me.

"I wanna be part of your life. All of it. If this means having dinner with you and your crew in a probably overly expensive restaurant, so be it." I flashed him a grin. I had no intention of disrupting all his plans. "All jokes aside, count me in. Carter Hills, will you be my date tonight?"

His mouth met mine, twinkles dancing in his eyes. "It will be my honor. June wants to take you shopping. She's excited to have you around. She called while you were asleep. If you prefer, we can go together, or she can pick up something for you to wear tonight and ask for it to be delivered here."

I scrunched up my nose. "I'd like to go with her. If that's okay. I'm still figuring out this whole *is it safe or not safe to go out* thing. And I love to have a girlfriend around. Saunders lives on the other side of the country, and June and I always have fun together."

"I knew you would fit right in with my people. In no time, you'll get used to asking Taylor to come with you. Choose whatever makes you happy, okay? No pressure."

Carter kissed the tip of my nose and wound his arms around me. With my face buried in his chest, I breathed him in. All male, cedarwood, and pine. My favorite smell. Every last bit of tension in my body from last night vanished.

———

June and I spent the afternoon together. Like I'd told Carter, I loved the idea of having a girlfriend around when I spent time with him and his crew.

Just like last time, June took me to stores I would've never ventured into and made me try on clothes I never would have imagined wearing, even in my wildest dreams. Pieces I could never afford on my own. My eyes bulged at the price tags hanging from every single item, from designer sunglasses and tiny clutches to dresses and shoes.

"June, I can't shop here. It's way over my budget. We should go elsewhere. I'm sure there's a mall within a few miles. It's more my scene, and I would be more comfortable shopping there."

"April, you don't have to worry about it. I'm on strict orders to buy anything you want or might need. All of this seems like a lot of money for gals like us. However, believe me when I say Carter can afford this without even blinking an eye." She squeezed my forearm gently. "I swear. Don't fight me on this, or I'll be the one he scolds."

"He scolds you?"

"Let's just say if we don't agree, he will tell me. In a stern voice. I do the same with him, so don't worry. It's part of our dynamics. Anyway, pick a few outfits you like and try them on."

"Carter has already bought too many expensive clothes for me. This isn't right. I don't like the idea I'm taking advantage." I gestured all around the pricey store with one hand.

"You're not. Believe me, I'm now proficient at recognizing people who do, and you're nothing like them." My friend's eyes drifted from me to the saleslady approaching with a tray of champagne glasses, her face so tight it only added to my uneasiness. June stopped her with a single lift of her index finger. The lady froze, her wrinkle-free face expressionless. *Botox or years of training to be a snob?* I couldn't tell. "Carter will kill me if I let you walk out of here without an outfit for tonight."

I sighed, my gaze circling the store once more. I dropped my shoulders and blew out a long breath. "Fine, but it's the last time I'm doing this. I'll talk to him. Next time, we're shopping at the mall, and I decide where."

In a small, hipster coffee shop downtown, June and I stopped for a bite over a cup of tea after we were done with shopping.

She fidgeted with a napkin and sucked in a breath as she locked her eyes on mine. "I'm sorry, April, if I wasn't too eager about your dating Carter at first. We were still dealing with the aftershocks of the whole Savannah Prince fiasco when you came around. I was being a bitch on purpose, but it wasn't personal. The timing sucked... Anyway, I'm sorry, and I really love having you around."

Since our first encounter in Nashville, things had changed for the better between us—*a lot.* These days, she genuinely seemed thrilled to enjoy my company. Carter's entire team had warmed up to my presence. Even Riley. I didn't blame them for watching out for him, though. Now that I knew more about his past, I understood their wariness.

Another knot in my stomach slackened. Her words went straight to my heart. "You're not so bad yourself," I teased. "I had no idea what I was getting into back then. Just know that I'm grateful you have Carter's best interests at heart. I really am. You and me, we're past all that, and I value our friendship."

She linked her arm with mine as we exited the café a little while later, and we strolled around town for another hour.

When I got back to the hotel, I sank into the couch,

exhaustion sitting heavy in every part of my body. Sprawled on my back, I closed my eyelids. If I stayed immobile, I could probably fall asleep in no time. A fog enveloped my mind. My limbs relaxed. And soon, I stopped fighting and fell into a deep slumber.

I woke up to Carter's lips brushing mine sometime later. "Tired?"

My eyelids weighed tons, and it took a superhuman effort to peel them open. Squinting, I took in my feet propped up on the coffee table. How tired had I been to fall asleep with my shoes on? Oh God. Did I also have drool at the corner of my lips? To avoid further humiliation, I wiped my mouth with the back of my hand.

Blinking in an attempt to reboot my brain, I rolled my shoulders back and straightened my position. "Not anymore." I tugged at the collar of Carter's shirt and drew him to me, claiming his mouth. He caged me between his arms, deepening the kiss. I lost myself in the feel of him. The minute a deep groan left his lips, my entire body woke up.

———

It was a little over midnight when we came back from the exquisite dinner Carter treated his crew and me to. My mouth was still salivating thanks to the *crème brulée* I had for dessert.

Our night had been amazing. Everybody treated me like I belonged. Carter's smile grew wider every time he introduced me to someone new. We weren't just having dinner with his team, but producers, musicians, roadies, and more. The entire time, my man rested his hand either on the small of my back or entangled our fingers together.

I wore an off-white cocktail dress, with lace sleeves and

bodice, which ended just above my knees and hugged all my curves. It was elegant, yet feminine and simple.

Ankle-strap heels and a small gold velvet clutch, that June insisted I needed, completed the look.

Carter whispered dirty things to me from the moment I put the dress on, so it was safe to say he approved of my choice.

Wearing dark jeans, he had traded his usual plaid shirt for a black one with the top two buttons undone. On him, the casual outfit looked kinda chic.

Hand in hand, we entered the suite. After changing into lounge clothes, we sat on the living room couch.

"Did you enjoy tonight?" He played with the tendrils of my hair while I shifted until my head rested against his stomach. He reached for my hand and peppered kisses all over my knuckles.

"It was perfect. Thank you. For everything."

"It was the first time I could introduce you to everyone officially. It feels right to have you by my side."

We said nothing for a beat, the silence comfortable between us.

"Can…can I tell you something?" I asked after I fished out some courage from deep inside me.

Carter tilted his head, eyebrows lifted, worry flashing in his smoky-gray irises.

Words flew out of my mouth. Stuff I'd kept inside for so long tumbled out. I talked. A lot. I told him about Travis. How I met him. How we fell in love. How the Bensons welcomed me like a daughter.

His grip on my hand tightened as I spilled it all out. I had opened the floodgates, and now I had no idea how to stop confiding in him.

The nostalgia of my past asphyxiated me. I forced the words out, needing to explain everything once and for all.

"Except with Saunders, I never talk about Travis. He lives in the part of my heart I buried deep down and rarely visit. For the longest time, it hurt too much to even think about him. Everything I did, everywhere I went, reminded me of him. What followed was a long stretch of darkness that clung to me for quite some time. I'm good now. I'm thriving again, and I don't feel so lost anymore. I am secure enough to be in a relationship." We exchanged timid smiles. "I'll cherish the memories of him and me forever, but they don't haunt me like they used to."

"Wow, I had no idea." He rubbed the skin of his nape with his long fingers. An emotion I couldn't name filled his eyes, and I feared what he would say next. "April, if you're still in love with him, I-I can't compete. I'll never ask you to choose. It wouldn't be fair. I can see how much he still means to you. Travis was your first great love. If you're in contact with him and you wanna see if there's still something between you two, I won't stand in the way. I will fight for you, for us, night and day, but I won't be the guy preventing you from being fully happy again."

"You love Dahlia. You'll always love her. But I don't see her as a threat. Perhaps a little at first but not now. You don't look at her the same way you look at me."

"That chapter of my life is closed. However, you welcomed the Bensons back into yours, April. You told me yourself they are family to you. I'm not blind. I can see how the mere mention of Travis affects you. He seems like a nice guy. One day, he'll realize his mistake and will want you back. I know I would… You two have a history together."

My blood turned to ice, hearing the doubt in Carter's voice. He only had doubts when it concerned my love for him. After being burned by the women in his life, I could understand his fears and reservations. I sucked in a sharp breath and told him everything. Every detail I withheld even from him. The good, the bad, and the ugly.

"Travis is dead, Carter. He'll never come back. He ended his own life… Three years ago."

Carter straightened underneath me. "Fuck. I knew the Bensons had lost a child, but I always believed it was a daughter—"

I sat onto his lap and shook my head, my own emotional overload smoldering inside me. "He suffered from a variant form of Creutzfeldt-Jakob disease. It's super rare. That's what the fundraiser was about the other day." The lump in my throat, hard as a rock, pressed against my airways. "I was aware he'd do it…that…that he'd kill himself, and I didn't stop him. I loved him too much to refuse him his last wish. He was sick and was losing the use of his body and mind. His condition deteriorated quicker than what the doctors expected. He refused to be a prisoner of his own body, waiting for his mind to fail him." I buried my face in Carter's chest, and sobs tore through me.

He pressed his lips to the top of my head and hugged me, blanketing me in his arms. The one place I felt safe these days."I'm here, April. I'm sorry. I didn't know. Don't cry. I'm not going anywhere. It's okay. I love you. Fuck, I spoke too fast. I panicked and thought you were having doubts about us. Shhh. I'm here. I'm always gonna be here for you. As long as you'll have me."

My entire body quaked in his embrace.

Carter held me, his inner strength pouring through me. I focused on the beating of his heart, and slowly I relaxed against him.

The tears gentled, and I smiled as a memory flashed in my mind. "We even got married before he passed away."

Carter flinched. A subtle movement, but one that revealed the shock of my admission.

His heartbeat raced under my cheek, but he fastened his arms around me instead of letting go of me.

"He proposed on a Wednesday, and we eloped to Vegas the next Saturday. I even bought a white dress because I wanted our wedding to be…to be perfect. He died the following weekend…" A new batch of emotions washed through me. "One week after our wedding." My cries ripped my chest into so many pieces I feared nobody could ever sew them back together. "I let him die, Carter. I did nothing to stop him. And I…and I didn't warn his parents either. They never said a heartfelt goodbye to their only son. Sometimes, it feels like I killed him myself. From that day on, the Bensons started to hate me. They fought me over everything, and I lost the only real family I had ever known at the same time I lost my husband."

Without interrupting me, Carter brushed my damp hair away from my face, kissing my tears away.

"The Bensons said they were sorry for blaming everything on me. Near the end, Travis distanced himself from his parents. I had nothing to do with it. I even tried to put some sense into him at first, but my grief and fears clouded my better judgment, and so I did what he asked of me, not thinking about how his parents would feel."

I yanked free from his embrace, desperate for space to breathe, and crumpled to the floor. My tears burned my eyes, the scorching stream carving its way down my cheeks.

"I will love him forever, but I love you more. You're here. He's not. You're alive. You're beside me right now." I took a long, shuddering breath and grabbed his hands. "Travis showed me how to love. How a family should be. How people should treat me. That I'm worth it. You're showing me what passion should be like. And also, how to live. How to feel. How to thrive. How not to be afraid. I love you so damn much, Carter Hills. You'll always come first in my heart. There's no doubt. Travis is ancient history. You own my heart. All of it. I will always choose you. You're my present. And my future. You're my soul mate."

He talked to me, but his words got buried under my heart-wrenching sobs.

Carter sat on the floor beside me and comforted me until I had no more tears left in me. Without a word, he lifted me in his arms and took me to the bedroom. He laid me on the bed and wrapped his arms around me, his heated stare full of promises. We stayed like that for a long time. Until desire grabbed hold of us and we undressed each other with frantic need. Kissing me senseless, he made love to me, showing just how much he loved me and how invested in us he was. Not that I doubted it, though. But this caring and generous side of him always appealed to me. His love glued together big, broken chunks of my heart. It sewed my torn chest back together. His eyes never left mine as he moved in and out of me. I shivered underneath him, and with tenderness, he kissed my pain away. Every single piece of it. Afterward, he spooned me and covered my naked body with his, a blanket keeping me safe. Entwined, we never broke apart.

I fought a yawn.

My man tightened his grip on me. "Sleep, April. I'll be here when you wake up. I'll always be here to watch over you. I love you." His warm lips landed on my cheek, and once more, he wiped my sadness away, replacing the withered parts of my heart with colors and dreams.

Rolling onto my back, I looped my arms around his neck and pulled him close until his face rested against my chest.

We said nothing. No words could express how I felt. I had revealed a big piece of me tonight, and the remnants of the weight I'd been carrying around for the last three years dissolved completely.

Soon enough, peace filled me, and Carter's heartbeat rocked me to sleep.

———

The next day, at lunch, Carter and I sat on the couch in our suite, our legs entangled, inhaling the Mexican food we ordered. Burritos, tacos, rice. We had one last night left in Seattle before driving to Vancouver, and we were trying to make the most of it.

"April," Carter began after a stretch of silence, "I just wanna say I'll never want my career to come between us. I'll never ask you to deal with what you're not fully comfortable with. You don't have to give any interviews. You don't have to walk the red carpet or come to every event. As long as I know you're there somewhere, cheering me on, it's good enough for me." His eyes glistened. "As long as I can kiss you whenever I want and bury myself in you in my dressing room, my trailer, or my hotel room and at home, whenever we feel like it, I'll never complain about anything." He winked at me, and I dissolved under the intensity of his stare.

"Carter, I wanna be beside you. No matter what. I take my role as your most enthusiastic fan very seriously. I love you. Nothing could change that."

"I love you like crazy." I heard the smile in his voice. "But I also don't want you to feel like your own career doesn't matter. Because it does. A lot. I want you to thrive and live your dreams. I'll always be your number-one fan too. Whatever you wanna do, I'll always support you and be right there to hold your hand. We're in this together."

We continued to eat in silence, lost in our thoughts.

"When my brother died, my parents blamed the entire world," he confided. "They still do. They never got past it. Each day, they're choosing to live locked in the past rather than moving forward, scared they're betraying Jeff by being happy. What I'm trying to say is that I can understand Travis's parents. It doesn't excuse what they did, but I know firsthand what losing a child can do." He swallowed the last bite of his burrito, his gaze lingering in the distance.

"Where are they now? Your parents?"

"They retired to Costa Rica. We never talk. They lost two sons that day. I tried to stay in touch…for years. I used to visit them whenever I had the chance, but I stopped some time ago. To this day, they still refuse to have a relationship with me. At first, I fought it—resented it even— but eventually, I accepted things for what they were. I'm sad for Jack, though. He'll never get to know his grandparents. On rare occasions, they send gifts for special events, but that's the extent of it."

"I'm sorry, Carter. It's not fair to you. Or to Jack and Dahlia. Your parents should always support you, root for you, be proud of you, love you the way you deserve to be loved. Unconditionally. Even as an adult."

"They did. For a long time. But the truth is that my mom has always had a soft spot for my brother. He was her favorite son. You and I, we're not so different after all. Our families turned their backs on us when we needed them the most. It's not fair, and it's selfish as fuck. I strongly believe we were meant to meet one day. I'm glad you walked into my life before I turned fifty, or I would have been sad to miss all those years by your side." He paused and swallowed, before looking at me. "Our pasts don't matter anymore." He twisted halfway and pulled me onto his lap, his arms circling my waist. "I'm not letting go of you."

"You really mean it?"

"Yeah. Every single word. This connection we share, it's unique. I strongly believe it's a *once in a lifetime* kinda thing. Fate bringing us together. And also...I meant to ask you... Would you consider coming to live with me full-time?"

I gasped, not sure I heard him right. "You—? Are you for real?"

He nodded. "Nashville or Green Mountain. Your place. Or anywhere else. Wherever you decide. Your choice."

My pulse sped up, and I clutched my chest to quiet my wild heart. Ohmygod. I was dreaming. This couldn't be true. "Huh... Wow. I don't know what to say. I-I can't just barge into your life and impose myself. That would be wrong, and you would hate me in no time. I know better."

"April, it's *our* lives. I'm the one asking. Don't overthink everything. If you're not ready to jump in, I'll give you time. However, if you think what we have is worth giving it a real shot, then please barge into my life, make demands, and rock my world. We've been living together for almost two months. I'm aware in the grand scheme of things, it hasn't been *that* long, and I've been burned before, but I'm not ready to say goodbye. We need more time. To figure out how to navigate this reality. This, you and me, it feels right. And real. More real than anything I've ever experienced."

"Carter... I..." My heart wanted to say yes. As much as my head warned me to think it over. That it was too fast and that I wasn't ready. That leaping into the unknown was risky. Deep down, I had no valid excuse to refuse. Agreeing to this crazy nonsense burned the tip of my tongue. Could I really do this full-time again? Live with someone else? Share my life, my heart, and my bed every day and every night?

Carter ran his knuckles down my cheek. "Life has hurt us both. I'm tired of wasting mine. It is too short not to chase after what we want or what we think is best for us. I'm all in."

My eyes found his. I could see all the love, the trust, and the lust in them.

"Fairy, you're everything I've ever wished for. And everything I never thought I needed."

I blinked. My heart swelled in its cage and banged against my ribs, asking to be freed. "You're sure you're ready for this? For all of me?"

"April, I've been waiting for you all my life. I always knew something was missing, but I wasn't sure what it was until you appeared on my front porch, frozen, needing my warmth…and my love." He brushed his lips over mine. Butterflies took off in my chest. Heat rolled down my spine. "I'm yours. For as long as you'll have me. Think about it, okay? The offer won't go away."

42

APRIL

The day after Carter's concert in Vancouver, we strolled around the city. Nobody cared about us out here. Yesterday, we took the ferry to Vancouver Island, and on the way back, we stood on the deck and admired the sunset, Carter wrapping his arms around me from behind. For three days, we enjoyed each other. Here we were, a normal couple, with no fame hanging over our heads.

We were packing our stuff in the hotel suite, overlooking Vancouver Harbour, when Carter surprised me with a white box.

"What is it?" I asked, my curiosity getting the better of me.

He led me to the loveseat beside the bed, in front of the panoramic window, and rotated his body to face me.

"I saw this the other day, and it reminded me of you." I tilted my gaze up and saw twinkles in his eyes. With my breathing on pause, I untied the black ribbon and opened the lid. My hands shot to my chest at the mere glimpse of what lay inside the velvet box.

I blinked. Once. Twice.

A pink diamond tennis bracelet with the words *My Absolute Favorite Color* etched on the lock.

The last few words of the song he wrote for me.

My eyes filled with tears.

I touched the delicate piece of jewelry like it might break under the pads of my fingers.

"Carter, this is beautiful." I leaned forward to kiss his lips. "I can't accept it, though. It's too much. It must have cost you a fortune."

"April, I want to spoil you. I know you don't like the idea of it, but from time to time, please let me. It makes me happy."

"As much as I love you, I'll never be okay with your spending money on me. Listen, living with you is one thing. But I'll never let you pay for everything. In case you haven't noticed, I'm pretty independent. I love small hotel rooms better than suites. I prefer tacos over fancy dinners, and I don't think I've ever bought more than a handful of pieces of clothing worth over fifty dollars. Thrift stores and vintage boutiques where you find rare pieces nobody else wears are my favorites."

He curled his fingers around my neck and pulled my forehead to his. "I value your independence. I do. And I love the fact that you're your own woman, and I'll never try to change who you are. This time, though, please accept it. See this as a moving-in-together gift. I'll downsize everything you don't feel comfortable with. Cars, hotel rooms, anything. I want you to tell me when I overdo something. It might take me a while to adjust, but I will. I promise. I'll do anything for you because I love you so fucking much."

We kissed—like it was the first time, or maybe the last —and I warmed up to his gift. The most beautiful thing someone has ever gifted me. After a song. Nothing could ever beat the song.

I breathed easier at the realization. Carter agreed to meet me halfway. It was everything I could ever ask for.

After we left Canada and Carter's managing team flew back to Nashville, the two of us, along with his security detail, spent three more days on the road before flying back home. *Home.* I loved the sound of it. My heart did flip-flops in my chest every time I thought of Green Mountain as my home. Once I agreed to move in together—officially—we discussed all our options for infinite hours. We voted to stay in Green Mountain for the time being. I wanted to live in Music City at some point, but not now. Green Mountain had become my favorite place, and I loved it there. Carter also admitted to being happier while living there, so the decision suited us both. The idea of us spending more time together, far from everyone else, weighed heavy in the balance. I cherished my privacy a lot, and so did my rock star of a boyfriend. In my mind, Carter wasn't Carter Hills, the country music god, but the handsome guy next door whom I fell head over heels in love with. Somehow, our story still felt like a dream I would wake up from one day.

"I never believed I'd say this, but I prefer the quiet life of Green Mountain over the city," Carter had said last night. "It wasn't the case before. I used to thrive in a busy environment. Now I feel more at peace when I'm far away from the hustle and bustle of life. Nashville, with its small city vibe, doesn't compare to bigger cities like New York or Miami, but still, I'm content living in the mountains."

He didn't say it, but knowing Carter, he also preferred living close to Dahlia and Jack. They were his family, so it made sense to stick around for a little longer.

On the flight back, after waking up from a restful nap, I caught a hint of a smile on Carter's lips as our eyes met. The way he looked at me, with so much passion in his eyes, always stole my breath away. He leaned in and pressed his mouth to mine, and gleams of desire flickered in his stormy-gray irises. "April, there's something I gotta tell you. Well, two things."

I tipped one eyebrow, prompting him to continue.

"The first one is that I rerouted the flight and we're landing in Nashville instead of Green Mountain so Taylor and Ed can go home sooner."

"And the second?"

Carter shook his head. "I won't tell you now. Not here. It can wait. I just wanted to put it out there. In case I chicken out later." He forced a smile. For a split second, a thick fog clouded his gaze before his eyes showered me with love.

Shards of fear tickled my spine.

Angst crept inside me.

Did he change his mind about us? Sweat pearled on my nape. Should I be worried? Would he realize I wasn't good, pretty, or cool enough to be part of his world? I zoned out for a minute.

Carter must've noticed this because he inched closer and captured my lips, the delicious pressure of his mouth on mine sending a thrill through me. "Don't worry, Fairy. It's not about us. You and I, we're good. More than good."

I relaxed under his warm stare.

Whatever Carter wanted to talk about, it must have been serious because he had his *I'm all business* look on his face and wrinkles around his eyes as he discussed his next engagements with June over the phone. But then he glanced my way, and the power of his stare liquefied me in my seat, messing with my head—and my heart—and I knew we'd be all right, no matter what.

Wanting to feel his heartbeat against mine, I got up to sit onto his lap. Carter's arm closed around my waist, and he held me flush to his chest, his head resting in the crook of my neck, while he finished his call.

"April, we'll get your things from your apartment when you're ready. This is real. Us. We're the real deal," he said once he was done, angling his body so we now faced each other.

"We're crazy." I wound my arms around his neck. "But I love us the way we are."

I rubbed the diamonds around my wrist between my fingers. A flutter of excitement stirred in my belly. Carter had no idea how his words meant more than any jewelry he could ever buy me.

I breathed in deeply, a sense of calm washing over me, and wondered how and when I had gotten so lucky.

We landed in Nashville and parted ways with his bodyguards, after my boyfriend reassured them we were going straight to his place downtown and he'd call them if required.

All my limbs were still heavy from my nap. Carter laced his fingers through mine, and I rested my head against his shoulder on the cab ride.

"Finally alone," he said between yawns. "Do you want to spend the night here? Could be fun. We could drive home in the morning."

I nodded. "I'd like that. Let me check with Saunders if she can watch Bernice for a little longer."

"Okay." He dropped a kiss on the side of my head, and we remained silent for the rest of the drive.

My tongue tied itself in knots, and my jaw dropped

when my feet touched the hardwood floor of Carter's penthouse. The amazing view of the city skyline from his top floor took my breath away. "Wow. This is impressive," I exclaimed, standing in front of the panoramic window overlooking the city. "You used to live here?"

My man inched closer, a lopsided smile lighting up his face. He enveloped me in his arms from behind, kissing my temple. "We said we'd wait, but we could still live here. Whatever you want."

I shrugged and spun around to face him. I looped my arms around his neck, twisting strands of his hair around my fingers. He let out a groan, the sound awakening my body like it did each time.

"Maybe someday. Right now, I'm happy in Green Mountain with you."

For dinner, we ordered from the Thai place down the street and sat on pillows on the floor in the living room. I loved how we could be so homey together. As if we'd been living under the same roof for years.

Since we landed, Carter had been a lot quieter than usual. He grabbed my plate and chopsticks and discarded them on the coffee table beside us. A flicker of fear passed through his eyes, and he scratched his forehead with his thumb.

Dread piled in my stomach. Whatever he wanted to tell me, the subject clearly made him nervous. I just hoped it was nothing bad because I wasn't sure how I would be able to deal with it otherwise.

"April, what I'm about to tell you, I've never told anybody else before. I've been keeping this to myself for a long time. It has haunted my nights quite often and some-times, my days. I'm sure there are people who suspect something, but no one has ever broached the subject with me."

My heart rate spiked. All traces of amusement had left his face.

"We're moving in together, and I don't want any secrets lingering between us. You told me about Travis, and now it's my time to tell you the truth."

"You've been married before?" The words left my mouth before I could think twice.

Carter shook his head and kept his gaze down. He took a long and deep breath and raked his fingers through his hair. "Okay, I've already told you I was in love with Dahlia for years." I nodded. "She started dating my brother when we were still in high school. It crushed me. That's when I started writing songs. To deal with my heartbreak. To get over her." His Adam's apple bobbed, and I would've given anything to relieve the pain carved into his features.

I felt his sorrow—like sharp thorns strangling my heart.

Carter dragged his hands over his face and averted his gaze for a long minute.

I kneeled between his legs, my hands squeezing his icy ones. The opposite of their usual warm temperature. "Whatever it is, I'm here, and I'm not going anywhere," I repeated his own words to him. "We're in this together, remember?"

He cleared his throat and continued, "Jeff, my brother, was deployed during our first world tour as Carter Hills Band. He came back a changed man. Most nights, when he was away and we were on tour, Dahlia crawled to my room in the middle of the night and cried for hours, fearing something would happen to him overseas. For as long as I could remember, Dahlia and I had been sharing a bed, and even as a kid, I used to sneak out and climb through her window every other night. Anyway, when he finally made it home, safe and sound, he'd lost his spark. Whatever he'd experienced over there changed him.

Forever. Around us, he'd act like nothing happened, but dark stuff passed through his eyes every time he thought we weren't looking. Things weren't easy for them at home. He often acted out over stupid stuff and withdrew to his garage for long hours. He didn't want to lash out at her… I knew my brother. He loved Dahlia with all his heart, but things were strained between them. We were all convinced it was the beginning of the end for them. He refused to get help, and it poisoned everything around him. Then we left for our second world tour. He didn't join us this time, which was unusual. I learned later Dahlia had asked him to stay behind because they had grown distant, and she didn't want him around. By then, their relationship was nonexistent, but neither one of them was ready to sever the last thread linking them together. They were apart a lot anyway, so they lived parallel lives most of the time. They also fought a lot. Even with thousands of miles between them, they couldn't get along the way they used to."

Carter brought our joined hands over his eyes, hiding the only window to his soul from me.

"A month before the end of our tour, Dahlia came to my room. It was a spur-of-the-moment thing, and we were young and stupid. For a night, we both craved the comfort the other could provide. For a short glimpse of time, I thought she would end things with Jeff for good and run away with me. The next morning, my brother showed up, surprising us on the road, and he stuck around for the rest of the tour. It…it killed whatever fantasy I was living in."

I bit my lower lip, refusing to interrupt him, the gears of my brain overworking under the weight of the confessions Carter just shared. I had no idea what to think of all of this. I already knew he had been in love with Dahlia, but his story was more heart-wrenching than I'd ever imagined it could be. I ached to protect the man I loved. Carter said he had never told anyone about this. How had he lived with this secret for so long? My heart broke for him, and I blinked the hot tears building up in my eyes away.

When he continued, his voice had dropped to a whisper, and I centered my focus back on him, hanging on every word. "On the last night of the tour, after we gave one of the best performances of our lives, Dahlia told me she was pregnant. Minutes later, she quit the band. My entire world crumbled at that instant. I begged her to raise the baby with me because I believed her relationship with my brother couldn't be salvaged. This was our chance. I wanted a future with her. A family. Everything. I remember how Jeff beamed that night. Like he used to. Like my big brother was back from the dead. Dahlia told me he'd proposed, and they were getting married. I couldn't believe it. Every piece of my life was shattering in front of me, and there was nothing I could do to stop the hemorrhage." His voice quivered when he continued. "I started drinking. A lot. To numb all my feelings. My pain. We had a few months off before going back to the studio. I…I didn't enjoy the break. I'd lost the woman I thought I'd marry someday and my band. Stud quit soon after Dahlia did. He had other dreams. I ended up…I ended up alone. Heartbroken…and lost. Everything I had worked so hard for was slipping through my fingers, and I felt powerless."

His voice cracked on the last word.

"I attended their wedding, wasted. Jeff and Dahlia loved me too much to say something about it. They let me be. Dahlia told me the other day she'd told Jeff about us before the wedding. That's why they didn't chastise me for my lack of manners. I barely remember anything about that day. I sucked as the best man. By then, whiskey and I had become best buddies. Up until Jeff died. I never said goodbye to my brother. To the best friend I've ever had. He tried to reach out after the wedding, but I always had a million reasons to push him away. Seeing him happy hurt too fucking much, and I was ashamed of what I'd become."

Kneeling, I lifted my upper body up and curled my hands behind Carter's head, pulling it down to my chest. His forehead rested between my breasts. Could I kiss all his pain away? Could I repair his heart with my love?

"I woke up from my path of self-destruction when Dahlia stood on my front porch one day, broken, telling me Jeff had died the night before." He snorted. "After he got back from the gym. All night, I'd ignored her calls. She must have tried at least two hundred times—fuck, I was stupid. And selfish. I even let my phone die on purpose. I'm such a..." He remained quiet for a long moment.

My brain overheated with silent questions. An icy shiver rolled down my back.

"After Jeff passed, I never touched another sip of alcohol again and changed my life overnight. I hate to think his death was my wake-up call. Anyway, after cleaning up my act, I promised myself to never fall off the bandwagon again. Dahlia and the baby had no one else to look after them, so I stepped in. I owed it to my brother."

Carter leaned back but kept his head hanging low. A guttural sound taking root in the dark corners of his soul escaped his lips, and every cell of my body vibrated. Down to my toes. His bloodshot eyes, glassy and unfocused, met mine. His handsome face had transformed into a roadmap of pain and sorrow. My lips traveled all over his skin, kissing it, healing the distress and grief that had settled there.

Breathing some air and courage, I asked the question hanging on the tip of my tongue. I wanted to know. It wouldn't change anything, but after such a confession, I deserved the truth.

"Is Jack your son?"

Carter straightened his back as if a puppet master had just pulled on the wire attached to his head and yanked it up. His throat rippled, like he'd just swallowed a scorching rock. The hurt shadowing his features nailed me to the floor.

"I…I don't know. Nobody knows. There's this paternity test—"

"The envelope under your pillow?"

He nodded. "I've never looked at the results. Dahlia gave it to me after his birth. She refuses to know unless I'm the one who tells her. I'm scared, April. It's been eating me up alive for the longest time. I believed I was okay not knowing, but lately, it's been nagging at me more than usual. Like I gotta know, but at the same time, I'm not sure I'm ready for what it says. Whatever the results, it won't change how much I love him. That I'm certain of. He's my blood, whether I'm his biological dad or not. He's mine to care for, no matter what a piece of paper says. Even if he's Jeff's, until Nick came along, I'd been the only father figure in his life since his birth."

His throat worked on a swallow as he remained silent for a whole minute.

"I should've opened the envelope years ago. The more I wait, the harder it gets. It's just… Back when he was a baby, the thought he was mine freaked me out. My brother had just died, and it would have been messy to expose the truth. That's why I never did it. To protect him…and… and Dahlia…and myself too. To protect my own feelings. Also, I didn't wanna shake the ground and rock our lives more than they had already been. Nowadays, I'm more detached, but it still eats me up inside sometimes…not knowing…and yet I'm too chickenshit to do the right thing. Well, the right thing *for me*. To appease my heart and my soul with the truth once and for all. But what if knowing and doing what's right for me spirals and affects those I love? What if it changes our dynamics and nothing is ever the same afterward? Am I too selfish by not considering the bigger picture? Dahlia never felt the urge to get to the bottom of this. She's convinced Jack is Jeff's, but she also says he's a part of me. That he's the result of our complicated and beautiful relationship….the best of each of us.

"Growing up, the three of us were this inseparable trio. Dahlia was my bandmate, my best friend, and my brother was…well…my brother. But also, my other best friend. And she loved us both, just not in the same way." He let out a sarcastic laugh and shook his head. "Took me years and a lot of therapy to understand that bit of information. Anyway, Jack is just a kid… The last thing I want is for the truth to impact him. Or for him to resent any of us when he grows up and learns about all of this. He'll have questions… I would too if I were him. Maybe he should be the one to find out…to get to the bottom of this…if that's what he wishes for. When he's ready. He has Nick now. And me. He has all of us, loving and caring for him. Maybe Dah is right, and it's not important to find out… Fuck, I'm rambling, but there are so many *what-ifs* swirling in my head. The only thing I'm sure of is that I don't wanna jeopardize everything."

"Carter, whatever you decide, you're allowed to know the truth if it matters to *you*. Other people's opinions shouldn't matter. Nobody will ever hate you for caring. And Jack will never blame you for looking at the results. He loves you. That much is evident. It's not selfish to ease your heart. Dahlia wouldn't have given you the results if she thought you didn't deserve the truth. But she gifted you the choice. Use it wisely."

"I-I love him so much… Why can't I make up my mind?"

"Then listen to your heart. There is no rush. Nobody said you had to deal with this today or tomorrow. Carter, you're amazing. You're honest, and you're strong. I won't tell you what to do. It's your decision. But whatever you decide, I'll hold your hand if you need me to. I'll stay tall by your side, no matter what. I'm here. With you. And I'm not going anywhere. You have my word. And for what it's worth, that little boy worships the ground you walk on. I haven't spent a lot of time with him, but from what I've seen, he cares about you as much as you care about him."

"Thanks."

"I'm only speaking the truth. Nothing you do or say, or even the result of a genetic test, will come between the two of you. Don't worry about him. Kids are resilient. And when he grows up, the truth may come out as a shock at first, but he'll understand. He may need some time to come to terms with the reality of it, but he will. Because, in the end, he'll know deep down all you guys ever did was to love him. With every piece of your heart. When life threw you a curve ball, you and Dahlia made the most of a situation and turned it into a precious gift. *Family.* By blood or not, it's still as precious. And if someone can vouch for it, it's me. Family is priceless, no matter the form. People who care about you, especially when you're down, and won't abandon you when things get tough. DNA means nothing. It's just a molecule that carries our genetic pool. It's not a foolproof guarantee of love and acceptance. It won't make people stay beside you or force them to hug you when you're sad. And it won't prevent them from abandoning you when they shouldn't. I've been there. You've been too… Even though my parents both ditched me before I could even comprehend what love and family were all about, a part of me is glad they did. Because if they hadn't, I might not be who I am today…and I might not be here with you."

"You really believe that?"

I nodded. "Yeah. Right now, I wouldn't change a thing. The hurt, the joys, the tears, the smiles, it all brought me to this moment."

"April, I love you."

"I love you too."

He lifted me until I straddled him. Framing my face with his hands, he kissed me with everything he had, slow and fast. Hard and soft.

Another fragment of my heart slid into place as my love for him grew bigger than I thought possible after his heartfelt admission.

43

CARTER

An incessant buzzing dragged me out of sleep. I cracked my eyes open, and without lifting my head from the pillow, I scanned the room. For a second, I wondered which city we were in. *Green Mountain.* Oh yes, we were back here. The room was still sunk in darkness. How early was it? I rubbed the heels of my hands over my heavy eyelids, trying to chase away my grogginess.

Buzz. Buzz.

I cocked my head to the side, savoring the sight of the woman sharing my bed. Beside me, April was deep asleep, oblivious to the sound that shook me out of my slumber.

Buzz. Buzz.

I cursed under my breath.

Can someone shut this off?

The buzzing stopped. Finally. I flipped onto my side, slipped an arm around her, and drifted back to sleep within seconds.

Buzz. Buzz. Buzz. Buzzzzzzz.

I tensed. *Fuck, it must be an emergency.* Damn it.

In the dark, I reached out toward the nightstand, my hand sweeping across its surface for my phone. Not there. I scrunched up my face and squinted. Where was it? Images from last night flickered through my mind, and a sly smirk tugged at my lips.

Buzz. Buzz. Buzz.

Buried under the comforter, I wiggled to the edge of the mattress and bent over. I swept my hand across the hardwood floor until my fingers brushed against yesterday's denims. I gave them a shake, and my phone hit the floor with a dull thud. I grimaced as the lit screen flashed, blinding me.

I cleared my throat, ready to bark at the person disturbing our peaceful sleep.

Rubbing my hands over my face, I hoped to galvanize my brain into action.

June? I fumbled with my hand-eye coordination as I tried to tap the screen to accept the call, and I ended up missing it. My eyes flared. Twelve calls. I'd missed twelve calls?

What the fuck.

I scrolled through the missed-call log and saw they were all from either Riley or June.

What happened this time? In my love-induced daze, did I do something that could have alerted the press?

I scratched the side of my head. Nothing. I couldn't think of anything that would have set them off. I'd kept a low profile and stayed under the radar for the last two months—well, mostly—and I couldn't think of a single incident that would justify these vultures being hot on my ass.

Last night, April and I went to a bar on the outskirts of town with Dahlia and Nick. Could it be about that? Nah. The lighting was shitty, and we sat in a dark corner booth, out of sight of the patrons. I even wore a beanie as a precaution. Anyway, I doubted I caught anybody's attention. Green Mountain folks were usually pretty chill and didn't care about me.

"'Someday You'll Fly' is about Jack, isn't it?" April had asked on our drive back home, her small fingers laced through mine. She wore her hair in a half-updo and a knitted black dress that hugged every curve, paired with her cowboy boots. She looked hot. The server failed to keep his eyes off her all night. So much that I thought he would slip her his number by the time Nick paid the check.

Heat had filled my stomach, and I eyed her sideways before nodding. "Everyone assumed I wrote this song about a girl. How did you figure it out?"

"I don't know." She had shrugged, her gaze fixed on the road before us. "Sure, it makes an incredible love song, but there's something about it that's raw. It expresses the kind of love I assume people only experience with their children… Something unique. Children see life through a different lens, and it's precious. It sucks we lose it growing up. Your words—those are the things I'd say to my child. They're beautiful."

How could April get me without my having to explain anything? How could she see beyond the lyrics?

Maybe it was the fact she was an author herself and understood the magic of words. Or perhaps she got me with all my complexities. Plain and simple.

Yeah, she connected with my soul like nobody else ever did.

The idea of figuring out her pen name and reading one of her books grew on me. It was about time I immersed myself in her world too.

Buzz. Buzz.

Oh yeah, my stupid phone. A million scenarios played inside my head as I accepted the call.

"Damn, Carter, I thought I'd have to drive all the way to the mountains to wake up your naked butt." June's tone startled me. She never yelled at me at five in the morning.

"Whoa. Back off a second, would you? Wait, I'll go downstairs," I whispered, eyeing April to make sure she was still asleep.

After sliding my legs into a pair of sweatpants I grabbed from a drawer, I tiptoed out of my bedroom, angst creeping along my spine, and reached the first floor without a sound.

"Okay, talk." I sat on a kitchen stool, one forearm sprawled on the counter and the other clutching the phone to my ear.

"Carter, it's everywhere out there. Magazines, newspapers, morning shows. We have over a hundred requests for interviews all over the globe. I believe it's better if I deliver the news myself. It's a big clusterfuck—"

My hair stood on end on my arms, and cold sweat beaded on my nape. What did my crazy ex do this time? She was the only person I knew with *vengeance* as the middle name. "What is it about? Tell me." I cut June short. My back tensed. My shoulders too. I leaped to my feet and paced the kitchen, my fingers running through my hair, a sense of déjà-vu tightening my insides.

"April, Carter. She's been portrayed as a gold digger who's after you and your money."

My shoulders dropped forward, and I relaxed my stance. A loud chuckle exited my mouth. "That's ridiculous, June. The media should get a life. I'm tired of their nonsense. They better keep their mouths shut, or I'll sue them." I let out a sigh of relief. "Next time, don't wake me up for stupid stuff. It can wait until I'm up."

I was about to hang up, but she kept going. "Did you know about Travis Benson?"

"Yeah. The Bensons' son she dated in college?"

"They didn't just date. They got hitched. Did you know he was wealthy and they never signed a prenup? He died under mysterious circumstances a week after their secret nuptials."

I rubbed my temples and exhaled my annoyance through my nose. "Okay, June, you know I love you. A lot. But this is a pile of crap. Travis Benson didn't die mysteriously. He was already dying when he ended his own life." I clenched my jaw for a second, and let go. "It's nobody's business why they got married. For God's sake. Since when did you start listening to such gossip?Anyway, I already knew all about it."

"Carter," June softened her voice, "I love April. I do, trust me, but maybe she has some secrets you don't know about. We don't want them to impact your career…and both your lives. You've been through enough already with Savannah." A weird, rough growl tumbled from her mouth. "There are websites, lots and lots of them, dedicated to hating her. People want her gone from your life, Carter. It's pretty serious. People are threatening her— death threats. She's not safe. From experience, you know how crazy fans can get. Even the police have gotten involved."

"The police? People are nutcases. I repeat, they should get a life instead of meddling in others' private businesses. Why would anyone have an opinion on my dating life? How does it concern them? People spend way too much time on things that really aren't their business. Who tipped the press? Nobody had leaked her name up to this point. Why now? What changed?"

"We don't know. We're trying to sort this out."

Riled, I hung up and threw my phone across the room. Still pacing, I tugged at the roots of my hair.

A mass formed in the back of my throat, and it messed with my breathing. I'd had my share of fake stories over the years, but none of them had ever made direct threats to someone I loved. Even Dahlia didn't get those kinds of threats when people fabricated stories about her while she was pregnant with Jack.

Six years ago

"Carter, I'm scared. They are everywhere. It's worse than when it was to get pictures of us in our everyday lives. Now they are following me around, harassing me everywhere I go with their insensitive questions, and even spreading rumors about my baby. Can't they let me mourn in peace? Haven't I been stressed enough lately?"

"They are vultures." I strangled my phone as if it had wronged me, trying to contain the distress spreading through every fiber of my being at the idea my best friend was being harassed by the press after everything she had endured.

Dahlia's red-rimmed eyes through the small screen of my phone showcased her despair. The sight of her, heartbroken and hopeless, twisted my insides.

"Now they chase me wherever I go and ask me all kinds of personal questions. One reporter even asked me if it was a PR stunt and told me I should provide proof I was pregnant for real. I'm twenty. My pregnancy was enough of a shock when I found out, and now I'm a widow too. All in the span of a few months. I'm done playing their games. It's sick. People are sick, Cart. They are scaring me. I don't feel safe anymore."

"Dah, we can get you more security. Don't be afraid, okay? We'll deal with this. You'll never be alone, I swear. You two are my top

priority, all that matters in my life. We'll fight them. We'll talk to my publicist and my lawyers. Whatever it takes. Don't worry. Please. You know I won't let anything bad happen to you two. Never." I would never let anyone hurt Dahlia or the baby. If anything happened to them, I'd never forgive myself. They were my family and mine to protect. And I would do anything in my power to make sure they felt safe and secure.

"No. I don't want extra security, Cart. I'm tired. My heart is in pieces. I crave the silence and the calm. Above all, I wanna be left alone. I need room to breathe and land back on my feet. Soon I'll be a single mom, and it's not how things are supposed to be… How they were supposed to be… That was never the plan." The words quivered out of her mouth, her voice filling with heartbreak. Some things I wished I had the power to heal so she would smile again. Even if it meant interchanging my brother's and my fates.

Tears pooled in her eyes. In the last month, I'd seen her break apart more times than I thought I would in a lifetime. My usually opinionated, caring, and strong best friend had become a ghost of herself. Every day, I had to make sure she ate enough and slept through the night after the doctor told her she was getting too thin and that exhaustion would impact her health and the baby's if she didn't find a way to quiet her mind at night. She turned down all drugs that could've helped her due to her pregnancy.

"I'm aware." When Dahlia was around, I tried to put my own grief on the back burner to be there for her. She didn't need me to fall apart too. No, I had to be the strong one this time. To lift her up when she couldn't do it herself. "But you don't have to be afraid, Dah. I'm here. I'll always be here. And I can raise the baby with you. I'll provide everything until you're better and can do it yourself. You won't have to worry about anything. We'll figure it out. Together. Like we've always done all our lives. It's you and me, remember? There's nothing we can't do when we're doing it together. Take the time to heal your heart, and then we'll come up with an action plan. Something that suits both of us…and the baby."

"I know, but I can't do this right now—I'm sorry, Carter. It's so messed up. It feels wrong to ask you to drop everything to take care of us. That's not your job."

"But what if…?"

"No. Stop. There are no what-ifs, *Cart. I know you don't believe me, but I am right. I can feel it. Call it female instinct or motherhood, or whatever, but I have no doubt."*

"Dah, don't say that." Tears prickled the corners of my eyes at the reminder of the mistake that had jeopardized our relationship in the first place, but I blinked them away. Dahlia was a mess, and I promised myself I would keep my feelings locked down when she was around. For everyone's sake. *"I want to be there for you two. I* will *be there for you two. Every step of the way. It's not even a question."*

"I know…but, for a while, I wanna do this on my own. That's what I need. I thought about it, and I'm moving away. I weighed the pros and cons, and being far from all this shitshow is my only wish. And to be on my own for the very first time. To get better without anyone or anything interfering in my life and my choices. I gotta learn to be independent…and resourceful. Jeff and you have always been there to care for me, protect me, and make sure I was okay. I love you both for being my anchors and my family since I was just a little girl, but it's time I take control of my own life back. Carter, don't try to make me change my mind. If you love me, you'll let me go. For now. By myself."

"But Dah—" My world shattered for the umpteenth time in just a few months. This—her leaving—was a nightmare. A fucking joke. Something I wasn't ready to deal with. I had lost my brother. I couldn't lose her too. Dahlia had been by my side since even before I could walk and talk. Before I could even hold a guitar. She was the best part of me. Always had been. I didn't know a life where she wasn't present. And I didn't wanna find out how it felt. Air stuck in my lungs on its way out. I was suffocating, unable to breathe.

"Carter, listen to me. You'll always be in our lives. Forever. But

right now, I have to leave and put a stop to those nasty rumors. I don't want my baby to grow up in a world where tabloids spread rumors about his parents or insinuate things that are false for the sake of enter-tainment. I'll call you once I'm settled so you can visit. I'll be in Green Mountain. You know how much that place means to me. I found a house…in the mountains. With a yard big enough for the baby once he's old enough to have a swing set. It will be good for me…for us… all of us." She paused. "And Cart? Don't give the media any power over you, okay? Prove to them you're better than everything they say about you. Accept Riley's offer and get back onstage. You've been away long enough. The world needs more of your music. It's beautiful. And powerful. Heal their troubled souls, one at a time, with your heartfelt lyrics and spread love to their hearts. Prove to yourself how successful you can be on your own. Keep shining, Carter. Always. You were born for this. And don't worry about me. I'll be just fine. I promise. And I'll cheer you on even when I'm not around. Goodbye, Carter. For now."

She hung up, and my heart escaped my chest and crashed on the pavement.

After I lost my band, my brother, and my fucking purpose, I was now losing my best friend too. If I lived in Nashville and they lived in Green Mountain, how would I make sure she and the baby missed nothing? How would I make sure they were safe?

My sense of control was slipping away, and I couldn't hold on to it. No matter how hard I tried.

How could I stop my life from shattering at every turn? I was tired of feeling helpless and being sad. A new form of darkness spread through me, and I couldn't tell if it was fear, anger, or something far worse.

———

The memories of the day Dahlia left me pinched my heart. My episodes began right after. The ones where I had to tire myself physically in order to keep the peace inside me and resist doing stupid, impulsive shit.

I'd train for hours, run a marathon, or lock myself in a room for countless hours, barely eating and sleeping, and create an entire album in just a few days, all in an attempt to put my mind at ease.

And until a few weeks ago, I'd been doing good. I had succeeded at keeping them away for the most part. Then April walked into my life, and my buried insecurities resurfaced. A part of me knew it meant I was afraid to lose her too. They were not episodes of sadness or helplessness this time around, but more like *how am I supposed to deal with my emotions* and *not let fear rule my life* types.

Taking a deep inhale, I calmed myself, doing my best not to let today's news affect my mental health and to keep my calm through all this. April needed me, and I had to be there for her. To be strong when she was hurt. Yeah, I could do this.

After making sure she was still asleep upstairs, I picked up my phone that was still on the floor and dragged my feet to my home gym. Stripping only to my boxer briefs, I did a skipping rope workout followed by some weightlifting. When I turned my device back on, I clicked on the email June had sent that contained over two dozen links to articles about April. I rushed to the bathroom across the hallway and emptied my stomach after browsing through a few of them. People knew nothing about us, and yet, they were spreading all these lies, claiming them to be the truth.

Whoever tipped off the media about April was out for *my* blood. The interviews with the unknown sources—which I believed were all the same person—screamed revenge. Savannah Fucking Prince. More than ever, I could bet my life on it.

April was on the receiving end of all this hatred

because of what Riley, Taylor, and I had done to my ex. She was retaliating.

I raked my fingers through my hair and wiped my mouth using the back of my hand.

All this would annihilate April. It would shake the foundation of our relationship. Our relationship was new, but I was convinced it could resist the earthquake as long as we stayed united in the face of this media frenzy.

No matter how much I tried to push them away, doubts still crippled me.

For the first time, I had no idea how to make things better. Not even all my money could make the story go away. My lawyers were already taking the proper steps to deal with all this, but the truth was that it was already too late. There would always be traces of these lies somewhere out there. My body was sore as I made my way to the second-floor bathroom. Under scorching water, I prayed this was all a nightmare. My skin tingled. I swallowed the bile down my throat.

Fresh out of the shower, with a towel wrapped around my waist, I made my way to the laundry room and got dressed, just in time to accept June's call.

"We haven't issued a statement yet. The PR firm is drafting one as we speak. Can you ask April to go over it and decide what she's comfortable sharing about her marriage to Travis Benson? I'll send the draft to you as soon as I receive it."

"Yeah, fine." My anger sliced through my words. "Was it Savannah?"

"We don't know for sure. Carter, for now, be with April. She'll need you. It's scary to see your life being dissected for entertainment when you're part of this industry, but when you're not, it's unthinkable and destructive. It's an invasion of privacy. I'll call her later and reassure her we're doing everything we can to protect her."

"Thanks."

"And please, Carter, answer your phone when we call."

I made my way back downstairs. I kicked a chair's leg on the way and cursed at the pain. Hopping on one foot, massaging my aching toe, I slouched down on the couch, my insides burning like boiling lava. On my phone, I read other articles about April. Whoever had done the research was thorough. There were pictures of her younger self partying, out with friends, in college, high school, and on some vacations. April didn't have any social media accounts, so they had to dig further to get those. She was beautiful with her long, braided silver-blonde hair. And so young. Her eyes bore an innocence they didn't possess anymore. But they also had these flecks of sadness that were still there nowadays. When I flipped to an image of April and Travis together, my heart tipped over in my chest. I studied them. In the picture, they smiled at each other, looking carefree, and so damn happy. April's baby-blue eyes sparkled. When I had met her, the spark was nonexistent. I liked to think I had brought it back to life. No matter what, now that it had returned, I never wanted it to fade again.

Whatever people thought they were entitled to, no one was going to mess with my relationship. It was the only thing that made sense in my life right now. I wouldn't sacrifice it for anything, and I wasn't about to go down without a fight.

The sound of April's footsteps down the stairs triggered a fresh wave of nausea. I steeled my back, not sure if I was ready for the shitshow to begin and for the truth of the situation to come out.

I held April close as she sobbed, her tear-dam bursting at the news. I didn't know how to mend the cracks it left behind. When she had joined me downstairs, beautiful with sleepy eyes and pillow wrinkles stamped on her face, she read my mood like an open book the moment our eyes met. She caught the alarm in my gaze and the restlessness in my twitching movements. I explained everything the best I could, and even though I gave it my all to downplay the whole thing, she didn't buy it. It didn't help when Saunders called, panicked, to make sure she was okay.

Saunders told April how bad things were without shying away from the harsh reality.

"The entire…the entire planet hates me. They hate me. They…they want me…ohmygod, they want me dead, Carter. They—" Her sobs drowned the last words.

This was bad. We all knew it. People would chase her down. They would try to get her to talk and snap pictures of her. They would make up stories to keep the buzz going. Every media outlet on the planet would gut her. They would dig out every bit of dirt about her, her family, or the Bensons in order to keep the scandal going. They would follow her every move.

My fans, the crazy ones, wanted her skinned alive.

Riley, June, the lawyers, and the PR people were all on their way here to meet with us.

"We'll fight back. Nobody messes with the people I love." Yeah, I wasn't one to kneel in front of those gossip rags.

With the pads of my thumbs, I dried her eyes, and my lips took hers in a slow kiss. If I couldn't comfort her with my words, I'd comfort her with my touch. With my love.

I'd never let anyone hurt this woman. They'd need to kill me first.

April's mouth let me in, and my body did all the talking. We needed to connect. Deep and fast. I sensed her slipping away. No way, I wouldn't let it happen. When everything turned to hell six years ago, I let Dahlia go. I wouldn't make the same mistake with April. She meant everything to me. Every chunk of my heart belonged to her. I'd never be whole again without her by my side.

In the time we'd known each other, she had become my entire world. The one who brightened my days and made my nights a safe haven.

Who put a smile on my face.

Who made breathing easier.

Who made my life brighter.

Who gave a sense to my existence.

With every sweep of her tongue, every caress of her hands, every moan from her mouth, a distance settled between us. I deepened our kiss. I held her tighter.

Don't go.

With every stare, every breath, and every beat of our hearts, April slipped further away from me—from us. I intertwined our fingers, hoping she'd hang on to me. I could be her lifeline. I would never drop her hand.

Please hold on tight, Fairy. Cling to me. I'll brave the storm for both of us.

I trailed kisses down her throat, swallowing her sobs and hoping to decrease the intensity of her pain.

We held on to each other as I thrust in and out of her, carving my love into her heart. I wanted to remember how she felt, how she tasted, how perfect she was for me. We never broke eye contact. I threaded my fingers through her hair and grazed her lower lip with my thumb, tracing its length.

Lost in her embrace, I made love to her. I put my heart out there. Every tiny piece of it. Raw and fragile. Strong and steady. Every beat was hers. Like a shining star shining through the night and leading the way back to me, so she wouldn't get lost.

By the time we both reached our climax, my muse was gone. Physically, she remained here, underneath me, but mentally, she'd left me. Lost and confused, and broken and desperate, her eyes never lied. Her body convulsed under mine. Our orgasms took us further apart instead of uniting us. Walls of ice rose around her. Thick. Sturdy. I doubted I'd ever be able to break through them. I saw her behind them, but I couldn't reach her. I couldn't hold on to her heart.

Mine bled. The hemorrhage threatened to drain all the good in me.

Unable to process the idea I'd already lost her, I kissed her with everything left in me, wanting to hang on to her for a little longer, not ready to lose her just yet. To lose us for eternity. I buried my head in her bare chest, the rhythm of her heart rocking me back to peace, and the air coming in and out of her lungs reminded me how alive I'd become with her in my life…with her in my arms.

April combed my hair back with her fingers, sending shivers down to my toes.

My own sobs broke free, and she tightened her grip around me, her tears streaming endlessly.

The air between us thickened, void of the usual sparks of desire.

We stayed like that, connected both physically and through our shared pain, for a long time.

She, crying.

I, holding on to her, hoping she'd come back to me.

Today… Tomorrow… One day…

Eventually.

44

APRIL

"Let me drive you home." Carter's low and hoarse voice rattled my heart, and more pieces scattered around in my chest.

I wanted to leave before the entire calvary got here. I inhaled through my mouth, forcing the bile to stay down, my gaze locked on his. I hugged myself, while he stood three feet away, his hands shoved into his hoodie's front pockets, his head hanging low, and his chest quivering with each breath. We were both facing each other in the entryway, and yet it felt like we were standing miles apart. I craved to touch him, to lose all sense of myself in him. One last time, or until the end of time. But I knew better than to stretch the unavoidable. Instead, I stayed rooted to the spot and blinked back my tears. Soon, I wouldn't have any left. Every cell in my body felt raw and sore. If I agreed to Carter's driving me, then I would have to say goodbye to him again later, and I wasn't sure I would be strong enough to go ahead with it if I waited any longer.

"I'd rather not," I said, shaking my head. *Yes, please*, I wanted to scream, but I remained silent instead.

Carter flinched and placed the heels of his hands over his eyes, underlined by dark circles. "Fuck, April. Am I supposed to let you leave without fighting back? Come on, work with me here. Do you believe I'll ever let those psychos hurt you?"

I pinched my lips together and averted my gaze. "You don't get to choose for both of us." I sounded heartless at the moment, and I hated myself. My emotions were ping-ponging inside me, and I was aware my decision to leave might seem harsh right now, but how was I supposed to protect myself from all this media-induced craziness? They had photos of me wearing a bikini back in college, one at a frat party while I was drunk and dancing the night away, another at Nana's funeral. All my life, even the most precious moments, had been turned into public interest. The worst part was that people were commenting on them as if they were entitled to—like it was their business or their job. It was the most humiliating thing I had ever gone through in my life. My relationship with Travis had been dissected, turned into a circus where strangers decided whether our love was real, and whether I had ulterior motives for being with him. Some even went so far as to suggest I had killed him, just because he passed before the illness that had been slowly stealing his body and mind could end his days.

All this shit was also impacting Carter. He had just gotten off that two-year-long relationship where his personal life had been invaded. He didn't need a do-over. If I stayed, it would hurt him. Personally and professionally.

My main goal was to protect the man I loved. Leaving was the only logical solution to put a stop to it. Once I was gone, they would no longer be able to weaponize my past to hurt him. They would have to find something juicier to pursue. No matter how many times I tried to explain it to him, he had refused to see things my way, stating he would fight the press for both of us.

Carter wiped his runny eyes with his sleeve.

My vocal cords had become useless. Anyway, I had nothing more to say. If I did, I would shatter and now, I had to be strong. For my own sake. And his.

"Fairy, say something."

I lifted my eyes toward him in slow motion. Sorrow must have traced every line on my face.

"Please. Talk to me."

"Carter, I'm a burden to your career. The press hates me. Your fans hate me ever more. Don't you get it? I have to leave." My words were sharp, the opposite of the crumbling chaos inside me. "It's what is best for both of us. You may not realize it right now, but give it a few days, and I'm sure you'll come to understand."

"No, you don't have the right to say things like that." His harsh voice jolted me. "Listen to me. You are not a burden. Leaving isn't the solution. Let's take a few more days and see how this plays out."

"No. We've already been over this. I won't change my mind." *Please tie me up, kidnap me, prevent me from running away.* "I'm going home whether you like it or not."

"Home? I thought you said Green Mountain was your home…" His stare burned through me. "I believed *I* was your home. You said so yourself." He was testing me. Testing my restraints. I wouldn't break. I could be strong when required.

I pinched my lips together and remained silent because I had nothing more to say. I was at a loss for words. Yes, Carter had become my home, and the idea of going back to Ginger Creek weighed heavy in my chest.

His tone hardened, his eyes now deep, dark holes.

"Then Taylor will go with you. He should get here soon. Don't leave without him."

I wanted to refuse, but I no longer had the strength to fight. My swollen eyes burned from all the tears I'd shed. My mouth was dry and my heart, a pile of dust rotting inside my chest.

I nodded, my insides a sinking mess. "Fine."

Would I get over our breakup one day? *No. Maybe. Never.*

I had welcomed true love twice in my life and lost both men.

This time, I had learned my lesson. Nobody would ever come near my heart again. It'd remain frozen forever. This —saying goodbye—hurt so bad that I didn't want to feel like this a third time.

In an attempt to escape his heavy stare, I pivoted on my heels. "Carter, I have to go. I'm sorry." With the sleeve of my sweater, I wiped off my eyes and sniffled. *Classy.* I refused to show him I was about to fall apart and that nothing would ever be right again in my life once I walked out of here. "I'll love you forever." I risked one last glance over my shoulder.

He locked his eyes on mine. Wild. Angry. Wretched. We faced each other for a long minute, neither of us brave enough to break the silence. His chest rose and fell. Without a word, he stalked closer, gripped my shoulders, swiveled me around, and wrapped his arms around me. He tucked my hair behind my ears, cupped my face, and leaned forward, his focus unfaltering and filled with hurt. With our foreheads pressed together, we breathed the same air. Thick and charged with electricity. Carter pulled me close, and devoured mu mouth. With hunger. Love. Lust. And anguish. I lost myself in his passion. Was I an idiot for leaving him? No. I was doing what was best for him. I was saving his career. The idea comforted my heart a little. I kissed him back. For all that had been and for everything that could have been.

With both hands, I fisted his sweater, holding on to him as if he was the only weight keeping me from drifting away. The one thing that made sense in my life. The calm in my storm.

The sound of screeching tires resonated outside, and our attention drifted to the window. The wild beat of my heart deafened me. I traced my lips, hoping I could tattoo our last kiss forever on them.

Go, April. Before you can't find the strength to move.
Now.

I stepped back, releasing my grip on the man I loved more than life itself, and a new stream of tears cascaded down my face. I cocked my head to the side to avoid facing him and the hurt I could read in his gaze, refusing him access to my soul.

I reminded myself again that I was leaving to protect his career. To protect him. Because that was what you did when you loved someone, you made them a priority. You saved them when you had the chance.

We tried, we really did, but his world could never be mine. I needed to walk away and give him his freedom back so that he'd keep shining.

"April—" He erased the distance between us and leaned forward to claim my mouth one more time. The kiss stole every molecule of air from my lungs, shaking the not-so-sturdy walls I had erected around my heart. Taking my palm in his, he escorted me to the car, his hand strangling mine.

He backed me up against the steel frame of Taylor's black SUV, his tall self towering over me. His stormy-gray eyes were glossy, and I tried to burn to my memory how they made me feel when locked on me one last time. "You're in no state to drive yourself, Fairy. Ride with Taylor. I'll send your car to you in a few days." He caged me between his arms and sighed, his eyes closed. His Adam's apple worked. "April, don't go." His voice sounded like a low plea. "Please. Stay and we'll figure this out. Together. I'm dying here. I won't survive losing you."

Every word he spoke stabbed my heart, and I was turning into a crying, bleeding mess.

I looked away and lowered my head.

Carter lifted my chin with one finger. I forced myself to meet his gaze and shook my head. "Sorry," I said, emptying my lungs. "I can't do this."

His face turned to stone, and he avoided my gaze as he opened the door for me while Taylor put my bags in the trunk and Bernice's carrier on the backseat—it now seemed pointless that Taylor had made a round trip to Ginger Creek to pick her up two days ago. My boyfriend—ex-boyfriend, ohmygod, even in my mind it sounded terrible—buckled me in and kissed me, his lips anchored to mine for long seconds. With the biggest inhale possible, I filled my lungs and my memory with his scent. Cedarwood, pine, and my man. A combination I would forever associate with him. Carter closed the door after me and stepped back, his gaze unfocused. Our tears had mixed, their saltiness lingering on my lips. I wanted him, but not at any cost. The idea of being dragged through the dirt and torn to shreds for the sake of entertainment made my stomach churn. If I stayed, our relationship would jeopardize everything he'd worked so hard to build, and I'd never allow that. Walking away was the only option, the only way to put a stop to all of this. But how many times would I have to remind myself of that before it finally sank in?

Taylor and he exchanged a few words, then the bodyguard slid into the driver's seat. He rubbed my shoulder in a comforting gesture but said nothing. There was nothing left to say anyway.

Maybe having him around wouldn't be such a bad idea after all. At least until the madness lessened. How would I defend myself if someone showed up on my doorstep or the media tracked me down? I had no clue what to do. I was so out of my league here.

The cops promised to investigate the death threats, but I preferred having Taylor around just in case. I trusted him.

Curling up on the leather seat with my arms hugging my folded knees, I watched Carter shrink into himself, with his hands stuffed into the pockets of his washed-out jeans, rocking back and forth on his heels, through the side mirror until he became so small that I could only perceive his cabin in the distance.

Since the shitstorm had hit us in the morning, he had begged me to stay more times than I could remember.

He had begged me to fight by his side.

He had begged me until his voice cracked.

What he didn't understand was that I was a liability to him and his career. People would soon forget about me if I disappeared. Yes, Carter could bounce back without me around. The longer I stayed, the harder it would be for him to make everyone forget about me once I left. I had to be realistic here. Eventually, they would chase me away. Better now than later, when we got too deep into our relationship.

A cry, an animal-like shriek, exited my mouth. I had broken his heart, and mine, after I promised I'd never do so. That I'd never leave him, and that nothing would ever come between us. Now that the entire world hated me, my words seemed trivial.

I was just another woman to abandon him, to make him feel as if he didn't matter, and yet, I couldn't stop my escape.

A truck honked behind us. It bypassed us from the left at full speed on the narrow mountain road. Taylor and I spun our heads toward the driver's window.

Carter. What was he doing?

His hand hit the horn two more times, and he mouthed *Pull over*. I noticed his knitted brows and thin lips, and the crater inside me deepened.

Taylor stopped the car behind Carter's on the side of the road, and my man sprang out of his before Taylor could shift the SUV into park.

I exited the vehicle on wobbly legs.

We crashed into each other in the middle of the road, our bodies craving each other's touch.

Carter stepped back and dropped to one knee on the gravelly ground. He caught my hand between his. His irises darkened, taking my soul hostage. "April, we belong together. I didn't believe in love before I met you. But now I can't imagine not having you in my life. How can you walk away from us? You're my muse, my fairy, my soul mate."

My hand flew to my mouth as hot tears ran down my cheeks.

"The sun will never wake up again if you're not in my life. We're meant to be together. We're a perfect match. Life is only worth living if you're around…if we do this together. I'll never forgive myself if you walk away. I don't care about fame. We'll move to Greenland if that's what you desire. I promise I'll cheer you up when you're down and care for you when you're sick. And I promise to love you every day. I want to be your muse too. Our story is just beginning. You're an author, so you know no book ends after chapter one. I'll never distract you again with sex when you're in one of your creative flows. I'll read every line you write if you let me. Fairy, I love you so damn much. My knee hurts like hell right now, but I'll kneel before you every minute of every day on a bed of blazing nails if that's what it takes to keep you in my life. Come back to me."

His squeeze on me tightened, and his eyes shadowed further.

Carter sucked in a breath. "April Simmons, will you marry me?"

My breathing hitched, my heart stopped, and tremors shook my body. From behind my curtain of tears, I stared at the ring he drew from his back pocket. An emerald-cut pink diamond surrounded by a halo of little diamonds on a rose gold band. It was beautiful, and absolutely perfect.

The man I loved stared at me, flickers of hope flashing in his eyes.

"When did you get this? You're out of your mind." I kneeled before him, taking his hands in mine. I wanted to say *Yes*. To scream it for the entire world to hear. I wanted to jump into his arms and kiss him senseless until our lips bled. To hold on to him until we were old and gray. To take a leap of faith and say *Fuck you* to the rest of the world. Instead, I inhaled the most painful breath I ever took. "Carter, I'm…I'm not right for you. Don't you see that nobody wants us together?"

"What about us? What about what *we* want?"

"I wish it was that easy, but it's not. Love can't fix everything. Our worlds don't blend." I lowered my gaze to the ring box. I skimmed the diamond with the tip of my finger. My words weakened. "This is the most gorgeous ring I've ever seen, and I'd love for it to be mine." The flow down my cheeks intensified, and I dried my tears with the sleeve of my sweater.

"Please, April. Don't go. You said nothing would ever make you walk away from me."

"Oh gosh, this is the hardest thing I've ever done in my entire life." I breathed in. "Carter, you're my soul mate too, and for a moment, I really thought we were it. That I could—"

He glared at me, his lips pursed, his body stiff. "April—"

I placed a finger over his lips to silence him. My heart died at that moment. It detached from my body, and the last fragments disintegrated into nothing. My hands trembled. Hiccups left my mouth. I was dying a slow death.

"I'll never love anybody else," I said between heartbreaking sobs, "but I can't stay." I brushed my lips against his. "Breaking your heart was never my intention, I swear, but I can't go through this. My privacy has been invaded. For the rest of my life, pictures of me, *private pictures*, will be online. Being seen with you is a thing, but this is another level of crazy. I feel violated, and I can't look past it. They want me dead or wish I never existed… I-I just can't… It's too much… Nobody is safe as long as I'm around. Jack included. Set me free, Carter. If you love me, you'll let me go."

He leaned into the kiss, letting it consume us, and nodded, his forehead pressing against mine and his hands framing my face. Boulders heavy with regret and loss pressed down inside me.

He tried to speak, but the words came out croaky, so he cleared his throat. "You…you're free. I can't force you to be with me. To accept this life. I understand everything you are saying. Just know… I'll never love anybody else either,

Fairy. You're the one for me too. I'm sorry our timing isn't now."

We clung to each other like we were drowning. The wreckage in my chest devoured everything inside me. His breath whistled on its way out. Once again, our tears mixed as our last seconds together ticked by.

Without another word, Carter rose to his feet and moved aside. "Goodbye, April."

I hauled myself back into the SUV and doubled over in pain. What did I do? I was a terrible person. *Remember why you're doing this. His career. His freedom.*

"Are you going to be okay?" Taylor asked, his face etched with worry.

I shook my head.

Carter stood on the side of the road, his shoulders slouched, his face pale, his hands stuffed into his pockets. His eyes stayed fixed on us as we passed him. I saw the pleading in his gaze. It shattered my heart all over again. I mouthed *I love you* to him, with my fingers molded in the shape of a heart.

A void grew within me. I was empty. Wrecked. Dead inside. Nothing would ever jolt my heart back to life again. With my head buried in my hands, I sobbed. For ten minutes or four hours. I didn't know. When I opened my eyes again, we had just crossed the North Carolina state line.

One quick glance at my phone later, and I sank deeper into my seat. The selfish side of me wished Carter had sent me a message or called. He didn't.

Realization hit me. Hard.

We were over.

45

CARTER

"Breaking news, April Simmons, Carter Hills's new love interest, has a shady past. She's well-known for dating millionaires and ripping them off. Folks, if you thought Hills's antics were a thing of the past, I have news for you. We won't stop hearing about the bad boy of country music just yet. I guess making headlines isn't new to him, so we shouldn't be surprised. Want my opinion? Carter Hills should go back to recording music and stay away from crazy fangirls."

———

"Savannah Prince is heartbroken over the news that Carter Hills dumped her months ago to date April Simmons, known for benefiting from the money snagged from her rich lovers. It's not the first time Ms. Simmons has pulled off this kind of sham. When she was twenty-one, she tried to rip off her rich husband, who died under mysterious circumstances one week after their secret nuptials. Ms.

Prince worries for Carter Hills. She fears his sex addiction is blinding him to a relationship that could hurt him in the long run and leave him in debt. Through a press release, Carter Hills has denied the story, stating that the false accusations could lead to a lawsuit. We're still waiting to hear from Ms. Simmons herself. Stay tuned for more details."

———

"Carter Hills is not out of the woods. Best known for bad press and scandals in the last few years, he has relapsed. This time, by dating a gold-digger after his money. The one he himself called his muse a few weeks back. The hashtag *golddiggerapril* has been trending since late last night. Carter Hills's fans are clear. They want the new ladylove out of the picture. The country star should focus on his music, the thing he has a God-given talent for, and avoid dating for a while. Or until he gets his life back on track. We interviewed Savannah Prince, his ex-girlfriend, who's worried about him."

"I'll always love Carter. He's been acting erratic for over a year now. Carter, if you are hearing me, please get professional help. I've done everything in my power to assist and take care of him, but it wasn't enough, as you can see. I met Ms. Simmons once. You could easily see she had a tight hold on him. She crept under his skin and messed with his head…and his better judgment. Carter is not the same man I used to date. He's lost. Carter, no matter what is going on in your life, I love you. I always will."

———

The TV remote hit the floor before I could process what I did. I screamed my pain, my anger, my distress. "Enough with this life."

My team had left thirty minutes ago. I hadn't had time to deal—really deal—with the aftermath of this nightmare until now.

I had lost April. I had fucking lost her.

She ran away, scared and broken. I couldn't even hold it against her. No doubt I would've done the same if I'd been in her shoes. My world sucked. It could take you to the top one day and destroy you and everything you loved the next. I had promised her I'd always protect her, and I failed. I fucking failed.

I cursed, opening the kitchen cabinets in search of a whiskey bottle. My mouth watered. The urge to drink my weight in liquor hadn't been this strong in years. With my foot, I kicked the last cabinet door shut, my search futile, and came back to my senses. Drinking wouldn't do me any good—the last time I let alcohol consume me, I lost myself in the process. Drinking myself into oblivion wouldn't bring the love of my life back nor would it make the media shut their fucking mouths about our relationship.

They could say anything they wanted about me. I didn't care anymore. However, April didn't deserve any of it. The things the gossip rags said about her or the names they called her couldn't be further from the truth.

My mind was a dizzying whirlwind of thoughts.

How could April leave me behind? After everything we'd both been through. We were it. I could tell. She promised she would never leave me, and yet, she ran away at the first instance. I couldn't find it in me to be mad at her, though.

The air I breathed, laced with fury, scorched my

larynx. I paced across the entire first floor, unable to stay still. April's scent lingered in every room.

Why were all the women in my life walking away? What was it about me that made me so unlovable they couldn't stick around?

Doubts crippled me. I thought I had dealt with the insecure part of me once and for all a few months ago. Still, how could I believe otherwise when I had yet another proof? Fuck. This wasn't the end. I would fight. In the past, perhaps I didn't fight enough for those I loved. I would change the narrative this time. I wouldn't let the circumstances dictate my love life.

With my phone in hand, I typed fast.

ME

April, come back to me.

Don't leave.

We'll figure this out. Together.

I'm not losing hope.

I wrote countless text messages but erased them all.

This couldn't be happening. My device burned my skin, and I hurled it against the living room wall, shattering the screen.

"Fuck," I growled. Breaking my phone wouldn't do me any good if April ever tried to contact me. If she ever changed her mind. Damn it.

Why was I losing my cool? What good had it ever done in the past?

Breathe in. Breathe out.

Breathe in. Breathe out.

The lead in my stomach drew all my organs down, piling them into a mushy clump.

My head pounded. My breathing hitched in my lungs. A wave of dizziness hit me, and I braced myself against the wall.

If you love me, you'll let me go. That was what she said. Those were the same words Dahlia had spoken to me the day she announced she was moving across the state. History was repeating itself. Fucking joke.

An episode was coming. April's leaving had triggered the anxious part of me. Nothing I could do would prevent it. My stomach was tied in a web of knots, and I balled my hands in fists, my palms turning into a bloody mess as my fingernails tore my flesh apart.

My heart had been ripped out of my chest.

Trampled on.

Left for dead.

Darkness blanketed me, and I lost touch with everything around me.

———

I leaned forward, hands pressed to my knees, chest heaving as I struggled to catch some much-needed air. Every breath skinned the lining of my lungs. I shut my eyes and enjoyed the spring breeze across my face. Breathless, I sat on the ground, over a patch of dried pine needles. With my knees folded and my ankles crossed, I looked around. The last traces of winter had melted away.

Should I go back to Nashville? April had left a week ago, and my cabin seemed empty without her. I could still smell her lavender perfume in every room. Yesterday, I came home after running errands and pictured her in the den, a cup of tea in hand and Bernice curled up in her lap. The other morning, I patted the bed when I woke up, hoping I'd dreamed the whole breakup and that she was still asleep beside me, the need to feel her warm body against mine overwhelming. Mirages. None of it was real. I let out a soul-breaking howl. I screamed until the back of my throat tingled and my body collapsed. All this pain, this sadness, cast a shadow over my entire life. My hopes. My dreams. My future.

I lifted my arm and checked the time on my brand-new phone, strapped in an armband around my biceps. June had ordered the new device after I shattered the other one. *Ten twenty-one.* I'd been running for over two hours. Where did I get all this energy from? I'd barely eaten anything all week and could count the total number of hours I'd slept on one hand. My house was a three-story garbage kingdom. Dirty clothes and used food containers lingered everywhere. Who had time to clean or do laundry with a broken heart? Not me. Most nights, I avoided my bedroom as if it were haunted. Sure enough, April's ghost was everywhere.

A woman with blonde hair tied in a high ponytail that swung down her back passed me, her little white pooch tugging on its leash. We exchanged polite smiles, and she gave me a slow once-over. She grimaced, and I cocked my head to avoid her judgmental stare. I knew I looked like hell. But I couldn't care less.

Perhaps this new look would keep the vultures at bay.

A shiver ran through me. My clothes, drenched in sweat, stuck to my skin. Without moving from the ground, I tipped my head back and closed my eyes so the sun, peeking through the tall pine trees, could warm me up.

After a moment, the adrenaline left me, and I felt lightheaded.

Images of April driving away flashed behind my closed eyelids. I held my breath. My pulse hammered against my ribs. She fucking stole my heart. Every piece of it. My chest was carved empty. A dark cave full of thorns.

Acid filled my mouth, and for a second, I feared I'd throw up. I dropped my head between my knees.

Breathe in. Breathe out.

My burning eyes and pounding head made it hard to think straight. I couldn't even remember the last time I showered or shaved.

My hands trembled.

I tried to swallow my anxiety, only to choke on my saliva. A blazing rock sat in my stomach.

April. I had to talk to her. See her. Hug her. I'd given her enough time. I was ready for her to come back home. To come back to me.

Yeah, last night, I had concluded she had run away because she was scared, and I would never hold it against her. The media circus had decreased in the last few days. What this entire fucked-up situation and the time apart had proved was that we belonged together. That we hadn't moved too fast when we chose to give our relationship a try. I was done waiting for good things to happen in my life. I wanted to be in the driver's seat and run the show from now on. Thus, I had decided that if there were a chance she still loved me and believed in us, I would bring her back.

But before making a move, I needed a plan.

My fatal mistake had been to give up and let her go. What if I'd held on to her tighter? What if I'd made her sit down with my team? They were used to dealing with these types of situations. She would've realized people cared about her. Maybe it would've reassured her. My head spun, too many *what-ifs* swimming around.

Taylor was giving me daily updates, and I knew she was as miserable as I was. April left because she believed if she extracted herself from my life, my career would be less impacted. How could she believe my career was the most important thing in my life? I understood why she did it, but she was wrong about everything else.

My life meant nothing without her in it. It had lost all its magic. Yeah, I was ready to bring it back. Every single shimmer.

My legs grew stronger after a moment, and I resumed my run. Instead of going back home, I turned around and headed for Dahlia's.

I reached her front door and let myself in without knocking. After kicking my shoes off, I pounded through the house.

Dahlia was here. Somewhere. My patience was a brittle thread, ready to snap at the slightest touch. I rushed upstairs and found my friend in her bedroom, wrapped in a towel, wet hair clinging to her shoulders.

"Carter, dear God, you scared me. What are you doing here?" She tightened the towel around her and eyed me with a frown. "You could've knocked. Or called. Or waited outside my room," she criticized gently, folding her arms over her chest.

"Sorry, Dah. I…it…couldn't wait. I gotta talk to someone, or I'll go crazy." I ran both my hands through my hair. "I'm losing it."

"Go downstairs, make some tea. I'll meet you in a minute."

I groaned but did as she said. I couldn't seem to stop my head from spinning. My thoughts scattered, impossible to catch or hold. Maybe it was the lack of sleep, or maybe I was really going nuts.

Busying myself in the kitchen, I tried to calm myself down. I was tracing the wood pattern of the countertop with my index finger when my best friend joined me.

"Carter, relax. You're making me dizzy." Her eyes traveled over me in slow motion. "When was the last time you actually slept?" Worry passed across her eyes. "Or showered?"

I gazed around and shrugged, clueless.

"These episodes aren't healthy, Carter. You've been having too many of them lately. Have you seen a doctor? Called your therapist?"

"I don't need a fucking doctor or Diaz, Dah. I need her," I barked. Her eyes widened. "I'm sorry. I didn't mean to yell at you. My head is a mess." I paced the room, my fingers interlocked behind my head.

"Have you talked to her?"

"No," I muttered, dropping my shoulders forward. "Taylor keeps me updated every day." The reason I made a detour to come here returned to my conscious mind. "Dah, I…I asked her to marry me." The words escaped my mouth and left a trail of fire in their wake.

Her jaw slackened. "You did?"

"Yeah…and she walked away nonetheless." I sighed, the air rushing from my lungs burning my trachea. "She fucking left."

"Carter, this is big. What did she say?"

"She's afraid. She thinks she'll screw up my career if we're together. How could she believe that? I-I haven't been able to work since she left. I can't even touch a guitar without thinking about her."

"Is this what you want? I mean, to marry her?"

"No, I'm just pussy-whipped." I groaned. "Be serious, Dah. I refused to have sex with her in Nashville because I didn't wanna ruin what we could have. Part-time wasn't an option. So, what do you think?" My words felt like red hot lava on my tongue.

"Carter, you and April are good together, but you haven't known her for long—"

"You're better than this, Dah. You should be the one defending her right now. They're doing to her the same thing they did to you when you were pregnant with Jack." I shook my head and snapped my jaw. Was she for real? "Dah, they chased her away." I plopped down on a kitchen stool and grabbed my mug with both hands. "They ruined us."

"I know. I'm sorry. I didn't mean it like that. I just don't want you to get hurt, that's all. In all honesty, you're more yourself around her than with anyone else I've seen you with over the years."

A long silence stretched between us.

My sinking heart withered, and its blood pooled into my stomach.

"With April, I can have it all, you know. Love. Dreams. Family. She's the one for me, Dah." I cleared my throat, emotions tightening it. "When we're together, sparks fly. It's deep, it's electric, it's real."

She stared at me for a moment, her forearms resting on the countertop.

I looked down to avoid her gaze and chugged my tea like it was whiskey.

"What are you doing here then? You should be with her, Carter. She should be the one you say those words to."

"What if she refuses to talk to me? What if she doesn't want to be in my life anymore? What if she thinks I'm not good enough for her in the long run? She already said no once. She left even when I opened my heart to her…" I jumped to my feet and paced the kitchen—again—fisting my hair. "I cannot barge into her life and make demands. She has to want it too."

"Are you going to spend the rest of your life wondering

about *what-ifs*? You're Carter Hills, for fuck's sake. You don't shy away when you believe in something. You face it straight on. How do you think you've made it this far in your career? Because you don't take *No* for an answer. And if someone throws a punch at you, you fight back. Find your girl and show her what she's missing. You deserve to be happy. When will you realize that yourself?"

"I'm tired. Every time things settle down, another bomb explodes. Sometimes, I wonder if making music is worth all this. The fake news, the stalkers, the press, the rumors. I don't think I can do anything else, but I'm also not sure if I want to keep doing this. I'm over having my love life dissected for nothing else but other people's entertainment."

"Take a break, Carter. Be with your woman. Enjoy life and lie low. God knows you deserve it. You've been spreading yourself thin for years. Have fun for once."

I raised my eyes to stare at her.

"Why not? April is good for you. When she's around, you're relaxed. You're focused. You're smiling. Be happy and a bit selfish for a change and see where it takes you."

Dahlia stood on her feet and inched closer to me. She wrapped her arms around me and hugged me with all her strength.

"Thanks, Dah. I needed this. A wake-up call. Why are you still dealing with my fuckups after all these years?"

"Because I love you. And I always will. And Carter? Have you opened the envelope and seen the results? Is not knowing the truth keeping you from moving forward in your life? Maybe it's time you put all your doubts to rest. Whatever it says, I'll respect your choice."

I nodded, my head buried in the crook of her neck. Dahlia kept her arms locked around me for an infinite minute. Her embrace acted as a calming blanket. One by one, the knots in my stomach loosened. "I'm still debating whether to open it or not… April and I, we…huh…we talked about it… Even though a part of me wants to know, I'm not sure it's the right thing to do. I love how things are between all of us. You, me, Jack…Nick. I gotta think about it a bit longer before I do something I can't take back…"

Dahlia took a step back, studying my face. "You discussed Jack with her?"

I dragged a hand over my face and hung my head forward. "Yep. I told her everything. She made me see things from a different perspective. Told me that family isn't all about DNA, but about the people who truly care for you and love you. With no conditions. Like you and me. We're family and always have been. No matter what goes down in our lives, we're always there for each other. It's precious." I lifted my head to search her eyes. "Thanks. For always being there for me, Dah. Even when I was a wreck and you had to pick me up piece by piece. You never complained or chased me away. And when you were hurting too, you still found time to make sure I was okay. I never told you how much it meant to me. How much… how much it still means to me. You didn't have to, but you did out of the selflessness of your heart."

She reached for my hand and squeezed it between hers. "Carter, you were the single most important person in my life growing up. You were there for me too. All through everything. You reassured me every time we walked onstage and I was freaking out. You always provided me with a shoulder to cry on or strength when I lacked it. You always held my hand when I had doubts and cheered me on when I was taking chances. You took over after Jeff's death without questioning or demanding anything in return. You showed up and spent nights rocking Jack to sleep and fed him bottles so I could catch up on some rest even though you had a concert in Europe the next day. You flew home more than a dozen times because he was sick or *I* was sick, so you could care for us. You love my son like your own. You drop everything without blinking twice if I ask you to. And because of that, I know, in my heart, you and April will be okay. Your separation, it's just a hiccup in your journey…a moment apart to figure stuff out. Your relationship is a whirlwind. Perhaps it's a good thing you both have some time to assess what you really want. I know the conditions are not ideal and it's a clusterfuck out there, but you've been through so much to stop fighting this time around. And if I recall, you panicked and ran away too when you were overwhelmed by your own complicated feelings not so long ago, no? You were a mess. Give April the same benefit of the doubt. I'm pretty sure if she's the one, she's already rethinking the whole disappearing act by now. I swear it'll be all right. You need her more than you need me. I'm proud of the man you've become."

"Huh…Dah… What if she doesn't take me back? I can't imagine—"

"Positive thoughts, Cart. First, you gotta sleep. Eat and take care of yourself before you make a move."

Uncertainty and confusion swirled in my mind, and I had no idea how to turn it off.

My eyes fought to stay open.

I blew out a breath. "Can I crash here? I can't go back home. I'm…so…I'm so exhausted."

My friend nodded, tugged at my hand, and led me to the guest room. On my back, I collapsed on the mattress.

"I'll be here when you wake up. Then you'll shower, because you smell, and get a haircut."

Dahlia lay down beside me and pressed her head to mine, and we entwined our fingers, our hands resting between us, the same way we did when we were kids. Her comfort brought me peace. My pulse slowed down. My limbs grew heavier, and I drifted off to sleep.

When I woke up, the room was dark, but I could see a splinter of light through the drapes. How late was it? I turned the bedside lamp on and looked for my phone. It wasn't here. I stood on weak legs and made my way downstairs. I had no idea how long I'd slept, but from the golden sunlight coming through the windows, it seemed like morning. I found my phone connected to a charger in the kitchen. *Eight twenty-six.* Had I been knocked out for over twenty hours? I rubbed my fists over my eyes, chasing the sleep away from my face.

"Finally, you're awake," a little voice spoke up from behind me. "Mama said I shouldn't make noise because you were super tired."

I spun on my heels as Jack sauntered my way, and I crouched down to hug him. "Hey you." His presence erased the last traces of uneasiness swirling inside me.

He wound his tiny arms around my neck for a second before stepping back. "Oh, you smell bad."

Damn, I forgot I didn't shower after my run yesterday. I tugged at my shirt collar, bent my head, and took a whiff. My stomach churned. Yeah, I smelled like old sweat and despair.

"Sorry, buddy. I'm still groggy from my nap."

Jack snickered. "It wasn't a nap. Mama said you were hibernating because your heart is broken. She's right because you sound like a bear when you snore."

I chuckled. "Let's see if this bear fears water," I said, pointing my thumb to my chest. I dropped a kiss on the crown of his head and hurried into the guest bedroom to shower. When I came out, a pile of clean clothes waited for me on the bed. A hoodie and a pair of sweatpants. I was glad I'd left them here the time I watched Jack when he had a nasty stomach bug and kept throwing up all over me while Nick and Dahlia were away for the weekend.

When I returned to the kitchen, Nick was cooking breakfast.

"Just in time. Here, take a seat," he said, sliding a plate in front of me on the island.

Jack propped himself up on the stool next to mine and leaned in. "Hmm, you smell nice now."

I ruffled his hair. "Thanks, bud."

Dahlia walked in. "Morning, Cart. You look better. Come see me upstairs when you're done. I'll trim your hair." She kissed her son on the cheek. Nick caught her elbow before she left the room and kissed her, placing his hand over her belly in a protective, yet tender way. They exchanged the kind of smile only soul mates shared.

Another knot loosened in my chest. Dahlia was right. It was time I got my own family. I couldn't insert myself in theirs forever.

"Nick, I'm sorry for barging in here yesterday," I said, casting a glance down. "I should be able to deal with my own"—I picked a better word since Jack sat beside me—"stuff." I sighed.

"Don't worry about it, man. We're here for you. Whenever you need us. I know how going through hell feels. Remember why I came into this town. Back then, I was a mess and craved the chance at a new life. Never say you're sorry for having a hard time, man. If anyone gets it, it's us."

"Yeah. You're right." I inhaled a jagged breath. An idea took root inside my head, and I pondered it for a moment, until a light flickered in the dark cave my existence had turned into. "Actually, I might take you up on your offer. Soon."

"Anytime." Nick clapped my shoulder and took the seat

on my right. "Just tell me when and where and I'll be there." When he moved to Green Mountain and Dahlia and he got together, our relationship had a rocky start. Nowadays, I recognized he was perfect for her, and I was happy to consider him my friend too.

Jack, Nick, and I ate in comfortable silence while Dahlia busied herself making tea.

After she cut my hair, my best friend drove me back home. "Promise me you'll fight for what you want and deserve," she said.

Jack spoke up from the backseat before I could reply. "Carter? If you're too shy, I can talk to April for you. She loves me the most because I'm small and super cute. And she's *my* fairy friend, so she'll listen to *me* better."

I turned around in my seat and ruffled his hair. It was our thing. "Okay, I'll keep that in mind, buddy. I'll call you if I need a wingman." I whirled around to face Dahlia. "I love you both."

I kissed her cheek and climbed out of her car, giving myself a pep talk.

Dahlia rolled down her window and waved at me as she drove away. "Good luck, Carter. Keep me updated. I have faith in you."

———

In the media room, sitting on the tan leather sectional sofa, I watched one of Savannah's interviews with the press while talking to June on video chat. My hand itched to hurl my phone at the eighty-inch screen hanging on the wall, but I knew better. I wasn't a violent guy, and I wouldn't turn into one because of her. Nah, I would never give her the satisfaction. My jaw flexed, and I exhaled through my nose, trying to keep my composure.

Every word coming out of her mouth was a lie. Again. We hadn't talked in months. Our last encounter was at the fundraiser in New York, and even back then, we never even exchanged a single word. We ignored each other all evening, even though she attacked April the moment I walked onstage. Why was she telling people we were just on a break? Why couldn't she move on and harass someone else? I thought I already loathed my ex-girlfriend, yet my hatred toward her worsened every time I heard her name or saw her face.

I hoped April wasn't watching TV or believing the load of crap coming out of my ex's lips. She didn't need to be hurt more than she already was.

June's brows furrowed. "Stop. No more phone tossing." I sighed. Even through a video call, she missed nothing.

"I won't. I'm just tempted. Please get her to shut her mouth." Savannah Prince was done bullying her way into my life. "Enough with all this circus. I'm sure she's the mole. She has traitor written all over her plastic face."

June's eyes lit up. "We all believe it as well. I'll see what I can do. Maybe she needs us to refresh her memory about what's in it for her if she badmouths you."

"I have to give it to her, though. Using April to attack me is a low blow, but she's not badmouthing me directly. Perhaps she's smarter than what we all have given her credit for. Anyway, let me know how it goes. Or if you learn anything."

"I will. Gotta go. Someone is blowing up my phone. Bye."

We hung up, and I buried my head in my hands, my elbows propped up on my knees. Once the discomfort in me lessened, I grabbed my phone and punched a number.

"Hey, it's me. We need to talk. Call me back later tonight. There's something I want to run by you." A pause.

"Sure. Talk to you later, man." I hung up and punched a second number. "Hey, man. I'm calling about your offer. Can we talk tomorrow? I might require your help." A long pause. "Yes. Perfect."

For the first time in a week, my heart didn't seem so dark. A spark of hope grew inside me.

I shot to my feet, ready to put my plan into action.

46

APRIL

I unlocked the door to my apartment. Two steps inside, and it already suffocated me. Had it shrunk? It'd been twelve days since I broke things off with Carter and came back to Ginger Creek, fractured in more fragments than I could ever count. Since returning, I'd been feeling like a stranger in my own home. Every minute of each day I missed his presence, his scent, his laughter. And his love. My life lost all colors when I drove away from Green Mountain.

I wanted to disappear. To hide. To keep clear of the tornado's winds. Yet, it felt wrong to be here on my own and not fight alongside him.

But then I remembered that as much as I loved him, I wasn't cut out to live in the glare of his fame. Where it was dark and ugly. It had ruined me after only a few weeks. How bad would it have gotten after years? No amount of pure, raw, once-in-a-lifetime kind of love could fix what I went through. For the rest of my life, there'd be articles about me online. Lies waiting to be forged. Personal pictures belonging to my past.

Despite everything, I couldn't seem to let go of the love we shared.

Things were confusing, to say the least. I was okay with my decision to walk away…sometimes. Or maybe I was feeding lies to myself to justify my actions. I had fled Green Mountain without giving Carter and his team a chance to disclose their plan of action. Did I make a mistake? Why couldn't I just move on and be done with that chapter of my life? Carter and I had fun while it lasted, but it was about time I accepted that it was over. That *we* were over. Yeah, I had left to save his career and his reputation. To protect him. Or had I left to spare my own feelings? Dizziness made my head spin. What had I done?

I ran to the bathroom and made it just in time to relieve my heaving stomach. I'd been doing this for the past two days. Tears welled up in my eyes. I slid down until my back pressed against the wall, folded my legs, and buried my head between my knees, my breathing ragged as air scraped through my raw throat.

When I turned my back on Carter, I thought I'd die. Now I was surviving on the last piece of my heart beating in my chest. I clung to it with all the strength I had left.

A soft knock on the door startled me. "April, are you okay?"

"Yeah…huh, I'll be out in a second, Taylor. Thanks for checking on me." Talking hurt the scorched lining of my throat. With my hands, I pushed myself up from the floor to stand in front of the mirror and splashed cold water over my face. "I'm a mess," I said to my reflection, the image of someone I didn't recognize. Swollen lips. Bloodshot eyes. Pale complexion. Reddened nose tip. I brushed my greasy hair back with my fingers and tied it in some sort of half-knot. There. Better. I wanted to give myself a pep talk, but when I parted my lips, nothing came out. I sighed, my hands clutching the sink.

Tomorrow will be better.

Three hours later, Saunders appeared on my doorstep, her arms filled with cupcakes, tacos, and wine.

"That's why we're best friends," I said as I let her in. For a second, I wondered if Taylor had called her to the rescue. I didn't care, though. Saunders always had the right words to light up my dark moods.

"I thought it was because, in junior year, I flashed my boobs at a bouncer so that he'd let us in at the Wet Shirt concert." She raised an eyebrow.

I nudged her on the side, and my lips curled up for the very first time in almost two weeks.

I remembered that night. I was wearing a tiny, metallic-blue skirt and four-inch heels. Wet Shirt was Travis's favorite band, and they were playing in a bar a four-hour drive away. We'd never have made it inside because the line-up was half a mile long. Without missing a beat, Saunders flashed the bouncer, and he let us in. I might have told her that night she'd earned her best friend title for life.

"You're smiling, Bubble Head," Saunders observed with a grin as she rummaged through a kitchen drawer for a cork opener while I fixed our plates with food.

After I came back to Ginger Creek, my best friend had slept over the first three nights because I was unable to take care of myself without breaking down. I had nightmares in the darkness and woke up crying. Poor Taylor. He must have not known what to do. The breakup had reopened the wounds of losing Travis all over again. I was reliving the pain I had gone through before, and I had no idea how to make it stop hurting this time. I missed Carter. I needed him.

He made my life better.

He knew how to calm me down. How to comfort me the right way and how to patch my broken heart or make me laugh.

I missed every single thing about him. Even the way he snored when he was exhausted.

Since I begged him for a clean break, we hadn't talked since the day I left.

He contacted his chief of security twice a day—Taylor confided in me one night after I asked him for the truth.

Every day, his bodyguard asked me countless times what he could do to help me heal my broken heart.

The answer was simple: nothing. No one could make things better. Except Carter himself.

In college, when we learned about Travis's illness, I did my best to avoid crying in front of him. I did it at night when he was deep asleep, in the shower when I was alone, or in my car in-between classes, where no one could witness my heartbreaking sobs.

After Travis passed, all the unshed tears I had kept inside for so long came out. I cried nonstop for weeks. No matter what I did, I was inconsolable and believed, at some point, I could die of a broken heart.

At this moment, I wondered if it was still a possibility.

I lost the only two men I allowed myself to love utterly and completely because of circumstances I had no control over. I lost them both when I needed them the most.

This time though, my heart would never heal. Carter was alive, not buried six feet under. I would see him from time to time on a magazine cover or on the news. I would hear about his shows, his album releases, or his dating life unless I moved to a cave. I would hear his songs on the radio...and *my song*, too, since it had been released as his new single. Given that the pain hadn't lessened in the twelve days we'd been apart, it confirmed we were the real deal, and deep down, I had the certitude I'd never loved another man the way I loved him.

"Hey, Taylor. Come, join us." Saunders invited my friend slash bodyguard slash roommate to eat with us.

Taylor shook his head, a lopsided smile grazing his lips, and sat beside me. This was my new normal. The three of us—four when Reed joined us—sharing a meal together.

An hour later, my best friend left, and Taylor disappeared to his room to call his wife. After I cleaned up the kitchen, I retreated to the living room and slouched down on the couch, trying to put my thoughts in order. The hammering in my head had transformed into a roaring headache, and I massaged my temples with the tips of my fingers. Thinking was exhausting. Making plans in my mind was too. I yearned for a break, something to keep me busy and prevent my brain from going haywire all the time.

A chime on the screen of my laptop caught my attention. An incoming email from Jill, my agent. I'd forgotten I had sent her a complete draft a few weeks ago. It wasn't the final version, but it was good enough to provide a solid overview of the story and kick off the editing process.

With a shaky finger, I clicked on the message.

April, I've submitted your draft to the publisher, and they're happy with your work. I've attached a document with your editor's notes. She should be in touch with you in a few days.

Like I told you on the phone last Thursday, I know your life is a mess right now, but I'm here if you need to talk.

Hold on. The cyclone will pass.
Jill

A ghost of a smile peeked out at her kind words.

My life was lackluster. Nothing got me raring to go these days. Not the pink-glazed donuts Saunders brought me every morning or the hot chocolate Taylor learned to prepare the exact way I liked it.

Not the moon high in the sky at night. Or the cuddles with Bernice under a blanket on the sofa while we watched a movie.

But this, knowing I had battled insomnia and written something my publisher liked, filled my heart with specks of hope. Perhaps the sun would shine again someday. Just not today.

Taylor finished his phone call and joined me. "Anything I can do?" he asked.

I forced a small smile his way. "No, I think I'll take a nap. There are leftovers in the fridge for dinner. You know the drill. I'll see you later." I moved to my feet and squeezed his forearm as I passed him.

I hid in my bedroom and shut the door after me.

Buried under a pile of blankets, I counted the minutes. Sleep never came.

My hyperactive mind refused to shut off.

For the umpteenth time today, my thoughts wandered to Carter. I wondered what he was doing, where he was, how he was holding on.

The pictures of him in my mind faded a little more with each passing day.

My stomach rumbled, and the tears returned.

How would I survive?

The entire planet hated me with a fierceness I never knew could exist toward someone you'd never even met.

And the worst thing? People now hoped Carter would reunite with Savannah Prince. In her interviews, she called me a mistake, a slip-up, and a bump in the road.

Amazing.

One tabloid depicted me as a bloodsucker only ruled by rich men's wealth.

One blogger called me "The Money Whore." I cringed at the painful memory.

The day after I left Green Mountain, June contacted me. We went over some statements and papers together, while Carter's legal team was managing the *fuck-up*, as they called the situation I put all of us in.

I was the fuck-up. My life was. My entire existence was.

Carter had done nothing wrong, except falling in love with a girl like me. *With me.* With the wrong woman.

June tried to comfort me. "Give it some time, April," she'd said. "It will go away. Just let us all do our job."

Something had shifted between us. I could hear it in her voice. Her tone was sharper. It missed its usual warmth. I couldn't blame her. The press had depicted me as a witch who wooed rich guys and made them fall in love with her, married them, and stole their money. The first one died a week after we'd eloped, nothing to ease the public opinion about me. People feared I'd ruin Carter somehow. June told me once she'd do anything to protect him. She was a woman of her word. Knowing he was in good hands calmed some of my inner turmoil.

A wave of nausea hit me, and I rushed to the bathroom.

I was tiptoeing back to my bedroom when I heard Taylor on the phone, his voice low. I drew in a whistling breath, unable not to eavesdrop on his conversation.

"No, she isn't doing better. There was no threat today, though. That's good." A pause. "She barely eats and never goes out. I do most of her errands or Saunders does." Another pause. "I understand." A long pause. "Nope, I don't think so." He sighed. I'd never heard Taylor sigh before. Usually, he kept his composure intact, no matter the situation. He showed no emotion, kept his face unreadable, and his back straight. "Sure, I'll keep you updated. Good night."

Carter.

I wanted to talk to him.

To kiss him.

To ask him to suck all my pain away.

To heal my broken heart.

I wouldn't contact him, though. Not now. Not ever. The wounds required time to heal, and talking to him would only make the process harder and lengthier.

Tomorrow will be better.

My body grew heavier, and just as I was drifting to sleep, memories of my past became vivid in my head.

"You can come closer, baby. I won't break," Travis whispered as he opened his arms to welcome me into his embrace. "I need to hold you one last time." I tiptoed toward the bed and sank my body into his. Travis took a whiff of my hair. My throat closed up. No words could come out. "April, promise me you'll keep living. And that you'll never let other people kill all the goodness inside you. All your dreams."

I tried to picture Travis as his old self. His healthy, happy self. With a hint of mischief in his irises. Just the way I wanted to remember him forever. Tears prickled the back of my eyes.

I raised my arms, trying to touch every part of him. To memorize every inch of him.

His lips found my temple. "I'll always be here." He pointed to my heart. "And there," he said, pointing at the sky. "You deserve to be happy. That's all I've ever wanted for you, baby. Don't be afraid. I'll forever watch over you."

"I love you," I said, the words dissolving on the tip of my tongue.

"I'll always love you. Be brave. Be fearless. And listen to your heart."

I opened my mouth to speak up, but Travis crashed his mouth on mine, stealing all the oxygen from my lungs. Hours bled together.

Three days later, he was gone. Forever.

In my sleep, I thrashed, kicking the sheets, trying to hold on to the memory of him for a little longer. I missed his words of wisdom. His contagious optimism. "

Travis. Travis." I called out his name but in vain. He was gone.

A thick cloud blanketed me. He wasn't here. It was all a dream. A figment of my imagination. Our last moments together that I had often replayed at night after his passing. This time, though, it felt real. Like it wasn't just my mind playing tricks on me, but a message I had to grasp.

Nor ready to be alone in the dark, I shut my eyes, trying to go back to the moment.

I heard his voice, deeper than it used to be. More assured. Like a grown-up version of the man I once loved. Even though I looked around, I couldn't see him. It wasn't a memory this time, but more like he was comforting me in his own way from wherever he was. My voice of reason. "Reach for your dreams, April. You deserve the best. Never settle for less."

All the air exited my lungs, and I woke up with a start. I rubbed my hands over my eyes. I'd dreamed of Travis, and it all seemed so real. I scanned my bedroom. For half a second, I wondered where I was. Reality sunk in. I was back in Georgia. Not in Green Mountain with Carter. Reality tightened around my heart like a band. The dream replayed in my head, and a hint of a smile curved my lips. I relaxed—a tiny bit.

I'd promised Travis I'd never stop living. What was I doing? I was letting life—and people I didn't even know—

stomp on me, without fighting back. Travis's last words sowed a seed of courage within me. Ready, or almost ready, to stand up and fight for my honor, I sprang out of bed with newfound determination swimming inside me. I was done being a crestfallen version of myself.

Choosing to bring back joy into my life and to feel confident again, I touched up my hair color, making the pink shimmer, treated myself to a long hot shower, and dressed in real clothes. No more dirty, faded hair, stained shirts, and yoga pants. With a lighter heart, I applied a little makeup to hide the dark circles around my eyes and added a pop of color to my ghostly-white complexion.

Taylor sat in my kitchen, reading the newspapers on his tablet, a cup of tea set beside him. He preferred coffee in the morning, but some of my habits had rubbed off on him since he first came to live with me, and now he often drank tea instead.

He raised his eyes when I walked in and nodded his approval.

What could pass as a smile stretched my lips.

"Today, I'll deal with my life," I said, a tiny flame of confidence igniting inside me. "I'm ready. Time to regain control of my own destiny." Yeah, I could do this.

"I'm glad you're doing better. Whatever you need, I'm here for you."

"Thanks. First, I'll call Mrs. Benson. It's long over-due." The Bensons were collateral damage in all this mess, and I intended to apologize for the scrutiny and bad publicity my relationship with Carter had brought them. After all, I was the one who'd gotten involved with a rock star.

Not them.

Not Travis.

Me.

I'd show the world their webs of lies wouldn't destroy me.

I ate breakfast with Taylor while we discussed my plans. I didn't care if he shared everything with Carter. He was Taylor's boss and his friend first. He had more rights over him than I did.

After Travis's death, I had grown a thick skin. This time, I would have to grow a thicker one—an armor.

No one would belittle me. I was April Simmons and I was a strong and independent woman. It was time to stand up for myself and show the world I wouldn't be intimidated so easily.

———

Saunders arrived before noon for our Saturday baking session.

"I tried to call Mrs. Benson three times, but it always goes straight to voicemail. Do you think they're being harassed by the press?" I winced. "Or they hate me?" Were they ghosting me just when we'd finally made up?

"Don't worry about them. You've got enough going on right now. Give them some time. I'm sure they'll come around."

I shrugged. "Yeah, but I'd feel better knowing they're all right. Maybe I'll drive to their place in a few days if they don't return my calls. Just to make sure." I wiped my flour-dusted hands on a plaid kitchen rag. "Where's Reed? You two have been joined at the hips lately."

My best friend poked me in the ribs.

"Ouch, Saund. That hurts," I grumbled, laughing.

I closed my eyes and inhaled the peace all around me.

Warmth danced in my chest. My old self had made an appearance today, and the boulder living in my stomach had shrunk a little. I blew out a cleansing breath. Maybe I could really do this—take back control of my life.

"His brother is in town, and they had some 'guy stuff' to deal with," she said with air quotes. "I refuse to partake in their sibling shenanigans. They're back to being twelve-year-olds when they're together. Anyway, I much prefer spending my Saturday with you. I missed you when you lived with… She lowered her voice and wrinkled her face. "Sorry, didn't think it through."

"It's okay, Saund. We can talk about it…about him. I gotta be able to say his name without breaking into pieces." I sucked in a shuddering breath.

"Well, have you talked to *him*?"

I shook my head. "Why would I? It'd just complicate everything. I don't know where I stand anymore." An invisible clamp tightened my stomach. I closed my eyes, refusing to crumple in tears today. *You are regaining control of your own destiny*, I reminded myself. "I changed my mind. Let's not talk about him. Not yet at least. Gimme a little more time. Anyway, last night I dreamed about Travis… One of our last days together. It seemed so real, like he was here with me."

"Remember that time we went camping by the river during sophomore year?"

"Ohmygod, that was epic. It was Travis's idea. Such a horrible one." I laughed so much I had cramps.

"He always had terrible ideas. Like all the time. I never understood how he could come up with those." Saunders hiccupped, laughing in tandem with me.

That day, Travis, Saunders, and I went camping with some friends. My boyfriend came up with the brilliant idea to go tubing down the river. "It will be an easy ride," he'd said. Yeah, right. We ended up in some sort of rapids, and my tube tipped over. I struggled in the water for a minute and lost my bikini top as I tried to swim toward the river-bank. For the rest of the afternoon, I sat onto Travis's lap, and he had a blast hiding my naked breasts with his hands since I had no way of covering myself up. Fun day, indeed. When we hiked back to our campsite, Travis removed his swim trunks so I could conceal my upper body. Butt-naked, my boyfriend had trekked the entire way back with the tube before him, hiding his junk from our friends.

"What about that time we skinny-dipped in the stream and Travis locked all our belongings in the car and ended up running around town naked to find a phone to call his dad, who had a spare key? Somehow, he always ended up bare-arsed."

Tears rolled down my cheeks. A mix of happy memories and *I miss him so much* tears. I dried them with my floury hands, creating clumps all over my cheeks.

"Oh, Bubble Head, you look terrible," Saunders remarked, pushing my hair away from my teary face.

"Thanks, girl. I've been called worse." My happy tears switched to sad ones. I stepped back. Against the wall, I slid down until I collapsed on the kitchen floor.

Saunders dropped down next to me, her legs stretched in front of her, her side pressed against mine, and draped her arm around my heaving shoulders. "Oh, April. It wasn't supposed to make you cry. I'm sorry. Don't you think you should call Carter? Maybe you need to get some sort of closure. Or maybe you should patch things up with him. You're a mess."

A weak laugh escaped my mouth. "We fell in love. It wasn't planned. We never talked about the damage it could inflict on both our lives if the press got involved in our rela-tionship. I never thought they could be so nasty."

"Nobody ever plans to fall in love." My best friend

pushed her blonde hair back. "If you could change one thing, what would you do differently?"

The thought simmered for a long minute.

"Nothing… I wouldn't change a thing. I loved us the way we were." Sobs drowned my last words. "We were it, Saund. When we were together, I forgot who Carter was outside those walls." I covered my face with my hands. "I wasn't in love with a famous country star, I was in love with a man. Life gave me a second chance at love, and I blew it. It won't give me a third one. I don't like fame. I like simple, normal things. Almost boring. I'd never want him to rent a stadium for my birthday or fly me to Italy for a night just because he could afford it. I want home-cooked dinners and movie nights by the fireplace. Carving pumpkins together on Halloween. I want Christmas mornings in matching PJs. Breakfast in bed and painting the kitchen wall on a Tuesday night just because we feel like it."

"We should get you drunk. I think drunk April would tell Carter Hills those things."

Bernice came to rest on my lap, and I petted her, drying my tears with the fingertips of my other hand.

"Have you ever asked him if he wanted those things too?"

I shook my head, tears blurring my vision. "What difference would it make? His fans hate me. Being with me isn't good for his career, Saund. It could be dangerous for him…or for the people he cares about. He told me stories…about his crazy fans. Imagine if Jack became collateral damage. I would never forgive myself. And I won't ask him to choose."

"I think you'd be surprised. From everything you've told me, I doubt Carter sees you as a liability in his professional life. The guy asked you to marry him, bloody hell." My friend moved to her feet and held out her hand for me to grab. "Let's get your makeup fixed. It will make you feel better."

I nodded and held on to my best friend as if only her touch could heal everything broken inside me.

Saunders did more than fix my makeup. She curled my hair and added a side-braid. "You gotta change."

I lowered my gaze. Flour was dusting my clothes.

She rummaged through my closet and let out a wolf whistle. "Whoa, this is the dress? The one from Nashville?"

"Yeah," I said in a low voice.

"The one from the elevator?"

I nodded again, my cheeks warming up. I'd forgotten I told my best friend about the elevator sex. I grimaced mentally.

"Girl, no wonder your hot piece of man couldn't stay away."

With my lips tight, I forced a smile.

"Sorry. I didn't mean to—"

"I won't cry. No more messing up my mascara. This morning, I promised myself I would stop letting other people affect my life and take away my control. I'm not supposed to break down anymore. I'm supposed to be a strong and badass bitch and not let anyone annihilate me."

"You did? I knew something was different when I arrived earlier. I was wondering what had changed. I'm glad you're ready to get your groove back. My girl is a fighter. Let's teach the world a lesson."

"Which is?"

"That you are a strong and badass bitch and won't let anyone annihilate you."

I burst into a fit of laughter. "When you say it like that, I can't really disagree."

"April Simmons hasn't said her last word. How does it sound?"

"Perfect."

"Now get dressed, we have more baking to do."

I changed into a pair of black skinny jeans and a white cotton shirt. "How do I look?"

"Beautiful."

We baked for another hour, then fixed ourselves something to eat.

Taylor joined us after we both begged him to sample our food.

"You ladies can't feed me anymore. Eating is all I've been doing lately. This has to stop."

The three of us chuckled, and it felt awesome to laugh again.

"April, I told you home-baked food is my weakness. Stop torturing me."

"Well, that's the fun of being my friend, Taylor. Sweets every day."

Later, Taylor went for a run, and Saunders and I baked two more batches of cookies and half-a-dozen apple pies. It was after seven o'clock when we hung up our aprons.

"Bubble Head, I have to get going. Plan nothing tomorrow. We're going to the spa. My man scored us two last-minute spots with hot-blooded massage therapists. Big, magical hands working wonders to unknot every tense back muscles." She winked. "Taylor, will you be able to drive us?"

Reed owned Blue Ozone, the hottest spa in town. People waited over three months for an appointment. Now and then, he fixed Saunders and me up with VIP treatments. We often got massages on a whim or mani-pedis.

"Sure," Taylor said. "What time?"

"Huh…let's say nine in the morning. We'll relax in the hot tubs, then have lunch. Massages are from one to three in the afternoon. Oh, and Taylor, Reed says you can hang out with him. He's taking the day off. Anyway, girls' day out will last all day."

My friend was setting our spa date without even consulting me, acting like I wasn't even around.

"Guys, I'm right here, in case you forgot."

"April, I'm not asking you if you want to go because you'll find a hundred reasons to refuse. You need this. You're tense, and it'll be good for you to relax for a few hours." Saunders kissed me on the cheek. "I'll see you tomorrow. Taylor, would you walk me to my car? I hate thinking people out there might be spying on us." She shrugged, and Taylor followed her.

Through the living room window, I watched as Saunders talked a mile a minute and Taylor nodded, the two of them laughing about something she said. I smiled at the idea my friends were all getting along.

Tomorrow was spa day, and the more I thought about it, the gladder I was that my best friend was forcing me to go out and have some fun. I needed to get out of the house more often, and getting massages seemed like the perfect way to do it.

The idea of relaxing and soaking in the hot tubs sent flutters through my stomach—the good kind—the ones that had been missing lately.

Saunders was right.

I deserved a day of pampering.

———

"Oh, right there. Yes. Oh God, this…this feels good." Big, muscular hands—just as Saunders had promised—kneaded, rolled, and wrung my muscles. I blew out a long breath as my back became the playground of a deep-tissue massage.

"If I didn't know you better, Bubble Head, I'd think you're having an orgasm, three feet away from me. Disturbing."

Lying on my front, my laughter caught in my lungs, and it sounded more like a cough. "You brought me here, Saund. It's all your fault. Reed is a genius for booking us a couple's massage."

I scrunched up my nose. From the hole in the massage table, all I could see was my therapist's feet. When he massaged my neck, his scent reminded me of Carter. Cedarwood and pine. The candles burning around the room and the massage oil diluted the smell. Thank God.

My muscles relaxed, and, bit by bit, so did my brain. The aromatherapy acted like a truth serum and untied my tongue. "I dreamed about him last night."

Saunders cleared her throat. "You did?"

"Yes. In my dream, I agreed to marry him, and we were having a small, intimate wedding in a barn." I released a slow, deliberate breath, my shoulders easing into it. The therapist kneaded my back some more, forcing me to relax even further. "It was…it was perfect."

"What are you saying?"

It took me a minute to straighten my thoughts. "I-I don't know. I want what we had, but—" Strong thumbs rolled the skin of my arms and stretched my fingers. "Oh, yes. More, please." How could my hands be so tense?

"Girl, you ran away from this. Are you having second thoughts?"

"What if leaving was a mistake? What if HN was my happy ending? I should have fought for us. Did I fuck everything up?" I bit my tongue. "I've drained the well of my tears, and now my mind keeps questioning everything. This morning, I almost called him. Just to hear his voice…

because the sound of him is enough to fix everything broken in me."

We both remained silent for a full minute.

"All I wished for was to protect him and his career so he wouldn't be affected by whatever lies the press fabricated about me… I realize now that I didn't give him a real chance. I panicked and fled, and now that the dust has settled, I feel like I was in the wrong. I'm not sure if I knock on his door, he'll still want me, though. I broke his heart, Saund. I left him to deal with this shit all by himself after I promised him that nothing would ever make me wanna leave his side. Now I feel like a liar. And I'm not… I'm not a liar. I don't deceive people. That's not my M.O. With him, I've been happier than I've been in years. How could I throw it all away? I should be able to stand up for myself and give the world a giant *Fuck you* and show them they don't scare me. And yet, I'm still here, in this town, wondering if I'll ever get over my heartbreak instead of doing something to make it all better. I feel so stupid right now." My own words echoed in my head, and I felt even more foolish. "Forget I said anything."

Shivers ran along my spine, and I tensed. The therapist was massaging my feet, the same way Carter did so many times. A wave of nostalgia hit me. I missed him more with every passing day. How could everything in my life keep reminding me of him?

"April, you're not stupid. You're in love." Saunders paused. "What are you going to do? You're in or you're out? Make up your mind and stick with your decision."

"It's not that simple. I wish I knew—" I closed my eyes and tried to quiet my thundering heart. I inhaled, pushing my wild, inner turmoil down. I slipped my hand between my face and the headrest and dried my eyes with my fingertips. I shouldn't be crying. Yesterday, I had promised myself I'd be strong. Saunders was right. I had to make up my mind once and for all and stick with the plan.

"Okay, ladies, please flip onto your backs," Saunders's therapist said after a long pause.

I clutched the white sheet to my chest and carefully rolled over. For half a second, I blinked, trying to adjust to the dimly lit room, but ended up closing my eyes again. I could fall asleep right here. From the head end, firm hands placed a warm cloth over my eyes and massaged my scalp, moving slowly to my temples and the tight muscles of my jaw. They drifted to my shoulders and collarbones. Saunders had promised our therapists would be hot. I only caught a glimpse of hers, and she hadn't lied. Tall, broad shoulders, olive skin, curly raven hair, full lips. He looked like an underwear model. Hopefully, mine was as good-looking. Knowing Reed picked him, he had to be. My massage therapist had entered the room late, and since we were already face down on the tables with the white sheets draped over our legs and bottoms, I didn't have a moment to admire his masculine charm before he got to work.

Next, my therapist cradled the weight of my head in his hands and pressed on the pressure points at the base of my skull with his fingertips.

I purred like a kitten.

Saunders snickered. "Last time we came here for a massage, you weren't as vocal."

"Because it wasn't as good as it is today." Magic Hands knew exactly what my body craved. He pinpointed every knot and transformed them into mush.

Soft, warm lips brushed my forehead from above, and I jumped at the sudden touch. *What the hell?* Did I just imagine this? I stiffened my back. The therapist slid his hands down my arms and laced our fingers. I held my breath. His lips grazed mine—again, pressing down from above

I jerked into a sitting position and opened my eyes, clutching the sheet to my chest as the washcloth slipped onto my thighs.

My heart banged inside my chest at the audacity of this man. "Who do you think you are?" I screamed, anger slicing through my words. I twisted my upper body sharply, eyes locking onto the therapist taking advantage of me.

My jaw went slack, my chest frozen as if my heart had stopped.

I blinked. Once. Twice. A thousand times. "When… Why… How… What's happening?"

My lips quivered into a smile.

Carter curled his hand around my nape. "April."

I sank into the depth of his stormy gaze.

His lips parted, and I stretched my arm to graze them with my fingertips. My entire body quaked at the sight of him, so close to me, so real. "Were you here the entire time?"

He nodded.

"You heard everything I said."

He nodded again, his gaze locked on mine.

"Reed agreed to this?"

Carter nodded a third time. "He's a great guy. We spent the day together yesterday."

Yesterday? Wasn't Reed supposed to be with his brother? My pulse raced.

"And Saunders?" I ignored my best friend lying on the massage table three feet from me. I couldn't break eye contact with the man standing in front of me, clad in the spa's black uniform.

"We talked. She's the one who came up with this spa idea, actually."

"You called my best friend?"

"April, I love you. There's nothing I wouldn't do for you. I want to take care of you. Be by your side through the good and the bad. I can't promise the press won't target us ever again, but I can assure you I'll do everything in my power to protect you. Fairy, I never want to sleep without you for the rest of my life. You make everything better when you're around. You're the woman I've been looking for all my life. Nobody else gets me the way you do. I should've fought harder for us the other day."

My hands flew to my mouth. My eyes overflowed with warm tears. "I should have never run away. I'm sorry I did. This won't happen again. I'm a fighter. I-I'm not a quitter. I know now it was stupid and selfish. I panicked, and I regretted my decision from the get-go. I was just too proud to admit it…even to myself."

"I'll never let anything bad happen to you, and you'll always come first." His eyes shone with unshed tears. "You're not only my muse, but my best friend too." He walked around the table and sat next to me, grazing my hand with his long guitar-player fingers. "April, I'm tired of fame. I want a quiet life with the woman I love. You're everything to me. You're all that matters. Even music is dull without you around. You own every chunk of my heart and every piece of my soul."

The fractures of my heart, the ones that had been bleeding for two weeks, sealed. The hemorrhage inside me stopped. My organ, now revived, beat joyfully in my chest, and I breathed easier. "Carter, I—"

"Let me finish." He dropped to one knee and grabbed the small rose-gold velvet box from his pocket.

I gasped, and a grin brightened his gorgeous face.

"I sang it to you that night in Nashville, and I'll sing it to you every night for the rest of my life. I'm mesmerized by you. You are the rainbow I never knew I needed. You're my compass, my muse, and my other half. Babe, I'll never let you go. I just want you to know I want my life to be pink like yours. You're my absolute favorite color. I love you like I've never loved anyone before, April Simmons. This time, I'm not taking *No* for an answer. Will you spend the rest of your life with me?"

The "Pink and Country" lyrics had never sounded so right. At this moment, they spoke to me in the most meaningful way.

My eyes watered.

My heart throbbed.

My blood warmed.

My chest expanded.

Carter was here, on one knee, sparkles in his eyes, offering me his love.

"April, I want you to be my wife. I don't care about anything else. I would give away everything I own for a chance to have you in my life for another day. But I won't be satisfied with just one day. I want forever with you."

He was offering me a happily-ever-after.

I pulled him up to his feet. "Carter Hills, I love you. That hasn't changed. I love the man you are, and I don't care whether you're rich or poor, famous or not. I won't win a Grammy for my singing talent, but believe me when I say I'm crazy about you. The day I walked out of your life, I stopped breathing. When you're not around, my heart forgets to beat. Ohmygod, I've missed you so much."

He dried my soaked cheeks, and I let out a high-pitched laugh.

"So, Fairy? Are you coming back to me? Forever this time?"

Between laughs and sobs, I cleared my throat. "Yes. I wanna be your wife, even though it sounds crazy and rushed. The only time I feel truly alive is when you're by my side. There's nothing I want more than to grow old with you and call you my husband. I'm tired of the darkness. Keep shining because it makes me the happiest woman on Earth. And please, never let me walk away from you ever again. I don't know how to deal with your world, but I want you to teach me. My heart is yours and so is my entire being. I belong with you. I belong to you."

Carter crashed his mouth on mine. Hard. Fast. With no restraint.

Home. Carter Hills was my home. His lips jolted my heart back to life. All the shades of gray disappeared as he brought the whole spectrum of colors back into my existence.

"Oh, wait, the ring. I'm doing it all wrong."

"No. It's perfect. It's us. Pink and Country."

Carter kneeled again and slid the emerald-cut pink diamond ring onto my finger. I choked on my breath. It was even more gorgeous than I remembered.

Stunning. Perfect. And all pink.

"I wanted to get a custom design, but when I saw this in Seattle, I knew someone had created it just for you. It's an exquisite piece, just like you. One of a kind. Designed by the owner herself."

"Wow, I love it. It's beautiful." I extended my hand and admired the ring sparkling on my finger. *My ring.* "Wait. Seattle?"

"Long story short. I saw it displayed in a small jewelry window and got it, hoping that one day I'd give it to you."

Saunders and her therapist tiptoed out of the room, but I barely registered their departure, still in awe, facing my man. I couldn't believe he had been giving me a massage for the last hour. His lips captured mine again, and I melted in his arms.

A loud gasp passed my lips when he lifted me in his arms, and the white sheet around my body pooled onto the floor. "Carter."

He silenced me with one more sweep of his tongue. "Shhh, April. Let me kiss you. You've deprived me of oxygen for days. Don't let me die. Please revive me."

My lips curled against his. My boyfriend was gifted with words, and every declaration of his love sounded like poetry—a fact my heart couldn't resist.

He tangled his fingers in my hair and kissed me like a starving madman.

My body heated up, an ache building between my thighs when his fingers dug into my ass cheeks, and he drew me closer. I ground against the hard part of him, my panties and the black cotton pants he was wearing the only barrier between us. The friction alone was enough to take me to heaven.

"I can't believe you're here," I whispered, leaning back to watch him, arms circling his neck.

"Believe it, because I'm not leaving unless you're with me." My fiancé crashed his lips onto mine, and the next thing I knew, it was morning, and I was waking up in his arms, in my bed, a permanent smile etched across my face and my entire body deliciously sore.

47

CARTER

I lay in bed, one arm folded under my head, and the other draped around April, still asleep against me, her head resting on my chest and her pink hair spread around her angelic face. The morning sun's rays glowed through the window, illuminating her features. Last night, once we came back to her apartment, we were in such a hurry to get naked that we never thought about closing the blinds.

Saunders's idea to transform me into a therapist had worked wonderfully and became the longest foreplay known to humankind.

Yesterday, Reed and I had arrived at Blue Ozone mid-morning. After I had put the spa uniform on, I hesitated to go forward with the plan because I looked ridiculous. The fabric stretched too much over my upper arms, and the pants were just long enough to cover my ankles. Reed didn't have a larger size, but we made it work, somehow.

For a long minute, I had stood in front of the room with my hand around the doorknob, pausing before going in, not knowing how April would react to my presence.

From the outside, I tried to look casual, unaffected, but my insides were a chaotic mess, and each intake of air made me dizzy.

Reed approached and tapped me on the shoulder, relieving me of my qualms. "You've got this, man. April loves you. Trust me."

His words, full of confidence, supplied the last shred of courage I was missing to enter the room.

My lips curled up as I recalled the look on Saunders's face when she had tipped her head up from the table, seeing me ease into the dimly lit room. She had stifled a chuckle as her eyes had scanned the length of me, but then she winked, and all my lingering doubts vanished.

I should've known April's friend would come up with a scheme if I asked for her help. From what I'd gathered over the past few weeks, April and her friend never did things like everyone else. They always put their personal spin on everything. April had told me about their college days and recent shenanigans, and I had to admit, her friend had balls of steel.

The moment my hands had touched my woman's skin, I thought I'd combust. Her flesh felt softer than I remembered. Fireworks had blasted inside me the entire time I kneaded her muscles and my palms traveled all over her body. Massaging her had been an exercise of self-control.

A million sensations had rushed through me, and the emotions I had bottled up while we were apart had threatened to explode all over her with every passing second.

To be ready to play the part and not be unmasked, I'd arrived in town the previous morning and had spent my day with Reed as he taught me the basics of massage therapy. Simple techniques that would help me to pull it off.

The more I massaged April's tenseness away, the more

my uneasiness faded and the more my hands found their rhythm.

At some point, she started moaning stuff like "Oh, right there," "Yes More," "Oh God, this feels good," and I almost revealed my identity, not sure how long I would last in that role because my body reacted to the smallest things when it involved her.

Men doing massage therapy as a job were saints. It was pure torture.

April was my sin and my muse, but also my weakness.

As she had shared her dream of marrying me, her doubts about leaving me, her desire to be with me, and her fear that I had moved on, her revelations had captured all my attention. I hadn't missed a word of the girls' heartfelt conversation. In my head, I thanked Saunders for encouraging April to open up about her feelings for me. The more relaxed April had become, the more she had spilled her heart out.

I had listened to her admitting how she believed distancing herself from me was the only option to help me and my career through the media storm. It pained me because it was the opposite. The best thing for me was being with her. Waking up by her side and sharing my life with her. Being able to kiss her and hold on to her when everything else made no sense.

Unable to resist the orgasm-like sounds coming out of her mouth any longer, I had kissed the crown of her head. My pulse had slowed a little when I closed my eyes and breathed her in. Every nerve in her body had tautened, and I'd chastised myself for giving in, unable to keep playing the game anymore. The moment I ran my hands down her arms and laced our fingers, everything inside me quietened, except for my heart. It throbbed so hard that I feared it'd jump out of my chest. When I fused my lips to hers, the room had blurred, and it felt like coming home after the longest world tour. Familiar, safe, and exciting.

I hadn't planned to propose right there, but somehow, I couldn't stop the words from tumbling out of my mouth.

With her sleeping body still nestled against mine, I caressed her bare arms, the dip of her shoulder, the side of her neck, looking at her. We'd been apart a couple of weeks, and it felt like a lifetime. My gaze drifted to her ring finger, the pink diamond shining in the morning light. I hadn't dreamed the last twenty-four hours. It was all real. We were doing this. Getting married, flipping the finger at everyone who wasn't on board with the plan. It was us against the world.

April stirred in her sleep, and I held my breath. A minute later, her eyelids fluttered open, and her blue eyes landed on me."Morning, HN." Her lips shaped into the most blinding smile. All aimed at me.

"Morning, Fairy. Slept well?"

"Yeah. I had the most incredible dream. I don't know what's going on with me, but I keep having dreams these days. Anyway, this one was the greatest one I'd ever had."

"Wanna tell me more about it?"

She flipped onto her front and rested her chin over my chest, staring straight into my soul. "There was this guy. Tall, dark hair, skillful fingers. A musician...I think. Or maybe a singer. I'm not sure about the details. And there was this girl. For the longest time, she believed this guy was an ass, but a really handsome and sexy ass, I must say. Anyway, they had a whirlwind romance, and one day, the guy pretended to be a massage therapist to sweep the girl off her feet because she was afraid and had run away from him. Biggest mistake of her life. It took her a little while to realize her wrongdoing. The guy searched for her all over the country, and when he finally found her, he proposed to her, offering her a ring she could have only dreamed of."

"And what happened next? I'm sure there is an ending to that dream."

"Yes. She kissed him. Because she missed him so much and only felt alive when he held her in his arms. She said she was sorry for pushing him away, and they made up. He then loved her for hours, erasing every single trace of fear left in her heart. She agreed to move in with him and told him that one day, she'd like to have a family with him because he was the greatest person she had ever met, and she'd seen him in action with children before. Big turn-on, by the way. She promised to never run away ever again and that she would be better at not freaking out when they were challenged in the future."

"And?"

"They lived happily ever after for the rest of time."

"And what happens now?"

"She goes back home with him because it is the only place that makes sense to her. And they grow old together."

"I like it. A lot." I propped myself up and kissed her, pouring all my love for her into that kiss. "You're ready to come back home with me?"

"Yes. You are my home, Carter. Wherever you go, I'll follow you."

Home. Yes, April was my home too.

———

That afternoon, April, Saunders, Taylor, and I were packing April's apartment. She was coming back to Green Mountain with me. For good. As she told me earlier, she was coming home.

"I thought you'd call a moving company and get them to deal with all the boxes and heavy lifting, HN," she teased.

"No. We can do this. Riley would die of a heart attack right now if he saw me. But I like the idea we're doing this together. Like normal couples do."

April looped her arms around my neck. "I love you, Carter Hills. Thanks for doing boring stuff with me." Her grin woke my body up. "It means a lot."

I fished my wallet out of my jacket pocket and handed it to Saunders. "Okay, guys. Use my credit card and go grab some food. Anything. I request some alone time with my fiancée."

Taylor smirked. "You know I already have a card, right?"

"I don't care. Take both. Go crazy."

Saunders led Taylor outside. "We'll pick up Reed from the spa on our way back, so you sick lovebirds will have a full hour to yourselves. Go, be filthy animals. I'm proud of you."

I scooped April over my shoulder and padded to her bedroom. Her sweet laughter ignited the alpha in me. I put her down on her feet next to her bed. "Get naked, woman. I gotta show you just how much I've missed you one more time."

Last night, we barely slept. We made love twice and caught up the rest of the time, facing each other on a pillow, spread naked on the floor, topless in April's kitchen gulping apple pie, or piled up in her tiny bathtub.

April peeled off her white fluffy shirt and shimmied out of her cobalt-blue leggings. I undressed before she even had time to unclasp her white lace bra.

Unable to wait another second, I fisted her hair and devoured her pink-painted lips while I eased my index finger inside her. She moaned in my mouth as her warmth clung to my digit.

"Fuck, I can't believe I'll get to do this for the rest of my life. You're mine. All of you."

I lifted her up and entered another finger inside her, spreading her wetness over her folds. Our mouths never broke apart when, after the first orgasm hit her, I laid her on the bed and thrust inside her. Prickles spread all over her skin under the pads of my fingers.

"I love you, Carter."

I rammed into her faster. She dug her fingernails into my flesh. My movements became erratic. I pounded harder, faster. Sweat lined my spine.

April's entire body stiffened underneath me, and her eyes rolled back as my name parted her lips on a cry. "Please love me forever. Never let go of me again."

"Never."

I trailed kisses from her lips to her navel, sucked on her diamond-hard nipples, and flicked her earlobe with the tip of my tongue.

Unable to go slow, I pushed into her. My vision blurred. I lost contact with everything else around me. The familiar tingle spread inside me.

April's arms held on to me as we moved in sync, both of us lost in a pleasure-induced state we couldn't escape from.

I rocked my hips once more, and we came together. I kissed her before collapsing over her, breathless and spent.

With a stretch of my arm, once my heartbeat calmed down, I picked up my phone from the nightstand and checked the time. "Good news. We still have thirty-four minutes left. Let's take a shower." My tongue lingered on the tender flesh of her neck, licking and sucking.

Once on my feet, I hauled my fiancée over my shoulder and carried her to the bathroom.

"Feeling possessive, HN, or you think cavemen are sexy?"

Something sounding like a chuckle mixed with a groan escaped my mouth, and I smacked her naked ass. "I'm making sure you can't run away. If it means being a caveman, so be it."

I lowered her to her feet as I fiddled with the knob of the shower to adjust the temperature.

"And what about those handcuffs you promised?" April arched a brow, and my pulse picked up as a bunch of filthy images played in my head.

"Don't tempt me right now."

For the next twenty minutes, we let the pleasure consume us, our mouths insatiable and our hands traveling all over each other's wet skin under the hot stream until the water ran cold and we had to exit the confines of the shower.

Half-dressed, I slid April's sweater over her head, stealing a kiss as I did so.

She trailed kisses down the length of my throat, and I shivered, my body going rigid, ready for another round.

We hadn't made two steps into the living room when the front door burst open, and Saunders rushed in.

Beside me, April's eyes widened as she took in her friend. "What's wrong, Saund?"

I put my shirt on and raked my fingers through my still-damp, untamed mass of hair, trying to look respectable.

"Good. You guys are done. Sorry I barged in here." Saunders halted, shut her eyes, and crinkled her nose. "Damn it, I didn't think. I could've seen things I wasn't ready for. Thank God you're both dressed and decent."

She sighed and looked at us. "Where was I? Okay, sit tight, Bubble Head. You too, Country Bloke. This is huge."

April frowned.

"Jenna, my accountant, called me because she knows we're best friends." Saunders stopped, catching her breath.

"Saund, you're freaking me out right now. What is it?"

I wrapped one arm around April's tense shoulders, pulling her against me. Whatever her best friend was about to say, I would be her moral and physical support. We exchanged a glance, and I noticed the color draining from her face.

"Speak."

Reed and Taylor walked in at the same time.

"Did you tell them?" Reed asked with an arched brow, pointing at us, a bag of Chinese food in his hand.

"Tell us what?" I asked, my patience growing thinner by the second.

"The Bensons. They gave an exclusive interview an hour ago. To *Sixty Minutes of Truth*. They talked about you. Travis. The foundation. Everything. They defended your honor, girl. Nobody will ever hate you again after the way they portrayed you. Jenna told me she cried through the entire interview. Did you know they would do this? Have you finally talked to them?" Saunders asked.

My shoulders sagged, and a warm feeling ran through me.

From the way April was cupping her mouth and tears were brightening her eyes, I was sure she had no clue her ex-in-laws had planned to defend her honor on national television.

"They did?" she asked in a small voice. "They stood up for me?"

Saunders, Reed, and Taylor all nodded.

Saunders gripped April's shoulders and turned her so

they could face each other. "Jenna told me it was epic. She tried to call me when it started, but I'd left my phone in the car."

April and I stared at each other.

Reed broke the silence. "Hey guys, I looked it up, and we can re-watch the interview online. Let's have dinner, and I'll stream it on the TV."

My phone went off at the same time. *June.* "Carter, have you heard?"

I nodded as if she could see me from her end of the line. "Yeah, I did. I missed it, though. Was it good?"

"Are you kidding? It was amazing. You both need to watch this. I tried to call you half an hour ago, but it went straight to voicemail. Anyway, tell April I miss her, and I'll see you two soon."

We hung up, and the five of us gathered in the living room, hanging on every word from Mr. and Mrs. Benson, barely touching our food.

They called April a gem. A force of nature and said meeting her was the best thing that could have ever happened to their son. That she had been a daughter to them. They also said they had missed her in the last few years and were happy they had reconnected not so long ago, thanks to me. They finished the interview by saying they hoped April would keep in touch with them and that anyone lucky enough to meet her in their lifetime was destined to become a better person, because my girl had this magical way of impacting everyone she came across.

April sobbed the entire time, and I enveloped her in my arms, trying to bring her the comfort and love she needed. As soon as the interview wrapped up, I leaned back into the couch headrest, and the tension that had gripped me melted away. It felt as though a heavy weight had been lifted off my shoulders, and I was floating in relief.

"I told you, you are magical," I murmured in her ear. "See? I'm living proof that you inspire people to be better."

I kissed her cheek, and she leaned into me, her body going soft. For the rest of the night, we ate, chatted, and laughed with our friends, the air in the room light and festive.

It was ten the next morning when we finished bubble-wrapping and boxing up all of her belongings. Pop music blasted from the speaker in the living room—just for my sake. A new song began, and I winced when the chorus started. It reminded me of our playlist conversation the first time we drove to Nashville together. That episode of our lives felt like a lifetime away.

April's smile widened like she could read my mind. "What? It's catchy."

I shook my head and planted a gentle skiss on her forehead. "If you say so…"

She nodded once. "I do."

"Don't worry. I still love you."

Married life would be fun. And entertaining. I had no doubt.

"The moving truck will be here in one hour," Saunders informed us, walking toward us from the kitchen, a cup of tea in hand. "I can't believe you're moving, girl. I knew it was coming, but I never thought I'd find it so hard." She dried her eyes with a tissue.

The moving truck was actually just a trailer Taylor had rented and hitched to his SUV. We were doing this the old-school way—the way April liked it.

"You and Reed will forever be my family, Saund. But now, Carter and I will be a family too. Don't worry. We'll visit each other all the time." April hugged her best friend for endless minutes, and both women turned into a giant crying jumble.

Reed joined me and tapped my shoulder as I watched them, my hands stuffed into my pockets and my feet frozen on the floor. "Women," he said. "You'll get used to these two. Don't worry. It's not as bad as it looks. They're quite adorable once you get accustomed to their antics."

My phone chimed. "Gimme a sec." I grabbed the device from my back pocket and glided my thumb over the screen to unlock it.

JUNE

Look at this.

Dozens of links to web pages and social media accounts were devoted to April and our relationship. T-shirts with "I love April," "April + Carter," and other catchy phrases were now available for purchase all over the internet. April inched closer, and I turned my phone around to show her the frenzy surrounding us.

A wide smile tugged at her lips, chasing away all traces of her breakdown. "Ohmygod. People are crazy. Yesterday they hated me, and now they are worshipping us."

If she thought it was funny, then it was all that mattered. Stupid fame. It was so unpredictable. The boulders that had taken root in my stomach when April left me fragmented to dust. We'd be okay.

JUNE

And you're still number one.

For the third week in a row, "Pink and Country" had topped the charts.

Hopefully, my life was turning around, and all the bad

stuff would stay in the rearview mirror as we looked into the future.

> JUNE
>
> I have over fifty interview requests in my inbox as we speak.
>
> They want to interview both of you. I already said no. The new PR firm will take care of it. Don't worry.

The media would have to wait for a very long time if they wanted to talk to me—or my fiancée. I wouldn't address my private life publicly, not now and never again. I'd learned my lesson the hard way.

Camping in April's apartment for one last night, we looked like teenagers on a budget.

We had set the mattress on the living room floor and transformed a box of cereal into a bedside table. There was no other furniture left.

I had sent Taylor to the hotel for a second night in a row, wanting the entire place to ourselves.

We lit up candles and ate tacos sitting on a blanket on the floor.

We made love in the kitchen, in the shower, and against the wall in the bedroom walk-in closet.

"Carter, no big wedding, okay? Friends and family only. Something simple. No fancy shit."

I tipped her chin up with a finger. "As long as I have you, nothing else matters. Anyway, there're just a handful of people I'd like to invite, so it'll be perfect. And April?" Her eyes met mine. "I've been thinking. No more world tours and sold-out stadium concerts…at least for now. I can't say I'll never do those again someday, but not in the next year. All I want is to be with you. I'll do small-venue gigs like the one in Nashville instead." My lips found hers. "Right now, I'm taking the next few months off." I claimed her lips in a slow kiss. "I want to be with you. Build something together. Adopt a dog. Get pregnant. Or whatever we desire. I want us to be a family and for you to focus on your career and fulfill all your dreams."

"You're done with tours? You sure?"

"Yes. For now, my focus is elsewhere. I want to lay down roots and make our life together my top priority. It's what feels right."

"I love you so much."

My hands found her hips, holding her in place, as I sealed my words with a mind-blowing kiss.

"Don't change for me, Carter. I love you just the way you are. But thanks for saying all those things." She pressed a hand to my heart. "You're hot when you care."

"Are you turning into a groupie, Ms. Simmons? Oh god, I can't wait to call you Mrs. Hills. Are you changing your last name?"

She kissed me. "I've thought about it. I'm not sure, what do you think?"

"Whatever makes you happy." I deepened the kiss as I slid into her. I slid home. Where I belonged. "The truth is that I'm tired. I need a break from all this circus. I need you. All of you. And only you."

Her head fell back, and I grazed the column of her throat with my tongue. She squirmed underneath me, and we both went over the edge together, our bond stronger than ever.

"Barn wedding?"

She poked my chest, and her cheeks turned a bright shade of red. "Oh, I forgot you had a front row seat to my dream recap the other day when you pretended to be a massage therapist."

"So?"

"I don't care as long as you look at me with those eyes when I walk down the aisle."

48

CARTER

"Keep your eyes closed. No cheating."

April muttered something I didn't quite catch.

"Come on, Fairy, play with me here." Clamping her elbow, I led her inside the cabin. April hadn't been here in more than two weeks. But right now, it felt as if she'd never left. Once we passed the threshold, I freed Bernice from her carrier and kicked the front door shut. We moved further in. "Okay, one step to your right." We halted. "Now turn ninety degrees to your left. Perfect." I sucked in a breath. April stiffened under my touch. I circled her and caught her lips between mine before stepping back. "Ready? Open your eyes."

I couldn't contain my excitement for another second.

Beside me, April stayed silent, her eyes rounded and her lips parted in shock.

Tension invaded my shoulders, and ice crept up my spine. Would she like it? "So? Huh…what do you think?"

She twirled on herself, and when her face met mine. Her eyes glistened with tears, barely held back. She rushed into my arms, and I relaxed. A little. "Carter, ohmygod. It's... Wow. I-I don't know what to say. I can't find the words."

I leaned back and framed her face with my hands. "You're happy?" A guy needed some reassurance here.

"You're kidding, right? It's everything I've ever dreamed of." Her voice cracked. "You did all this for me?" Her arms tightened around my midsection. "You know you're the absolute best, right?"

"I love you. You make me the happiest man on Earth, and I want this room to have your colors. And your energy. When you left, I couldn't cross the threshold because I couldn't deal with the fact you wouldn't be inside if I walked in."

I scanned the den. With Nick's help, I'd transformed it into an office for April. Or rather a creative space. A place just for her. I knew it was her favorite room in my house— *our house*—so I'd created the perfect writer's nest. A soft, striped rug in shades of gold and pink. A white desk stocked with every shade of paper and pen I could find. A new and improved hanging chair with fuzzy colorful pillows. A rose-gold velvety lounge chair. A wooden bookshelf, that Nick custom-built, along a wall that I filled with novels, biographies, art, and picture albums. A guitar sat in the corner, just in case April ever felt like trying her hand at writing lyrics.

She traipsed around the room, brushing every surface with her fingertips. "I love everything about it, Carter. I can't believe you sacrificed your den for me."

My heart swelled in my chest, and I prowled in her direction, sweeping her off her feet, ready to christen her new office. "There's no sacrifice when you're involved, Fairy. And this isn't my den. It's ours. It's our house now."

———

"You need to get dressed. I have a surprise for you," I announced a month later as I dried my hair with a towel, exiting our hotel room in Atlanta. We drove here yesterday afternoon after I pretended I had a meeting in the city. At April's request, we had booked a king-size bedroom, smaller than our walk-in closet at home. It was simple, yet cozy. A white duvet, a dark-green carpet with bronze patterns, and an en-suite bathroom comprising of a tub-shower and a vanity sink. No fancy double-size round bathtub or glass shower. No kitchen—then again, we never used it while staying at the hotel—no living room, and no panoramic view.

"A surprise? You've already created the perfect space for me at home. I'm still not over it."

My pulse picked up. "The office was just an appetizer. Now let's get ready."

Thirty minutes later, we stood on the sidewalk, April's back facing the wide building.

"Listen to me, Fairy. Since you won't accept gifts or anything money can buy, I hope you'll accept this."

A lineup of about a hundred people stood outside, waiting for the doors to open.

"What's this?" she asked, her voice trembling. "Atlanta Convention Center," she read aloud, half a statement, half a question, as we approached the entrance. "You're having a show here?"

I shook my head. "Just wait and see. Do you trust me?"

She nodded and slipped her hand in mine for reassurance.

"Then follow me."

We intertwined our fingers, and with a baseball cap over my head and my shades on, I led April inside through the side entrance. A security guard with buzzed ginger hair in his mid-thirties asked us for our passes. I fetched them from my pocket and handed him all three. I bit a smirk when his eyes ping-ponged between the name written on my VIP pass and my face. I might have used the name "Clay Stephenson" when I filled out the form. I thought it sounded author-like when I chose it. The security guy scratched the side of his head and looked at something on the pad in his hand. Finally, he motioned for us to enter, with Taylor hot on our heels.

April's grip on my hand tightened as she took in the entire room."Carter, what is this?"

I opened my arms and motioned her further inside. "April, I'm proud to offer you your first book signing. You told me once you never had one. I made a few phone calls, met with your agent, talked to your publisher. And—"

She jumped into my arms. My heart liquefied and pooled at my feet at the sheer enthusiasm I could read on her face. "You what? How did you do this?"

"Turns out the organizer is a huge fan." Her eyes flared, waiting me for to explain. "I didn't buy my way in, I promise. But in exchange for a few pictures and a couple of autographs, she agreed to meet with me. She gave me twenty minutes to convince her why she should make room for you at the event, especially since it was already full and you'd turned down all their invitations in the past." I acted as if it was no big deal, but inside, I was a nervous wreck. A pile of mush. I was hoping April would be on board with all this.

"What did you tell her?"

"All about *Amelia's Kingdom*. How King Edward portrayed the perfect antihero in book one, only to become the kingdom's savior in the sequel. Your story is such an emotional ride. It's brilliant."

"Wait. You read my books?"

"Babe, I didn't just read them. I researched them too. Found online forums devoted to your story and chatted with your most dedicated fans. There are thousands of them. It's amazing, the world you've created. Anyway, after talking to them, I came up with more reasons to convince the organizer that you belong here. All I did was state the truth. You *do* belong here."

She stared at me, her mouth agape, and her eyes so big that she looked like a doe caught in the headlights.

"Are you mad? Did I overstep here?"

She cleared her throat. "Mad? Carter, how could I be mad? I'm bewildered. I'm excited. I'm…I don't even know what I am, but mad isn't it. Jill and I discussed doing some events like this for a while. Before…before you, I wasn't ready. But now? Now I think I am."

"So, you don't mind people knowing you're Avery Davis, which, by the way, I love a lot?"

She shook her head.

"You told me once you cherish your privacy, Fairy. I know dating me has fucked this up for you, but so far, your pen name hasn't come up anywhere. If you prefer to stay anonymous, we'll go. It was part of the deal I made with the organizer."

She stood there, not saying a thing. After a minute, she laced her fingers through mine. Her lips parted.

My heart cartwheeled, and I held my breath, waiting to hear her thoughts.

"After everything we've been through, I'm done being afraid."

Warmth rolled down my back, and I breathed easier knowing I hadn't overstepped.

"How did you find out my pen name? Because if I

remember correctly, I told you I'd have to kill you if you ever did."

I raised my hands in surrender. "No need to kill me. You're not the one who told me. I figured it out on my own…and maybe with Reed's help. Don't forget, he and I spent an entire day together. Guys talk, babe."

She snickered, hiding her grin behind her fist. "Gosh, you always find new ways to amaze me." Her eyes found mine, and she wrinkled her face. "Maybe I'll let you live because you're kinda cute and you organized this," she said, gesturing around with a hand. "But only this time, though."

"Thanks. I'm relieved my life is safe." I slid the back of my hand across my forehead, and we both burst into a fit of laughter. "April, I love you. You're amazing. Listen, this is your day. I want you to make the most of it. You've always been understanding and selfless about my career. All I'm saying is that it's my turn to do something for you." I inhaled, my lungs filling with a mix of oxygen and pride. "Are you ready?"

She bobbed her head with determination.

Yep, that's my girl.

Hand in hand, we entered the room. It had twenty-foot-high ceilings, navy-blue rugs covering the concrete floor, vivid yellow tablecloths, and yards of bookshelves filled with the most popular fantasy novels on the market. Colorful and enlarged book covers and life-size cardboard cutouts of some of the main characters of those books covered the walls. I didn't have enough eyes to take every-thing in. I wasn't some fantasy genre expert, but I knew, without a doubt, fans would love this event. Magic filled the air. As we neared April's appointed table, her agent Jill met us. She was a short woman with medium-length chocolate-brown hair and eyes even darker. I held out my hand for her to shake. If it weren't for her, I might not have succeeded in getting April a table here today.

"Nice to see you again, Mr. Hills." She pivoted on her heels to face my fiancée. God, I loved that word. "You've got yourself a really tenacious boyfriend, April," she said as she hugged her. "You're lucky to have him in your corner. I'm glad we're doing this together. It's about time to let the world know you're the talent behind *Amelia's Kingdom*. I can't wait for book number three to be out. Just wait until you see the cover the graphic designer sent over." Jill grabbed April's shaky hand. "Let's do this."

April eyed me sideways, and I nodded.

I caught her elbow and brushed my lips over hers. "Go shine, Fairy. I'll be right here if you need me." I wasn't about to steal her thunder. She'd worked too hard to get here. She offered me a shy smile as I stepped to the back of the room where Taylor waited for me.

For the next six hours, I watched the woman I loved talk to her fans, take pictures with them, and sign so many books that I feared she'd be short by the end of the day. The entire time, we exchanged glances and grins. To see the fondness on my woman's face, I would sit in this uncomfortable chair forever. When she spun in her seat and grinned at me, her eyes full of love and awe, it took all my inner strength not to scoop her over my shoulder and carry her back to the hotel.

I mouthed *I love you* instead, and we eye-fucked each other for a moment. As usual, the electricity between us could light up the entire convention center.

When did I get so lucky?

My heart was full. Since I'd met her, every single lost piece had come back and built up my most precious organ again.

"Do you want a little privacy?" April asked.

We'd been back in Green Mountain for three days. After the book signing, we spent a month in Hawaii and the next in Oregon because I wanted Stud and Belinda to meet April and get to know her for more than just a few days. As expected, she fit right in with my friends. They all fell in love with one another the moment they met.

April used this time off to work on her book. It was being proofread right now.

Life was good. Our lives were wonderful.

"Please, stay." Sitting on the edge of the bed, I studied the torn envelope, tracing the letters of my name in faded black ink with a fingertip. "Okay. Let's see what's inside." I rubbed the back of my neck. My throat was itchy, my mouth dry, and my heart was in a muddle.

April stood in front of me, and her hold on my hand tightened. "Listen to me, Carter. You've been avoiding this moment for six years, and it's unhealthy. You need to make up your mind once and for all, so you can move on. Face the music."

I frowned.

She shook her head and sighed. "No pun intended, Country Boy. Let's do this."

She pressed a kiss to my shoulder, and I couldn't help but catch her contagious grin. "I love you, HN. No matter what's in this envelope, or how you handle it, it will never change how I feel about you."

Carefully, like it might explode, I tore the flap open.

With my girl by my side, I found the courage I desperately needed. I held my breath as a letter and a smaller sealed envelope fell into my hands, the one I knew contained the genetic test results.

My heart jackhammered in my chest, and my hands trembled.

April unfolded the letter and placed it back in my hands. "Here."

With a quivering breath and a shaky voice, I read it out loud. She deserved to know everything it said, as much as I did. We were in this together. For better or for worse.

Dear Carter,

I'm giving you this because I owe you the right to know the truth.

Regardless of the results, nothing will change between the three of us. Jack, you, and I are family, now and forever. I'll respect your wish, whatever you decide to do in the light of the results, if you choose to look at them. Knowing how stubborn you are, I'm pretty sure you're older now and still debating if you should open the envelope or not. Even if you and I aren't together, your love for Jack will never change. You'll always love him like your own. You'll be (or were) there for his first steps and on each birthday. Someday, you'll teach him how to drive and mouth the pickup lines when he's old enough to get a girlfriend. You'll comfort him when he's heartbroken and show him how to transpose his feelings into music. I just know you two will bond over this. It's written in the skies. Every time my eyes land on his long fingers, I think of you. I hear you saying he has the fingers of a musician.

Carter, I know you. Like nobody else. But if you're thinking about the test results all these years later, it's because you need to know. You owe it to yourself. You'll forever be haunted if you don't find out. If that wasn't the case, you would've gotten rid of this envelope a long time ago...or the day I gave it to you. I don't need to know what it says because in my mind, and in my heart, Jack is all ours. Yes, he's the perfect mix of two awesome human beings I was lucky enough to call my best friends growing up. Two men I loved with my whole heart and still do after all these years. Two men who loved me enough to stick by my side through it all. Even when I messed up.

I'm sure Jack will inherit your drive and talent. His humor and patience will come from Jeff, though.

It's time for you to live your life, Carter. To spread your wings and be free. It's time for you to love and open your heart. Someone special will enter your life when you are ready. Never let her go. You'll need her as much as she'll need you. She'll be fearless and beautiful.

She'll have the biggest heart, as big as yours, and challenge you to be the best version of yourself. Hold on to her with all you've got.

Never stop shining, amazing star, your light makes all of us better.

I'll love you forever,
Dahlia xx

I reread the last part twice because tears clouded my vision, and I missed a few words. April sniffled beside me, and she looked as much an emotional mess as I probably did.

It was as if Dahlia had predicted, when she was barely twenty, how our story would unfold—as though she knew April was the perfect match for me, my soul mate, and that she'd enter my life only once I was truly ready.

I twisted the sealed envelope between my fingers, hoping I was making the best decision right now.

"Have you decided what you're gonna do?" April asked.

"Yep." My heart tumbled in my chest, and my body temperature rose. A giant, messy ball seemed to bounce in my chest as all my thoughts collided. "I...I won't look at it."

"You sure?"

I nodded. "Yes. I am. I've been replaying your words in my head. About DNA not being a gauge of love and acceptance but just being a variable determining our genetic pool. Once I realized my resistance to the results stemmed from fear, I no longer felt the need to know. No matter what the results say, it won't change my love for Jack or his love for me. I'll always consider him my son. From day one, I was there for every milestone, every birthday, everything that counts. Even if he were mine, I would never fight his mama for custody. No matter what, the truth wouldn't have made her fall in love with me over all these years.Perhaps Jack is the result of our special relationship, perhaps he is my brother's son. In the end, I would like to believe, as she said, that he's a bit of all of us. That he's the result of so much love."

"He's lucky to have all of you as his parents."

"In a way, I hope he's Jeff's because it means my brother gets to live through him, but somehow, I had always hoped he was mine too. I wanted to be a dad since the day I found out Dah was pregnant. I never knew how bad I craved a family of my own until he happened." My eyes filled with a new batch of tears. My heart healed as the pain I'd been carrying around vanished. My mind quietened. My entire body relaxed. I was okay with my decision. "I'll give the results back to Dahlia. One day, if Jack wants to know, it will be his to decide. It has to be *his* choice."

"I'm proud of you." April stood between my legs and wrapped her arms around me. She leaned closer, and her warm breath tickled my cheek. "Carter, what if I told you, you are going to be a dad again?" She cocked her head to meet my eyes, a slight blush reddening her cheeks, her eyes watery, and a soft curve lifting one corner of her lips.

I wiped my tears with the hem of my shirt.

She intertwined our fingers and stared at me, waiting for me to say something.

"Are you kidding? Because if you are, it's not funny." I swallowed the lump blocking my airways and blinked a few times to clear my foggy vision.

She huffed out a breath. "I found out two days ago."

"What? You did? And you didn't tell me? Why?"

"Because you said you were opening the letter today, and I didn't want to steal this moment from you. It took you six years to find the courage to go through with it. I'm telling you now. I can't hide the truth anymore. I just hope it's really what you desire."

I rose to my feet and lifted her into my arms, burying my head in the crook of her neck, her lavender scent filling my nostrils.

I cradled her cheeks in both hands, lost in her baby-blue irises. "It's everything I want. It's us. It's upside down. It's messy. It's beautiful." I laid her carefully on her back and lifted her shirt over her head to press a kiss to her belly. "Hold on tight, baby girl. Daddy needs to show your mama how much he loves her."

April's head sprang up from the mattress. "Baby girl?" she asked with a tipped brow.

"Yeah. I dreamed about her the other night. She'll look just like you. I thought it was just a dream—" My voice stuck in my throat.

April nodded twice. "It's happening."

In one swift movement, I yanked her pants and panties down her legs and buried my face in her sweet wetness. My tongue teased her, one stroke at a time. Her body shivered as I devoured her with my mouth.

My fingers found her center and dived in and out of her at a fast pace.

When she arched her back and whimpered, I believed I would come in my pants. "Fuck, you're gorgeous."

"Oh, Carter, don't you ever stop." She fisted my hair and settled into the rhythm.

I grinned as I worshipped every inch of her with my tongue.

April came undone and convulsed in my arms. She rode her orgasm, writhing in bliss on our bed.

I finished undressing her and hovered over her naked figure, teasing her lips. I seared into her, her core clenching around my swollen erection the moment I plunged in. My mouth and hands attacked her perky breasts, my tongue playing with her puckered pink nipples. I kissed my way down from her neck to her navel, tasting her.

Her body shuddered against mine, and she looked gorgeous with her shiny eyes and the pink hue coloring her cheeks.

I positioned myself over her, fixing her gaze, lost in the ocean of her eyes.

Our mouths danced together as I thrust into her with fieriness and love, not giving her time to catch her breath.

April pushed my chest with both hands, and I knew what she wanted. Clamping her hipbones, I flipped us over until she straddled me. "Ride me, Fairy." I watched her naked glory setting the pace, entranced by the movement of her hips rolling over my groin, toying with every thread of my self-control. Pleasure built inside me, and unable to endure her sweet torture anymore, I pulled her toward my chest and drilled into her with everything I had. "Come for me."

Her body undulated over mine, my palms traveling all over her back, caressing her flesh.

"I love you, HN."

I cocked one brow, halting my movements. "Wanna tell me what it means?"

She blushed, her eyes lighting up. "Nah, I think I'll keep that piece of information to myself, *Hot Neighbor*."

My smiled reached both ears. "I knew I was irresistible back then."

"You were an ass." She peppered kisses across my chest. "But a very handsome one, I must say."

"I think I just fell in love with you all over again. Hold on tight, Fairy." I rolled April onto her back and hiked her legs up over my shoulders. She lifted her hips to deepen our connection and hooked her hand around my neck, keeping her eyes locked on mine. I sank into her. Faster. Stronger. I curled my fingers behind her neck and claimed her mouth again. Hungrier. April's fingernails grazed the skin of my chest, my biceps, then my stomach. The sensation sent a bolt of electricity to my pulsing cock. I rammed into my fiancée, pressing my forehead against hers. Gravity left me. I was floating. I was drowning. I was being consumed by all of her. My body turned into a blazing inferno. My heart constricted, and it burst open. April climaxed, and I followed suit, both of us breathless and grinning like little kids.

"Let's get married next month. I don't want to wait. This," I motioned the space between the two of us, "is forever." I captured her lips with mine, and with our bodies tangled together, we drifted into sleep.

EPILOGUE
CARTER

Five years later

"Georgia, don't pull your brother's hair." My little girl had drive. She was the perfect mix of her mother and me. Nobody pushed her around. In fact, she did most of the pushing—a habit we'd been working super hard to break. And she had enough energy to light up a small town. Georgia came as a blessing in our lives. She had April's blonde hair and my melted-steel irises.

Tennessee, our toddler, who had April's baby-blue eyes, had inherited his height from me. At two, he was already taller than most kids his age. My friends had nicknamed him Li'l Carter.

Tennessee was more laid-back than his sister. He preferred music to running around. I often kept him in a baby carrier while recording new music. It soothed him. The same way it had always soothed me too.

April and I never moved away from Green Mountain.

And we never rented the other two cabins next to ours again, keeping them for our guests instead.

We still owned an apartment in Nashville but not the penthouse. After we got married, we bought a smaller place, something cozier—with old, exposed brick walls and wood beams across the ceilings. It had an industrial yet rustic charm and was more kid-friendly than my bachelor pad. We loved having our own place for the nights we spent in the city.

April and I named our children after the states where our lives had changed for the better. The one where we fell in love and the one where she agreed to spend the rest of her life with me.

I lifted my daughter into my arms. "Come on, honey, it's Mama's birthday. Let's go get her. Grams and gramps will be here soon." I nuzzled her neck and kissed her rosy cheeks.

"Daddy, I love you." Those four words were my pride and joy.

Saunders, Reed, and Hunter, their three-year-old son, joined us on the deck, Stud, Belinda, and their children in tow. Before we could make it inside, Georgia asked to play with Hunter—they were inseparable, just like their mothers. As soon as she landed on her feet, my daughter grabbed her friend's hand, and they disappeared with Kimmie toward the playhouse Stud had built for the kids the last time he visited. From his highchair, Tennessee raised his arms, and I picked him up, holding him close to my heart. His dark-brown baby hair tickled my chin, and I dropped a kiss on the crown of his head.

My wife exited the house, her three-month baby belly visible through the fabric of her soft-gray maxi dress, looking as beautiful as the day I met her in these woods, bantering with me about what an ass I was.

My hand found her waist, and I pulled her in for a kiss. April lifted the baby from my arms and greeted everyone.

Dahlia, Nick, Jack, and Violet turned the corner of the deck and sauntered in our direction. Violet ran into my arms, her red pigtails bouncing on both sides of her head, the sight reminding me of her mama at the same age. "Uncle Carter." She dropped a wet kiss on my cheek, and her eyes glistened as I twirled her around. Once I put her down, she scurried away, joining the rest of the children.

"Hey, son," I greeted Jack when he neared me. Now older, he looked so much like Jeff. The striking resemblance was troubling but also comforting in a way. He wrapped his arms around me, and I did the same before planting a kiss on the side of his head.

After I gave the paternity test results back to Dahlia, five years ago, I started calling Jack, *son*. The ghost of the genetic test results no longer lingered between us. I didn't fear calling him mine as if one day a piece of paper would shatter our bond and tell me I wasn't allowed to love him as my own. Deep in my heart, I still believed Dahlia suspected she had been right all along about who Jack's biological father was, but we never spoke of it again. She also never asked me not to call him *son* after I started. The first time the word passed my lips, she cried as much as I did. She was right the day she said *Together, we were too emotional*. She even told me she was relieved I wasn't fighting the connection anymore.

Even after all these years, April's words still rang true in my ears. Family wasn't about blood, but rather about love and acceptance. Through the years, Dahlia and I had built our own big, uncommon family—one I couldn't imagine my life without.

My children were on board, considering Jack their big brother too. Jack was still very close to my wife, as she went from being his fairy friend to his confidant. Someone he turned to whenever his other three parents were not cool enough for his liking.

It was all good. *We* were all good.

Never again would I let a piece of paper dictate who I belonged with.

I stepped back and pointed inside with a thumb. "You know that song we recorded last week, I finished the arrangement. We'll listen to it together later, and you'll tell me what you think. By the way, the new bridge you came up with is fire. Just sayin'." Dahlia was right again when she predicted Jack and I would bond over our love for music. It was our thing whenever he came over, and we jammed in the studio for hours together. The kid had raw talent.

"Cool. We could send it to Uncle Riley for a demo." His smile split his face in two. Jack told us on his tenth birthday he wanted to pursue a music career once he grew up.

After Riley heard him sing once, my manager kept joking that he would one day sign him. Dahlia wasn't excited at the idea. After all, she'd been trying to shield Jack from this life and its effects since she'd learned she was pregnant when she was still a kid herself. I reassured her that it wasn't a done deal and that we would talk about it later, when Jack was old enough to understand the baggage this life came with. In the meantime, I would teach him everything I knew. In case it was his destiny too.

"You know the drill, buddy. We'll talk about it when you turn sixteen. As far as I know, you're only eleven, so we have plenty of time."

"Almost twelve."

I ruffled his hair the same way I'd always done. "Yeah, well, not quite. Enjoy being a child for now."

"Whatever." He rolled his eyes and followed Tristan, Stud and Bella's son, when he saw him waving from the opposite side of the deck. His teenage years would be a lot of fun.

From a distance, Dahlia and I exchanged one of our glances that bore more weight than our words could. She mouthed *Thank you*, and I blew her a kiss. She winked, then turned to her husband. Yeah, we would catch up later.

"Grams," Georgia yelled, running toward the corner of the deck, capturing my full attention. I spun on my heels just in time to witness Grams and Gramps walking our way, my wife beside them.

Georgia tugged at Grams's hand, while Gramps picked up Tennessee.

"When did you get here?" I asked.

"Last night," Gramps said.

April glared at them, a warning frown etched on her face. Five years later, she still hated the sharp turns down the mountain roads at night.

"We were safe, dear. We promise. Don't worry so much about us," Grams said, squeezing April's forearm. "We arrived around nine, but we went to bed as soon as we got here. We should've called. I'm sorry."

April neared Grams and pulled her into a warm hug. "I'm glad you made it safe and sound. Next time, don't drive up here at night. And if you do, please let us know."

Grams patted my wife's cheek and nodded. "I promise, dear. We went to town early this morning to have breakfast at the same eatery Dahlia had recommended last time. That's why we're late."

"You're just in time," I said. "Are you staying here for the whole month?"

"You bet we are. We missed you all so much," Gramps

said with a large grin. The kids hadn't seen their grandparents since Tennessee's second birthday last month. Gramps leaned forward and kissed my wife's cheek. "Happy birthday, April."

She hugged him, smiling.

"Give me this little monster," I said, lifting my son from Gramps's arms.

After they defended her honor and character on national television to the world—the day after our engagement—April and I had welcomed Mr. and Mrs. Benson into our family. Permanently.

They were destined to be part of our lives. They became the parents April never had growing up and the grandparents our kids needed in their lives.

And they both had accepted me as a son.

April believed Travis was the reason we all found one another. I liked the idea he chose me to love her forever.

My parents never came around. They still lived in Costa Rica. We invited them to our wedding, but they never showed up. Now and then, I sent them pictures of the kids. Once again, their rejection hurt, but I'd grown an even thicker skin in the last few years, so I didn't let it shatter me the way it had when I was younger.

I had my own family now to keep me completely busy. The one I had chosen.

The one that brought me joy and unconditional love, not defined solely by the DNA we shared.

Nowadays, I was still making music, but the way I liked it. Small concerts. Most of them acoustic. Nothing that kept me away from home for more than two nights when the family couldn't join me on the road.

I still hated fame, but now I embraced it on my own terms. I wasn't its prisoner anymore. The rich and famous lifestyle never suited me anyway, and April loathed it as much as I did. I preferred my low-key existence a thousand times over.

After my wife came back into my life, I never had another destructive anxiety episode again. I had learned to handle the stress and adjust to the changes in my lifestyle. Listening to myself, instead of being a by-product of who other people expected me to be, played a big part in it. Sharing my life with April had helped me to sever the last chains life—and my past—once held over me. She challenged me to be better and not let my overwhelming emotions dictate my actions. Whenever my thoughts began racing, we would sit down, talk things through, and she would reassure me, helping me see the situation from a different perspective. She still had that special calming power that washed over me whenever I became agitated. With her unconditional love and support, I had learned not to let my deafening thoughts control me anymore.

Through the years, April and I found our pace, and our peace, as a couple, as a family, and as artists, and never looked back. We were the best team I could've ever dreamed of. We completed each other in every aspect of our lives.

"Carter, it's time for your toast," Dahlia said, bringing me back to the present. Everyone we loved—except June, Riley, and their families, who couldn't make it today— stood on the deck facing the valley, our entire wedding party. I took in every person, reminding myself of how lucky I was to have all of them in my life. In our lives. I watched the kids running around and laughing, and a renewed sense of calm filled me.

I raised my glass of water. "Thanks, all y'all, for joining us today to celebrate the birthday of the most exquisite woman in the entire world. Fairy, I still love you a little more every day. You're the sun to my moon, the yin to my yang, the white to my black, the good to my bad. I've told you a million times that I love you, and I'll tell you a million more. Nothing in my life makes sense without you. You're the reason I found my place in this world. And my peace. You once told me I showed you what passion was. I'm telling you today you've shown me what living should be. And what happiness should feel like. I'm the luckiest man alive, and I wouldn't wish to be anywhere but here today. Just say the word, and I'll marry you all over again. Happy birthday, Mrs. Hills." The small crowd cheered.

"It's not fair to us, Carter, you're a songwriter. I think I'll hire you to write my wife's next birthday wishes," Reed said.

Saunders rolled her eyes and elbowed him in the ribs.

We all laughed.

"Sorry, ladies, Carter is mine," April said while running into my arms to kiss me. "*I am* the luckiest woman on Earth," she whispered in my ear.

I kissed her back, and for a minute, the world around us disappeared.

"Yuck, that's gross," Georgia said as she wrapped her little arms around us.

Tennessee wrinkled his face and babbled a "Yucky."

Everybody burst out laughing.

April stepped back, her grin beaming across her face, and picked up our son as I squatted to lift our little girl.

My wife extended an arm, and Jack joined our little love bubble.

"I love you guys," I said as I drew my family into my embrace.

———

"You'll never guess who just signed a tell-all book deal," April said, standing next to the bed, as I entered our bedroom after checking on the kids to make sure they were both deep asleep.

From behind, I wound my arms around her. With her back against my chest, I nestled my head in the crook of her neck, my palms resting flat on her burgeoning belly. "Who?"

"Savannah Prince."

I choked on my breath. I hadn't heard that name in years. After the whole *dragging April into the dirt* episode, Savannah got a taste of her own medicine. Producers dropped her from two blockbusters that were meant to catapult her career to stardom, and she'd been acting in only-for-TV movies and other small projects since then. The last I heard, she was bartending in a dive bar in LA to make ends meet.

"You're kidding, right?"

"I wish. Jill told me she heard Savannah got paid a lot of money to dish out dirt about other celebrities. I'm pretty sure you'll be in her book. Or maybe we'll both be. Who knows? She hated both of us." April sank her body into my chest, her cheek pressing against mine.

I sighed and narrowed my eyes. "I can't believe she's still a head case after all this time. Guess she didn't learn her lesson." I shrugged. "Please don't worry about her." I doubted Savannah would include a chapter about me after what happened the day I walked away from her. If she had any judgment left, she would leave me and my family out of it. For her own good.

April cocked her head so I could look at her face. "I won't. I'm sad for her. She'd do anything for attention, fame, or money."

My lips found the flesh of my her neck, and I tickled it with the tip of my tongue. She squirmed, and I tightened my arms around her. A moan passed her lips, and I was a goner.

April ended our makeout session when she turned in my arms. "Did you send that stroller back?" she asked, the skin of her neck blotchy, thanks to my short stubble.

After photos of April and me with wedding bands and a visibly pregnant belly surfaced a few years back, she had designers gifting her clothes and companies sending her baby stuff. My wife sent back every single item. Two pregnancies later, she still returned every single item they sent us, hoping she would wear it and talk about it. She had strong principles, and no one could ever buy her with money or with free, overpriced items.

I stopped fighting it a long time ago. Except for the tennis bracelet I gave her when we moved in together and her engagement ring, April barely ever let me buy her jewelry or other expensive gifts. Instead, we used our money to launch a program to help young artists pursue their dreams. We started the foundation that funded the program, and I helped manage it in between other engagements. April dedicated a few hours a week to helping those teenagers too.

I nodded. "The stroller. The crib. The clothes. All of it. Now can we go back to what we were doing? My dick has been hard for you all day. He's been patient enough, and I think he deserves some fun and a treat."

April cupped my erection over my denims, and a whistle escaped my mouth.

"God, you feel good," I said. "Let's get the birthday celebrations started."

She chuckled and kissed the side of my throat. I shivered, feeling my restraints slacken.

"I love you when you talk dirty, Country Boy." She swiped her lips with her tongue, and I almost shot my load in my pants right there. This woman robbed me of all my self-control even years later.

My sex-brain took over, like it did every time she was close to me, and I ground against her hand as a deep, guttural groan formed in my throat. "Fuck, Wife. You're killing me."

"You've seen nothing yet, Husband."

April unbuttoned my denims. Was she taking her time on purpose? Fairy could be evil when she put her mind to it. Her eyes met mine, and she gave me an innocent look, chewing on her lower lip. I let my eyes roam over her figure, burning every detail to memory. She sat in the armchair set in the corner of the room, pulling me to her.

"It's your birthday. I should be the one spoiling you."

She freed my cock and leaned forward, her tongue playing with the tip.

"Damn. Don't make me beg—" My phone went off, and we both froze. "What the fucking hell. It's like ten o'clock."

My wife released me and fished my phone out of my back pocket. Her brows bunched together. "Riley."

We both stared at the device as if it were a grenade we were supposed to diffuse.

"It could be an emergency," she finally declared, her cheeks still flushed from our foreplay.

Curiosity got the best of me. "Fine." I tugged at her hand, and she followed me as we both sat on the edge of the bed. I accepted the call while she curled her hand around my hard flesh, pumping me with slow, agonizing strokes.

My throat bobbed, and I tried to project nonchalance when inside I was a ticking time bomb.

"Hey, Carter. Glad you picked up. Listen, I know you don't want to schedule any shows until after the baby is born, but I may have something you could help me with." My manager spoke fast, not giving me time to say anything.

"Talk." That was all I could say as waves of heat rippled through me.

April kissed my jaw and mouthed *Is everything all right?*

I shrugged as my hand landed on her ass.

"I have three talented musicians I want to sign. They remind me of you guys when you started the band."

"What's the catch?"

"They hate one another. Too many egos. Too much drama. They refuse to work together. They'd be a killer group if they give it a chance. You know I'm always right about these things. So, I was thinking, I want you to mentor them."

"You want me to babysit your new pet project?" I asked, lifting my brows. "I'm listening."

April's eyes widened, and she released my dick.

"Yes. You already have your arts program going on. I'm sure you can squeeze them in. You could use your old freaking-out spot, that you turned into a recording studio, to work with them. I'll rent it. I'll even rent one of your cabins for a few months and move them there. I know you don't usually get involved with the program, but what if, this time, you did? As a favor to your favorite manager and business partner." He paused, probably to let the idea sink in. "Carter, you're the perfect candidate to get these kids to see their full potential. What do you think?"

I could feel the excitement in Riley's voice. Maybe this could be fun after all.

Beside me, April frowned. An idea flashed through my head as I looked at my wife.

"Ry, April is working with this crazy talented lyricist right now. I'm sure we could bring her on board. What if we cut a couple of demos, get your kids to work together, and see how it goes? If I like their sound, we could bribe them with the promise to open for me next year. Maybe it would convince them to agree to your *make them hostages until they fall in love* plan. What do you say?"

"I like how you're thinking, my friend. I knew you were the man for the job. Let's talk tomorrow. I have a few tasks to go over first thing in the morning. Say hi to April for me, and tell her I'm sorry again I missed her birthday."

"Tell Devon we say hi, and we'll come over next weekend as planned."

We hung up, and I lifted April into my arms until she straddled me. I hooked my arms around her waist and told her about Riley's and my conversation. "What do you think?"

"Are you sure it's a great idea? Summer is quite shy and not really a people person."

I brushed her lips with mine. "It could be good for her. My gut is usually right. If she refuses, I'm sure my wonderful and amazing wife will help us out. After all, she won a country music award for Best Song two years in a row, thanks to her incredible songwriting talent."

April squirmed on my lap as I let her robe fall back and cupped her naked breasts. "And she's a bestselling author, so words are her playground." I leaned forward to suck a nipple into my mouth. "But her body is mine."

She moaned, arching her back and pushing her chest against my starving lips, speaking between harsh breaths. "You're sure about this?"

"Babe, we'd have a new project together until the baby comes. It could be fun."

She dissolved in my mouth when my lips found hers.

She looped her arms around my neck and angled her head. I trailed kisses from her chin to her collarbone. "You're right, Carter. It'll be good for Summer to get her talent out there. She's incredible and doesn't even know it. Perhaps it will give her the confidence boost she needs. I'll talk to her on Monday."

"You better wait till Monday because right now I have a project for the two of us. It involves my dick and a very naked you." Another idea flashed through my mind as my hands landed on her belly. "How about Dakota?"

My wife stared at me, questions written across her face. "For the baby?"

"That's where you got pregnant," I replied. Hugging her against me, her soft breasts molded to my hard chest. "Remember the concert I gave in the old warehouse and the lovemaking under the stars afterward?"

A smirk lit up her face, and flickers of mischief shone in her eyes. The memory of that night was enough to make her arousal soar. She was probably already damp by now. "How could I forget?"

I kissed the tip of her nose.

"Dakota…" She said the name out loud, testing how it sounded. "Dakota Hills. I love it, Carter. It's perfect."

"It's settled." I pulled her into my arms, kissing her neck. She laughed her heart out. I slipped my hand under the waistband of her pink lace panties, and she liquefied under my touch. "Now tell this little fellow to stay put because his daddy needs to show his mama how much he loves her."

Time stood still. Our breaths quickened, and our heartbeats synced. As they always did when we loved each other. With fierceness. With lust. With tenderness.

With love big enough to shake the planet out of its axis.

Thank you for reading the conclusion to Carter and April's beautiful and emotional love story.

Keep reading for an exclusive bonus scene

Wedding Day

April walked down the aisle with Saunders by her side, looking like a vision in her white dress. Wavy pink hair—same exact shade as the painted lips I was dying to kiss—baby-blue eyes framed with mascara-coated lashes, and a smile that could bring me down to my knees right here at the altar.

A halo of glittery light glittered around her as she erased the distance between us.

My throat bobbed as my eyes locked with hers. How could I ever look anywhere else? Fairy's spell on me was everything I'd ever wished for. Dahlia—dressed in a long emerald gown hugging her pregnant figure, her hair loose down her back—and Stud—dressed in a black three-piece suit—were playing some song I couldn't even hear over the pounding of my heart.

I rolled my shoulders back, trying to hide how tense I was. Jack, the ring-bearer, walked down the aisle first, dressed in a black suit identical to mine. He offered me a giant smile that rippled through me. We fist-bumped when he reached me, then he took his seat next to Nick on one of the white wooden garden chairs.

With shaky fingers, I pinched the bridge of my nose, blinking back my tears. But it wasn't enough. Moisture filled my eyes.

My heart did some funny flips inside my chest.

April's glossy eyes met mine.

My lungs seized, but I compelled them to keep working.

April's lips parted, and she mouthed, *I love you.* Right there, I could have stopped the ceremony and stolen the bride.

My bride.

I didn't care about our friends and family being here at this exact moment. Nah, I just wanted to be with her—only her. Buried deep inside her. Imprinting myself with her love. Blanketing her in mine. Nothing else mattered anymore.

She stopped before me. I blinked back more tears and sucked a big gulp of air, needing to oxygenate my brain. Saunders dropped a kiss on her cheek and whispered something in her ear. A smile as bright as the noon sun lit up April's face. And then, as I stood there with my hands linked before me, she turned her focus back to me. I felt the laser intensity of her love in her gaze. No one had as much magnetic pull on me as she did.

All my heartstrings snapped at once.

My heart defied gravity.

It floated in my chest.

Free. Light.

And happy.

I stepped forward and held out my hands, waiting for her gentle palms to meet mine—the final act of trust. Her warmth shot through me, and my need to touch her anchored deep. The electricity from her traveled down my spine. Leaning in, I curled my hand around her nape, pressing my forehead to hers, just as we'd always done. "You're beautiful, Fairy." I brushed her lips with mine, and she smiled against my mouth. "Let's do this because I can't wait to love all of you later."

April gasped, her eyes sparkling like the most precious diamonds. "I love you."

My heart floated a little higher as the words left her mouth. The one I couldn't wait to claim as mine.

The ceremony was short and sweet. We didn't need long and complicated. Nope, it wasn't our thing.

"April, you may now read your vows," the pastor said in a low voice.

My bride gestured to Jack to join her. He rushed to her and placed a piece of paper in her hand. My heart swelled at the sight of them together. April kissed his cheek and said something that made him giggle. Once Jack returned to his seat, April's eyes zoomed in on me.

All of me.

Only me.

"Carter," she offered me a shy smile, tears now filling her eyes, "or should I say HN?" My insides tied in a knot. One with a big pink ribbon. "When I came to Green Mountain for a month-long vacation, I never imagined I'd meet my destiny. The town and the cabin charmed me right away, but when your eyes landed on me, it felt like coming home after a storm. You were the shelter I never knew existed. The one I never knew I needed. I have no idea how I spent so many years without you by my side. Every minute with you is amazing. You make me want to be better, stronger, and happier. Carter, you are the star I'll always follow when the night is dark and the sun that will always shine on me when I'm cold. Someone I really admire sang, 'You and me, we're cut from the same tree; You and me, we're a forever love story.' Today, I'm telling you that our souls are cut from the same tree, Carter, and that we'll be a forever love story. I love you a thousand times more each day, my Handsome Neighbor." April winked at me, and I stifled a chuckle. "And I'll love you every second for the rest of my life."

She retrieved a tissue from the décolletage of her dress —which made our little wedding party laugh—and patted her cheeks, doing her best to avoid ruining her makeup.

"Here, let me," I offered in a breathless whisper as I dried her tears. Well, most of them.

My finally joined heart thundered in my chest. April's love making the seams slowly disappear.

Never loosening my grip on her hand, I took a step back.

"Thanks," my about-to-be wife said, grinning through her tears.

"My turn, I guess," I said, my fingers closing on the square of paper in my pocket. I breathed in, trying to calm the jitters inside me. My body temperature rose, and I welcomed the clouds concealing some of the warm sun's rays. "Fairy, falling for you was the best thing that ever happened in my life. For a long time, I thought my heart was a rusty piece of steel, too rough to love or ever be loved. With your smile, your gentleness, your sass, and your strength, you've charmed your way into there," I said, pointing to my chest. "You brought colors into my life when I thought I was destined to live a black-and-white existence for the rest of time. You changed everything I thought I knew about love and showed me every one deserved to be happy—even me. I thought I'd lost you once, and I almost bled to death that day. But I also realized that, in order to have you in my life, I needed to be ready for you…all of you. That I needed to recognize I was enough and worthy of your heart—and your love. Every day with you helps patch the pieces of my broken heart back together—something I thought was unattainable for so long. April, I'm a better man because of you. Nothing seems impossible when you're beside me. Neither happiness nor reaching for my dreams."

I held tight my grip on her hand, and she squeezed back, her touch powerful enough to heal all my scars.

"Today, I'm standing here before you, asking you to trust me with your heart. Forever. And, in exchange, I promise to always cherish and handle it with utmost care. We both lost people we loved deeply in the past, but without them passing through our lives, we wouldn't be standing here right now, promising to love each other for eternity. Because Pixie, you and I, we're in this together for as long as our souls shall live. Wherever you go, I'll follow you. And if you get lost, I'll find you. Every single time. Because that's how soul mates work. They fight until they reunite. Over and over again. April Simmons, in front of all our friends and family, I'm telling you there's no one else for me in this world. My heart is yours. Now and until the end of time."

I choked on a sob, and when I met April's face, there was a stream of tears rolling down her cheeks. Fuck her mascara. My eyes scanned the small crowd. Everyone was a teary mess. Stud and Belinda. Saunders and Reed. Dahlia and Nick. Riley, June, and even Ed and Taylor had moisture in their eyes.

We exchanged rings. And when the pastor said, "You may now kiss the bride," I lifted April into my arms and kissed her, without a care in the world that brides and grooms weren't supposed to kiss this way. Pixie's lips parted, giving me full access to her mouth, and my tongue danced with hers. I grazed her cheeks with my thumbs, soothing her tears.

"God, I love you," I said against her quivering lips.

April's arms tightened around my neck, tugging me closer, until our bodies fused together.

Breathless, I leaned back, lost in my woman's gaze. My wife.

I set her back on her feet, intertwined my fingers with hers, and walked down the aisle as our guests cheered us on.

***

Everyone made a speech. April reached for my hand under the table. Her warmth traveled through me, igniting my entire body. I basked in the happiness radiating from her.

In the middle of the dance floor, with my wife in my arms, I closed my eyes, trying to burn every little detail of that day into my memory. The way our bodies waltzed together. Her scent. The way her hand felt in mine. Her touch. The way her smile brightened her face. Her happiness. The way our hearts beat as one. Our souls.

Reed neared us, and we stopped. "May I have the honor of asking the bride to dance?" he asked with a grin.

April turned to face me.

I leaned forward and brushed my lips on hers, tasting the remnant sugar frosting of our wedding cake on them. "Go. I'll get the next one."

Reed led her away, and I loosened my tie as I watched them.

"Cart, can I get a dance?" Dahlia touched my shoulder from behind. I spun on my heels to face her.

"I've been owing you a dance for a very long time,

Dah. There's nothing I'd like more." My best friend's eyes clouded. "Come here," I said, drawing her closer and nesting my head in the crook of her neck. Dahlia's perfume filled my nose as she looped her arms around me. She fastened her grip around me as sobs rocked her body. "Don't cry, Dah. You were right. All this time. I'm sorry I didn't listen to you earlier. I found the one. It took me longer than I thought, but I got her. Everything is good. We're both where we're supposed to be."

She leaned back and wiped her damp eyes with her fingertips. She stared at me, and a small smile broke free on her tear-stained face."Never let her walk away, Cart. She's perfect for you. You're perfect together. I love you so much. My heart is full now that yours is overflowing with happiness too. That's all I've ever wished for you… That… that you'd be happy. I lost this happy version of you when we were fifteen and I broke your heart. I'm glad you got it back…that you're back. I've missed you so damn much, Carter Hills."

Dahlia's words shot another dose of ecstasy right through my heart.

"I'm here to stay this time. For good."

We exchanged one of our smiles that bore more weight than our words as we hugged on the dance floor.

———

"Ready?" I asked, my palm facing up, waiting for April to slide her hand into mine.

She bobbed her head. "Yes. I've been ready for a long time. I just can't believe this day is over." She was beaming, and I wanted to bask in her light a little longer.

I twirled my wife in a dance move until she landed in my arms, and framed her face with my palms. "I'm so happy." I kissed her lips and lowered one hand to her belly. "You're everything I've ever wished for and more, April Hills. Oh, I like the sound of it." She pressed her warm cheek into my palm. "Now let's get to our room because even if I'm exhausted, there is plenty more of you I plan to cherish tonight."

I traced a trail of kisses from the corner of her mouth, along her jaw, down her neck, and over her breastbone.

April melted in my embrace, a loud whimper escaping her quivering lips.

I ground my hips against hers. My wife's eyes fluttered as she tried to keep her balance. I clutched her waist with my fingers, the fabric of her wedding dress crinkling under my touch.

With my teeth, I nipped her lower lip, and her head tilted back, giving me access to the soft flesh of her neck.

"Carter...I-I..."

"I know, baby." With a single step back, I freed myself from the flustered woman who had taken my heart hostage and made it hers, then scooped her over my shoulder. Her laughter vibrated through every cell in my body.

When we reached the door of the cabin at the lakeside resort we'd booked for our wedding night, I lowered her to the ground. Our lips met, and time seemed to stop.

"Carter...just sweep me off my feet, okay?" April asked against my hungry lips.

With one arm under her knees and the other under her shoulders, I lifted her, honeymoon style, as we crossed the threshold of the room together.

I lay her on the white fluffy bed. "Love me, husband. Love me till we both can't breathe."

April wouldn't have to ask me twice.

I planned to love her—again and again—for the rest of tonight.

And the rest of our lives.

———

FREE bonus chapter
Want even more? Your bonus chapter awaits here
emmanuellesnow.com

———

Read False Promises: Carter's prequel story

Curious about the rest of their friends?
Read Cruel Destiny: Dahlia and Nick's story
Read Last Hope: Riley Burn's story

Grab them all HERE: emmanuellesnow.com

ACKNOWLEDGMENTS

When my editor offered to revisit this story (which was my debut novel), I jumped on the occasion. I remembered how in awe I was of Carter's and April's characters when they first appeared on the pages and how hard I fell in love with them both.

After everything they had overcome in their lives, they needed to find each other and embrace the happiness they both deserved. They were made for one another…not just on paper. *Blindsided* is book one in the *Heart Song* duet, and my new re-edited version of their love story.

Back when I wrote this book a few years ago, I knew it couldn't end there. It just didn't feel right. Carter and April and their friends and family had so much more to experience. Along the way, my country music standalone novel became a series that I'm so proud of. Fast forward a few years later and you can now see plenty of Carter and April in other books of the Carter Hills Band universe because they are the heart and soul of this world.

I want to thank my husband, without whom I wouldn't have started to write my first novel yet. You've always believed in me even back when we were young and clueless, and you've stuck by my side, no matter what. I love you. I'm lucky I found my soul mate early in life.

I also want to thank my kids. All four of them. You guys have been patient and selfless through this whole project and the many that came afterward, giving me the space I needed when my fingers itched to write one more page or one more chapter. The love and pride you show me every day are priceless. Thanks, guys, for being my biggest fans.

I also want to thank those people who helped me through this adventurous journey as an author.

Shalini. Thanks for sticking by my side and helping me write the best version of Carter and April's story and revisiting it when the timing was right. You're the best!

To my readers, none of this would be possible without you. Thanks for giving me the chance to do the thing I love the most—writing love stories.

Ashley, Miriam, and Sara, thank you for your help and unconditional support.

And to the Bookstagramers, influencers, Booktokers, Booktubers, who helped me share this book with the rest of the world, I can't tell all y'all enough how grateful I am.

Hope you enjoy reading this book as much as I did writing it.

Cheers
Emmanuelle

★★★★★ "This is not a romance, it is a story about first love, first heartbreak and growing up."

A compelling tale of love, friendship, and self-discovery that will tug at your heartstrings.

Start Dahlia's story now

———

Cruel Destiny

★★★★★ "Wow. Just wow. If that could be my review, that is all I would write."

★★★★★ "Emmanuelle has done it yet again. She found a way to slip into my mind and heart with her words and the creation of characters you can't help but fall in love with."

★★★★★ "This book broke my heart in the first twenty five percent and sewed it back together."

A story of healing, second chances, and the risks of opening your heart to someone new. Can they trust each other with their hearts, or will their pasts keep them apart?

Read Nick and Dahlia's love story now

———

Wild Encounter

★★★★★ "This is by far one of the most well-written book I've read this month. It is dynamic, intriguing, interesting, unafraid to go there and most of all touching."

★★★★★ "I personally wouldn't call this book JUST a romance novel because it's so much more. I 100% recommend it no doubt in mind."

A tale of passion and perseverance that will leave your heart racing and your spirit soaring.

Read Tucker and Addison's love story now

———

Last Hope

★★★★★ "This book was not only about the darkness but it was about pure love, hope, spice, family, and friendships on point with just the right amount without overpowering the storyline at all."

★★★★★ "Devon and Riley's story is a beautiful one with a lot of emotions. The subject matter is intense but it is handled very gently."

A tale of resilience and second chances in a world where love and danger intertwine.

Read Riley and Devon's love story now

———

Midnight Sparks

★★★★★ "The characters, the love, the humor, the steaminess, the emotions… it's everything I hoped and more."

★★★★★ "I think that is one Emmanuelle Snow's sexiest novels yet."

Welcome to the island where Holiday magic meets unexpected romance and a chance at a fresh start.

Read Gavin and Aisha's love story now

———

Fallen Legend

★★★★★ ""The love that grows, not only through tough angst but through unconditional moments had my heart. This is a spicy and riveting book"

★★★★★ "Emmanuelle Snow doesn't just tell a story, she creates an entire world."

A poignant and uplifting journey of hope, love, and the power of second chances.

Read Sam and Madison's love story now

———

Snowbound

★★★★★ "5 big stars from me for this amazing story. Absolutely loved it!"

★★★★★ "Emmanuelle Snow's stories are always full of angst, and Snowbound is no exception."

The intertwined lives of two strangers bound by fate in the midst of a snowstorm.

Read Anderson and Abigail's love story now

All available at emmanuellesnow.com

ABOUT THE AUTHOR

Soulfully Beautiful Love Stories

USA Today Bestselling author Emmanuelle Snow is a contemporary author of mature YA and New Adult love stories, who gives life to strong characters who'll fight with all they have to reach their life goals and find their own happiness.

Emmanuelle is in love with love. Especially complicated, deep, and passionate feelings that make a relationship extraordinary and complex all at the same time.

In her spare time, when she's not writing or reading, she likes to go on road trips—with her four kids and her own soulmate—watch movies, paint, or do some DIY, always with a cup of green tea in her hand and listening to country music.

She splits her time between beautiful Canada and the small US towns she adores.

Find all of Emmanuelle's books here:

emmanuellesnow.com

———

Want to connect with Emmanuelle online?

ALSO BY THE AUTHOR

CARTER HILLS BAND UNIVERSE

(suggested reading order)

Carter Hills Band series

False Promises

Heart Song Duet

BlindSided

ForeverMore

Whiskey Melody series

Sweet Agony

Second Tear Duet

Cruel Destiny

Beautiful Salvation

Breathless Duet

Wild Encounter

Brittle Scars

Upon A Star Series

Last Hope

Midnight Sparks

Love Song For Two Series

Read them all

emmanuellesnow.com

All available on author's bookshop

WILD ENCOUNTER

ADDISON

I slumped down on the couch of the posh hotel we were staying at all weekend and huffed, a wine bottle hanging from my fingers by its neck. Glasses were overrated, anyway. "That's it. I'm over men. I'm done." My childhood best friend snickered. "I'm serious, Dah. This time I mean it. You know I do."

I scanned the space around me. Large windows with a direct view of Nashville's busy streets below, high wooden beam ceilings, dark flooring, and handcrafted wood furniture. Chic and tasteful, with an unmistakable country vibe.

"Yeah, right. I'm sure you won't last a week. Two at the most," Dahlia teased.

My friend, and the bride-to-be, inched closer, and I zipped her up. Her cut-out mermaid gown was a gray-lavender hue and looked both sexy and demure, showing just enough skin without being indecent. Perfectly Dahlia Ellis.

Before I could sink back into my lazy position on the couch, she beckoned me with a finger to follow her. Sitting on the edge of the bathtub, I glugged the wine straight from the bottle and watched her apply mascara.

"Addi, there are good men out there who would appreciate your light. Don't punish all of them because you dated a few who were total dickheads." She grinned at her reflection, but it was meant for me. And it warmed my heart as she continued, "I'm confident you won't last in your quest to ignore them all when they turn on the charm."

"Laugh all you want, girlfriend. You'll see. Be prepared to be shocked. This time, I'm not backing down. Anyway, remember Felicia from college? She messaged me last week. It's destiny."

"The one you 'experimented' with?" my friend asked, curving her fingers into elaborate air quotes, her gaze fixed on her eyelashes in the mirror, not sparing me a look.

Another sip. "The same. We could have been in love and lived happily ever after. The timing was just not right back then."

"Huh, you said the same thing about Carter once. Besides, I thought women weren't your thing," Dahlia added with a quirked brow.

"It's not the same. And perhaps I changed my mind. Who knows? I might be into women more than men after all. Think about it, we should have been a couple, you and I. Everything would have been much simpler."

"You think?"

I shrugged. "We get along fine. And we're friends, so our relationship would have had a solid foundation. Look at you and Nick. Friends, then lovers. I believe that's the secret to long-lasting love. Back to business..." I sighed. "Felicia and I experienced some pretty memorable moments together. It's just Shawn happened to cross my path, and I couldn't resist him. Stupid me. Stupid men. I'm telling you their species is old news. You're lucky you found two awesome ones in your lifetime. What are the odds? God knows I've tried. I usually don't back down easily, but hey, maybe it's time I try something else. That I understand once and for all what life has been trying to tell me all these years…"

Dahlia shook her head, focusing her attention on me for the first time since I started the conversation about my disastrous love life. "Addi, you know how much I love it when you're not being overdramatic, right?"

I poked my tongue out, and we both burst out laughing. Peace washed over me. Dahlia Ellis had that effect on me. Her presence was always enough to ease all my doubts and bring a curve to my lips even when I didn't feel like expressing joy. "That's why you love me. I'm entertaining…despite myself. Anyway, where are the bridal shower festivities taking place? I can't wait to party the entire weekend. The distraction will do me good."

My best friend reached over and landed a kiss on my cheek, her eyes searching mine. Worry shimmered in them. "You okay?"

I nodded.

"You'd tell me if it wasn't the case, right?" I sensed the apprehension in her question.

"Always. You're the only one I willingly confide in."

With a warm smile that promised everything would turn out just fine, she went back to applying her makeup. "All over town. Tonight, we're having dinner with only the people closest to us. And tomorrow, a get-together with some of my good friends and the guys on a yacht before splitting up and maybe meeting them again later."

"Rewind for a sec. We're having your bridal shower with your future husband and his friends?"

"Yep. His best friend. Guys from work. That's the idea."

"Yeah, I should've been the one organizing the whole thing." Dahlia raised a hand, ready to argue, but I kept going. "For what it's worth, I'm sorry I let you down. I was really looking forward to throwing you the bachelorette party of the century."

A new weight grew heavy on my shoulders. In the fog of my latest relationship blowing up, I had lost focus on what really mattered. This time, my tears had knocked me out more than ever. But I was back now, and no way was I failing the girl I considered a sister again.

Dahlia pulled me into a hug. "It's okay. Don't chastise yourself. It'll still be fun. And you did plan most of the wedding already. You deserve a night off...to enjoy yourself... You, me, booze, music. And the man I love and his friends."

I leaned back, studying her for a moment. Dahlia had no ounce of evilness in her. She really meant everything she'd just said.

"What is it?" she asked, a frown marring her forehead.

"Real sweet, Dah. After I told you I was done with men, you're going to make me spend hours with a bunch of Nick's buddies. And alcohol. If I didn't know your heart, I'd think this was a test. To check my newfound determination." One more sip of wine. *Be strong, Addi,* I repeated in my head. I flicked my hand and pasted a smile on my lips. "Know what? It doesn't matter. I won't back down. I'm done with men, and I'll prove it to you. Tonight. I won't flirt, and I won't kiss. Nope. Nada. D.O.N.E. Just watch and learn, girlfriend."

I held out my hand, and we shook on it.

———

Read Tucker and Addison's story,
Wild Encounter, now

emmanuellesnowshop.com/products/wild-encounter

"Tucker freaking Philips!!! Wow! Emmanuelle Snow has written another beautiful, rollercoaster, sneakily emotional romance." (Goodreads)

"This is without a doubt Emmanuelle's best work yet!" (Goodreads)
Wild Encounter is book one in the **Breathless** duet. Read the first part now

Wild Encounter

emmanuellesnowshop.com/products/wild-encounter

Author's bookstore at emmanuellesnow.com